THE COMPLETE KOSKI & FALK Vol I

A. G. Hayes
with Raymond Gaynor

Savant Books and Publications
Honolulu, HI, USA
2020

Published in the USA by Savant Books and Publications
2630 Kapiolani Blvd #1601
Honolulu, HI 96826
http://www.savantbooksandpublications.com

Printed in the USA
Edited by Daniel S. Janik

Cover design by Daniel S. Janik
Cover image "Armageddon" by Pete Linforth from Pixabay
Cover image "Silhouette Agent" by Mohamed Hassan from
Pixabay
Cover images reproduced with permission

ISBN 9780999693834

First Printing April 2020
Library of Congress Control Number: 2020936674

NOTE: *Quantum Death* was published before its prequel, *Finding
Kate*. For continuity and clarity, however, they are presented in
order of their storyline in this collection.

TABLE OF CONTENTS

Book One:

Dedication

To my wife Connie and family, Michael, Patricia and Christopher, who encouraged me in so many ways to enable this story to see the light of day.

Acknowledgements

To author and poet Maggie Roth for her tireless advice and encouragement. My special thanks to Hollywood writer Lea Andrews and the Hungarian Grammarians and my agents, Gloria Koehler and Donna Eastman at Parkeast Literary Agency. Without them I still would be collecting rejection slips. Finally, special thanks to my editor, Mary Yamin-Garone, and her sharp eye for a comma being placed before a conjunction introducing an independent clause and my publisher, Daniel Janik, the "Man Behind the Curtain" I *did* listen to.

Chapter 1

The man in the tuxedo had an arrow buried almost to the fledge jutting from the left front of his white starched shirt. His right fist, crusted with dried blood, was clamped around the arrow below the flight, indicating he never knew what hit him.

In mortal pain, his instinct was to attempt to withdraw the foreign object he suddenly found embedded in his chest. Because an Indian arrowhead is perfectly configured to enter freely but not exit easily, that struggle merely served to rip his organs more severely as he endeavored to extract it. Flat on his back, the deceased lay in an old, wooden, cattle chute just off Centerville, a lonely road in Gardnerville, Nevada.

Special Agent Joseph Falk parked his World War II jeep just off the pavement on Centerville, killed the engine and slid from the vehicle. Falk was a handsome, chestnut-haired man in his thirties.

The collar of his deer-hide jacket was turned up to merge with the rim of a woolen cap that covered his ears. Together the garments sealed off the cold wind that rustled the sagebrush of Job's Peak, a jagged pinnacle of the Sierra Nevada Mountains that overlooked Lake Tahoe to the west and Douglas County to the east.

The moon was low, casting geodesic light across the sloping countryside. Falk mumbled to himself as he strode toward the Douglas County patrol car and the deputy sheriff. The lawman was one of three individuals who had preceded him to the location, evidenced by an old Plymouth sedan and a Cherokee parked alongside the highway, their engines still crackling as they cooled.

Falk had no idea why he was called to this crime scene. He was Reno FBI, Rover Division. This investigation was not his and he wasn't going to let it become his. The body was on Nevada Bureau of Land Management property. Being involved meant working with BLM agents and working with *anyone* right now flew in the face of Falk's brooding, fiercely solitary nature. He still was chewing on his wife's death.

"Morning," he mumbled to the deputy, introducing himself.

"Five-thirty," the man said with a sigh made visible by the cold air. "Thirty minutes to my official quitting time." He kicked idly at a rock and told Falk what Falk already knew. "This stiff is on BLM property, making this a federal case, which means a shitload of reports and red tape." He leaned against the door of his cruiser, arms folded over a paunch Falk guessed he'd been working on for fifty years. "I'll be lucky if I get off the job by noon."

Concluding that the man already had been at his job for too many years, Falk didn't offer so much as a shrug. "Who called it in?"

"Mr. Anonymous, about forty minutes ago from a pay phone up at the lake. Caller's probably seen too many TV shows depicting the person who finds the vic as the *numero uno* suspect."

Falk left the highway and scrambled through a gate, inhaling fresh, grassy aromas of pastureland. He climbed up the side of another cattle chute a dozen yards from the highway. Portable lights the deputy had strung along a fence separating the field from the pavement illuminated it.

"Good morning," Falk felt obliged to say to a woman he had never met but knew to be the Carson City Medical Examiner. It seemed she already had examined the body. She stood, nodded and pulled off her heavy latex gloves. "I'm Joseph Falk, FBI," he added. Under the glare of the bare bulbs, she looked thirtyish, beautiful but tired. Medium height and slim build, she wore a thick merino wool coat and a watch cap. Her dark skin was smoky in the early morning light.

She shot Falk a quick, absorbing look. "Millicent Maxwell, ME."

Standing beside her, a tall, rangy blond in his early thirties offered a nod in Falk's direction. "Wes Webster, BLM."

Falk had a preformed opinion of BLM agents in general. He mostly thought they could phone in the type of jobs they did.

"Don't see many killed that way," Webster said, nodding toward the arrow jutting from the dead man's chest.

Maxwell scribbled in her notebook and then looked up at Webster with a straight, brown-eyed gaze that didn't miss anything. "Right, not much doubt as to cause of death. He's been dead about forty-eight hours."

Falk leaned forward for a closer look. "Certainly not your regular, garden variety arrow."

"Also right." Maxwell pointed with her pencil. "In essence, a radio-controlled missile; the flight is thin, pressed aluminium."

Falk nodded. "Really?" He didn't attempt to disguise his surprise at Maxwell's apparent knowledge of an extremely unusual weapon.

She continued while Falk scrutinized the arrow. "You probably already noticed there's a fiber optic wire protruding from the end of the shaft, attached to a dime-sized disk. It's curved and fashioned to retain its aerodynamic shape."

Falk's eyebrows wrinkled upward. The woman had a keen eye

for details. "You sound like a weapons expert."

He thought she might imagine that her quick assessment intimidated him; bruised his male ego. A black, female medical examiner was not such a novelty anymore but her cool expertise probably ran up against its own prejudice in some quarters. Right now, he wasn't of a mind to care what she thought.

As if offering him a gracious out, she said, "In all honesty, I've seen one of these before…had a chance to study one."

"Where was that?"

"I can't disclose that information."

Falk stretched into a standing position, his large, slender hands resting lightly on his hips. He *did* have a prejudice against uncooperative, smartass medical examiners. "Pardon me?"

"Try the Carson City DA's office." She snapped her bag shut. "Nice meeting you, Agent Falk, Agent Webster."

Falk watched her nimbly climb down from the chute, seemingly unencumbered by her heavy coat. She got into the Plymouth sedan and drove off.

"She's new," Webster said. "Only been with the department a couple of months, I understand. From back east; Chicago I think."

Falk shrugged. He returned his attention to the body. "She call the coroner's wagon?"

"Should be here any minute." He watched Falk go through the man's pockets. "How the hell does a man in a tux end up in a cattle chute out here in the boonies with a high-tech arrow through his heart?"

Falk had just asked himself the same question. He reached into the inside pocket of the tuxedo jacket and removed a slim leather wallet, flipped it open and checked the driver's license. The photograph was indeed that of the dead man, Howard L. Kiley. The address, an expensive area in Incline Village, Lake Tahoe, was consistent with the tux and Rolex on his wrist. Robbery was not the motive. In addition to the Rolex, credit cards and cash were still in his wallet. His business card indicated that he was an attorney-at-law.

Falk folded and replaced the wallet and continued his examination. The only dirt on the victim's clothes was on his back, acquired when his body landed in the chute. The soles of his shoes were clean. Falk silently wondered if Webster had come to the same conclusion he had when Webster answered the unasked question.

"This is a dump job."

"Right," Falk mumbled. "Howard Kiley was nowhere near a cattle chute when the arrow pierced his heart."

Why was he killed this way and dumped here? Was he killed by Indians? He knew today's Native Americans were certainly more sophisticated than they were in the last century. Was it possible that they had created smart arrows and were killing people with them?

On the other hand, did someone simply want it to appear that way, to implicate Native Americans, at least symbolically? Falk was certain about one thing: whoever reported it did so to be sure the body was found. Another few hours and it would be road kill for carnivorous wildlife.

A BLM vehicle that arrived without sirens or flashing lights interrupted Falk's thoughts. The deputy's harsh voice immediately drifted up to Falk and Webster. "Your crew's here, Webster. You don't need me any longer. I'll have the lights collected later; almost daylight anyway."

"Thanks, you can go," Webster shouted. "I'll release the body soon as I'm through and stop by your office for the paperwork."

Falk watched the deputy wave and head back to his cruiser, no doubt thinking of the large breakfast he would soon devour at Sharkey's, where most locals went for good food and coffee. Falk climbed up the wooden slats to exit the chute. "Yes, it's your homicide, Webster. Body's on BLM land."

Webster nodded in the direction of the occupants of the BLM vehicle who got out and started toward them. "I've asked for video and still pictures."

A gray-haired man wearing a size 2X parka puffed up to the cattle chute, photographic equipment hanging from his shoulders like loose reins on a carthorse. Not long from retirement, Falk judged.

"Alex Spade," Webster said to the rotund man, "this is Special Agent Joseph Falk, FBI."

When Spade's eyebrows shot up, Falk said, "I'm not here officially." It was a wish and a statement. Falk was here because Tom Stewart ordered him to be. Stewart was his contact in Cerberus, a covert federal agency that employed Falk's skills and, to a particular, mentally well-defined degree, enjoyed his loyalty.

Stewart had called him at 4:15 that morning, apprising Falk of the attorney's body in the chute. It was the latest in a recent string of similar lawyers' deaths in Nevada and California.

"Check out the scene on Centerville Road," Stewart had said, "and meet me at the usual place at seven."

Falk left his apartment in Reno and headed south on I-395, through Carson City and to rural Centerville Road. He hoped checking out the body would be the extent of his participation but a hunch nagged at his heretofore impeccable intuition.

"Spade's a still expert," Falk heard Webster say. "He's been shooting crime scenes since they used Speed Graphics."

Falk noticed that Spade wielded a digital, strobe-equipped Nikon that he unslung then started shooting film. The camera snapped and whirred as he deftly captured all angles of the victim's deathly repose.

"Is Koski with you?" Webster asked.

Spade jerked his thumb over his shoulder. "Yeah, moving slowly. She's no morning person."

Later Falk remembered that assessment and added that Susan Koski did not appear to be an afternoon or evening person. In fact, his observations concluded she seemed to be merely going through the motions of living.

Koski looked like a teenager but was probably in her late twenties, dressed in a bulky snowsuit and baseball cap turned backwards. She casually approached the chute, hardly acknowledging Webster's introduction of Falk.

Koski was about five-one. She looked like a person whose bathroom scale didn't need to register a hundred pounds. She had short, raked-back, ash blonde hair, full pouty lips and was pretty in a natural, no-fuss way. Falk later learned she recently had engineered a lateral transfer to BLM from Las Vegas PD and that she did her job well. She may be the best videographer in the district. Due to a particular circumstance in her not-too-distant personal past, she vacillated between numbness and rage.

"Koski, go over everything, too, inch by inch," Webster instructed. "Cover the area around the chute first. Come up here when Alex is through. I'm pretty sure the body was dumped."

"Okay," she said in a disinterested, husky voice.

Falk watched for several more minutes as Koski silently obeyed, shooting with her digital Sony camcorder. She used her equipment with practiced ease, one eye at the eyepiece while the other seemed to be seeking out the next frame. He noticed her eyes, sea green, and the sort in which ships were wrecked.

A siren wail began in the distance and grew steadily.

"The morgue wagon," Webster advised. "They like to arrive in style."

Falk turned and walked to his jeep. He did not envy Webster. He seemed like a regular, possibly too youthful guy, having to work with a know-it-all medical examiner, a fat man salivating for retirement and a young, zombie-like videographer who probably couldn't be goosed into an emotion.

Falk looked at the clouds that snaked around the mountaintops. Not yet winter and the Sierra already had gathered weather that boded a harsh season to come.

Chapter 2

Yesterday Falk was in his element; seven thousand feet in the Sierra Nevada Mountains on an assignment for the Bureau's Rover Division. His jeep had churned its way over a rock-strewn trail, the purr of its well-tuned engine belying its appearance. Splotches of gray primer mingled with faded khaki paint made the vehicle difficult to see in the surrounding terrain.

That was how Falk preferred to work: alone, blending into twisted scrub, pitchy pines and craggy mountain outcroppings. He was a deep cover, roving agent for the little-known Rover Division, established after the government's 1993 debacle in Waco, Texas. Falk was a self-contained man, not unlike the OSS agents dropped behind enemy lines in Europe during World War II or today's Special Ops troops.

The federal government finally had become aware of its need

to improve covert observation and control over potential terrorists and rogue paramilitary groups. As a rover, Falk's job was to infiltrate such fringe assemblages all over the western states. His aim was to be accepted among the ranks of such factions, keep to himself and report whatever useful information came into his possession to the Bureau.

Today, Falk had been ready to head for Reno HQ to file just such a report when the global system mobile phone in his jeep rang. If not for the damned GSM phone that employed a Cerberus satellite and was used by Cerberus agents worldwide, he would be unreachable here in the mountains. "Falk," he growled into the receiver.

"Joe, Stewart here. We need to talk."

Tom Stewart was not only Falk's primary contact but also director of Cerberus, a federal government agency so top secret that few in the Bureau, CIA, NSA and even Homeland Security knew it existed. Stewart never called him unless it was important.

"Okay, Tom, what's happening?"

Stewart had scheduled a meeting with him for later today but he called this morning to inform Falk of the corpse in the cattle chute and changed their meeting to six a.m.

It was precisely six and still dark when Falk turned off the highway. Three letters in the flickering neon sign were out, leaving the stuttering message in garish pink to read: VA ANCY. CABI S WITH KITCHE S. Falk passed the pink anagram, bumped across the potholed parking lot and proceeded to motel cabin number eight. It was the last in a row of wooden cabins built when they were known as motor courts. He snapped off the headlights and eased from the jeep. As he neared the cabin door, it opened. No lights glowed from within.

"Come in," a deep, familiar voice said.

Falk entered and the door closed behind him. A second later, a low wattage table lamp came on, weakly illuminating the shabby two-room cabin. He crossed to a wooden table, pulled out a chair and eased his one hundred and seventy-eight pounds onto it.

Tom Stewart was a white-haired man in his late fifties, tanned and trim. He went to a gas burner and removed a coffee pot. "Coffee?"

"How long's it been brewing?"

"Long enough." Falk raised an eyebrow and Stewart caught his meaning, adding, "But not *too* long." He filled two tin mugs and handed one to Falk.

"What's the problem, Tom?"

Stewart lowered himself into a sagging easy chair. "I couldn't tell you on the phone yesterday but I got word that the Bureau is putting together an investigative team to look into what has now become the serial killing of lawyers. They want you to head it up."

He hurried on before Falk could protest. "This will be a new gig for you; not Quantico-controlled as you once were and not a solitary Rover Division agent. You will be out in the field and responsible for clearing up this mess. I wanted to give you as much of a heads-up as possible."

Falk set down his mug. "Why are they tapping *me* for this? I want to continue what I'm doing."

"They need the best and that's you. It's that simple. Yours was the first name that came up at the bureau chiefs' meeting yesterday."

Falk shook his head. "It figures they'd choose the one person who doesn't want the job." He paused and studied Stewart. "As always, I'm amazed at how much you know about what's happening at the Bureau."

Stewart grinned. "My ESP and I have a friend at Covert Transmissions, Domestic, both reliable sources."

Falk watched the play of humor on the man's face. Freshly open and honest one moment, Stewart's expression could evoke images of unfathomable darkness in the next.

The two men had met several years ago when Stewart recruited Falk for Cerberus. The name *Cerberus* was derived from the dog of Greek mythology said to have three heads and designated as keeper of the entrance to the infernal regions where the gods resided.

Those in the present-day organization who adopted the name believed it was their duty to see that America was protected from domestic insurgence, to sniff out foreign terrorists and to respond to any threatening intruder, internal or otherwise, with ferocity. Falk initially resisted initiation into Cerberus but ultimately he acknowledged the need for an organization that covertly supported America's security.

Falk's membership in the Rover Division was an added bonus to his recruitment and, in turn, he felt honored to lend his expertise to what he now believed was a vital tool in the future security of the country.

"Your Bureau control will call and give you the details of this assignment," Stewart went on, "but let me fill you in on what we know. You're not going to like it."

Falk resignedly tipped his chair back. "Okay, Tom, spit it out."

"You said you'd heard about the recent murders of California and Nevada lawyers so you know that, like the man in the cattle chute, all were killed by arrows to the heart."

Falk sighed. "You think the government believes Indians are to blame. So-called arrows are killing lawyers at a time when various Native American tribes are exercising their sovereign rights to open more casinos in the interest of self-improvement." He shook his head. "I'm not altogether convinced. You know these are not conventional arrows. They're more like guided missiles designed to look like arrows."

Stewart eyed Falk over the rim of his coffee mug. "Didn't you recently disclose that there have been reports of Indian militia maneuvers?"

"What I reported were scattered, disorganized, half-ass military-type maneuvers by some members of the tribes...more like bonding excursions, nothing menacing."

"But with the potential to organize, right?"

"Do we even have a *clue* Indians are killing the lawyers—any real evidence?" Falk gave him a skeptical glance and a slightly impatient gesture that indicated he still awaited the bottom line.

"So," Stewart said, "maybe the tribes have decided that no one is paying enough attention to them. Maybe they've decided to kick the pressure up a notch. Emboldened by economic security from their casinos, maybe to expand their gaming rights and thus obtain privileges they believe are due them."

He finished his coffee and set the mug down. "You may find it difficult to imagine a full-scale Indian uprising in this country in the 21st century, Joe, but I believe it's a distinct possibility." He leaned forward. "I don't know about you but that thought scares the hell out of me."

Falk let his chair return to all fours. "I don't know, Tom...all of this because of a few more casinos..."

"Casinos translate into money, Joe, which translates into

power—power to negotiate for…whatever…"

Falk got up and headed for the coffee pot. "Try this, Tom. What if it's not the Indians? What if it's somebody who wants us to *think* it is?"

"Okay, who then and why?"

"Well, the Nevada gambling cartel for one. They're dead set against any increased Indian gambling in California." He signalled with the pot but Stewart declined. Returning to his chair, Falk continued his thought. "The Nevada Mafia could have chosen this reign of terror against lawyers to scare the public into anti-Indian sentiments. The mob feels the pinch every time a Californian fails to cross the state line to gamble in Nevada. If they succeeded, it would keep millions in Nevada gaming and resorts."

Stewart seemed convinced of his initial argument. "From all accounts, the murdered lawyers were working *against* Indian gambling. That would put them and the Mafia on the same side."

Falk nodded. "That's the one thing that doesn't make sense. Then again, it's possible we're not dealing with an American Indian or a Michael Corleone. Maybe it's just one crazy son of a bitch who majored in archery and simply hates attorneys."

Stewart seemed to go along. "Or perhaps the killers are foreign terrorists with their own reasons."

Falk gave him a cynical stare. "You're pumping sunshine up my butt. You've already made up your mind as to who you think is responsible."

Stewart's lips turned into the bemused grin with which Falk had become familiar.

"In any case," he said, "the governor of Nevada has agreed to let the feds help solve this quickly. He wants to avoid using high profile agents in logo jackets. Naturally, local police are investigating. We and the Bureau trust their ability about as much as we trusted LAPD to nail O.J. or the Boulder police to arrest the person we all know killed JonBenet Ramsey.

"Moreover, if there's inside involvement the locals could be suspect. So, they're counting on you and a small, elite team to do the leg work...get the facts from the bottom up."

Falk rose and stretched. "When does this assignment begin?"

"You'll hear from Lester Carter at the Bureau tomorrow."

"I'll check in with you from time to time."

"No need. I'll know where to find you."

Falk had a few more questions. "Tom, how and why is Cerberus involved in this?"

Stewart stood and ran a hand through his thick white hair. "We're not actually involved at this point but as a Cerberus member, you know it's our responsibility to always be acutely aware of the balance of domestic power and any possible shifts in that power. Let's just say that the economy's suffering enough. We don't want to be surprised by an economic earthquake."

Falk generally felt Stewart had a habit of speaking in riddles, like a baseball club's general manager dancing around the subject of trading an iffy pitcher. This seemed to be one of those occasions. Rather than try to decode the man's thoughts, and since that seemed to be the extent to which Stewart was prepared to explain, Falk nodded and started for the door. "What do you know about this so-called elite team I'm supposed to get? Bureau agents or local?"

Stewart's eyes flickered as he went to the door and opened it for Falk to exit. "I don't know for sure but if what I'm hearing is correct, as I said, you're not going to like it."

Attorney Mark Sharpe stood on the balcony of his lakeside

home, smoking an expensive cigar. Six feet tall, almost two hundred pounds, the counsellor was as imposing a figure at home as he was in the courtroom. Clothed in a heavy brocade dressing gown, he gazed across Lake Tahoe, which shimmered in autumn's early morning light. Snow dusted the mountains rimming the lake. This was a dream location, his third residence and, unless the feds raised interest rates and the NASDAQ dropped even further, soon he would consider a fourth.

His wife called from inside the house, "Coffee's ready. Breakfast in five minutes."

Sharpe blew a smoke stream and watched as a light wind swirled it for a moment before it vanished. He entered the bedroom and was halfway across the room when something made him stop and return to the balcony. There was a cough of smoke from his last inhalation when the arrow thudded into his chest. He fell back against the wall. His knees buckled and he slowly slid to a sitting position on the balcony floor, a vivid, vertical track of blood tracing his descent.

Chapter 3

That night Falk's mind dwelt heavily on the moment of physical impact that each of the lawyers must have experienced in their deaths. The terrifying human condition of being unexpectedly hit by a lethal projectile. Then, in the wolf hours of the next morning, from nowhere, Falk heard not the twang of a bow string, but the sharp, deadly crack of a rifle. A bullet speeding in slow motion travelled inexorably in his direction. He was in a dense, surreal forest yet the bullet—red with a shine like dripping lacquer—kept to its steady trajectory. It didn't strike anything directly in its path despite trees that grew so closely together they seemed to inhabit the same piece of landscape.

Falk sat in the passenger seat of his Toyota and stared straight ahead through the windshield. He still saw the lethal bullet homing through the woods to his right, flashing in a beeline for his right temple. While he expected its arrival, he also was powerless to escape it. When it hit him, he felt a knife-like incision in the right side of his head and the world exploded.

He awoke.

He sat upright in his bed, perspiration weeping from his body, the sheets over and beneath him sodden with sweat. He turned and let his feet slide to the floor. He'd had the same dream many times in the past two years yet it was *not* his nightmare; it was Meg's.

He looked at the red glowing digital figures of the black square on his nightstand—four o'clock. He stood and ripped the soaking sheets from the bed. You could make soup with them! He threw them toward an overflowing hamper in the corner of the bedroom and grabbed his robe.

Over his usual weak coffee, he reminded himself of what the therapist, with whom he kept only three appointments after Meg's death, said: "It wasn't your fault your wife was killed."

Wasn't it?

They were returning from a day in the backcountry in their four-wheel drive Toyota when the engine quit. Despite his best efforts, he could not get the damn thing started. It was late afternoon and without a cell phone he had no choice but to walk to get help. Meg wanted to go with him but she had turned her ankle when hiking earlier in the day. Not a sprain but it was painful. There was no way she could walk the rough terrain.

Falk always carried emergency blankets, flashlights and the like so he made her comfortable and promised to return as soon as possible. He never saw her alive again. When he returned two hours later, she was dead; shot once through the head. The police were unsuccessful in determining who was responsible for what was ruled "death by misadventure." Whoever fired the shot most likely never knew they killed someone. The theory was that the shooter, using a high power Winchester, could have been a mile away when he fired, missed the intended wild animal target, and the bullet continued traveling until it struck Meg.

She'd been sitting in the passenger seat with the window open a few inches to allow fresh air in. When the bullet reached the Toyota, it had enough speed left to kill her, striking her right temple. The irony was that had the window been shut, the bullet, nearly spent, would merely have struck the glass, possibly cracking it but not with enough power to break it.

Falk headed for the shower. Going over it again did no good. He had to clear his mind. Lester Carter of the Bureau would call any minute to inform him of the assignment Stewart had generally outlined yesterday. In a cynical moment, he thought of the stinging lawyer jokes he had heard or read on the Internet and wondered if someone had really taken the quote from Shakespeare's Henry V1 seriously; "The first thing we do, let's kill all the lawyers."

As hot water cascaded down his body and attuned him to the day, he thought about the team to which he was assigned. He hoped they were a bright, dedicated group.

Chapter 4

In less than two hours Falk received messengered papers confirming his temporary transfer out of Rover Division to FBI headquarters in Reno. Carter, his bureau chief, had called briefly but had no details. He only informed him that Nevada State

Attorney General Donald Lovesy would be arriving at Reno HQ to meet with Falk and his team at three p.m.

Shortly before three Falk joined Lovesy and his two aides in a secure room on the second floor. The building supposedly was constructed to preclude any possible listening devices. Falk stopped before an eight foot square Plexiglas map of the United States that seemed portable and hung with temporary hooks. Lovesy faced a computer monitor, keyboard and printer on the table beneath the map.

"Marvelous device," Lovesy said to Falk, who watched as he tapped in the name Mark Sharpe and a code number two, both of which came up on the monitor. Simultaneously, the number two glowed blue on the black and white map in the area of Lake Tahoe, which was lit up in red, in the yellow-colored state of Nevada, where Sharpe met his demise.

"Marvelous device," Lovesy repeated. He hit one of the keys and the map went dark, then he tapped a button on the printer. A color printout of the previously lit section of the map highlighting the locations of all the recent lawyers' deaths slid out of the machine into his waiting hand.

Lovesy seated himself at the head of the table. Falk took the seat to his left just as the door opened and three individuals Falk recognized entered the room.

"I believe you all know each other," Lovesy said, waving a hand in the air.

Falk attempted to keep the sinking feeling he felt in his heart from showing on his face as he nodded to each of them.

The slim, stunning, African-American medical examiner was dressed in black linen overalls over a beige crewneck and a black Georgio Armani blazer. Gold chains adorned her neck and wrists and various rings brightened all but her ring finger.

BLM's Wes Webster's most involved assignment before now was probably hunting for a mountain lion that had killed a dog, some sheep and a nine-point buck out of season. Alex Spade, gray-haired and overweight, wore a permanently disheveled suit, his soon-to-be-retired Nikon hanging from his neck.

Then all heads turned as the aide who had stationed himself near the door responded to an exterior sound. He opened the door to admit the fourth member of what Falk now knew was to be his "elite" team. It also was the reason Stewart had warned, "You're not going to like it."

Susan Koski, the petite, slow, sauntering sensational blonde, wore black slacks, an oversized hand-knit turtleneck sweater with a mosaic design and black boots. Her eyes reflected a distracted Twiggy look. She slid into a chair next to Spade, set her camcorder on the floor and leaned back, crossing her hands on her lap as if waiting to be entertained.

Lovesy did not seem the least bothered by her late arrival but Falk remembered Spade saying that Koski was not a morning person. It was six minutes after three.

"Ah," Lovesy said, "so glad you all could join me." He gestured and one of the aides approached him with a sheaf of papers. "These two gentlemen are part of my staff," Lovesy said. It was clear that he did not intend to introduce them.

Portly Donald Lovesy, middle-aged, with a large, square mouth and a smile like a toothache, wore a too-tight suit, the jacket of which he alternately unbuttoned and buttoned, straightening and sucking in his girth on each occasion.

"Shall we begin," he said, aware that none believed it to be a question. "Needless to say, the governor is more than anxious to complete this investigation *yesterday* and to foil the media circus that can possibly result from it. As you know, the recent murders in Nevada and California were all committed with the same kind of weapon and each victim was a lawyer.

"The homicide investigation you are being asked to conduct will be quite visible, followed closely by print and broadcast media, an unfortunate and unpleasant fact. You are authorized to tell them nothing."

He paused and pursed his thick lips as he repeated, "*No thing.* Whatever you uncover is hereby classified top secret. *I* am the only one who gets a copy of whatever documents flow from this endeavor."

He paused again, quickly glancing around the table. "No doubt you've all heard rumors about who is responsible for these killings—the American Indians, the Mafia, radical Islamic militants, the Iraqis, the Russians, the Chinese…"

He waved a hand and let his voice trail off as he straightened and slipped the middle button of his jacket from its hole. "Whoever—we need to know the truth ASAP." He turned to Falk. "We'd like to see a thorough and timely 24/7 probe. You'll report the results directly to my office or to a contact Washington has assigned us—a man in the National Security Agency whose name and phone number you'll be provided with."

He pulled himself up in his chair and re-buttoned his jacket. "Questions?"

Maxwell said, "I understand the importance of the assignment, sir, and I'd be honored to serve. I'm a medical examiner, not an investigator. I'm not sure what expertise I could bring to such a team."

"My intelligence sources tell me that you're uniquely familiar with this type of arrow, that you have studied several…"

"Well, yes, extensively, in fact, but—"

"That fact, in addition to our desire to confine the team to those already involved in some way, makes you an ideal person to be pressed into service for your country in its hour of need."

Maxwell could only nod as the AG went on addressing Falk. "You will have full access to all files on the murders—electronic and otherwise." He squared the edges of a stack of papers in front of him. "Including those in California."

He deliberately stared at each person. "You will be under FBI jurisdiction until otherwise notified. Bear in mind the governor's insistence that this remain a top secret operation until brought to a swift and satisfactory conclusion. Do I make myself clear?"

A murmur of agreement echoed around the table. "Very well, now you will sign documents to that effect."

He handed boilerplate forms to each of them. "Read and sign these, please." As he collected the signed forms he said, "You will be given all the support you need from any state or federal agency that can be of assistance, including the Office of Homeland Security."

Handing out cards, he advised, "One number on this list, the NSA contact I mentioned—Samuel Ryland—you should have with you at all times. Washington has assigned him to oversee your investigation."

This was the first Falk had heard of Ryland. "Sir, does that mean we *report* to him?"

Lovesy unbuttoned. "No, not at all. I understand that Samuel's a busy man. He'll be around if you need him. If I need an update I'll call him. He'll be on the periphery.

"Well," he pushed back his chair and buttoned up again, "I'm sure you five will work well together. Thank you for your service."

The closest aide opened an attaché case and extracted a thick stack of files that he deposited on the table. Falk noticed they were stamped in red: AG Channels Only. "These are top secret." Gesturing to the computer, he added, "E-files are at your disposal." Then, with the two aides at his heels, Lovesy left the room.

Falk jammed his hands into his pants pockets and walked to the window. He felt uncomfortable for several reasons. For one, he was dressed in a suit and he was a man who looked and felt better in a sweater and jeans. For another, he had a question he decided to keep to himself. With his team being so "visible," as Lovesy put it, the media was bound to get interested and ask questions.

Yet he was under orders not to give them any information. If the fourth estate did not get answers in one quarter, they were motivated to query another. It was almost as if the reporters were being set up. Teased to ask yet denied access to answers, forced to dig deeper—why? He'd have to see how it played out.

Not speaking to the media or anyone else for that matter was okay with him.

He thought about what he knew of Lovesy. When the AG last ran for office he'd won by smearing his opponent at every opportunity. Now, Falk had to take orders from the man he considered an unprincipled politician.

It was a typical aspect of FBI employment that made Falk glad he belonged to Cerberus. It was an outlet for the frustration he sometimes felt over the tactics of the too-often bungling Bureau.

Falk stared down at the rooftops of Reno and sighed. That brought him back to his present problem, the four albatrosses Lovesy had hung around his neck.

Koski muttered in her disarmingly husky voice, "I suppose that once we've looked at these files we have to eat them," referring, Falk supposed, to the AG's remark regarding them.

Maxwell grinned but one glance at Falk sobered her.

"Damn," Spade groaned, getting up from the table. "I don't know what *I'm* doing here. Has anyone stopped to realize that I'm only days from retirement?"

Falk looked from Spade to Maxwell to Koski then to the tall, quiet BLM agent. "What about you, Webster? You got anything you want to gripe about?"

Webster looked around with a surprised expression and shrugged. "I'm cool."

"Good, because anybody who has anything negative to say about this assignment and who isn't ready to totally commit to it can get the fuck out!"

There was silence while Falk waited. Nobody moved. "Look, I didn't ask for you—any of you—but I've got you and we've been given a job to do." He returned to the table and sat down. "Let's begin by going over these files, shall we."

Three hours later Chinese take-out food containers were scattered on the table. Falk rubbed his forehead and gazed at the slumping assembly. "Okay, I think we've learned all we can from these and the computer files. We'll meet here in the morning, at which time I'll have worked out our first course of action."

"What if I'm needed in my department? Has anyone been assigned to take over for me in Carson City?" Maxwell questioned.

Falk opened up a file marked for his eyes only. "Yes. As of now, you'll be staying at a hotel in town. Some of your clothing already has been transferred by a female agent." He closed the file.

"I'll have a car take you there." He noticed that she seemed disconcerted that someone had gone through her personal belongings but he made a mental note that rather than complain, she opted for irony.

"Oh, a *female* agent," she quipped, "that makes it all okay."

Falk got up. "Okay, people, tomorrow morning, here, at nine sharp." He flipped open his cell phone. "I'll get your transportation, Maxwell."

Before he could dial, the phone rang. "Falk," he snapped. After a few moments he said, "Thanks" and disconnected.

He punched in a number and while it rang he informed his four hangers-on, "The Douglas County Sheriff's Office reports that, as with the others, the Centerville arrow contained no prints." He'd been hoping for a positive break but no such luck.

Falk stopped at a convenience store on his way home. When he returned to his jeep, a deep, familiar voice pronounced his name from the dark Lexus perfectly parked beside his vehicle. He turned and saw Tom Stewart at the wheel.

"Got a minute," Stewart said casually.

Falk rounded the back of the Lexus and slid into the passenger seat. "Tom, how in hell do you always know where to find me?"

Stewart offered his characteristic grin. "ESP and—"

Falk interrupted. "I know. I know—you have a friend at Covert Transmissions, Domestic, both reliable sources."

"You're going to want to know this." Stewart's head often moved from side to side as he spoke, his eyes alert to any movement near the two automobiles. "I just got word that a man who has been known to be connected to various nefarious activities in Nevada—nothing that can be proved, mind you—may be a mediator involved in the deaths you and your A-Team are investigating." He paused.

"Oh," Falk said coolly.

"He's known only as The Fox."

"The Fox? Aren't we cute."

"I know, conjures up old cloak and dagger images. If he's in any way involved in this business, however, he could be a formidable player."

Falk frowned. "Hold on a second. I've heard that name before."

His eyes went abstract as he related a chance encounter he had some time ago with an old trapper who had retired from his job at a mine up in the Sierra near Bowman Lake.

"I'd been hunting in the area and came across this guy and we shared a fresh trout dinner at his camp. This geezer told me that one day when he was still working at the mine, he overheard a guy talking on a cell phone as he sat in his car in the parking lot. The old guy remembered very clearly the words he heard the man say because, as he put it, 'They gave me the shivers.' The man on the phone said, 'This is The Fox. Kill our target.'"

"Did he see the man?" Stewart asked.

Falk shook his head. "I asked the same question. He said he only saw the back of his head—dark hair—as he drove away in a nondescript compact."

"Did he notify the police?"

Falk shrugged. "Said he thought about it and decided he might have misunderstood…that the guy may have been talking about an animal…about killing a fox…I don't know. I guess, finally, he figured he might have imagined it. Still, he never forgot it."

Stewart sighed. "Well, if there's anything to the old man's tale, all the more reason why you should be aware that this chap is out there."

Falk slid the information to one of the back burners of his mind. "Thanks. Anything else?"

Stewart put the key into the ignition and the expensive engine purred to life. "Just good luck."

As Falk climbed out of the vehicle, he thought about his A-Team and mumbled, "I'll need it."

Chapter 5

Nine o'clock the next morning, Falk silently pushed through a wave of print and electronic media reporters gathered outside the Reno office.

He entered the conference room, carrying a cup of coffee, and sat down. Webster was seated, reading the *Reno Gazette-Journal.* He lowered the paper, "Morning."

"Morning," Falk answered. He sipped his coffee and looked toward the door as Maxwell entered, followed by Spade. Falk turned to Webster. "I did say nine o'clock. Where's Koski?"

Spade wheezed as he lowered himself into a chair. "She sometimes has trouble with her car...and she's not a morning person."

"You said that yesterday," Falk snapped. From what he had learned about Susan Koski since their meeting last night, she may not give a damn. He was stuck with her, at least for now.

He needed a top-notch videographer on this assignment. He would try to be patient.

Falk was already feeling the smothering sense of company. He was doing exactly what he did not want to do: babysit this

BLM bunch. He was antsy to get this assignment over with. He wanted to get back into the field, where he was alone, where he was most dangerous and where the eternal distance between Meg and him lay lightest on his heart.

He looked around the room. He hated small talk but information collecting about those you had to work with was never a waste of time, even if it seemed trivial.

He'd read the bios on each team member that Lovesy supplied. At some point in the near future, Falk's life might depend on these individuals. He needed to know what was *not* in their files. He turned to Maxwell, whom he learned was single with only one living relative—a father in Chicago, an ex-cop to whom she never spoke or corresponded.

"Everything to your liking at the hotel?"

"It's okay. It's a hotel." She sipped a strong Latte Grande that she held in both hands for warmth.

"I understand you work with Police Chief Bud Vigo in Carson City. What's he like?"

"In his fifties, about five-seven, dark hair with a stupid bowl haircut and blue eyes that are so light you sometimes think he has no eyeballs."

Falk smiled inwardly. He got the smart-ass answer he expected but ignored it. "I mean what's he *really* like? They say he's tough."

Maxwell took another sip of coffee and seemed to relax somewhat, sensing what appeared to be a sympathetic ear.

"In truth, he's a bit obsessive—drinks, smokes and like so many Nevada natives who insist they never gamble—can't resist testing any slot machine he comes across."

Falk shook his head. "Smokes…that's really bad."

"And he smokes unfiltered cigarettes!" Her eyes rolled. "He says it's the chemicals in the filter tips that kill you." It was her turn to shake her head. "Regarding working with him, yes, he's tough. It took me a half hour yesterday to convince him to let his pilot and his precious department helicopter fly me to Reno for our meeting with Lovesy."

"Seems unreasonable."

She was back in the emotion she felt twenty-four hours earlier. "I made the point that it would give the chopper crew a break from nailing tourists on I-395 but he insisted he wasn't running a taxi service." She paused. "He finally acquiesced."

Falk glanced at his watch; five minutes past nine. "Why do you think he was so reluctant?"

She shrugged. "He's just naturally surly. It's as if something's always eating at him."

"Or maybe he wasn't thrilled that you were invited to that meeting and not him. Could be just plain professional jealousy."

She looked up at the clock on the wall. "Maybe."

Falk got the feeling that she felt she might have said more than she meant to.

"How long do you think this investigation will take?"

He sighed in sudden irritation and couldn't resist voicing the source of that emotion. "Depends on how soon her highness gets here and we get started."

At that moment, the door opened slowly and Koski entered nonchalantly. Her video camera was slung over her left shoulder. She held a Styrofoam cup of coffee in one hand. On her head was a soft white polar fleece snowdrop hat that framed her brooding face with a '20s flair. She carried a snow jacket and wore a long, heavy, natural-cotton turtleneck sweater that covered all but the legs of dark sweat pants.

In her quiet, inflectionless voice, as if she was offering no apology at all, she said, "Sorry to be late." Distracted, she rummaged in the purse that hung over her right shoulder. "I had car trouble."

Falk noticed Maxwell give Koski a lower-over-upper-lip smile. He made a mental note that the medical examiner either was the compassionate type or was good at faking it.

"We know you're not a morning person," Falk said, hoping the sarcasm he oozed punctuated his frustration. He glanced quickly around without making eye contact with anyone.

"I'll say this slowly." He didn't care that it sounded condescending. "It's important that you all fully understand my expectations for you as members of this team. Each of you has various skills and training. It's my job to see that you and I use those skills to maximum effect."

He turned to Maxwell. "Your medical training, familiarity with police procedures and knowledge of the arrows should prove invaluable."

Webster paid wide-eyed attention as Falk addressed him. "You'll be second-in-command in the event of my absence or incapacity. You're seasoned in various facets of criminal justice and have had hands-on confrontations with criminals at all levels in rural and urban settings."

Out in the air, those words sounded over-generous but surprisingly, Webster's file had impressed Falk. The Bureau of Land Management was an agency of the U.S. Department of Interior, managing 1.5 million acres in Northwest Nevada. Webster was responsible for a good portion of it.

"Spade and Koski, as photographers you're going to be very

busy. I'll want a lot of video and digitals for every situation in which we're involved."

Spade suddenly cleared his throat for attention. "I don't mean to sound...unpatriotic..." He paused and seemed to choose his words deliberately, a fact not lost on Falk. "I wonder if you have any specific idea as to how long this investigation will take. Due to my pending retirement, I mean...my wife and I having made plans to drive to Arkansas to visit her sister and all...The RV's ready to go." He laughed nervously and his round, chubby face reddened. "In two weeks I'm scheduled to be a senior citizen holding up traffic from here to Little Rock."

Falk managed a thin smile through gnashed teeth. "If all goes as I anticipate, Spade, we should all be back to our normal pursuits in a couple of weeks." Almost inaudibly, he added, "God knows, I hope so."

He glanced around the table. "Any more questions?" When there was none, he continued. "First, bad news. I got word earlier that a hang-glider pilot was found dead this morning near Spooner Summit close to Spooner Lake. It appeared to be an accident; he crashed into a tree. When rescue personnel got him down, however, they discovered he'd taken an arrow in the chest before he hit the tree. He was a corporate attorney moonlighting for a Vegas hotel against expanded Indian gambling."

Falk paused long enough for the others to assimilate the news. "Now, just because we'll be watched by the media and our movements reported doesn't mean we won't try to stick to standard investigative procedures.

"This morning we'll check out the locations of two killings. Webster, you take Maxwell and Spade and go to Spooner Summit." He handed Webster a map with the marked area.

"Scrutinize the terrain up there, particularly any spot that offers cover from which to fire an arrow. Spade, I want extensive digital photos. Koski and her equipment will go with me to the house at Lake Tahoe where…," he checked his notes, "Mark Sharpe was killed."

As she had in the Lovesy meeting, Koski sat silently, seeming to listen at times, distracted and aloof at others. In any case, Falk already had set a mental limit on how much time he'd give her to snap out of it.

"We should be at our initial destinations between eleven thirty and noon."

He reached into a case on the floor beside him, removed one of two phones and slid it down the table to Webster. He took out the second phone and placed it on the table in front of him.

"These have a closed frequency. Although they're cellular, they're the closest thing we have to a secure line with the ability to send and receive while scrambling and decoding."

Falk felt the need to translate for his BLM charges. "Meaning that when I transmit, it goes out scrambled, cutting down on the chances of a spurious signal being picked up by someone else. When you receive my message, your phone will automatically decode. Any questions?"

Koski chose this moment to offer sardonic appraisal. "Those Chinese are amazing."

"Made by Motorola, Koski, right here in the U.S. of A." He turned back to Webster. "I'll have Koski call you when we're done at the lake, then we'll switch locations. You'll examine the Sharpe crime scene while Koski and I check out the Spooner location. This way, if one of us misses something, hopefully the other will catch it."

He stood and finished packing his case. "We'll leave by the back door. Despite what Attorney General Lovesy said about our being visible, I'm not ready for the media sharks out front."

"Do we have any leads on perps yet?" Webster asked.

"Nothing," Falk said, "but that's what we're here for."

When the four walked out, Falk noticed that Maxwell initiated a conversation with Koski, the latter seeming to be hard pressed to hold up her end of the discussion. Webster had to slow down for the lumbering Spade. Frank wondered how in hell he was supposed to pull these dilettanti together into an efficient team.

The Kingsbury grade is a twisting highway out of the Carson Valley to Lake Tahoe. Cut through steep granite hills covered in pine and jagged rocks, it was an engineering masterpiece. Falk silently concentrated on the tortured curves while, beside him, Koski sustained a drum beat on her knees, as if listening to an inner rhythm.

"Why didn't you take Spooner Pass to the lake?" Koski suddenly asked. "Would have been quicker."

Up to this point she had said nothing. Falk actually preferred it that way. If he had to wet nurse a prima donna he'd just as soon do it in silence. "We'll go down Spooner on our way back," he snapped.

Koski mentally sang along with Carole King's "Tapestry" and tried not to think about what this guy's problem was. It was obvious he wanted her here about as much as she wanted to *be* here. She leaned back and closed her eyes.

When she had transferred to BLM eight months ago from Las Vegas PD after David went to prison, she felt sure that work would resurrect her from the walking dead. She found that she was unable to throw herself into her job as she once did, still stinging from the sadness and bewilderment of suddenly being alone after two intensely happy years with David. She wondered if the emptiness in her would fill up again.

David had not come to her as a knight in shining armor. She never wanted that. She wanted someone interesting, intelligent, kind and exciting. That David was all of that and more—tall, handsome with a disarming smile and explosive to an acceptable, intoxicating degree—was magnetic to her.

He was born in Tel Aviv in 1963 and trained to shoot and in the use and care of various weapons. When he was eighteen, his two older brothers serving with the army were killed in a skirmish in the Golan Heights. David and his parents immigrated to America where he drifted into law enforcement.

He was with Las Vegas Vice when Koski met him. She often speculated that maybe it wasn't something in his distant past that turned him—maybe it was his job. Dealing with those who fed on the warm rot at the bottom of society's slimy underbelly every day probably took its toll. Nevertheless, the true puzzle was in her. When she met David, she was on good terms with her instincts. She had complete faith in David's goodness and trustworthiness. No doubt she was wrong.

"Damn tourists! They don't bother reading the signs," Falk snapped, "and then they wonder why so many of them run off the highway."

The RV made it around the bend but the driver probably wished he had slowed down. As Falk reached the crest and began the downhill toward Highway 50 and Lake Tahoe, he intermittently glimpsed the lake; a cold blue gem.

He was bored, noting how telephone poles seemed to count

their passing, and decided to try to gather a little information. "You get a chance to speak to Maxwell yesterday when we finished for the day?"

"Not really. We merely exchanged a few words as we collected our stuff. Why?"

"She told me she saw another arrow similar to the one we checked out in Centerville but she didn't say where. Did she tell you?"

There was more traffic now as they neared Incline Village. Koski cranked down the window. "No." When she offered nothing beyond the one word, he lost the impetus to inquire further. He glanced at the clock on the dashboard. "Better check out your equipment. We'll be there soon."

"Okay," she said but he noticed she made no movement to follow through.

"Uh...?" raising his eyebrows questioningly in her direction.

"It's already done. My car might break down now and then but my gear is always ready to go." She restarted the drum beat on her knees and added, "So, if we count her arrow—which we can assume is tied to a murder—plus the one in the cattle chute on Centerville, the hang-gliding lawyer at Spooner, Sharpe at the house at the lake and the killings Lovesy told us about...that makes seven."

"Yes," he said in a businesslike tone, "it seems someone's taking all those lawyer jokes to heart." He slowed as a couple of teenagers carrying a canoe sprinted across the highway, dodging traffic in their eagerness to get to the water. "Keep your eyes peeled for the address. It should be a right turn."

They fell silent again and Falk was content to return to his own thoughts. They'd managed a little conversation but it was filler. He could not imagine himself ever having a protracted, give-and-take discussion with the woman.

Nonetheless, he did wonder about her. She was an enigma. He'd read her bio, knew that her parents were deceased and she had no siblings. She'd left LVPD to work for BLM nearly a year ago and held a BA in criminal science. She'd expressed her interest in BLM's Video Division and trained in videography at the FBI Academy in Quantico.

Koski was twenty-eight years old, unmarried, five-one, a little under a hundred pounds of perfect physical condition, with intelligence that would have allowed her into MENSA with IQ to spare. He also read her file from Quantico. The FBI attempted to recruit her on the spot but she refused, saying she enjoyed the wide open spaces. So did he but he couldn't think of another thing they had in common.

"There," she said, pointing, "second road coming up on the right."

He passed the first turn, checking the sign. "Mountain Mist Drive."

"Ours is Vista Point Drive," Koski said.

"Those colorful names add to the price of the homes," he said as he hung a sharp right and started up a steep hill lined with stately pines. The address they sought was the last house, almost at the top of the ridge. The slate driveway twisted like a gray snake toward the entrance.

He parked in sight of the front door and glanced back toward the lake. "Great view, like sitting in the treetops."

Shallow steps ran up to a double front entry flanked by plants and blooms positioned to give the entrance the ambiance of a cool grotto. Falk took in the gracious two-story house of rock and timber. "This place must be four thousand square feet if it's an inch." His words hung in the air while his disinterested companion chose not to comment.

As Falk and Koski entered the home on Vista Point Drive, Webster, Maxwell and Spade tramped through brush and climbed over rocks until they reached the area where the hang-gliding victim had died. Familiar yellow tape hung from the surrounding trees and bushes.

"I'm not sure exactly what we're looking for, Webster," Maxwell said. "Obviously, the police have already investigated this scene. We know he was hit with an arrow before he crashed into the trees. I'm not sure what else we can learn."

Webster leaned against a tree, loosening his tie. "Well, Falk apparently wants us to see—to *realize*—both the scenes, get a fresh perspective. You're a medical examiner. You know that details are important."

Spade sat on a flat rock in a tangle of cameras. He waved a pudgy arm at the surrounding trees.

"You want me to take pictures of…what?"

Webster moved toward two pines, pointing upward. "The vic apparently hit the top of these trees…note the broken branches there…and his chute must have tangled near the top. Falk said the sheriff's men had to pull the body down…probably about here."

He ground the heel of his shoe into the earth, which was carpeted with pine cones and needles. Spade joined him then, snapping shots of the area and the cathedral of branches overhead.

Maxwell approached the spot. "This crime scene has been trampled so badly that it's useless."

"There," Webster said, pointing to the disturbed bark on one of the pines, "investigating officers blazed the tree to mark the spot."

Gesturing in the direction of the dense forest beyond the partial clearing where he stood, Webster said, "The killer had to have been in there somewhere."

Maxwell followed his line of sight, standing pensively for a long beat, her natural curiosity involving her more in the details with each passing moment. "One would need to be quite adept just to navigate that dense area, let alone get off a good shot with a bow and arrow from there."

Spade let his Nikon slide to his side and he, too, appraised the surrounding woods. "What did the officers at the scene say about the trajectory of the arrow they dug out of the hang-glider pilot's body?"

"Nearly straight on," Webster replied.

"Straight on!" Maxwell exclaimed. "That would indicate the killer was on a level with the vic, like up in a tree when he shot the arrow." She shook her head. "This means we're dealing with an extremely powerful archer. Just to get his or her tackle—which we have concluded from the type of arrow must include some kind of sophisticated propelling device—up in those trees takes a lot of effort…and maneuvering a bow in such tight quarters…" She carefully picked her way as far as possible into the dense woods, dodging branches and strands of dead moss that hung from the trees, while Spade followed with his camera ready.

When they rejoined Webster, Maxwell said, "Of course, I'm more accustomed to examining corpses than forests but if you ask me, something's wrong with this picture. If an archer was up in those trees they must be some kind of contortionist. They didn't disturb a single pine needle."

Chapter 6

As they covered the crime scene, Falk was impressed at how efficient and professional Koski was once she actually became involved in her work; intuitively knowing which areas and items Falk wanted videotaped before he pointed them out. This did not make her a necessary asset, just an unavoidable one.

Now he stood on the balcony, scanning the view through a pair of powerful binoculars, searching for a likely spot from which an archer could perform with stability. "The killer had to be close enough and accurate enough to hit Sharpe in the chest first shot out," he speculated aloud. Koski, meanwhile, had switched off her recorder and stood by silently.

Continuing his magnified search of the trees, rooftop and surrounding area, he focused on a house on the opposite side of the hill, its red tile roof visible above the treetops.

"Ever shoot arrows?" he asked directly.

"Yes, when I was younger."

It did not surprise him that she was not curious about his query. "I was on an archery team in college. We almost won a trophy."

He lowered the binoculars and squinted at the red roof, wondering if it was too far away to accommodate the accuracy needed to kill with one shot.

"I say 'almost' because we had a hard night before the competition."

"Studying for finals?"

"No, we were so sure we'd win that we went out and partied all night."

Then the cell phone rang, its tone muffled from inside Koski's jacket. She produced it and flipped it open. "Koski here."

Webster's voice was tinny and loud and Falk could hear it as he stood beside her.

"We're ready to leave our location now," Webster said.

Koski looked at Falk, who nodded. "Falk says okay."

"We'll arrive there in the next half hour. This is an isolated spot to find. When you proceed toward Spooner you'll see a sheriff's deputy waiting in his car as you turn right out of Vista Point Drive. I've instructed him to direct you to the scene." The phone clicked off.

"That yokel," Falk sighed heavily. "He thinks *I* need help finding the location."

Koski shrugged defensively. "He probably just thought…in the interest of saving time…"

Oh, now she's quick to remark. Falk turned back to the rooftops fronting the balcony and pointed. "Pan across that ridge, a long, slow pan starting at the right. When you see the lake, come down until you get to that pink house, far left. See it?"

"Of course."

"At that point, shift to a close-up, retrace the pan back to the red tile roof and give me a one minute focused hold on the roof before you adjust to normal and fade."

"A full sixty-second hold on the roof will seem like an hour on tape. Sure you need that long?"

He took a deep breath. "I'm sure."

She positioned the camera, ready to begin.

"No," he said, "here…stand right *here.*" He tapped the rail and moved aside until she was in the approximate spot he had vacated. She turned, assessing the terrain he indicated. Looking over her shoulder, he took her arm and quickly moved her one inch to the left.

He felt an ephemeral shock that stung the hand that touched her and reverberated to other parts of his body. Quickly moving away, he said more gruffly than he had spoken to her before, "Start shooting."

Webster's car made its way around the lake. Spade sat in the back seat with his camera gear. Maxwell was in the passenger seat beside Webster.

Maxwell stared blankly at the passing rural scene, her mind going back to the time, less than two weeks ago, when she'd seen the first of the high-tech arrows. A hiker had found it embedded in a tree trunk in the hills near Wally's Hot Springs when his dog ran into the brush and he went after it. He noticed it looked different so he stuck it in his backpack and finished his hike. It was later, when he arrived home and was unpacking, that he examined the arrow more closely, noting the tail fin and electronic contacts. He was afraid that the arrow was an explosive device. Being civic minded he took it to the Carson City Sheriff's Office.

Maxwell, along with her boss, Police Chief Bud Vigo, and others at the office, examined the arrow. It was sealed in a plastic bag and placed in the evidence cage.

Maxwell shuddered and pulled the collar of her coat around her neck.

Webster glanced her way. "Too cold for you, Doc? I can roll up the window."

"No, I'm fine." It was not the cold air of late autumn. It was the fact that she knew the arrow had vanished from the sheriff's evidence cage without a clue.

Before that, she considered evidence bags as sacrosanct. Untouchable. Then one day, entering the caged room at the rear of the department, she noticed that the tagged plastic evidence bag containing the arrow was gone.

She reported it. She and Chief Vigo looked everywhere, questioned everyone but it was never found. After that, even when she was not at the office, she often wondered if someone was there, breaking in, absconding with other evidence.

"Almost there." Webster flipped on the turn indicator and eased into the left lane, approaching Vista Point Drive.

As Webster was making his left turn, Falk and Koski, having followed the squad car Webster had provided, turned off the main road onto a dirt trail running into a grove of trees near Spooner Summit. The deputy stopped and climbed out. He was thirtyish with a tired, weathered face and gray eyes that lacked any semblance of humor.

Falk nodded to Koski and they both got out from the car and joined the deputy. The deputy hooked his thumbs into his well-worn leather gun belt, turned his head to the left and shot a stream of tobacco juice into a clump of grass three feet away. "I was told to meet Falk and Koski," he mumbled. "That you?"

Falk nodded and the man said, "C'mon, I'll show you where they found the hang-glider." He walked away.

Koski was twenty feet behind Falk as they followed the man into the heavily wooded area. Koski said, "If I'd known this was going to be a trek, I'd have asked that we stop for something to eat first."

The deputy continued for several more minutes before he stopped and jerked a thumb over his shoulder. "She should walk into the clearing where the victim was removed from the trees. She can shoot the video at the same time. It will produce a more thorough picture. Then you, Agent Falk, can move in and she can pan your entrance from that angle to complete the shot."

Falk blinked deliberately. "Who does she look like? Steven Spielberg? This is not a movie we're shooting here, deputy."

Koski shot him an irritated look. "It is sometimes helpful later if you set up the scene, Falk."

Falk shrugged. "Go ahead. I'll wait here. Let me know when you're ready for my close-up."

Falk waited, expecting the deputy and Koski to walk no more than a hundred yards ahead. Soon they disappeared into the trees. Alone, he began to absorb the surroundings but a chill soon nudged him forward, straining to see where they were. He had gone about two hundred feet when he saw them.

Koski was on one knee, panning the ground with her camcorder, the sheriff standing behind her. The hair on the back of Falk's neck rose as if attracted by a magnet. Unaware of Falk's presence, the deputy removed an automatic from the inside pocket of his jacket and Falk saw the ugly shape of a silencer…

"Look out," Falk shouted and burst forward, his own weapon clearing leather.

Koski instinctively whirled as the deputy turned, surprised by Falk's yell. She rolled onto her side, kicking, knocking the deputy off balance. The pistol flew from his grip and Koski was on him, rolling with him across the ground.

In the next instant, they were up and the deputy swung a beefy fist, a glancing blow on her cheek. He plunged his knee into her ribs with a crack that sounded like splintering bone. Koski bent double, groaned and sank to the earth.

Now that the two were separated, the deputy pulled his service revolver from its holster but Falk got off a shot and the side of the man's head was blown away in a pink mist. He spun and staggered before his legs folded. He collapsed without a sound, the revolver still clutched in his hand. As Falk approached the grotesquely twisted figure with arms splayed on a blanket of pine needles, the man's left foot kicked twice in a final spasm.

Koski rose slowly, brushing earth and leaves from her clothes. "At Quantico," she said breathlessly, "we were taught that being in law enforcement and dealing with criminals didn't require any special talent. You simply had to understand how to handle fear." She picked up her cap that had spiralled from her head in the fight. "I guess I didn't learn that lesson very well."

Falk wiped the back of his hand across his sweaty upper lip. "Meaning you were afraid just now?"

"Terrified."

"Welcome to the club." He suddenly remembered the blow to her ribs and studied her face for signs of the pain he imagined she felt. "I thought I heard…your ribs?"

She reached inside her jacket and pulled out the broken cell phone. "You heard this crack." When Falk smiled, she added, "I know, made in the U.S. of A." She tossed it aside.

He leaned down, forced the revolver from the dead man's fingers and handed it to her. "Keep this. We're going to need all the help we can get." He looked down at the would-be killer one more time. "I knew there was something odd about this guy." He pointed toward the man's feet. She glanced down as Falk indicated that a man in a black sheriff's uniform wearing brown shoes and white socks should be suspect. "We've got to move fast before they try again."

"Before who tries again?"

"I have no idea but we can't go back to the office."

"Can't—why not?"

"Look, someone tried to *kill* us!"

"Why does that mean we can't go back to the office?"

Falk grunted. "The fewer people who know where we are the better."

"I know Webster arranged for this so-called deputy to meet us," Koski replied, "but surely you don't suspect Webster…or Maxwell or Spade for that matter."

"Not at this point. I'm sure Webster talked to the real deputy, who most likely was intercepted, maybe killed."

"What do we do now?"

Before Falk could answer, a voice behind them said, "You come with me."

They spun in unison and faced a tall bearded man holding an AK-47 at waist height. "Throw your guns into the middle of the clearing."

Falk tossed his automatic, nodding to Koski to do the same with the dead man's gun. He watched the man as he walked toward them. He had slick black hair, a compact build and looked fit and agile.

"This yours?" the man asked, picking up Koski's video equipment. When she nodded, he slung it onto his shoulder. Gesturing with the assault rifle, he commanded, "Keep your hands on top of your heads and walk ahead of me." As they obeyed, he looked back at the dead man and growled, "You'd never have been able to take him if I hadn't had to take a piss when I did."

A half a mile later, they came to a battered, grimy Chevy parked beneath the branches of a drooping pine. It was the kind of car you could leave on the street overnight with the keys in the ignition and no one would bother it.

The man gestured toward Koski with the Kalashnikov. "Open the trunk." He removed a silenced automatic from his jacket and held it to her head. He lowered the AK-47 and her video equipment into the trunk and covered them with a blanket, slamming the lid shut. "You drive," he told Falk, tossing him the key. "We'll sit in back. Don't try any heroics, Falk, or you'll lose your friend here. Understand?"

"Absolutely."

"Fine. Now listen up. Ahead, on your right, you'll see an old logging trail that exits onto Highway 50. When it does, turn right and head toward Virginia City. Move out."

Falk gripped the steering wheel and stared ahead, his mind chewing on the realization that he was what he swore he'd never be again: helpless—as he was helpless to save his wife's life. Meg's ghost was with him every morning when he looked in the mirror. Glancing in the rear view now, he doubled his fists, seeing their captor holding a gun to Koski's ear. The man returned his gaze maliciously, raising both eyebrows. Falk turned the key in the ignition and the engine rumbled to life. His hands on the wheel gave him hope, a sense of power, which, somehow, he'd turn to his advantage.

Chapter 7

Spade reloaded his Nikon. "I've shot a total of seventy-two pictures at Spooner and here. That enough?"

"That should be fine." Webster walked from the balcony back into the late Mark Sharpe's bedroom, sat on the edge of the bed and removed the Motorola phone from his pocket. Tapping out a number, he spoke as he waited for the ring. "We could get a late lunch. I know a little place on the side of the lake not far from here. Falk and Koski can meet us…" He paused and tapped out the number again. "Funny, I don't get a ring on his end."

Maxwell came into the room and began to pace. "Perhaps we should have purchased a Chinese model after all."

Webster flipped the phone shut. "We'll try him again from the restaurant. Let's go eat."

As they drove away from the location, a TV news van drove up the hill like a bloodhound following its relentless nose to the dead lawyer's lakeside home.

They were halfway through dessert when Webster looked up and saw a couple of deputies moving toward them between tables.

"Sorry to interrupt your lunch, Agent Webster," one of the men said as he stopped beside him, "but we need you to step outside with us." Maxwell and Spade exchanged glances.

"What's the problem?" Webster asked.

"We need to be outside, sir."

Webster pushed his chair back. "Wait here."

"Now what?" Spade grumbled as he watched Webster follow the two men from the restaurant, then returned to his apple pie.

Maxwell sipped her coffee. Instinct told her that this visit by the sheriff's department could be connected to their inability to reach Falk. Were he and Koski okay?

Spade was scraping his plate so as not to miss a crumb of crust when Webster returned.

"Bad news. They've just discovered the deputy I assigned to show Falk and Koski the hang-glider location—dead; locked in the trunk of his patrol car up at Spooner. Falk's jeep was parked nearby but no sign of him or Koski." Spade and Maxwell pushed their plates aside and rose. "There's a search party going over the area right now," Webster added. "Let's go."

When they arrived at the scene, local television and press were already nosing around. Spade and Maxwell followed Webster as he silently shoved through the crowd among shouted questions.

"The incident officer will issue a statement later," Webster said in the reporters' general direction, flashing his badge to a deputy who waved the three into the area.

Maxwell ducked under the line of police tape that cordoned off the squad car and surrounding area. She could see the trunk was open and a CSI photographer was preserving the dead body on film.

"How was he killed?" Webster asked the deputy.

"One shot to the head at close range." He shook his head. "Poor bastard was just doing his job…never had a chance."

Maxwell watched in silence as the crime scene investigators worked around and in the squad car. She had worked with CSI people and knew how determined they were in digging up clues that might otherwise be trampled on and lost. They were meticulous, able to coax a clue from the seemingly most insignificant evidence, painstakingly measuring minute distances and trajectories, utilizing everything from high-tech equipment to Q-tips.

She thought about how far the science of criminology had come since her father was a police officer in the '60s. As a child, she could sit and listen for hours as he related events of his days on the force. Forensics amazed him.

"I'm only a beat cop," he'd say. "What do I know? I don't even understand how those people in the lab can figure out what *type* blood it is let alone whether a blood spot on an object is old or recent, the angle at which the blood hit the object, the velocity of the blood as it hit the object…" He shook his head and added brightly, "Pretty soon the perps won't stand a chance."

As she followed the deputy through the trees, Maxwell

thought cynically that perps will always stand a chance and wondered if her father was still alive.

The reason she had not spoken to him in years flooded not only her mind but all her senses, stirring the old animosity. It was the killing of her best friend's father by her own father when Maxwell was a teenager. Her mind blinked at the thought and she managed to push away the chill of memory.

Suddenly Spade was at Maxwell's side. "They've unearthed another body a hundred yards away. We'd better take a look."

She shuddered, dreading taking that look, knowing that Falk and Koski had been in the area but she breathed a sigh of relief when she saw the dead man. Half his face was blown away but it was plainly not Falk. The corpse was dressed as a deputy but wore white socks and brown shoes.

"A couple of usable footprints here," Webster said to the deputy. "One set small enough to be a woman's. You took casts?"

The officer shook his head. "Not deep enough. Maybe CSI can work up something."

A member of the search party ran back into the clearing and reported tire marks indicating that a vehicle had driven through the woods and departed by an old logging road nearby.

Maxwell, Webster and Spade turned from the scene and headed for their sedan but not before a covey of men and women who incessantly cackled questions approached. Maxwell blinked to dispel the red dots that swirled in her vision as the reporters and TV news crews surrounded them, making their departure a flash bulb event. Now and then, one shouted question managed to isolate itself from the others.

"Doctor Maxwell, do you have any idea who is responsible for these murders?" a loud, deep baritone from the *Reno Gazette-*

Journal wanted to know.

"Not yet," she said as she kept walking. "We'll let you know when we do."

"Do you suspect Native Americans?" the deep baritone persisted.

Maxwell crinkled her brow. "No."

"So, you're saying that other than Native Americans are responsible?"

"No, I'm saying…" Another flash went off in her face and she realized that a photographer had caught her mid-sentence. "I'm saying that we don't know yet."

"Highly placed sources say that the Nevada Mafia has hired a team of terrorists to kill all who oppose the spread of Indian gaming," a female reporter insisted, pushing a microphone at Maxwell. "Can you confirm that?"

"No."

"Then you're saying that the Mafia is *not* responsible?"

Webster suddenly swept an arm in front of Maxwell, creating a path for her. "She said we don't have any information we can give you yet," he shouted in an authoritative voice Maxwell never heard him use before.

She turned up the collar of her heavy coat and buried her hands deep into the pockets as she, Spade and Webster climbed into their vehicle, wondering about the fate of their two companions.

Chapter 8

"Keep your eyes on the road," the man in the back seat growled at Falk. "We don't want any accidents."

Falk drove Highway 50, which wound down the wide sweeps

and curves descending into the Carson Valley. They were more than thirty-five miles from Virginia City. As long as he followed orders he and Koski would stay alive.

He glanced in the rear view mirror and caught Koski's vision riveted to the same reflective rectangle. He tried to read her eyes and realized that neither fear nor terror resided there. Her eyes were smoking; her lips pressed tightly together. She wasn't afraid. She was pissed off.

He slowed for the traffic light at 395. A couple more miles and they'd pass through Carson City. The light changed and he moved forward.

"As we go through Carson," the man said, "stay within the speed limit. Keep to the right and let anyone who wants to pass go ahead. Got it?"

"No problem," Falk muttered and in the next instant caught Koski's vision again. Her eyes rolled skyward in apparent frustration. What was the woman thinking? What would she have him do?

Koski silently steamed. When she started this assignment, she had been…well, she had overheard Spade call her "beautifully indifferent." Perhaps she *had* been apathetic. Nevertheless, she was involved now and wanted to get this situation over with— offensively and quickly. Falk liked to appear self-sufficient so why wasn't there some FBI magic he could pull out of a hat? They had come all this way and he had done nothing but obey the scumbag beside her.

Periodically throughout the journey the man pulled his gun away from the side of her head and rested it on his knee, always keeping it aimed directly at her. It was beginning to look as if deliverance was going to be up to her. She had to figure a way to get hold of that gun.

"What do you want from us?" Falk suddenly asked, moving his head slightly so he could see the man's face in the mirror.

"Doing my job."

"Does that include killing us like the real deputy your friend impersonated? Why didn't you just kill us back there?"

"Too many shots fired in those parts. We're going to Virginia City as ordered. A quiet town…a good place to…" his voice trailed off.

Falk shifted into low gear for the steep, winding hill that signaled the approach to Virginia City.

"Okay," the man said, "there's a side road coming up about a quarter of a mile on the right, turn in there."

Falk knew at once if he made the transfer to a deserted rural trail their situation would worsen. At least here, near the city, small as it was, there was the potential for help. The car suddenly gave a lurch as it jolted across a pothole. Falk glanced back and saw that both passengers had their seat belts fastened. The realization spawned an idea.

The highway dipped at an angle at the turn and the shoulder fell away to a deep trench on the right side of the road. Letting up off the gas, Falk immediately hit the accelerator, repeating this pattern several times. The old Chevy shuddered and jerked, stuttering forward.

"The engine's about to quit," Falk shouted. "According to the gauge, we're not out of gas. We've got a problem." He knew oncoming darkness made it difficult for the man behind him to see his feet and the situation he was creating. "You want me to stop?" he asked, his voice quivering with each alternate rev and sputter of the automobile.

Startled and aggravated by the sudden lurches, Falk's captor unhooked his seat belt and leaned forward, attempting to examine the dashboard for possible red lights that might indicate the cause of the trouble. Yanking hard on the steering wheel, Falk jammed the gas pedal to the floor in the same instant. The car lurched violently from the sudden acceleration and powered into a nosedive over the shoulder and into the ditch. The man's head was slammed against the window frame with a sickening crunch then whipped back and smashed against the doorpost.

Koski, still strapped within the security of her seat belt, reacted instinctively and grabbed the gun.

The tortured engine stalled and Falk turned and looked back. Their companion was out cold. Koski seemed shaken but unhurt. "You okay?" he asked.

She followed him from the wreck, the automatic in her hand. "You don't give a damn if I'm okay or not!"

Falk was stunned by her words.

She stopped and rotated her head and shoulders to relieve the tension in her neck. "Jesus," she went on derisively, "I was beginning to think you were *never* going to make a move."

They were back to square one in their relationship. "You're serious, aren't you?" Falk asked. "Did you forget what they teach at Quantico about hostage situations? Remain calm. Do not jump into actions that are not well thought out. Choose your moment carefully...Did you forget that?"

"I *never* forget—anything."

"Don't take everything so personally, Koski."

She reacted as if she had been slapped.

Falk didn't believe they were having this absurd conversation. All he could do was move on quickly. "Look," he said, keeping his voice under control, "let's both shut up and do what we have to do here."

He climbed out and headed for the trunk. "We're going to tie up our *faux* deputy and stuff him in the trunk." He lifted the lid. "You'll wait in the front of the car for the first vehicle that comes along. Tell them to take this guy to FBI Reno and they can take you back to whatever cave you hang upside down in each night."

He regretted it as soon as he said it.

In the gathering darkness and silhouetted by a faint glimmer of moonlight, Koski had what looked like smoke coming from her ears. It was only her warm breath in the cold air.

"Now *you* listen," she said, her voice low but more bitter than the wind. "I didn't ask to be put on this fucking assignment with you. It was thrust upon me. It's my job, which I happen to need right now but you wouldn't understand that. All you understand is your crippling, neurotic obsession with solitude. You exude it. I consider being able to read people to be part of my job and mister, you're an open book. Whether you like it or not, I'm in this now and I'm going to stay until we find out who's killing lawyers and why."

She paused and stood unmoving, the outburst having left her drained. "So, we're going to tie and gag this guy, leave him by the side of the highway with a note for whoever finds him, get this car out of the ditch and get back to Reno to connect with the other members of this so-called team."

Falk realized his mouth was open. It not only was what Koski had said, although it made sense on a level he'd explore later, but what he had been thinking. Preparing to leave this woman in the car. Of course, she would not have been alone but—worse—she would have been in the car with a would-be killer! If somehow he managed to—.

He took several deep breaths and then shrugged in a conciliatory way. She had him pegged but he, too, had been right. She was fighting a war with something, a war that probably would not end until she got something...or maybe until she gave something.

His dark brows arched mischievously. "Is there any truth to the rumor that a poor sucker in the Las Vegas PD put the moves on you too heavily and you yanked his balls off?"

Koski was silent before finally, striking a mental balance, she dropped her arms by her side and replied offhandedly, "Ask "her.""

Falk grinned. "Okay, we'll leave him here with a note." He took a sheet from a pocket organizer and began to write. "We can't get this car out of the ditch ourselves. It'll require a tow truck."

"You're right." She grabbed the assault weapon and her equipment from the trunk.

"What else is in that trunk?" he asked as he continued writing.

She rummaged around. "A rusty jack, jumper cables, chains, an old blanket. That's about it."

"Take the blanket," he said. "We might need it."

She did a double take. "An old blanket?"

He finished writing the note. "Help me get him back here."

Once the semi-conscious man was stuffed into the trunk, Falk made a slit in one corner of the note with a fingernail and forced the paper over the button of the man's shirt. It read: CALL FBI RENO. THIS MAN KILLED A DEPUTY SHERIFF. AGENT FALK, FBI.

Falk caught sight of a leather bag in the corner of the trunk. "Bingo! An *old* cell phone, the kind that rings, operated by battery or from the cigarette lighter in a car." He hung the bag around his neck, wrapped the AK-47 in the blanket and slung it over his shoulder.

As Koski gathered up her video equipment, Falk thought he was beginning to like the pint-sized pain in the ass but as for someone to rely on as a partner? She'd missed the cell phone and had not thought of using the blanket to conceal the rifle. As always, the only one he could truly rely on was himself. They started walking back to Highway 50.

Suddenly he grabbed her arm, pulling her deep into the shadows at the side of the road as a car approached. The evening was dark enough for the vehicle to require headlights, which swept a bright arc as it passed.

"Why'd you do that?" Koski asked, pulling her arm free from his grasp. "We've got to flag a ride to Reno and there's little enough traffic on this road."

Falk returned to the side of the highway and she followed. "Koski, hasn't it occurred to you that somebody knew that Webster arranged for a deputy to escort us to Spooner and that same somebody probably arranged for this guy and his partner to kill us?"

He did not wait for her response. "Whoever is killing lawyers also is out to get us and has the help of an insider—somebody *deep* inside. The best thing we can do right now is stay out of sight and continue the investigation on our own."

"What about Webster, Maxwell and Spade? Shouldn't we let them know?"

"If we contact them now they may inadvertently give us away. Maybe with us gone missing, it'll make them more aware of the danger they're in. Hopefully, they can make some progress on their end as to what's really going on." He didn't add that he had not ruled out any of them as suspects.

"Okay," she said, "what do we do in the meantime?"

"There's a group of old buildings on the hillside up there." He saw them when they drove past earlier and wondered if she had noticed.

"Old buildings?"

He felt some disappointment that she had not but he went on. "They looked like part of an abandoned mining operation. We'll lay low there until morning."

"Lay low in an old shed, all night. You know how cold it gets up here this time of year?"

"If our friend's pals track us down, we'll be a damn sight colder for a lot longer." He figured she got the point because she fell into silence as they rounded a bend and headed toward the hill.

After fifteen minutes of picking their way over rough, steep, stony terrain, they came to an old wooden shack that seemed sturdy. Moonlight found its way through the open door and allowed a dim look at the single room. The one window was paned though streaks of filth prevented a view.

"Must have been a storeroom at one time," Falk said. Constructed on a concrete slab, it contained a table, shelving along three walls and an old, wooden chair with three legs, for which someone had engineered a cure by propping a block of wood where the missing leg had been.

"Perfect hideout," Koski said sarcastically. "For sure, no one would expect two well-trained federal agents to hole up in here."

Ignoring her, he dragged a piece of cardboard from one of the shelves and pressed it against the grimy window. "Hold this cardboard until I find some kind of prop." He turned on the flashlight, finally located a couple of rusty nails and tapped them into the wooden frame with a piece of iron pipe. Then he placed the flashlight on the floor, partially covering the beam with an edge of the blanket, allowing a slither of light to illuminate the room.

Falk was removing the AK-47 from the blanket when suddenly he reached and switched off the light. "Listen!"

It was the throbbing sound of a car being driven very slowly that made Falk's body stiffen. Not a vehicle passing by on the highway, as others had. "I'm going to open the door a touch," he whispered. "Don't move, okay."

"Okay."

He leaned toward the door and inched it open a crack, the bottom dragging on the concrete floor. The engine sound was closer now. He saw headlights as the automobile crept slowly along the side road. Its high beams, wide and glaring, revealed the old Chevy in the ditch; the vehicle stopped.

Falk watched through the partially open door. Two men ran forward and checked the interior of the old car with their own headlights illuminating the eerie scene. Moving to the rear, they jammed an iron bar under the trunk hinge and levered up, forcing the lid open with a metallic groan, and lifted the wriggling body to the ground.

While one man ripped off the sign and read it, his companion removed the captive's gag and untied him. Wild gesticulations indicated a heated discussion, then one of them pointed up the hill in Falk's direction. He pushed the door shut but his body reacted to a voice in his ear.

"They figure we're up here," Koski whispered. She had been looking over his shoulder.

"I told you not to move and you said…" He stopped. It was no use. She would do as she pleased.

"If we stay here, it'll only be a matter of time before they find us. Let's use the cell phone and call 911."

"Koski, we're in a deserted shack on an isolated hillside outside Virginia City. I couldn't even give an exact location."

"Those operators use global positioning, don't they? They can pinpoint general areas at least. It's worth a try."

Falk did not have time to argue. He felt around the floor for the phone, not daring to turn on the flashlight. "Where is the damn thing?"

"Here." She reached into his jacket pocket where he had put it after taking it from around his neck and produced the leather case.

The silence was shattered abruptly as the phone rang. Koski gasped, dropping the phone but its ringing continued.

Lunging forward, Falk scooped it up, ripped the door open and flung the thing as far as he could into the night. The ringing diminished as it arced out over the hill, thudded to the ground and then stopped.

Falk swore softly. "Our friend told them we took the phone and that it wasn't the type to chirp or vibrate so they dialed the number to zero in on our location by the ring."

The first arrow thudded into a wooden shack nearby and a bright flash ignited into flames.

"Quick!" He slammed the door shut and scooped up the blanket, keeping the AK-47 at his side. "They're burning the buildings…firing arrows with incendiary tips." While Koski gathered up the rest of their gear, he said, "When I open the door, move fast, stay low and hug the side of the building. Go around back, keeping the building between you and the fires." He slid the door open, seeing hot embers sparkle and singe the night air.

"Be careful. I'll cover you. If you hear shots, don't look back, just keep going to the top of the hill and you'll see the lights of Virginia City."

She burst out, her equipment slung across her back. Falk lunged through the opening into the darkness and the smell of ruined wood. He nearly reached the corner of the building when— THWAK—an arrow slammed into the door. He glanced back as it hissed into action, spewing blinding white phosphorus and splattering the building with fire. He bounded, crouching, following the sound of Koski's boots as they scraped over the rocks.

The fires would be visible from the city less than a quarter of a mile away and the alarm raised. He did not want to be discovered by fire or police units. Everyone was their enemy now, even innocents who might lead their pursuers to them.

He was breathing hard by the time he caught up with Koski just below the rim of the hill. Hugging the earth, she fought back a cough in the choking air, the veins in her neck pronounced. He dropped to the ground beside her.

"If we go over the top," she rasped, "we'll be backlit by the flames."

He patted her shoulder. "Good thinking. We'll stay just below the ridge. Keep moving to the right toward that large outcropping of rocks. Ready?"

She grunted and together they moved, hunched shadows, farther and farther away from the fires until they reached the outcropping. Calling a halt, Falk sank among the monumental, cave-like boulders, listening for the slightest sound of a chase. Koski landed beside him.

"Stay here," he said. "I'm going to the top of the ridge and take a look."

"Okay," he heard her say as he fell to his belly and elbowed his way to the ridge. Cautiously raising his head, he saw only the lights of Virginia City glowing in the distance.

"Why would they attract attention by torching the buildings?" Koski had wriggled up beside him, her normally husky voice even smokier. "They could have just come up the hill and shot us."

"They knew we had the AK-47 as soon as they spoke to scumbag. Playing it safe…burning the huts in an effort to smoke us out into their path. They'll either assume that we were caught in the fire or they'll come looking for us again in daylight when the emergency units are gone."

They returned to the boulders and he handed her the old blanket. "I think we'll be safe here for the rest of the night. I'll take first watch while you try to get some sleep." He cocked the weapon and thumbed the safety to off.

Chapter 9

A radial engine seaplane banked over the Gulf of Mexico, early morning sunlight reflecting on the cockpit windows as the aircraft straightened direction for its approach. It swayed slightly in a light crosswind before touching down, its pontoons making a graceful feather of white on the blue-green lagoon. The engine throttled back, the sudden snarl startling a flock of flamingos from their wading and feeding to take flight, their outstretched necks resembling a squadron of supersonic transports.

The pilot made a wide, arcing turn, moving in close to a white, fine-grained beach. Big Pine Key was one of many in the chain stretching from Key Largo to Key West.

Palm trees crowded down to the sea, bright tropical flowers belied it was autumn in the Florida Keys. Before the propeller stopped, an inflatable Zodiac put out from the shore, its blunt nose curving upward, thrust forward by powerful twin outboards as it closed in on the seaplane.

A door in the plane's fuselage swung open and a powerfully built man with a strong face, a mass of red, unruly hair and dressed in a black jumpsuit waved toward the Zodiac that came alongside. The redhead, Rodney Eiker, a hard-boiled British soldier of fortune, sloshed gum from one side of his mouth to the other, chewing furiously, snapping and crackling it.

Ten minutes later, Eiker stood on the balcony of the hotel room that was reserved for him, overlooking the bay.

Rod Eiker was born in Manchester, England. At eighteen, he joined the British Army, served in the Middle East and Asia, then transferred to the Special Air Service at twenty-two. He relinquished his rank of sergeant, as do all non-commissioned or commissioned members of the British Army when they volunteer for SAS.

Time proved him an outstanding candidate in all phases of the elite service's strenuous training program. Posted to Belfast, Ireland, he re-earned the rank of sergeant in charge of a plainclothes detachment specializing in undercover and sabotage. Eighteen months later, he was commissioned first lieutenant and transferred to SAS headquarters, Hereford, UK.

Now, years later, Eiker had decided that this would be his last hire. Forty-three was old for the mercenary business.

He scanned the beach and surrounding area, remembering the day he was approached for the assignment. It was in the Green Man, a small pub on O'Connell Street in Dublin. Halfway through a pint of Guinness, Eiker felt a tap on his shoulder. He recognized the man as a mercenary recruiter he'd seen in other places around the world; a man who generally sought the best professional killers available. Eiker moved with him to a table in a dark corner of the pub. Two pints later, the deal was made. Two days later, Eiker flew to Miami, then here.

Now the phone rang and he went back into the room and plucked it from a side table.

"Yes?" he uttered in a voice lower and as unlike his own as he could manage.

A nondescript male voice softly asked, "Have I reached the party to whom I am to be connected?"

Eiker's quirky sense of humor made him wait to answer. It was the prearranged code question but it suddenly sounded so asinine that he was tempted to reply in the negative and hang up. Instead, he answered in the also prearranged counter code. "Yes, the green man."

"Right," the voice said, satisfied. "Get some rest. You'll need to be up early. You'll return to Miami tomorrow morning. Sorry about the circuitous route."

Eiker grunted, familiar with backtracking to avoid a tail, and the man continued, "There'll be a first class ticket to Las Vegas in the name of Taddington—an alias I understand you've used in the past and for which you have appropriate identification—at the Delta Airlines desk at Miami International for Flight 145. Someone will meet you upon arrival and take you to your meeting."

"Right," Eiker said and immediately hung up. He crossed the room again, glancing at his reflection in the wall mirror. Instinctively, his hand went to his left ear, which had an old scar and a mangled lobe—a constant reminder of a debt incurred in Nevada years ago and yet to be paid.

The next day, a black BMW and driver awaited him at McCarren International in Las Vegas. Eiker was familiar with the city and enjoyed the ride along Tropicana Avenue that paralleled The Strip, past the intersection of Paradise and Desert next to the Convention Center.

He looked forward to meeting with his new employer, who hired him for about the price of an American League baseball pitcher. His new boss also managed to stay at the top of the pyramid that was the Nevada Mafia.

Chapter 10

The view from Tony Villachi's penthouse made the lights of Las Vegas appear to be twinkling jewels scattered across a black velvet display cloth. Villachi, however, was not a man to appreciate the aesthetic beauty of this display, only that it represented money and power painfully attained through ulcers, irritable bowel syndrome, diverticulitis and hypertension.

He pulled deeply on his Havana cigar, turned from the window and took his seat at the head of a long cherry-wood conference table, the gleaming surface of which reflected the faces of six men; the core of Nevada's gambling interests.

"Gentlemen," he mumbled as cigar smoke seeped from his nostrils, "I called you here to give you yet another example of why I sit at the head of this table while you are on the sidelines, so to speak." His pause gave the others a chance to redden, exchange glances or nervously sip from water glasses.

Attaining riches and power had not served to produce contentment, good health or a polished veneer to Tony Villachi's weathered appearance, frail body and rancorous personality. He was a short, small-boned man with thinning, stubborn gray hair and awning eyebrows. It was said that Villachi's wife also was from humble beginnings. She wallowed in her husband's wealth, a heart of gold type who gloried in the glamour with which the aging don surrounded her. Acquaintances secretly dubbed them "Happy and Grumpy."

The insiders at Villachi's table attributed the campaign of terror against lawyers to the don. In fact, it was hatched in the mind of The Fox; that was how The Fox wanted it. The Fox did not require a powerful, high profile presence. He preferred it to appear as if others were making the decisions when, in reality, it was the other way around.

"Hasn't it occurred to any of you," Villachi grumbled, "that there is money to be made in the fact that most of our local legal beagles are *against* the spread of Indian gaming because, like you, they want to keep as much money as possible in Nevada?"

He paused, his head steady while his eyes swept around the table but no one spoke, awaiting his point. "What would *you* do?" he growled. "How would *you* feel if you were a Nevada lawyer and your fellow attorneys were dropping like flies just because they opposed Indian casinos?"

This time he only paused for a nanosecond. He was getting to his bottom line and didn't want to take the chance one of his colleagues might guess what he was about to suggest and steal his thunder. He leaned forward. "You'd shit your shorts and scream for help, for Chrissake!"

Some of the men simply nodded. Others' eyes evidenced that they had begun to fathom the fortuitous circumstance to which Villachi alluded. The old don continued.

"Every lawyer in this state who's done anti-Indian gambling work is looking over their shoulder right now, wondering if they'll be next. They know better than to count on the local police." He stabbed his cigar into a large, smoked glass ashtray at his elbow, enlivened by his own words. "These people need *protection…*"

A heavyset man in an expensive suit to Villachi's left pounded the table, getting the message. "And *we're* going to provide it!"

Another middle-aged, overweight man frowned. "You're saying that we're going to ask *them* to pay *us* for protection against…what we're doing to them?"

Villachi eased back in his chair. "You bet your sweet ass we are."

The others began to get it and speculated aloud as to just how such extortion could be arranged.

Heavyset's deep baritone drowned out the other voices. "We'll need out-of-town, high-tech muscle to enforce payment… somebody who, if caught, can't be traced back to us…maybe somebody from the fuckin' Russian Mafia or—"

"Hold it, hold it, for Chrissake!" Villachi rankled. "As usual, I'm one step ahead of you." He looked into each face, appreciating the moment. "Tomorrow I'm meeting with a kick-ass British mercenary with a reputation for putting together the kind of small, efficient group we'll need to persuade our…esteemed…" Villachi lingered, "members of the bar that they need us on their side."

A tall, ascetic-looking man leaned forward and turned toward Villachi. "Harry's right, Tony." He nodded toward the middle-aged man who had questioned Villachi's logic. "It doesn't make sense that we're paying big bucks for somebody to do lawyers and, at the same time, we're going to hire a high-priced outsider to *protect* them."

Villachi's face reddened and his dark, cool eyes locked on the man. "Nobody's *really* going to protect them, Frank. We're just going to make them *pay* for it." He snorted and made eye contact with the others.

Satisfied they were all on the same page, he attempted to lighten the mood. "Jesus, Frank," he elbowed the man good-naturedly, "you one of those people who dimple your chads instead of punching 'em all the way through?"

A ripple of laughter went around the table and Villachi took the moment to get up and wave toward the full bar at one end of the room. "Stay, all of you...relax...have a drink. I wish I could join you but..." he patted the spot where his ulcers resided and let his words trail off.

Yes, Villachi thought as he left the room, the idea of extracting protection money from the lawyers was his inspiration; a serendipitous outgrowth of the terror campaign that even The Fox had failed to recognize.

Villachi was concentrated on that campaign. To date, his associate in Carson City had handled it pretty well; as yet no one had come up with any real suspects in the killings. The associate, however, only had one more job to do, then that aspect of the operation would phase out. It was time for the big guns.

The British soldier of fortune was perfect. He would operate in and out of state and could not be connected to Villachi in any way. He'd scare the shit out of the local lawyers until they paid through the nose and increase the pressure on the Indians, believing—as did those saps in the conference room—that Villachi's true objective was to stop the spread of Indian gambling.

Chapter 11

Maxwell sat in her Reno hotel room, nursing vodka over ice. The neon lights of the "Biggest Little City in the World" glowed outside her window. It had been two days since Falk and Koski disappeared. In the short time they were together during their briefing with Falk, she had quickly formed a fondness for the two.

Younger than Maxwell, Koski was what Maxwell called gritty, quick, capable but with a 'tude. Instinctively, Maxwell felt that the petite-size footprints at the scene in the woods were Koski's. She hoped to God that Falk and Koski were not in serious trouble.

Why hadn't they contacted the rest of the team? Webster could be reached at his office most of the time, fielding questions by increasingly irritated reporters. Why didn't Falk and Koski call? Had they, for some reason, determined that they couldn't trust the others? Certainly, they could trust *her*...and Spade and Webster...

She paced a few minutes before settling down again, awaiting a call from Webster as to their next move.

She decided to pass the time by reading a noir detective novel she purchased in the lobby gift shop. Her admiration for authors who wrote darkly about what they had lived in their professions was high. She wished she could do it, the prospect seen as scoring a double whammy in the marketability department. Not only was she a medical examiner, she also might be one of the few female African-American MEs writing in the genre.

Alas, she had long ago dismissed the idea as preposterous. She had never even taken a creative writing class. Beyond that, she firmly believed there already were too many writers and not enough readers.

She was reading the first chapter of the novel when the phone rang.

"Hi, Doc." It was Spade. "Got a minute?"

"Sure, Alex. What's up?"

"My wife and I were wondering if you'd like to have dinner with us here at the house. We're only ten minutes away. I could pick you up at the hotel."

She was both surprised and pleased at the offer. "Sure we wouldn't be breaking some federal rule?" she asked, mocking the many admonitions they'd received about secrecy.

Spade caught her meaning and laughed. "Don't think so. At least we haven't been forbidden to fraternize. Webster can reach you here. Will you come?"

"Certainly, give me a call from the lobby." She hung up and went to a mirror, running her fingers through her short, thick hair, wondering what to wear. She kicked off her terry mules and padded into the bathroom. Five minutes later she was ready. In a zip-front denim dress from J. Peterman and white NB 800 walking shoes, she slung an indigo boucle cardigan over one shoulder.

Now she looked for the right purse. She'd made up her mind as soon as the team was formed never to go anywhere without her Walther P38, which she both needed and reviled. Registered to carry the weapon in Nevada, she felt lost—even dining at a colleague's home—without the sense of security it offered.

She reached into a chest drawer beside her. She extracted her hand, as if stung. The gun's very presence stirred painful memories of her father. If she kept the gun available, would she, too, one day commit the unforgivable? Once this assignment was over she would officially dispose of it. Meanwhile, she'd tuck it down into the purse she chose for the evening and forget it existed.

Maxwell found she was at ease with Spade's wife, Flo, whose home-cooked meal was a pleasant break from hotel food. During the evening, Spade seemed careful to keep his part of the bargain with the government; there was no talk of the investigation or the missing agents. As far as Flo was concerned, Maxwell was in Reno doing routine work with the PD.

"When Alex told me you were stuck alone in a hotel room I said we must have you over."

They were seated in the living room; Maxwell on the sofa, Spade in what was obviously his chair, a well-used recliner. Flo dispensed coffee from her chair next to the coffee table. "I did wonder why you had to stay in town when you live in Carson City. I know so many people who commute every day."

Maxwell and Spade exchanged glances. "It's only for a few days," Maxwell lied, as she accepted a coffee cup from Flo. "Sort of a get-together…need to be on the spot, so to speak."

"That's the government for you. Alex will be retiring soon and it'll all be behind us. Right, hon?"

Spade smiled from behind his coffee cup. "Right," he said emphatically.

Maxwell excused herself to use the bathroom. While she washed her hands, she decided to peek out the window, idly curious to see the backyard. Switching off the light, she peered out. As her eyes grew accustomed to the darkness, she saw several small evergreens, a few bare deciduous trees, a patio and a medium-sized lawn featuring a Mexican fireplace with an Arizona flagstone surround.

Suddenly her peripheral vision picked up a quick movement where the fence and garage met. She pulled back automatically before easing forward. There it was again. Someone was out there. She had a moment of indecision.

Considering the events of the last few days with Falk and Koski gone missing, she shouldn't take any chances. She couldn't bring herself to reach into her purse. If she had, she would only fling the weapon from her, abhorring its hold on her instincts.

She saw the movement outside again. A darkened figure detached itself from the bushes and monkey-walked toward the house, hugging the garage wall to remain in shadow.

She envisioned the living room with French doors opening onto the patio...the drapes pulled back...light streaming out into the darkness, making perfect targets of those in the living room.

She opened the bathroom and quickly slipped out into the dark, narrow hallway. She had to think fast. If she went back into the room she, too, would be on the stage of light...Then she walked into Flo.

"Oh," Flo exclaimed, "there you are. I was wondering if you were having trouble with the flusher. Sometimes we have to jiggle the handle—"

Maxwell stopped her by grabbing her arm. "Do you have a phone in the bedroom?" Flo's face registered such surprise and fright at the sudden question that Maxwell had to repeat herself. *"Do you?"*

"Yes but—"

"Get on it right now. Call 9ll. Tell them someone's breaking into your house and they're armed. Hurry!"

She pushed past Flo and raced to the end of the hallway adjoining the living room. Standing back from the entrance, she could see Spade in the recliner and called softly, "Alex, come into the hallway, *quick*!" He looked up as if unsure he'd heard. "Now," she hollered. "Move it, Alex!"

The urgency in her voice removed his doubt. He flung himself out of the chair in the exact instant the sound of breaking glass split the air. He lunged into the hallway, stumbling and falling to his knees.

Righting himself, he wheezed, "What the hell..." He looked back into the living room and, after a moment of realization, gasped, "Where's Flo?"

"She's okay...on the phone in the bedroom, calling 911. I saw someone in the backyard moving toward the house." She peered into the vacated room. "Son of a bitch!" she said, hearing Spade inhale convulsively beside her. An arrow was buried in the upright portion of Spade's recliner, which backed up to the shattered French door. The ugly point of the arrow was jutting almost a foot through the back of his chair. Shards of glass were strewn across the carpet.

"Alex, are you all right?" It was Flo calling from the bedroom.

"Go talk to her," Maxwell said, "but keep her in the bedroom for now. Do you have another phone?"

"Only the car phone. Why?"

"I changed purses before I left the hotel and my cell is in there. I'm going to call Webster. He's in command in Falk's absence. He'll want to be here when the cops arrive."

Breathing heavily, Spade went to a sideboard and picked up the car keys. "Here, you'll have to switch on the ignition to make the phone work."

"Alex...can you hear me?" Flo wailed from the bedroom.

Maxwell grabbed the keys. Pausing to look around to be sure the assailant was not in the area, she bolted out the front door.

She reached Webster at FBI Reno and told him what happened.

"Can you remove the arrow from the chair?" he asked.

"I don't know. I can try."

"*Do it*. We don't want the local law enforcement officers

messing with it."

"If I remove the arrow what do we tell the cops? The glass door is shattered...glass all over the floor...there'll be a hole through the back of Alex's chair that'll be difficult to explain."

"Think of something," he replied and the phone call turned to the buzz of a dial tone.

"Thanks a lot."

Maxwell returned to the house. She went to the living room and quickly extracted the arrow from the chair. The projectile was identical to the others. The seemingly indestructible weapon had suffered no discernible effects from the force of smashing through the tempered glass and the chair. It crossed her mind that whatever the arrow was made of should be used in automobile construction.

She raced out to the car and placed the arrow under the back seat. As she did, she noticed a blanket and scooped it up. Returning to the house, she told Spade about her call to Webster. She placed the blanket over the recliner, being careful to cover the front and back of the upright portion.

"Alex," she said, "quickly, tell Flo to sit in the chair. Ask her to not move, just sit and keep her mouth shut while the police are here. Can she do that?" Still visibly shaken, Spade nodded numbly. "Good," Maxwell continued, "I'll answer all questions when the cops arrive. I'll say you and Flo are too shaken up."

"You...you'll have that right," he mumbled and headed back to the bedroom and Flo.

Webster arrived, playing the visiting friend, just as the dumbfounded police officers were leaving after checking the grounds and writing the incident off as a bizarre attempted break-in.

When Flo went to put on a fresh pot of coffee, Webster turned to Maxwell. "That was inspired…putting the blanket over the chair…having Mrs. Spade sit there." Maxwell shrugged but there was some pride in her face.

"Webster," Spade asked, "what are we going to do?" His body language signaled fatigue and apprehension. "Obviously, whoever is killing lawyers is out to get us, too. They could come back and finish the job." He shook his head. "The last few days on the job and Flo and I are in danger of winding up dead."

Webster put a hand on his shoulder. "I'll put you up in a hotel and arrange for the house to be secured." He sank into an easy chair. "I have an update on Falk and Koski. An abandoned car was found in a ditch near Virginia City. The police have given us reason to believe that Falk and Koski were in the car, at least for a time."

"Any idea where they are now?" Maxwell asked.

Webster shook his head. "It's possible they might still be hiding somewhere in the area."

"Why haven't they contacted you?" Spade wondered.

"It's my hunch that Falk feels there's a leak in local law enforcement. He's taking no chances. If they did manage to escape from whoever was transporting them, they'll probably lay low for a while and then get in touch with us in person."

Flo entered, carrying the tray with cups and a coffee carafe. "A nice cup of hot coffee will make us feel better." She placed the tray on the coffee table.

Webster smiled disarmingly. "Mrs. Spade," he said, "Dr. Maxwell, Alex and I have an important assignment that may take us out of town for several days. Maybe it would be a good idea for you to get away, too…" He turned to Spade before Flo had a chance to reply. "Don't you agree, Alex?"

Spade opened and closed his mouth twice before finally muttering, "Yes, good idea." He turned to Flo. "I wouldn't want you here alone…if we have to be out of town. You can visit your sister in Little Rock since we were going to do that soon anyway."

Flo's eyebrows shot up. She was about to say something but Webster took quick command of the moment. "I'll arrange for you to fly. Alex can pick up your ticket tomorrow morning."

"Well…" Flo started.

"Good…great," Webster said and set his cup and saucer back on the table. "That's settled. I'll call and reserve the ticket tonight… round trip from Reno to Little Rock with the return date open." He stood and started for the door.

Maxwell gathered up her purse and jacket with renewed respect for Webster. His usually quiet, ingratiating manner could morph into a firm, take-charge approach when required and there was no competing authority.

Smiling at Flo, Maxwell said, "Thank you for a lovely dinner. I hope you have a nice trip."

Flo smiled, bewildered, and shrugged.

At the door, Webster turned to Spade. "I'll contact you shortly. I'll arrange for you both to stay at the Hilton tonight. See you at the office at ten a.m."

Maxwell shot a final look at Spade, who looked as if a tornado had swept through his life; no doubt he wondered when he would stop spinning.

Chapter 12

Falk slumped against a boulder, his head propped against another, as he watched dawn streak pale light through weakening darkness, a rippling pink tint fringing the edges of low gray clouds.

Winter soon would claim the mountains, bind them in white, freeze them solid and allow a frigid silence to settle until spring.

He had stayed awake for his last four hours of guard duty and was stiff, cold and hungry. His mind had been busy trying to make sense of the two *faux* deputies who tried to kill them. Who hired them? He must get some answers today.

He looked back, scanning the hillside in the distance where buildings had stood and only charred beams remained. The shed from which they escaped was only a pile of ash, wisps of smoke curling from its ruins. The odor of burnt wood hung in the early morning air.

He ducked quickly, seeing two firefighters on clean-up duty less than a hundred yards away, poking the ashes with long hooked poles. Koski, startled by his sudden movement, jerked awake. He pressed his hand on her shoulder.

"Stay still."

She rubbed her eyes, raked her slender fingers through her tousled hair and mumbled, "If I don't eat soon, I'll stay still, all right. I won't have the strength to get up."

She rolled over and squinted up at him. "How about *I* go into town, get something for us to eat, pick up a few groceries, while you steal a vehicle—"

"*Steal* a vehicle…?"

"*Commandeer* a vehicle, then. Isn't this a national emergency?"

He looked down at her. He wanted to kiss her. They had spent the night together, curled up among the rocks. They had faced death and survived. Perhaps it was because this complex female, with compelling green eyes with tawny specks, was capable of delivering a judo chop and being soft and vulnerable. She snapped open her hand, displaying an empty palm. "How much money do you have?"

A few minutes later, Falk watched her hike over the hill. She had picked up a stick and now swung it casually, looking like an early morning hiker headed toward the slumbering town. They agreed he would follow into town five minutes behind her and find a car to steal.

Once she was out of sight, he felt a strange sense of loneliness. There was a time, only hours ago, when he would have gladly left her and gone off on his own. Now it no longer was an option.

Once in town, Falk turned to the right down a side street, crossed the parking lot behind an old wooden church and noticed a large, black hearse parked under a carport across the street. The sign on the building read: TIDAL AND FLYNN UNDERTAKERS.

Hefting the blanket with the rifle rolled inside, he ambled closer to his objective. Seconds—and a few deft moves in the art of hot wiring—later, he was behind the wheel with the motor running. He checked his watch as he pulled onto the highway.

He was to meet Koski outside the store in three minutes. He heard the sound of a vehicle in the distance. It came up fast behind him. He shaded his eyes against the sun, higher now, a weak, late autumn sun, and glimpsed the automobile. It dipped over a rise shortly before dropping out of sight for a few seconds, cleared the second rise and came into full view.

A rush of adrenaline subsided when Falk saw it was an old pick-up truck, the object of past fender benders, one of dozens to be seen in and around the area. The relic roared past him, its muffler rattling, spewing a pale blue plume of smoke behind.

The clunker had just passed out of sight when Koski left the store, looked both ways and crossed the street. She took no notice of the hearse but scanned the highway for Falk and a fast car. He drove slowly up to her and stopped. She tensed, cautiously eyeing the highly polished vehicle. Recognition dawned as Falk swung open the passenger door. She jumped in fast and he took off.

"Well," she said sarcastically, "this is certainly a nice, low profile vehicle."

Her hair had captured the brisk morning air and when she settled in the seat beside him the hearse smelled fresher. "Figured it wouldn't be missed for a while," he offered in explanation. "You don't see too many funerals this early in the morning."

She held up a white paper sack. "Hot coffee and four bacon sandwiches."

He could have guessed bacon; the sweet, smoky aroma helped dispel the scent of formaldehyde that permeated the vehicle's interior. "Unwrap me one," he said then added, "please." She silently obliged and he stared ahead, chewing, his mind deep in thought. He finished the sandwich and gulped some coffee.

"Honestly," Koski said between bites, "do you really think we can get very far in a stolen hearse?"

Falk shrugged. "Someone said, 'There are those who dare and those who don't, and those who don't sometimes get slaughtered anyway.'" He smiled, pleased that he remembered a quotation appropriate to the occasion. "We'll ditch it once we get to Carson City."

She eyeballed the ignition wires hanging from the steering column. "Marksmanship and grand theft auto were my two best subjects at Quantico, too."

He reached into the bag and started on a second sandwich as they crested a hill. He saw the Washoe Valley in the distance. He laid out his plan between mouthfuls. "Another fifteen minutes and we'll be in Carson. We'll park this monster in a church parking lot in town. Then—"

Suddenly, the two-way radio crackled to life. "Unit one, unit one, do you read?"

"I *knew* it!" Koski growled. "They've already discovered the hearse is missing."

Falk grunted. "Do they really expect us to answer?" He had an idea. "Koski, what else did you buy at the store?"

"Odds and ends in case we had to stay on the road; canned goods, bread, ham, fruit, a few power bars."

"Did you speak to the cashier...think she or he would remember your voice?"

"I was the only customer; they'd just opened. She'd probably remember my face but not my voice...I barely spoke."

"Good. Answer the radio."

"You want me to answer the radio," she repeated dryly.

"Yes but be vague. Say you had to get up to Tahoe in a hurry...some family emergency or some such."

"What! Why?"

"For God's sake, Koski, if they think you're on the way to Tahoe they'll head in that direction." He couldn't believe he had to spell it out for her. "Then we can make it to Carson without the Nevada Highway Patrol on our tail. We have less than ten miles to go." He reached for the microphone and handed it to her. "Wing it."

It was obvious that she still resented taking orders but when she chose to follow them she did it well.

A short time later Falk drove into the parking lot of a small, granite stone church in Carson City. He disconnected one of the wires hanging from the steering column and the engine shuddered to silence.

"Where to now?" Koski asked as she scooped up the groceries.

Falk carefully gathered up the blanket. "To a place where they don't ask questions as long as you pay the bill." She followed as he swung out of the hearse and strolled down a side street out onto Highway 395.

"What place?" she asked, taking two steps to his one in order to keep up.

He replied nonchalantly, as if there wasn't any reason for her to raise an eyebrow, "To a motel."

Chapter 13

At nine in the morning pedestrian traffic on Highway 395—less than a block from the state building in Carson City—was double its normal volume. Civil servants rushed to their cubicles to contend with miles of red tape caused by the flurry of activity from yet another lawyer's demise.

Two FBI agents, in suits distinguished enough to be laid out in, hurried toward the silver-domed Capitol building. The tails of their jackets flapped with their stride. Increased aircraft activity in the area also was becoming the norm of late. The cacophony of a regulation chopper's rotors passed overhead going largely unnoticed.

A man in an empty shop doorway watched the two agents and surreptitiously maneuvered a small device until the red dot it controlled bobbed across the back of one of the agent's jacket.

"Yeah, well, I'm a lawyer, too," the unsuspecting, targeted agent was saying. "My wife doesn't even want me to leave the house in the morning…"

The dot moved in small concentric circles and stopped where a vital, vulnerable organ lay beneath the jacket's wool threads…"and my kids, they've seen enough about "killing arrows" on the six o'clock news to scare the shit out of them…before this, I thought I was too young to retire but right about now all of that Salsa Saturday and Bingo Monday stuff is beginning to sound—" He never finished his sentence as the dancing dot determined its mark at the lower tip of his left shoulder blade.

The second agent might have heard the deep, thick *THUMP* that accompanied the arrow into his companion's heart. He might have seen the blood splatter out of the man's chest onto the beige coat of a woman walking six feet ahead but no one will ever know because he, too, was hit and fell.

"Relax, Don. Agents Falk and Koski going missing only serves to heighten the media's interest in them," claimed Nevada Senator Albert Reinecke. He had made one of his rare visits to Attorney General Lovesy's office and was forced to wade through a sea of reporters to get there. "After all, that was the initial intent."

"I don't like it, Albert," Lovesy said, his red, prickly face slick with sweat. "As ordered, I specifically formed this team to be highly visible at each of the crime scenes…to show the public that we have dedicated professionals on the job. Now, with the two best agents on the team missing, the heat's coming back to my department, defeating the purpose. The news hounds have worked themselves into a frenzy."

"Ah, relax," Reinecke repeated. "Publicity is what we want. All this helps to stoke the fires and put more suspicion on the Indians. He glanced toward the flat screen television set on the wall and leaned across Lovesy's desk, pressing a button on the remote.

A local anchor pictured over the "Breaking News" banner, which was above the crawl at the bottom of the screen, had reported the arrow killing of two FBI agents near the Capitol.

"We expect to have further comment from State Attorney General Donald Lovesy soon," the reporter said. "To date, however, Lovesy has said only that he has a top-level task force investigating these senseless killings. Meanwhile, local Native American leaders, encouraged by remarks from Democratic State Senator Albert Reinecke, are demanding a face-to-face meeting with the governor, claiming that hate and racism are being directed at local tribes—"

Reinecke hit the mute button and turned back to Lovesy with a slight grin. "We couldn't get more ink and air time if we'd hired a press agent."

It was three in the afternoon but Lovesy and Reinecke each held glasses of scotch in their hands. Lovesy set his down and twisted in his seat, his fat knees squeaking against the wood inside the kneehole of his desk.

"I repeat. I don't like what's happening, Albert. Washington has assigned this guy from the NSA, Samuel Ryland, to oversee this investigation. What if he finds out too much?"

Reinecke's voice was steady. "Then you'll have to take care of the situation."

Lovesy's squirming intensified. "When I agreed to be a part of this—and I *only* agreed because I was convinced that halting the spread of Indian gambling would keep Nevada financially strong— I was given to understand that there wouldn't be any killing."

Reinecke's eyebrows shot up. "None of your team has been killed, Don. At least as far as we know."

"Others have, including two of Tony Villachi's men, thanks to their own bungling. I guess agents Falk and Koski proved to be too much for them." He sipped his neat Johnny Walker Black and shook his head. "No, I don't like it, Albert. I don't like the whole thing."

Senator Reinecke was a tall, polished man in his sixties, widowed, with three grown children. He wore large gold rings on his fingers, expensive leather shoes and wool suits. Accustomed to political maneuvering, his face was capable of simultaneously registering self-importance and humility.

Through the years, it seemed that events conspired to bless him with what he most admired—power. In fact, it was his adroit manipulation of the state machine, coached by The Fox, that allowed him to rise in the political ranks until he emerged from nonentity to stellar social and political status.

No one knew about this manipulation. Ostensibly, Reinecke was a champion of Native American rights. The Washoe Indians owned nearly twenty million acres of Nevada. Reinecke, by exhibiting shrewd political prowess, controlled the Washoe tribe.

He was the natural choice to channel the political end of The Fox's campaign against lawyers. He appeared to be aiding the Indian gaming cause, while in fact he weakened it from within. In this way, Reinecke retained control over the tribes and The Fox retained control of Reinecke. Additional impetus for the senator to join forces with The Fox was the fact that Reinecke was dipping into the reservations' tills for years and The Fox knew it.

Reinecke stood up and slowly rubbed a manicured index finger across his sleek, silver mustache. "We don't have to *like* any of this, Don. We just have to do it."

Reinecke turned and left. One of Lovesy's aides immediately

replaced him in the room.

"Sir, the reporters are waiting for a statement, sir," the young aide said nervously.

Lovesy stood and buttoned his jacket over his ample girth. "Kid," he said rhetorically, putting on a forced, philosophical air, "did you ever stop to think that ours is a planet of shit, a stinking outhouse dangling from a rightfully exploding universe?"

"Yes, sir." The aide apparently was accustomed to the AG's rambling, sardonic view of the world. "The reporters, sir…what do we do?"

Lovesy straightened his tie. "We give them a show. There always has to be a show, kid."

Reinecke got back to his office and called Villachi, using his scrambler line, as he always did when being publicly connected. The conversation was brief and one-sided.

"We'll have to do something about Lovesy. He's sweating heavily and the odor will ultimately attach itself to us." There was a grunt on the other end and the line went dead.

Chapter 14

Maxwell was already in Webster's office at BLM Reno when Spade arrived, breathless as usual, and trimmed with camera equipment.

"You get Flo off to Arkansas all right?"

Spade nodded as he sank into a chair. "Yeah, she's excited about it, despite the fact that she's worried about me."

"Worried?" Webster asked. He poured Spade a mug of coffee from a carafe atop a filing cabinet.

"It's funny," Spade said, accepting the mug. "She never had reason to worry about me on the job before but now, after last night, she's afraid this assignment will be my last in more ways than one."

Webster showed obvious concern. "Alex, I'd hoped you would allay any fears she had before she left. Didn't you assure her that you weren't in any danger?"

"I may have not sounded too convincing. I've been married to Flo for thirty years." He paused and sipped his coffee. "She may be naive but she's not stupid."

"Married to you that long," Webster said with his personable smile. "I'm not too sure about her."

Maxwell was in her thirties and single by choice but a part of her silently longed to be in a relationship like what Flo and Alex shared. She immediately corrected her thoughts: relationships were what you had with friends and family. Marriage was a partnership or else it didn't work.

"What's your take on long-term partnerships, Webster?" She had heard that he was thirty-seven, divorced, with no children. It was said that he led a quiet, self-indulgent life in which he sometimes partied hard but was dedicated and good at his job. This morning he looked a little bleary-eyed, as if he had worked late on this assignment last night or had too many beers with his friends.

He smiled with slight embarrassment, signaling his discomfort in discussing his feelings. After a moment he said slowly, "I think it takes a lot of work to make that tiny, inner magic —that can happen in the blink of an eye—last a lifetime."

The frankness and depth of his response impressed Maxwell. She also noted that he quickly changed the subject.

"I've already had two interesting phone calls this morning," he said. "Virginia City Police report that Koski was probably there yesterday morning. The owner of a small grocery store on the edge of town said a woman fitting Koski's description came in and bought coffee, sandwiches and some miscellaneous items. At the same time, a hearse was stolen from a nearby mortuary."

"A hearse!" Spade exclaimed.

Webster nodded. "It was found later in a church parking lot in Carson City."

"What about Falk?" Maxwell asked.

Webster downed the remains of his coffee. "The store owner said Koski bought two coffees, which leads me to conclude that Falk stole the hearse while she bought the provisions."

Maxwell sighed. "At least we know they're alive…or were…"

"So, we're going to Carson now?" Spade asked.

"Not *we*, Alex," Webster said, getting up and sitting on the edge of the desk, facing him. "Maxwell and I need you to stay here in the office." He gestured toward the well-worn couch and the adjoining restroom. "You'll be our base of communication as we try to find Falk and Koski," he paused for emphasis, "which means you cannot leave this office for the next few days."

Spade nodded, looking around. Maxwell thought he was somewhat relieved to have a desk job for the duration.

"Webster, you said you had two interesting phone calls. Who was the second?" Maxwell asked.

He glanced up at the white-faced clock on the wall, its black hands indicating 10:14. "We're having a visitor any minute. We get to meet the man from the National Security Agency Lovesy told us about…who is supposed to be overseeing—"

A light tap on the door interrupted him and all three looked up as the door opened.

"Excuse me," the man who leaned in said in a deep, soft voice. "Your secretary wasn't at her desk so I…"

"Come in, come in," Webster said, rising and extending his hand.

Maxwell took in the details of the NSA agent as introductions were made.

Samuel Ryland was of medium height, in his early forties and dressed in a dark, conservative suit. His hair was black; his face handsome, with a wide forehead, aquiline nose and dark gray eyes softened by a smile that Maxwell thought suggested gentleness and sensitivity.

With two quick strides, he closed the space between Maxwell and himself and took her hand. His palm was cool and smooth as he touched her. She thought his grip lingered a moment longer than necessary in its hold and was timed deliberately.

They took their seats. Ryland preferred to stand.

There was a sense of decisiveness about him, a firm set to his shoulders and a confident attitude that seemed to signify a career man at the NSA.

He said, "I know you're busy, as am I, so I'll keep this brief. Basically, I need some points clarified." He turned to Maxwell. "Doctor, tell me about the arrow that was turned over to you at the sheriff's office in Carson."

It was the embarrassing episode that she and her boss, Chief Bud Vigo, avoided discussing. "I placed it in the evidence locker myself after I examined it," she said, more defensively than intended, "but it subsequently disappeared."

"It was never recovered?"

"Not to my knowledge."

"It was the same as those found in the bodies of the dead lawyers?"

"Yes, employing an electronic guidance system."

They all turned then at a sudden interruption by Roz Newton, Webster's secretary, who had returned to her area and heard their voices.

"Oh," Roz said as she stepped inside the room, "we have a visitor." She turned intelligent blue eyes to Ryland. "Coffee?" she asked in the intimate way that came naturally to extremely physically attractive women.

Maxwell had wondered aloud to Webster earlier as to what secretarial attributes Roz possessed. He seemed indifferent to her striking looks, insisting that she was efficient and possessed extraordinary "people skills."

Now Maxwell scrutinized Roz with Webster's assessment in mind. She was a tall, leggy blonde, about thirty, a little over the age limit to be wearing the Jennifer Lopez outfit she had on: tight, powder-blue sweatshirt and super low-cut, leather-lace jeans. Maxwell thought her a curious mixture between soft-core dream date and, from what Webster said, a master's degree.

"No, thank you," Ryland answered and Roz retreated to her area. The J.Lo logo emblazoned in rhinestones on her butt pocket caught the light of syncopation as she moved.

Webster rose and closed the door. Ryland continued as if no interruption had occurred.

"I'm assuming the arrow embedded in the tree was just a miss of some kind…that some lawyer who was hiking in the area had a lucky day."

"I thought that, too," replied Maxwell.

Ryland nodded and included the two men in his next question. "We've been attempting to factor the range these arrows can cover. Does anyone have a guesstimate on that?"

"I'd say approximately five miles," Webster responded as he

returned to his chair behind the desk. "The last few hundred feet could be under the control of a preset homing device. Whoever has control of these missiles has a pretty sophisticated piece of hardware."

"Yes," Ryland agreed, pacing the floor, "in fact, it may be worse than we thought...we've concluded that these so-called arrows probably have nuclear capability."

Spade, who had been silent until now, let his mouth fall open. "Nuclear!"

"Low-yield, of course," Ryland said, "but potent enough to be termed a nuclear strike if used on almost any type of infrastructure. We can be thankful our enemy hasn't chosen to use the arrows that way."

Webster shook his head. "Does our military have anything like it?"

Ryland scoffed. "Dealing with Middle East terrorists, *Star Wars* systems and LGBs—laser-guided bombs—the Pentagon hasn't put much effort into developing laser-guided arrows." He stopped pacing. "Webster, any news on the rest of the team? I heard about the incident a couple of days ago with the man impersonating a deputy out near the lake."

Webster related the incident at Spade's home the night before. He also relayed what he heard from the Virginia City PD a short time ago and his belief that it was indeed Falk and Koski who "borrowed" the hearse and left it in Carson City. "Doc and I are about to head out to Carson now."

Ryland started toward the door. "Good. Hopefully, their trail won't be too cold."

"Mr. Ryland," Maxwell said, her words delaying his exit, "do you have any information about the man who was playing deputy sheriff...the man who apparently killed the real deputy out near Vista Point?"

"Not a clue." He shook his head. "Keep working on it." Then he was gone.

Webster accelerated to the maximum speed limit as he and Maxwell headed out Highway 50 toward Carson City. After a few minutes of Clint Black and some other C & W artist with whom Maxwell was unfamiliar but surprisingly enjoyed, Webster turned the radio off.

"Doc," he said, "I owe you an apology."

"Oh?"

"Yeah, when we talked for the first time, at the cattle chute where the vic in the tuxedo was found, I can honestly say I figured you for a wise-ass know-it-all. I suspected that either you and Falk or you and I might commit a major act of mayhem against the other before this assignment was over. I thought here is a woman I'll remember long after lunch."

Maxwell's warm brown eyes smiled but she remained silent.

"Well, anyway, I was wrong," he continued. "You're okay. You think like a cop, a good one, and have what I call mental agility and I admire that." He paused, nodding approval of his own words. "I just wanted to put that out there."

"Thanks, Webster." Something in what he said moved her to go to a place she generally avoided and never went voluntarily. "My father was a cop."

"Really? Where?"

"In a small Chicago suburb where I lived until I was seventeen." She had begun and, without any further word from Webster, simply started down the slippery slope of recollection. "God, I loved my father. I was an only child and as a kid, I was so proud of him. I listened to him tell about this or that which happened on his beat, about how he and his partner collared a perp, how they unearthed clues that led to solving cases. To hear him tell it, he was cop, detective, DA, judge and jury, all rolled into one."

"Ah," Webster interjected, "that's why you're into those detective novels."

"Maybe," she said, then went sullen, sucking on her bottom lip before she could go on. "When I was a senior in high school, my father, who had hardly ever unholstered his gun during his previous ten years on the force, shot and killed a brother...Mr. Peck, father of my best friend and classmate, Barbara."

"Oh, wow," Webster exclaimed, no doubt cognizant that he may be privy to thoughts that few, if any, had heard before.

"I *still* don't see why he had to *kill* him." Maxwell's voice quavered and she paused to bring it under control. "Everybody said it wasn't his fault. Apparently, Mr. Peck was a thief with ties to the mob du jour. An official Internal Affairs investigation exonerated my father of any wrongdoing. They found that Mr. Peck drew on my father while committing a robbery and my father fired in self-defense."

As he concentrated on the highway ahead, Webster tried to decide how he should weigh in on this subject. "That must have been tough on you," he ventured, "a teenager in high school...a very fragile time of life...and your best friend's dad...Yet, you couldn't blame your father if—"

"But I *do* blame him. Why *shouldn't* I? *He* did it. *He* killed Barbara's father...and ruined my life." Again she steadied her voice. "Oh, my friends at school didn't exactly persecute me but I believed they somehow blamed me. I felt that my mere presence among my classmates after that was a constant, bitter reminder of the tragedy that traumatized the whole school."

Webster handed her his handkerchief and drove silently, concluding that the situation Maxwell described had been a bum rap all around.

Maxwell dabbed at her eyes and slowly relaxed, pushing her thoughts back into perspective. "I managed to finish out the year and graduate…went off to college. I did go back now and then, mostly to see my mother, but she died five years ago and I haven't been back since the funeral." She handed back the limp, damp square of white cotton. "Nice hanky."

Chapter 15

Falk and Koski checked into a motel room next to the Greyhound bus stop on Highway 395 in Carson. A small parking lot and a liquor store anchored the rundown building. Falk sat on the edge of a sway-backed double bed and lowered the blanket roll to the floor. As he did, one side of the blanket opened and the Kalashnikov clattered to the floor with the sound only an ugly, lethal weapon can make. He picked up the rifle, along with the remaining items Koski had purchased in Virginia City—cans of corn and beans and several power bars.

Koski nodded to her video equipment. "For all the good this has been, I could have left it in the shack on the hillside instead of schlepping it all over Nevada."

"Just be sure to keep it in working order," Falk insisted. "I've a hunch we'll need it."

Koski wrinkled her nose and looked around the dismal room. "You get the blanket. I get the bed. How long are we going to be holed up here?"

"Just long enough to get some equipment together."

She shrugged. "What kind of equipment?"

"Snow gear. I want to check out an area near Bowman Lake where I came across an armed force of American Indians in training exercises a few weeks ago. They were on their own land and generally tolerated my nosing around. I'd like to rule out—or rule in—their involvement in these murders once and for all." He fished in his pocket for some change. "In any case, it's the last place anyone would think to look for us."

"*Us*? You've decided that I might be needed."

Needed? He certainly was not ready to admit that. "You might be *useful*," he corrected and handed her some quarters. "Look, I'll make my call for gear and wheels from the motel lobby. You go to the liquor store and call Webster. He knows the Sierra pretty well. Tell him to meet us three miles up the Bowman Lake road off Highway 20 before it joins the I-180. Tell him to come alone. I want Maxwell in her hotel in Reno in case we need the connection there."

He checked his watch. "It's almost five-thirty. Tell him to meet us at eight. He should look for a camper parked at the side of the road."

Koski nodded. "Who are you going to get the gear and camper from?"

"Someone I can always count on to deliver." He had one more order. "Tell Webster not to say anything on the phone and tell him to be on time or we go without him, no matter how well he knows the mountains."

At the liquor store, Koski got through to Webster's cell phone. "Don't say anything, Webster. Just listen."

When she finished relaying Falk's orders, Webster responded, "But Maxwell and I are on our way to Carson now—"

"Webster!" Koski snapped, stopping him. "I just said Falk doesn't want you to talk on this line." She sighed. "Look, you have plenty of time. Take Maxwell back—she'll understand—and meet us as Falk instructed."

"Right," he said without further protest and the dial tone hummed on the line.

Webster made a quick U-turn and headed back to Reno. Maxwell looked surprised and asked where they were going. Webster brought her up to date and she was naturally disappointed, being out of the loop, but she respected that Falk had his reasons.

"Where are you, Falk and Koski going?" she asked.

"Into the mountains," was all he said, although he probably saw no reason to withhold the exact location from her.

Through the smudged window of the motel room, Falk saw a dented, dusty camper truck drive into the parking lot and stop. A young man got out, looked around and walked into the liquor store.

"Stay here," Falk said.

Koski went to the window. The store had two entrances, one to the parking lot and the other to the street where a Greyhound bus was picking up passengers. She watched Falk go to the driver's side of the truck, remove the keys and lock the door. He opened the camper's rear door and climbed in, only to reappear in minutes, carrying a large, bulky canvas bag. The bus turned onto Highway 395 and the camper driver nodded in Falk's direction from inside the bus as it gained speed and headed south.

"Like I said, my man always delivers," Falk said, re-entering the room.

"That young guy is your man?"

Falk ignored the question as he swung the heavy bag onto the bed then tugged open the heavy-duty zipper. "The camper is equipped with food, five-pound, goose-down sleeping bags, ordnance...everything."

Koski took another glance out the window at the ratty vehicle. "Doesn't look as if it will make it to Bowman Lake."

"Looks can be deceiving. It'll make it." He quickly checked out the sack's contents, which included an alcohol compass, a small Primus stove, enough dehydrated, individually wrapped meals for three people for six days—supplementing the canned goods already in the camper—three personal packs containing first aid supplies and toiletries, including non-freezing liquid soap.

"In the camper I saw three, one-piece, white coveralls, a couple changes of nylon mesh underwear, lightweight silk gloves to be worn under padded mittens with trigger slips and vacuum insulated boots."

"Sounds like your man *did* think of everything."

Falk reached back into the pack. Wrapped in an oilskin pouch near the bottom of the bag was a thoughtful addition: a Glock 17 9mm automatic with a loaded 17 round magazine.

"In the right hands," he said, "this is capable of placing five-shot groups inside a 2.5-inch circle at a range of 25 yards."

"Right," she said, disappointed, "but there's only one of them." When he nodded, she shrugged. "Oh, well, those can openers are always jamming anyway."

Falk went into the bathroom. He had extracted a small manila envelope from the bottom of the canvas sack. Falk's name was written on it in a scribble he recognized as Tom Stewart's of Cerberus. He had asked Stewart a question when he called for the camper. He hoped the note contained the answer. The message read: IT IS RUMORED THAT UNDERWORLD UNSUBS TO MEET ON LEVEL 15 OF MINE NEAR BOWMAN. PURPOSE

UNKNOWN. BOLO. IN ANSWER TO QUESTION RE MINE, DEED TRACED (WITH DIFFICULTY) TO INDIAN NAME "MUKUAMP." T.

"Mukuamp?" Falk whispered to himself. He had hoped for something more specific. That name, however, sounded familiar... something Falk heard or read in the past. He sighed. He had no idea what the cryptic rumor of a meeting at the mine meant or who the unknown underworld subjects were. Moreover, why were they meeting at the mine? Did they have some connection to the Indian militia members Falk himself was planning to investigate?

On an abstract level of understanding, this information tied into his unformed thoughts. Yes, he would BOLO—be on the lookout—for anyone and anything that posed a threat. He tore up the note, flushed it down the toilet, then returned to the room where Koski had finished repacking the bag.

"Now what do we do?" she asked. "We've got some time before we meet Webster."

He decided to do something he seldom did—share his thoughts. "A couple of things bother me about this operation," he said. Koski sank to the bed and he sat in the only chair in the room. "According to Lovesy, we were supposed to be visible but silent, right?"

"Right."

"What does that suggest to you?" Koski shrugged, not sure where he was going. "Ever go duck hunting?"

"No."

"When you hunt ducks, you put a brightly colored wooden duck in plain sight to attract other *real* ducks. The wooden version is called a decoy."

Koski rolled her eyes. "Fascinating."

"That's *us*, Koski. You and I and the whole team. I'm convinced we were meant to be decoys from the start."

Her expression turned serious as she realized what he was saying. "But why?"

"To give the public evidence that something is being done about the lawyers' deaths—while something *else* is being done in another place."

"What? Where?"

"If I knew the answers, I wouldn't have to sound out the situation. I might even go so far as to say that we're expendable."

"Are you saying that people in our state government are using us...maybe even trying to kill us?" Koski's forehead furrowed beneath her silken bangs.

"I'm saying that their plan was to put us out there, cut us loose and if we got killed in the process...so be it. By disappearing and going off on our own, we must be, to put it mildly, frustrating them royally."

"You think that Lovesy...?"

"I don't know anything for sure yet—but he certainly has a stake in this. To halt the spread of Indian gambling in California would keep the state that pays Lovesy's salary fiscally strong." He shook his head. "If you try to mentally round up all the usual suspects, everybody's questionable."

He leaned back in the chair. "I have a friend in the Bureau of Indian Affairs with strong ties to the Indian nations. A Native American chief in Arizona mentioned a name that rang a bell with me: Senator Albert Reinecke of Nevada, chairman of the powerful Ways and Means Committee and outspoken champion of Native American welfare.

"The senator has been the driving force behind increased

funding for all Indian tribes in the state for the last ten years. The report indicated, however, that there hasn't been any significant improvement in the tribes' way of life. In fact, in many instances, conditions have worsened. Millions in aid targeted by the Interior Department for them is going…where?"

Koski was propped against the headboard with her arms folded across her chest. "That would suggest that Reinecke is getting rich off Native Americans. He wouldn't want them weakened…blamed for the killings."

Falk's vision was abstract. "At least not publicly," he mumbled, "or at least not *voluntarily.*" His eyes narrowed slightly and he looked at her. "Another thing: why would the tribes need to resort to murder to get more casinos in California? Governor Gray Davis endorsed, and the voters passed, Proposition 1A in March 2000, which initially envisioned small casinos in remote rural areas but in fact resulted in mega hotel casinos.

"Then in January 2001, President Clinton signed legislation that allowed the building of the San Pablo Casino on Interstate 80 between Oakland and Vallejo. It was the first Indian casino to operate in a major urban area in Northern California. As I recall, Davis even signed an agreement with sixty tribal leaders to legalize gambling on nearly all large reservation lands in California."

"That's true," Koski said. "I remember when California's Miwok Indians announced their intention to build a $100 million casino hotel along U.S. 50."

Falk nodded. "There's even an Indian gambling operation adjacent to the entrance to Yosemite National Park, for God's sake. Indian gambling is not only increasing in California but all over the country."

Koski leaned forward. "So, if your last statement is a defense against the Indians having motivation to kill the anti-gambling lawyers, it's an indictment against the people those lawyers represent, which means a large portion of the public that's against gambling. On the other hand, Nevada's organized crime, which opposes any gambling pie they don't have a piece of…top echelon officials in Nevada state government who want to protect the status quo—like, possibly, Reinecke and Lovesy here in Nevada—and God knows who else."

She sighed and let her back return to the headboard. "Which of these scenarios are we buying into and if we're decoys, for what?"

Falk's vision rested somewhere in the space between his eyes and the wall. "I'm not sure yet." He paused. "I'm pondering the motivations of those *who else* people you mentioned. Casinos are popping up everywhere—creating traffic problems, environmental concerns, etc.—but they're changing the very character of rural communities…"

"Environmental concerns?"

"In some California communities, local authorities have warned there isn't enough water in the areas to meet the needs of local homeowners and the casinos…that wells are running dry."

"What's the Indians' response to that?"

"Pretty scary. They flatly state that under their agreement with Governor Davis they are not obligated to obey California environmental laws."

Koski was surprised. "Do the non-Native American Californians know that?"

"Even if they do, there's nothing they can do about it."

"Doesn't California have a gambling commission to regulate all of this?"

"Yes but I haven't heard of any substantial regulation or oversight on their part. Some tribes even refuse to disclose how many slot machines they intend to operate in any given casino."

"So, you're saying that *lots* of disgruntled citizens have what you might call motivation to want to make the country afraid of Indians?"

"I'm not sure what I'm saying. For now, remember that we trust no one." He silently hoped to figure out the answers before it was too late. He bent forward in his chair and checked his watch. "Time to meet Webster."

Her green eyes narrowed and her head tilted to one side. "Who, by the way, we can't even be sure is someone we should trust." She got up from the bed. "Are we being paranoid?"

Falk got up and slung the canvas bag over his shoulder. "I only know that this situation is more complicated than it first seemed. There's more at stake here than the spread of Indian casinos. Native Americans suddenly represent something a lot more threatening than a few more slot machines."

Chapter 16

Koski sat silently in the passenger seat of the old camper listening to the *clack-clack-clack* of the turn indicator as Falk switched to the right lane and exited Highway 20 onto the lonely Bowman Lake road and their prearranged rendezvous with Webster.

The farther they moved into the backcountry, the more remote the rest of the world became. On Highway 20, despite little traffic and miles between exits, there were homes in the distance. Their lighted windows were beacons in the darkness. Now, trees and bushes were their only companions and the exterior isolation heightened a sense of camaraderie in the warm truck.

In the glow from the dashboard, Falk's strong features softened as he glanced her way. A spontaneous, friendly, disarming smile turned up the corners of his mouth. A tenderness long denied welled up inside Koski and dismayed her. She immediately pushed away her emotions, trying to deny a girl-like shyness that remained.

The voice inside that had dogged her since David's arrest and imprisonment whispered in its darkly feathered way. *You can't trust your instincts, Susan. You're in danger of reading something into a situation that isn't there.* She thought of David doing time at the Ely State Pen in the high desert for stealing and selling eight pounds of coke.

"A penny for your thoughts," Falk said softly.

She shook her head dismissively. He didn't really want to know despite their protracted conversation in the motel room; that was business, not personal.

A muscle quivered at his jaw. "Okay, a nickel then."

She decided that conversation might be a good thing right now. "To be perfectly honest, I was thinking of my ex-significant other doing time up at Ely because he and a bunch of other rogue cops were caught dealing."

He nodded. "I read something about it. Was it a bum rap or was he really involved?"

"Oh, he was involved all right. Up to his nostrils."

"Ah, a user; signed his own arrest warrant."

Koski made the conscious decision to relax and spoke comfortably, as if she were talking to herself. "It's not that he didn't respect the law initially—he did. He revered it, as if it was a god and he was its prophet. I imagine that once you place yourself in that role nothing can stand in your way. Eventually, a warped sense of survival—his own—grew out of that philosophy. He lost the sense of shame that most people naturally feel if they think exclusively of themselves. Ultimately, all but the most superficial feelings became subordinate to the sense of power David derived from his work in Las Vegas Vice. It was so intoxicating that it was difficult to turn off when he came home at night."

She paused but Falk's interested silence encouraged her to go on. "I should have questioned the paradox; he could be gentle and kind—not boyish; he was never that—yet polished, slick, duplicitous."

She shook her head. "Damn! I never saw it coming. Until that day, I was sure I could read people, had passed Psychology 101 with flying colors, yadda, yadda, yadda...What a fool I—" She stopped abruptly, thinking she already said too much.

Falk's voice was low and soft. "Do you still love him?" When she didn't answer immediately, he added, "I think it only fair to tell you that in my last life I was a lie detector."

She sighed. "I don't think I ever did." Then she turned to the window. "If we can be mistaken about so elemental an emotion as love what feelings can we trust?"

Falk noticed she reached into the breast pocket of her jacket, as if to extract something. The hand lingered for a second but came out empty. He'd seen her do this before, reminiscent of a person who fingered a charm for luck, touched base with a treasured trinket or brushed a Buddha's belly.

He had a sudden, overwhelming desire to take her in his arms. In response to her question about trusting one's feelings, he wanted to reply that such were not so elemental but that he trusted his and they seemed to involve her more and more.

Webster came up behind them, the lights of his jeep blinking, and Falk pulled to the side of the road. Further conversation with Koski on the subject of feelings was fatefully interrupted. Perhaps that was a good thing.

Chapter 17

Because his pale hand trembled, Donald Lovesy slowly raised a glass of scotch to his lips. He sat at his desk and stared at the flat screen on the facing wall. The impact of his part in the horror hit home as he caught the breaking news on television.

"Attorney John Hamlington and the three-member staff of his law firm were found dead in Sacramento today. The firm represents more than a dozen Northern California card clubs and various Bay Area charity organizations whose card rooms are struggling to stay open amidst new, flourishing Indian gambling facilities." The co-anchor managed an appropriate pause before continuing. "Police will only say that all four individuals, each in a separate office in a high-rise suite Hamlington leased, were killed by arrows."

Lovesy continued to hold the glass, unable to drink. Disgust at himself and his fear increased the tremor. When his private line rang, the glass jumped in his hand, blotching amber liquid across his desk and its contents. Even the phone was his enemy now.

"Lovesy," he grumbled. There were the usual gulps and gurgles from scrambler equipment and then Tony Villachi's deep growl came on the line.

"Morning, Don. In your office bright and early, I see."

Lovesy thought that the bastard, whose tone was usually grumpy, sounded as if nothing happened; as if four more innocent people hadn't just lost their lives. "It's all a show, Tony," Lovesy said honestly. "I'm here in body but not in spirit."

"Chrissake!" Villachi seemed surprised at his associate's bad humor. "I take back the bright and early remark. Why so glum?"

"I just turned on the TV and learned about that attorney, Hamlington, and his staff in Sacramento. I imagine your people are behind this?"

Villachi sounded indignant but controlled. "What a thing to say, Don. My people wouldn't do—"

"Oh, no, not your people. You're right. You wouldn't use anybody who can be traced to you. I'm sure you *imported* the talent for these atrocities." He paused and tried to drink, again unsuccessfully. "When is the slaughter going to end, Tony?"

Villachi's voice turned to ice. "I'm gonna chalk this conversation up to angst and pretend you never said that, my friend. I'm calling because you'll need to meet with Reinecke and me this morning. There are a few things we need to touch base on…make sure we're on the same page."

Lovesy knew not to refuse. One word from Villachi or Reinecke and he'd be revealed as a co-conspirator. He sighed heavily. "I suppose I can clear my calendar—"

"Good. Reinecke will send a car for you."

The phone went dead in the same instant that his intercom buzzed. "A car is here from Senator Reinecke's office, sir," his private secretary said.

"Thank you." Why hadn't Albert called himself? Lovesy seldom dealt directly with Villachi, which was as he liked it. Consorting with the Las Vegas don—even on a secure line—was not something the state attorney general was—or should be— comfortable doing. Beads of perspiration formed on his forehead. He wanted to go to this meeting about as much as he wanted to undergo the bypass of his blocked left carotid artery scheduled for next week. He had no choice; a situation he found himself in a lot lately, a situation he hated.

He put on and buttoned his jacket. When he started through his secretary's office on his way out, he said, "Push back my meetings for about an hour."

"Yes, sir," the middle-aged woman said. "You'll probably want to take the private exit, sir. The outer office is full of reporters...you can imagine...four more deaths and no word on the missing members of your investigative team..."

"Buzzards," Lovesy muttered. "Everybody's thirsting to be first with the worst." He turned and went back into his office and was passing his desk when his private line to the governor rang.

"Donald." The governor's voice was high-pitched and crisp. "You've talked to local law enforcement officials. This vendetta against lawyers continues to spread. Should it become out-and-out terrorism against the citizens of California and Nevada, are you satisfied that sufficient high alert security is in place at the Capitol and every major state and federal facility in Nevada?"

Lovesy gripped the glass of scotch and managed to down the liquid. The sensation was exhilarating, spreading from a fiery explosion in his mouth and throat to every part of his body. His mind cleared. "Yes, governor, I am." He took a deep breath, poured another couple of fingers and added an ice cube from the leather bucket. The cube cracked and crackled and he quickly moved it away from the phone, hoping the governor hadn't heard.

"What about the dam?" the governor asked. "If whoever these terrorists are—and I'm beginning to doubt they are Native American weekend militia warriors—should decide to play havoc with Hoover Dam and that 726-foot-high concrete wall holding back twenty-seven million acre feet of the Colorado River was damaged..."

"Not a chance, governor. The dam is totally secure; has been since September 2001...the National Guard is there and—"

"Speaking of warriors, Donald, it wouldn't be a bad idea to..."

Lovesy nodded at his directives as the governor continued, "Yes, governor, I'll call General Stone of the National Guard...a squad of men will be deployed...yes, sir, immediately."

Concluding the conversation with more assurances to the governor, Lovesy finished the remainder of his drink and made a brief call to an old friend, General Rocky Stone of the Nevada National Guard. Then he walked to the back of his office. Touching a panel on the wall, he waited while a pocket door disguised as wood paneling slid open. He walked through the opening, which returned itself to the appearance of a seamless wall behind him.

Soon Lovesy sat slumped in the back seat of Reinecke's limo, staring out at the city. Traffic was light but Lovesy was aware of an air of expectancy surrounding the moment. The car felt uncomfortably warm...maybe the scotch...It was more than that. He reached for the intercom and asked the driver to cut back on the heat.

He cursed silently and pressed the button to lower the window beside him to allow a cold draft to sweep into the vehicle. He removed a handkerchief from his pocket, wiped away a film of perspiration that had collected on his upper lip and leaned back in the seat. Reinecke and Villachi should know the governor wanted a National Guard unit deployed to monitor the militia camp where Bowman Lake bordered Nevada and California. Lovesy should have called them immediately. No matter, he would see them in a few minutes; he'd tell them then.

The limo slowed and stopped for a traffic light near the Nugget Casino a few blocks from the Capitol.

The target was perfectly placed. The window of the limo was partly open, giving a powerfully built, redheaded man and his partner, poised behind the tinted windows of a parked car at the corner, a clear view of the attorney general and the red dot moving down the side of his face. It settled just above his collar. At this range it was a cinch. The arrow flew fast and true, thudding into Lovesy's neck and pinning him to the seat. He was dead before the light changed.

Chapter 18

During his meeting yesterday with Tony Villachi in a secret place behind the counting room in one of Villachi's Vegas casino hotels, Rod Eiker, British mercenary par excellence, was given a goal and a nearly bottomless budget. He also was informed that how he accomplished that goal was pretty much his business, within reason. It was the way Eiker preferred to carry out an assignment; unencumbered by moral or fiscal considerations.

Villachi's unnamed associate in Carson City had completed phase one of the campaign with the killing of the two FBI lawyers outside their offices at the state building in Carson. Eiker had picked up the torch, solved what Villachi called "the Lovesy problem," contracted out an assignment in Sacramento and had an important personal date in Reno at noon today. Now he would begin the campaign to collect extortion money from frightened Nevada attorneys.

Eiker first chose the prominent Nevada law firm of O'Connor,

Cox and Brace that occupied three floors of opulent office suites at the top of a twenty-five-story steel and glass tower in Las Vegas. Here, amid muffled legality, associates and soft-spoken executive secretaries generally ministered to the absolute power of Ralph O'Connor. He leaned toward rejecting the mob's offer of security against death by an arrow through the heart.

Eiker had secured a blueprint of the high-rise and a schedule of the members' appointments.

He planned his visit for nine a.m. on the day all the firm's attorneys met in the twenty-fifth floor conference room. Eiker and two of his men entered the building in predawn darkness, bypassing the security system with ease. Earlier, he had carefully handpicked these men, flying them to a rendezvous point in the desert midway between Vegas and Carson City.

With only a few hours to prepare them for this assignment, Eiker was forced to push the envelope but he was satisfied they were the best local talent available. Now, the three were dressed in state-of-the-art anti-terrorist attire, clad entirely in black clothing and body armor, black Kevlar helmets and shatterproof goggles. Flame-resistant Nomex balaclavas protected their heads and faces. Their assault vests and leg pouches held an assortment of grenades and other gear, a terrifying sight to the uninitiated.

Eiker's dramatic plan was to be hidden in the drop ceiling of the conference room when the meeting began. One of his men carried a portable laser beam guidance system. In addition to his regular weaponry, Eiker toted a bow and two arrows. Having had only a short time to practice with the unusual weapon, Eiker and his archer had nevertheless mastered the skill needed to work as a team. Their third man was assigned to toss a low-powered Flash bang concussion grenade into the room when Eiker gave the order to plunge from their hiding place behind the ceiling panels.

Eiker had fitted a length of flexible fiber optic tubing through a small hole in the ceiling tile and attached it to a palm-sized TV. Then he plugged the whole assembly into a battery pack attached to his vest and he and his men, balanced on beams, waited silently.

Soon a sharp, clear picture of a bevy of male and female barristers appeared on Eiker's tiny TV screen as they entered the room and took their seats, sipping coffee and awaiting the main man. The sound of a grandfather clock striking nine floated up through the ceiling.

"Good morning," O'Connor's voice boomed as he entered the room. Eiker adjusted the tube and held on the large Orson Welles look-alike as he seated himself at the head of the table. "Before we consider regular business, let's take a moment to discuss our in-house security. As you know, we have spared no expense to ensure that we have the best available. Nonetheless, some of you have suggested that in light of the recent killings, it might be prudent to consider the, shall we say, *particular* type of security offered by a local gaming and resorts organization."

One of the partners gulped a handful of pills, downed some water and mumbled, "Nothing but the old protection racket. They want to take advantage of us. Gangsters, all of them."

O'Connor nodded. "My sentiments exactly."

Another partner leaned forward and said in a solicitous, negotiating tone, "These people you call gangsters happen to be, for the most part, our bread and butter. It's possible they're only thinking of our welfare."

"Our welfare, my foot!" It was obvious the discussion was over. O'Connor reddened and banged a fist on the table intermittently as he spoke. "It's nothing short of extortion (thump) and I for one am appalled that you'd even consider going along with this strong-arm tactic. I will not (thump) be—"

Eiker tapped his closest companion's shoulder and whispered, "It's show time."

The man kicked at a ceiling panel and tossed his Flash grenade down onto the center of the conference table. An ear-splitting roar and a flash of blinding light accompanied Eiker and his men as they landed on the large, long slab of glossy mahogany, terrifying everyone in the room. Women screamed. White-faced men sat, unmoving, with their mouths agape, fingers gripping the arms of their chairs. The third member of Eiker's team jumped lightly to the floor and stood in front of the door, his Uzi submachine gun covering the room. Eiker nodded and his archery partner took an exaggerated stance with the laser transmitter, snapped on the switch and with a flourish placed a red dot on the panelled wall.

"A preview, counselors," Eiker said, his voice ringing through the room, "of what can happen if certain people ignore sound security advice. The lawyers whose demise you've read about in the newspapers," he continued, "were dispatched in the following fashion." He held the arrows aloft. "Laser-guided shafts. The victims were marked with a laser dot aimed by an accomplice while a second person fired the arrow."

The smoke from the Flash bang had cleared and the red dot on the wall was visible to all. "The shooter," Eiker continued, "could be, and in most instances was, out of sight of the target. The arrow was released and by the wonders of modern electronics, homed in on the little red dot." He paused and smiled perversely. "Just like the laser-guided bombs the Yanks use in Afghanistan and Iraq."

Eiker's man moved the dot from the wall and centered it on the forehead of a terrified attorney sitting at the far end of the table. The dot slowly went from one lawyer to another, bouncing around the table until it stopped and held on O'Connor's chest.

"No one is safe," Eiker said menacingly, "once the bead is drawn on the victim." He nodded across the room to a large oil painting of O'Connor's great-grandfather twenty feet away. His partner moved the laser dot onto the subject's forehead and held it motionless. Eiker notched an arrow into the bow, aimed in a direction deliberately to the left of the target and released the arrow. The twang of the bowstring was still in the air as the projectile was corrected in flight then veered to its goal, thudding into the forehcad of the likeness of the law firm's illustrious founder.

"I think you get the point," Eiker said in O'Connor's direction. He and his companion jumped from the table and backed toward the door. "Don't attempt to exit this room for one hour after we leave; it will be booby trapped." He flicked his eyes to the oil painting. "You may keep the arrow as a symbol of our determination." His crooked, boyish grin slowly transformed his face. "Someone will be in touch regarding the premiums due on your new insurance policies."

Outside the room, Eiker led the way to a freight elevator he had wired earlier with a hidden bypass switch to override its normal operation. Closing the lift's gate, he activated the override and spoke an order into his wrist microphone as they continued non-stop to the basement.

Like clockwork, a van pulled up to the back door as the three men exited the building and climbed aboard. Within minutes they were on The Strip and headed back to their desert location, where

Eiker would reveal the details of their next and infinitely more dangerous assignment.

Chapter 19

Sitting in her hotel room in Reno, Maxwell put down the book she was reading and switched on the television to a local news channel. A co-anchor announced the lead story: the murder of Nevada's Attorney General Donald Lovesy. His two closest aides and private secretary were being interviewed, extracting their fifteen minutes of fame by tearfully proclaiming that the AG was a kind, honest, optimistic straight-shooter who didn't have an enemy in the world.

A meeting that the governor convened at his mansion less than an hour earlier resulted in his announcing that martial law was in effect in Nevada until further notice. The governor also expressed his sorrow at the loss of the attorney general, promising his killer would be brought to justice.

"Enough!" Maxwell said as she depressed a button on the remote and the television screen went black. She was angry, sad, uneasy, frustrated and curious. Why Lovesy? Yes, he was the state's chief law enforcement officer but there was someone ready to step in and take his place. What would Native Americans—or anyone—gain by killing him? At that moment, she sorely longed to talk to her teammates.

The phone rang and she grabbed it eagerly.

"Dr. Maxwell?"

She thought she recognized the deep, powerful voice. "Mr. Ryland?"

"Yes, but call me Samuel, please. How are you?"

She felt relieved at the sound of a familiar voice and decided to be honest. "A little antsy, a little angry...I just heard about Attorney General Lovesy."

"Yes, it seems so senseless."

Maxwell sighed. "I also think I've got cabin fever."

"Cabin fever, why?"

"My part in the investigation at the present time is to stay here at the hotel in the event I'm needed but so much is happening out there..."

"Where is Falk? Have you talked to him?"

"I haven't the faintest, except that he, Koski and Webster are headed into the mountains somewhere."

"Well, look, I just flew in from HQ at Fort Meade and I'm about to have an early lunch with Lester Carter. He's not only an old friend but Falk's bureau chief here in Reno. Would you care to join us? I'm not far from your hotel. I can pick you up before I collect Lester."

Maxwell's inclination was to jump at the invitation but she had her orders. "Thanks but Falk—"

"He has my numbers. If he doesn't get you there he'll probably check with me, in which case I'll say I insisted that you get out of the "cabin.""

His reassuring words were all Maxwell needed. She concluded the conversation and was ready before Ryland arrived.

Fifteen minutes later they were seated at the Steak House in Harrah's on North Center Street.

Lester Carter was a short, thin man who looked like he was in the habit of skipping meals. He was pale, with fine features and curly light hair that tended to frizz around the edges like Gene Wilder's. Maxwell soon realized that the man's lean body was probably due more to an overactive metabolism than Weight

Watchers' meals.

Carter had devoured a deep-fried Monte Cristo sandwich, fries and coleslaw and was working on a large wedge of apple pie.

"Nice place," Carter said, glancing around. "When it comes to steak houses, you can't beat Binion's Horseshoe on Fremont Street in Las Vegas. If you haven't tried it for dinner, you should."

"I remember it, Lester," Ryland interjected. "You and I ate there years ago."

"Oh, yes, that's right." Carter turned to Maxwell. "I forget how far back this guy and I go. Anyway, Binion's Steak House has the best prime rib this side of Texas." He put down his fork and gestured with his thumb and index finger. "I swear, it's at least two inches thick…rare…tender…" He shook his head. "It'll cost you but worth every penny. The restaurant's on the twenty-fourth floor and the view—"

"Lester," Ryland interrupted softly, "you should know that I got word a few hours ago that FBI Reno is under investigation."

Maxwell silently watched Carter as he discontinued scraping the last vestiges of pie crust from his plate and studied Ryland's face. Despite his responsible position at the Bureau, Maxwell got the impression that Carter was a man whose biggest challenge in life to date was how to avoid a second mortgage on his home.

"You're serious?" Carter asked Ryland.

"Dead serious, I'm sorry to say."

Maxwell leaned forward and whispered, "The NSA is investigating the FBI?"

Ryland smiled slightly, enough for Maxwell to see his strong, sparkling white teeth. "Actually," he said, "the FBI will be doing an internal investigation of its own field offices."

Maxwell looked around. "Should you be telling us this?"

Ryland's dark, solemn eyes softened. "Probably not." He looked at Carter. "A heads-up among friends."

Carter nodded, then wiped his mouth and put his napkin down. "I hate it when that happens," he complained. "Internals always disrupt routine...morale drops to zero...everyone's pores are dissected under a microscope."

"Including yours?" Maxwell asked.

"Especially mine, Doctor. They start at the top and work their way down."

"Sorry, Lester," Ryland said. "I know you have enough to deal with right now without contending with a witch hunt." He signaled for the check and turned back to Maxwell. "Bad news for you, too, I'm afraid. If the scuttlebutt is correct they'll also be digging into the sheriff's offices in Carson and Virginia City."

It was Maxwell's turn to be surprised. "If there's someone connected to the murders working in the Carson City office, I'll be more than shocked." She shook her head. "I guess I can't blame them for checking out everyone—whoever's behind the killings might have internal access—but my boss, Chief Vigo, and his deputies...the other personnel...they're all honest as the day is long."

Mention of her boss made her wonder how Vigo was doing without her. She resolved to call him when she got back to the hotel. Surly bastard that he could be, she missed him.

"If you ask me," Carter was saying, "it's an import that's doing the lawyers. If I was heavily involved I'd check out an ex-agent from the Mossad's Saudi Arabian desk, Tamar Aderet. She has the brains to mastermind something like this." He paused and finished the last drop of coffee in his cup. "Of course, there's the British mercenary with whom I have a history..."

"British mercenary?" Ryland asked.

"He uses several aliases but his name's Eiker, Rodney Eiker."

"I've heard that name," Ryland said. "What kind of history are you talking about?"

Carter said, "Several years ago my partner and I caught him and a couple of his men red-handed near Hoover Dam. They had nearly three hundred pounds of stolen plastic explosives and several hundred detonators. We spotted them and called for backup but decided not to wait.

"When we broke cover, our perps opened fire and in the ensuing gunfight, Eiker's men were killed. He got away but not before I got off a round that caught his left ear." Carter paused and grinned slightly. "I didn't get the son of a bitch but I can guarantee that his ability to wear a diamond stud in that lobe was seriously impaired."

Maxwell silently took back her earlier assessment of Carter as untried.

"Think he's here in this country?" Ryland asked.

Carter shrugged. "You might want to check that out."

As the three walked back to Ryland's car, Maxwell felt grateful for the advance warning Ryland had provided about her office being under investigation. She felt no compunction to act upon that information. She was guilty of no wrongdoing and was certain Vigo was equally unstained.

Maxwell would remember the next few minutes the rest of her life, in flashes collaged upon the background of her mind.

The three approached the car. Ryland took out his remote and pressed a button and the alarm chirped. He opened the door behind the driver's seat for Maxwell while Carter walked around the vehicle to the front passenger door.

Maxwell did not see the red dot of light that moved across Carter's shoulders, lowered slightly and remained fixed, burning to penetrate its chosen spot. Before ducking to sink into the back seat, Maxwell heard a sound like the rushing wind captured by a large bird as it fluttered to earth. Something made her glance toward Carter. His eyes were like a deer's impertinent question as it stares out of the darkness.

Maxwell later envisioned the arrow's passage as it pierced the illuminated dot on Carter's back, tore through his left lung and sliced through his aorta, stopping only after it passed through the front of his chest and pinned him to the car.

"*Jesus*!" Ryland breathed and Maxwell felt his hand shove her into the car. His head whipped around, desperately scanning nearby vehicles. Several rows away, one surged from its spot and screeched toward the other end of the parking lot. Ryland sprang behind the wheel and started the engine. Backing out, he stomped on the gas and careened across the lot, burning rubber in a cloud of stinking smoke, so intent on pursuit as to be oblivious to Carter's body.

Maxwell was unable to move, speak or breathe. She saw Carter, still pinned to the passenger door, face pressed against the side window, blood pumping from his lips, his eyes retaining the eternal question.

Ryland had to swerve in an attempt to avoid another automobile but Maxwell heard the sickening crunch of metal and bones as Carter's body hit the car, snapping him free from the shaft.

Ryland shouted, "*God damn son of a bitch*!" as he braked the car and pounded the steering wheel. The suspect car had disappeared, merging into the flow of traffic. For a second he was undecided whether to go back for the bloody pulp that was his friend lying in the parking lot. Making a decision in the next instant, he pressed the accelerator to the floor.

Maxwell groaned and passed out.

Chapter 20

Falk, Koski and Webster spent the night in the camper on the deserted trail off Highway 20, splitting the hours into shifts so that one was on watch while the others slept. They were on the road by dawn. Webster followed in his jeep as they neared their destination. Falk steered out of a long S-curve and checked the rear view mirror again, expecting to see the jeep but it didn't appear.

"Webster," he said to Koski, "he's not there."

She looked back. "He was right behind us…"

Falk slowed the truck, not highly concerned. Their companion might have had to stop for one of the many deer in the area that crossed to get to water…might have had to take a leak…

He drove to the right shoulder and waited and then turned off the engine. It was silent except for the ticking from the hot engine manifold. Thirty seconds passed and then Falk reached into the glove compartment and grabbed the Glock.

"Something's wrong. Wait here. I'll be right back."

Koski watched Falk in the side mirror as he jogged back along the side of the road. She pulled the collar of her jacket around her ears and squirmed deeper into the seat. With the heater off, a chill was already seeping into the vehicle.

Suddenly she jerked to attention. A gunshot cracked the freezing air, echoing across the mountains. She immediately reached for the AK-47 she had stowed behind the driver's seat, opened the door and slid out, cocking the weapon. The metallic sound was particularly harsh in the still, cold air as it slid to the killing position. Crouching with her back to the camper, she eased toward the rear, allowing herself a clear view of the road. She could not see Falk. She would wait sixty seconds…Then she heard a sound in the direction Falk had taken. The crunch of footsteps… but no voices…no sounds of conversation…

She took a deep breath, then crawled beneath the vehicle, gripping the automatic weapon in front of her, never taking her eyes off the empty road. If there had been an ambush she did not intend to walk into it. She wriggled closer to the right back wheel and pressed the butt of the cold weapon against her cheek. Then she saw them.

Webster and Falk rounded the bend, walking toward the truck, hands on their heads.

Several feet to one side and to the rear, a stranger had the drop on them.

Koski fingered the fire selector switch and it softly clicked to automatic. *Son of a bitch.* She watched as the three came closer. The stranger was silent but directed Falk and Webster with his weapon to continue toward the camper. Soon they were so close that Koski could have reached out and tapped the toes of their boots.

"Open the door," the man commanded. "Tell her to get out, hands on her head."

Falk opened the driver's door, letting it swing wide, surprised himself to see there was no one inside the vehicle. The man moved a few steps closer. Koski could see his weapon, a SPAS, Special Purpose Shotgun, Model 12. The swine could blow the damn camper apart with that kind of ordnance. He spoke again.

"I know there were three of you. Where is she?"

Falk sounded calm. "There's no one else here, I tell you. Take a look."

The man gripped the shotgun and moved slowly, until he was only inches from Koski. She zeroed in on his boots, legs and belt buckle.

"Unless you tell me where the woman is," he snarled, "I'll shoot one of you, now. My orders are to bring you in. It's no problem for me if I have to kill one of you."

Falk asked, "Whose orders?" not expecting a response.

The man grinned with sadistic wickedness as if, having the upper hand, he could afford to divulge a titillating portion of a secret. "Some Limey with a fat wallet." His face closed then and he demanded, "Where's the woman?"

"I don't know," Falk said honestly.

Koski saw the man's boots shuffle impatiently in Webster's direction.

"If I shoot your friend here, maybe that'll help you recall. Get over here," he commanded Webster, "away from the truck. I'll count to three. One…"

Oh, God! Not daring to breathe, Koski positioned the AK-47 and took aim at a spot a few inches below the man's belt buckle and waited, praying he would change his mind.

"Two…"

She saw Falk's feet shuffle slightly, too. Was he preparing to dive at their captor? The man stepped back, however, and she heard the chilling, metallic rattle of the shotgun being cocked; her own finger tightened on the trigger…

"Three—"

The automatic weapon roared and kicked against her cheek,

the sound deafening in the close confines of the truck's underbelly. The raw, acrid pungency of cordite filled her lungs. The man's shotgun was flung across the clearing and dropped unfired into a mound of boulders more than twenty feet away. His body fell to the ground, ripped from groin to sternum.

Webster and Falk stared at her in disbelief as she wormed from beneath the truck and staggered to her feet. Gravity collected in her legs and for a moment she couldn't move. Then she ran headlong into Falk's arms, burying her head in his chest, stifling a gag as bile rose in her throat. She killed a man. "He was going to kill Webster," she stammered, "I...I had to...to..."

Falk held her close. "It's okay," he whispered. "It's okay." She remained in his arms, shaking and drenched in sweat.

She couldn't know his thoughts; that he marveled at her toughness, as tough as they come, yet she was like the soul of a sparrow, fluttering in his arms.

Finally she pulled away. "Why would he..."

"I don't know." Reluctantly, he released her.

She realized she had reached into her inside jacket pocket for the postcard she always carried. As if the inked writing beneath the laminated surface was Braille of love, she gently smoothed her fingers over it. It was the last communiqué from her parents before they perished in a train wreck five winters ago—a touchstone of her courage representing the fiercest test of her life to date. It was a test that had taken all her mettle to survive.

Touching this material memory of a moment of loss had become more than a habitual reaction to distress. Suddenly aware that Falk and Webster had noted the card and the pressing of her fingertips across it, she quickly tucked it back into the folds of her jacket.

"He got the drop on me," Webster said, continuing their discussion as if Koski's action had not intervened. "He just seemed to materialize from the side of the road back there…" He paused and offered his hand to her, saying, "Thanks, Koski, although thanks doesn't begin to cover it."

She smiled weakly. "It's covered."

Falk walked over to the body splayed in the dirt. Sinking to one knee, he went through the man's pockets. Keys, wallet. "Nice," he said as he turned him over before removing a Bowie knife from a leather sheath attached to the man's belt and positioned out of sight in the center of his back. "This guy routinely expected trouble." He picked up the wallet and quickly flipped through it. "About sixty dollars cash…no ID."

"No ID," Webster repeated.

Falk grunted. "Yeah, a pro, a hit man." He replaced the wallet in the man's pocket and headed for the camper.

"Ride with you or take my jeep?" Webster asked.

Koski watched Falk tuck the AK-47 behind the seat in the cab. "May as well leave the jeep," he said. Then he added something Koski thought she'd never hear him say. "It's best if we all stay together."

As he eased the camper onto the highway, Falk asked, "Webster, being in BLM you must know a little about the Native American population. How many of them are there in the United States?"

Webster was surprised by the question but had a ready answer, "Close to three million."

Falk whistled. "Three million?"

"Yes and I recently read a report that the Census Bureau expects that number to triple by 2050."

"Do you know how many total acres of land they own in the West?"

"Well, let's see...The Navajo reservation is the largest in the country, with 16 million acres in Arizona, New Mexico and Utah..."

"Sixteen million acres," Falk interjected in Webster's pause. "That's a lot of land to control."

"Pyramid Lake became a 475,000-acre Paiute Indian reservation way back in 1874," Webster went on. "The Washoe tribe owns almost 20,000 acres in Nevada."

"Twenty thou..." Falk grimaced. "Thanks, Webster. That gives me some idea of what we're looking at here." He paused and added, "Right, Koski?"

"Right," she said weakly. He took his eyes off the road long enough to watch her brow wrinkle as she tried to establish a nexus between Webster's answers and Falk's remark.

"One more question, Webster. Are there any Algonquin Indian tribes living in the western part of the United States?"

"They're mostly concentrated in the New England states."

"Yeah, I know about those in New England. Well, thanks again." He reached into the pocket of his heavy jacket and produced a folded road map. "If you promise to refold this correctly later," he said lightly as he handed it to Webster, "I'll let you be our guide. I basically know the area I want but it'll help if you pinpoint it exactly for me."

Webster silently flipped open the folds as Falk continued. "The camp I visited near Bowman Lake, where some militants of the local tribes go to train, is on the premises of an old, inactive gold mine. I crudely marked it on that map." Falk's concentration on the winding road did not preclude his wondering aloud. "How did that guy know there were three of us?"

Koski shrugged and Webster replied, "Beats me. I didn't even tell Roz I was going to be with you."

"Roz?"

"My secretary." He was silent for a moment, then added, "At least I don't *think* I told Roz…"

Chapter 21

Tony Villachi and Senator Reinecke arrived at the mine at eleven on the morning following Lovesy's death, summoned to a meeting with The Fox. As they walked from the parking lot toward the high, steel mesh fence surrounding the premises, Reinecke looked down at his runty companion. He adjusted his steps to accommodate the frail man's minced stride and asked, "Been here before, Tony?"

Villachi took a long draw on his cigar. "Never."

The guard at the entrance recognized the senator and pulled open the tall gate, nodding a silent greeting.

Glancing around at the rows of run-down, mostly single-story wooden cabins, Villachi mumbled, "Can't say I'm impressed. Seems deserted. I thought you said some of the local Indians pow-wowed here."

Reinecke grinned at Villachi's politically incorrect phrasing but didn't mention it, not wanting to let the mobster know that Reinecke considered him gauche.

"The Native American militia members only train here on weekends." He pointed toward a two-story structure at the back of the facility.

"It's all supposed to be quite harmless. When I was here on a Saturday I was allowed to observe maneuvers taking place in that building. It actually was quite frightening: Indians armed with weapons made in Israel that were a cross between Russian-built AK-47 assault rifles and American M-16s. Don't ask me how they happened to have those weapons. I was told they were practicing what they called "shooting and ducking."

"First one man then another would run up and down the stairs, covering himself by firing live bullets while being shot at by a machine that fired rubber bullets…bullets that can do a lot of damage if they connect at close range. I suppose it was good exercise as well as good practice."

"Chrissake," Villachi said, "sounds like they're preparing for war."

Reinecke shrugged and ran a manicured index finger across his silver moustache. "In any case, the training camp is just a cover."

They had reached the main entrance to the mine; a large, stone building, the earthen path to which was edged with uniformly sized, white painted rocks. Faded letters on a weathered sign above the door read "Colonial Mine." The guard stationed just outside the door waved them through.

Reinecke leaned toward the gangster at his side and said, sotto voce, "It's rare for The Fox to call a meeting at his headquarters."

Villachi shivered and tugged at the collar of his calf length, black wool coat. "Some kind of emergency, I suppose. Just what we need." He paused and looked up at the senator. "What do you mean the camp is just a cover?"

Reinecke's slight, condescending smile betrayed the pleasure he derived from always being on top of events. "Even the Native Americans who train here don't know of the secret sanctuary beneath the camp. They only know there once was an operational gold mine beneath the surface.

"Now a skeleton crew maintains the main shaft and fourteen lower levels at the eccentric, unknown owner's request, despite the fact that veins of the precious ore were depleted sometime back in 1956. Federal authorities concentrate on militant Indians, who are allowed by the landowner—even encouraged—to train here above ground."

Villachi grunted. "I know that even though mining operations ceased, BLM agents, state safety inspectors and other bureaucrats inspect it periodically. You telling me there's something they're missing?"

While they continued into a long hall, Reinecke went on as if he was a tour guide. "The Colonial Mine ownership passed to several different companies until 1966. The present owner is listed as a legitimate corporation. That owner, however, created a level fifteen and turned it into what he refers to as "Control"—the exclusive headquarters from which he manipulates events that he imagines will one day allow him to…to…"

Villachi was getting impatient with talk. "To what, for Chrissake?"

"I don't know exactly…some sort of grand plan. I wish I did know The Fox's ultimate goal."

Villachi was pleased there was something Reinecke didn't know. Villachi, however, also wasn't able to fathom The Fox's motivations. Villachi did know that the senator's ambitions were to continue to build his own power base and save his own skin. He went along with the scheme to discredit the Indians because The Fox had him in an awkward position. He led Reinecke to believe that in the end there would be increased money in Indian aid, much of which would find its way into the senator's pockets.

Villachi also was aware of the single-minded motivation of his friends in the Nevada organization: to create enough fear in the public's mind to halt the spread of Indian gambling and keep Las Vegas' coffers full.

Nevertheless, Villachi's associates, like Reinecke, didn't get it. There *was* no way to stop Native American tribes from overrunning the United States with casinos.

Like his associates, Villachi had fought that battle initially; until he recognized the odds. His Sicilian mother didn't raise foolish sons. There was only one thing to do. "If you can't beat 'em..." If there was finally to be a substantial Indian pie, Villachi would get a piece of it.

Quietly, singly, he began injecting millions of his own money and money from the organization into the pro-Indian gambling referendums in California and other states. For now, he would be the Indians' silent partner.

One day, his vision of the entire country being one big Las Vegas would come true. Despite whatever plan The Fox may have in mind, Villachi would let his associates in on his coup. This would further ensure his place at the head of the table in his Las Vegas penthouse for years to come.

Meanwhile, he would back the campaign *against* his Indian friends, convinced that the more pressure they felt, the more readily they would feel obliged to share a wedge of the ultimate dessert when the time came.

"This place is spooky," Villachi grumbled, his unlit cigar moving from one side of his mouth to the other. He began to breathe laboriously, taking two steps to Reinecke's one in the dimly lit hall. The walls were lined with old sepia aerial and ground photographs of the mine in its earlier days, pictures of bearded, moustached men with picks and shovels, dressed in dingy clothes, boots and round domed hard hats. At the end of the hall, a guard ushered them into a steel cage elevator that dropped at a stomach-churning velocity in total blackness through a shaft drilled through solid rock. The lift jolted to a halt in a lighted horizontal tunnel fourteen hundred feet below the earth's surface. A heavyset man in clean street clothes opened the iron-trellised door and waited for them to step out.

"Each of you take one," the man said, indicating a row of numbered laminates hanging from wall hooks. "Wear them around your necks at all times. This enables security to know how many persons are below the surface in case of an emergency. You'll be reminded to replace them when you leave." He opened a wall-mounted cabinet and issued each man a hard hat with a battery-operated lamp attached.

"As you see, we have lights along this gallery." He indicated the low wattage bulbs hanging from the rocky, cave-like ceiling every fifty feet. "This lighting system is used throughout the mine's galleries. The lamps on the hard hats are for the tributary areas in drifts and stoops where there is little or no overhead illumination. You probably won't need them but in case of emergency…"

"Stop saying *emergency*," Villachi grumbled. "What are drifts and stoops?" he muttered. Crude mining terms were beyond the realm of his comprehension.

"In mining terms, a drift, sir," the man explained patiently, "refers to any horizontal passage. It's also known as a gallery or level of the mine that follows, or once followed, a lode or vein of ore. A stoop is an area where the miner has to kneel or stoop due to the lack of height in the tunnel."

Villachi then asked, "How far is it to this control center?"

"About a mile, sir."

"You mean we're expected to walk a mile through this tunnel?"

"No, sir." He gestured toward the ground where narrow gauge rails ran through the center of the gallery. "There'll be a tram along in a few minutes. Here it is now." The man turned to Villachi, "And don't light up that cigar, sir."

The old don grumbled. "Hey, you think I'm stupid." A steady hum filled the air followed by the rhythmic clatter of iron wheels on the track.

"No, sir. Stay close to the wall until the tram comes to a full stop."

The tram consisted of an electric engine and three high-sided ore carts with wooden seats and entry doors cut into the iron sides that had been converted for passenger use.

"Keep your hands inside the cart at all times," the driver grunted as they climbed aboard.

"I feel like I'm on a kiddie ride at Disneyland, for Chrissake," Villachi rankled in Reinecke's direction. His companion was silent, apparently thinking it uncouth to complain.

When they reached what looked like a solid wall of rock, the track U-turned and the tram stopped. The driver slid out, signaled the others to follow and walked to the wall. He waved a hand before an unseen sensor and a door in the breakaway rock wall opened, exposing a brightly lit stairway.

"Chrissake," Villachi said, "what next?"

"Only six steps, a landing, then six more steps," their guide explained as he led them down the stairs to another door. A keypad on the left wall glowed beneath a soft red light. "Protection against unwarranted approach," the guide explained and then punched in a sequence of numbers and symbols. The red light flashed to green and the door opened to Control—a connected series of rooms—the hub of a multi-million dollar operation governed by The Fox.

Two male technicians sat at a security console against one wall of the cavernous main room and concentrated on a bank of screens fed by cameras positioned throughout the facility. The feeds were crisp and in color. All critical interior areas were covered and exterior robot camera eyes panned desolate areas of the mountainside. Except for the movements of security guards, there was no activity.

"From that console," Reinecke advised, recalling his previous visit, "the operators monitor all levels of the mine 24/7." He removed his hard hat and set it on a large round table in the center of the room, then sank into one of the twelve ample swivel armchairs surrounding the table. "No one gets near this mine without a technician at the monitors knowing it. I'm told the security systems are so sensitive they can detect two flies copulating a hundred yards away."

"Copulating?" Villachi repeated quizzically.

It seemed distasteful to Reinecke that he should have to resort to such common terms. He said softly, "It means *fucking*."

The man who had been their guide gestured to a tray of glasses and a water pitcher on the table's mahogany-finished surface. "The Fox has asked that you make yourselves comfortable. He'll be arriving shortly." He turned and left by the door through which they had entered.

Following Reinecke's lead, Villachi discarded his hat and sat at the table. "Albert," he said in his frail baritone, "I'll take some of that water."

Reinecke, accustomed to being waited on, nevertheless reached and poured a glass of ice water for the older man.

"Who else is supposed to be here?" Villachi asked.

Reinecke shook his head. "The message I got only mentioned an urgent, top-level meeting."

Villachi sipped his water and wiped away a little dribble that ran down one side of his chin. He glanced around the room. "Some setup." The floor was marble. Three of the windowless walls were concrete, designed to accommodate the technology the room contained. The third wall, however, was glass, behind which could be seen an interior garden, replete with tropical plants, a small pool and a waterfall.

"Nice touch," Villachi added.

Reinecke nodded toward a phone on the table with one red and several unlit white buttons. "I understand the phone system has a bypass setup whereby a call can be made from here to anywhere in the world. For anyone attempting to trace the call, however, it will be recorded as having originated from another state or country."

Villachi raised his gray awning eyebrows and nodded. He was impressed. Pointing to a bank of computer terminals against the wall to their right, he said, "I'll bet people in every federal agency in the country would give their right arms to hack into that intelligence control system." He glanced at the ceiling. "This place seems to have everything but a cone of silence."

The two sat quietly for a moment, then Villachi glanced at his Rolex and in his grumpy way said, "Well, where is our esteemed boss, for Chrissake."

Reinecke, ordinarily very much at ease in any given situation, was antsy, unaccustomed to being kept waiting and thus determined to make the time pass in conversation.

He leaned toward his companion and whispered, "I don't know if there's any truth to it but I heard that years ago a demolition expert worked on the construction of this control center and other parts of the mine. He planted explosives in the infrastructure's concrete. They can easily be detonated in the event Control is in danger of being overtaken by an enemy force."

He took an empty glass from the tray and eased back slightly. "A sort of scorched earth policy, you might say."

Leaving his listener with an assessing expression, he rose and went to a wall at the back of the room. He opened a cabinet containing a three-tiered Lazy Susan liquor assortment and swiveled one section until a bottle of Johnny Walker Black came into view. He poured some into his glass and glanced at the clock on the wall. He had no idea as to why The Fox had summoned them here. Suddenly it bothered him that he, like Villachi, had never seen The Fox, never actually heard his voice.

Here he was, a so-called top-level player in this scheme, yet his dealings went through an intermediary—an unrecognizable voice on the phone. On his previous visit to Control, like now, he had waited for The Fox but the meeting was cancelled. The Fox was unavoidably involved in an emergency and could not join him.

He returned to the table and Villachi. "So, you have *no* idea why we've been summoned here, Tony?"

Villachi chewed on his cigar before deciding to answer. "My guess is that it has something to do with our British import."

"Eik—" Reinecke started to say but caught himself, glancing at the technicians across the room who were engrossed in their work. "What *about* our British import?"

Villachi shrugged. "Like I said, it's just my guess but I'll wager that the boss thinks it's time to call our friend off, that the point has been made and that people are starting to turn against the...the..." he searched for the right word..."proliferation of Indian gambling—"

Villachi stopped in mid-sentence. He and Reinecke turned at the sound of someone entering the room, walking confidently, seemingly familiar with Control, heading toward them. It would seem reasonable that both men at the table might make parallel observations.

Police Chief Bud Vigo, whom they knew as a loud, surly man given to overt gestures, was unattractive, of medium height, fifty pounds overweight and oval, with a bowl haircut and bangs. His light blue eyes were so pale that from where Reinecke and Villachi sat, it appeared they had no pupils, held no clue to his soul.

Villachi thought Vigo had never appeared to be overly ambitious or overly bright, yet...Could it be?

Villachi whispered, "Bud Vigo—The Fox?"

Chapter 22

Earlier, heavy dark clouds had swollen the sky. Now cold rain turned to sleet as first the temperature fell, then snow. Falk switched on the wipers, clearing two paths on the windshield but beyond their sweeping jurisdiction, whiteness gathered.

"Should I call Spade?" Webster asked, reaching for his cell phone.

"Call Spade?" Falk demanded, surprised. "Why?"

Webster shrugged and pulled his empty hand from his jacket. "It's just that when I talked to him earlier, he asked me to keep him...he and Maxwell are naturally..."

If it had not been necessary to concentrate on the slick

highway, Falk thought he might have reached over and choked Webster. "What do you *mean*, 'When you talked to him earlier?'"

Webster raised his eyebrows and leaned back, keeping Koski's head between himself and Falk, staring straight ahead. "He called this morning," Webster said, "when you and Koski were still asleep and I was on watch…just to see how we were doing and to bring us up to speed about Maxwell."

"Goddamnit, Webster! *Nobody* is supposed to know where we are or what we're doing."

Koski started to say something but Webster, trying to justify his actions, stammered, "Don't tell me you suspect Alex Spade of being—"

"Whether I suspect Alex Spade or you or anyone else of anything is not the point. That cell phone of yours and Spade's could be tapped into by now. Damn! *Never* use it again unless I specifically tell you to." He sighed and brought his frustration under control.

Koski turned to Webster and whispered, "Webster, you are sooo off this island." Immediately seeing that her attempt at flippancy did not ease his humiliation, she asked seriously, "Since Alex has talked to Maxwell, how did he say she's doing?"

At first reluctant, Webster finally relaxed and briefly told about the incident at Spade's home and how he narrowly escaped death when an arrow was shot into his recliner. Then Webster related Spade's account of Maxwell's luncheon with Ryland and Carter, following which Carter was killed and Maxwell taken to a safe place to recuperate.

Falk could not believe it. Carter was dead. He had known his bureau chief for many years—a small man with a big heart and keen dedication to his work. "Why?" Falk demanded aloud. "If all this is about killing those who are against the Indians why kill Carter?" Certainly, he thought, Carter had made enemies in his profession. It was a given at that level of Bureau stratification.

Falk and Carter had held private conversations, some—unfortunately not enough—in which they exchanged their own personal "most wanted" lists. Now Falk tried to remember those on Carter's list who might want to kill him but it was no use. It took too much time and acute concentration to recall.

"And you heard about Lovesy?" Webster asked after a long silence.

"We've been a little too busy staying alive to catch the eleven o'clock news, Webster," Falk snapped. "What about Lovesy?"

"He was killed by an arrow, too…in a limo on his way to a meeting with Senator Albert Reinecke."

Falk cursed. Not that he believed Lovesy's death was of a particular loss to the world as compared to Carter but any man's death, as someone once said, diminished us all. Now there was another puzzle. If, as Falk and Koski had speculated earlier in the motel, there was a connection to Lovesy and the arrow killings, why did his co-conspirators kill him?

Koski turned to Falk. "Maybe we were wrong about Lovesy."

"Or maybe he simply outlived his usefulness," Falk replied.

All three fell silent. There still were so many questions and so few answers.

Webster, occupied intermittently with the map during the past hour, took one last look at it. They had climbed to twelve thousand feet. The snow-covered highway snaked into woods heavily furred with age. "According to your map markings," he said, "we're close to the mine now…little less than a mile." He deftly refolded the topographical map and returned it to Falk.

"Okay," Falk said. He let the vehicle crawl a short distance farther, dropping into deep ruts, climbing over small rocks that had rumbled down the steep cliffs at the side of the roadway. Finally, he pulled to the dextral side of the one-lane gravel road and killed the engine.

Without the rumble of the snow tires, hum of the motor and blow of the heater and defroster, the sudden muteness seemed big and palpable. The temperature dropped immediately.

"Time for a little reconnaissance," Falk said, opening the door. A furious flurry of snow flew and eddied into the truck as he slid out, the Glock in his hand.

With a curtness meant to discourage debate, he quickly added, "You two stay together until I get back." He pulled the jacket collar up around his neck.

Koski slithered from the seat and jumped out beside him. "We're joining you," she said with her usual determination, her cheeks pink with eagerness and cold.

Webster watched them, unmoving.

It was Falk's habit, his nature, his job to reconnoiter on his own, damn it. He certainly didn't need a nursemaid on this little side trip. He pointed an index finger directly into her face. "You'll join me when I'm *ready* for you to join me."

With an exaggerated pout, she scrambled back into the truck beside Webster, extracted the AK-47 from behind the seat, laid it across her knees and folded her arms.

Even with Webster there, she suddenly looked vulnerable. The automatic only served to punctuate that danger might be all around them.

"Okay," he growled and led the way into the woods.

"Hey! I've been to this mine before, months ago," Koski

whispered, as she and Falk huddled by the steel mesh fence. "I didn't recall until we got close to it."

"Do you know who owns it?" Falk asked.

"Some veiled corporations, DBA some other corporation's statutory client trust account...in other words, who knows."

"Why were you here?"

"BLM got a request to check out a complaint from some small independent miners in the area. They were concerned about water usage, the possibility that streams were being diverted."

"What happened when you checked it out?"

"Not much, we made recommendations, they complied and we left."

"Were they diverting streams?"

Webster, who had been scouting the area behind them, emerged from the trees and crouched next to Koski. Having heard Falk's question, he added, "I remember reading the report. We couldn't prove anything."

"Oddly enough, though," Koski said, "we suspected some diversion near an old mine entrance that went unused for years."

"You mean near an old mine shaft?"

"No...it was a horizontal entrance, an adit. The miners dug into the side of the mountain, their path slanting downward until they reached what they called the "working face," the actual wall of rock that contained the vein they were mining. Later the practice was discarded in favor of sinking a shaft." She smiled slightly, as if pleased that her work at BLM gave her opportunity to enlighten Falk.

"I knew that," he said. "So, what did you do?"

She shrugged. "As Webster said, we couldn't prove anything. The old entrance looked unsafe to me. We went several hundred feet into it and then got the hell out. We ordered them to re-timber the roof and shore up the walls."

"And did they?"

She shrugged. "I assume so. We never re-inspected. We were told to take their word…orders from someone above our lowly station." She paused. "Come to think of it, I could find that entrance now…take us right into the mine."

Yes, Falk wanted that. Suddenly he felt a presence behind him. He pivoted and saw two National Guardsmen approaching—rifles at the ready.

"Drop your weapons," one soldier commanded quietly, not wanting to be seen or heard by the guard at the mine's main gate several hundred feet away. He gestured impatiently, his dark eyes threatening from beneath the rim of his white camouflaged steel helmet.

Falk let the Glock slip to the ground and Koski's AK-47 followed suit.

"Damn!" Falk mumbled as they turned and raised their hands. They were led back into the woods.

Five minutes later, seated in an old cabin, the trio faced a bored-looking officer whom Falk recognized as Colonel Staudinger of the Nevada National Guard.

Once identifications were established and Staudinger notified Command of the three interlopers, the officer seated himself behind an old table he used as a desk. "What are you three doing in this dismal place, Agent Falk?"

"My team was assigned by Attorney General Lovesy to investigate the recent deaths of lawyers in the state. We're up here to talk to the Indian militia who train in the area."

Staudinger nodded. "Weekend warriors; they only train on

weekends."

"The actual exercises, yes but we thought some of them might be around."

"You say Lovesy requested your investigation?"

"Yes."

"Mine, too," Staudinger said. "Before he died, he called General Stone, who ordered me and two platoons up here." He shrugged. "It seems that our mission is moot. We haven't found any increased activity in the vicinity and, as you see, the mine's nearly deserted."

"You went into the mine itself?"

"No, not yet." He paused and added, "The powers that be are concerned about the kind of press we get. Everything must be low-key here. Should an incident occur, we don't want the media to get wind of it and come up here. They'd shoot video, decrying the tragedy of poor, misunderstood American Indians, who were doing nothing more than bonding in this bucolic setting and being attacked without provocation, blah, blah, blah. It's obvious that all's quiet right now. We thought it best to observe for the time being... see what develops."

Falk studied Staudinger, a tired old soldier who would most definitely fade away when the time came—and that time was not too far away.

The sound of helicopters thwacking low overhead drowned out any further conversation and the communications officer burst into the cabin.

"Received nothing on the radio, sir," the breathless man reported. "No warning of approaching helicopters. Unidentified, sir...they came out of nowhere."

Falk followed the colonel and his lieutenant as they raced

outside, staring up as an unmarked chopper passed over the wooded area and continued to the east.

"The first one already has dipped out of sight," Staudinger snarled just as the second vanished below the tree line. "Raise Command and ask them what the hell's going on. Tell them we received no notification of impending aircraft."

He stormed back into the cabin and went to his desk. "Take a patrol and scout the area where those birds landed," he commanded his lieutenant. "Find out who the hell they are and what they're doing here." He gestured toward Webster and Koski, who had been sitting silently the past few minutes. "Stay put," he ordered, as if they had made some threatening gesture.

Falk had a premonition that the colonel's luck was about to change, and Falk and his two companions' with it.

Following the violent death of Lester Carter, Ryland decided Maxwell should be housed in a secure location until the case was over. He chose a little-used military hospital at the U.S. Navy "Top Gun" Fighter Weapons School near the city of Fallow east of Reno.

Maxwell raised her eyebrows.

Ryland gently touched her arm. "I want to be sure you're safe."

She stood at the window in her room on the second floor and stared out at the rain. Already she was bored out of her mind. The weather channel predicted that rain would turn to snow before the end of the day. It also reported that snow was falling in the higher elevations.

More than ever, she was frustrated. She decided to tell Ryland that she must either get back into the investigation or return to her job in Carson City. Instead, she called Alex, who also confessed to being bored at his assigned location, Webster's office. At least Alex was contributing. He was being helpful by keeping her apprised of the others' activities. Thanks to Alex, at least Maxwell knew that Falk, Koski and Webster were alive...or *were,* early this morning.

Chapter 23

"What!" Bud Vigo said harshly to Reinecke and Villachi when he walked into Control and saw the look of inquisition in the men's faces. "I'm only ten fucking minutes late," he exclaimed, thinking his tardiness was the reason for their silent inquiry. He flailed his arms in the air. "Do you have any idea what kind of precautions I have to take to be sure I'm not tailed when I come here?" He sat down.

"It's a good thing the boss doesn't call us here often." When Villachi and the senator were still silent, no doubt reassessing their hasty assumption that Vigo was The Fox, he went on. "Where's the boss?" He glanced around the room. "Ya know, I was here once before. Had to pick up some instructions that he didn't want to have delivered...never did see him...the guy's a fucking phantom." He looked at his watch. "He'd better show pretty soon. I got a life, ya know."

Reinecke looked at Villachi. The older man broke into a grin while Reinecke laughed out loud, turning to Vigo. "We thought that *you...*" Reinecke started to say but decided that it was too absurd a premise to bother mentioning.

Vigo turned toward the technicians seated at the monitors thirty feet away. "Any activity topside we should know about, fellas?"

Realizing they were being addressed, the older of the two replied, "Activity normal at all levels, sir."

His attention remained riveted on images of the main gate,

the interior and exterior of the entrance building.

"Maybe so," Vigo fretted, "but something doesn't feel right to me."

It was two years ago when The Fox incorporated Bud Vigo into his grand scheme. Vigo knew he was a perfect candidate for the job for several reasons. He was police chief of Carson City with clout and access to local law enforcement resources. He was a stubborn, determined man who didn't covet the limelight like Reinecke. Once persuaded, Vigo could be relied on because he was a man whose past could be used against him.

Vigo, in his late fifties, was married for twenty years to a woman he loved and who gave him six children. On one occasion, however, he succumbed to a weakness in his groin for a teenage girl and The Fox had learned of the liaison. When The Fox required an associate in Carson City to begin implementing phase one of the campaign against anti-American Indian lawyers, he only needed to meet secretly with Vigo and remind him of the tabloid-type details of his single, unfortunate amour.

The subsequent association with The Fox had altered Vigo into sycophantic submission, and chain-smoking, dramatic passive-aggression. He and his well-bribed helicopter pilot had done exactly as instructed from the start. Their only misstep was the arrow that missed a hiking lawyer and ended up in the tree near Wally's Hot Springs.

Vigo had retrieved and destroyed the arrow from the evidence cage where Maxwell had placed it. Since then, any attempt to keep the murder weapons a secret was forgotten in favor of getting his job done.

"What feels wrong, Bud?" Reinecke asked.

Vigo rubbed his chin. "My contact—that high, singsong voice

that gives me all orders from The Fox and, for all I know, could be The Fox himself—ordered me to pull back right after the demise of the two FBI agents in Carson. Then there were the murders in California, then the FBI man, Carter and Lovesy—"

"Carter!" Villachi made the exclamation but it might have been Reinecke; he, too, was that surprised. "I *know* Carter," the don said. "He's been around awhile. What happened?"

If Vigo wondered why the two men were surprised at the news that foul play had befallen Carter but exhibited none regarding Lovesy's fate, he did not stop to ponder it. "Poor son of a bitch was killed in Reno on his way home from lunch with the Carson City ME and a NSA man."

"Chrissake," Villachi mumbled.

"Yeah," Vigo agreed, "that's what I mean. Things are out of control...maybe even out of The Fox's control."

Villachi slumped solemnly in his chair, chewed on his cigar and wondered if he had created a monster by hiring Rod Eiker.

"Trouble!" one of the technicians at the security monitors barked. He and his companion tensed in their chairs as a klaxon alarm pulsed in the air.

Vigo, Reinecke and Villachi, in that order, rose from their chairs at the round table and immediately rushed to the console.

The monitors that had slumbered earlier with benign images of routine, seemingly unneeded, security, now flashed with activity as the alarm sounded throughout the facility.

"Shit!" the younger technician spat as his vision zeroed in on two unmarked helicopters landing in a clearing the size of a football field away from the mine's outer fence. Seven men, obscured by falling snow and indistinguishable in their snowsuits, jumped from the aircraft. Loaded down with weaponry, they dispersed to a staging area at the tree line.

"What's happening?" Reinecke insisted, echoing the concerns of his companions.

If the technician he addressed knew, he didn't have time to answer. A red phone on the wall by his ear shrilled and flashed with stroboscopic intensity. He lashed out his left hand and grabbed it.

"Yes, sir," he said crisply. Listening silently for a minute, he repeated, "Yes, sir." Holding the phone away from his ear, he relieved his partner's apprehension by nodding toward the screen that displayed the helicopters and saying, "Friendly…they're okay." Then he handed the phone to Reinecke. "The boss wants to speak to you."

"Albert," the soprano-like voice on the line said without preliminaries, "I've just learned that minutes before his demise, Lovesy ordered National Guard troops to the mine at the governor's request. Not because they had any idea we were to meet there—your ass is covered—but as a precaution against any possible militant Indian gathering.

"I've instructed our British friend—because he's the only one who can do it—to get you and our associates out before the troops start nosing around." The voice paused and said pointedly, "That's *all* that son of a bitch is authorized to do. I'll be in touch once you're back in your office." The Fox hung up before Reinecke could respond.

As instructed, Eiker had earlier arranged for himself and his six-man team to be combat-equipped at their desert location, picked up and flown to a clearing near the mine. Now he instructed the men to remove the mortar tubes from the aircraft and ready them for use. Although Villachi initially hired him, Eiker soon learned that his orders came from a singsong voice that reached him on his cellular phone from various public phones. The last call reamed him a new asshole for killing Carter, which was a personal score Eiker needed to settle.

It was now imperative that Reinecke, Villachi and Vigo be safely spirited away to prevent any possibility of their being found and questioned. How Eiker accomplished this was up to him. In his flamboyant fashion, he decided not only to rescue the three men but also to eliminate the National Guard troops.

The Fox's last words to Eiker were, "If you fail to get the three men out safely, the last installment of your fee will be forfeited."

While his men prepared the mortars, he pulled slightly on his maimed left ear lobe, savoring the satisfaction that the man who was responsible for that affliction had paid the ultimate price for branding Eiker with a constant, visual reminder of the failed Hoover Dam episode years ago. He turned his eyes to the cool flakes that melted on his warm cheeks. "Let it snow, let it snow, let it snow," he sang softly. No adverse element Mother Nature thrust at him could smother the inner fire that the anticipation of battle inflamed in him.

The sound no soldier experienced in combat ever forgets assailed Falk's ears. "Get down!" he shouted, grabbing Koski's arm and yanking her to the floor. Webster, Colonel Staudinger and two of his men reacted, too. They hit the deck in the same instant a thunderous explosion ripped one side of the cabin apart. A gusher of bright orange flame leapt out of the ground a few feet from the office, throwing rocks and debris through the air.

"Mortar attack!" Falk hollered, pulling Koski up by her jacket. Both jumped through the gaping hole where the wall was seconds earlier. He was vaguely aware of Webster vaulting through the air beside them.

As his two companions dove for cover behind a tree, Falk looked back at what was left of the cabin. He saw Staudinger sprawled face down on the floor. He whirled and lurched back inside but he knew the colonel was dead as soon as he rolled him onto his back. A piece of window glass had severed his throat as if sliced with a knife. Falk whispered an Amen to the man's life and removed the 9mm from his holster.

"Mayday…mayday…"

Falk turned in the direction of the distress call. The radio man lay on the floor ten feet from him, one side of his body a bloody, amorphous mass. "Mayday—," the shell-shocked man repeated into the transmitter as his intestines spilled onto the floor before his mouth gaped and he lapsed into final silence.

Falk heard the sound of another incoming round and burst from the cabin as it hit the remains of the roof and exploded. What was left of the cabin went up in a searing sheet of flame along with several more of Staudinger's men nearby.

Falk dove behind the pine tree that sheltered Koski. "You okay?" She nodded but her hands, pressed to her ears, trembled. "Webster," Falk called to the figure lying on his stomach, his face buried in the snow. "Webster!" Falk started to go to him but Webster slowly raised his head.

"I'm…I'm okay," he rasped. A burning slab of wood from the demolished building lay beside his head. Groggily, as if just awakening from sleep, he slowly pushed it away.

The staccato repetition of automatic gunfire sounding in the distance led Falk to speculate that whoever mounted the mortar attack also was attempting to wipe out Staudinger's lieutenant and the small unit sent out earlier to investigate the choppers. Falk said a silent prayer that the dead radio operator's "Mayday" got through to someone.

A third round whistled in, landing a few yards from the remains of the cabin. When the debris from the explosion settled, Falk slowly raised his head. The mortar fire came from the direction where the helicopters had landed near the mine. Damn! He sorely wanted to get into that mine but the crackle of automatic gunfire was closer now.

"What'll we do?" Koski asked. "Whoever mounted the mortar attack will move in…"

Falk looked up into a flurry of falling flakes. The sky, a deep dove gray and pregnant with more snow, seemed to reach down and touch the earth. Unless they found a place to hide and keep warm, they would freeze to death before the day was over. The Sierra Nevada gave no quarter to the unprepared.

"We'll get back to the camper then decide our next move."

Fifteen minutes later they were inside the camper. Falk got the motor running and kept the revs high until he was sure the motor wouldn't stall. He eased forward slowly.

Koski shivered. "Where will we go?"

"I noticed a trail running into the woods a couple of miles back that's wide enough for us to squeeze this old beater into until the storm lets up." He switched on the wipers, squinting through the fan-shaped clearings at clumps of snow that stuck to the blades and then slid down the glass like fat, white slugs. He switched the blades to high as the flakes thickened.

"What the hell happened?" Webster asked, his voice vibrating as the truck's right front wheel dropped in and out of a rut.

Falk was pleased to hear Webster asking questions. He had

been concerned about his dazed demeanor immediately following the attack. "I'm not sure who they are yet," Falk replied. "In the meantime, we don't want them to find us."

Webster put a hand to his head. "We don't want them to find us," he repeated.

When they reached the small trail, Falk headed the vehicle into it and stopped. "Koski," he said, "you take the wheel. I'll guide you into the trees and bushes as far as you can go." He turned to Webster. "There's a shovel behind your seat. Use it to break away some good-sized branches we can use to cover the camper."

Following Falk's directions, Koski drove the truck deep into the forest and stopped. She opened the door against protruding tree limbs and squeezed out.

"Good," Falk said, "now we'll camouflage it some more. The snow will do the rest." Snowflakes that had melted and run off the warm hood of the vehicle now found acceptance as it cooled.

Webster walked through the brush to collect branches and scrub, his gait slow and hesitant.

As Koski sighed and leaned back against the camper, Falk silently moved closer to her. She turned a tired face up toward him and, squinting against the barrage of disintegrating whiteness, she asked, "What are our chances of getting out of here?"

He moved nearer, his boots crunching in the snow. He stopped inches from her. "Not bad."

Emotion ordained physicality. She was acutely conscious of his stance now, which emphasized the force of his thighs. Something stirred in her, a blazing locomotion of awakened embers that compelled her to move…

She twisted away. "I'd better see what I can do to secure the gear," she said, her hood falling to her shoulders as she raked a hand through her hair and climbed into the camper.

Falk nodded slightly to himself. He had better help Webster, whose camouflaging efforts seemed to be flagging.

Ten minutes later the camper had melded into the white foliage. Falk backtracked through the trees to where they had turned off, assuring himself that their tracks were already nearly covered by snowfall. In less than an hour no one would know they had driven through the area.

Returning to the camper, he found Webster bent double beside the rear wheels, one arm to his forehead.

"Webster?"

"Headache..." the lanky younger man stammered. "Dizzy..." Falk grabbed him just as he passed out.

Chapter 24

The interior of the camper was crowded, in disarray and smelled of wet clothing and canned food they had devoured. Their jackets hung from wall hooks, boots scattered in various places and three sleeping bags snuggled together on the floor. After gaining consciousness two hours earlier, Webster was asleep in his bag and Falk and Koski seated on theirs.

Koski shot a twinkle of sympathy in Webster's direction. "I'm worried about him."

Falk nodded. "He was conscious after the attack...able to carry brush and tree limbs."

"He didn't want to be a burden to us..." She turned to Falk. "Even when consciousness is *not* lost, symptoms of a concussion can show up hours later." She sighed. "I hope he's going to be all right." She eased down to her back on her sleeping bag.

"He will be," Falk said, trying to sound optimistic as he

twisted and lay on his stomach beside her. Gently, slowly, he ran an index finger over the back of her hand. He repeated it and she silently allowed his touch to continue.

"Are you familiar with the term "bundling?"" he asked.

"Isn't that something people did back in New England in Colonial times?"

"Right, when two young people were ready to start courting, their parents let them bundle. That is, lie side by side but in separate bundling bags. That way they couldn't get into too much trouble, unless, of course, they were ingenious and determined."

She smiled but her expression turned serious. "May I ask you a question that may be too personal, in which case, just say so?"

"Anything." He continued to trace concentric circles on the back of her hand.

"Who is Meg?"

The question surprised him, although he had known since the night they spent together near the burning buildings on a rocky hill outside Virginia City that one day he would tell her about Meg. "Where did you hear that name?"

She sighed, "When I was on watch last night in the camper, before we started up the mountain. You called her name in your sleep."

He nodded. "Can talking about the past change it?"

"Of course not, but sometimes it can give one perspective, maybe even perception."

He cleared his throat and turned over to his back, hands under his head. "Meg was my wife. She's dead now. It happened two years ago…"

Speaking in low tones so not to wake Webster, and pausing intermittently to assure himself there were no exterior sounds, he related the events surrounding Meg's accidental death that day in the woods; events he often relived in sweaty nightmares and in the accusing light of day.

When he finished, she slowly lowered her head to his chest. "You've been blaming yourself," she whispered, her green eyes gleaming, "yet you know it wasn't your fault."

That's just *it*. It *was* my fault." He felt the old agitation rising. "I *left* her. I left her there in the woods—alone." He rose up on one elbow and Koski pulled away. "I…I never expected…" he went on, "I hurried…I ran all the way back…she'd be afraid of darkness…of a bear maybe but never…" He stopped.

"Guilt is such a destructive force. Joe, we're not responsible for everything that happens in life. We can't be. None of us is that powerful. Did it ever occur to you that you might have returned earlier, got into the car and been sitting there with her when it happened? Would you still blame yourself?"

His head rolled from side to side. "I know. I know…bad things happen to good people."

"You can apply all of the clichés but the bottom line is that it was an accident."

Falk glanced away from her. "If I believe that there's no one to blame…and the hurt goes on."

"It goes on anyway. Maybe you have to learn to manage it." She touched his chin, forcing his face back to hers and her voice was soft. "Freud said that guilt is the way our super ego punishes us for violating its standards."

"Meaning?"

There was amused tenderness and understanding in her eyes. "Meaning you should stop punishing yourself."

Webster stirred and groaned and the two sat up and turned to him. "Oow…" he moaned, opening his eyes and raising both hands to his head.

"How bad is it?" Koski gently inquired. "We have morphine in the survival kit."

"No," Webster mumbled, "I'll be okay."

Koski lifted his head and put a cup of water to his lips. After a sip, he turned over and closed his eyes again. "Just need a little rest…" He was asleep in less than a minute.

Koski turned to Falk and whispered, "He has to have expert medical attention, Joe."

Falk shrugged into his heavy, hooded jacket and turned up the collar, explaining as he did, "I have to get help. It's possible the Guard's "Mayday" got through and that area is swarming with troopers."

"It's also possible there are no reinforcements or they're all dead." Koski was not in an optimistic mood.

"A chance I'll have to take." He glanced from her to Webster and back. Damn! He didn't want to do this. He hated to leave them. In the beginning, he resented having to take them along. That was so long ago…eons, it seemed. They were an important part of his life now, like family; they were his.

"You'll be safer here than with me," he said, as if she had protested his leaving. He gently ran a hand up and down her arm. *Oh, God, it hurt his heart to leave her.* He reached into his pocket and handed her the 9mm he had taken from Staudinger's dead body. "Here."

She pushed it away. "You'll need it."

"If I'm lucky, I'll only need stealth for this assignment." He held her gaze pointedly. "Don't leave this camper for any reason, understand?"

"Okay."

His eyebrows pulled together in a frown. "You have a way of saying 'okay' to an order and then doing as you damn please."

"Okay," she repeated in a way that said she meant it. She quickly stuffed some power bars into a small backpack. "You'll need all the energy you can get."

Struggling into the backpack, he said, "Take care of yourself and Webster until I return." He paused and then added, "I *will* return."

She put her hands on his shoulders and lightly turned him away from her. "I know you will, Joe."

Chapter 25

As Falk vanished into the pines amid lightly falling snow, Koski closed the camper door. She had to keep busy as her mind tried to assimilate the emotions of the last few minutes. She began sorting through the survival kit, finally finding what she was looking for: a plastic tackle box full of miscellaneous items. She located glue and a roll of twine and set about making a crude trip wire mechanism using odd pieces of metal, which, carefully connected, would touch each other and sound an alarm if disturbed.

Holding a section of the twine, she stretched her arms apart and surveyed her handiwork—three tin plates, two aluminum mugs, an assortment of metal fishing lures and five metal tent pegs. She had placed a dollop of glue on each of the knots to assure they remained in place.

Gently shaking the twine, she created a jangle of sounds reminiscent of a wandering group of Hindu musicians. None of the sounds awakened Webster, yet she quickly lowered the noisemakers to the floor to quiet them.

She exited the camper and returned in minutes, removing her gloves and breathing on her numb fingers to warm them. Her alarm was set, concealed beneath brush but with enough clearance to allow the noisemakers plenty of room to do their job.

Webster still slept, breathing quietly, his face pale. Koski settled down beside the window, the 9mm in one hand. Her empty hand slid into her inside pocket and she fingered the laminated postcard that was suddenly in it.

It was five years ago when her mother and father took their last and fatal train trip through the Northwest. As the train began its descent from thirteen hundred feet to the Christmas card beauty of Klamath Falls, Oregon, the tracks suffered an inexplicable defect. Two sleeper cars derailed, tumbling into a deep, diamond-ice ravine, killing twelve people, Koski's parents among them.

As was their habit, they had sent their only child a postcard from Eureka, California. That fateful mailing arrived in Koski's mailbox two days after their funeral. She had laminated the card, which depicted a photograph of Eureka's historic Old Town on its obverse, and always carried it near her breast.

She glanced out the camper window just as a small sliver of sunshine briefly sliced through the falling snow and clouds, igniting the icy tips of a stand of spruce. She tucked the memento gently back into her pocket and decided to concentrate on the silent clearing outside, praying for Falk's quick return.

Falk was sweating, notwithstanding the cold. It began to snow more heavily, bringing the eerie silence that had a tendency to dull the senses. He bent and scooped up a handful of freshly fallen snow and took it into his mouth, bit by bit. He knew that eating snow wasn't wise but the continual gasping for breath as he plodded through the gathering drifts exposed the membranes of his mouth to the air and quickly extracted their moisture. Exertion, coupled with high altitude, became a race against fatigue and dehydration.

Because clots of glassy old ice hid beneath the new layer of snow, he slowly and cautiously made his way to the site where Staudinger's cabin had been.

As he rounded a large noble fir, two men seemed to rise out of the ground, their weapons aimed at his head. These were not National Guardsmen. They were U.S. Army Special Ops soldiers and the one hauling out a pair of Flexcuffs before Falk could explain himself had cold blue eyes and an attitude.

Chapter 26

"What do you mean, we have to leave by a secret exit a mile away," Reinecke demanded of the big redhead in hard hat and Kilimanjaro coat. He suddenly had entered into Control with two of his men, AR-18s slung across their shoulders. "We're aware that The Fox sent you to get us out," the senator went on, "but our cars are in the parking lot. Why can't we simply drive away?"

"Because my orders are to get you out *safely and secretly*," Eiker snapped, "and there are still a couple of National Guardsmen out there somewhere. My understanding is that you don't want them to see you. I'm also assuming you don't want them to *kill* you."

"Kill—Why, they have no reason to kill *me*...to think that I —"

"You don't know what they're thinking," Eiker barked.

"Chrissake," Villachi grumbled, pushing his cigar to one side of his mouth and pulling up his collar. "Let's just go!"

Vigo, anxious to get out by any means, started for the large double doors through which they had entered.

"This way, sir," one of the technicians said and Vigo stopped and turned. The young man pointed to a five-foot vertical cabinet against the wall to his right. Turning back to the console, he reached down and depressed a button recessed beneath the working surface. The cabinet opened like a door, revealing a five-foot rectangle of darkness.

"You'll need your hard hats," the technician who seemed to be the senior of the two said. "The lamps atop the hats will be your only illumination."

Vigo and Reinecke scrambled to retrieve their hats but Villachi, his fragile neck and shoulders bobbing in protest, said, "I'll walk behind you all and follow your lights."

"So, where does this black hole go?" Eiker demanded of the men at the console. He retained his hard hat but checked his gear for the added insurance of the flashlight he found there.

"This unlit passage connects to an old entrance that hasn't been used for years," the older man said. "The pipes that provide our pirated water supply run beneath it. Here in Control we're just below the area once considered to be the working face of the mine, where the original vein of gold was worked.

"The passage you'll follow will gradually slope uphill until you reach a wooden ladder running vertically through a natural, chimney-like cleft that rambles up through the mountain to the surface on a ridge east of the mine. It's a long climb but you'll be well outside the fence that surrounds the mine proper. After that you're on your own."

As he was about to turn away, he added, "By the way, three months ago there was an earthquake, a strong one, up in the

Mammoth Lake area. I was told that the old slant entrance to the mine—the one on that ridge you're headed for—lost some of its ceiling timbers. Repairs were made but it could be dangerous should anything…Well, good luck."

There was a moment in which all six who were about to depart stood still and looked at each other, their faces darkened with doubt.

Then the other technician shouted, "Helios!"

"Say again," Eiker commanded.

"*Helios!* Helicopters! One…two…" As he counted, the others raced to the console. "Three…four. Four U.S. Army Blackhawk's approaching the perimeter are circling at three hundred…two hundred feet above the main gate…"

The senior technician hit a large red button on the console, activating loud alarm klaxons attached to the walls throughout the mine. Then he began answering phones as each security station reported in.

"Shit!" Eiker raged, "One of those National Guard assholes got a Mayday through. The Army's sent in the fucking A-team."

"Oh, my God, the United States Army," Reinecke said, his face waxen. "They mustn't find me here—" He grabbed the front of Eiker's jacket. "Get me out of here!"

Eiker threw off the senator's sweaty hands and studied the monitors, two of which captured the threatening rotorized aircraft descending through the falling snow. A reconnaissance team was already rappelling down from the first, dispersing to the shelter of the mine's outbuildings. "Shit!" Eiker repeated.

Reinecke's face turned white. "For God's sake, Eiker, don't you have a contingency plan? Didn't you *expect* the possibility of —"

"I had no reason to expect the fucking United States Army," Eiker said, cutting him off.

"One more thing," the senior technician said loudly but calmly, "If our situation here gets critical, which is unlikely, but… my orders are to destroy the mine." He paused to be sure they understood the import of his words. "If you hear a steady, shrill red alert whistle, you'll only have twenty minutes to clear the perimeter."

"Oh, my God," Reinecke moaned.

Eiker signaled his two men toward the passage and then turned to Reinecke, Villachi and Vigo. "Come on, let's get your sorry asses out of here."

Once the six men had vanished into the darkness, the senior technician closed the door and refocused on the console. For a moment the two were silent, their vision caught on the screens before them, which now displayed dozens of arctic-suited soldiers rappelling down ropes that dangled from still hovering helicopters.

"What happens if the soldiers find level fifteen…Control… us?" the junior man asked.

"They won't." The man's eyes darted from monitors two through five that offered underground level views and revealed more Special Forces with ready rifles racing through the galleries, rounding up security guards, exchanging small arms fire with those who resisted.

"They're through on levels six and eight," the younger man shouted, panic rising in his voice.

"Chill," his companion commanded firmly. "We've always known this day might come. We're well prepared for it."

"But *look*. They're already in the main elevator shaft." Sweat moistened his upper lip. "The commander probably has maps of the mine and can trace the galleries, entrances and exits…"

"Control's not on any map, you idiot. They don't know about level fifteen." As he made deft adjustments, snapping switches and viewing the intense activity at each descending level, the older man also began to lose conviction. Then he saw two security men on level fourteen draw their pistols and fall to the automatic gunfire of the invading troops. A third guard surrendered and stood trembling and gesturing wildly, no doubt offering whatever he knew of the secrets of the complex.

"Holy shit!" the younger man shrieked. "We're gonna get fucking killed."

"Hold it," one of Eiker's men shouted, his voice resounding above the cacophony of pounding feet as the six men raced through the dark tunnel. "Man down."

Eiker led the column now. He stopped, turned and rushed back past Reinecke, Vigo and the second guard. The latter was helping the Mafia don to his feet.

"You've got to keep up, you son of a bitch," Eiker shouted. The old man already was breathing heavily and it hadn't been five minutes since they left Control. He concentrated the beam of his flashlight on Villachi's face. "We've got almost a mile to go to that exit."

Villachi shoved the light away and swiped at the mud on his overcoat and pants. "The ground's slippery, for Chrissake," he grumbled, steadying himself against the rock wall. "I slipped."

"Well, don't slip again." Eiker turned to his man. "Take his arm. Keep him upright and moving." He ran back to the front of the line, muttering, "I don't have time for this shit."

That Falk was FBI didn't seem to impress the Special Ops soldiers who found him plodding through the snow. His disclosure that a female BLM agent and her wounded companion were stranded in a camper less than a mile away, however, piqued their sense of responsibility. One had switched on the squad intercom attached to his right chest and requested and received permission to check out Falk's story.

Falk stood next to Koski in an abandoned lodge a quarter mile west of the mine, facing a flint-eyed, fortyish officer. He was U.S. Army Colonel Alvin Cromwell, Commander of a Special Operations Force. Cromwell's unit, consisting of four six-man teams, had deployed here after Staudinger's troops were wiped out by mortar fire. They had flown Webster to a Reno hospital. Falk could only hope that his concussion was not as severe as Falk and Koski initially feared.

"Look, Colonel," Falk said, "we've told you everything we can." Throughout the informal interrogation he and Koski had just undergone, they were helpful but provided only general information. "Like I said, and as our credentials attest," Falk continued, "we're federal agents on a high-level assignment, the details of which we've been sworn not to divulge." He displayed his most innocuous smile. "We're here because we have reason to believe that at least one suspect in our investigation may be at the mine."

Koski's eyes widened slightly, hardly betraying her surprise at this disclosure.

Falk turned to her. "Right, Agent Koski?"

She sucked in her bottom lip and said without conviction, "Right, Agent Falk."

Colonel Cromwell swiped a finger under his long, narrow nose and spoke crisply but with amusement. "It isn't irritating enough that my deployment is in the Sierra Nevada in near-winter but I also have to suffer with wannabe G-men..." He looked from Falk to Koski..."G-Persons."

He sighed. "Yes, well, you should know enough to take orders, I imagine. And, to reiterate mine, you both are to be airlifted out of here as soon as I'm sure I don't need the chopper." He kicked at a chunk of dirty, encrusted snow-ice that had been tracked into his command post. "I can't take the chance of non-military personnel jeopardizing my operation."

"Colonel," Falk protested, elbowing Koski's arm, "Agent Koski, being with the Bureau of Land Management, is familiar with this mine. She has intimate knowledge of areas that can be helpful in this regard." Less gently, he nudged her again. "Right, Agent Koski?"

"Yes...right." Koski cleared her throat, this time prepared to step up to the plate. "You said you have troops in the mine, correct, sir?"

"Yes, they're engaged and encountering extreme resistance, I might add."

She continued, "Well, sir, your troops no doubt have general knowledge of the mine but are they aware of a particular, old, forgotten surface entrance? The entrance that would provide an ideal escape route for anyone—like whoever launched the mortar attack on Staudinger's unit—who may be inside and trying to get away even as we speak."

She paused long enough to be sure she had his attention. "No doubt, you'd want to have such an entrance covered, sir. I know where it is. I've been there."

Falk was silent, watching Cromwell deliberate, running a finger across his upper lip. He would be skating on thin ice, allowing a civilian female to be involved in a dangerous operation.

It was tempting. Seeing Cromwell's indecision, Falk decided that it was time to feed the commander enough insight into Falk's conclusions to gain trust or at least gain an advantage that might make Koski and him more valuable.

"Colonel," he said, assuming a more solicitous tone, "Agent Koski, a videographer, has something on video that might be extremely interesting to you." He pointed to Koski's video equipment that he had insisted she bring when she and Webster were taken from the camper. He turned to her. Koski's surprise was less subtle than earlier, her recovery slow. "Ah…yes." She nodded. "Right."

Colonel Cromwell waved his assent and two crisp young uniforms helped Falk and Koski sort out cables and hook them up to a portable battery-operated color monitor. Koski tentatively switched on the camcorder, glancing at Falk for a clue as to what exactly they were about to demonstrate but got none.

The video shot on attorney Mark Sharpe's balcony at his home at Lake Tahoe came up on the screen as Falk set the scene for Cromwell. He fast-forwarded to the outdoor shot he had requested at the time in which Koski panned and held for a full minute on a red tile roof opposite Sharpe's home. Hitting the pause button, he leaned forward and tapped the screen.

"There." He ran the tip of his finger across the tile roof. "See them?"

Cromwell squinted at the screen, his steely eyes searching for what he was supposed to see.

"Nice work, Agent Koski," Falk said, looking at her. He couldn't help himself. He had discovered that he enjoyed putting her on the spot. He knew that she, like Cromwell, couldn't possibly make out the feature he indicated. Without knowing precisely what he or she was looking for, no one could. Yet, he calculated that she could take the teasing.

"There they are," he repeated, gesturing toward the screen. "See them? Clear as day." Koski's eyes never moved from the screen.

"Of course," Falk continued, "when enhanced they will be more readily revealed. Nevertheless, those, Colonel, are marks made by a helicopter's landing skids when it hovered above the red tile roof for a few seconds and accidentally touched down on the tiles. The helicopter was equipped with a sophisticated firing mechanism used to project the arrow that killed the lawyer living in the home next to this one."

Cromwell turned from the image. "But a helicopter?"

Falk snapped off the video. "No doubt Sharpe came out onto the balcony, wondering why a helicopter would be hovering so low, when the arrow was fired from the aircraft into his chest."

"What about the neighbors? Wouldn't they have seen and heard the copter?"

"Not necessarily. Many of the homes in that area are only used on weekends and only for a portion of the year."

Cromwell stood and started to pace. "Who is in possession of this phantom helicopter?"

"We have an idea," Falk said, his head nodding to include Koski, "but I doubt—"

""*We*" don't have a clue, Colonel," Koski interrupted honestly. "My partner here might have an idea but *I* don't."

Falk let his eyes half flicker to her but went on casually. "In any case, I doubt we'd find it. By now it's probably hidden or the mechanism dismantled and the chopper no doubt easily converted back to standard."

Cromwell shrugged. "Where does that leave us?"

Falk's reply was hard edged, "In the middle of a conspiracy of national magnitude."

The Colonel stopped pacing. "What do you mean, mister?"

Falk did not intend to disclose all of his suspicions but if he was to get into the mine, he needed to throw out enough breadcrumbs for Cromwell to want to follow the trail.

"Colonel," he said, "I suspect that from the start, my task force and I were decoys, meant to be seen investigating—and thereby giving credence to—the supposition that Native Americans are killing lawyers. It seems there also are others who oppose those Native Americans' gambling rights."

He paused and raised a forewarning finger in the air. "While my team and I were supposed to deflect attention, someone was busy setting the stage for something a lot more sinister than the growth of gambling casinos."

Cromwell returned to his chair, aware he was being made privy to intrigue on a grand scale. He put his elbows on his desk and made a steeple of his fingers. "And that is…?"

"If I knew that, this investigation would be over."

The Colonel's mobile phone interrupted and he took the call. "Roger, Major," he said with quizzical satisfaction and hung up.

"I only know," Falk continued, "that I was given a tip that some important people were meeting at the mine. I suspect at least one of them is connected to the killing helicopter we just talked about."

Cromwell snorted, "Important people, here?" He nodded toward the phone. "That call was reporting that all fourteen levels of the mine are secure at this time. To date, my troops found only maintenance and security personnel. There is no evidence that anyone who might be considered important in a military or political sense has been there."

"As you no doubt know, Colonel," Falk said, "there's a saying in the intelligence community that goes: 'The absence of evidence is not evidence of absence'."

Cromwell nodded. "Yes, well, they're still searching for those responsible for the mortar attack and expect to have them in custody soon." He paused and ran the finger across his upper lip, a gesture that Falk had ascertained was a sign of uncertainty. "I must say," Cromwell continued, "that the degree of resistance by mine personnel is puzzling. In any case, that bird is available now to evacuate you two."

Falk contemplated divulging the seed of suspicion that had sprouted in his mind earlier, when Koski mentioned the mystery of water diversion in connection with the old entrance. Now that seed was nurtured by the Colonel's mention of "all fourteen levels." Tom Stewart's note to Falk, delivered to him at the motel along with the gear and camper, had indicated a meeting on level *fifteen*. Stewart seldom made mistakes.

"Colonel," Falk said, bringing the conversation full circle, "what about the mine entrance…the one Agent Koski mentioned as a possible escape route?"

Cromwell sighed heavily and stared at him. "Can you guide some of my men to this secret entrance?"

"We can do—"

"*I* can," Koski interrupted, jumping to her feet— "Most definitely, right now."

Falk saw the Colonel's mouth momentarily twist into something resembling a grin. Cromwell turned to one of his officers. "Get these two equipped with snowsuits and vests right away. Take three men with you. Notify me when you find the entrance—but nobody goes into the mine. You got that?" The officer nodded and Cromwell turned back to Falk. "As soon as we have secured that entrance, you two are out of here, mister."

In the control room, the senior technician's mind burned with shock and indecision. How could this be? His had always been a quiet, mundane job in which he put in his hours watching monitors that, day after day, displayed a series of tranquil scenes that merely prepared him for more of the same.

He was trained how to react in an emergency. Indeed, he had sworn to die willingly here at these controls if necessary to keep the computers and files generated by The Fox's crusade from falling into the wrong hands. He fully understood that should invaders threaten Control, his responsibility was to implement the plan.

The demolition packs were in position at every level of the complex and would have to be activated. The time-destruct mechanism then would count down the minutes until those strategically placed explosives destroyed Control and the rest of the mine with it. Nothing must remain that could lead authorities to The Fox or other players in his campaign. Even now—when it seemed possible that the government's elite fighting force might actually discover level fifteen—the man could not believe that he must set that final plan in motion.

He glanced at a particular monitor and saw soldiers standing at the false breakaway wall that separated level fourteen from the stairs leading to the lowest level. It was a matter of time before they drew the critical conclusions; ten or fifteen minutes to get through the outer door. He already had delayed too long.

He sighed and turned to his companion, who was screeching

and imploring by turns. "It's time," he said calmly. "I'm setting delay destruct for..." he concentrated on the Seiko on his wrist..."two p.m." He glanced at his companion, who fidgeted silently now, his mouth agape.

"Synchronize your watch," the senior man commanded. "It's one-forty...now." He snapped open two red-capped metal covers flush with the console surface and simultaneously pressed the two recessed buttons. A high-pitched whistle shrilled through the facility. He jerked his head in the direction of the concealed door and pressed its release button. "Go!" he commanded. "You've only got twenty minutes."

Jumping up, the terrified man grabbed his coat from a hook on the wall. "What...what about you?" he asked before he stepped into the black aperture.

"I'll be along. It's my job to be the last to leave."

Chapter 27

"Oh, no," Reinecke screamed. All six men in the gallery stopped running. Their ears filled and burned with the sound of the shrill red alert whistle of which the technician had warned.

"We've got less than twenty minutes to find and get up that ladder," Eiker shouted, reacting quickly. "Move it!" He dashed forward. His flashlight and the lamp on his hard hat cast bobbing, erratic streamers of light into the dark passage ahead.

He ran full tilt; Reinecke, Vigo, Villachi and the two guards at his heels, their footfalls, wheezing and fear echoing with the sound of the whistle off the damp, dark walls. For a time, they made swift progress, despite the steady uphill slant of the rock and earthen floor. Then Eiker heard the guard at the rear shout something indistinguishable. Waving Reinecke and the others past him, he waited for the guard, who halted his labor of dragging the frail Villachi along with him.

"Somebody's coming behind us," the guard said, catching his breath.

Eiker listened long enough to distinguish two footsteps. "It's just one man."

He turned and shouted to the other guard, who stopped abruptly and came back. "You take up the rear position," Eiker ordered. He nodded to the darkness behind them. "If he's Special Forces, kill him."

Eiker raced to return to the head of the column of desperate men. In minutes he heard voices from the rear and turned to see the junior technician from Control flying past the rear guard. His eyes wide with terror, the young man now shoved past Villachi and the guard who upheld him, nearly knocking Vigo and Reinecke down, too, in his race to be first out of the tunnel. Eiker merely watched as the terrified youth flew past him, his forward pitch so impatient as to be in danger of becoming a stumble.

Eiker and the others raced on. Finally, without slackening his gait, Eiker dared to glance at his watch again. "Two minutes," he wheezed, hope sinking. Maybe his watch was not exactly coordinated with that of the man in Control…maybe his was fast… maybe—

His light caught horizontal shapes on the right wall beyond the runner, little more than a hundred feet away. They were wooden rungs…built into the side of the wall…*the ladder*! Then the shrill alert whistle died. Eiker and the others halted and froze. There was a moment of silence; indeed, breathing itself halted.

Three simultaneous surface explosions blew open the earth beneath the mine's main gate building and surrounding areas, spewing large chunks of wood, cement, metal, snow, dirt and shards of rock and boulders into the air.

Black smoke plumed upward with fragments of timber and other debris that returned to earth with the damp, lightly falling snow. The earth jolted and trembled, as similar explosions rocked all underground levels of the old mine, coughing more torn and twisted matter into the atmosphere.

Cromwell's soldiers stationed outside the perimeter of the fence watched the instantaneous destruction of the mine in horror, knowing that many of their fellows bled in final agony inside.

The explosions came in the instant Eiker's vision had fixed on the ladder that represented the exit and freedom. He looked up as an old, neglected ceiling timber several feet ahead jolted and split instantly. It was followed by others that cracked and splintered and, in a roar, fell with rock and earth, collapsing the tunnel before his eyes. Only his exceptionally responsive reflexes, burying his chin in his chest and letting the hard hat take the brunt of the falling debris, saved him.

The force of the explosion behind them as Control erupted sent a rush of air like a wall into the frenzied group of men, plunging them, screaming, through the air and headlong into each other.

Minutes earlier, Koski's unerring sense of direction had led Falk and four attendant soldiers to a spot on a hillside less than a mile due east of the mine where they halted. Only the sound of sporadic gunfire in the distance had attested to the fact that the Delta unit had moved farther into the mine complex.

"There it is," Koski said, pointing to what appeared to be no more than a concentrated overgrowth of shrubs. "It probably hasn't been disturbed for months."

"Let me," Falk said and started forward but Cromwell's serious lieutenant stopped him.

"Let *us*," the officer insisted, as much protectively as representing an order. The four men pushed through the dense, snow-covered vegetation. It was no more than a five-foot-square opening on the side of a hill, reinforced with timber and covered with a fine mesh screen.

The lieutenant pulled a flashlight from his utility pack. He had led Koski, Falk and his men twenty feet into the entrance. Now he trained his flashlight beam into the black abyss. "There are wooden ladder rungs built into—"

He never finished his sentence. He was knocked to the ground by the percussion of smoke, dust and dirt that erupted like molten lava from the black hole as explosions rocked the earth for miles around.

In the instant of the explosions, Falk turned and lunged through the air to Koski, carrying them both as far as possible from the belching hole.

Eiker, forced to his knees by the power of the blast, was pummeled with fragments of wood, rock and other debris, as dust and smoke continued to whirl through the passage, burning and scratching his eyes, nose and throat. Then he heard Vigo cough.

"What the fuck happened?" Vigo's voice was thick from the dust he had inhaled. "I thought if we got this far—" Then another paroxysm of coughing overtook him.

Eiker shook his head. His flashlight was gone, blown from his hand, and his shoulders ached from being hit by a piece of falling timber. His hard hat was still on and he sensed that he was generally unharmed.

"Don't move, Vigo," he said. Hearing no other voices, he

moved his head to illuminate the area but only swirling dust beams were revealed. "Reinecke...Villachi..." he called but got no response.

Squinting through the dust and smoke, he spat out a mouthful of dirt and moved ahead slowly. Then the beam reflected on the head and shoulders of the guard who had been assisting Villachi. The already expanding pool of blood flowed from a massive and life-ending slice to the guard's jugular, the offending knife of splintered wood still embedded in his neck. His lower body was buried beneath a jumble of rocks that had dislodged from the ceiling.

Now there was movement around Eiker as dazed figures groped haphazardly in the chaos, trying to focus. He saw Ray, the other guard, who sustained cuts and bruises but was not seriously injured.

"Eiker..." It was Reinecke's voice. Eiker trained the miner's lamp on his hard hat in the direction of the sound.

"It's Villachi..." Reinecke rasped between coughing spasms.

Eiker turned his head to light the area Reinecke indicated. The settling dust allowed him to see the frail body crumpled against the jagged wall. It was the old don, all right, although he was hardly recognizable. His head, not sheltered by a hard hat, lay open. Blood mixed with pieces of bone and brain splattered the dusty ground.

"Debris from the blast killed him," Eiker said without emotion, "sucking away the soul of a gambler to join his ancestors. Bad luck."

A quick survey of the tunnel confirmed what Eiker already had surmised. The explosion had deposited ruined sections of the gallery in front and behind them. Eiker, Ray, Reinecke and Vigo were marooned in a pocket of thick, musty air between that portion of the passage leading to the now destroyed Control and the ladder, the condition of which Eiker couldn't know.

He was thankful for one thing. The water pipes the senior technician had mentioned buried beneath this tunnel apparently had not broken, at least not in this section. The men would have drowned. Eiker thought of that technician, who must have been the last to leave Control and never had a chance of making it out alive.

"Okay," Eiker said, "we've got to work fast." Any minute, he figured, residual cave-ins could occur. He gestured toward the wall-high heap of rubble that separated them from the ladder. "Ray and I'll start clearing this passage. Senator, you and Vigo find a place to sit that's out of our way. You'll need your strength once we're out of here."

He grabbed a slab of wood and, using it as a fulcrum, threw all of his strength into rolling a stubborn boulder that had been part of the ceiling from his path. Beside him, Ray's body twitched at a sudden rumble overhead that caused a small landslide of dirt and stones to rattle into the narrow confine. Ten minutes later, they had scraped and clawed their way to the top of the heap and achieved an opening between it and the ceiling large enough to wriggle through and escape.

"Thank God," Reinecke breathed.

Eiker scoffed, "Reinecke, you're always invoking the deity. Whatever gives you the impression that God would ever intercede on *your* bloody behalf?"

On the other side of the wall of rubble, they discovered what must have been the body of the technician who earlier shoved past them on his way to be the first one out. He was literally flattened by an I-beam and only his broken, twisted extremities and the litter that followed its violent descent were visible beneath it.

Eiker stepped over him and rushed to the ladder, testing its strength, finding only several of the lowest rungs unusable. He looked up into the shaft. From what was visible through the smoke, he determined that it had sustained little damage and that it contained about a hundred rungs.

"Good luck," he said to Reinecke and gestured for him to ascend first, followed by Vigo, Ray and Eiker himself. Being last to leave the deadly passage in this instance was no heroic courtesy. Eiker knew that The Fox wanted Reinecke and Vigo alive, if possible. He would get out somehow but these milquetoasts needed special consideration.

Chapter 28

Following the explosions, Falk and Koski wanted to descend the ladder the lieutenant saw in the mine opening but the officer reached Colonel Cromwell on the squad intercom. In turn, Cromwell ordered massive reinforcements in the wake of the explosions and commanded his men and their two charges to stand clear of the entrance until those reinforcements arrived.

As they waited, the soldiers rested on boulders that had resembled large marshmallows before the men swept the snow from their surfaces. Like Falk and Koski, they were in white snowsuits that, when they were still, nearly masked their presence in the silent scene in which snow had ceased to fall.

Falk and Koski paced slowly but impatiently. Looking down the hillside toward the smoldering mine, she asked, "What do you suppose happened?"

He shook his head. "From the locations and totality of the explosions it appeared that they were deliberately triggered from within the mine…no accident."

"So, you think whoever was in charge rigged the place to self-destruct in the event of any hostile intrusion. Who do you think that was?"

"I don't know yet."

In an effort to avoid being surprised later, she replied, "But you do know *something*. I can tell. What have you figured out so far?"

"That we're getting closer to The Fox." He had told her what he knew about The Fox and that Stewart suspected that person may be involved in the lawyers' deaths.

Suddenly Falk turned, having caught movement at the nearby mine entrance. Koski and the others followed him in the direction of the hole. His instinct was to draw his weapon but Cromwell had confiscated it. A weapon didn't seem necessary, however, when Falk saw the weary, unarmed man who emerged.

"Senator Reinecke," he said, not entirely surprised.

Reinecke wheezed and coughed as he staggered into the cold air, puffs of dust and dirt attending his emergence. "Now," Falk whispered to Koski, "what do you suppose Reinecke is doing here?"

Koski caught sight of the next man to surface. "Bud Vigo!" she exclaimed, recognizing Maxwell's boss, the Carson City police chief. Vigo lumbered from the hole like a bear coming out of hibernation but he was panting, doubled over in a fit of coughing.

On later reflection, Falk would have to admit that their recognition and tacit acceptance of these two men were greatly responsible for what happened next.

It wasn't until the final two men jumped from the hole with their ready AR-18s aimed at them that the military men became aware of their critical misreading of the situation.

Nothing that followed could be misinterpreted, however. The appearance here of Reinecke and Vigo served to confirm the hunch Falk had nursed for days. It was as if the lens through which he viewed the puzzling investigation suddenly cleared and all but a few remaining pieces fit together. Obviously, Reinecke and Vigo were two of the unknown subjects Stewart referred to in his note. Who were the others?

The militia's mistake allowed Reinecke, who might not have been a physically fit or courageous man, to exhibit a skill he possessed in abundance—quick-wittedness. "We..." he began, trying to read the group's faces, "we were taken prisoner by this..." he nodded toward the big redhead, "this terrorist and brought here to this godforsaken place to...to..."

Apparently, Falk mused, the senator's quick thinking had its limits.

Vigo jumped in to assist, as well as to salvage himself, no doubt. "Exactly," he said, "we were taken hostage at gun point and forced to divulge official police and state secrets to aid this man in his scheme to murder all the lawyers in the state. You have no idea —"

"Save it," the redhead commanded, not commenting on his companions' allegations. Something in his inflection gave Falk the impression that he was English.

After patting down Falk and Koski and finding no weapons, the big man with one mangled ear lobe walked over to the soldiers, whose faces burned with the acrimonious fire of those who have been outmaneuvered. Their rifles hung at their sides.

"My name is Eiker," the Brit said.

A bell rang in Falk's head. Yes, he had heard of the man...not on the Bureau's Most Wanted list but somewhere in one of their databases…maybe on the ITL, the International Terrorists List.

"We'll take your weapons now," Eiker said. "Ray," he summoned and the bald, bearded, thick-necked menacing man came forward to carry out his leader's order.

The first two troopers immediately opened their hands and let their rifles thud to the soft snow. The third hesitated only slightly then followed suit. The lieutenant seemed to be measuring something.

"I said *now*," Eiker repeated.

Without taking his eyes from Eiker's face, the soldier let his rifle fall to earth. Then, as Ray bent to gather up the weapons and Eiker let his eyes flicker momentarily to the others, the officer's right hand foolishly whipped to his hip and pulled a 92F Berretta automatic.

He got off one round—a hurried, ineffectual shot—before Eiker's automatic blazed. Hit, the soldier nevertheless brought his gun down from recoil to squeeze off another round. Eiker's storm of bullets punched into his body and he lurched back, taking several more rounds in the head.

The soldier standing beside him, a youngster with visages of the acne of puberty still evident on his face, turned toward the lieutenant, as if to keep him from going down—a ridiculous, spontaneous reflex. Eiker chose to read it as an attempt to grab the handgun and fired, killing him along with the veteran.

Eiker calmly looked at the dry clip in his AR-18, thumbed the clip release, then reached into his belt and drove a fresh clip home.

Falk was aware of a profound silence there on the hillside among the pristine sparkle of trees iced in white. Koski had involuntarily screamed during the exchange of gunfire. Now she, too, was silent, malevolence in her eyes trained on the redheaded killer.

Reinecke and Vigo were obviously shaken, too, as if questioning whether they had chosen the right side in this fight. If what Falk suspected was true, it was too late for the duo to question their choice. They committed to the wrong side long ago.

His rifle always at the ready, Eiker herded them into a tight group and addressed Falk and Koski. "Just exactly who the hell are you?"

"Bureau of Land Management," Falk quickly offered, trying to make their presence here as benign as possible, at least for the time being. "Sent to do an inspection in the area of the mine when suddenly there were these explosions."

"What's Land Management doing here? I thought you Yanks had something called the Bureau of Mines."

"We do. However, there appears to be a water dispute...our jurisdiction."

Eiker seemed to buy it but Falk figured that he did so either because he didn't have enough time to probe further or because it didn't matter. He was not the type of man to accept anything at face value if it were pertinent to him. Falk thought something else about this Limey. He obviously had the opposable qualities of detached calm and exploding urgency; often juxtaposed in a hired killer.

"Okay," Eiker said and turned to Koski. "I need to rendezvous at Bowman Lake in exactly two hours. You and your friend here, being BLM, should know your way around the area enough to lead me there."

Eiker chewed his gum slowly. Its sound snapped crisply in the cold air. "You have the right to remain silent," he said, "in which case, I have the right to kill you."

"You expect *me* to help *you*?" Koski said slowly and levelly. "I would regard that on a par with feeding an alligator in hopes that he would eat me *last.*"

Falk stepped forward. "Look, Eiker, I'll—"

Bud Vigo, not sure what Falk's response would be, was already in the act of bursting between them. "I know the area well, Eiker…I have a cabin near the lake…I'll show you how to get there."

In that moment Falk thought that Vigo probably did the only decent thing he had done in years. Maybe because Eiker was his ticket out of here. Maybe because his stomach couldn't take the prospect of more dead bodies in the snow.

Eiker shrugged. "How long will it take us on foot?" he asked Vigo.

"A couple of hours if we hurry and don't get more storms."

"Then let's move out."

Koski's green eyes blazed anew. "You're just going to leave them here? There are wolves and coyotes in these woods. They'll —"

Eiker dismissed her with a wave of his gloved hand. "Don't worry your pretty head. More troops will be along to collect them soon—too soon." He turned to his partner. "Ray, Vigo will lead." He gestured with his rifle to Falk, Koski, Reinecke and the two remaining soldiers. "You follow Vigo and Ray will follow you. I'll be…everywhere."

Before they stepped into the encompassing forest, Falk looked back down the hillside at what remained of the mine.

Regular Army troops, several fire trucks and other first response units converged on the scene of blazing rubble. Special Forces units were probably on their way to the hillside entrance

Falk and the others had just left.

Once more, Falk glanced back toward the entrance and the two brave, fallen soldiers. Before this day ended he would avenge their deaths.

Chapter 29

Maxwell jumped when the phone rang. This room in the military hospital in Fallon had been her home for the past twenty-four hours and she'd had no calls.

"Webster!" She was jubilant to hear his voice.

"Didn't Alex tell you I was transferred here from the hospital in Reno?"

"No, Alex hasn't called me in two days. I assumed he either had no news or was told to discontinue broadcasting our whereabouts...if he even knows our whereabouts." She paused. "How are you?"

"I'm fine now."

Maxwell detected a great tiredness in his usual, congenial tone. "'Now?'"

"I had a moderate concussion that kept me hovering in no man's land for a while but I'm...it's a long story. Look, I just discovered that only a couple of rooms separate us. Want some company?"

"Of course."

By the time Webster arrived and gave her an account of the mortar attack near the mine and his, Falk and Koski's detention by the U.S. Army, he was thoroughly exhausted. He looked around the militarily sparse room; a hospital bed, a portable tilt-top table and two comfortable arm chairs. A scarlet duvet woven with gold thread lent an ambiance of personality to the room. "I don't have a pretty bedspread like that on my bed," he said, as if deprived.

She smiled. "Are there patients in any other rooms on this floor?"

"No and the nurses' station is unattended, too. This place is more like a hotel than a hospital."

"Well, at least we're safe here," she said sympathetically.

"Yes, but our being safe doesn't help Falk and Koski."

He slumped in one of the easy chairs and Maxwell thought of the strong, take-charge man he was the night at Alex Spade's home when an arrow was nearly buried in Alex's back. "I understand your frustration," she said, "but what can we do?"

He stood up suddenly, reached into the pocket of his western style shirt and extracted a small piece of folded paper. "I'm going to call Ryland…tell him that we need to get back into action, that…" His words trailed off and he weaved slightly, repositioning his feet to steady himself.

"Whoa!" Maxwell said and was at his elbow, urging him gently back into the chair. "I think you need another day of rest."

A quick, light tapping on the door made them both turn toward the sound.

"Ryland told me that nobody knew I was here," Maxwell whispered. The tapping repeated, louder.

"Maybe we should see who it is," he said.

She got up and stood by the door. "Who is it?"

"It's Roz Newton, Wes Webster's secretary. Do you have a moment, Dr. Maxwell?"

Webster roused with recognition, started to get up but Maxwell waved him to stay in his chair. She couldn't explain it. It was as if somewhere some hidden evil had stuck its head out of a hole and she shivered. Looking back at Webster, she mouthed,

"How did *she* know I was here?"

Webster shrugged naively. "I might have mentioned..."

Maxwell rolled her eyes. "Why do you want to see me, Roz?" she called out.

"I have some information you'd be interested in. It's about Agents Falk and Koski."

Maxwell envisioned Roz as she had seen her in Webster's office several days ago—Roz and the J.Lo jeans with rhinestone pockets. She had seemed harmless and Maxwell had no reason to mistrust her. Nevertheless, events of this investigation had heightened Maxwell's vigilance. She decided to ask one more question. "How did you know I was here?"

"Wes told me, of course. In fact, he sent me."

Maxwell was chilled that her seemingly unfounded suspicion was confirmed. She turned and walked back to where Webster had silently risen from his chair, his mouth hanging open.

"You *sure* you didn't tell her to come here for any reason?" she whispered.

He nodded blankly, unable to comprehend Roz's motives. "I'm sure."

"She doesn't know you're here. She must think you're in your own room." She walked back to the door. "Look, Roz," she called, "I was just about to jump into the shower. Why don't you come back say, in half an hour?"

They both stared at the door. Maxwell could almost feel the woman's anger. Then there was the rattle of the doorknob and Maxwell was grateful she'd had the foresight to lock it after Webster arrived. Finally, hearing Roz's heels clicking along the corridor, she sighed and walked away from the door.

"She's gone." Would she be back? That depended on what she

had in mind. If she did come back, what would Maxwell do?

Inexplicably, she thought of her father's words when she was young. He was speaking of preparedness. "Don't assume everybody wants to hurt you but expect it."

"We should call security," Webster said.

Maxwell started pacing. "I'm not sure…I don't even know if we can trust *them*. We could call Ryland but I doubt he's close enough to do us any good." Every ounce of her being resisted her next thought but finally inbred preparedness prevailed.

"I'll be right back," she said and went to the bathroom, pulled off her skirt, jacket and panty hose and slipped into a robe and slippers. Carefully, fighting disgust, she removed the Walther from her purse on the countertop, checked that it was loaded and cocked and then thumbed the safety to off.

Draping a thick bath towel over her right arm, she arranged the folds to conceal the weapon. When she returned to the room, Webster was standing by the door and pronounced what she had expected.

"She's coming back and it's been less than ten minutes…" Moving away from the door, he glanced up at the overhead light Maxwell had turned on earlier to expel the gloom of the dark afternoon. He instinctively hit the wall switch, which extinguished all but one low wattage lamp. He crossed to Maxwell and protectively placed an arm around her shoulders. "Don't worry," he whispered. "I'll protect you."

Maxwell knew he meant it but she was aware of the slight sway of his body against her own. The footsteps paused at the door and she heard the jangle of a key in the lock. Maxwell could think of only one purpose that would make the woman this determined. She curled her finger around the trigger of the automatic and waited, unsure if she could pressure that trigger if the need arose.

Chapter 30

It was late afternoon and a white sift fell on the Sierra again. Falk felt apart from the other seven people in the straggling column, his mind constantly assessing the chances of his and Koski's escape before they reached Bowman Lake. The Brit was a tough opponent in a battle of wits and strength yet, like any man, he had weaknesses. Falk watched for one to show itself. Only moments ago, Falk remembered where he heard the name Rodney Eiker.

The ITL listed him as a freelancer, for sale to the highest bidder. Now he'd been hired to extricate Vigo and Reinecke from the mine before the Army found them. "Hurry it up." The Englishman's voice cut through the cold air from his present position at the end of the column. "I won't look kindly on anyone who makes me late for my rendezvous at the Lake."

Falk figured that Eiker, like any good warrior, never underestimated the enemy. One of Cromwell's units could be in the surrounding hills. That reflection might be reassuring to Koski, Falk thought, and he whispered, "Once the Delta troops discover the two dead soldiers and our tracks, they'll locate us." Koski, preceding him in line, nodded silently. Snowflakes tumbled around them as the wind, up to fifteen miles per hour a short time ago, dropped to zero and the still air grew deathly cold.

Falk thought of how he reassured Meg in her time of need before he left her in the vehicle in which she died. He quickly barred the haunting memory. He had not failed Meg and he would not fail Koski.

Then he realized Koski was not waiting for anyone to fail her.

She had dropped back slightly, putting some space between herself and Vigo. "Psst," she whispered, turning her head so that her voice travelled back to Falk.

"Yes?"

"The direction we're travelling will put us in open country soon." Falk nodded silently. "We want to get to Bowman in one piece," she said. "That Delta team could wipe us *all* out."

"The Brit will kill us anyway when we get to the lake." Falk was sure of this. Earlier, Ray had covered the column while Eiker and the two captive soldiers went into the woods. Two shots rang out and Eiker returned alone.

"We can lose Eiker when the time is right," she said.

"We can?"

"Of course." She paused. "Right, Agent Falk?"

"Right," he answered, noting that he had not seen her reach for her postcard in hours.

She turned and called to Vigo. "Tell our fearless leader that I can show him a better way to Bowman so we don't get picked off like rabbits out on the open slopes."

Eiker heard and walked ahead to Koski.

Falk positioned himself at Koski's side and, for the first time, took a close look at the man. Late forties, he guessed and younger shape. His left ear was deeply scarred and there weren't any laugh lines around his eyes, which were deep blue, flashing like Novas.

"I had a hunch taking you along would eventually pay off," Eiker said to Koski. "What's on your mind?"

"If we're being tracked by the Army, and I've no doubt we are, they'll sight us easily if we tramp across an open slope."

Eiker considered her comment. "So?"

"So, if we walk straight down the mountain we'll reach the

tree line, which will afford cover. Scrub pines overlap ridges that by heading northeast, will take us within yards of the lake where dense tree cover is available."

"You can find your way through the woods?"

"Definitely."

"You lead then. I'll be right behind you but remember, any false moves and—"

She waved him away. "I know. I know. I saw the movie."

Soon the weary column plodded through scattered underbrush, evergreens and interspersed deciduous alders. All was silent except for the occasional slap of snow falling from an overloaded branch and the soft squeak of powder underfoot. They travelled this way for thirty minutes before Falk heard Reinecke complain of muscle fatigue and their leader called for another brief rest stop.

Falk huddled with Koski next to a giant pine, seeking to give, and get, warmth. "We must be almost there," he said.

She pulled the collar of her jacket tightly around her throat. "We'll be over the ridge in less than twenty minutes and then we're basically at Bowman."

As a sudden spurt of wind whirled icy streams of snow from the powdered surface around them, Falk thought the Englishman would eliminate the excess baggage.

The column started moving again, making slow but steady progress. Falk saw two Delta men on skis cross in front of a stand of aspens, visible only for a split second, less than a hundred yards away. Eiker saw them, too. Falk watched him scoop up a handful of snow and lob a snowball at Ray, who was behind Koski at the head of the column. Ray spun around and saw Eiker tap the top of his head and point in the direction of the skiers.

Falk lurched behind a giant pine, whipping his arms around Koski and taking her with him. The others also dispersed and hit the ground among the dense trees.

"Soldiers," Falk whispered, his breath creating a cloud between them. "White suited and on skis."

"How many?"

"I only saw two…probably part of a split six-man team."

"We're only ten minutes from the lake," she said softly.

"Isn't there a Ranger Station somewhere near Bowman? We could call Ryland from there."

"Yes but we'll have to go around—"

Suddenly he clapped a hand over her mouth and pulled her deeper into the drift beneath snow-laden branches as an Army captain and a two-man team passed within five feet of them moving eastward.

When they had gone, Falk whispered, "Obviously, that team is not equipped with heat sensors."

"I'm thinking that maybe it's not such a good idea, hiding from Special Forces. After all, they're the good guys."

"I know, but we have work to do and we can't do it if we're detained in another session with Cromwell."

She nodded. "Or if we're dead."

He pointed to the edge of the woods. "They came from that direction so we'll head out that way." Moving from tree to tree and using all possible cover, they reached the border of the thickest tree growth. Falk peered across the white expanse of mountainside and saw the troopers' discarded skis sticking upright in the snow.

"We're out of here," he whispered. "Those skis are fitted with military bindings and designed to adjust to nearly any boot size and type." Within minutes, the two were ready to push off.

"Look!" Koski said, pointing to the tree line. Bud Vigo was running and stumbling toward them.

"Chief," Koski said, "are you all right?"

Falk was silent. Apparently, Koski had bought the story of how Vigo and Reinecke were hostages of Eiker. For the time being, Falk let it seem that he did, too.

"I saw you two leave and took a chance," Vigo said, sucking air and looking back over his shoulder.

"Where's Senator Reinecke?" Koski asked.

"Still hiding…with Ray and Eiker," he wheezed, "among the trees."

"What was he doing at the mine, anyway? And—"

"Koski!" Falk glared at her. "Later." He turned to Vigo. "You ski?" Vigo nodded. "Then grab a pair—hurry."

Falk pulled the remaining skis out of the snow. "No sense leaving these for anyone pursuing us." He tucked them under his arm.

Silently they hissed over the snow like low-flying gulls, leaving the woods behind. Soon Falk let the excess skis go and watched them race like stoats down the mountainside and vanish from sight. He heard the rattle of automatic weapons in the direction from which they had come but he stabbed the snow with his poles and never looked back.

Eiker took down two of the soldiers at nearly point blank range, having watched them approach from the hiding place he chose because it afforded an ideal crossfire condition for Ray. The remaining trooper of the first half of the team was fast and took cover, returning fire with amazing speed and accuracy.

Bark chips flew from a tree inches above Eiker's head. He rolled away to his next cover, a downed evergreen half hidden by fallen branches, as snow was whipped up by the fire of two Special Forces troopers. They had popped into view with astonishing speed, reminding Eiker of spring-loaded targets on a firing range. He snaked behind the log, one bullet tearing the heel from his boot.

Ray waited until he was sure he had the sharp-shooting trooper lined up. Then his finger froze on the trigger. There was a sound near him—something barely heard...but felt...He pivoted. "Wha—" and saw Reinecke. The senator had been crouching behind a nearby tree, afraid to move, afraid not to move. Either unaware of the trooper in Ray's crosshairs or oblivious to all but his need for the safety of an armed companion, he suddenly stood and took two steps in Ray's direction, alerting the sharpshooter to Ray's position.

The soldier fired, strafing a six-foot path in the bark of the trees around him. Pain, like the whack of a sledgehammer, seared Ray's left upper arm but he knew instantly that the bullet that found him had not tunnelled deeply into his flesh. He shot a malignant glance at Reinecke, who had taken cover beside him.

Eiker, having pinpointed the shooter when he fired at Ray, reacted swiftly, turning his AR-18 on the soldier in time to trigger twice, silencing the man forever. Then he took another blast of bullets from the two who had pinned down his position, but the domino effect continued. Ray let loose a barrage of bullets in their direction, firing until no fire returned.

Eiker took off, bent double, sprinting between trees for two hundred meters. He stopped, fell into firing position and waited. He assumed that Ray would leave the shivering Reinecke behind, bolt in the opposite direction and wait.

The Delta captain of the final three-man unit was the next in Eiker's sights. He squeezed the trigger, his AR-18 roared and the captain, hit in the throat, spun in a spray of blood, his life wrenched from him. Before disappearing into the trees, the two remaining troopers opened fire, raking the branches inches above Eiker's head.

Ray saw one of the remaining soldiers finger the squad communicator attached to the right side of his suit. If he got through to Command, he would give away their location. Inching forward, Ray closed in on the man who was moving out of the trees.

This would have to be a wet job. Sliding a bone-handled knife from its sheath, Ray stealthily crept through the soft snow. To kill the man without a sound would prevent the remaining trooper from gauging their location. Ray lunged. Before the soldier had time to react to danger, the razor-sharp knife had found its way to his jugular.

The snap of a twig behind him caused Ray to spin around. The remaining trooper was there, his body levelled into a combat stance, rifle angled in Ray's direction. Ray lurched sideways and blood spouted from the side of his left shoulder, yet some part of his mind registered amazement that he was still alive.

The sight of his fallen companion had diverted the soldier's aim. In the next instant, in the soldier's pause to assess what obviously was an advantage, Ray bolted to his feet and lunged savagely at the man, slamming him to the ground and knocking his weapon from his grip.

The soldier recovered quickly; a Bowie knife was suddenly in his hand. Grasping the wrist of his attacker, Ray brought his knee up into his groin. The soldier grunted and groaned but never lost the grip on his knife. Before he could duck and avoid it, the blade swept across Ray's face, laying it open from below the right eye to the top lip.

Blood gushed into Ray's eyes as he spun sideways to avert a second slash but it sliced through his snow jacket and cut a gash in his side. The trooper was built like a door. Ray would have to rely on speed and agility in this battle of blades but his wounds were slowing him down.

Clutching his knife in the classic position, he jabbed upward with all his strength, hoping to plunge the blade into the attacker's groin but the thrust was deflected. Again, Ray stabbed upward but the big man pitched to the side and the knife only caught the threads of his snowsuit.

Ray's hands were slippery with blood; the same vital fluid poured from his face and shoulder. He was losing strength, the knife now alien in his weakening grip. Turning his head, he saw the trooper leap, too, and his knife sliced down through Ray's collarbone on its way to his heart.

Eiker broke through the trees in time to see Ray receive the mortal wound. The soldier turned, his knife dripping with blood and in that instant Eiker fired from the hip. The trooper took the shots full in the face and his head disintegrated.

Slowly crossing the clearing, Eiker stopped and looked down at his dead companion. Then he fell to one knee and removed the knife from Ray's bloody grip. "I'll keep this in memory of a warrior," he said softly.

Tucking the weapon into the inside of his jacket, he turned and walked back into the trees. Where in hell was that pitiful excuse for a man, Reinecke, and Vigo and the two BLM agents? This battle was not over.

Chapter 31

Roz Newton was suddenly in the room and in her hand was a silenced Sig Sauer automatic.

True to her J.Lo image, Roz wore a tight tee and a denim miniskirt under her long tan leather coat, exaggerating her leggy appearance. Her blond hair was long, straight and wispy. She nodded at Webster.

"I was *afraid* I'd made a mistake when I answered Dr. Maxwell's last question. I knew by her response that I'd given myself away and that you were probably here." She kicked the door shut with her heel. "It's convenient, actually, you both in the same room."

Gesturing for them to move to the bed, she saw a *noir* paperback novel on Maxwell's nightstand and referenced its title. "You two are about to take the big sleep."

"But *why*, Roz?" Webster asked gently, adopting the tone of a negotiator. "Why do you want to kill us? How are you mixed up in all of this—?"

"I'm not *mixed up!*" she interjected defensively, mistaking Webster's remark.

Her response, however, was telling. Maxwell guessed that here was a young woman whose defense mechanism was a hair trigger; she hoped that her firing finger was not.

Maxwell's own finger was steady on the trigger of the Walther beneath the towel draped over her right arm.

Roz smiled then laughed, a full-throated laugh delivered through very white teeth and cherry red lips. It crossed Maxwell's mind that perhaps Roz was mad.

"I'm in this for the thrills, Wes," Roz said, "and the money and the experience." Her eyes flickered to the automatic in her hand. "This is something I've always wanted to do.

"My mother shot my father when I was six..." It was as if she was talking to herself. "I've played it over and over in my mind." She paused and seemed to reach to the bottom drawer of her madness. "It's time for an empirical experience."

"Look, Roz," Webster said, "if it's a question of money—I know BLM doesn't pay you much—I'll see what I can..."

Her shrill, crazed laugh stopped him. "I'm getting more money for these few minutes than BLM could pay me in a lifetime." She levelled the gun and her finger began to pressure the trigger.

Maxwell seemed to watch rather than experience what happened next, as if viewing an out-of-body experience. The Walther discharged twice. Maxwell was less than three feet from her would-be killer when the shots sounded.

Jolted back, Roz staggered and fell—a stunned expression on her face. Possibly her last vision was the blackened holes in the fluffy, white bath towel draped over Maxwell's arm.

Then there was a thunderous roar in Maxwell's ears, like dark, enormous wings flapping inside her head. She couldn't think. She couldn't speak. She couldn't breathe. She sank to the bed and cried uncontrollably.

Once Webster had recovered from shock and wrestled back the sensation to vomit, he sat down beside her and waited while she blurted out her feelings between giant gulps of breath and tears.

He hugged her close, "It's okay, Doc."

Maxwell thought of her father and how he must have felt after killing her best friend's father. She had never fully considered her father's point of view in that incident. How lonely he must have been; how desolate her estrangement from him must have made him...and had made her. New tears—swallowed instead of shed when she was seventeen—spilled from her eyes.

The sound of feet pounding along the corridor announced the arrival of security personnel and others who heard the shots. Webster reached out with one hand and flipped the wall switch. The illumination reflected in the hanging mirror beside them heightened the red-gold bed covering beneath them.

In Reno, Samuel Ryland received the news that the mine near Bowman Lake had suffered numerous internal explosions. Special Forces under the command of Colonel Alvin Cromwell also had sustained heavy losses, both at the mine and in battles in the surrounding forest. Within thirty minutes, Ryland arrived at the mine via NSA helicopter and was shown into Cromwell's makeshift office at the old lodge.

"Colonel Cromwell, do you think there's anything left underground to find...to help us piece together what in hell was down there that the mine's personnel were ready to die for?"

Cromwell shook his head. "No, what wasn't destroyed in the initial explosions is burned or buried under tons of rock and rubble. It's like Ground Zero down there."

An FBI representative who had arrived minutes ago with his entourage asked, "Colonel, we had reports that Senator Albert Reinecke and Carson City Police Chief Bud Vigo were in the vicinity of the mine. Do you have any information as to their whereabouts?"

Cromwell shook his head. "Negative at this time."

"What about FBI Special Agent Joseph Falk and BLM's Susan Koski...do you have *any* idea as to the condition of the civilians or those agents?"

"After the explosions, I dispatched a six-man search team that is still somewhere in the field. At last report, the team had encountered heavy small-arms' fire, apparently from some of those civilians you're all so worried about." He ran a finger across his tight upper lip. "I have commenced an air search in the area and more troops are on their way there."

A knock on the office door stopped further conversation as one of Cromwell's men appeared, snapping a crisp salute. "Report from one of the tracking and reconnaissance copters, sir. Three bodies sighted in a heavily wooded area less than 1.6 kilometers from Bowman Lake. T&R are awaiting reinforcements before putting down, sir."

Cromwell sighed. "Soldier, be sure you get this order loud and clear. I want whoever is left in those woods taken alive. We don't know the good guys from the bad in that bunch and I need some answers. I want them all taken alive."

Ryland was on board the next search helicopter. Seated beside the Army pilot, his senses seemed extraordinarily enhanced. He keenly felt the movement of air as it mapped its path around the aircraft. He ran a hand across his bronze forehead and through his thick ebony hair. His eyes, dark gray and solemn as an owl's, scanned the woods of worry below. Where were Falk and Koski? Would he find them before one of Cromwell's other units did? "I want them taken alive," the Colonel had said.

I want them dead, the voice in Ryland's head whispered.

Memories, like strange wind whistling down the long tunnel of time, filled him and an old love of happy predestination burned more brightly than ever in his heart. Since he was a boy in New England he had listened wide-eyed at his grandfather's knee to tales of his great-grandfather. He was an Algonquin chief.

Hearing tales of other elders of the tribe, he took seriously the sobriquet with which his father dubbed him: *Mukuamp*.

In the Algonquian language of the early Massachusetts Indian tribes, the word meant "big man" or "chief." Although he remained Mukuamp in his heart, he legally became Samuel Ryland at age eighteen. The name was unimportant and a convenience he had fingered from the Yellow Pages.

When he attended college in Oklahoma, his introduction to the Plains Indians deepened his kinship with other tribes and pride in his forebears. Some of them still cursed the white man and harbored vengeance in their hearts. They strengthened his resolve to become a twenty-first century leader.

A law degree from Harvard furthered the opportunity for him to envision his long-term goal. From the days the United States Cavalry drove the buffalo, the Comanches, Kiowas, Crows and other tribes from Oklahoma's Southern Plains, Mukuamp's people —for now *all* Native Americans were Mukuamp's people—had been forced to succumb to the realization that their glory days were over. Worse, their culture had lost its ability to evolve.

For years, Mukuamp had schemed and plotted that the greatest moment in their history was yet to be; that the journey to the second golden age of the Native American awaited only the broad eagle's vision and careful silent planning of a truly big man.

For hundreds of years, it seemed beyond his people's reach. Now it would come to pass. It required the singular vision and leadership of a man who was a chief in the bravest, most tenacious and highborn sense of the word.

His grandfather and great-grandfather's words lived only in memory. Mukuamp remembered their curse of the white invaders. He retained the image of a proud past that would come again. Not as it once was, not in the form of fierce, painted, breech-clothed hunter-warriors but as suited, economically, politically, legally and technologically savvy leaders under the administration of a man who would give new meaning to the term *Commander-in-Chief.*

This was not an overreaching statement of Mukuamp's aims. Certainly, in the newly configured world he envisioned, his would be a more powerful position than any *president* ever enjoyed.

It would take time, more time now since the mine complex was lost and the human scaffolding he had carefully constructed with Reinecke, Lovesy, Vigo and the others was deconstructed. As long as his own identity remained protected, however, he could begin again. One did not tear wine from the vine; the rebirth of a nation required ripening.

Chapter 32

The topography was erratic as the three skiers neared the lake; in one moment glacially flat, in the next a hill heaved before them. On the lake, slate gray waves broke into small angry whitecaps and fingers of thin ice crept out from the shore.

Falk, with Koski ahead and Vigo behind him, bent deeply for more thrust and speed, the increasing wind driving him on and stinging his face. For several minutes he was wholly absorbed in the pure act of sailing over the snow, lost in the peaceful surroundings.

Then something impelled him to look back. He caught a glimpse of Vigo disappearing at a confluence of slopes, heading toward the eastern shore.

"Koski!" Falk shouted. When she did not respond, he repeated, "*Koski*," shouting over the wind. This time she heard and circled back.

"Where's—" she started and stopped.

"That's right...he said he's got a cabin up here somewhere." Falk was convinced that Vigo was connected to the lawyers' deaths and that he was at the mine to meet with his co-conspirators regarding some new offensive.

"We're going after him," he said.

"Why?"

"Vigo's dirty."

"No." It was a statement.

"Listen, what else explains the disappearance of the arrow in Carson City...the one Maxwell said was found in a tree and that she placed in the evidence cage? Moreover, Maxwell told me Vigo has access to a helicopter, a helicopter he guards carefully. It's the one that I'm convinced accidentally made the marks on the roof where Sharpe was killed." He paused. "He may even be The Fox."

"Bud Vigo, The Fox?"

"I'll explain later. Let's go."

Following the firefight, Eiker quickly scoured the area and found a terrified Reinecke huddled at the base of a tree, banked in snow.

"Looks like we're all that's left," Eiker said, urging Reinecke through the trees. "I'm saving your arse, senator. I could easily leave you here and let the Army shoot you." He gave the older man an extra shove. "We're due to be picked up by a chopper at four p.m. and I have no intention of missing that flight. So, if you want to stay alive, hustle, old chap."

They hadn't gone far when Eiker heard a low-flying helicopter approaching. He shoved Reinecke toward a rock outcropping and they huddled beneath huge overhanging boulders, not daring to move. Finally, Eiker raised his head cautiously.

"That Army pilot is searching for signs of life, concentrating on the ski tracks we saw."

Once the aircraft passed from view, he shoved Reinecke forward. The senator, who was exhausted and breathing erratically, stumbled and Eiker had to drag him up from his knees. Eiker cursed silently. He must keep this bastard alive long enough to get the last installment on his wages for this bloody gig.

Believing he had lost Falk and Koski, Vigo discarded his skis and raced to his four-room cabin on the lakeshore. Once inside, he went directly to a wall phone and dialed a number. "I'm at my cabin. Pick me up mid-lake as soon as possible."

He hung up and hurried into the bedroom. He kicked aside a woollen rug and lifted several floorboards. He reached down and removed two oilskin packages. Unwrapping one, he uncovered a bolt-action shotgun, the Marlin Model 55 goose gun designed for killing migratory waterfowl at high altitudes. It was a rare but extremely lethal weapon. Vigo loaded the shotgun and scooped up four extra shells, grabbed the second package and hustled out of the cabin and down to the boathouse. Inside, he considered the two-seater Jet Ski he kept there, knowing it was fast.

He figured his chopper to be here in less than fifteen minutes. He had no wish to freeze before it arrived and sitting astride that bucking sport craft in this weather…he thought not. He opened the double wooden doors facing the lake, removed the canvas cover from the outboard motor of his fourteen-foot aluminum fishing boat, slipped the cumbersome package beneath the seat and yanked the outboard motor lanyard three times. The engine sprang to life. Cold wind stung his eyes and nostrils as he steered through the sheer film of ice and out into deeper water.

The original escape plan called for him to fly out of Carson City to a safe house up at Mammoth Lake. Now it had to be

Bowman instead of Carson. He didn't like changing plans that increased the chances of fickle fate stepping in. Glancing back at the shore, a split second of curiosity as to what happened to the two agents flickered through his mind. Something told him they would show up.

Falk and Koski broke from the trees just as the sound of an outboard motor kicking over roared in the cold air.

"Shit!" Koski swore, seeing Vigo seated in the stern of his boat and moving out into the lake. "Where are Cromwell's choppers when we need them? They could easily get him from the air…"

"We've got to find a boat and go after him," Falk growled. In the time it took him to finish his sentence, she was gone.

In the boathouse, Falk stared at the sleek blue and white Jet Ski bobbing gently in the water, Koski astride its double banana seat.

"Koski, that's not a boat."

"But it sure as hell can catch that thing Vigo's puttering in."

He had only a second of indecision. "You're right." He grabbed her and pulled her from the seat, straddling it himself. "You stay. I'll go."

"Okay," she said and slid into the seat behind him.

He rolled his eyes and hit the starter. There was a shattering roar as the powerful engine came to life and the machine leapt forward and headed for the open water.

Soon they were a quarter of a mile out on the lake, a white plumed rooster tail gallantly arcing behind them. The openness of the lake conspired with the wind to whip the air from their lungs and Falk's hands tingled with the cold.

He moved his fingers to increase blood circulation. He had to be ready to react when the moment came. Ahead, he saw Vigo's boat, which had a discouraging head start. Notching the throttle wider, he hurled the sport craft across the freezing lake, the bow wave breaking beneath the shark-like nose with the distinct thudding and pounding beat of fiberglass on water.

All of a sudden, Koski was beating on his shoulder and shouting in his ear— *"Behind us! Vigo's chopper!"*

Falk snapped his gaze in the direction she pointed and saw the sheriff's helicopter skimming the surface less than a quarter of a mile behind them. "Hold on!" He yanked hard on the handlebars and the Jet Ski responded in time to allow an arrow to flash past and bury itself in the lake water. He was relieved to realize that this time there was no extra man in the aircraft and no laser-controlled beam to assist the arrow's flight. The odds still were not good. They were unarmed against an arrow-spitting helicopter.

A second arrow flashed from the bird's underbelly, snaking toward them like a serpent's tongue. It embedded itself in the fiberglass hull of the Jet Ski less than an inch from Koski's thigh. Falk pulled to the right in a tight turn, dipping the starboard footrest underwater and causing the nose to lurch upward, nearly bringing the craft to a halt. Then, jamming the throttle wide open, he turned left and hurtled through his own wake.

Vigo was only yards in front of them now but the helicopter skewed into a tight turn and danced in place. Its blades were a wild wash of motion as a rope ladder was lowered toward Vigo's boat, which slowed slightly. He glanced back at the bucking Jet Ski and reached for his goose gun.

"Koski," Falk shouted, "get ready to take over. I'm going alongside. When I jump, pull away at once." She had no chance to reply before Falk powered alongside the fishing boat.

The dangling ladder momentarily diverted Vigo's attention. He was thrown off balance by the boat's rocking in the powerful prop wash from the aircraft's rotors. It was long enough for Falk to throw himself across the few feet separating them. He grabbed Vigo by the leg, the momentum of his leap knocking the police chief down in the boat. Koski pulled away and then throttled down almost to a stop.

Falk took a glancing blow to the right cheek from the barrel of the Marlin 55. He felt himself rock back against the side of the boat, blood running from a gash in his face. Vigo tried to steady the gun to aim, but Falk lashed his right foot out, delivering a scissor kick that caught Vigo's groin. He grabbed himself and screamed in pain.

The helicopter dropped lower; the ladder swung inches in front of Vigo's face. Releasing the gun and grabbing wildly at the rungs, his fingers connected and the pilot immediately started to climb.

Falk scrambled toward the goose gun and scooped it from the floor, his fingers numb with cold, fumbling with the unfamiliar mechanism. The chopper was gaining altitude fast and Vigo, uttering a sound between a rattle and a wheeze, clutched the ladder for dear life, his legs flailing as he desperately tried to ascend by getting a foothold on one of the slippery rungs.

The unsteady boat on the wind-whipped lake was not an ideal platform from which to fire but Falk spread his legs for balance and took careful aim at the helicopter's engine compartment. Steadying the 36-inch, full-choke barrel of the Marlin, he fired. Quickly working the bolt and sliding the second round into the chamber, he took a fast aim and pulled the trigger. The shot hit the engine. Grabbing extra shells from the floor, he got off one more shot before losing his balance and nearly toppling into the lake.

Vigo grimly hung onto the ladder as flames billowed from beneath the engine cowling, licking downward, driven by the thrust of the down draft from the aircraft's blades. The yellow flames licked at Vigo's hands as he twisted from side to side in an effort to escape the searing heat. Falk righted himself and took careful aim at the man dangling from the chopper, sighting in on his neck. Nevertheless, this kill was not to be his.

When flames suddenly met fuel, Vigo's helicopter exploded into a fireball, erupting with a vast thunderclap of searing heat felt by Falk and Koski two hundred feet below. Killed instantly by exploding debris, Vigo dropped, his fingers clutching scraps of the ladder as he fell, legs flapping wildly in space.

The shattered remains of the copter hung in midair for a few seconds before it dropped, slamming into the lake. It boiled and bubbled on the surface then sank from sight, trailing steam and smoke and leaving only an oil slick and jetsam in its wake.

Koski eased the Jet Ski alongside the aluminum boat. "Your face…you're bleeding!"

Falk swiped at the blood. "Superficial, head to shore." He moved to the rear seat of the fishing boat and pulled the outboard to life. It was on the way back to the boathouse that he noticed an oilskin package jutting from beneath one of the seats.

Back inside the boathouse, Falk secured the open craft, reached under the seat and removed the oilskin covering from the second package, revealing a bow, four laser-guided arrows and a handheld laser guidance system.

"Wow," Koski gasped, "the whole enchilada."

Falk had the laser system working within minutes, aiming the red dot on the inside wall of the boathouse. "Aim the dot at the target...and the arrow hones in on the dot," he purred. "Fantastic weapon but it takes two to tango with this."

"Nothing wrong with that, Joe." She could not remember when she began to call him by his first name; it just happened.

Falk refolded the covering over the equipment and glanced around the interior. "We'll just leave it in here for the time being." He placed the bundle on a shelf near the door and they hurried toward the cabin.

As he walked, Falk pondered what he knew. Only one piece of the puzzle remained and it would not be as simple as fitting the last piece of a jigsaw into a remaining void.

Eiker and Reinecke kept a screen of trees between them and Vigo's cabin as they approached the boathouse.

"Don't make a sound," Eiker hissed. He and the senator had seen the chopper go down in flames, watched the man and woman return the Jet Ski and fishing boat to the boathouse and enter the cabin. "We'll take the fishing boat." Eiker held the side of the boat as Reinecke gingerly stepped in. "Here." He handed two paddles to Reinecke. "We'll paddle out a way before starting the outboard. Might as well have as much of a head start as possible."

Moving to the Jet Ski, he pulled the key from the ignition and dropped it into the lake. Snapping open the engine compartment, he reached in and ripped out a handful of electrical wiring, totally dismantling the ignition system. He returned to the boat and climbed in, released the lines, took one of the paddles and pushed out into the lake.

"Paddle," he ordered but soon took over himself, seeing Reinecke's strength failing. When he judged that they were far enough from the cabin, he pulled the outboard to life and steered eastward, slowly increasing speed.

Chapter 33

"You must be exhausted," Falk said to Koski, once he checked out the cabin. "I'll make a call and get us out of here." The cabin was small and comfortably furnished in a style somewhere between shabby chic and early New England. The living room had an old pot-belly stove.

Falk went to the antique wall phone but hesitated. "Damn! I'm not sure who we can trust at BLM…or the Bureau for that matter. I'll try Ryland." He dug into his shirt pocket and extracted a folded piece of paper. Lovesy had given them three numbers for Ryland. Falk chose the cell number, waiting as the old rotary dial slowly returned after each digit.

Koski shivered noticeably, eyeing the stove. "I think I'll fire up this relic." She took newspaper and kindling from a large version of a Vermont maple sugar bucket. She stuffed them into the stove, struck a wooden match and touched the flame to the edge of the paper. She added the kindling, adjusted the damper on the stovepipe and rubbed her palms together as if to hurry the heat.

Ryland answered on the first ring.

"Agent Koski and I are in a cabin on the east shore of Bowman Lake," Falk said after identifying himself. "The cabin's owned by Chief Bud Vigo of the Carson City—"

"Yes, I know of it," Ryland interrupted. "I'm in an Army chopper nearby."

"Good. Look, I'm not sure who we can trust at BLM Reno anymore or who I should contact at the Bureau—"

"No one," Ryland quickly put in over the static on the line. "I'll take care of all calls. Stay where you are. We'll be there in a few minutes."

After he hung up, Falk turned to Koski, who was placing a log on the fire. "Ryland's on his way. He'll notify the Bureau."

"What'll we do next?" She turned her back to the stove. "Is this case closed?"

"Not by a long shot." He paced the floor, frowning darkly. "I've worked out a rough what and why scenario about the case but I don't have a "who" yet."

"But I thought Vigo was The Fox and if—"

He stopped at the window and looked out at the lake. "I've failed. The mastermind is still out there."

"No!" When he turned, she shot him a chastising glance and added an aside. "Friends don't let friends go on guilt trips." She slowly twirled back to the stove, staring at the fire through the door's tempered glass window. "Maybe Webster, Maxwell and Spade have come up with something." She sighed. "I wonder about them." Turning again, she looked at him. "I wonder about *us, too.*"

He sank into a large, low swivel rocker with tan and white plaid upholstery and honey-toned wood. The cabin was warming up and he noticed a blush on Koski's cheeks. "*What* do you wonder?" he asked.

She casually moved a few steps closer to the rocker. "After all the excitement of this assignment, what could ever possibly get our adrenaline flowing again?"

Looking at her, he wondered if his eyes gave away the longing in his soul. He held out his hand. "*I'll* get your adrenaline flowing."

She took his hand then slipped onto his lap and slid her arms around his neck. He thought about how she handled herself in the crises they had been through. "I like the way you get angry instead of being afraid," he said softly into her ear.

She nuzzled her nose against his neck "I like the way you get afraid instead of being angry." She immediately pulled back and faced him. "Only *kidding*!"

He kissed her, a sweet, lingering kiss at first but her lips parted beneath his own and a rush of warmth went through his body...Then he heard the thwoping of rotors. "Ryland," he said with a sigh as he gently pulled away.

"Damn!" Koski whispered, still holding his eyes. They rose and as they started for the door she said, "I'd like a rain check on whatever was about to happen back there."

"Mmmm..." he purred and touched her hand. "You got it."

When they opened the door, the helicopter had already put down in the only open space in the area beyond a dense palisade of birches. Ryland had deplaned and approached the cabin, offering his hand. "Samuel Ryland."

Koski's greeting was half-hearted. She shook his hand.

Falk nodded. "Thanks for coming for us," he said as he turned back into the room. "I'll bank that fire and we'll be with you in a sec."

Ryland walked past them into the cabin, stomping snow from his boots. "Oh, no rush."

Koski cried, "The chopper— It's leaving!"

The cabin door was still open and Falk looked out just as the aircraft lifted off. "What—" he began but Ryland waved away their concerns.

"Not to worry. He was low on fuel when I got your call. I told him I'd wait here with you while he refueled. He'll be back within the hour."

Falk closed the door. "That the only bird available?"

"Apparently so," Ryland said as he lowered into a straight-back chair. "This man isn't going to be easy to track. He's a well-trained pro."

Koski sank into the swivel rocker and added, "And a cold-blooded killer."

It was Ryland's turn to nod. "You have the United States Army to thank for giving you the opportunity to escape from that English mercenary."

"You know about him?" Falk asked.

Ryland shrugged. "It depends on what you mean by 'know about.'"

"You said 'English mercenary.' I assumed that if you knew he was English and a mercenary you'd had some contact with him."

"No, no." He stretched, as if feeling the warmth of the fire. "I must have picked that up in a briefing."

Koski swiveled slightly toward Ryland. "Have you received any word on Webster, Maxwell and Spade?"

"I inquired about them several hours ago. They're fine."

"Really!"

He smiled at her almost childlike curiosity. "Really," he replied. "Spade is at home and Webster and Maxwell are safe and recuperating in a secured environment. Webster's expected to recover totally from the concussion he sustained."

Under the flattering light of Koski's attention, he briefly outlined the incident of Lester Carter's death following his luncheon with Ryland and Maxwell at Harrah's and Maxwell's relocation to Top Gun.

As Ryland spoke, it occurred to Falk the extent to which this man had been there for Falk's team—and, in the process, privy to at least some of the entire team's movements.

"You've been a regular Johnny-on-the-spot for them," Falk

said when Ryland paused.

"You might say that." His modesty was polished.

"And you, a man probably constantly in demand at NSA headquarters at Fort Meade...privy to top-level security information...on call to the president himself no doubt..." He paused, watching Ryland's face and then went on. "When I stop to think about it, it's amazing that Koski and I are fortunate to have the privilege of your...magnanimity." He lingered on that last word and felt Koski turn the lighthouse of her eyes in his direction.

Ryland got up and moved away from the stove, his heretofore perfectly maintained composure slipping slightly. "I'm not sure I understand your point, Falk."

When he had watched Ryland deplane and walk toward the cabin, it was obvious to Falk that the man was of Native American descent. Now he noticed how dark and slick his hair was. Falk recalled the old trapper he had shared a fish dinner with in the woods years ago and the description the trapper gave of the person he heard on the phone in the mine's parking lot.

That recollection spurred Falk on.

"Don't you see the irony of it, Ryland? A man highly placed in national security. A man so powerful that even the Nevada Mafia would probably kiss his ring. A man with access to instant transportation to hop around the country at will; in fact, a man in *charge* of overseeing the investigation into the lawyers' deaths... Should such a man turn out to be the very brains behind those killings...well, you see where I'm going with this..."

Falk stood up, wanting the advantage of being on his feet.

Koski didn't move or speak.

Ryland compressed his lips then released and licked them. "I don't like what you're insinuating, Falk."

"Oh, I'm not insinuating. To insinuate is to suggest indirectly. I thought I was frankly laying out the foundation for a plan to ultimately take over the United States from within."

A muscle rippled along Ryland's jaw and his dark gray eyes flared.

"Take over?" Koski said almost inaudibly.

"Take over," Falk repeated firmly, "big time." Cocking his head slightly, he continued to look directly into Ryland's eyes. He remembered something Tom Stewart had said at their meeting in the motel with the flickering neon sign.

It was Stewart's oblique reference to his and Cerberus' part in this investigation. Cerberus' responsibility was to be "acutely aware of the balance of domestic power and any possible shift in that power." Stewart, therefore, must have known—or at least had a hunch—about a grand plan although he had no idea at the time that it was *Ryland's* plan.

"We don't want to be surprised by an economic earthquake," Stewart had said and added, "You may find it difficult to imagine a full-scale Indian uprising in this country in the twenty-first century, Joe, but I believe it's a distinct possibility."

Now Falk realized the phenomenal proportions of the earthquake Stewart feared and Ryland had in mind.

"Let's see if I've got it right," Falk began. "I've been informed that there are approximately three million Native Americans in North America, hardly enough to take over a nation of better than 280 million. It's certainly not enough to take over in the traditional sense of that word or even in the sense that the events of September 11, 2001, envisioned."

He paused and turned his head but not his eyes to his partner. "I'm sure you've guessed, Koski, this new threat is not only about how many Native Americans there are and how many casinos they own but about the land on which those casinos are located. They're located on Indian reservations, of course; reservations that belong to the Indian nations. In addition, Indian nations are *sovereign* nations—technically, independent nations within the United States.

"Think about it, Koski. If, through vastly extended gambling and the dollars it creates, the tribes were to be *truly* unified—under a determined, powerful, intelligent and charismatic leader—they would be able to operate as the independent nations they are."

His head turned back to Ryland. "Abetted by lawyers of all races whose loyalties are moot so long as the financial remunerations are sufficient. These independent nations could make their own laws...mint their own money...organize and train their own militia..."

He paused to assess Ryland's reaction, which evidenced that Falk was indeed on the right track before he went on. "The United States as we know it may find itself surrounded by wealthy, independent Indian nations.

"Other state citizens couldn't even enter, say, without visas. These nations could trade with whomever they wished...import and export goods with foreign countries at their discretion, despite regulations and embargoes set up by our present government to the contrary. They will be able to generate their own gross national product into the billions." He glanced in Koski's direction. "You can see the disastrous ramifications."

Koski did not move, stunned by the chilling potential. "That would rip America apart," she whispered. "*Worse than* the situation created in the Balkans back in the 1990s. The federal government couldn't do anything about it."

"Nothing," Falk replied. "These nations could choose as allies various miscreant countries of the world that will leap at the opportunity to send their troops, requested by the tribes, to protect and serve their interests. Imagine Chinese, Iranian or Korean troops on our soil." He paused again, getting confirmation from Ryland's silent, smoldering look. "How am I doing, Ryland?"

Ryland's demeanor switched to a pretense of indignant consternation. "It's your theory, Falk."

"That's not the whole of it," Falk continued. "For years public records have proved that millions of dollars appropriated by the federal government for the tribes every year never trickled down to the reservations for which they were intended. Under this new federation, as more Native Americans come out of law schools and more money is available to them, suits will be brought against the federal government for unlawful disbursement of funds.

"I suspect that the class action suits would dwarf those brought against the tobacco companies and nearly bankrupt the government. What was left of the United States would be strangled in many ways. Lawyers working for the tribes have already taught them how to protect and sell their water rights to towns and cities who once took their water for granted. The American public doesn't even realize that the takeover has begun."

"But," Koski said, looking for a positive aspect, "these scenarios only make sense if the tribes were *empowered*, infused with the big bucks more casinos would generate. The campaign we've seen—killing the lawyers who are working *against* the tribes —would have the opposite effect and turn the public against the American Indians, resulting in *less* support for their gambling and the tribes in general."

"To say that demonstrates your gross ignorance of the weakened American psyche," Ryland growled. He suddenly seemed puffed with pride, willing to participate in spelling out the details of his plan. He was eager for his two companions to understand the grandeur of the strategy he continued to see as achievable and the tactics involved in that achievement. "Are you not aware that the liberalization of America begun in the '60s was completed in the late '90s and continues today, despite the surge of traditionalism that was sparked after September 11? It is a common joke in other countries that when an American sees a badly beaten man lying in the gutter, he doesn't say, 'We need to find the person who did this and punish him.' They say, 'We need to find the person who did this; *that* person needs help.'

"This perverse form of reverse psychology will work mightily for my people. At the conclusion of this campaign, when it is proven that Native Americans were not to blame, when they are shown as the innocent victims of hate crimes planned to make them look bad, public empathy for them will rise to new heights… a bump in the polls, so to speak. New laws will be put into place to protect their civil rights. My people will enjoy more freedom than ever before."

"*My people,*" Koski said softly as she got up and walked to Falk's side. "Of course…"

"Meet Mukuwamp, Koski," Falk said. "Would-be sachem of the Algonquin Indian tribe, owner of the Colonial Mine, a.k.a. The Fox."

Ryland scoffed. "The Fox, a silly sobriquet my associates hung on me." His dark gray eyes narrowed. "How did you uncover my tribal name?"

"ESP," Falk replied. "I also have friends in Covert Transmissions. I was born in Connecticut; we had our share of Algonquin Indians. I went to school with one, in fact, and remembered that Mukuwamp means "Chief.""

Ryland straightened and his head rose defiantly, his vision momentarily lost in the space between himself and the ceiling. "The Sovereign Commonwealth of Native Americans," he pronounced. Lowering his gaze to Falk, he continued to interpret his vision. "One nation, under Mukuwamp, free to establish its own justice, ensure its own domestic tranquillity, provide for its own common defense...with liberty and justice for all Native Americans."

A sliver of ice ran down Falk's spine. Suddenly he thought about the Army chopper that had brought Ryland and wondered if it would return. He had no ready weapon. There was a chance that Ryland didn't have one either. He wanted to keep him talking until someone arrived who did.

"So, it's all pretty clear now, right, Koski?" Falk said. When she was profoundly silent, he went on. "Abraham Lincoln's words were to be prophetic, 'If America ever falls it will be from within.' You had to love the prospect, Ryland. You would ultimately take the country back from those who stole it from you."

Falk sighed and shook his head. "Not only was my team a farce, meant to evidence that something was being done, even as we were being prevented from doing it, but also this whole thing about making the Indians seem guilty was a smoke screen to eventually *help* them, to lure already perverse public opinion to your will."

"We're professionals, Falk," Ryland said matter-of-factly. "We all know that now and then someone has to sacrifice. Like in baseball, not everyone is given the signal to hit a home run; sometimes somebody has to bunt."

"And the weekend militia members at the mine also were just

pawns in your game. They never dreamed their maneuvers meant anything, didn't know that you meant to eventually build them up into a true fighting force. Their vision probably didn't go beyond the equation that more casinos equal more money equals more rights. They're not farsighted enough to envision their new wealth being used to reconfigure the entire United States of America."

"Few of my people are farsighted enough," Ryland scoffed. "In fact, I expect my plan will meet with passionate resistance among all the tribes but no matter. They'll come around once I make them aware of the big, attainable picture."

Falk shook his head. "Getting the Nevada gaming people involved was good. They'd be more than happy to make the Indians and the prospect of more of their gambling establishments look threatening. However, even they didn't grasp the whole concept, did they? Their limited sights were probably set on keeping Nevada's coffers full. You alone were the brain trust, pumping out individual components, never disclosing to one exactly what the other's part or the final outcome would be."

Ryland seemed comfortable now—too comfortable—as if he had a trump card and could afford to reveal more details of his scheme. "Except for Villachi," he said. "He knew that nothing can stop the expansion of Indian gambling all over the country so he wisely decided to opt for a piece of the action."

Falk rasped, "And Reinecke?"

"The worst kind of thief, who sees more money for the tribes only as more money and power for himself."

"Bud Vigo's part was to do the actual killing," Koski interjected, "with arrows projected from his helicopter." Her husky voice grew scratchy in extreme anger. "You're nothing more than another terrorist."

Ryland snorted. "Yes, well, Vigo was the perfect grass—a man with one foot in the police department and the other in the underworld. Useful but in terms of evolution, I placed Vigo one step behind orangutans." His twisted smile faded but no readable emotion took its place. "Speaking of killing, I understand from Cromwell that you killed Vigo."

"Not really," Koski responded, imaging Vigo hanging from the rungs of the helicopter's ladder as the aircraft above him exploded. She added venomously, "Although we gladly would have."

"I assume you orchestrated Lovesy's death," Falk queried. "Why?"

"He was a weak link on the verge of falling apart." Ryland glanced around the room, suddenly impatient with further conversation.

"One more question," Falk said, a new rise in anger tightening his throat. "My Bureau Chief Lester Carter also was my friend and a man who I doubt ever harmed you. Why kill him?"

Ryland's vision flickered to the floor then back. His voice carried a tenor of regret.

"He was my friend, too, that hot-headed English son of a bitch!" He looked away, shaking his head. "I called the meeting at the mine for the express purpose of discussing how best to terminate his services."

"Eiker," Falk said with vehemence, "the Limey gun for hire. But *why* did he kill Carter?"

"As we saw," Koski put in, referencing the unarmed soldier at the mine entrance on the hillside, "that bastard doesn't need a reason to kill people."

"He and Carter had a history," Ryland offered. "Some time

around the attacks of 9/11 Carter apparently thwarted some mischief Eiker had planned for Hoover Dam. Apparently, Eiker just decided it was payback time."

"It figures," Falk growled.

This brief moment of near camaraderie, in which all three individuals knew a common enemy, caused Falk to momentarily drop his mental guardedness. That he had no ready weapon did not mean he had no defense against one should it be produced; heightened mental alertness might help him spontaneously devise an effective strategy. Ryland's hand shot into his jacket and came out with a .38 caliber, blue-steel, snub-nosed Smith and Wesson.

Falk nodded regrettably. "I should have figured you for a gun." His hand slowly reached out and tucked Koski behind him. "But not a woman's gun," he finished.

Ryland was unfazed by what was obviously meant to be a denigrating remark. "It'll serve the purpose."

"Don't be a fool, Ryland. The Army chopper will be back any minute."

"By the time it is, you'll both be in the past tense." He moved toward the door, his back to it. "Eiker—pain in the ass though he is —can be handy. Even as we speak he's directing our pick-up aircraft here."

"But you said the Army chopper would be back," Koski insisted, stepping from behind Falk, her cheeks scarlet with anger.

"I lied." A subtle, almost playful grin rippled across his lips. "I needed to be sure Eiker's copter could pick me up without being challenged so I sent the pilot away."

"Well," Falk said with acerbity, "at least your plan for the great Sovereign Commonwealth of Native Americans has suffered a fatal blow. Too many of the dominoes have fallen and there are still people like Reinecke and others who, to save their own asses, will bring you down."

"No, this has only been a temporary setback. Even if all the present plans were to be exposed and abandoned—which is highly unlikely—I have here the only two people who could and would expose me. If I were to be eliminated, young warriors who are now making their way through law schools will one day take up the standard. They will see that my labor of creating a true Indian nation comes to fruition." He waved his .38 toward the door, "Hands on your heads, outside."

Falk's mind raced as they walked out the door and toward the boathouse. Maybe when he and Koski didn't return with the pilot, Cromwell would figure something was wrong and send another aircraft. Maybe one of the choppers out searching for Eiker and Reinecke would come this way. Maybe—what was he thinking? He knew better than to hang his hopes on maybes.

Eiker spotted the small, fast-moving Bell 205 skimming the lake's surface. His recovery team was running right on schedule. He headed the fishing boat into shore and up onto a narrow beach, jumped out and shouted for Reinecke to follow. The helicopter sank earthward, raising a squall of snow. Eiker bolted for it then stopped. Reinecke barely moved. He gasped for breath and clutched his chest as he stumbled toward the aircraft.

Eiker cursed and grabbed him, pulling him aboard with the help of the co-pilot. As the Bell rocked and ascended on a bearing toward Vigo's cabin, the senator slumped to the floor and leaned back against the fuselage.

"This guy we're picking up had better be ready," the pilot shouted over his shoulder. "We've got another storm *and* the Army to consider."

Scanning the sky for any sign of pursuit aircraft, Eiker sighed and leaned back; all clear. His contract was almost fulfilled. He'd be glad to put this assignment behind him. Glancing across at Reinecke, he saw the senator's head slump on his chest; his lips were flabby, agape and tinged in blue. Eiker knew the signs. The exertion had been too much for a man accustomed to a soft lifestyle. Could Eiker resuscitate him if his heart gave out?

That was too much bloody bother. The Brit champed furiously on his gum. Would he collect his final payment if he didn't have this trophy? Why not? He had performed well. Without the last installment due him, he had enough to retire nicely but he wanted it. He could insist that the situation was beyond his control, that the senator died of natural causes, which would not be altogether false. He decided to risk it.

"Open up," he ordered the co-pilot. Reaching under Reinecke's arms, Eiker dragged him to the door as the other man, mechanically following orders, unlocked and opened it. A blast of freezing air took his breath away.

"Look at it this way," Eiker said to Reinecke's ashen face, whose eyes were like half dollars now, facing two deaths, "I'm saving your family the expense of hiring a school of lawyers to defend you." He shoved the limp but resisting body out, watched it quiver downward and thump into the center of the lake. He yanked the door shut.

Chapter 34

"Open the door," Ryland commanded. Falk slowly pulled the boathouse door open and waited. Ryland nodded, "Inside, you, too, Agent Koski."

Once inside the boathouse, Falk saw that the fishing boat was gone and the Jet Ski's cowling was open, exposing frayed remains of ripped out wiring.

"Characteristically thorough," Ryland said, "that's Eiker's style. He wanted to be sure he didn't have a tail when he went to meet the copter at the rendezvous point."

As he trained the revolver on them with his right hand, he smashed the left side of his fist against an ordinary looking wallboard. A spring door snapped open to reveal a slender, vertical cabinet in the wall. Falk's sense of frustration notched up when he saw Ryland extract an AK-47 from its groove in the cabinet, checking to confirm it was loaded.

"I've made use of Vigo's little vacation spot in the past, unbeknownst to him, of course." He took two extra magazines from the cabinet and stuffed them in his jacket pockets. "My absentee host was equally unaware of certain precautions I took…" He paused and raised his eyebrows at Falk. "Why so surprised? I'm an NSA agent." He slung the weapon across his shoulder. "Face the lake, Falk. Keep your hands on your head."

Falk looked down at the icy water a couple of feet below the inside dock and felt the irony of sweat in the stubble of hair on his upper lip.

"Kneel," Ryland barked.

Falk slowly eased to his knees, aware that Ryland was watching him closely. Good, it might allow his attentiveness to Koski to waver, in which case she might find an opening—

Then, as if reading Falk's mind, she did. A sudden lurch to the right, a duck and she was a blur as she turned and slammed a sweep kick that dislodged Ryland's right kneecap with the crunch only distressed bone can produce.

Ryland wailed in pain and went down on his left knee. He had the strength and presence of mind, however, to retain his hold on both weapons.

Reacting instinctively, hoping to catch the man off balance before he could fire, Falk lunged forward, ramming a shoulder into him with sufficient force to knock him back toward the door. Ryland fired the gun as it slipped from his hand and fell into the lake, the bullet missing Koski by inches. In the split second in which Falk halted to assure himself that Koski wasn't hurt, Ryland scrambled from the boathouse, retaining the AK-47 that dangled from his arm.

Falk was at the door in a flash, prepared to pursue Ryland. Instead, he shouted, "*Down!*" and quickly back-pedalled, slamming the door shut and flinging his body sideways to avoid a succession of shattering blasts that signaled Ryland had recovered control of his Kalashnikov.

Chunks of wood blew inward as the door was riddled with bullets. Falk rolled back toward the prone Koski, bullets seeming to sense him, to etch his shape as they raked the building. His eyes desperately swept the interior for cover but there was none. "*Over the edge,*" he shouted and they both dropped into the freezing lake water, clutching the dock, as Ryland continued to blast the boathouse. Bullets ricocheted off metal tackle boxes, cans and bottles, exploding shelves and thudding into the far wall.

"He'll run out of ammo soon," Koski said through chattering teeth.

"Not soon enough. He took two extra magazines, remember."

"Shit!" They were silent for several seconds. Finally Koski whispered, "He stopped."

"Could be reloading, I'm going to try to see where he is. Stay put." Pulling up, he raised his head over the edge of the dock and took a fast look around. "Jesus! The walls look like Swiss cheese."

"You can't go up there," Koski warned. "He'll see you through the bullet holes."

"Chance I'll have to take." He pulled his body over the edge of the dock and, propelling himself on his elbows, slithered toward the door, his body leaving a wet trail across the floor. The silence reinforced his courage. "I'm going to open the door just a crack," he whispered. "Remember, you stay there."

"Okay but I'm about to freeze to death."

Raising his body to a crouch, Falk moved to the right of the door and slowly eased the battered exit open an inch and then two.

Nothing. No violent retort followed his tentative movements. He thought how a cowboy from the Old West would have removed his hat and slid it into the open space to draw any potential fire and pinpoint his enemy's location.

Falk didn't have a hat but he had gloves and an old broom stood in the corner behind him. He stuck a glove on the broomstick and used it to force the door open several more inches, pulling his body back to the wall. Still no response.

He glanced around the interior once more, searching for anything he could use as a weapon. His vision fell on a shelf and the oilskin package he had found in the boat and placed there earlier. At the time, he wasn't sure why he felt compelled to hide it there; some instinct he didn't understand but for which he now was grateful. He seized on it as his next strategy.

Turning to call to Koski, he discovered she was already there, drenched and shivering with the cold, crawling toward him. "I can't see him," Falk said, "but I have an idea." He unwrapped the bow, arrow and laser equipment and tested the laser, shining the red dot on the back of the Jet Ski for a second before snapping it off.

There was no way he could do this on his own. It would take the two of them to pull it off. Koski was sodden and cold. Was she up to it? In that second of doubt, his mind instantaneously rewound through the many occasions in the past few days when she outperformed any agent he had ever known, and he put uncertainty away forever.

"We're going hunting," he said. "Since you were on the archery team, you take the bow and a couple of arrows. I'll handle the laser. Remember, you don't have to hit the target by careful aim. Shooting in the general direction will do as long as I place the laser beam on the target. We'll have to be quick. The element of surprise is all we've got against the AK-47."

She nodded. "First we have to find the bastard."

Suddenly Falk put a finger to his lips and pointed upward. Her eyes flickered to the roof and she listened intently. There was the unmistakable sound of someone limping across the snow-covered wood shakes. "He's crossing the boathouse to the wide entrance facing the lake."

Falk whispered, "A flanking maneuver; he plans to surprise us from behind." He handed her the bow and two arrows. "If we hurry, we can get out." Easing the door open slightly, he took one quick look around. "There," he whispered, indicating a fir tree twenty yards away. "Go!"

Koski bolted through the snow with Falk at her heels. They dove into the snowdrift at the base of the fir. From this vantage point, Falk had a clear view of Ryland, who didn't see them as he hobbled across the roof, his attempt at furtiveness made almost comic by his lumbering gait.

"Notch up one of those babies, Koski," Falk said and she quickly strung an arrow and held the bow in readiness. Activating the laser device, Falk projected a red dot up the side of the boathouse, dancing it in Ryland's direction. Another second and he would have his mark in his sights.

Then Ryland slipped and fell. In one second he was a target, in the next, a flashing blur in a cloud of snow that dropped from sight on the opposite side of the building.

Falk snapped off the laser. "Son of a bitch!" Ryland may have broken a leg or been otherwise injured, or was he still able to play the most dangerous game?

"Koski, go back to the boathouse, opposite to where he fell. If he's not hurt and comes around the building, I'll make sure he sees me. When he does, I'll put the bead on him and you take him out."

Like Falk, Koski was tired and rightfully uneasy, considering the disparity of weapons between them but she nodded without question and took off.

The laser device was similar in shape to that of a light sporting rifle with a telescopic sight. Falk had little understanding of laser technology beyond knowing that most were battery-powered.

Amplified light created in the form of a beacon shot through a crystal to emit an intense, direct light beam. Falk didn't need to understand the device; only make it work. He waited until Koski took up her position, then he edged from behind the tree and eased toward the building, using what cover he could.

A burst of automatic gunfire abruptly splintered the branches above his head. Falk dove to the ground hard and rolled in the snow, a volley of bullets coming at him in a wide spray. Ryland had survived his fall and was alert enough to spot Falk before being seen—so much for the element of surprise.

When there was a pause in the gunfire, Falk started to inch

his head around the tree trunk that sheltered him. Again, bullets splintered limbs and showered him with pine needles. He needed Ryland to show himself. Koski needed her target. He saw her, crouched beside the boathouse wall, opposite Ryland's position. Falk cursed silently. Pinned down this way, he couldn't simply step out and draw Ryland's fire; death would be the inevitable result of that.

His sodden snowsuit was crusted with ice. Immobility increased his sense of cold and threatened to numb his mind. He desperately sought an answer. At first, the drone of a helicopter in the distance did not register on a conscious level. When it did, Falk knew that *it* was his answer.

By the sound of its engine, he knew it wasn't Army but a smaller aircraft, the one meant for Ryland's rendezvous. Ryland would have to make a run for his transportation out of here. Falk eased his head slightly around the tree for another look and all hell broke loose.

A blizzard of bullets split the side of the tree inches above Falk's head, ripping free a splinter of wood eight inches long and sending it plunging deep into his left bicep. No sensation at all, he thought. Then numbness gave way to fiery, agonizing pain that pumped through his entire arm and the laser device slipped to the ground.

Gritting his teeth, he reached across with his right hand and yanked the dagger-like shard from his flesh. Somewhere deep in his consciousness there was a sense of relief. The jagged, wooden missile had struck bone but didn't break it.

Sound signaled that the chopper was overhead. Ryland *must* show himself. Falk looked up. It was Eiker all right, the shock of red, unruly hair plainly visible in the plane, back to collect his superior. Ignoring his wound, Falk retrieved the laser with his good hand...

Ryland was running, half dragging the leg Koski had dropkicked earlier. He made for the clearing behind the stand of birches where the chopper was about to put down.

Knowing Koski waited with the bow and arrow, needing the guiding beam that only he could provide, Falk lifted the laser with his right arm, resting the barrel against the side of the tree for support. The laser dot bounced across the clearing, the red pinpoint seeking its mark. Exhausted and cold, Falk fought for the calm determination he needed. Concentrate...

Ryland was one hundred feet from the chopper. Then fifty... twenty...ten...

Steady the laser...Falk leaned against the tree, his motor skills not attending the command of the neurons that fired in his brain. *Concentrate! A deep breath...Zero in on the objective*...He could almost hear the fast arrhythmic beat of Ryland's heart as the man prepared to climb into the aircraft. *Steady...Hold the dot steady between his shoulder blades...Now shoot, Koski, shoot!*

The arrow flashed across the clearing like a heat-seeking missile, thudding squarely into its target. Its impact rocked Ryland, piercing his heart and taking portions of that organ with it on its journey through the front of his chest. He managed to stay on his feet for a few seconds before his knees folded and he dropped to the ground. The Fox died bleeding out, like any other hunted animal.

Falk slumped against the tree but not before he glimpsed Eiker, saw the Englishman yank the chopper door shut and order the pilot out of the area.

"Damn!" Falk cursed. Eiker no longer had a dog in this fight;

he simply wanted to get away. Falk had a score to settle with the mercenary that went beyond the cold-blooded murder of the young soldier back at the mine entrance and the two others he killed on the trail. A man like that, who killed with impunity, was the antithesis of the very essence of Falk's ideals.

The practice of killing for killing's sake bred weakness in humankind. Men like Rodney Eiker had a part in killing humanity itself. Falk did not know why, how or when but he knew that his and Eiker's paths would cross again. Falk looked forward to that meeting.

Then Koski was kneeling beside him, assessing the extent of the wound in his arm.

"Oh, God," she said at sight of the flow of blood. Inverting one of her gloves, she pressed it hard against the jagged gash in his flesh and it stuck. "We need—" She quickly unzipped the front of her drenched snowsuit and reached inside toward her right side, beneath her sweater. Using her right hand to push her left elbow farther in, she reached the clasp she sought, then withdrew her hand and a black lace bra.

"This'll do," she said with an exaggerated swagger in her voice as she fashioned the attractive tourniquet around his arm, tucking the "C" cups in at the edges.

Falk looked from his extraordinary Florence Nightingale to the darkening sky. No more search planes could fly over the isolated area this day.

He struggled to his feet and leaned against Koski, his attention caught by the sudden sound of a pack of whining engines. First there was movement beyond the trees. Koski's eyes followed his gaze as the growl grew louder. Then half a dozen snowmobiles burst forth from the woods, snarling in their direction.

Falk had no idea if these white-suited visitors were friend or foe but it didn't matter. He and Koski were through running for today. He took her hand as the lead machine slowed to a stop nearby. The man slid to his feet and removed his helmet.

"Colonel Cromwell!" Koski exclaimed.

Falk never imagined he would be happy to see the crusty old bastard again. "To what do we owe this pleasure, Colonel?"

Cromwell's lips turned up into the quirky grin Falk had witnessed earlier. "You two were like bees in my bonnet, so to speak," he said, and ran a finger across his upper lip. "I missed you."

Wincing at the sight of the wound in Falk's arm, he ordered one of his men to break out the first aid kit and brandy. "I was concerned when the chopper with Ryland came back without him or you. One of my men reported smoke from the cabin's chimney, which we were told was vacant." He nodded toward the snowmobiles. "We were losing the light so we had to resort to using these monsters—"

"Excuse me, sir," a young soldier returning from the clearing by the birches said. "It's Mr. Ryland, sir. He's dead."

Cromwell's forehead creased in several places. "What in hell happened, Falk?"

Falk shook his head. "It's a long story, Colonel." He wondered if Cromwell—or anyone—would believe Ryland's ominous plot when Falk relayed the details. If not, as Mukuwamp had said, another warrior would take up the banner…the threat was still out there.

He watched the soldiers lift Ryland's body and drape it over one of the mobile units. "You got him, Koski," he said, turning to her.

She shrugged and bobbed her head, as if to amiably take issue with his remark. "I got him…you got him…we got him…"

Glancing at the black lace tourniquet, which had been removed in favor of a more traditional one and displayed for all to see, Cromwell shrugged and said, "Whatever works."

Chapter 35

Two days later Koski drove to a dinner engagement at Alex Spade's home. Falk was seated beside her with his left arm in a sling. Approaching vehicles flashed past, light snow reflecting in the glare of their headlights.

Koski said with a sigh, "About the Tribes…what happens now?"

"The lawyers take over, reducing life to the vernacular of their trade. As Indian gambling continues to increase in California, lawyers on both sides will work together to ensure that California *and* Nevada continue to profit." He checked his watch and switched on the radio. "I nearly forgot…the president is supposed to be speaking to the states' governors and the nation."

"In a further development on the domestic front," the distinctive voice said, *"I'm happy to report that a home-grown terrorist plot to overtake the government of the state of Nevada by killing lawyers and creating economic chaos was thwarted this week."*

"Overtake the government of the state of *Nevada*!" Koski said, incredulous. "They're watering this down to a *local* problem!"

Falk gently shushed her as the president continued.

"To those Native Americans who believe that, as a race, they were unjustly targeted or accused in the attorneys' deaths, I state my regret. I want to reiterate what cannot be stressed enough: We

are all Americans, any American who persecutes or discriminates against another American based on race, religion, age or gender is committing a crime and they will be dealt with accordingly.

"Finally, I have appointed a blue-ribbon committee to thoroughly investigate the allegations that monies allocated to the Native American Trust Fund have been misappropriated."

Falk angrily switched off the radio. "They're not making it a *local* problem. They're not making it *anyone's* problem."

Koski seethed, "They're just sweeping it under the rug. I don't believe it."

"I suppose they figure there's no sense stirring up the Tribes who, by Ryland's own admission, didn't know about his plan. Left alone, they'll probably go along as they are for years. They're in the catbird seat and don't know it."

"What do you mean?"

"The individual members of the Tribes would probably be happy just running the new gaming establishments and raking in the big bucks. But if…when…another Ryland comes along and sees that army of fat cat casino owners sitting there, ready to be introduced to another grand plan for "economic chaos," who knows what will happen."

"The American public has the right to know about Ryland's plot," Koski insisted. "It was aimed at the heart of our republic. People should *know* that."

"The president probably thinks they can't take it and he's right. Since the War on Terrorism began they've heard nothing but bad economic news, along with anthrax, possible dirty bombs and other terrorist alerts. Maybe Americans have reached a saturation point where they just can't handle more bad news."

"That's the point at which we become even more vulnerable

to enemy attack."

He smiled and flexed his left arm in its sling, attempting a more comfortable position. "Not exactly," he said pointedly, lightening the conversation. "There are always those of us who get pissed off instead of afraid. Right, Koski?"

Her solemn expression turned playful, too. "Right," she said graciously and signaled, veering into Spade's driveway.

Falk thought of Tom Stewart and Cerberus. Like a sort of early-warning system, their wakeful diligence would ensure that new threats to the country were swiftly recognized and dealt with. Were he to take the time to explore it, Falk would have to admit that one slightly disquieting aspect of Stewart's part in this nagged at him.

If Stewart initially saw the potential for the Commonwealth of Indian states that Ryland envisioned, and it seemed now that he must have, did he also feel that Falk and his team could be set up…perhaps killed? No, he was being absurd. In the future, he would revert to focusing only on the positive aspects of his revered organization.

The American president's image, viewed by direct satellite broadcast, faded from the flat-screen plasma television set in Eiker's suite at the Grosvenor Hotel in London. Eiker lounged back in a leather chair. He slowly swirled a glass of warm brandy, reached for the remote and lowered the volume, at the same time that the phone rang. He picked it up and heard a soft but firm American voice.

"My name is Tom Stewart. I understand you're a highly professional mercenary."

Book Two

Dedication
To Keith G. Nelson: Over the years, we climbed many a steep hill together.

Acknowledgements
My publisher, Daniel Janik; my editor, Mary Yamin-Garone; my book cover artist, Kristin Arbuckle: Thank you for your combined talents in making this book possible.

Chapter 1

VIENNA, WINTER, 1945

Nikolia Youmatoff didn't know exactly where he was but a sense of impending doom filled the dark, dank vault. He recalled hearing a church bell chime but Vienna was full of churches. His companions had unloaded the army trucks and dragged dozens of sealed crates into the vault and stacked them alongside hundreds of obviously valuable objects.

That night, Youmatoff suspected, they stored away a supply of riches that could have been sufficient to sustain starving Ukrainian farmers for decades.

Youmatoff could clearly see Reichmarshall Herman Goering's white pigskin face by the flickering candlelight as he sat behind a gray steel desk at one end of the musty crypt. Wax from a thick ocher candle rimmed and dripped down onto the ornate candlestick. Goering held a blueprint on which he scribbled the word, *"Uberholt."* Youmatoff's limited German translated it as "obsolete," though he wasn't sure. Goering then refolded the blueprint and slipped it into a leather bound book. He opened a desk drawer, picked up the compact wire recorder sitting next to the candlestick and gently placed the recorder in the drawer.

Several soldiers and an officer were overseeing prisoners of war crouched on the floor at the far end of the vault. The prisoners were replacing flagstones they had moved. The officer reached down and turned a key then indicated they lower the last stone into place. The POWs were part of a group that had delivered the wooden crates and unloaded them into the sepulcher-like space. Youmatoff's assignment was to carry boxes of books for the Reichmarshall.

The officer approached the Reichmarshall, saluted, handed

him the key and returned to his men. Goering took the peculiar shaped key and slid it beneath the cover of the volume holding the blueprint. He placed the book atop other books in a box on the desk.

Youmatoff saw him tap the book and Goering said something Youmatoff interpreted as *"Here's the blueprint to the future."* Youmatoff didn't have time to ponder as Goering pushed back his chair, heaved his bulk up and surveyed the area of treasures. A smile twisted his lips and he slapped his thigh with a golden Field Marshal's baton.

"Bring that box of books," Goering told Youmatoff as he strode from the vault.

What Youmatoff did next was done without premeditation. Picking up the book that had held Goering's attention, Youmatoff removed the key and slipped the book into the front of his thin canvas shirt. He tipped the candle and splattered a mushroom edged blob of wax on the desk, placed the key in the wax and pressed a perfect impression.

He moved to the entrance, looked back and saw one of the soldiers reeling out what appeared to be copper wire. A voice from outside cursed at Youmatoff to hurry.

The moon was high. He saw they were in an ancient square that was unfamiliar to him. A German SS officer took the box of books, placed it in the trunk of Goering's staff car, slammed the trunk shut and got into the car. A second later it roared out of the square.

Youmatoff felt the weight of the book inside his shirt. The original key *and* the wax impression were in the pocket. "The secret to the future" was in his care.

He was alone in the empty square. Suddenly pistol shots

sounded from within the vault and Youmatoff knew at once the other prisoners had been executed. Terror-stricken, he fled into the darkest shadows and bolted from the square.

Chapter 2
RENO, NEVADA, WINTER 2009

"Believe it, Joe. We still use foot soldiers in the game of espionage, even in today's political correctness and electronic wizardry."

Henry Stevenson was a taciturn silver-haired man in his early sixties with a face that was easily forgotten. He leaned back in his executive chair and rested his chin on the tip of a pyramid made by his long slender fingers. He observed the reaction of the two agents he had summoned to his office.

Special Agent Joseph Falk nodded. He was handsome, chestnut-haired, in his thirties. He'd heard the 'Atta-Boy' speeches plenty of times. They never changed. "We were beginning to think we were the only two left." He indicated the petite blonde female sitting beside him.

"I understand." Stevenson collapsed the pyramid, slid open a drawer, removed a large envelope and laid it on the desktop. "An old investigation is being reopened that has, over the last few weeks, become an extremely troublesome problem for United States' foreign policy." Stevenson paused. Susan Koski's green, tawny-speckled eyes were trained on him as he continued. "Tom Stewart has ordered that you two meet with him right away."

Stewart was director of Cerberus, a covert agency named for the dog of Greek mythology, said to have had three heads and served as keeper of the entrance to the infernal regions where the gods resided. Those who had adopted this name believed that much of the U.S. was in danger of falling into the external regions, the gutters of humanity. Cerberus was clandestinely funded and supported by an anonymous cartel of intelligence personnel known only to the president. Tom Stewart was the head of the agency. Officially, Falk and Koski were FBI special agents assigned to liaise with unique units of the Office of Homeland Security. That had given Tom Stewart the ability to spirit them into Cerberus. Stewart had used their talents in several demanding investigations over the last three years. All were resolved successfully.

Stevenson checked his watch. "You're booked on a Lufthansa flight tonight." He tapped the envelope and pushed it across to Falk. "Airline tickets and a letter Stewart wants you both to study enroute. He'll give further details of the assignment at a briefing when you arrive in Vienna."

Dinner had ended. One or two reading lamps glowed in the cabin of the 747 as Koski and Falk read the letter.

In Canada, Nikolai Youmatoff entered a small clearing and paused, having put six miles of Ontario's majestic forestland between himself and home. That's what he called his now vacated log cabin and the neighboring town. The fact that he would never see home again gave him a rush of exhilaration although he'd been happy there until Ann died.

He looked up at Twyla Point and its narrow cascade of water splashing its solitary way down to Ring-of-Moon Lake. There it would continue on to the snarling Lower Rips River then make a watery curl and finally join other waterways to the Great Lakes region.

Youmatoff lowered himself to a small rock outcropping and dusted off a layer of the last snowfall. Thoughts of the prayer book, the key and the blueprint nagged at him even though he had disowned them. He had mailed them to the man who saved his life at the conclusion of the war.

In the end, the souvenirs of a long ago night in which he had been obliged to assist the Nazi, Hermann Goering, meant nothing to him. His pursuers, he feared, wouldn't believe that. They would think he knew more. He shook off these thoughts and looked around him.

Smell preceded recollection of the day he and Ann had last trapped in this region and rested here. A gentle Chinook wind off the eastern slopes of the mountains had mixed with the stonewashed flax scent of her hair. This fresh, seedy smell now made him quiver for her touch. He reminded himself that Ann was gone and he was adrift, alone.

As Youmatoff rose and headed deeper into the forest, farther from the Canadian Mounties dispatched to detain him, he was prepared to acknowledge that Ann's death and the withholding of children were fate's unquestionable foresight.

Chapter 3

It was 6:30 a.m., December 11th, when Falk and Koski cleared customs at Vienna's Schwechat International Airport.

Koski scanned the rows of faces waiting outside the gate. "Do you see him?" Many were drivers holding handwritten signs with the names of their pick-ups scrawled across them.

"Not yet. If I know Tom Stewart, he'll find us before we see him."

As they walked toward the airport's main entrance, a nondescript young woman suddenly appeared beside Falk. She spoke perfect English. "Follow me. There's a car waiting." When

Falk and Koski didn't respond immediately she added, "I'm Mr. Stewart's driver."

The large glass doors automatically slid open and they followed her out into the icy December air of the city dubbed "Paris on the Danube." She quickly led them to a silver gray Mercedes with tinted windows parked at the curb. Inside, a thin, impeccably dressed man in his late fifties with hair the color of the Mercedes greeted them.

"Good morning, Joe. Good to see you again." He shook Falk's hand and turned to Koski. "I'm Tom Stewart."

"Susan Koski." She offered her hand.

Falk watched his partner take quick measure of the man. She would find his grip gentle, two-handed, emanating an inner strength that belied his age. His voice was soft, his vocal pattern deliberate, carefully calculated to reflect thoughts that had sufficiently germinated. She would later confess to Falk that her initial impression was that Tom Stewart was slick. Over time, a deeper understanding of the man would reveal the profound compassion and integrity Falk admired and had come to rely on.

Stewart leaned forward and addressed Falk. "I've booked you both into the Romischer-Kaiser Hotel. I'll be staying there for a few days then move to a different location that I'll pass on to you. We'll have breakfast in my suite at eight and I'll update you on the situation." He gave Koski a final nod. "Your luggage will be along in a moment."

Forty minutes later they entered the hotel through the revolving glass door. Falk was impressed with the old-world atmosphere: potted palms; thick, damask, rose-colored carpets; highly polished burled woodwork; gleaming brass. A birdcage elevator slowly moved aloft through a lacework of black wrought iron.

"Wow," Koski remarked as they followed the porter with their bags to the elevator. The cage gradually made its sedate, well-oiled ascent.

Falk checked his watch. "Just enough time for a shower, shave and a clean shirt." They were shown to adjoining rooms on the third floor. "Give me a ring when you're ready," he said. "We'll go down together."

Koski paused in the doorway. They had traveled without the usual courtesy accorded to law enforcement personnel. Their weapons were broken down and secured in locked carrying cases. Stewart wanted no extraneous paperwork or evidence of their arrival in Vienna.

"Joe, I feel naked without my weapon." She spun away with a smile and entered her room, closing the door behind her.

Falk entered his room. He was mesmerized by the luxury of a bygone era. A high, ornate ceiling added a sense of vastness to an already large room. Tasteful furniture was arranged to enable easy conversation around the burning coal fire in a marble fireplace. Then the phone rang.

"You have a desk in your room?" Koski's voice was almost a whisper. Falk glanced around.

"No, I don't."

"Check in the other room, should be one."

He moved to the next room and saw it—a small writing desk against one wall. Returning to the phone, he affirmed her hunch.

"Good, check the top right-hand drawer. There should be something there to dispel that naked feeling. See you in a bit." The phone clicked off.

Falk opened the drawer and saw a Beretta 92F in a shoulder

holster. Boasting a 15-round magazine, the Beretta weighed in at 2.52 pounds fully loaded. He lovingly slid the weapon from the holster. It had been recently cleaned and lightly oiled. He reached into the drawer, removed a fully loaded magazine and snapped it into place, experiencing a sense of security at the business-like *click*. He cocked the piece, hefted its weight, set the safety and placed it back into the smooth leather holster, wondering why he hadn't checked out the rooms and their contents.

Koski had, heeding one of the most basic rules of Quantico training. He silently swore. Before he met her he'd been a loner, working in the Bureau's elite Rover Division. Then he was paired with Koski on a couple of assignments—operations in which he'd come to rely on her. Now, minutes into their present mission that had the potential to be even more dangerous than the others, she once again demonstrated her skill, discovering the weapon she was obviously meant to find while he took time to admire the furnishings.

Because he no longer worked alone and wasn't required to rely solely on himself, he had become one-half of what he once was. Had he also become lax, dependent? Was he, in his late thirties, in danger of losing his edge?

He sighed and shrugged off the notion. That he had fallen in love with Koski and she with him tended to abrogate all other considerations. He headed for the shower, wondering just what kind of mission Stewart and Cerberus had in mind for them.

Two years ago Falk resisted initiation into Cerberus but ultimately, like Koski, he acknowledged the need for an organization that covertly supported humankind's highest aspirations. Dressed, refreshed and with the Beretta snugly fitted beneath his arm, Falk was ready for breakfast and whatever else

Stewart had on the agenda. There was a knock at the door.

Koski patted the left side of her jacket. "Did you have a gift in your drawer, too?"

Falk took in her mischievous grin and the sparkle in her green-eyed gaze. Special Agent Susan Koski, with her tousled haircut, dressed in a black pantsuit over a heather gray turtleneck sweater and wearing black leather boots looked as if, were she slightly taller, she should be strutting down a Paris catwalk.

He put his arm around her shoulder. "Sure did, gorgeous. Let's go."

Falk rapped sharply on the door to Stewart's suite. It opened immediately.

"Come in, take a seat," Stewart said in his soft voice. "I've ordered breakfast, full American, none of that continental coffee and croissants. You'll need a hearty meal to begin this day." He indicated two easy chairs opposite his desk.

"From now until this assignment is completed, you doctors of archaeology are part of a four person team sponsored by the Smithsonian Institute. My cover is director of archaeological activities assigned to liaise with the Viennese city. We'll have the cooperation of the local police and Interpol. Our Embassy won't know anything of our true mission. Because you two aren't known in this part of the world the chance of being recognized is slim."

The short, snappy instructions signaled the urgency of their new assignment to Falk.

"Do we have any idea where in the city Goering might have hidden his plunder?"

Stewart smiled wryly. "Not really. We know where we thought it might be back in 1975. We just never had the opportunity to look for it."

A knock at the door announced room service. Stewart called out, "Come in." A white jacketed waiter entered, pushing a well-appointed food trolley. He quickly arranged the breakfast and left.

Stewart continued the briefing as they sat at the table. "I want you to listen to this while we have breakfast." Stewart removed an iPod from his pocket, inserted it into a speaker cradle and turned it on. A man's educated and well-modulated voice began.

"It was in the sandwich of time between the end of World War II and the winter of 1975 when events took place in Vienna, Austria, that continue to affect world powers today. My father, Dr. David Benson, was in Vienna that year, attending the third reunion of a group of partisans of which he had been a member during the latter part of the war. In 1945, those freedom fighters joined with local insurgents to resist the Nazi invaders.

"The night of the reunion my father was killed by an unknown assassin. One of the partisans, Lego Moyzisch, had addressed his fellow reunioners, telling them how he had saved a Russian officer's life, a prisoner of war held in a displaced persons' camp outside of Vienna.

"The Russian knew that if he was sent back to Russia he'd be shot for becoming a German prisoner. Lego, a Czech, was also a DP, working as an interpreter in the American Army orderly room at the camp."

By giving the Russian forged papers stating he was Polish, Lego had saved the man's life. In return, the grateful Russian—Nikolai Youmatoff—told Lego a secret he learned while a prisoner of the Germans: the approximate hiding place of Herman Goering's spoils of war, gold and treasures worth countless millions. The hiding place was there in Vienna. "I traveled to Vienna in 1975 to claim and return my father's body to California. It was during that time I was coerced into using my knowledge as an archaeologist to organize a covert team and search for Goering's loot. I was led to believe I was doing a service of national importance. The assignment was short-lived, however, due to political infighting between the Austrian government and Washington.

"The Austrian Socialist Party was running Kurt Waldheim for president of Austria. Due to his secret capacity as a Nazi officer during the war, Waldheim wanted no spotlight turned on that aspect of his past by attempts to search for loot pillaged by the Germans that might be unearthed in Vienna at that time. There was one other factor.

"Reliable sources reported that if the cache being sought was in fact the fabled Goering plunder, there was the possibility of finding a so-called "Judas List." It's a compendium of individuals and organizations that had secretly helped finance World War II that Goering reportedly compiled. They intended to increase their manipulating power over world finances for generations to come, control the future United Nations and selected member nations after the war.

"This so-called "Judas List" was planned to undermine America's Armed Forces by manipulating them to undertake a major part in mindless military actions throughout the world and the support of despot dictators." After a soft sigh he continued. "Deliberately orchestrated civil war and unrest also became part of the devilish plan. I, of course, cannot confirm or deny the existence of such a list and it would be beyond the scope of my interest."

Respectively,

Mark Benson

Stewart turned off the iPod. "Here in Vienna is a place called the Dorotheum. Founded in 1707 by Emperor Joseph I, it's a cross between a museum and an auction house. Four times a year experts, dealers and private parties from around the world meet to purchase important works of art or to merely observe the going prices." Stewart paused. "It's believed that the Goering treasures could still be hidden somewhere below the cellars and foundation of the Dorotheum."

"Wouldn't the loot have been discovered long ago?" Falk asked.

Stewart took a bite of food and shook his head. "During the war the vaults beneath the Dorotheum, along with all Vienna's major museums, were emptied of valuables that were then hidden deep in the Bavarian Mountains.

"The Dorotheum remained empty throughout the war. The story goes that Goering saw it as a perfect hiding place and secretly had the loot taken to Vienna and buried beneath the empty building. Allied bombing toward the end of conflict damaged the Dorotheum. Extensive rebuilding was carried out at the conclusion of hostilities. An attempt to find any so-called loot was made at that time but there was no sign of hidden treasure."

Falk cleared his throat. "What about the "Judas List" Benson mentions? As I see it, Benson's bleak economic ruminations aside, the possibilities that a combination of people and organizations whose names are supposedly on this list, who not only supported Hitler and manipulated the past but also are controlling world events and finances today, is a serious thing to consider."

Stewart watched Falk over the rim of his coffee cup but said nothing. Falk continued.

"The part about the U.S. and our Armed Forces being maneuvered into taking part in mindless actions throughout the world are certainly true. For God's sake, we've watched it happen.

There may be something to it, Tom. Such a record may be real. For almost 80 years people have pondered how Adolf Hitler went from a lance corporal in World War I to become dictator of Nazi Germany by 1933. Who backed him? Where did the massive financing and materiel come from that permitted them to create an army, navy and air force in secret that took the allies seven years to bring to final surrender?

"The years between 1914 and Hitler's rise to power were fraught with intrigue that may still be at work today; arranging for another mad man to repeat even worse atrocities on the world."

"If the listing exists, Joe, we must be the ones to find it. The main reason for the sudden urgency to locate that damn list is due to a report we received a matter of hours ago at Cerberus.

"During the Nuremberg War Crimes Trials there had been a report that Goering made a fruitless attempt to make a deal with one of the American trial judges that he be executed by firing squad, not hanged as a common criminal if found guilty.

"Goering rebuffed, tried blackmail, saying when allowed to speak in his own defense in court he would announce the location of the list. He would reveal how Hitler and the National Socialist Party had been supported and by whom and how the same people arranged for a new Fourth Reich to arise within the next 75 years and attain world domination."

Stewart took a deep breath. "Herman Goering never had his chance to speak in court. He was found dead in his cell, a so-called suicide by cyanide."

"Good God," Falk exclaimed. "Are you saying it wasn't suicide?"

"Look at it this way, Joe. Goering was in a maximum security cell and searched daily—inside and outside of his body. Security was provided 24/7 by specially trained military police personnel. One from each of the four powers—American, British, Russian and French.

"A letter written by an 85-year-old veteran just before his death was mailed to the White House by his wife. She discovered it among papers in his desk." Stewart held up his hand as Falk started to speak.

"The man had been a guard at the prison in Nuremberg. He was ordered to give Goering a cyanide pill to make it look like suicide. Evidently, Goering decided it was better than dying like a common criminal because that's how his death went into the history books."

"Did the letter indicate who gave the order?" Falk questioned.

"No. He simply wanted us to know that if what Goering said about a new group of maniacs taking over the world was true the list had to be discovered—fast. The time frame mentioned was about up."

Falk looked grim. "It ties in with what world economists have said for years, that early in the twenty-first century massive takeovers will have narrowed down all power to certain mega corporations. They would run everything, including heads of world governments and the world economy."

Stewart cocked his head and his eyes narrowed. "If such a list does exist, Cerberus has decided it could have been preserved in an unconventional form, not simply written on a piece of paper. Goering would have planned its use as any extortionist would. He'd make it unique and in a virtually indestructible form... perhaps a wire recording..."

"What's a wire recording?" Koski asked.

"The father of the tape recorder," Stewart explained. "Wire

recordings were widely used by the German Army prior to tape. Sound was recorded onto a magnetic wire held on spools. The wire could record and play back sound, with marginally good quality. Goering would have used a German machine manufactured during the 1940s, a German microphone, wire, spool—German everything."

Koski shook her head. "I had no idea there ever was such a device."

Falk was intrigued. His mind had raced ahead to a fantastic conclusion. "What if a dirty tricks 101 contingent, like a radical Islamic, Israeli, Russian or Palestinian group, finds out about this?"

Stewart's expression darkened. "We believe they have. Our latest report is Mikhail Brasinov's thugs have wind of the loot."

Falk stared at Stewart before saying, "Brasinov, that psychopathic Bosnian mass murderer? I thought he was on the run from the United Nations' War Crimes Commission."

"Right. And believed to be hiding in the Czech Republic, possibly in Brno," said Stewart. "We also have it from a reliable source that he became aware of the list shortly after we were advised by the letter. Brasinov is well protected and will remain hidden. I don't have to tell you that his men are a brutal group of sinister paramilitary thugs that killed and raped their way across Bosnia. They'll show no mercy."

Stewart rose from his chair and crossed to the desk. He seemed exceptionally relieved that the earlier conversation was behind him, yet there remained an edge of uncharacteristic nervousness in his manner.

"This is going to be a tough assignment and a difficult race to be first to the unknown site," Stewart continued. "You're both anti-terrorist experts and, make no mistake, that's what we're up against.

We know Brasinov is working with an Islamic terrorist group. It's doubtful you'll ever personally confront him but his right-hand man, known only as Pasha, will be leading the search."

Stewart pushed back from the desk and went to the window. He stared out at the rooftops of Vienna, his back to his companions. "I've arranged your passports and other necessary documents authenticating the Smithsonian connection. They state that you're traveling with an official American archaeological delegation visiting Vienna to study stolen works of art and peruse the possibility of other undiscovered works around the world.

"One other thing, you'll be working with a newcomer to Cerberus, a man you both know from your participation in the Nevada-California investigation. Cerberus chose him solely because his talents fit our needs. He'll be backup for you in the event Brasinov's men get too close or outnumber our estimate."

Stewart turned and faced them. "I know I can put my full trust in your ability to forget past differences and accept Rod Eiker as a working member of Cerberus. His participation in this venture comports nicely with our desire to succeed."

Falk couldn't believe it. "Eiker! You mean he's on our side now? That son of a bitch caused us more trouble than any ten men did. He almost killed Koski and me. He'd sell his mother to the highest bidder. Tom, what are you thinking? The man's a vicious killer."

"I understand but he works for us now."

"What exactly will Eiker's role be in all of this?" Koski asked.

"To be there at the end... In case we need him."

Falk's mind flashed back to those bitter winter days when he and Koski had fought their way across the High Sierra—through snowbound forests, matching wits with crooked politicians,

Nevada gambling cartels…and Rod Eiker.

Falk turned to Koski and knew by her expression that she shared his disgust.

Stewart noted their reactions. "To quote Emerson, 'As there is a use in medicine for poison so the world cannot move without rouges.' Get some rest, both of you. You have a difficult assignment ahead."

After the agents left, Stewart sat in his chair, leaned back and closed his eyes. "Joseph Falk," he said aloud. "You always manage to give me a few anxious moments."

The assignment he had given Falk and Koski was only part of the big picture. If they succeeded in locating the list, 'The Global Village' and 'International Community' loving politicians worldwide would be looking for new jobs.

Chapter 4

"Fisher's Antiques," Emma Lewis announced, picking up the phone.

"If Pasha arrives before I get there," John Steele said gruffly, "have him wait."

Emma acknowledged his order, hung up the phone and wondered how she had allowed herself to become enmeshed in Steele's latest scheme. Indeed, why had she deluded herself for years into believing that he was her friend? His conduct in the last few days tended to indicate otherwise. She felt used and didn't like it.

She walked back to the small office area of the antique shop that still bore the name of its founder and took a photograph in a silver frame down from a shelf. She studied the familiar picture wistfully. "Oh, Aunt Louise," she whispered, "if only you were here. There's so much I wish I knew."

Emma had inherited the shop and a small upstairs apartment on the Am Numarkt in Vienna from her Aunt Louise, who died two years before. Her aunt had opened the shop after World War II, deciding to remain in Vienna rather than return to England.

Emma had spent time with Louise on many occasions since she finished school in England. There were postcards at Christmas, phone calls—and then the news of Louise's death and that Emma had inherited the shop.

Emma was thirty-four. She'd been working as a teacher for a small, private school in Oxford. Since she had broken up with her fiancé two weeks before being notified of the inheritance, the shop seemed a timely diversion. Being a woman who made up her mind quickly, she had quit her job, flown to Austria and assumed proprietary duties all within a month.

The only child of deceased parents, she had no family in the U.K. and believed that no one would particularly miss her. She studied the five figures in the group photograph.

Her aunt had fought alongside a rugged band of partisans who found their way to Vienna shortly before Russian troops "liberated" the city in 1945. Louise, in the center of the picture, was nineteen then, looking like a Cossack princess, dressed in buckskin trousers, black turtleneck sweater, boots and a bandoleer of bullets slung across her chest.

On her right was a tall, handsome man wearing an American Army cap, his jacket displaying the Medical Corps insignia. His soulful eyes stared at the camera while his chin reflected strong determination. Emma turned the picture over and read the names Louise had neatly printed on the back, corresponding to their positions in the photograph.

The American was David Benson. On Louise's left was John Steele, tall, blond, tanned and leathery, smoking a stub of a cigar, dressed in crumpled and patched Canadian battle dress and wearing a pair of German Army boots. A Sten gun was across his chest.

The remaining two men were older. Far left was Horst Ekel, the oldest. White-haired, with tufted Franz Joseph side whiskers, Ekel was frail and brittle. He also was the owner of the Romischer-Kaiser Hotel where the group had held their reunions in 1955, 1965 and the last in 1975. Horst more resembled an old watchmaker than someone who worked with local insurgents defying the Nazis.

To the far right stood Lego Moyzisch, the tough, barrel-chested Czechoslovakian displaced person who had joined the group and fought his way to the outskirts of Vienna.

Emma placed the photograph back on the shelf. She knew that David Benson had become a noted archaeologist after the war and that, like Louise, was deceased. Horst Ekel was gone, too. She knew nothing, however, of the fate of Lego Moyzisch. It occurred to her that she now regretted never having inquired about Lego's present circumstances.

It was possible that John Steele was the only surviving face from the old photograph.

When Louise died and Emma arrived in Vienna to assume ownership of the shop, Steele met her at the airport. An antique dealer himself, he was a helpful and comforting companion during those early days.

Over time, he had become ever-present, insinuating himself into her otherwise solitary life. Recently she had begun to feel smothered and controlled. Then she learned about Steele's involvement with Pasha and his intention—and apparent need—to involve her.

It started a few days ago when he mentioned millions of dollars lying around, there for the taking. All Emma had to do was follow orders. He would attend to all the details. It was a sure thing, he had said; actually, the belated continuance of a plan put into motion by Lego Moyzisch when he last spoke to Steele, Louise and the others at the 1975 reunion.

Steele was quick to point out he had never asked anything of her. He had been there for her from the day she arrived in Vienna and introduced her to influential individuals in the antique business. He went so far as to intimate that because he had literally saved Louise Fisher's life on more than one occasion in the 1940s, a certain amount of loyalty was owed.

Emma hadn't been privy to the details Steele was working out with his Arab friend, Pasha, but a cold feather of fear had perched on her shoulder the last few days. One that refused to flutter away.

Chapter 5

Over the years, John Steele had not only dealt in *objet d'art*, he also collected a circle of scurrilous business associates who were involved in everything from antiques to assassinations.

Mikhail Brasinov was now one of those associates. Brasinov needed Steele's skills to recruit the right people to locate Goering's treasure. Brasinov also had discovered a new piece of information that was little known at the end of WWII.

During the ethnic differences between Serbs and Muslims in Bosnia, Brasinov had ordered the torture and death of thousands. One of those was a man who tried to save his life by trading the true account of who stole the Africa Corps' payroll during WWII in return for his freedom. Brasinov agreed and was told the story.

The Africa Corps, under the command of Field Marshal Erwin Rommel, plundered North Africa and Egypt of their art treasures with thoroughness typical of the German Army. They took everything. Millions of dollars worth of art cunningly transferred to German custody via the Luftwaffe at the height of the North African campaign, when it was almost impossible to get enough fuel and ammunition to fight the war.

Rommel had been furious. He was a soldier taking orders. At the same time he knew Goering was responsible for flying the treasures out of the Middle East while his troops were fighting with less than enough supplies.

Rommel complained and Hitler recalled him to Germany. It was while Rommel was there that the Africa Corps' payroll vanished.

Arabs had no use for trusts in paper money so it was decided the Corps be paid in gold. The gold, along with other treasures, went to Goering's lair—Carinhall, a great country mansion. A monument to his first wife and a symbol of his own aggrandizement, it was but a stopover on the way to Vienna.

The man who told Brasinov the story of the heist was shot in the head, hands tied behind his back and tossed into a mass grave.

The doorbell jangled and Emma glanced up to see John Steele standing in the doorway.

"Any word from Pasha?" he asked, striding across to a small table that held a coffeepot.

"No, John." Emma felt her stomach tighten at the mention of the man's name. Steele noticed her agitation.

"Listen, Emma. I've explained this to you before. Sometimes we have to do business with people we don't like. That's the way it is."

"We don't have to do business with mass murderers," she complained. He had told her just enough to ensure she would pass along messages from Pasha, who used her shop as a communications center. She didn't want to know more.

"Look at it this way," he said as if trying to lighten the mood. "Pasha is simply a man trying to start a new life after losing everything in the Bosnian conflict. Remember, Emma, there were some 200,000 people killed in that war. Pasha didn't kill them all and he didn't start the war."

Emma turned away and busied herself with paperwork. She wished she could ignore the sense of loyalty she felt for Steele. However, it wasn't only a matter of him befriending her when she came to Vienna and supporting her while she was learning the antique business, it was his connection to her past and his prior devotion to Aunt Louise and the others in the group of partisans. She owed Steele on many levels.

Steele poured two cups of coffee, set one on her desk and remained standing as he sipped his. "I told you Pasha can help me arrange for the right men to go after what your aunt and I were informed of back in 1975 and what we're entitled to. I have maps, books, papers and plans, everything they need."

Emma couldn't help herself. "Everything except the muscle and guts to find it yourself, is that it? What do you think Aunt Louise would think of you now, going into business with Islamic terrorists?"

She saw the anger rise from within him like a hot flame, burnishing his cheeks. For a moment, she thought he might even strike her but he needed her, at least for now.

"I won't even bother to answer that, Emma. I've made an

agreement with these people and I intend to keep it." He pointed at her with the coffee cup. "If I don't, both you and I will be killed. It's that simple."

Emma remained silent as he banged his cup on the desk. "I'll be at my apartment if Pasha shows up or calls."

He turned and walked out of the shop, the bell jangling furiously as the door slammed shut.

At his apartment on Wahringer Strasser, Steele was slumped in an easy chair, finishing a potent drink still waiting to hear from Pasha. He watched as Rosie Wimmer sorted a pile of papers at a desk next to the window. Rosie was pretty, mid-thirties with long, straight, dark hair. She wore little makeup and had a nice figure.

"Get me another drink, Rosie," Steele grunted.

She looked up from her work and a slight frown creased her forehead.

"Just make the drink," he barked, reading her disapproving expression. The phone rang and Steele scooped it up. "I'll be here," he said and hung up. "That was Pasha. He's coming over."

"Do you want me to make sandwiches?" She looked over her shoulder as she dutifully mixed his drink.

"No, this isn't going to be a social meeting. Once he gets here you can take those ledgers to the shop." He took the drink from her and sipped thoughtfully.

Rosie Wimmer had worked for Steele for more than three years. She had her own apartment in the city, supplied by Steele, and ran the larger of his two antique shops. She knew her business and was well liked in the trade. Steele knew Rosie silently fantasized that one day he would ask her to marry him. Steele enjoyed the game. He took care to let his intentions be undecipherable. The doorbell chimed.

"That must be him," Rosie said. "I'll get it." She went to the door and Steele heard voices in the hallway. He finished his drink in one swallow and eased from the chair as Rosie led Pasha into the room.

The man Steele knew only as Pasha was a thin-framed, middle-aged Arab with a pale coffee-hued face devoid of animation. He carried a leather briefcase. His heavy-lidded eyes were black as scorched oil and unlit by inner warmth, his voice a rasping whisper as he acknowledged Steele.

"Herr Steele." Pasha spoke good English with only a trace of an accent.

"Can I offer you refreshment?" Steele asked.

"No, thank you. I can only stay a moment."

"Please, take a chair."

Pasha seated himself but remained stiff, his back straight and inches from the backrest. "There is a group of archaeologists—a delegation from America—due here seeking government information on lost, stolen and missing art treasures from World War II. Do you know anything about them?"

"No. Then again, there's always some group or another here in Vienna looking into missing art objects. It's ongoing."

Pasha continued, "We believe the delegation is backed by American Intelligence."

"Then I suggest we move quickly, the sooner the better."

"That's our intention. Brasinov demands we start at once." Pasha snapped open his briefcase and removed a package wrapped in brown paper. He outlined a detailed set of instructions, ending with, "Do I make myself clear?"

Steele assured Pasha he understood fully. Pasha nodded, rose from his chair, went to the door and waited for Steele to open it.

He touched Steele's shoulder but not with assuring camaraderie. "We will prevail in this endeavor." He left before Steele had a chance to say how much he was already beginning to doubt it.

Chapter 6

Falk and Koski's second briefing took place in Tom Stewart's car. He handed a package to Falk sitting in the back seat with Koski. "Here are the passports for you and Dr. Koski and a phone number where you can reach me any time." Stewart eased the car forward.

Falk stuffed the package into his jacket pocket. "Are we certain this guy Steele is working with Brasinov?"

"Yes, Steele has been under our surveillance for years," Stewart replied. "That man has been more useful to us running loose than if he'd been on our payroll. Yes, we're certain."

"How long has Steele been watched?"

Stewart stopped at a red light. "Since before the Bosnian conflict."

Falk's eyebrows arched. Cerberus certainly believed in long-term surveillance.

Stewart continued. "There's someone else we've kept tabs on for a number of years. Nikolai Youmatoff, the Russian officer whose life was saved by the Czech, Lego Moyzisch. We're aware Lego provided the Russian with forged papers." The light changed and they moved forward.

"Army Intelligence checked Youmatoff out through usual procedures, made sure he was not a plant, then, in 1945, they shipped him to Canada where they could keep an eye on him. I understand he's still alive and very spry at over 80 years old."

Falk and Koski swapped glances and Koski remarked. "Hell of a long time."

"You think so?" Stewart replied.

Falk smiled wryly. "This was usual for the Allies, I take it—packing a man off somewhere, fitting him with a new identity and telling him to keep his nose clean until needed or..."

"Of course. In 1975, shortly before the third reunion of Dr. Benson and Louise Fisher's group, Youmatoff surprised us. He sent Lego a package. We thought it somehow was connected to the location of Goering's plunder, some information Youmatoff hadn't divulged. We planned to intercept it but there was a bungle of some sort and the package got through."

Falk winced. "We have no idea what it was?"

"Apparently it had no meaning in terms of the Goering business—could have been a knitted sweater for all we know. Evidently Lego said nothing at the reunion that would attach any significance to the package."

"Were the Communists also watching Lego at that time?" Koski asked.

"Absolutely. He'd been held in a displaced persons camp run by the Allies at the end of the war. That always worried them."

Falk stared out the window as Stewart deftly threaded the car through evening traffic past the Opera House. "Did they attempt to do anything about the package?" Falk questioned. "Could they have intercepted it?"

"I doubt it. They knew there'd be a reunion every ten years. Like us, they figured that in time anything important would turn up. We know they were watching very closely in 1975 but, as you now know, nothing happened except for Dr. Benson's death. Then the Austrian government asked us to leave."

"And this operation has gone into effect now because something *has* turned up?"

"Yes, Joe. A few days ago Youmatoff sent Lego another package. This time we intercepted. It was an old blueprint to the original passageways under the Dorotheum. There was no note from Youmatoff but we figure Lego knew who sent it. Youmatoff had drawn a straight horizontal line crossed by three Xs in the margin. It was the way prisoners of war identified themselves in the camp where Youmatoff and Lego met."

Stewart glanced at Falk through the rearview mirror. "We made the obvious assumption. We copied the blueprint and sent it to Lego. He has no idea we saw it. We also contacted the special branch of the Royal Canadian Mounted Police. We expect they'll have Youmatoff in hand soon at which time we'll find out what, if any, other pieces of the puzzle are needed to find the treasures' exact location."

Koski looked over at Falk. "I'd say, so long as you have the blueprint all that's needed are people with special skills in architecture and subterranean foundations, modern and historic, plus degrees in Gothic design and history."

Stewart smiled. "Your associates from the Smithsonian have all that. They'll be here by morning."

"All the years you were waiting," Falk said, "following Steele, playing cloak-and-dagger with the Russians, you must have had a clever agent close to the action."

"We played cloak-and-dagger with others as well. Our agent was Louise Fisher. She was good, all right; damned good."

"No one ever found out who killed Dr. Benson?"

"No," Stewart replied.

Then his killer is still out there, Falk thought. If they got wind of the present activity involving the rumored treasures they would be burning to get involved.

Chapter 7

One thousand and seventy-six miles from Vienna as British Airways flies, a single light shone from the second-story window of a three-story brick boardinghouse squeezed between two others on a quiet back street.

This was Number Nine Cable Street in the town of Southport, Lancashire, on the northwest coast of England.

Rodney Eiker listened to a Rolling Stones CD and did sit-ups. He was starting his second set of a hundred when the muffled tune on his cell phone emitted from his jacket hanging on the back of a chair. He got to his feet with the grace of a gymnast and plucked the phone from the pocket.

"Yes?" He listened intently, his face registering no emotion. "Very well. I'll find it, no problem." He snapped off the phone and returned it to his jacket, crossed the sparsely furnished room and turned off the Stones mid-song.

The room was quiet except for the ticking of a cheap wind up alarm clock on the table.

Rod Eiker was forty-six. He was born in Manchester, England, an ex-SAS soldier who had seen bloody action from Belfast to Beirut. Now he was a freelance soldier of fortune whose last assignment had been in the U.S. It involved a murderous plot designed by crooked politicians and a Nevada gambling cartel.

His assignment completed, he escaped the country, leaving a trail of death and destruction in his wake. It was to be his last job. He had earned enough to retire and he did, until he received a phone call from Tom Stewart shortly after he returned to England.

Cerberus had been impressed with his skills even if they had been used against the U.S. government. Stewart offered him complete immunity for his crimes in America on the condition he work for Cerberus. If he refused, he would be dead within a few hours.

Eiker had no choice but to agree. Now, a year later, the phone call had directed him to report to Stewart at the Bristol Hotel, Vienna. He was to fly out that evening from Manchester International.

Chapter 8

December's bitter cold had crept deep into the stonework and flagstones of the ancient church, making the air difficult to inhale. A bent figure dressed in black lit a wrought iron rack of candles with a long wax taper at the foot of a marble statue.

Smoke from the taper curled heavenward, its waxen odor sharp to the senses as it contacted the freezing air. The figure turned and the dancing flames of the flickering candles in their red glass containers reflected on his pallid skin like a thousand points of hellish light. Heaven would never shine in an incandescent way on the face of Pasha.

Steele waited until the man in black snuffed the taper and then began his slow walk toward the back of the church.

They met in the apse beside the great wooden door. Pasha spoke first, his voice hushed and harsh. "You have information about the American team?"

Steele checked his watch. "Two hours from now I meet with a man who knows who they are."

"What's his name?"

"Jack Switzer, attaché at the American Embassy here in

Vienna."

"Brasinov is anxious. He doesn't like to wait." Pasha pulled open the door. He slipped his repellent self from the house of God just as an icy draft of air entered.

Snow gently sifted down onto the city's steep rooftops as Steele and Switzer left the Dorotheum, walked across a square and stopped beside the ornate stonework of the Donner Fountain.

Switzer was scared. He operated in fear, with fear, through fear and by the use of fear.

Intimidation of those he commanded came naturally as did his own obsequious behavior in the presence of those from whom he took orders. He knew he, his wife and child would live only as long as he followed those orders and was useful.

Steele pointed across the square to the Capuchin Church. "Know much about that place, Switzer?"

"Of course, exterior is Romanesque and Baroque that has effectively superimposed itself upon Gothic in some of the church's interior decoration."

"What we're looking for isn't in any textbook," Steele growled as he glanced around the almost empty square. "When are the Americans expected?"

"Two are due tomorrow morning."

"Shit."

"Two are already here. They arrived early."

"Who are they?"

"Drs. Joseph Falk and Susan Koski," Switzer replied. "They're staying at the Romischer-Kaiser."

"Who else at the Embassy knows of their arrival?"

"No one, not even the Ambassador. I was contacted by our man in Washington because of my role in this endeavor."

Together they walked through falling snow. Steele glanced toward Saint Augustine's, historical burial place of 54 urns in the Herzgruftelkammer (The Heart Crypt) containing the hearts of the Habsburgs. "We're being watched, Switzer, but keep walking. We're going inside to meet someone."

They continued the rest of the way to Saint Augustine's in silence. As they entered, Switzer felt the penetrating cold mix with a dank odor of age and dampness.

The door swung closed behind them with a dull, resounding thud. They crossed the vestibule and Switzer peered around the interior of the church. Initially, all he saw was a dim gray light sifting through the stained glass windows.

When his eyes grew accustomed to the gloom, he focused on the red votive light at the side of the altar. As they moved forward, his shoe struck the side of one of the pews. The sound was amplified in the silence and echoed up the stone columns, curved with the arch high into the transept then faded away into space, as had a million hymns over ages past.

"Sit down, Mr. Switzer." Pasha's rasping whisper gasped from the darkness of a pew. Steele guided Switzer to a seat.

"How much time do we have?" Pasha asked.

"Two will arrive in the morning, early. Two are already in Vienna at the hotel Romischer-Kaiser."

A low rattle not unlike the growl of a wild animal sounded from Pasha's throat. "Then you will fetch *those two* to me—here, tonight."

Outside an American Express tour bus trundled through the square, evidently late from a city tour. It turned onto Dorotheegasse and past the front entrance of the Dorotheum. A few tired faces peered out at the slush-ridden street, reflecting little interest. No doubt they had seen the city's main attractions at night and an insignificant side street had nothing to offer.

A young boy looked out at Steele and Switzer and grinned. A fat-faced man with a chewed, unlit cigar glanced over his shoulder. The hydraulic brakes hissed as the bus stopped at the corner then merged into the flow of city traffic.

"Good night, Switzer," Steele said as he walked into the darkness. "We'll be in touch." Switzer turned up the collar of his raincoat and walked in the opposite direction, certain of Steele's last statement.

A limo pulled up outside the Hotel Bristol. Rod Eiker tipped the driver and was on the sidewalk before the door attendant reached the vehicle. "I can manage," Eiker said. He hefted his leather carry on and walked through the revolving doors into the warmth and elegance of the foyer.

The Bristol was one of the few great hotels left in the world, a haven from modernity and its accelerated pace. Eiker sensed the heady atmosphere of another time period seeping through his skin as he strode to the desk.

The desk clerk swiveled the register for Eiker to sign. Once the formalities were over, the tall, neat man with a reserved smile slid a key across the polished counter. "Room 312. Enjoy your stay, Herr Eiker."

Eiker nodded, picked up the key, walked to the elevator and jabbed the Up button.

In his room, he tossed his bag on the bed and went to the window. He noted a few people hustling in and out of the subway entrance on the corner near the opera house, which was dark. He closed the drapes, removed a toilet case from his bag and entered the large, tiled bathroom.

A tired face stared back from the mirror. Despite his body's extraordinary physical condition, his facial reflection reminded him that he was getting a bit old for the game. He turned on the cold water tap and cupped icy water over his face, gasping at its sting. He was drying his face when the phone rang.

He picked up. "Good evening, Eiker."

"Who's this?"

"Mifflin, Harold Mifflin. Tom Stewart is unable to meet with you. He asked if I would fill in for him. Do you have time for a drink?"

"Sure, why not?"

"I can be at the Bristol in, say… ten minutes?"

"Okay, the bar then, ten minutes."

After Eiker hung up he went to his field kit, removed a plastic 9mm and placed it beneath his pillow. The Marakov that Stewart's limo driver had supplied was in his shoulder holster and needed a slight adjustment, as did his tie, and he was off.

He walked the deep carpeted hallway to the elevator and contemplated this man Mifflin, remembering a face-to-face with him in Hong Kong. Like Eiker, Mifflin had a reputation for getting things done, not caring how he accomplished them.

Although he was sure Mifflin's determination stopped short of his own. Harold Mifflin had become a legend in the CIA, perhaps more feared than respected. Eiker also recalled hearing that Mifflin had retired several months ago and supposedly was living in Southern California raising roses.

The sound of Gershwin softly playing on a piano in the bar took his mind off Mifflin for a moment as he glanced around for a table. It was still early, plenty of choices. Eiker opted for a table against the wall facing the entrance. As he sat down he wondered where Mifflin's men were. He had no doubt they were already in place.

"I'm expecting someone," Eiker told the waiter. "Heavyset man. Can't miss him. When he arrives bring him a double Jack Daniel's. I'll take a double scotch, splash of soda, no ice." The waiter nodded and left.

Eiker was halfway through his drink when Mifflin appeared at the entrance, peering into the smoky gray air, a battered felt fedora pulled down over his forehead. He looked only slightly older than the last time Eiker had seen him.

A stubby man a little over five six, he'd planted his stumpy legs apart as if ready to do battle, a jutting jaw reinforcing the demeanor. Winston Churchill look-alike, Eiker thought as he waved. The solid mass of mankind stomped across the room to his table. The waiter with the double JD was there immediately.

Mifflin doffed his hat and nodded at the drink. "Nice touch, Eiker." He tossed the fedora on the floor beside his chair and wrapped a brawny hand around the glass. "Cheers." He took a long, masterly swig then offered his beefy hand across the table and Eiker returned the handshake.

"You haven't changed much, Harold."

Mifflin gave a low, rumbling laugh. "Liar." He finished his drink and signaled the waiter for another round. "I never thought I'd be briefing you. I thought you were a freelancer."

"I was." He gave a sardonic grin. "But I couldn't resist Tom Stewart's invitation."

"Yes, well things change, don't they?"

"CIA drum you out, Harold?"

"No, just the regulation retirement. I'm a consultant now."

"You almost nailed my arse in Hong Kong."

Mifflin nodded. "Only your dramatic leap onto the Star Ferry saved your ass."

They were silent for a moment, remembering when they had been on opposite sides. The waiter delivered two more drinks and left.

"Now here we are, partners, so to speak." Fifteen minutes later Mifflin had given Eiker the rundown on the operation to date and Eiker's exact part in its potential conclusion.

"What you propose will be damned tricky," Eiker said, his cool eyes mirroring the risks his mind calculated, "if even possible."

"You can do it," Mifflin stated flatly. "Probably the only man who can." Nodding immodestly, Eiker downed his drink and called the waiter. "Coffee, strong and black."

Chapter 9

Falk and Koski were enjoying a nightcap in the bar at the Romischer-Kaiser. A waiter approached their table and informed Falk there was a messenger from the American Embassy waiting in the lobby and that the courier said it was important.

Falk and Koski exchanged a glance as Falk pushed his drink aside. "Be right back." He followed the waiter between the tables.

In the lobby, the waiter indicated a man of medium build in a raincoat sitting next to a Chamaedorea palm. Falk nodded and moved in the man's direction.

Switzer got to his feet and flashed his ID. "Jack Switzer, American Embassy. Sorry to bother you so late Dr. Falk but the Ambassador needs to see you at once."

Falk glanced at the ID. "Wouldn't a phone call have done?"

"Afraid not, Doctor. The Ambassador thought it wise not to

trust the phone on this one." He gave a weak smile and looked around as if antsy to get on with it.

Falk eyed the man carefully. It was obvious he was nervous and on edge. "You okay?" Switzer glanced back toward the bar then to Falk. "Okay, sir?"

"Yeah, you seem edgy."

Switzer quickly put on what looked like a genuinely tired smile. "Possibly due to working a sixteen-hour day, Doctor. The Ambassador has had me on the go getting everything in order for your team from the Smithsonian. Won't be any rest for me until we have you all together and ready to go."

Falk knew at once that something was wrong. Stewart had emphasized the Embassy was in the dark as far as their assignment was concerned. "I'll get Dr. Koski." He started back to the bar.

"No need, Doctor. I'm sure she'd rather relax here at the hotel. We won't be long."

Before Falk could answer Koski emerged from the bar and headed toward them.

"What's up? Everything okay?"

"I was just telling Dr. Falk that there's no reason for you to come along." Switzer glanced at his watch. "It's getting late. You have a busy schedule tomorrow."

Koski opened her green orbs wide and beamed them directly at Switzer's elusive eyes. "And you are?"

"Sorry," Falk said. "Kos, Dr. Koski, this is Jack Switzer, American Embassy."

Koski simply nodded then turned to Falk. "I'd rather go along. I'm not tired."

Falk reconsidered his initial impulse. If this was a trick it would be wiser if Koski stayed behind. At least she would be able to inform Stewart of what happened.

"No," Falk exclaimed. "You should turn in. We do have a busy day tomorrow. Besides, you were going to call your Uncle Tom, remember?" Falk checked his watch. "Better do it soon or the time difference will have him fast asleep."

Koski met Falk's gaze, her intelligent eyes registering awareness. "You're right. I forgot the time difference."

"Shall we go?" Switzer asked as he moved toward the door. "I have a car and driver waiting outside." Falk felt assured. Koski knew where he was headed and with whom. Nonetheless the feel of the automatic in the shoulder holster gave him added assurance.

Koski watched them leave and headed to her room to call Tom Stewart. As she entered the old-fashioned birdcage elevator, a man slipped in beside her just as the concertina door closed.

A black Mercedes waited at the curb outside the Romischer-Kaiser with its engine running. Switzer pulled open the back door and stepped aside for Falk to get in.

As he folded into the interior, the soft *PHUTT* of an air-propelled tranquilizer dart was the last thing Falk heard before slumping into a thick, swirling blackness.

Slowly, through a gradually rising sense of consciousness, Falk realized he was no longer in Switzer's car. He struggled to focus. It was a dimly lit room with a high, beamed ceiling that was as cold as the lump in the pit of his stomach.

A meager, cracker box room with a bare, concrete floor and little furniture, it was reminiscent of a cell. Falk saw Switzer sitting at a small wooden table with his back to him and the room got meaner.

"Where am I?" Falk asked.

Switzer turned. "Ah, you're awake." Then there was the sound of an iron bolt grating and a door swung open. Koski was ushered in, her hands cuffed behind her back, flanked by a man and a woman.

Struggling to get to his feet, Falk discovered he was tied to the chair and didn't have the strength to stand.

The man who just entered came over and crouched in front of Falk. "My name is Steele. I have no doubt you've heard my name mentioned since you arrived in Vienna." He straightened to his full height. "If you really *are* doctors of archaeology all well and good. You'll be an asset. If, on the other hand, you're not, you're going to have to continue to play the part. I know few genuine archaeologists who carry automatics in shoulder holsters."

"In any case, we could use your help. I have all we need to start the search—maps, architectural plans of the Dorotheum— original and those used for rebuilding after the war. No doubt I know more about the area we're going to search than any of your people from the Smithsonian."

Falk cursed silently. "Why do you need us?"

"I'm working with someone who has no patience. He expects me to provide an expert and I said I would. That's you, Doctor. Dr. Koski will remain a hostage until we have achieved our objective. After that you'll both be free to go."

Falk was more alert now. His vision was clearing, enabling him to see across the room to Koski and the attractive, thirtyish female beside her with medium brown hair pulled back in a tight French braid. Her basic black dress was cut high at the neck and just below the knee. It was clear from her pained facial expression that she wished she was anywhere but here.

"You won't get away with this, Steele," Falk said. "You'll be the first one they look for. You're too well-known."

"Being well-known and being found are two different matters and I have no intention of being caught. I've looked forward to what we're about to do for too long."

He started to pace as he continued. "Beneath the *Innere Stadt*, the inner city of Vienna is a labyrinth of passages dating back to Roman times. I have a starting place—a vault beneath the Saint Augustine Church—and a monk whose knowledge of the subterranean secrets of Vienna is legend."

Switzer seemed compelled to add what Falk thought might be making him so edgy. "There are others besides our friend Brasinov looking for the treasures."

"He's right," Steele said. "Seems some hard asses in the Czech Republic got wind of what we and Brasinov are up to and want in on the deal. So you help us get to it first and you and the lady doctor can go home. No problem."

No one knew where Falk and Koski were and wouldn't for some time...if ever.

Falk replied, "What guarantee do we have you'll let us go after this is over?"

"None. You'll have to trust me." Steele went over to the woman next to Koski. "You two ladies are going to be close for a while. I'd better introduce you. Emma Lewis meet Dr. Susan Koski."

Chapter 10

Steele kept an automatic pressed hard into Falk's ribs as they walked down a side aisle in Saint Augustine's. A stand of flickering red candles cast jagged shadows of their bodies on the wall.

"Hold it," Steele said touching Falk's shoulder.

Out of the gloom a figure came toward them; a man dressed

in the dark, flowing robes of a monk, the cowl pulled forward covering much of his face. He made a brusque, beckoning motion and led Falk and Steele down the aisle to a brass gate on one of the side altars. The gate yielded to his touch and they followed him up three shallow steps and around behind the altar. He pulled his cowl aside and looked around. Seemingly satisfied they were alone he turned his attention to the stone altar. Falk heard a soft click then Steele and the monk leaned their weight against a section of the altar that creaked open.

The aperture was barely wide enough for a man to squeeze through. The monk went first then Falk entered into the black, dank cavity. Steele was last in. Falk heard him grunt as he pulled the stone slab shut behind him.

"Okay, now listen." Steele's voice sounded muffled inside the narrow passage. "This leads to a vault. Downward incline all the way. Keep your hands on the walls. Don't worry about your head. There's enough room above us."

There was a sputter and flare of a match followed by a pungent odor of brimstone. Falk glimpsed his own distorted shadow on the rough-hewn stonewall before the match fluttered out. The monk reached beneath his robe and removed a flashlight, switched it on and its beam stabbed through the blackness.

They walked for several minutes during which Falk was aware of the sound of dripping water and the walls were wet beneath his fingertips.

"Hold it."

It was the first time the monk had spoken and Falk noticed there was no trace of an Austrian accent. Steele took the flashlight and held the beam on a studded iron door. The monk rattled keys as he worked on the lock.

The monk grunted. "Got it. Go, slowly."

Steele shoved Falk forward. In doing so he dropped the flashlight, smashing the lens on the stone floor. Cursing, Steele fumbled his way into a small chamber. A second match hissed and Steele touched the flame to a thick stub of candle on a small table.

They were crowded into some kind of crypt but the weak glimmer of candlelight permitted Falk a glimpse into the gloomy corners. He stiffened when he saw a pallid human foot protruding from the shadows.

Steele picked up the candle and crossed the room. The light exposed another foot and legs before casting its flickering disclosure on a man bound, gagged and stripped to his underwear. The captive's eyes were filled with terror. Falk concluded that he was probably looking at the real monk.

"Grab a chair, Falk," Steele said and Falk seated himself at the table. "This guy has the information you'll need." Steele gestured toward the bound monk and ordered his bogus counterpart to return the "bathrobe."

The impostor did so. As he slipped off the heavy vestment, Falk saw he was fully dressed. The shivering cleric, who was shoeless, grabbed the garment and pulled it on watching the trio in terror.

"Okay," Steele said jerking his head toward the hapless cleric. The pretender monk hit the churchman across the mouth with the back of his hand, hauled him to his feet and pushed him into a chair across the table from Falk. The man trembled as a trickle of blood oozed from one corner of his mouth.

Faux Monk, as Falk designated the impostor in his mind, spat out rapid-fire German. The terrified man shook his head and made some reply that *Faux* Monk translated.

"He says he'll die first."

"Fine," Steele rasped. "Tell him he has no idea how slowly and painfully I can make him die. Advise him he'll be responsible for the deaths of two other innocent people who will never see another Christmas and that isn't the Christian way."

Falk watched the monk. Vague instinct told him the man understood what was being said but remained silent as *Faux* Monk went into a guttural onslaught, punctuating his point with a solid smash to the man's head.

"Goddamn it, Steele," Falk roared. "Call the ape off. He'll kill him."

Steele feigned shock. "Why Dr. Falk, such language in a place of worship."

"You mean, crazy, son of a bitch. You enjoy this." Falk itched for the chance to slam his fist into Steele's face.

"Control yourself, Doctor. That guy," he jabbed a finger toward the holy man who lolled back in his chair, "could be your ticket home. He must give us information and assistance."

From what he could see of the poor bastard, Falk figured he was in no shape to give much of anything. The man who had done the punching pulled the monk's head up.

"He's out cold."

"Damn!" Steele's fist came down hard on the table. It was the first time Falk saw Steele overtly agitated, the first time he'd seen a crack in that all-too-smooth exterior. It was good to measure a man's limit. It was the first step in defeating him.

Steele was dammed good and recovered quickly. He reached under the table and picked up a package wrapped in brown paper. Tossing it to the center of the table, he stood back.

"Take a look inside, Doc. Tell me if it's any good."

Falk reached out, pulled the parcel toward him then slowly tore off the wrapping. What he saw surprised him. It was a Carmelite edition of a *Book of Hours* in mint condition. Falk opened the heavy leather cover and studied the first page.

The inscription indicated the prayer book had belonged to the Bohun family in 1390. Each page was illuminated with drawings of angels and cherubs, birds and snakes, blessed icons and words lettered in gold. Falk's knowledge of antiques was limited to auctions and estate sales his now deceased wife used to drag him to but he had seen similar books and guessed this one to be nearly priceless.

Steele leaned close to Falk, his breath hot and sour. "You and this pope hopeful should have a nice chat tonight." He straightened. "It better be the kind that produces information we can use otherwise you're getting a preview of your own tomb."

Steele moved toward the exit and *Faux* Monk followed.

"How the hell am I supposed to talk to him?" Falk shouted. "I can't speak German."

Steele grinned. "Then try Latin."

"What is it I'm supposed to find out?"

"Back when those books were made, hidden messages, clues if you will, were placed in the wording or the pictures. Families used them as a cryptogram for their secrets. You'll find it's written in Latin, Greek and Arabic. It's like a Rosetta Stone in book form."

"Then why leave me in here with this person? Take the book and have someone decode it."

Steele neared the table and pointed at the monk. "His expertise is in ancient books and writings. Your expertise is in archeology. Put your heads together and see what you come up with."

"And where did the book come from?"

"The Czech Republic," Steele replied. "That's all you need to know."

Falk was about to question Steele further but he left the crypt and slammed the iron door shut behind him.

Falk pulled the missal toward him; his own macabre shadow looming against the cold stonewalls as he studied the book. Closer inspection confirmed his initial determination that it was a Gothic missal over seven hundred years old.

The monk moaned, regaining his sensibility. Dizzily, he lifted his head and wiped his bloody mouth with a trembling hand. Falk glanced up. "Do you speak English?"

The monk's voice was low, traces of fear still evident in his eyes as he answered, "Very little."

Falk sighed. "Good. We must find a way out of this hole."

The man shook his head and remained hunched over the table. "There's only one way." He nodded in the direction of the small iron door.

Falk took the candle, crossed to the wall and scrutinized the door inch by inch. He found no way to open it. Returning to the table, he tapped the missal.

"Where did this come from?"

"I don't know," the monk replied.

Falk slid the book across the table and held the candle close, enabling the man to see the detailed workmanship of the rare and valuable object. He watched his eyes, expecting a reverent reaction to the tome's significance and beauty. There was none. Was he still dazed from the pounding he had taken?

Another possibility crossed Falk's mind. Was he a genuine monk? Would a monastic that knew the ancient books and details of the passageways beneath the city not recognize the value of a fourteenth century prayer book? He was formulating his question when they both heard it: the sound of the iron door rasping open. One perfectly placed shot struck the monk squarely between the eyes and Falk was grabbed and dragged twisting and kicking from his chair. At some point he dropped the book. The last thing he remembered before everything went black was the monk's blood splattering across the tabletop.

Chapter 11

Koski, desolate and silent, sat in the same small empty room that Steele and Falk had left earlier. Emma was seated beside her with a quavering .45 aimed in Koski's general direction. It was evident to Koski that Emma was an unwilling accomplice in this affair. Trained to read faces and body language, Koski had witnessed the woman's resolve waiver several times, the anguish of indecision visible in her silent expressions.

Nevertheless, Koski had concluded it was time to neutralize Emma and get out of there when Steele burst through the door.

"Where's Joe?" Koski demanded when she saw Steele was alone.

"Don't worry. He's safe." Steele poured a cup of coffee from a thermos on the table and cradled the mug with both hands.

Koski watched Emma, who closely eyed Steele as he sipped the brew.

"Something's wrong, isn't it?" Emma asked. "Where is he, John?"

"He's tucked away in Saint Augustine's Church working on our project."

Emma's eyes widened. "You most likely were followed."

Steele smiled sardonically. "We were *not* followed. Falk is safe in a vault with a monk deciphering a Gothic missal."

Emma was on her feet more nervous than ever. "God, Steele, you've fallen into a trap. We're all as good as dead!"

"What the hell are you talking about?"

"Whoever's in that vault with Falk is no monk." Emma's high voice cut the air in the room. "I'll bet my life on it."

Steele laughed. "Then you'd lose, my dear. One of my men captured him in the church earlier, took his robes, hid him in the vault, dressed himself as the monk and stayed at the church until I arrived."

"When was this original monk put into the vault?"

"Couple of hours ago, why?"

Koski noticed that Emma's nervousness was waning, her voice gaining confidence.

"John," Emma asked, "Did you ever mention the loot to Rosie Wimmer?"

Steele hesitated a moment, sipping his coffee. "Yes, what of it?"

Emma gave a bitter laugh. "You tipped off the Israelis via Interpol. The "monk" you left with Falk no doubt was an Interpol plant. Someone else already has the real cleric."

Steele was dumbfounded. "You must be nuts. Why the hell would she go to Interpol for Christ's sake?"

"John," Emma replied sarcastically, "Rosie Wimmer has been an informer for Interpol for the last five years."

"I don't believe that."

"Just because I've been accommodating to you over the years doesn't mean I've been dumb or blind. I've learned a few things. The head man at Interpol-Vienna is Franz Kutna. He and Rosie

Wimmer are members of the *Urgun-Zvilumi,* a group dedicated to searching out every last living Nazi of any consequence and finding any remaining Nazi caches hidden during the war."

Steele's face blanched as Emma continued. "Kutna was planted in Interpol, the perfect job for his life's mission."

"How do you know this?"

"Did you think Rosie and I never talked? If you continue with your plans you'll have tough competition. Get Falk back here. Maybe we can work together as a team but I doubt you'll find him. I think you've botched your first move and if I'm right we're sitting ducks. My guess is either the Israelis or the Czechs have him."

Steele's jaws clamped tight. He had to be sure. "Stay here. Shoot her if she tries to leave." He left the room, slamming the door behind him.

Koski and Emma faced each other in silence.

Chapter 12

It was shortly before dawn and a frosty mist hung over Vienna as the man driving the snowplow squinted in the glare of his headlights. The plow knifed its way through the snow, pushing it aside like a curvilinear wave in a sea of foam. He was thinking of a warm breakfast when suddenly his plow jarred.

He jammed on the brakes when he saw a body slide up with the pile of snow, twisted in a praying position on the mound the plow just created. The driver's hand shook as he switched off the chugging engine.

When the police arrived, he talked to the officer while the revolving blue light atop the patrol car split the darkness with hypnotic intensity. An ambulance pulled up, its siren growling to a halt. The medics removed the body from the snow bank and placed it on a gurney.

As the emergency vehicle drove off, the plow driver crossed himself and said a silent prayer for the poor monk who died with no shoes on.

Chapter 13

When John Steele re-entered the room where Emma and Koski waited, his face was gray. Koski could tell at once that Emma had been right. *Oh my God! Joe...*

Steele didn't look directly at them as he spoke. "Someone has been watching the church," he mumbled. "The vault's empty."

"What's happened to Joe?" Koski demanded.

In her first outward gesture of compassion, Emma gently touched Koski's shoulder. "We'll find him," she said. Then she turned to Steele, her deep blue eyes clear and determined. "I think you'll agree we'd better leave here immediately—separately, a few minutes apart."

When Steele didn't reply but stood frozen in indecision, she went on. "Don't you see, John? If we stay together we're all in danger. Pasha's men will easily hunt us down."

Koski paused, wanting to sprint into action yet needing to see how this conversation played out. At the mention of Pasha, Steele's peevish eyes took on a furtive, feral look but he didn't move.

"If we split up," Emma continued, "we may have a chance to stay alive. If not..." Her voice was pleading. "It's our only hope, John. You know Pasha's people will kill us if they find us." Her last words were finally persuasive. "You failed them."

"Okay!" Steele thundered. He rushed to the door and turned briefly. "But I'm not giving up on finding the loot, Emma, remember that. I'll find it if it kills me." He flung the door open and fled the room.

Emma slumped into a chair, the automatic slipping from her hand to the floor. "Thank God he didn't insist we go with him," she murmured. Her entire body began to shake. Koski walked toward her, her own knees feeling slightly weak with momentary relief. She picked up the gun, unafraid now of any threatening response from Emma.

"Oh, God, I'm so sorry…I don't know why I ever listened to John or thought he was my friend…It's just that I…" Her voice cracked. "I felt indebted to him and I thought…"

"Emma," Koski said, stopping her. "It's okay. You'll be okay now. If I were you I'd get out of town."

Chapter 14

Falk tried to open his eyes but the pain in his head said to forget it. He was dimly aware that he was upright in the back seat of a moving vehicle and his wrists hurt badly. He opened his eyes slowly. He was in handcuffs and Jack Switzer sat beside him.

Falk groaned and turned to the window. A snow-covered landscape flashed by in a reel of almost endless monotony, broken now and then by bare trees and stonewalls. Soon it would be daylight. He had no idea where he was or where Switzer and the driver were taking him.

The car, a black Peugeot, slowed to let a horse-drawn cart loaded with empty potato sacks plod through a crossroad. The driver of the cart barely noticed them from under his woolen cap and continued his slow pace. The car dropped into low gear and went around the cart with a snarl of exhaust causing the horse to rear, almost jerking the driver from his perch. Falk closed his eyes as the car fishtailed on the slick, icy road, regained traction and howled off down the bleak curving road.

In her small apartment above the antique shop, Emma Lewis concluded a phone call and grabbed the coffee pot in the same moment the car containing Falk was racing out of town.

Emma placed the pot on the table, saying, "All Rosie could tell me was that her people put a watch on my place." She poured steaming coffee into two antique mugs. "We're safe for the moment. Rosie said Dr. Falk was last seen in a car with Czech diplomatic plates. They were heading northeast out of the city."

Koski set down her mug. "Northeast—you mean the Czech Republic?" Her first thought was to contact the American Embassy but Stewart had warned them against talking to the Embassy or anyone else.

"Rosie and Kutna have alerted Interpol," Emma began but Koski interrupted, not listening. "I'm going after him."

Emma gave her an incredulous look. "If he's being abducted into the Czech Republic...forget it, Susan."

"What do you mean?"

Emma was almost apologetic. "For one thing, if you're caught you may spend the rest of your life in an East European prison. There's also no guarantee you'll find him and..."

"You operate an antique shop, Emma," Koski said. "How many guarantees are there in your business?"

Emma shrugged.

Koski downed her coffee. "The business Joe and I are in offers none but that doesn't stop us from doing it." From the quizzical expression on Emma's face, Koski figured the woman was trying to juxtapose no guarantees with the field of archaeology. "No matter," Koski said and got up.

Emma put on her coat. "C'mon, we'll take my car."

The first sign of daylight was breaking as they drove across the awakening city. "We'll catch the morning train to Bratislava," Emma said, "transfer to a local to Kuty, a small town at the fork of the river across from Hohenau. I know someone there who will help us."

They fell silent. Koski slumped back and stared ahead. In five days, it would be Christmas. She thought of candles, trees with many colored lights, warm wax and bayberry, the message of peace struggling to preserve itself. She pulled her coat tighter around her as Emma turned into the parking lot of the Nordbahnhof railway station.

Walking into the old, cavernous station, Koski saw the grime and gloom of an age long past mixed with modern. There were the usual harried early morning travelers one saw on every railway platform, their faces a combination of happiness and harassment. Koski herself was bewildered at the last few hours. Normally she would have easily adjusted to foreign surroundings, been able to cope with any situation. This time she found herself in a limbo of uncertainty.

Was it that she was in a strange country and unable to speak the language or turn to any friendly agency due to the secrecy of her mission? Or was it simply that she was lost without her partner, without his encouragement and optimistic outlook…without his touch?

Emma tapped her elbow. "Wait here. I'll get the tickets."

"I'll come with you."

"No, stay. It's too easy to remember a couple of women buying tickets." Emma crossed the station platform and entered the ticket line.

Koski watched, marveling that Emma, a small antique shop

owner, had such unusual shrewdness about things like two women being noticed. She went over to a bookstall and browsed through magazines. She could look at the pictures if she couldn't understand the words.

Emma appeared with the tickets. "Let's get some breakfast. We have time."

Koski nodded and wondered what paperwork, if any, they might need to cross into the Czech Republic. They entered a busy café and found a table.

"You hold the table," Emma said. "I'll get the food."

Koski waited, visa and passports on her mind. Had Emma, in her rush to get out of the city, overlooked this important consideration?

Emma returned and planted bread rolls and small packages of butter and jam on the table then got the coffee. She laughed and sat down. "Phew. I'd hate to see this place during rush hour."

"Emma..." Koski broke her roll and buttered it slowly. "I don't think Americans can cross into the Czech Republic without papers of some sort and I don't have any."

Emma nodded. "I know. Pass the jam, please."

Koski's surprise was evident. Here she was, certain she was going to dash Emma's plans and she calmly asked for the jam.

"On the train," Emma said, "later in the journey, after we cross the border, there will be the routine ID check. Rosie has the word out ahead of us. Don't worry. You'll get through."

Koski decided it was time to talk to Emma about her connection to this Rosie character. "What did you say the name of Rosie's organization was?"

Emma shushed her. "Forget I ever mentioned it." Checking her watch, she announced it was time to go.

Emma led the way out of the café. As they passed through the ticket gate, a large man in a leather trench coat, whose demeanor conjured up images of secret passwords and invisible ink, oozed his way into a nearby phone booth although they never saw him.

"They're boarding the train to Kuty now," he reported then hung up and wheezed out between the wood and glass concertina doors.

Once on the Vienna-Bratislava-Prague-Bahnoffenlocalstutz, the two women found a compartment and sat down. Emma checked her watch. "Nice timing. The train leaves in eight minutes."

Koski grew increasingly uneasy having to rely on Emma, a woman she had only just met yet whose instincts and knowledge she sorely needed.

Chapter 15

The clock on the dash of the Peugeot indicated they'd been driving nearly two and a half hours. The pain in Falk's wrists from the unusually tight handcuffs was agonizing.

They had turned off the main highway at a small town called Wilfersdorf. Now he saw a sign at the fork in the road: Hohenau 35 Km. The driver swung the car in the direction of Hohenau and they flashed through the village of Angern.

Through a row of leafless trees, Falk glimpsed a roadside shrine with a peaked slate roof and a statue of the Virgin. Off to his right was a fair sized river, its fast-flowing center edged with ice. The road followed the river for miles and he grew weary of watching the slate gray water. His mind filled with the possible logistics of escape. If the chance came, he was ready.

Switzer spoke to the driver. "I'll make my contact call when we get to Hohenau. Give us a chance to get a hot drink." The driver nodded.

"Christ, Switzer, these cuffs are digging into my flesh!" Falk said. "When do I get them off?"

"Maybe never. Sit back and enjoy the view."

Falk's arms also felt as if they were coming out of their sockets. "What the hell do you think I'm going to do, jump from the fucking car?" Falk wanted to escape not splatter himself across the pavement. He would wait until the odds were in his favor.

His wrists twisted painfully in the restraints. "If I wind up in the hospital with an infection I'll be of no use to you bastards." He saw a flicker of concern in Switzer's cold eyes. "Look." He lifted his arms "I'm not kidding."

What Switzer saw seemed to make an impression. "Okay, while we're in the car." He reached over and slipped the key into the steel manacles and Falk eased out of them. The blood started to circulate as he rubbed his chafed wrists until they retained a bluish color.

"Any damned tricks and you'll be dead, no matter how much we need you. Understand?" Switzer reached across and checked that the doors were firmly locked.

The car stopped and Falk saw the red and white pole indicating a railway crossing projecting across the road. There was a dull, off-key clang of the crossing bell and a train hurtled past, windows blurred, wheels clattering. Then it was gone, followed by silence until the creak and groan of the crossing pole went skyward in a series of jerks and came to rest in a present arms position.

"We're making good time," the driver called back to Switzer. "That was the Vienna-Bratislava-Prague Bahnoffenlocalstutz."

Falk leaned back in the Peugeot as it bumped over the

railroad crossing and down a second-class road. He thought about what the driver just said—Bratislava-Prague.

Christ! He was in the Czech Republic!

When did they cross the border? He must have been out cold when they did. He saw a sign: Hohenau 5Km. He was getting closer and deeper...but into what? He had no idea. All at once he knew he didn't want to find out.

The narrow road ahead wound up a steep hill. There were thick groves of trees on his side of the car—woods that came almost to the edge of the highway. The car would have to slow considerably to navigate the curves and make the ascent. It was a chance.

Switzer must have read his mind. "Make a move to get out of the car and you'll be dead before you hit the ground."

"You think I'm dumb enough to try? I don't have a clue as to where the hell I am."

Falk's reply must have satisfied him because when Falk slammed the heel of his hand into Switzer's nose he took it full on. Falk felt the bones crunch.

The driver of the car half turned and pulled his gun but the road was slick, the bends tight. He couldn't handle both. The vehicle swerved erratically. Falk lunged, grasped the gun, unlocked and opened the door in one synchronized motion that surprised even him.

Lunging from the automobile, he landed in a clump of snow-covered bushes. The driver lost control, swerved and crashed. Falk heard the smash of metal as he leaped to his feet and bolted into the woods.

He ran until the air in his lungs felt like fire. Afraid he would pass out and be found, he stopped and slumped against a tree, his chest heaving. He listened for sounds of pursuit but all he heard was the pounding of his own heart. He had to keep on the move, force himself to go deeper into the woods.

He realized he still gripped the Walther P38 automatic he'd taken from the driver. He stuck the weapon in his pocket, the reassuring weight tugging at his jacket. Ahead, past the woods, he saw flat country and a wide, metallic-hued sky.

He thought of Koski in Vienna. Was she able to escape and get word to someone? He realized she didn't have anyone to contact. Stewart had checked out of the hotel Romischer-Kaiser, telling them he'd be in touch from a new location. Koski was resourceful but...

He felt a stab of pain in his left leg from the hard landing. Still he had to go on. Leaving the safety of the woods, he crossed a field and came to a narrow dirt road. The snow was soiled and sparse. Puddles encrusted with thin gray ice and frozen earth showed through in spots. Falk limped passed a fork in the road where little more than a cow path intersected. He glanced back over his shoulder repeatedly but saw no one. That was when he spotted the tire prints frozen into the earth.

At first he thought they were car tracks but then realized they belonged to a motorcycle. He scanned the area: silence and the ever-present, bone-chilling cold.

Cautiously he approached the next bend in the rutted track. On the right was a long stretch of pines, their twisted trunks curved southward from years of prevailing north winds. Even now, with no breeze to stir the icy air, the trees looked tormented, clinging to the frozen earth by the tips of their roots that strained upward in a shapeless tangle.

Glancing to his right he spotted a farmhouse set back from

the lane, almost hidden by undergrowth and scrub. Bleak as it was, Falk was tempted to go to the door and seek aid. Instead he continued until he saw weather-scarred outbuildings with some rotting in sections. One structure that once was a barn caught his attention. A solid thick wall on one side and the tile roof seemed intact over most of the frame. Ancient clay tiles patched in spots and clumps of grass sprouted from the roof at random intervals.

He had to rest, needed a place to hide for the night. Clambering over a rock wall, he dropped to the other side and crawled toward the barn.

The bulky wooden door was unlocked but had warped over the years. He had to strain to make it give. Inside he smelled the odor of rotting vegetation as he warily limped to a dark corner, gathered scraps of hay, piled them into a heap and squirmed inside, the Walther next to his cheek.

It was dark when he awoke. His watch had stopped, the luminous hands showing twelve twenty-five. It probably broke when he jumped from the car. His stomach growled. He crawled to a broken window and peered out at a bare, frosty meadow illumined by the moon riding midway overhead. He figured it was around two or three in the morning.

Again his stomach protested. He reached out and plucked old wheat straws stuck to the sill and chewed the stems. In the distance, Falk heard the sound of a train whistle tugging at the cold night air and thought of its warm compartments and fresh brewed coffee.

The whistle faded. He leaned his forehead against the grimy windowpane and thought of the dirt road and motorcycle tracks. If it was a police patrol it would search this area, these buildings. Cold fingers of uncertainty walked down his spine. He decided to move on.

Chapter 16

Koski stood in line at the ticket gate at Kuty. She watched her traveling companion hold out both tickets to a uniformed collector who took them without a second glance. Together they walked across the platform and out of the building.

Emma scanned the busy city center and pointed. "Good. Here comes a number seven bus. It'll take us right to their front door."

"Whose front door?"

"C'mon, let's go," Emma said. They ran across the street and were among the last to board, swaying down the aisle as the bus pulled away. They found two empty seats and sank into them, each with a sigh.

They didn't notice a black Skoda sedan make a U-turn in the city square and tail their bus, staying about three car lengths behind.

Koski was tired. "Okay, Emma. Where exactly are we going?"

"A place on the Rijnove Revoluce," she whispered. "There's a small grocery shop with an apartment above it. We'll be safe there."

"What about Joe?"

Emma shook her head as if to discourage conversation. Koski obliged, allowing Emma to concentrate on the stops to be certain they didn't miss theirs.

Two men boarded the bus at the next stop and took seats behind them. Koski felt an inexplicable chill as they slowly walked past but she didn't want to distract Emma, who concentrated on the street signs and didn't dare say anything in English.

The bus lurched to a stop. As it pulled away one of the men tapped Emma on the shoulder. He spoke English with a thick Slavic accent.

"You both will get off at the next stop."

Koski felt ominously lightheaded. Her heart pounded. She wasn't in her element and that pissed her off. She turned and glared at the two burly men.

"Do as I say." The man who spoke smiled in Koski's direction but his eyes had as much warmth as an asp.

Emma turned to Koski. "Don't worry. It'll be all right."

Don't worry!

The men followed them off at the next stop. Immediately the black Skoda pulled up at the curb and Koski and Emma were ordered in.

The man who had been silent sat in back with them and asp-eyes slipped in next to the driver. Their back seat companion removed a Magnum .357 from his jacket and rested it on his knees.

Koski's green eyes flashed. "How dare you think you can hold us? I demand we be taken to the American Embassy at once." She knew she wasn't supposed to involve any embassy but under the circumstances she had to try something.

The man nodded. "You'll be taken to Brno and interviewed by internal security. Don't worry. If all goes well you should be flown back to Vienna tonight."

He muttered something in Czech and the car picked up speed. Reaching into his pocket, he removed a slim, silver cigarette case and snapped it open. He reached back and offered it to Koski then Emma but both ignored the gesture. He smiled, extracted a cigarette and lit it. "Enjoy the ride to Spilberg."

Koski thought the name Spilberg rang a bell. They were now

on the outskirts of Kuty headed for Brno. Within hours they would be under the control of Czech Internal Security at Spilberg Castle, a residence with a history going back for centuries. It was a notorious history not improved by the present covert occupants.

Koski wondered about Falk. Where was he? Was he safe? She gazed out the window and her mind tried to devise a way to extricate Emma and herself from the mess.

Was it possible that Rosie Wimmer and her people knew of their capture? Her stomach began to tighten and for the first time she considered the possibility of not getting out of this situation alive.

Chapter 17

Switzer, his nose bloody and sore, made his contact at Hohenau, reporting the loss of his prisoner. He was enraged, afraid of the consequences of failure, aware that the bartender, polishing glasses behind the bar, surreptitiously glanced at him. Then, probably reminding himself that glasses and drinks were his job, not trying to second-guess what obviously was internal security business, the man turned away.

Switzer slammed the phone back on the hook and left the building cursing that his cell phone had no coverage in the mountains. He crunched through the snow to his car where the driver was attempting to pull the twisted metal fender away from the tire.

Falk moved cautiously through the freezing dawn. Any minute he expected to hear the sounds of an early morning patrol. Instead, the only sounds were squawks of quarreling blackbirds that seemed to consider him a threat to their scavenging.

Two purple finches planed toward the ground, their wings

skimming the snow. As they banked skyward, their calls faded as they gained altitude and sped across the pearl gray sky.

Falk suddenly crouched when he heard the threatening growl of a motor in the distance. He ducked instinctively into the brush and pulled the Walther from his pocket.

He had an excellent command of the road from his position behind the hedgerow. When he saw the stubby green-gray armored car and its ugly 75mm jutting like an accusing finger from the turret, he knew that if those in the vehicle spotted him his P38 would be of little use.

The menace slowly ground its way through the mud and ice. Falk remained stock-still until it rounded a bend and passed from sight, the sound of its motor fading. Falk bolted in the opposite direction. He had covered about twenty yards and was running full tilt when he ran straight into a kneeling figure—Switzer!

With his eyes unblinking, Switzer's face was a wolfish grin. "Good morning, Dr. Falk." A long barreled, blue-black automatic pointed at Falk's face. Behind him, two uniformed soldiers threatened him with automatic carbines.

Falk sank to the ground and tossed his gun to one side. In that moment he almost didn't give a damn if they fired.

Switzer rasped, "Very wise, Doctor. I had hoped to shoot you for resisting arrest." Switzer's tone was nasally from the plaster cast across the bridge of his nose and both eyes were black and blue. He gestured to the soldiers to pull Falk to his feet and recuff his hands behind his back. "This time they stay on until we get to Brno."

The armored car that apparently hadn't gone far returned and pulled up beside them. A young officer poked his head out of the turret hatch and saluted Switzer. They exchanged a few words.

"Okay, Falk," Switzer said. "We're going for a ride."

The soldiers tossed Falk up on the vehicle's rear engine deck as if he was a sack of potatoes. Switzer climbed up beside him. The soldiers walked behind as the armored car got into gear and slowly moved down the rutted track. They covered about two miles and halted at a railway stop near a loading platform with a small hut and water tower.

Switzer snapped. "We get off here."

A soldier reached up and pulled Falk from the deck. He fell in a heap to the snow-covered ground. The commander snapped a salute to Switzer and ordered his vehicle on its way.

"A train is due in half an hour and has orders to pick us up," Switzer explained as Falk tried vainly to struggle to his feet. "You'll be in an interrogation room in Brno in two hours."

Three soldiers came from the hut dragging a tarpaulin. They tossed it over Falk and rolled him against the side of the wooden shack.

Chapter 18

Rosie Wimmer was worried. She had returned to her apartment from the antique shop nearly an hour ago and still no sign of Steele. He should have returned by now. She poured herself a drink, crossed to the window and gazed out at the city aglow with Christmas lights. She sipped her brandy, aware of nagging concerns.

At the sound of the door opening she whirled around then froze. A dark, handsome man in a long leather overcoat and a green Tyrolean hat stood there with a gleaming Voroshilov revolver held rock steady and aimed at her heart.

"Please," he said, "remain calm. I'm here to help you."

Rosie looked from his Omar Sharif brown eyes to the gun, neither of which shifted an inch. She leaned against the wall. Rosie Wimmer was not easily scared. She had dealt with all kinds of killers.

Two men came in after Omar and closed the door behind them. Now, she thought, I could get nervous. "What's this about?" she insisted.

"Follow them." He flicked his revolver and the men headed for the bedroom.

She noted a professional detachment in the men's eyes. In the bedroom, one of them approached the bed, slid the mattress to one side with great care and stood back. He pointed to a compact, well-designed bomb strapped to the bed frame. A timing device set to activate in three hours was visible.

"That's for openers," Omar said.

Rosie's thoughts raced toward an explanation but there was none.

He swung open a clothes closet door and with the tip of his revolver moved aside the lapel of the leopard-skin coat that Steele had given her for her birthday.

"Had you removed your coat from the hanger…" He made a gesture denoting a puff of smoke.

Rosie stared at the hideous booby-trap for a long moment before she began to tremble. Realization robbed her of control and she sank to a chair, shaking feverishly.

The man took a cloth coat from a hanger and placed it around her shoulders. "Sorry, there was no other way." He gently urged her toward the door. "We have to get you out of here."

They left the apartment and took the elevator to the garage. They walked to her Mercedes in silence. The tall, handsome man held Rosie's arm as one of the others opened the door and released the hood latch. Another raised the hood and stood back.

"Let's say you left the apartment," the man beside Rosie hypothesized, "never sat on the bed, never disturbed the leopard coat. You would have died on this spot when you started your car." He pointed to a neatly wrapped package snuggled against the engine manifold. "Nothing new, but damned effective."

Rosie attempted to save her sanity. "How do I know you didn't set all this up?"

He smiled and shrugged. "You don't. But why would we?"

A silver four-door BMW drove up and slid to a halt with a soft squeal of tires. The back door opened and Omar gestured politely for Rosie to enter. She did so, staring blankly ahead as they followed and the car moved swiftly out of the underground parking structure. They had topped the ramp and were about to turn into the flow of traffic when a vivid flash of brilliant orange exploded from the garage. Rosie saw this reflected in the rearview mirror. Her mouth dropped open as her mind dizzied off into space.

Omar settled back in the seat. "We decided not to defuse it," he explained. "This will give Steele something to ponder."

A light snow began falling over Vienna as the BMW worked its way through the late afternoon traffic.

Falk was in agony. Wrists handcuffed and ankles bound with rough hemp, he lay on the ground beneath the tarp outside the shed at the railway stop. Switzer and the soldiers huddled inside. Wind slashed across the countryside, driving swirling snow before it.

Finally a train whistle in the distance prompted those in the hut to appear. A soldier released Falk's ankles and hauled him to his feet, leaving his wrists enveloped in the freezing, twin circles of steel.

"I'll be damned glad to be rid of you," Switzer snarled and gave him a shove. The whistle screamed louder, closer. A steam engine, like a huge black monster, clanked and hissed to a stop with a screech of metal-on-metal beside them. It was a passenger train of six carriages. Faces peered out of frosted windows at the unexpected stop. A fat man in a blue serge uniform and a peaked cap with red braid stood at the top of a set of three wooden steps.

He nodded and smiled when Switzer called up to him, showing large, yellow teeth.

Switzer propelled Falk up the steep steps. The fat man laughed and Falk smelt an onrush of garlic and sausage breath as he pushed past the man's barrel shape. "Left, through the door," Switzer ordered. They entered a postal car where men stood at long tables sorting mail. The workers glanced up but quickly returned their gaze to the sorting table.

"Sit on the floor, back to the wall." Switzer carefully rechecked the cuffs. "Don't try anything. There's no way out of here until we get to Brno."

Falk sank to the floor and eased his head back against the splintered wood. A jolt and the car began to move. At least it was warm in the train, Falk thought, and closed his eyes.

Chapter 19

Steele stood outside his cordoned off apartment building and played the part of the distraught tenant. He was concerned about Rosie who, someone said, had been seen walking to her car earlier.

"Hey!" he shouted in German to a nearby police officer. "I live here. What the hell is going on?"

"Explosion in the garage," he clipped. "No one can enter until cleared by the authorities."

Steele heard someone call his name. It was a neighbor.

"Steele," the man said excitedly, his face troubled. "They say it was Rosie's car that exploded."

"Oh my God." Steele slumped slightly against him.

"Get the man in charge," the neighbor called to another officer. "This man was living with the woman who..." He looked sympathetically at Steele and left his remark unfinished.

Steele admired his own performance. He was coming home like an innocent. Johnny Depp himself could not have given such a stellar performance.

A young soldier led Steele to the building's entrance. "Wait here."

Steele stood, looking desolate and alone, as emergency crews passed, pulling hoses and barking orders.

Captain Gunther Vlad of Austrian Military Intelligence greeted Steele with a curt nod. "You are a fortunate man, Herr Steele; fortunate to be alive." He removed a thin, black cigar from between his lips. "My condolences."

He extracted a crumpled note from his pocket and glanced at it. "On the death of Rosie Wimmer. We understand she was in the car. The vehicle has been totally demolished." He returned the note to his pocket. "A close friend I take it?"

Steele replied solemnly. "We were to be married. What exactly happened, Inspector?"

"Captain," Vlad corrected. "When explosives are used in a crime the Army takes over." Vlad screwed up his eyes and moved the cigar to the other side of his mouth.

"Herr Steele, explosives were found in your apartment. Perhaps you could answer some questions for me."

"I'll do anything to help find the devils that killed Rosie..."

Steele let his voice trail off and it cracked with what he hoped simulated emotion.

"Expert work, Herr Steele," Vlad said.

Steele stiffened, thinking for a moment that Vlad knew. "You know…you know who did this?"

Vlad shook his head. "Not yet but we will." He blew a stream of smoke skyward. "Do you have any enemies?"

"Not that I know of. Should I?"

"You *are* a businessman."

"To the best of my knowledge I have no enemies—business or personal."

"The car in the garage, was it yours?"

Steele cleared his throat. "Yes, a company car for my fiancée."

"I see." Vlad stared at the floor. "Does the name Emma Lewis mean anything?"

Steele felt his stomach twist. "Emma? Sure I know her, know her well. In fact, we're in the same line of business. She has a place here in Vienna."

"Place?"

"Yes, an antique shop on the Am Numarkt."

"Do you see her socially or just to do business?"

"Mainly business. Why do you ask?"

"Routine. So you are both in antiques." Vlad smoothed his uniform jacket. "Do you have friends in the Jewish Liberation Movement?"

Steele shook his head. "I've never heard of such a group."

"I see. Political groups are of no interest to you?"

"I have no feelings one way or another. My business is selling other people's dreams so to speak. Living somewhat in the past renders me unaware of contemporary politics."

Vlad contemplated the stub of his cigar. "I see. Perhaps it's also possible, is it not, for one to become immune to feelings, become like antiques, simply awaiting the best offer?" He didn't wait for an answer. "Your apartment is safe now. Thank you for your cooperation. I'll be in touch with you soon."

Steele headed to the elevator and his apartment. He didn't like the questions. What did the son of a bitch mean he would be in touch soon?

Chapter 20

It was late afternoon when the train Falk was on arrived in Brno. Slowly it clanked into the gloomy, old railway station, past rows of stone and brick houses, grimy warehouses and buildings looking more drab and dull than ever in the early dusk of an equally dreary winter day.

"On your feet, Falk."

Falk struggled to get up. Two men in raincoats entered the railroad car and, at Switzer's nod, led Falk off the train and along a dank, poorly lit platform to the entrance beside the ticket master's office. A black car waited at the curb. Switzer hurried Falk into the back seat, flanked by two men. Switzer sat beside the driver.

As they weaved through traffic, Falk caught brief glimpses of the city. Stopped at a traffic signal, he saw a large, ornate fountain surrounded by fruit and vegetable stands lit by the flickering yellow glow of paraffin lanterns. Peasant women hooded in dark shawls bent over their produce.

When the light changed and they left the tranquil scene behind, its memory, contrasted with the prospect of his destination, deepened Falk's gloom at the thought of Spilberg Castle.

Switzer had filled him in on its history dating back to 1278—grim tales of torture chambers and hideous instruments of physical torment. At each turn of the zigzag climb up the hill toward the ominous castle, he glimpsed the fortress from various angles. None was inviting.

It was dark when they swung into the spacious, gravel courtyard and drove past the front entrance to a small entry virtually hidden at the far left of the massive stone structure. Falk, Switzer and two of the men entered an undersized anteroom containing two soldiers and an officer. Switzer finally removed the handcuffs.

"You won't need these in here." He grinned maliciously. "No place to go." He nudged Falk with his elbow. "Perhaps I'll see you again, Doctor. I have to await orders." His eyes blazed with acrimonious fire. "Whatever is decided, I look forward to the pleasure of killing you first chance I get."

Falk took a step toward him but the two soldiers gripped his arms. Switzer laughed and left the room. The officer barked orders and the soldiers opened an inner door and shoved Falk through the opening.

"Where are you taking me?" Falk demanded.

"To Commissar Victor Horidecki, Minister of the Interior," the officer said in perfect English. "He will interview you."

Anger fueled Falk's irritation, overpowering weariness that itself was bone deep. "And if I don't *want* to be interviewed?"

The soldier to his right lashed out with his gloved hand. Falk reeled from the sharp blow to the side of his head and the two renewed their grip on him. They walked for what seemed like miles along bone-chilling passageways until they finally stopped outside an oak door recessed into the thick stonewall. The officer knocked and a muffled voice bid them enter.

It was a large, warm, well-furnished room. Floor to ceiling tapestries hung on one wall beside a huge open fireplace where a log fire burned. A wood-paneled wall held ornately framed oils, dimly illumined by concealed lighting.

Behind a decorative desk, an old man was busy writing by the light of a brass reading lamp with a lime green shade. He glanced up and waved the soldiers and the officer back against the door.

"Please sit down, Doctor," Horidecki said in a soft almost amiable voice. "You must be tired." They exchanged appraising glances.

"You're damn right I'm tired. I want to know what the hell I'm doing here. I want to talk with someone from the American Embassy. Now!"

Horidecki smiled. "Self-righteous indignation when all else fails. Well done, Doctor."

Horidecki was pink-faced, had closely cropped gray hair and deep, lightless brown eyes. He leaned back in his chair and studied Falk from beneath shaggy gray brows.

Falk was becoming angrier by the second. "I was brought into this country against my will. I have certain rights and you're damn well aware of that."

Horidecki unhooked a pair of steel-rimmed glasses and laid them carefully on his desk. "My dear Doctor. I'm afraid you're now a missing person."

"Why was I taken from Vienna?"

"We decided it was an advantage from our standpoint. It gives us a certain benefit to be on home ground, less chance of interruption. At any rate, Brno isn't that far from Vienna." He leaned back. "Had you not decided to play the hero and run off into the woods we could have had this little talk yesterday and you'd be back in Vienna at this moment."

"What do you want?" Falk slumped in the chair, the warmth of the fire sabotaging his crisp demeanor.

Horidecki opened a box of cigars, bit the end off one and spat it into his wastebasket. He snapped a gold plated lighter to flame and sucked the cigar to life in a thick swirl of smoke. "Did you ever do any fishing in the United States?"

"What are you getting at?"

"I suppose when you fish in America, as anywhere, you use bait. Well, Doctor, you are our bait." The end of the cigar glowed. Tapping away the ash, he continued. "We in the Czech Republic know about the secret hiding place—not the exact location but the approximate site of Herman Goering's last act of mystery. We desire to be the first to locate it at all cost."

"Why?"

Horidecki showed obvious surprise at the question. "Surely you know that aside from its financial value such a discovery would, in itself, be a reward."

"Give me a break," Falk snapped. "I've been through hell the last couple of days and I damn well know it's not been for the benefit of mankind or crowds who visit the museums."

Horidecki blew a smoke ring toward the ceiling and smiled. "You're right."

Chapter 21

On the floor of a freezing cold cell in Spilberg Castle, Koski and Emma slept fitfully, huddled together for warmth against the whitewashed stonework. They shared a threadbare blanket hardly adequate for one.

Koski snapped her eyes open at a slight sound and remained motionless as the door slowly creaked open on dry, rusted hinges and stopped. A bulky guard lumbered in.

"Wake her," he told Koski. "I'll take you to the director now."

Koski shook Emma, who came awake gradually, stiffly. She was tired and disheveled.

At the door, Koski turned to a soldier outside and said flatly, "I'm an American and she's British. We want to see our consulates."

He stared at her, not understanding, then moved his carbine, directing her forward. Exchanging futile glances, the women obeyed and were led to Horidecki's office.

Falk looked up as the door opened and his jaw went slack. He pushed from his chair and toward Koski but a guard intervened with his rifle, training it on Falk.

Falk spun to one side, grabbed the rifle and gave a fast twist, dropping to one knee at the same time. The guard lost his grip on the weapon and Falk jammed the butt into the hapless guard's throat. He went down without a sound. Falk turned just as the second guard swung the butt of his weapon at him. The swing stopped midway by a command from Horidecki.

Falk shoved the guard aside and swept Koski into his arms. "You okay?" He stroked her hair.

"Yes, yes, I'm all right."

They kissed and as he pulled away she said, "Joe, Emma and I were trying to find you. What happened?"

Falk placed a finger on her lips. "Later." He turned to Horidecki. "Both of them stay with me. You want me…they're part of the deal."

Horidecki smiled. "Such devotion. As much as I would like to concur with your demand, it cannot be. Let me explain…"

"No explanations. The three of us or no deal."

"Joe," Koski said softly.

"We're together and we're going to stay together."

Horidecki sighed. "Doctor, allow me to make myself clear. My objective is to persuade you to locate whatever artifacts were stolen from Egypt. In turn, my government will hand them back to Egypt in the name of the Czech Republic. If I fail the three of you will die."

"If you fail your government mister, all four of us will die," Falk spat.

Horidecki said nothing. He was aware of the price he would have to pay.

Falk continued. "You need me, Horidecki. Get the women back to Vienna. Let them check in with their consulates and I'll be your man." Horidecki shook his head.

"Let me try," Emma said. She quickly spoke to Horidecki in Czech, gesturing emphatically. It soon was clear that an argument in his own language did little to move the hardened official.

Horidecki crossed the room and pulled a silken cord beside the marble fireplace. There was an immediate knock at the door.

"Come," Horidecki said. A soldier entered carrying a large manila envelope that he handed to his superior. Horidecki removed a letter opener from a desk drawer and slit the seal.

Without removing the contents, he looked at the trio and spoke. "A man named Lego Moyzisch hasn't been seen at his residence for several days. His wife would appreciate hearing from him. You see, she's in protective custody until he returns."

He tapped the envelope. "We have something that once belonged to him. We do all we can to locate any of our missing citizens who might need our help."

Falk remembered that Lego was one of the partisans mentioned in Mark Benson's letter. He saved Nikolai Youmatoff's life.

Falk scoffed. "That's how you help? Throwing their wives in prison?"

Horidecki said something to the officer, who immediately ordered the soldiers to escort Koski and Emma from the room.

In a flash of movement that Falk barely followed, Koski twisted away from the man and chopped the side of her right hand into his clavicle. Seizing the moment, Falk lunged at the second soldier, who spun instinctively and brought his gun butt down, grazing Falk's head. He slumped to the floor.

"Joe!" Koski cried and fell to her knees at his side. Falk shook his head and slowly climbed to his feet. Koski gently ran her hand along his cheek. "We'll make the bastards pay."

Horidecki rose from his chair. "Enough! Doctor, perhaps now you won't make the mistake of underestimating my determination." He lowered back into his chair. "Handcuff these reckless women and take them back to their cell."

Another armed guard had entered and Falk was forced to watch helplessly as Koski and Emma were handcuffed and dragged from the room.

"We don't have time to waste," Horidecki continued. "There are too many others interested in our fishing expedition. I'd advise you to listen carefully."

He paused and studied Falk. Deciding the effects of the blow had subsided, he went on. "We need Middle East trade, Doctor. It is imperative to our growth, our existence. Our country produces the finest weapons in the world. Our Skoda Works can meet every military requirement of the Middle East and its neighbors. They need our industrial output. We need hard currency."

He drummed his fingers on the desktop before picking up the envelope. "You're being given the chance to be instrumental in a project that will enrich the lives of millions." He removed a folded sheet of paper from the manila envelope. "Look at this."

Falk took the sheet. It was a blueprint. He recognized the word *Dorotheum* among other German words on the plan. The blueprint was of the foundations of the Dorotheum, a detailed plan of the original structure. His eyes caught a penciled marginal note scribbled in Latin. It was a reference to the *Book of Hours*. The same one he had been studying when hauled from the crypt and the monk was shot to death. How did this scribbled note connect to the actual prayer book? He was becoming more curious. He handed it back. "What do you want me to do?"

"The physical prowess you and Doctor Koski demonstrated here tonight makes it clear to me that you're not archaeologists as represented. Nonetheless, I'm sure you were chosen for good reason." He slipped the blueprint back into the envelope. "This will be waiting for you in Vienna along with instructions."

Falk figured things couldn't get much worse, but then Horidecki said, "Switzer will drive you back tonight."

Chapter 22

A tide of dusk rose in the mountains and across the sky on the second day of Nikolai Youmatoff's trek. He walked diagonally through Canada's wilderness and continued determinedly along an old trap line.

Despite his more than eighty years, Youmatoff's genes were pooled from stout peasant stock and living a woodsman's life had kept him hardy. He broke over the crest of a beech-covered ridge carpeted with week-old virgin snow and wound his way down into an alee depression beneath a cliff where he halted.

He relieved himself near a tree, his stream leaving scattered yellow-rimmed cavities in the snow where his aim, as it seemed destined to do in his waning years, wandered. Hunger gnawed at his innards. Under the overhang, he swung the pack and bedroll from his shoulders. He dug into the rabbit skin interior of the hide pack, extracting utensils, a rusty grate and an old tin pannikin.

Soon fire crackled to life under the grate he had suspended between two rocks and he fed the flame with a handful of dry spruce. A portion of the white fish he had angled earlier boiled in butter and water in a pan. A cloud of odorous steam filtered up and was lost in the blackness above his small pool of firelight.

After the meal, Youmatoff eased back against an old birch and stared into the fire. His dark blue wool cap pushed up above his ears and the red bandana knotted at his throat hung loosely.

With a boot toe, he nudged some birch bark into the faltering flame and it flared anew.

Youmatoff wondered what happened to the others in the vault that night. Of course Goering was dead, but what of the rest?

He sat in companionable silence with the woods for several minutes then spread his bedroll in the sheltered "V" between two bulky boulders beneath the cliff. He wasn't wholly concerned about the Mounties. This was his milieu and he knew how to cover his tracks. Still inexplicable sounds persisted in the woods.

Before closing his eyes Youmatoff spit tobacco into his palms then rubbed the juice liberally over his face to ward off black flies and other pests while he slept.

Tomorrow he would be moving into areas of the forest of

which he knew nothing. He looked up at the black mass of unfamiliar Caribou Peak silhouetted against the slightly lighter sky. If he didn't become hopelessly lost, he would be out of the woods and in Ottawa in less than forty-eight hours.

Chapter 23

After Koski and Emma were escorted from Horidecki's office, they were ushered to another cell in Spilberg Castle. It was small and freezing with a narrow window set high in the wall overlooking the courtyard. Two rickety cots, filthy straw-filled mattresses and twin lumpy pillows were the accommodations. A dim low wattage light bulb shed a weak glow over the disheartening scene.

When the iron door slammed behind the exiting guard, Koski bent and tested the mattress. It was hard and dank. "No frills," she groaned. She shook out a thin, moth-eaten, gray wool blanket. "I'm so beyond tired." Stifling a yawn, she sank to the edge of the cot. "Don't worry, Emma. It's too damn cold for bugs. Get some rest."

Eventually they fell into a fitful sleep. Koski moved restlessly at the sound of a car starting in the gravel courtyard. She pulled the musty blanket to her chin. In a few hours it would be dawn.

Falk, his wrists again in handcuffs, sat between Switzer and a formidable guard in the back seat of a black, four-door Skoda that drove out of the castle courtyard and headed down the winding hill toward the inner city of Brno.

He watched tall, dark stone buildings pass in a monotonous array. Thin moonlight from a gauzy crescent moon glimmered like silver water on the frost covered slate rooftops. There was nothing to prepare him for what happened next.

A tearing crash of metal conjoined with shattering glass and a shuddering jolt and one side of the car was instantly gone, sliced away. The driver, who moments before had been a living, breathing human being, was now a mass of bloody pulp. Switzer had half-turned, his features frozen in shock before vanishing in a red smear of his own blood, jagged steel edges of the car retaining fragments of his flesh and clothing.

When the jarring, shattering, insane moment passed, Falk saw the road beside him where the other half of the car had been. He gulped and fell sideways onto the asphalt.

He was alive amid a tangle of metal, blood and snow. Then he saw the gleaming, knifelike edge of the snowplow that had severed the Skoda and three men appeared out of the darkness.

"Hurry," one said, shining a flashlight beam on Falk, unlocking the handcuffs and pulling him to his feet. "There's little time."

Falk dazedly looked back as the man led him to the fountain in the square. He saw the guard who had been sitting next to him in the car groggily trying to get to his feet. One of the men beside Falk ran back to the wreck and shot the guard twice in the back of the head.

Falk leaned back against the curved stone rim surrounding the fountain, his heart thumping wildly in his chest. Water cascaded from the fountain, the wind catching and sending it in a fine spray of sparkling mist that turned to frost in mid-air. A distant clock chimed 5 a.m.

"Who are you?" Falk asked weakly.

"We're here to help you get back to Vienna."

Falk shook his head to clear his thoughts. Was he hearing right? "You mean…you arranged that crash?"

The man nodded.

"Help me? I *was* on my way back to Vienna! How the hell did you know I wouldn't be in a different seat? I could have been the one smeared all over the pavement."

"Seating arrangements never change when prisoners are transported by car. This is a disciplined country." He steered Falk to a car standing in the shadows. "There's no time to waste." He and Falk scrambled into the back seat and the man with the ready pistol drove. A light, icy mist began to fall.

"My name is Horst," the man beside him said. "We had to eliminate Switzer. He'd have killed you five miles out of town."

Falk rubbed his red, swollen wrists. "Half an inch either way I'd have been eliminated with him."

"Sometimes we have no choice."

"Horidecki won't be pleased."

"No. Switzer was one of his best men."

"And you, Horst, in what intriguing international scheme of yours do I figure?"

"I work for Colonel Zhilin." He tossed a .45 onto Falk's lap. "Know how to use that?"

Falk looked at the automatic. What he wanted were answers. "Who's Colonel Zhilin?"

"It matters nothing to you, Doctor. You didn't answer me about the gun." Horst took the gun back and began a discourse that sounded like the Colt .45's manual.

"Why do you want me to have the weapon?"

Horst shrugged. "It's your choice."

Falk thought he'd play the game. "Okay, say I take this. If I try to use it, it backfires and blows my head off, right?"

Horst remained stoic. His ears moved back and forth a centimeter, nothing else. "Doctor, you have a devious mind."

"Look, pal, after what I've been through I'm lucky to still have a mind. I don't trust a soul, so take your gun and shove it."

"I was offering it as protection. There's a possibility we could be intercepted before we cross back into Austria." He flipped the weapon back onto Falk's lap.

The car turned left and Falk saw a street sign that read, Ulice 9Kvetna. He wondered what it meant.

As if reading his mind, Horst said, "It means the Ninth of May Street in English."

Some things, Falk thought, gained in translation.

"By the way, Doctor, the gun wasn't loaded." Horst tossed the ammunition clip to Falk, who knew all along that it wasn't loaded. He said nothing as he slipped the clip into the handle, chambered a round and set the safety.

The car suddenly started to slide on the slick, icy pavement, and the driver made the mistake of slamming his foot on the brakes. The rear end slid to the left, the front to the right, and the vehicle slid off the road. Falk felt the front wheels go down off the deep shoulder with a shuddering thump and the car came to a stop.

"Damn!" Horst said.

The driver got out, surveyed the situation and reported the bottom of the car was marooned on the frozen shoulder, leaving the rear wheels without traction. They could dig the axle free but it looked as if the engine block was cracked. He recommended phoning someone to pick them up.

"Use your cell phone dumbkopff. Wait here till they arrive then meet us in the church," Horst ordered. As he opened the door and they climbed out into the cold morning air, Falk slipped the .45 into his jacket pocket.

Horst pointed across to the Church of Saint James and its

three-hundred-foot steeple. Turning to Falk he said, "There's an early mass. No one will bother us."

Chapter 24

Inside the Church of Saint James it smelled of incense, dampness and old age mixed with chilling cold. The early hour congregation was small. Two lit candles on the altar indicated a low mass being said by a tall, thin priest and a sleepy-eyed altar boy.

Horst nudged Falk and indicated a scared and timeworn pew.

Falk had an uneasy feeling. It was as if he was a hostage inside the church. He knew he had to get away, free himself from his so-called rescuers. His gut feeling told him this Colonel Zhilin probably represented another faction bent on finding the treasures and they needed the expertise they believed Falk had.

Once they figured out he couldn't or wouldn't help them…he had to make a run for it as soon as the chance presented itself.

The altar bell rang, indicating communion. Falk watched the mostly elderly congregation get stiffly to their feet and step into the aisle for the walk to the altar rails. This was his chance and he took it.

Slowly he rose and pushed into the aisle, joining the line of communicants. His move took Horst and the other man by surprise. Glancing back, Falk saw them talking as they, too, stepped into the aisle and were separated from him by more than a dozen people.

A side entrance caught Falk's eye. Moving into an empty pew, he quickly crossed to the side aisle and headed for the door. It was large and old with a huge, wrought iron doorknob…and locked tight.

Horst and the other man followed to the side aisle. Realizing Falk was trapped they took their time. Falk knew he had to escape out the front door. As he turned, he saw the man with Horst reach into his shoulder holster and the hole in a dark round barrel looked directly in Falk's direction. His gut feeling had been right!

A parishioner bumped the man, gracing Falk with a few seconds in which to act. Removing the .45 from his jacket, he released the safety and aimed, steadying his right wrist with his left hand in the classic weaver stance and squeezed the trigger—all in one quick movement. His next realization was that his head remained on his shoulders meaning the gun hadn't been rigged. It didn't make sense. Why had one man given Falk a perfectly usable gun and his companion try to kill him?

The sound of the discharge boomed like a cannon inside the church. Falk's aim was true and the man with the gun never got off a round. He stood for a second with an astonished look on his face, a small hole in his cheek beneath his left eye. Then he turned in a jagged, twisting movement that allowed Falk to see where the back of the man's head once was. Horst, splattered with gore as his companion hit the back of the pew, slid down and crumpled across the kneeler.

Falk bolted for the main door, out and down the steps before the churchgoers' horrified cries rose to full effect.

He ran with the fear of God in his soul. He had killed a man in a holy place. Otherwise, he would be lying back there. He continued to run, not knowing in what direction, his heart pounding in unison with his footsteps. A clanging bell sounded. He jumped back as a three-section streetcar rocked noisily past. He had nearly stepped in front of it. For a moment he was tempted to run after the tram but it was too late.

A narrow side street presented itself. Knowing he had to get off the main road Falk went down it like a sprinter. He ducked into a doorway as a car pulled across the end of the street, blocking his path. A second car sealed off his only other escape just as he was about to turn back. Two men got out and crouched behind the car, leaving the doors open. Falk's mouth was dry, his chest heaved uncontrollably.

He could shoot it out. The shots might bring help. Yeah, right. Who would help him? He glanced up at the tall, stone structure five stories high, one of a block of buildings running about five hundred yards to the end of the street.

The roofs were steep with dormer windows and brick chimney pots. Smoke curled from a stack of chimneys to his right. If he could get into the building and up to the roof… perhaps there was a chance of escape over the rooftops. He tried the door behind him…Locked!

Then he heard Horst's harsh and metallic voice over a bullhorn. "Come out into the center of the street with your hands up, Doctor. You're surrounded."

Chapter 25

Falk remained squeezed back in the doorway. "No way," he yelled. "Come near me and I'll shoot the first bastard I see." He scanned the windows of the barracks-like building opposite.

"Throw out your weapon," Horst shouted. "You haven't gotta chance."

Falk grimaced. Horst might be right but Falk was tired of being ordered and used. He wouldn't be subjugated by the likes of Horst again. "Forget it, Horst. You wanted me to have a gun. I intend to keep it."

All at once Falk saw what might be a chance. Across the street, a metal door in a long brick wall opened and he caught sight of an inner courtyard. Two women with scarves over their heads and wicker baskets on their arms came out. Their heads were bent together, collars up against the cold and completely unaware of the drama in the street. As they stepped clear of the door Falk made his move.

He bolted, no more than a blur to the men at the end of the street. Shots rang out and both women screamed. A bullet splattered against the wall and a piece of plaster clipped Falk's chin as he went headlong into the courtyard. Falk headed for the nearest door and darted up an interior flight of stone steps. The sound of gunfire caused windows to open and heads to appear. Falk reached the first floor and from a small balcony saw one of the two cars come screeching through the gate.

He faced a second flight not visible from below and double-timed them. His legs trembled with exertion. Ahead were the last few steps to the rooftop. Suddenly a door opened and a woman looked out. Their eyes met and locked. She opened her mouth to scream but fell silent when Falk pointed the .45 at her face.

Pushing her back into the apartment, he followed and closed the door. He didn't try to speak, simply signaled for her to sit at the table. She was about fifty, small and thin with bright blue eyes wide with fright. After checking to be certain they were alone, he eased back a lace curtain a few inches and peered down into the courtyard.

There were the two cars and a third was coming through the gate. Men were scattered in all directions, several with cell phones to their ears. One heavyset man scanned the buildings through binoculars. As Falk watched, the binoculars moved in the direction of his window. It seemed as if the bastard was about to look directly at him. He quickly let the curtain swing back into place. Horst would no doubt start a door-to-door search that would leave little chance for escape.

He tucked the .45 into his jacket pocket and held out his hands to show the woman he meant no harm. For the first time he realized how he must look to her: stubble of beard, blood on his chin, red-eyed and gaunt from the experiences of the last few days. He tried to smile as he backed out through the door into the passage, knowing that if she opened a window, stuck her head out and yelled it would all be over. Before he could decide if he should gag and tie her up, the woman spoke in a thin, hesitant voice.

"You are American?" Falk nodded emphatically. She went to the door and looked up and down the passage. "Don't go to the roof. What you call?" She whirled her hand over her head.

"Helicopter?"

"Ja! So—it soon be here…you never get free."

Falk knew she was right. Once on the roof, a helicopter hovering overhead… he would be a sitting duck.

In broken English she whispered, "Do not tell of me…go to stairs, down. Then to the basement go…" Her words trailed off.

Falk smiled broadly. "Thanks…*danke*."

Her door closed behind him without a sound and he headed for the inside stairs. He was halfway down the second flight when he heard it. Someone was coming up. He pressed back against the wall, the .45 at his side. Whoever it was was in a hell of a hurry.

Falk raised the automatic and aimed at the open stairwell as a man came around the corner. He stopped in his tracks. It was a young man in his early twenties, big and muscular, his biceps straining his shirt-sleeves. They stared at each other for a second then the sudden clatter of a low flying helicopter broke their mental connection.

Falk made the mistake of shifting his eyes for a split second and the man was on him like a lunging animal. Falk saw a blur, felt his head snap back as the man rammed into his gut with a terrible force, slamming him back against the concrete wall like a rag doll. The .45 wrenched from his hand.

For a moment the attacker seemed undecided whether or not to shoot but the helicopter came closer, the blades echoing and making a slapping sound outside the building. The man turned and ran up the stairs. Whomever he was running from must be a bigger threat than taking a chance on the rooftop.

Falk decided the man's pursuer could be close behind. He cursed and listened. The stairwell below was silent. The sound of the chopper above indicated a turn for another pass across the building.

Down at the end of the street Horst was thinking, *Good, Doctor. No matter where you run, no matter where you try to hide, the electronic homing device planted in that .45 will send me a loud and clear signal as to your whereabouts. You may as well wave a flag or send up a flare.* He smiled at his own cunning.

Chapter 26

The signal Horst received from the transmitter in the gun indicated that Falk had started down the stairs, changed his mind, turned and made for the roof.

In fact, Falk was slowly easing down the stairs, ears tuned for the slightest sound. He made it to the basement and, through smudged, eye level windows, viewed the courtyard. The men stood in groups, all staring at the roof as the helicopter edged in, hovering like a hawk poised to kill. It swung in close to the rain gutter, moving with deadly efficiency—an instrument of colossal, shattering power.

The young man darted from behind one of the chimney stacks. He twisted and turned, slithering on the slates then rolled behind another chimney. The chopper made an adjustment and edged closer, its Perspex nose dipping as it maneuvered into position.

The target suddenly stood up from behind a red brick chimneystack, both hands grasping the automatic. Falk saw the gun jolt and knew the man was firing. What kind of man was this? He fought as if defiance alone was the measure of courage.

Then a figure leaned from the helicopter and the barrel of a machine gun caught a glint of light. Falk's stomach twisted as the powerful weapon let loose a furious fusillade jerking the man back against the brickwork. He slumped, rolled onto his face and slid down the steep roof. For a few seconds the rain gutter slowed his descent then it gave way and they fell together. The body hit first, a shower of debris falling on and around him in the courtyard.

The man had fought and died alone, a fate to which Falk now seemed condemned. Though Falk didn't even know him, he was aware of a sense of bereavement.

The helicopter moved over the building and out of sight. On the ground, Horst's men ran toward the crumpled remains like a pack of hounds at a foxhunt.

Falk pushed the window open, crawled out and fled the scene while Horst and his men's attention were still on the victim in the courtyard.

Chapter 27

Koski opened her eyes and turned toward the faint tinge of daylight filtering through the cell window. In the distance a cathedral clock chimed 6 a.m. as Emma stirred awake.

Sitting motionless in a nearby chair was the guard who had been with them since their return from Horidecki's office. She was a gaunt woman with a sharp-featured face, dressed in dark leather knee high boots and a black denim uniform.

Koski swung her legs over the edge of the narrow cot. "I've got to find a way out of this place, Emma."

Emma shivered and sat upright on her cot. "But we'd be shot if we tried to escape." Her voice quavered with an inner chill.

"We may be shot if we don't. I'm not betting on these people returning us to Vienna. Once they get what they need from Joe, who knows? We'd better find a way home on our own, no matter what we have to..." She was stopped in mid-sentence by the guard's sudden interjection.

"I speak your language. I can understand what you say." She adjusted the holstered pistol at her hip.

"Fine. May we go to the bathroom?" Koski asked politely.

"You will only leave the cell with me. One of you will remain at all times. You cannot leave together."

Koski rose slowly and approached the woman. "Soon it will be Christmas." It was a soft, controlled voice designed to elicit sympathy. "Our families...our little children will be worried about us. Is there any way we can be allowed to communicate with them?"

The woman was silent, staring ahead. Koski threw her hands up in a futile gesture and returned to the cot.

Emma jumped up and began pacing and wringing her hands. Until then, Koski hadn't been aware of the extent of her panic.

"We're going to die here in this rat hole, Koski. I just know it."

She had been a rock since they separated from Steele: *We're going to my place. Pass the jam. It's too easy to remember a couple of women buying tickets.* She had seemed possessed of extraordinary skills and courage. Now she was coming apart at the seams. Koski reminded herself that Emma, after all, was not trained at Quantico. She sighed. "Emma, how do you happen to know Rosie Wimmer?"

Emma nodded as if there was no longer any reason for secrecy. "I met her through John. She's basically the only female friend I've made in Vienna." She hugged the blanket around her as she continued to pace. "She lives with John. It was inevitable that we would become friends, I guess."

"But it's more than a social relationship isn't it?"

Emma stopped walking and sank to the cot, lowering her voice to a whisper. "She has asked for my help on occasion… to pass along a message…let a friend sleep on a blanket on the floor of my shop, the next morning the person is gone, that sort of thing.

"It seemed harmless. Nevertheless, I swore to tell no one, not even…especially…not John. Now I see why she asked that. Rosie, despite the fact that she's in love with him, must have known he couldn't be trusted." She jumped up again. "In the end *I* gave away Rosie's secret…to John. Oh, God, we're going to die here!" Koski glanced at the guard, who was gauging Emma's behavior."What does it all mean? What are we dying for?"

The guard unsnapped her holster and rested her right hand on the butt of the pistol. "I warn you. If you attempt anything I will kill you."

"It's okay." Koski jumped up and waved her palms between the two women. "It's okay," she told the guard. She led Emma back to the cot. "Don't worry," she whispered. "I'll think of something." Loudly, she said, "We don't want the nice woman to do anything we'd all be sorry for." Her own words brought a light to her eyes and she turned back to the guard. "We should all get along...learn to coexist. No sense making it more difficult than it is."

Emma threw Koski an uneasy glance at this turnabout. The guard flicked her eyes in their direction but said nothing.

Koski walked closer to the sentinel. "Today, even in your country, the walls have ears. I'm sure there are those who know of our capture, perhaps will let it be known to the West if we were killed..." She paused before the woman. "Am I right?"

The blow landed with vicious force, crushing into Koski's chest and driving the air from her lungs. Pain, as if a red hot rod was plunged into her breasts, made her sway. Her vision was blurred. Gasping for air, she slumped to her knees and rolled onto her side.

The guard was on her feet, knees bent, hands rigid, fingers slightly curved in classic karate stance. She aimed a kick at Koski's head but her target turned in time to deflect the blow with her shoulder. It was a reaction beyond primordial instinct, one learned from years of extraordinary training honed by the practiced teachings of experience.

Koski's hand grabbed the woman's ankle, gave a fast twist and a short jerk and the guard was down beside her. She yanked the woman's head back with all her strength, made a swift half roll and, slamming her arm across her opponent's windpipe, gave two quick jerks. There was a soft splintering sound, a slight arching of the guard's back and she was still.

"Dear God!" Emma exclaimed as she knelt beside Koski and stared at the face, the bright mouse eyes bulging from their sockets.

Koski pulled herself close to the door, placing an ear against it. "Thick doors...no one heard." She looked at Emma silent and staring. "We've got to move fast." Emma nodded numbly but made no reply. "You dress as the guard. You're about the same size and can speak the language. There's a chance we can make it."

Koski pulled at the boots, the body inching across the floor with each tug. "Grab beneath her arms and hold her still." Koski tugged until the boot slid off. "Now the other," she hissed. Emma wasted no time and was soon dressed in the uniform. She tucked her hair beneath the peaked cap, pulled on the still-warm boots.

"Let's get her on the cot," Koski whispered. Together they lifted the body to the mattress and covered it.

Koski placed her hands gently on Emma's shoulders. "You okay?" Emma nodded. Not really, Koski thought, but under present conditions she dare not take time to distinguish between killing and *killing.* "Listen, you tell the guard outside that you're escorting me to the bathroom."

Emma banged on the door. "Guard!" It opened immediately. A man stuck his head in and snapped to attention with a smart salute.

"Allow no one in until we return," Emma said in her most authoritative Czech, miming the dead woman's deep, guttural tone. She pointed toward the mound of humanity on the cot. "I want her to stay right here." The door clanged shut behind them. Ahead was a dimly lit passageway with low wattage bulbs hung at long intervals. Hopefully, muted light and dark shadows would work in their favor and lead them to freedom.

"We'll make it," Koski whispered.

Chapter 28

John Steele switched on the lights in his apartment following his encounter with Captain Vlad. No doubt the authorities had searched but he had to be certain. He went to a small desk and sat. Pushing in on the center drawer until it would go no farther, he eased it back slightly then gave it a hard shove forward. He was rewarded with a soft click.

He looked into the space where his knees had been. To the right, almost at floor level, the edge of a shallow drawer projected an inch from his right shoe. Quickly reaching down he removed a small key. Next he took a magnifying glass from a cubbyhole in the desk and scrutinized the key.

It was still there, a hair-like filament across the grooves. He grunted in satisfaction. If Military Intelligence had found the key and made an impression the filament would be gone. It was an old trick but one that still worked. He tossed the key in the air and caught it. He needed a drink. He was recapping the decanter when he saw it—a quick flash, a reflection from the crystal stopper in the lens of a concealed camera.

He knew better than to react. Play dumb, he thought. He sipped his drink. The crafty bastards…a camera flush mounted in the wainscoting and he had showed them everything! Damn.

He returned to the desk with the key in his pocket and shuffled through some papers. When his drink was finished he went to the bedroom and closed the door. This room also could be under surveillance. He removed a pair of slacks from the closet. As he laid them on the bed, he slid the key beneath the mattress and changed his clothes.

Why would Vlad go to the trouble of hiding a camera in his apartment? Perhaps it wasn't Vlad. He opened the apartment door, set the lock and left.

As he walked toward the elevators two men approached from opposite directions. They followed him into the elevator and the door slid shut with a soft hiss. The hair on the back of his neck rose.

Chapter 29

It was 7 a.m. when Rod Eiker phoned a woman named Lisa Winkler. Lisa was the type who fit into the lectures Eiker had drilled into him many times while serving with British SAS:

Aside from its professional practitioners, Intelligence draws its personnel from a vast reservoir of people. Traditionally, journalists play an exceptional role if only because they are professional collectors of information. This is recognized by most espionage agencies around the world.

Lisa was perfect; a freelance journalist on the international beat who guiltlessly worked both sides of the street. She grumbled and turned onto her back, exposing her full, nearly naked bosom. Her hand reached from beneath satin sheets and located the phone. "Who is it?" she growled. Her demeanor softened when she recognized the voice. She fluffed self-consciously at an improbable mass of orange red hair. "Well," she cooed, "this is a nice surprise."

"Lisa, my dear, sorry to bother you so early…"

"Rod Eiker," she interrupted and fell into a husky, seductive drawl. "You can bother me in bed anytime. Where are you?"

"Here in Vienna. Lisa, I need some information," he said more abruptly than he intended.

Her lower lip slid out. "Only for you would I make conversation so early in the morning. What is it you want to know…and the answer is probably yes."

Eiker smiled inwardly. "Are you familiar with a man named John Steele?"

Lisa crinkled her brow. "Yes, I know of him. A Canadian living here for many years. He owns a couple of nice antique stores. Looking for a trinket? He's very expensive."

"More than a trinket. My business with him has to do with quite a collection."

"I had no idea you were interested in antiques."

"There are a few things you don't know about me."

"Yes, well, that can be corrected. When will I see you again?"

"That was my next question. Are you free for dinner say around the twenty-sixth?"

"If I'm not, I will be."

"Shall we say seven-thirty? I'll pick you up at your place."

"Wonderful. I look forward to it." She paused and added, "Eiker, you're not the first person this week to ask about Steele."

"Who else?"

"Interpol. What's he done?"

"I have no idea. I've heard he has a lead on some interesting pieces of Middle Eastern art."

"Hmmm…I guess that answer will have to do. See you on the twenty-sixth."

As soon as Lisa broke the connection she placed a call to Franz Kutna, Interpol Vienna, and immediately connected

"Good morning, Lisa. What can I do for you?"

"It's about Rod Eiker. He's after all he can get on John Steele."

"What does that renegade want with Steele? I'll check it out right away. Thanks." He replaced the phone and flicked ash from the end of his cigarette. He took a long drag then dropped the butt into the dregs of his coffee cup and rose.

"Magda," he called to his secretary as he shrugged into his overcoat and passed through the outer office. "Take messages. Be back in an hour. If anything comes up you can get me at the Kartendome."

Magda smiled. It was the first time in days he had taken time to get a meal.

Kutna walked two blocks to the Kartendome. Little by little things were falling into place. He entered the building through the back door into a large steamy kitchen.

Fritz saw him and waved. "About time, Franz," he called in a booming voice. "Wait there."

Fritz Lubbe, owner, chef, host to some of Vienna's most famous personages, pushed his well-rounded bulk between worktables, dodging cutting blocks, steaming vats and bubbling cauldrons of aromatic food until he was facing his dear friend.

"You look terrible; far too thin and tired." He shoved aside a pile of dishes on a nearby table and waved to one of the cooks. "You also smoke too much and don't eat enough." He pulled two chairs forward. "Sit down."

Kutna sat and leaned forward across the table. "Fritz, get word to our people in Brno. We must find an American by the name of Joseph Falk and bring him back to Vienna."

A deep bowl of goulash, a large mug of thick, black coffee, half a loaf of dark bread and a dish of butter came to the table and slid in front of Kutna.

"Eat," Fritz urged, "for me."

Kutna smiled and glanced around the kitchen, satisfied that the clamor made it impossible for the place to be bugged—a safe place to talk business, Mossad business. Kutna continued.

"This is vital, Fritz. We've been sitting on top of a Nazi treasure trove since the end of the Second World War…right here in the city." Kutna tore off a piece of bread. "Now there are many after it, including that war criminal, Brasinov. Rod Eiker also is sniffing around town…God knows who else."

He dipped the bread into his goulash. "We want Dr. Falk. We need him. The Czech's have grabbed him, taken him to Brno, to Spilberg. It's not going to be easy."

Fritz nodded. "It never is, my friend."

In her apartment, Lisa Winkler poured a second cup of milky coffee. She knew she was onto something good if she could just piece it all together. There was Eiker asking questions and Czechs sniffing the air of international intrigue. What did Eiker mean about Middle Eastern art? She intended to find out…fast.

Chapter 30

Falk stood at the fringe of a crowd of pedestrians waiting to cross a busy street in Brno. He felt like a lost tourist who had missed the bus. The light turned green and the early morning commuters surged ahead. He followed until he was on the opposite side of the square, near the railway station.

They had taken his money and ID while he was a prisoner in the castle. He knew that without money he couldn't take a train. He had to think of something.

Then he saw the car. A new low-slung, bright red Maserati was weaving through traffic, its perfectly tuned engine growling. His eyes followed as it turned a corner, the driver scaling down through the gearbox like a musician, engine notes reverberating, causing heads to turn and eyes to glaze with envy.

The Italian auto eased to a stop half a block from Falk. A final rev and the engine died. The driver stepped from the machine, crossed the sidewalk and entered a three-story building.

Eyeing the car, Falk sauntered toward the building, an old residence converted into offices. Two of three polished brass plates fixed into the stonework beside the door were in Czech, the other in English. Jan Michalavitch Travel, Ltd., Falk read. Was the man in the car Michalavitch? The brass seemed old, the man young.

A small crowd of admirers who had gathered around the Maserati dispersed slowly as Falk moved in for a closer look.

"Like it?" a voice behind him asked.

Falk spun around, surprised to see the driver. "Yes. How did you know I speak English?"

"You're American, right?" Before Falk could answer the man added, "Perhaps I can be of assistance."

"Are you the police?"

"No. I'm Jan Michalavitch. My office is upstairs. I saw you reading my plate. I thought I'd talk to you since I can always use the business of an American."

Falk liked his approach and decided to be blunt. "I was thinking of stealing your car."

"I see." Michalavitch's gray green eyes were alive with curiosity. "This is a new Ferrari-designed 4.2-liter V8. It makes 390 horsepower and 332 pound-feet of torque. You have picked a very expensive Maserati to steal. Perhaps I was right. You could use the services of a good travel agent."

Falk ran a finger gently along the curve of the hood. "It looks like business is pretty good."

"Oh, it's not mine. I'm driving it to Trieste for a client. I came by my office to pick up some papers. Actually business is rather slow."

Falk got the message. Jan was open for a deal in cold cash, especially American dollars. "What would it cost to drive me to Vienna?"

Jan gestured toward a nearby coffee shop. "Let's get a coffee. Maybe we can arrange something."

They were sipping coffee when Jan leaned close to Falk and in a hushed tone said, "I could arrange for you to steal the car. That way I'd be protected by my client's insurance company."

Falk looked up from his cup. "How much?"

"One thousand American paid to my bank in Munich."

"Sorry, I don't have a cent. No credit cards, checks, nothing."

"What do you mean?"

"I have no passport, no identification. Everything was taken from me."

"You were robbed?"

"You could say that. The police took everything when I was arrested."

"Oh." Jan's interest faded. He shifted uneasily in his chair obviously regretting the encounter altogether.

Falk decided it was time for more desperate measures. "Sorry, Jan. I'm on the run." He lowered his voice to a confidential tone. "I'm going to ask you not to make any sudden moves."

Jan regarded him, questioning, then his gaze followed Falk's arm down to his hand in his pocket. "I have a gun here," Falk said. "It has a full clip except for one round I used when I killed the cop as I made my escape."

Jan was unnerved but reacted coolly. "What are you saying?"

"I must insist you take me to Vienna."

Jan gave a sideways glance. "How do I know you have a gun?"

It was a "B" movie tactic that Falk didn't believe in a million years would work but he did it regardless. With a point of his finger in his jacket pocket he motioned toward the door. "Trust me."

Jan didn't move for a full five seconds then he scraped back his chair and stood, all signs of the friendly wheeler-dealer gone. He tossed a few coins on the table.

"Good," Falk said. "I've always wanted to ride in a Maserati." As they walked out, he nervously fingered the innocuous air in his pocket.

Chapter 31

Koski and Emma hurried through the dark corridors and came upon a small door with a cracked window. Koski twisted the knob and the door opened to a walled courtyard. On the far side a soldier huddled against a door, his head sunk into his upturned coat collar, a rifle slung over his shoulder.

"Keep walking," Koski whispered. "See that guy? He's half asleep. You're an officer. Tell him to open the door."

Emma never missed a beat. She walked up to the unsuspecting guard and tapped his shoulder. He jumped. Seeing her insignias, he came to attention as Emma let loose with a stream of Czech, dressing him down for being less than alert. "Open the door," she ordered.

The soldier fumbled with his keys, unable to open the door fast enough for her. He snapped a salute as they walked through. Emma knew the Czechoslovakian Army had left Spilberg castle back in 1959, marking a definite end to its military era.

In 1960, Spilberg became the seat of the Brno City Museum. It was evident that the Czech Republic secret police also had kept part of its infamous infrastructure for covert needs.

Once inside Koski knew they'd have to move fast. They entered a long, brightly lit corridor with highly polished floors and doors on either side. "Check the doors on that side, Emma. I'll check these."

"Empty office," Emma said after opening the first. When she opened the next, she whispered over her shoulder, "A janitor's room full of cleaning supplies."

Koski was at her side at once. She pushed Emma in and closed the door behind them. "Lock the door," she said and did a quick appraisal. Coveralls and assorted clothing hung on wall hangers. Rubber boots, buckets and mops filled one corner. The room smelled of soap and floor polish.

"Grab one of the coveralls and a pair of boots," Koski said. Emma nodded and started pulling off the guard's uniform. She wrapped it and the boots into a tight bundle and pushed them out of sight behind some buckets.

"These smell like fish," Emma said, sitting on the floor and pulling on what looked like painter's boots.

Koski wiggled into coveralls. "Grab those two cloth caps... should go well with these."

Emma reached up and flipped the caps off the hook. "Mop or broom?" she asked, handing Koski a bucket.

"Mop, let's go." Koski opened the door cautiously and peered into the hallway, "All clear."

They started down the corridor, boots squeaking and slapping. Ahead were the front entrance and freedom. An elderly white-haired man sat in a ticket booth inside the hallway, staring out at the mesmerizing winter landscape. They passed him without a second glance. His job was to sell tickets to tourists coming in, not detain two shoddy janitors going out.

Both women breathed a sigh of relief when they reached the outside.

"Can you ride a bike?" Koski asked, nodding toward a group of bicycles leaning against a wall. Emma nodded. "It's possible," Koski said with an ironic smile, "we're about to become the first ever to escape from Spilberg Castle on bicycles."

Koski cautioned as they approached the bikes. "Act like it belongs to you. Put the bucket on the handlebars, lay the mop across them, get on and follow me. Don't look back."

"This thing doesn't have any gears!" Emma complained as they started pedaling. "I'm used to a ten-speed."

"It's downhill into the city. You can coast."

Koski was right. Within a few hundred yards the road turned into a steep downgrade. They stuck their legs out, turned up their toes and with buckets swinging raced like kids through the cold morning air.

Once at the bottom, however, they had to crank hard to keep the heavy bikes moving.

Emma gasped. "Where to now?"

"Vienna."

"On these?"

"No, but we can't go near bus or railway stations. Soon as they find out we're gone, the city will be crawling with secret police. Our only chance is to steal a car. Do you know the way back to Vienna?"

"Yes. I've driven it several times but stealing a car...."

"Pull up here, ahead, near that shop. And no more talking. I doubt there are many English-speaking cleaning ladies around here." They wobbled to a halt. Koski lifted her bike onto the sidewalk and set it against the side of the building. Emma followed.

"Leave the bikes here," Koski whispered and faced the shop window. "Keep your eyes on the merchandise."

Emma suddenly rattled off a sentence in Czech and pointed to some object as an elderly couple paused to stare into the second-hand shop window. Koski feigned interest in stacks of old dishes covered in dust, cans without labels, a velvet jacket with moth-eaten sleeves and tarnished brass buttons at the cuffs.

Soon the couple moved on. When they were out of earshot Koski said, "Okay, I'm going to get us transportation if I can find an unlocked car."

Emma's heart beat wildly in her chest as she affected interest in a wooden wine rack full of empty beer bottles and a stuffed weasel with one glass eye peeping out from a stack of old felt hats. She passed her tongue over suddenly dry lips. It seemed an eternity before a car reflected in the glass as it pulled up at the curb behind her. She turned quickly and hopped in and Koski hit the gas pedal.

Koski knew it was coming. "Where did you learn how to steal a car?"

"Same place I learned to kill with my bare hands."

Emma shook her head. "Must have been *some* neighborhood you grew up in."

Koski smiled. "Which way to Vienna?"

"Make a left turn onto Jakubska Avenue, three blocks straight ahead then right and head west across the city."

Five minutes later they passed within half a mile of the barracks-like apartment from which Falk had made his escape earlier and the young man with a stolen gun lost his life.

Koski swore softly as she stopped behind an old truck stalled in the center of the road. The driver waved his arm in a passing motion but she couldn't squeeze past.

"Hold on. We're going to do a U-turn." She pulled hard on the wheel and the tires spun as the car began a 180-degree turn but halfway through a police car came cruising down the street.

Koski waved to the male officers, smiled her sweetest, completed her turn and kept going. It worked. The police officers waved back, one shaking his finger as if admonishing a child.

"Who said chivalry is dead," Koski muttered and headed out of town.

Chapter 32

Colonel Zasztol Zhilin, seated at his desk at Czech Military Intelligence headquarters in Brno, scribbled his signature on some correspondence and placed it in his out-basket. The intercom buzzed. "Yakov is here, sir."

"Send him in." He signed two more letters before glancing up at the short, over fifty, rumpled looking man who approached his desk.

Yakov stared down at his superior's bald, egg-shaped head. Zhilin's piggy eyes were magnified by the lens of his heavy horn-rimmed glasses perched on the end of his large nose.

"Tell me, Yakov," Zhilin raised his pale blonde eyebrows, "the man killed on the roof when you were after the American, who was he?"

Yakov moved uneasily and rubbed a hand over his patchy gray hair. "He had no ID, sir."

Zhilin glared. "He was armed with an automatic fitted with a transmitter. One of our latest?"

"Yes, sir."

"No one knows who he was or how he happened to be carrying the transmitter?"

"No, sir."

"Stay on it, Yakov. I want some answers." He lowered his head in dismissal.

"Yes, sir." Yakov started from the room.

"Tell them to send in Horidecki," Zhilin called as Yakov reached the door. "I believe he's been waiting to see me."

Yakov nodded and left as Horidecki pushed by him.

Zhilin's eyes flashed to Horidecki. "Sorry you had to wait. Police business…you understand."

Horidecki recognized the slap. He had been kept waiting because Zhilin considered it a psychological advantage, another indication of the constant power struggle between them.

He conceded Zhilin's skills in certain diplomatic areas but he wasn't the sort of man Horidecki considered a useful member of the country's united front. Zhilin's credos were action and force. The Colonel, however, outranked him—a powerful weapon in the Czech Republic.

"Please sit down," Zhilin said. "Now about the American doctor, Falk, and the two women. I understand you had them at Spilberg."

Horidecki felt a flush creep up his face but he made no response.

"My information is that you interrogated the prisoners then allowed them to escape from an armed escort." His eyebrows pulled together in an almost pained expression as he continued, "And the two women…on bicycles!"

"They were out of my jurisdiction, Colonel."

Zhilin waved contemptuously. "You'll be held responsible

until it can be determined who was at fault."

A muscle in Horidecki's jaw twitched visibly. "You're free to go about your business." He got to his feet slowly. "Colonel, one of my best agents was killed in a car crash...an important link, a well-placed double agent."

Zhilin peered over the top of his glasses. "Who was that?"

"Switzer," replied Horidecki.

Zhilin grunted. "Too bad. Do you have someone to replace him?" He reached across his desk, fiddled with some papers and continued. "Preferably someone in Vienna?"

"Yes, Colonel, of course."

"Who would that be?"

"I'm not at liberty to give you that information, Colonel."

Switzer's death hadn't fazed Zhilin but now he looked up and the flickering light in his eyes betrayed a sudden lack of composure. "What do you mean? You must tell me who the new agent will be."

Horidecki took a deep breath. "It's not my choice, Colonel. I have no recourse. My orders come from a higher power."

Zhilin leaned forward, his face crimson. "Unless you want to be placed under arrest right now, you'll tell me."

"It's out of my hands, Colonel." Horidecki said almost apologetically. "Certainly I would tell you if I could. We've known each other too long to have secrets between us. You see, Vasilkinik swore me to silence."

Zhilin eased back in his chair. "Vasilkinik spoke to you?"

"Yes, sir, before I left Spilberg to come here."

Zhilin was silent for a moment. Rudolf Vasilkinik was a highly placed politico. A well-known, likable man, he could well be the next president of the republic.

During the destalinization movement in Prague in the spring of 1968, a young Vasilkinik had stood beside Alexander Dubcek, comrades in arms. Vasilkinik was capable of uniting the country in the twenty-first century through a combination of socialism and western style democracy—state medicine and pensions, free education, inexpensive consumer goods and automobiles. Zhilin, for whom the old order of fear was the only way of life, detested Vasilkinik. He was desolate at the thought of Horidecki being on speaking terms with the man.

Zhilin picked up a pen and returned his gaze to the stack of papers on his desk. "Very well, I'll leave it to you to inform me when the time is right…when you and *Rudolph* feel it's safe for me to know."

"Thank you, Colonel." It wasn't enough for Horidecki. He had to push it. "I hope I can still call on your office if I need assistance."

Zhilin put down the pen and spread his hands on the top of the desk as if assessing his fingers then raised his disquieting gaze to Horidecki.

"Call me any time, old friend." He let his teeth show a little. "I'd be hurt if you didn't."

Horidecki nodded politely, turned and walked to the door. He had won this little battle with Zhilin and savored the taste of it. Nonetheless, he knew the war was still on. Zhilin said he was free but Horidecki felt about as free as the three prisoners he had allowed to elude him.

Chapter 33

Koski and Emma had made good time getting out of Brno. They were on the E7 heading for Vienna.

"I'm going to pull over and get out of these coveralls," Koski said. Emma had shed hers miles back. "After that we find a place to dump the car."

"Dump it! But…"

"At the next café stop," Koski said as she pulled to the side of the road and stepped out of the coveralls. "Twenty-four hour café stops have large parking lots, plenty of cars, trucks…be an age before an abandoned car is noticed."

"What do we do then?"

"I don't know yet." Koski started the car and pulled back onto the E7. "I just have this feeling it's time to make a change." They had driven a few more miles when she pointed. "There."

Ahead was the standard European road stop. Cars and trucks were parked around a huge modern complex of buildings that catered to the weary traveler.

"Excellent place to hide a stolen car," Emma said as she noted the number of vehicles.

"How much farther to Vienna?" Koski asked.

"About a hundred kilometers."

They entered the restaurant, found a table and ordered sandwiches and hot chocolate. Halfway through her meal Emma leaned across the table. "Don't look now but there are two men over there who've been eyeing us since we came in."

Koski stiffened. "The police?"

"No. Don't turn around."

"What makes you so sure they're not cops?"

Emma feigned a look of indignation. "I can read male body language. Trust me. These guys are looking for action not an arrest. I'm going to give them one of my most irresistible smiles. When they come over I'll ask if they're heading for Vienna."

Koski smiled inwardly at Emma's immodesty. "Okay but what if they're not?"

Emma shrugged. "We'll give them the brush-off."

Chapter 34

Falk drove through the center of Brno, keeping with the flow of traffic. The Maserati was a dream to drive and heads turned as they passed. Falk was hiding in full view and there was something extremely exhilarating about it.

"Jan, point me in the direction of Vienna. If we're stopped tell them I've lost my voice—laryngitis."

Jan gave him a disgusted look. "Even if I do the talking, they'll want your driver's license. Better I drive."

Falk shook his head. "No way. I'll take the chance on being stopped, making a run for it if I have to, just the directions, please."

"Follow this road to the E7 Highway."

"How far is that?"

"About five kilometers," Jan muttered. "You're a fool if you think you can get away with this."

"Maybe it's because I am a fool that I'm still alive."

The traffic was thinning as they drove out of the city.

"Who are you?" Jan asked.

"I'm a guy who fell into the middle of an international mess—and is trying to get out of it."

Jan didn't ask for further explanations. They were now in open country cresting the top of a long hill and had an expansive view of the surrounding landscape. It looked like a scene from a Christmas card.

"Give me an overview from here." Falk eased the car to the side of the road. "I want to have it in my head."

Jan looked across the rugged hills. "Down into the valley…" He pointed to the right. "…the highway runs parallel to the river all the way to Austria."

"Any other roads when we get to the E7?"

Jan shook his head. "There's an old road that runs closer to the river but it takes longer. Very few people use it anymore. The E7 is best."

Falk gazed in the direction Jan had indicated. In the distance, at the bottom of the hill, he saw the old road running to the left. If roadblocks were to be set up, the E7 would be the most likely. He eased back onto the highway and started down the hill.

When they reached the intersection, Jan's attention was focused in the distance. Falk turned left. The car responded beautifully, not a sound from the tires as they made the sudden, hard turn. Jan jerked forward in surprise.

"No! Stop! Turn back."

Falk stared ahead to a clear expanse of roadway. "Relax we're taking the scenic route."

Falk would later learn the reason for the warning. He had turned onto an old escape road leading to the ten-and-a-half-mile track of the Grand Prix of the Czech Republic. Ten-and one-half miles of twisting, hairpin turns beside the River Svratka.

The first twist came up fast. Jan stifled a yell and Falk pulled the car through the bend. This time the tires screeched but held the road. His arms nearly wrenched from their sockets but somehow he controlled the wheel. He said a silent prayer of thanks that the automobile was a masterpiece of engineering, responding like a thoroughbred.

Jan found his voice. "You'll kill us! This is a racetrack!"

Falk knew he couldn't just jam on the brakes. He backed off

the gas as the road suddenly dipped in front of him. The car was airborne for several feet, trees and hedges flashing past in a blur. As they landed, Falk cranked the steering wheel and slid into the next curve. He tromped hard on the accelerator to save the rear end from spinning out. The engine howled in mechanical ecstasy and took the bend without a shudder. More luck than good driving.

Falk remembered the Grand Prix ran each August when the roads were in perfect condition. He was driving on snow and ice. He slowed some, alert for any sudden changes in the road.

Jan saw it first. He groaned and pointed a shaking finger. A yellow helicopter with black markings on its fuselage flew low across the fields and was heading straight for them.

"Stop the car at once!" Jan screamed, "Or we'll be gunned down like dogs."

Falk eyed the chopper and decided they could be gunned down no matter what they did. The track ran through deep woods, the trees converging overhead. Falk's hurried conjecture was that the chopper couldn't fly through them. He jammed his foot on the gas. The tunnel of trees grew closer by the second. He had wondered how fast the car could go. He was about to find out.

He hit another dip in the road flat out as if indifferent to the disaster rushing up at them at a speed of 150 KPH and climbing.

Jan gripped the dashboard, teeth clenched and eyes closed, probably wondering how long it would take to retrieve his body.

A few seconds later the slash of the aircraft's blades hissed above them. Next they were in the tunnel of trees, the chopper out of sight. Falk spied the other end of the cathedral of trees about a kilometer away. That's when he realized the chopper didn't need to fly through the trees. The damn thing was waiting for them at the other end, dancing a few feet from the road like a colossal winged insect.

Falk's hands remained steady, his foot solidly on the gas pedal. The chopper pilot kept his craft pointed directly at them, tail swishing from side to side. Beside Falk, Jan moaned and sank to the floor, covering his ears with his hands.

Through the bubble nose of the chopper, Falk saw the blurred faces of men. The one next to the pilot was turning, poking a machine gun through the port window and taking aim. The pilot lifted the machine just as the car's left fender sliced under the landing skids. There was a shudder of attempted correction from the helicopter but it was too late.

The sound of the helicopter engine changed pitch, going from a roar to a shriek as the stress of the violent maneuver caused the machine to stand on its tail. Falk saw the rotors working like a runaway windmill. Then, as if in slow motion, the chopper gave itself to a maelstrom of invisible force and dropped to earth like a stricken, dying falcon. There was a blinding flash of orange as the gas tanks blew and a greasy, black tower of curling smoke rose from the spot. Jan put his head between his knees and threw up.

Chapter 35

Falk kept his foot firmly on the gas. He tried to be rational. No doubt, the helicopter had radioed for backup and it was only a matter of minutes before another picked up the chase. It wouldn't be tough to find a bright red Maserati in the snow. He had to keep going…and fast.

Jan wiped a hand across his mouth. He was no longer the free, flippant travel agent of an hour ago but a man fearing for his life. "I… I know this racetrack." Jan nodded forward. "There's an escape road that runs into the woods. Up there. About 300 meters."

Falk knew about escape roads. He had seen a film of a driver named Ken Miles, who saved his own life many years ago at Tory Pines in California. After a spinout, he'd driven his MG onto just such a forest clearing. Falk pressured the gas. "Right or left?"

"Over there on the left," Jan shouted. "See it?" He pointed and Falk picked out the narrow strip of earthen track, a mere slash in the trees. It was studded with errant saplings and shrubs that had sprung up since last August's race.

Falk's thoughts merged. He wasn't sure whether he was driving the car or the car and the rough frozen road were driving him. A young pine came at him like a fastball whistling down the grove toward the center of home plate. He swerved sharply to the left and it passed inches from his side. Finally he threaded into the ever-narrowing tract of land, braked hard and stopped.

Jan stared at him with open admiration. "Jesus, Mary and Joseph!" he said. Falk felt a strange camaraderie stir between them.

Jan climbed from the car. "Our best bet is to find the river and get to the other side. It's going to be cold. There's a spare jacket on the back seat."

Falk nodded, reached over, retrieved the leather jacket and shrugged into it as he climbed from the car.

They both sank up to their knees in snow as soon as they stepped from the rutted, frozen track. With Jan leading, they trudged slowly toward the river. Falk cursed. They were leaving tracks a blind man could follow.

"Down," Jan suddenly hissed, falling flat. A split second later Falk also went face down. Hearing nothing, he lifted his head slightly and peered at Jan a few feet ahead on the side of a slight rise. Jan motioned him over. "Down there," he whispered. "See them?"

Falk squinted against the white glare of the snow. Two men stood beside a small wooden boat loading fishing gear.

"Yeah."

Jan never took his eyes off the men. "They could be our ticket to freedom." He got to his feet and dusted the snow from his clothes. "Follow me. Don't say a word."

Soon they stood on a ridge looking down at the fishermen a few meters away.

"Police," Jan called out in a loud voice. "Stay where you are."

The two men looked up and turned frightened faces in the direction of the voice. As Falk and Jan walked toward them, Jan whispered, "Say nothing. Just keep looking them in the eye with authority."

"We need to commandeer your boat…police business."

Jan was cool, official. "We'll take you across the river. Give me your names and addresses and the boat will be returned to you."

One of them hesitated for a second, exchanging glances with his companion. They were elderly, rural men living in a country that trained its citizens well to obey police orders.

Jan wrote their names on a piece of paper and the four got in the boat and crossed the fast-flowing water. The small outboard strained with unaccustomed weight.

Falk saw Jan look back, no doubt wondering if he would ever return to life as it was, aware that if caught, he'd be found guilty of abetting Falk.

The boat nosed into the riverbank and the fishermen stepped out. When Jan passed the fishing tackle to them, they shouldered their poles and walked into the woods without so much as a backward glance.

"Can we trust them not to talk?" Falk asked as Jan pushed off, steering with a single oar over the stern.

"They'll go home, say nothing. Police business is serious in this country."

Falk hunched forward with the cold. It was obvious Jan knew how to handle a boat. Maybe they'd make it after all.

Jan pressed hard with the oar, avoiding a suddenly looming coal black rock ringed with foam. "I used to fish this river as a kid, know every rock for miles. Downstream, however, will be different."

"Why not use the outboard?"

"We might need it later. Right now the current will do the job."

As they rounded a bend in the river, Falk saw something that caused a ripple of icy fear to pass through him. An armored car sat beneath a clump of pines, its 75mm gun pointing skyward.

It reminded Falk of the vehicle that had hauled him to the railway siding. Like an attentive cat at a mouse hole, it was silent, unmoving.

"They're all along the river, part of a regular patrol between here and the Austrian border."

"What happened to European unity? I thought borders were out. Do you think they saw us?"

"We must still be in the clear. No one has picked up our trail…yet."

As Jan deftly navigated through the cold, dark water, Falk fell silent, the word "yet" lingering in his ears.

Chapter 36

Kutna was still at lunch when Rosie Wimmer entered the

office and nodded to the receptionist, who smiled in recognition.

"He should be back any minute."

"Thanks. I'll wait." Rosie seated herself and started to thumb through a magazine. Kutna entered on page three.

"Rosie!" He brushed her cheek with a kiss. "Been waiting long? I wish you'd called. We could have lunched together."

"I came in just ahead of you…no time to call."

Kutna detected something wrong as he led her into his office. "Sit down, Rosie. You're trembling."

"I'm okay." She sat on the edge of the chair. "Steele tried to kill me."

"What! When?" He fell silent, brooding as Rosie related the story of the bombs in the apartment and her car. "The men who came into the apartment, who were they?"

"I don't know."

"You don't know? Rosie, they could have been lying. They could have set all that up."

"It crossed my mind but I don't think so."

"Why does Steele want to kill you?"

"He wants me out of the way. Remember he told me about the loot he was after."

Kutna nodded. "Do you think he knows you're Mossad?"

"It's possible but there's no way to find out now. Whatever his reason, I would have been blown away if I'd made a wrong move in the apartment."

"And these men just showed up and whisked you to safety? Were they from Captain Vlad's office at Military Intelligence? They're always involved in anything to do with bombs."

Rosie nodded. "Whoever they were, they drove me away from the apartment and I'm still alive. That counts for something."

"Yes, of course, but…" Kutna paced his office. "Did they say anything that might give us a clue?"

"No."

"Rosie, think hard."

"The leader looked like an Arab."

Kutna thrust his arms skyward. "That's it? He looked like an Arab—that's all?"

Rosie drooped in her chair. "Sorry."

Kutna sighed. "You've had a harrowing experience. Get some rest. We'll talk later. Stay here and stretch out on the couch if you like."

"I will take the rest. I feel safe here."

"Good. I'll be right back. I'm going to check the latest input."

Kutna entered Vienna Interpol's communications room. Beside a wall covered with state-of-the-art computer code analyzers, a gray-haired woman stood in front of a printer as it smoothly delivered a page. She glanced up and beckoned to Kutna. Together they read the message:

TEL AVIV INTEL CONFIRMS SERB SEPARATISTS INVOLVED.

Kutna swore, lit a cigarette from a crumpled pack and left the room.

Back in his office, he sat at his desk. Rosie was already asleep on the couch. He stared at the terse message that was in answer to his call to Israeli Intelligence. The prospect of those bastards getting into the search wasn't good news.

His phone rang. "Kutna," he growled. "Yes, I understand." He replaced the phone as Rosie sat up, awakened by the ring.

"That was about Dr. Falk. He's still on the run in the Czech Republic." He shook his head. "Colonel Zhilin of Czech security is breathing down his neck." Kutna leaned back, stretched his arms over his head, fingers entwined and pulled to release the tension across his shoulders.

Was he getting too old for this game? He turned to Rosie. "Sometimes, Rosie, I wonder why we spend our lives this way."

She didn't answer. She knew why. They were avengers, coiled springs of anger with the need for retribution. They always were ready to dispense biblical justice for the sins against their fathers and even worse sins by those who planned Israel's removal from the face of the earth.

Rod Eiker walked through the revolving door of the Bristol Hotel into the clear, frosty morning. The door attendant touched his cap and swung open the door of the limo at the curb as Eiker crossed the sidewalk. He folded into the warm, spacious interior. The door thudded shut, automatic locks meshing with perfect synchronization.

"Morning, Eiker."

Eiker acknowledged Harold Mifflin with a nod. He leaned back into the deep leather, his voice harsh with early morning throatiness. "What's today's drill?"

Mifflin replied, "To see Tom Stewart. Have a few things to go over."

"Suppose you heard about Horidecki."

"Yeah, I understand he was dead before his body hit the sidewalk on Sady Osvobozeni Boulevard outside Czech Military Headquarters."

"Apparently it happened so fast that no one could identify the vehicle."

The limo turned onto the Karnter-Ring and continued toward the Stadt Park. Eiker glimpsed the statue of Strauss through the trees.

Mifflin grunted. "I wonder where Falk is at this moment."

Chapter 37

The penetrating chill from the river oozed into the marrow of Falk's bones despite the leather jacket he had taken from the Maserati. He told himself that with luck they would pass beneath the bridge at the border in darkness. It was already dusk. A thick mist slid over the countryside like gray smoke, blotting out patches of the riverbank. The trees were distant skeletons, pointing in indistinguishable directions. At the helm, Jan memorized details of the river's path before the rolling mist overtook them.

"It will get even colder when the fog settles," Jan whispered. "That will be to our benefit. It will help deaden any sounds when we pass under the bridge." He dipped an oar, shifted his weight and the boat moved a degree to the left. "Most of the guards will want to stay inside for warmth. It's the eager guard trying to make grade that might see us… the one who stays outside."

Falk knew they were three hours from Austria yet being on the run in an alien country made each hour seem like a week. All at once, the sun, not seen for days, broke through a rift in the clouds and a hazy shaft of light touched the tips of the winter firs. A reddish glow reflected on the low-lying clouds. This lasted less than a minute and then was gone. Gray clouds swirled in, the sky and fog darkening for the night. The brief glimpse of sunlight lifted Falk's spirit. He was more determined than ever to escape.

In his reverie he didn't see Jan slip off his coat. In a flash the man was in the water. He piked beneath the surface and stayed underwater for some time. He surfaced a hundred yards away and swam with strong strokes toward shore. He would take his chances in the woods.

Chapter 38

In the café off the E7 Koski feigned surprise as she looked up at the large man who was suddenly beside her chair, encouraged by Emma's earlier smile. He was dressed in a tweed jacket and pants and a Tyrolean hat with tufts of white crinkly hair protruding above his ears. He removed his hat with a beefy hand, coughed and attempted to introduce himself in Czech then switched to fractured French. Finally he looked back at his friend, who simply smiled and held up his martini glass in a salute.

Emma sighed. In flawless German she asked if there was anything she could do for him. His eyes turned wide and interested at the sound of his own language.

"I was wondering if *we* might be of service to *you*." He pulled his heels together and bowed slightly. Since the heels didn't click the effort at gallantry was wasted.

"Do you speak English?" Emma asked.

"Of course."

Emma nodded toward Koski. "My friend doesn't speak German. It would be easier…"

"Certainly." He bowed to Koski as the man with the martini glass joined them.

"Allow me, ladies. I am Marny Fries and this is my associate, Herman Lansfeldt. We are computer reps for a large firm."

"Pleased to meet you," Koski said. "This is Mary Jones." She shot a fast glance at Emma, who went along with the introduction as if it were authentic. "I'm Daphne Hailey." She gave Herman the most profoundly interested look she could muster.

"We're trying to decide whether to take the bus or rent a car.

You see, our car broke down and it'll be a couple of days before it's ready. We have to be back in Vienna by tomorrow."

Emma nodded and lowered her eyes. Her long, dark, straight lashes cast lacy shadows on her face. Marny and Herman looked from Koski to Emma then to each other. Herman spoke first.

"As Marny said, we're in computers. We're headed to Budapest. I suppose we could go via Vienna..." He glanced at Marny who nodded agreeably.

"Ach," Marny said. "We travel all the time. We're known by all the security personnel at the borders and can make up the time later."

"I thought borders were a thing of the past," Koski exclaimed.

"They are. Nonetheless, the EU has started taking certain precautions since the terrorist actions in Madrid and London. It won't be a problem for us."

They pulled up chairs. "So," Marny continued, "you see, we can be of service."

Koski and Emma exchanged glances. Bingo! By the time Marny was on his third drink, he had cozied up to Emma and was leaning close, one hand lightly tapping her knee at intervals.

Herman promised to drive them right to their front door. His Mercedes had plenty of room. They would travel in style.

"It's very kind of you," Koski said seductively. "We don't know what to say."

"Our pleasure, my dear," Herman whispered. He tipped his glass to consume the last drop then led the way to a silver Mercedes that happened to be parked alongside the car Koski and Emma had abandoned.

Emma sat beside Marny in the back seat. Next to Herman in front, Koski was uncharacteristically chatty. Less than ten miles down the highway, Marny fell asleep, his head on Emma's shoulder. Koski looked back and saw Emma push him away.

Chapter 39

Colonel Zhilin was in a rotten mood. He still didn't have Falk. He glared as Yakov entered his office and stopped in front of his desk.

Zhilin screwed a cigarette into a long ivory holder and held it between his left thumb and forefinger. "Yes, Yakov?"

Yakov reached into the pocket of his crumpled raincoat, extracted a mangled book of matches, scratched a match to flame and offered it. Zhilin squinted as he leaned forward and placed the tip of his cigarette in the flame.

Yakov blew out the match. "I have information that will please you, Colonel."

Zhilin leaned back slowly and blew a thin blue halo toward the ceiling. "If you have good news, Yakov, it will be the first today."

Yakov had worked with the Colonel a long time and had learned to be direct. "The car in the woods belonged to a person in Trieste. It was being transported by a travel agent named Jan Michalavitch. The owner in Trieste is…" He removed a piece of paper from his pocket. "Antonio Valencia."

Zhilin waved away the smoke from his cigarette. "You have this man, Michalavitch?"

"No, but we have the car, sir. It seems the travel agent has eluded us."

Zhilin snorted and crushed out his cigarette. "That is what you call good news?" Yakov was silent and Zhilin continued. "I suppose he vanished into thin air like that?" He snapped his fingers.

"There were two sets of footprints," Yakov replied, "leading from the car to the river."

"Was the American, Falk, with Michalavitch?"

"Yes, sir."

At last Zhilin was interested. "How do you know that? What did you find at the river?"

"Footprints in the mud, sir."

Zhilin began to breathe heavily, his face pinched with annoyance. "I suppose you're going to say they were American footprints."

"Yes, sir, and those of Jan Michalavitch."

Zhilin virtually trembled. "Tell me, Yakov, how could you tell the others were *American* footprints?"

"Our deductions indicate he may have been in the car. We interviewed people who saw the vehicle leave Brno with two men in it. One of the descriptions fits Falk."

Zhilin leaned back in his chair and glowered.

The room was warm. The thick air drooped over Yakov like a damp cloth. "We checked to see how many people had been at the river's edge," he continued, "but it was impossible to say. The snow was trampled. We obtained a boat, crossed the river and examined the landscape on the other side. Again many footprints led off into the woods. It had snowed recently and the prints were almost obliterated...."

"Did you follow the prints into the woods?"

"Yes. They led to a road and then ended."

"Did you find the boat the two crossed in?"

Yakov hesitated. Suddenly he knew what the Colonel was going to say next! Why hadn't he thought of it?

Zhilin pounded his thick palm on the desk. "You dolt. There is no boat because our two suspects are on their way out of the country in it!" He grabbed the phone and shouted a stream of commands.

"Concentrate on the river between the place of entry and the bridge at Drasenhofen. I want searchlights, six boats with two men in each with battery powered lights and automatic weapons. These fugitives must be found!" He slammed the phone down and fixed an icy gaze on his shivering subordinate.

"Yakov, do you have any idea what it would be like to go through life without testicles?"

Yakov swallowed hard and backed toward the door. "I'll get Falk, sir. I will."

When he was gone Zhilin took out another cigarette and eased back in his chair. Once he had Dr. Falk it would be easy to capture the two females, or vice versa.

The headlights drilled into the inky blackness of the night as Herman's Mercedes jostled over ridges of ice on the highway.

Koski concentrated on the odometer as if her intensity could cause the miles to slip away more quickly. Herman, cigar clenched between his teeth, focused on the road. His fleshy face was etched in shadow by the orange glow from the dashboard. In the rearview mirror Koski saw Marny's head lolling back, mouth agape, snoring.

Koski suddenly stiffened. Behind, a flashing blue light careered up the highway. She glanced at Herman. He hadn't seen it. With as much control as she could manage, she alerted him. He slowly eased the car to the roadside.

With just the blue lights blinking, an armored car swept past them in a spray of snow, mud and ice. Thick treaded tires humming, engine growling, in seconds the vehicle became red taillights that vanished into the darkness as quickly as they appeared.

Herman steered back onto the highway. "You looked scared, my leibschen. Did you think they were after us?" He chuckled and nudged his elbow into her side.

She responded with what she hoped was a look of mystification. "I thought they were after you, Herman."

He shook with laughter. "You thought perhaps I was different than I have represented myself to be?"

She smiled coyly and thought, *No, Herman. You are exactly as you represented yourself to be. Moreover, I am feeling guilty, using you this way.*

Herman switched on the radio and a Brahms composition filled the interior. Koski settled back with a deep sigh. Where was the military going in such a hurry? If it was an all-out alert they would be checked at some point.

As if he had been thinking it, too, Herman rolled his cigar to the other side of his mouth. "We'll be in Austria soon. I'll find out what's going on."

Koski decided the less they asked the better. She knew he wanted to appear important, show her what a clever man he was. Poor bastard had no idea he was transporting two escaped prisoners.

"You know, Herman," her voice was a low, seductive growl. "I'm glad today's borders are not like the old days. The longer we're there, the less time we'll have at my place." She cringed inwardly at her own shameless innuendo.

The cigar went quickly from one side of Herman's mouth to the other as if on a string and Koski felt the car accelerate. There would be little time wasted in idle chatter with security. She glanced over her shoulder at Emma, who raised one eyebrow a fraction and gave an almost imperceptible shake of her head. Herman, intent on getting to Vienna, didn't notice.

Chapter 40

The limo with Eiker and Mifflin wound through a narrow road on the outskirts of Vienna in an area known as Grinzing, a popular tourist wine tasting destination.

"Here we are," Mifflin said as he heaved forward when the car came to a halt. "Grinzinger Weinbeisser."

"Straight out of *Hansel and Gretel,*" Eiker replied.

He stepped from the car. A picturesque lantern swung on a black wrought iron support above the scrolled entrance. Fanciful braids of ivy clung to the ochre plaster walls of the fairy tale structure. He surveyed the landscape.

Eiker nodded. "Actually, I'm impressed. An excellent strategic location. Difficult for any possible interloper to approach without being detected, yet advantageous to a speedy departure if one should be required."

Mifflin agreed. "That's probably why Stewart chose it for his temporary quarters."

"Thanks for getting here so promptly," Stewart said as they entered his office. He indicated chairs and jumped right into the briefing. "All we have on Falk as of this moment is that he's somewhere in the Czech Republic."

In less than five minutes Stewart had updated them on what he knew of Falk's passage from Austria to Spilberg Castle and subsequent escape.

"At last report," Stewart concluded, "he was driving a

Maserati that we believe was stolen from a travel agent in Brno."

"Christ!" Mifflin exclaimed. "He's a dead man if he's trying to get out of the Czech Republic in a stolen car."

"How old is the report?" Eiker asked.

"Less than two hours," replied Stewart.

Eiker rubbed his chin. "Could you arrange a meeting for us with Kutna at Interpol?"

Stewart pulled his laptop closer and tapped a few keys. "No problem."

Kutna was asleep, slumped across his desk. He startled and reached for the phone, "Yes," he said. "I understand. Send them along…glad to talk to them." He recradled the phone. What did American Intelligence want now? He ran his fingers through his hair, adjusted his tie. He thought of the computer printout he had read a short time ago. He needed all the help he could get.

Kutna ordered cappuccino. Less than fifteen minutes later Magda was serving it to Mifflin and Eiker, who were too antsy to enjoy it.

"Recalling some of your escapades around the world over the last fifteen years, Eiker," Kutna said, "I must admit I'm surprised to see you working with Mifflin."

Mifflin handled the response. "Our involvement in this matter is as private investigators, working for a large international insurance company whose name we're not at liberty to reveal."

Kutna opened a fresh pack of cigarettes, removed one and placed it between his lips. "Really?" he murmured, lighting up.

Mifflin leaned his rotund body forward and set down his cup. "Enough of this happy horseshit. Let's get down to business."

Kutna reminded himself that it was Mifflin's style to dispense with the niceties and roll on with all the tact of a Sherman tank.

"What do your people in the Czech Republic know about Doctor Joseph Falk's whereabouts?" Mifflin demanded.

"Joseph Falk?" Kutna bunched his brows.

"Let's not play games here, Kutna," Mifflin growled "We…"

"Look," Eiker cut in. "We could work with Interpol…or the Mossad or the IZL. We're all after the same thing."

"Interpol," Kutna said stubbornly and evasively, "will be happy to do whatever it can. What is your most recent information?"

"That he's in Brno," Eiker said, "driving a stolen car."

Kutna nodded. "I have someone working on the Falk matter. I should have word soon."

Eiker stood and eased his neck and shoulders. "By the way, do you have any idea where we can find John Steele?"

Kutna smiled wryly. "When I last spoke to Rosie Wimmer she wished he was in hell."

Eiker didn't take the time to question Rosie's emotional mindset. "If not there," he said coolly, "where else would you suggest?"

"You might try Military Police Headquarters. He attempted to kill Rosie."

Steele hadn't been detained. He'd been allowed to return to his apartment. Then, like a babe in arms, he had walked in and performed for a hidden, very candid camera.

Now the two men who joined him in the elevator tightened against him and he was hardly aware of the quick nip as the hypodermic needle sank into his carotid artery. He walked between them through the lobby to the street. When his body sagged, they supported him, lowered him into the back seat of a waiting Audi and closed the doors without missing a beat. One man sat in the back seat with Steele, the other with the driver as they flowed into the Viennese traffic.

As he slumped with glassy, blank eyes, a prisoner of Brasinov's thugs, Steele tried to remember how he got into this mess. His mind reeled back, taking him to the last time he saw David Benson.

It was a little after 3 a.m. the night of the last reunion in 1975. Steele had gone to David's hotel room and rapped on the door.

"Sorry, David," he said as he was allowed in, "but I have to talk to you."

"It's okay." David nodded wearily toward a chair.

"About tonight, the information Lego gave us on the location of the loot. I think we should go after it."

David shook his head. "Could be what Lego said is true but you know as well as I do how many legends there are about hidden war treasures." He stretched. "Besides, I have to take care of my work back in California."

"You mean you can afford not to." Steele's voice turned harsh and David was surprised.

"That's not the reason. I have patients who depend on me. I don't have time to spend searching for something that may not exist."

"But it *does* exist! I *know* it. You owe it to the rest of us to at least try…"

"Look, John, I'm tired. If you're worried about me knowing, don't be. I don't plan on telling a soul. We can talk more about it in the morning if you like, but I won't change my mind." He crossed to the door and grasped the knob. "I'm going to bed."

"Too bad you're so short on time." Steele was beside him. "Wish I could have counted on you. Since I can't, I don't think I can trust you to keep your mouth shut."

Steele remembered David's eyes, widened in shock. The good doctor started to say something before the lethal burst from the aerosol can atomized his face, but no sound came. He sagged into Steele's arms. Steele carried him to the bed then went to the door, being careful to use his handkerchief on the knob as he softly closed it behind him.

Steele's mind swam slowly back to the present as the drug spread insidiously through his system. Through a haze, he saw a group of Christmas carolers step into the street in front of the Audi.

They walked slowly, waving as they sang. Steele heard voices but the fog in his head disallowed his eyes to focus. When they did, he was able to isolate the lanterns the singers carried on long poles that cast a pale yellow light on the snow. He thought he heard, "Let nothing you dismay..." before the sound faded. He closed his eyes, fell into a deep blackness and was dismayed.

Chapter 41

Falk couldn't believe it. He was alone on the boat with no idea how he was going to escape. A freezing wintriness swept across the dark brocade of water as the Svratka River continued to swirl past the boat. Falk felt the dampness reach out and clutch him. A vaporous, sickle moon glimmered for a moment through heavy clouds.

He concentrated on what he had to do. If only he could make it under the bridge at the border that was close now. He no longer had the expertise of Jan, who had maneuvered the boat as if he was a Colorado River rapids guide.

Suddenly a brilliant lance of light from the riverbank stabbed through the darkness across the water. Falk was conscious of a gasp escaping his lips before he realized the beam had fallen short of the boat.

"Military!" he hissed, struggling to keep the boat beyond reach of the light as it scavenged the black surface.

Falk slowly inched his way back to the boat's stern. He could beach her on the other side and take his chances on foot. He knew he had to stay on the river as long as possible. In the forest, guard dogs would pick up his trail and his sense of direction could go haywire. He could cover more miles on the river than stumbling through dark woods in deep snow.

Falk was jolted from his thoughts by another stream of light, almost white in its intensity, that shot out of the woods and illuminated the water not fifty yards ahead of him. It seemed wide and solid enough to drive a Mack truck across and lit everything in its path. He was moving fast, heading right into it....

Falk leaned on the oar. The craft resisted, refused to answer at first and then slued across the flow of the river. The maneuver wasn't enough to stop him. He still headed toward the slab of light but broadside. The sandbank came up fast just short of the beam. Falk jammed the oar deep into a ridge of foam and bent his full strength into edging her aground.

He jumped, landed in the sand and mud and clawed forward, pulling the bowline with him. Struggling against the weight of the boat, he felt the rope slide through his hands, burning skin as he battled with the craft. The rush of the river sucked the boat in a slow arc toward the light. Twisting the rough line around his hand, Falk dragged himself to a gnarled tree stump.

A quick hitch and the line caught on the roots. It strummed as it tightened, grew taut, quivered and held. He pulled the boat to the sandbank hand over hand until the nose nudged the sand. He pulled the boat until it was secure.

The brilliant beams of light didn't move but poured forth steadily across the width of the river—sentinels at a line of demarcation nothing could pass without suffering the scrutiny of their deadly gaze.

Falk heard the sounds of dogs baying in the distance, muffled by the thick fog covering the countryside. What had Sandburg meant? Fog didn't come on little cat's feet. It came on the mournful wail of the hounds from hell. When the fog lifted his pursuers would see him.

"I don't intend to stick around until daylight," Falk mumbled. He fell flat just as the wide beam of light slowly started moving toward him. It crept closer, lighting every swirling wave, every curvilinear secret of the river's course.

Falk, his face pressed into the freezing mud, could almost feel the light through the hair on the crown of his head. Any second now...

A man's voice called out. Someone had ordered the light extinguished. Falk didn't move.

Two shots crackled through the frost laden air. There was a flurry of voices. Falk kept his face buried in the wet earth as the shouts faded, absorbed in the fog. Next there was a single shot then a lengthening, uneasy silence. It was pitch black.

"What happened?" Falk whispered to himself. Before he could formulate an answer, there was an eruption of machine gun fire in the woods nearby. Again he dug his face into the mud. A second burst ripped through the night, beating a tattoo of fear in Falk's head. Soon the sounds faded deep into the woods.

Falk lifted his head a fraction then buried it fast as the eerie light of a flare ascended above him, sputtering like a skyrocket. It reached its zenith, burst into a pale, shimmering, penetrating glare as it floated over the fog shrouded countryside, trapping him in the periphery of its ghastly glow.

The *brrrrup-brrrrup* of a machine gun rattled in the distance as the flare faded, hissed into oblivion and blackness and silence returned.

Quick, Falk thought, get the boat loose. He fumbled furiously with the ice covered knots. There was another distant burst of gunfire and an outbreak of barking from the dogs he and Jan heard earlier. The bursts were all ahead of him, which meant that Jan might be safe after all. The shooters must think they're still after two men.

Crazy, Falk thought, but it's almost as if someone was creating a diversion. The rope came loose and Falk leapt into the boat and pushed off. He only had a moment of comparative calm before he realized the boat was taking on water.

Looking down, Falk saw water sloshing around his feet. "Must have been damaged when I dragged it onto the sand bank," he muttered. He cupped his hands and tried to bale but it was no use. The water was coming in too fast. Despite his struggles to make the opposite shore, the boat became sluggish and settled deeper into the river with each passing second.

Falk peered into the darkness and wondered if he would make it to the opposite side before the boat sank. Suddenly the searchlight jabbed through the inky blackness. Falk raised his arms to cover his eyes. This time the light was full in his face.

The first shot came. Falk spun sideways too fast and went over the side, tipping the boat and plunging into what seemed like fathomless leagues of ice water. As his descent continued, he heard three muffled shots. It seemed as if Falk's lungs would burst as he swam for his life deep under the surface. He wasn't the swimmer Jan was. He knew he must climb for air.

Chapter 42

Three more strokes and Falk's head broke the surface. He was almost to the opposite riverbank, surfacing outside the range of light.

The searchlight played on the partially submerged boat as the wreckage swirled into a clump of overhanging branches and came to a rest on its side, water breaking across the remains. They'll be on it like a pack of wolves, Falk thought.

His feet touched the stony bottom of the river as its depth lessened. Grasping for tufts of grass, he clawed his way up the frozen riverbank, tree branches scraping his face. His clothes didn't freeze as the air hit them so he knew it wasn't as cold as it felt. He had to put miles between himself and the military…fast.

He rolled onto the flat ground and slithered like a snake into the underbrush. What had Jan said—easy to get lost in the woods, lose your sense of direction? He decided to follow the downstream flow of the river as long as possible.

Stiffly he got to his feet and stumbled along a narrow dirt path, using the thick brush and trees for concealment. He had to keep moving to keep his circulation intact. He knew hypothermia could kill him as surely as a bullet in the back.

He heard faint shouts from the opposite bank. They had been searching for two men. Soon they'd know that both had eluded them. He thought of Jan swimming for his life and the young man on the rooftop gunned down by the helicopter. He hoped fervently that Jan had made it to safety. He'd probably never know.

In his flight to freedom that was still far from won, Falk was responsible for the fates of these two and others whose fates happened to cross his own. There also was the possibility that Koski and Emma were still suffering captivity in Spilberg.

He clamped his teeth down hard on his lip and stumbled into the blackness. Like a hunted animal his ears strained at every sound. His eyes tried to penetrate the darkness.

Less than a mile from where he crawled out of the river, a flashlight beam looked him squarely in the face. He had heard nothing, had no warning. His heart pounded and his mouth went dry. Motionless, he waited for the bullet he was certain would tear into him. A strong masculine arm went around his neck, cutting off his air and a pistol barrel pressed into his ear.

"Don't move, Dr. Falk." The voice behind the flashlight was a woman's, soft, husky and authoritative. The arm eased just enough for him to breathe. The beam dipped, ran down his body and went out, leaving two amorphous red disks floating before his eyes.

When the limb around his neck loosened, he could breathe easier but was unable to speak for several seconds. His mind raced with questions. How did they know his name?

"Who are you?"

The woman moved closer and he saw her face. Pressing a finger to her lips, she whispered, "Follow me."

She turned and walked ahead, carefully picking her way between the trees. Falk followed, rubbing his neck, the man close at his side. After what seemed an eternity the man gripped his arm and pulled him close against a tree. The woman, silent as a cat, continued toward a small cabin. Falk and the man remained in the deep shadows and waited. When they heard two high-pitched whistles like the sound of a nightingale, the man pushed Falk forward toward a stone and log structure with two small windows and a chimney.

In the distance Falk heard water rushing and deduced that, in daylight, the cabin commanded a view of the river.

The door opened and the woman waved them forward. Inside smelled damp and musty. The woman covered the windows with heavy canvas before scratching a match. The acrid smell was sharp as she touched the flame to the wick of an old-style oil lamp. It flared to light and suffused through the room, affording Falk his first full look at his captors.

The woman was young. Falk guessed mid-thirties and of medium height. Errant strands of blonde hair straggled down under the edge of her black woolen cap. She offered her hand and although her wrist and hand were slender, her grip was firm.

"My name is Maria," she said in English. "He is Heinz."

Heinz nodded. He appeared to be a contradiction, resembling rough, peasant stock with the build and ability to kill but with eyes and a manner that reflected a polished modernity.

Falk started to ask more questions but Maria shook her head. "That's all you need to know about us for now." She left the room and returned almost immediately with a large towel and clothes that looked exactly Falk's size.

"Change those wet clothes. We can't light a fire. Smoke would give away our location." She handed him the towel. "Dry with this." As she left the room she added, "Hurry."

Falk removed his shirt and quickly rubbed his body with the rough towel. Heinz passed him a flannel shirt and in a few minutes he was dressed in a thick woolen turtleneck over the flannel shirt, ski pants and boots and a hooded windbreaker jacket.

Maria returned. "Our information was that you can ski. I hope that's correct."

"Yes." He turned to Heinz then back to Maria. "How did you know about me...clothing size, boots... everything?"

Maria was carrying a tin tray with two mugs that she held up to him. "It's our business to know. Drink this. It'll warm you." She handed the other mug to Heinz.

Holding the mug in both hands, Falk took a deep swig. It was like taking in liquid fire. The brew flowed down his throat and hit his stomach like hot mercury, raw country brandy. The warmth it generated thawed Falk's frozen body.

Heinz laughed and drank his in one long gulp.

Falk finished his and handed the mug to Maria. "Thanks. Now will you tell me who you are?"

Maria and Heinz exchanged a quick glance. "We're smugglers," she said.

"What do you smuggle?"

"People," Maria replied softly.

"You're going to smuggle me across the border?"

"No," Maria replied. "We're going to show you how to get yourself across. You're too hot. We can't risk ruining a network that has taken years to build." She nodded toward two wooden chairs and she and Falk sat down.

"You're going back to Austria with help from the Irgun," Heinz said, standing beside Maria. "Does the name Rosie Wimmer mean anything to you?"

"I met her once, briefly. As a matter of fact..." He started to say that Rosie was with that son of a bitch, Steele, but Maria interrupted him.

"She is one of our contacts in Vienna. That's all we can tell you. We wouldn't have been called in had you not decided to make a run for it at the church."

"What do you mean?" Falk asked.

"You ruined plan 'A' to get you back to Vienna when you escaped from Saint James. One of our men was planted in Colonel Zhilin's group. You would have been freed once you entered Austria."

"Who was your man?"

"His name is Horst."

Falk was dumbfounded. "That bastard tried to kill me…was responsible for the death of a young man…"

"Doctor," Heinz said gruffly, "every day there are operatives out there who die for the sake of this 'Underground Railroad' of ours. Horst couldn't do anything that would reveal himself to Zhilin's men. Let's not waste time debating moral issues."

Maria spoke softly. "You're very lucky we found you at the river. Our subterfuge threw them off, caused them to look in other directions."

"The shots… I sensed they were a diversion."

"A distraction by a well-trained guerrilla force."

She became very solemn and pointed admonishingly at Falk. "Listen very carefully to what we tell you. This time, if you decide to improvise, your life will be cut short."

Chapter 43

When Maria finished detailing plan "B," Falk wished he hadn't made a run for it in Brno. What he had to undertake seemed almost impossible.

"You're certain there's no other way?" he asked.

Maria shook her head. "Repeat what I told you. We must be sure you don't forget anything."

Falk inhaled deeply. "I'm to be taken from here and pointed in the direction of Austria. I'll be given a pair of skis and a wish for good luck in finding a rather vague contact who, hopefully, will be waiting for me among some equally nebulous trees just inside Austria. The only known obstacles I must avoid are mines, booby-traps, guard dogs and Czech military personnel."

He shrugged. "Other than that it's a piece of cake."

Heinz gave him a contemptuous look and Maria said coolly, "We didn't say it would be easy."

Falk reddened at the small sound of her voice. He regretted his flippancy. These people were risking their lives for him. Except for his brief stint with Jan, this was the first time since being in this godforsaken country that he felt genuine warmth from other human beings.

"Sorry," he said sincerely.

"You forgot to mention the package," Heinz told him dogmatically.

"Oh, yes, the package…to be given to my contact the minute we meet."

"Our man will be watching for you as you near the border." Maria's voice was gentle. "We must go."

Heinz turned down the lamp until its flame died. Falk watched the smoke curl to the ceiling. The smell of the extinguished wick triggered a memory of his childhood camping trips.

Maria removed the canvas from the windows and the gray winter dawn filtered in. She left the room and returned with a pair of skis. "If you couldn't ski, you would have no chance at all." She pushed them toward him. "They are waxed and ready to go."

Heinz eased the front door open and cold air rushed in, filling the cabin. Falk zipped up his jacket and looked at Maria.

"The package?"

"I'll give it to you when we get into the hills."

Together the trio moved slowly through the thick snow, Maria leading, alert as a doe. They traveled in silence for close to a mile. Then the sound of the river faded as they climbed higher toward the crest where the snow sprayed back in a mare's tail, tossed by the wind against the first light of the morning sky.

They halted at the top of a steep incline.

"Doctor," Heinz said, "be careful when you get down the mountain near the border. That is where the guard dogs will be— Hungarian Komondors that can tear a man apart in seconds."

Falk shuddered and slid his boots into the bindings.

"Open your jacket," Maria ordered. She slipped an oilskin pouch inside. "Remember, give that to your contact the *second* you meet him." She turned to Heinz and held out her hand to receive an automatic fitted with a suppressor.

"Take this." Falk tucked it into a side pocket of his jacket and pulled the zipper.

"Thanks," Falk muttered. He knew they wouldn't meet again.

Heinz patted his shoulder. "Hurry. There's no time to lose."

"Goodbye," Maria said and turned and went back down the slope.

Heinz pointed across the mountains. "It's a hard run. Don't stop if you can help it. See the small woods, there to the right..." Falk made out a small green patch in the distance. He nodded. "That's about five kilometers. Beyond is a meadow, deep in snow. Take care. There's a steep drop once you pass over it. Down the slope, past the bottom of the black scar that points like an arrow in the direction you must go."

"I see it."

"When you've passed the scar, you'll be very close to a military fortification and you'll enter a small forest. Go slowly, keep moving left. Do not enter the deep woods, understand?"

Falk nodded, trying to take in everything. Heinz continued. "It should take you eight to ten minutes to edge the woods then you'll come to a narrow stream. You can cross on foot. It should be knee deep this time of year.

"Bury the skis before you cross. The longer it takes them to learn how you got away, the better for all of us. Our man will see you long before you see him." Heinz paused and stuck out his hard, callused hand. Falk grasped it.

Without another word, Heinz was gone. Falk felt totally and utterly alone. He gripped the poles and slid his skis back and forth. He was going to get back no matter what it took. He would find Koski and Emma, too. Nobody was going to fuck with his life again.

He jammed the poles deep into the snow and leaned forward. The ground fell away beneath his skis and soon he was moving at top speed in a hiss of snow, the soft moan of the wind singing past his ears.

Shifting his weight, he made a *Stem Christiana* turn across the slope as a wintry sun edged over the tips of the jagged mountains. He viewed this as the beginning of the last leg of his journey home.

Chapter 44

A limo turned onto Dorotheegasse Street and stopped in front of the Dorotheum. Rod Eiker got out and looked up at the tall, imposing building housing the famous auction rooms.

Over the years, priceless objects had passed through these

rooms. How was it possible, he wondered, for Goering to hide the fruits of his pillage of Europe in or under the huge stone structure without them being discovered? Perhaps the next few days would tell.

"Wait for us," Harold Mifflin said and handed the driver a piece of paper. "Contact this number if we're not back in half an hour."

Glancing back along the street, Eiker saw a dark sedan in the shadows near the Capuchin Church and figured it was back up, if needed. He also noticed a small bistro in the same block with the name "Miljoo." The lights were on and faint sounds of music drifted toward them.

Mifflin caught his eye. "I have two men in there, too."

Together they walked to a side entrance of the Dorotheum that led through an arch into a small courtyard. A cold wind whirled in the corners, scuttling bits of paper over the cobblestones. Across the yard, a dim light shone over a doorway partially hidden behind a stack of packing cases. The door opened as they approached. Before entering, they were searched and their weapons taken.

"Hell," Mifflin protested, "this is like flying El Al!"

Dr. Yigael Herschel, a tall, gaunt man with a heavy gray beard and a slight paunch, stood at a wooden table, flipping pages of a large city map of Vienna. His expression was straight forward as if somewhere in his youth he had seen a profound truth and had worked all his life to illuminate it for others. He looked up as they entered and walked toward them.

"Sorry for the formalities. Routine. You understand. Your weapons will be returned to you when you leave." He stared at Eiker for a long moment then adjusted his glasses. "Mr. Eiker! This is a surprise. I never expected to see you again."

"Good to see you, General." They shook hands as Mifflin stood aside. "General Herschel, allow me to introduce Harold Mifflin."

Mifflin offered his hand but was silent.

"As you know, Harold," Eiker continued, "General Herschel's background includes being the former chief of the Israeli Defense Forces."

"Indeed I do. The general designed his plan of attack on years of research of the *Old Testament* campaigns and firsthand archaeological knowledge during the Arab-Israeli Six-Day War. He led his troops down long-forgotten routes to the east bank of the Suez Canal and victory."

"I'm flattered, Mr. Mifflin." Herschel turned to Eiker. "And this soldier of fortune has done freelance work for Israel on several occasions. Mr. Eiker contributed some very useful tactics to our military." Herschel waved them to chairs. "Now gentlemen, down to business." He seated himself.

"What began as a secret attempt to locate hidden war loot has turned out to be more than a treasure hunt between numerous hunters." He tugged thoughtfully at his beard before continuing. "Due to my many years as an archaeologist, my government has asked me to participate. We're bringing in Dr. Falk from the Czech Republic. He'll be here shortly. I also have been informed that Brasinov still believes Falk is the man who will get them to the loot first."

"Brasinov knows the Czechs kidnapped him," Mifflin said. "How do we explain his escape and return to Vienna? After all, mild-mannered archaeologists aren't the sort of people who can escape single-handedly from Czech Military Intelligence. And what did you mean when you said the war loot had turned out to be more than a treasure hunt?"

Herschel smiled thinly. "For now let me say there may be more information to be found other than Goering's gold. Brasinov will learn that the Czech Republic has taken an interest in the search, faked Falk's escape and that the American team from the Smithsonian has returned to Washington."

Mifflin grunted. "Disinformation."

"Perhaps," Herschel said. "I think you'll agree it is to our mutual advantage to pool our resources."

Mifflin was thoughtful for a moment as if to disagree but changed his mind. "You're suggesting a combined operation, Doctor?"

"Yes. We will do far better working together."

Eiker shifted in his chair. "Especially since so many others are getting into the game."

"Thank you, Eiker. I'd hoped you'd feel that way."

Mifflin squirmed and eased his bulk from his chair. "I'll go along with you, but it's against my better judgment."

Eiker understood Mifflin's natural reluctance. He, too, had instincts that whispered best when unencumbered by the views of others. Nevertheless, they had to go along with Herschel. Moreover, he was sure Mifflin was as impressed as he was by the fact that Herschel had found Falk.

Herschel offered his hand. "Thank you gentlemen. I'll see that you are notified as soon as Dr. Falk is in the city. We'll meet in a different location, of course."

Mifflin, who intrinsically mistrusted all who didn't have Cerberus as their base, smiled enigmatically and echoed, "Of course."

Less than five miles from the Dorotheum, on the third floor of Kanglerkrank-Zimmerstadt, in a nearly bare, dingy office, John Steele sat in a chair, leather straps pulled tight across his chest, arms and thighs. A guard was positioned on either side of the chair and Pasha sat on a stool facing him. The Arab's moist, clawlike hands held a leather shaving strop eighteen inches long and twice as wide as a normal shoelace.

Pasha, interrogator par excellence, ran his practiced eye over Steele. He analyzed his findings noting the stubborn chin—determined, even under sedation—and the hardened body that would take time to kill.

Pasha reached out and grasped Steele's jaw in a vise-tight grip. He waited until Steele's eyelids fluttered in pain then released him. Steele's legs jerked convulsively as the drug the men from the elevator administered still gripped him. Saliva ran from his mouth and dripped from his chin. A series of animalistic sounds began deep in his throat then died.

"My name…is…" he attempted but couldn't finish.

Pasha allowed an evil grin to split his parchment-like face, exposing ochre teeth to which threads of saliva clung. Leaning forward, he slowly slid the leather strop across Steele's face. "We want you to answer some questions…" Moving back, he raised his hand and brought the leather down across Steele's face with all the force he could muster.

Blood from the new wound oozed to the surface and streaked down Steele's cheek. "You are stupid, Steele. You were fooled by Switzer. You allowed Falk to escape and you were careless enough to be seen with a key. We want to know what the key is for and where you hid it."

Steele heard him, knew what he was saying but he couldn't

function or articulate his thoughts. The pain in his face was excruciating. The humming in his head made him dizzy. He groaned and fell forward, the straps across his chest preventing him from sinking to the floor.

"Steele," Pasha said, "I'll make you talk. I've never failed. Use your brain...or die slowly."

Steele made a weak attempt to reply.

Pasha rose from the stool. "I'll wait one hour. By then the effects of the injection will have worn off. Then you'll talk."

Chapter 45

The crack of a rifle shot echoed and re-echoed in the utter, snow blanketed silence of the mountains. Falk heard the crackle of the bullet forcing its way through the frosty air as it passed inches above his head. A sniper.

He crouched low, his buttocks touching the top of the skis as they flicked and vibrated over the snow. Leaning forward, he rounded his shoulders until he was a compact mass, except for the poles tucked under his armpits, extending beyond his body like the wings of a diving hawk. He didn't dare look back. Instead he kept his attention focused on the tips of the skis and the oncoming snowscape, every fiber of his body tuned to survival.

Shifting his weight, he flashed past a half-hidden tree stump. No tourist run. This was raw, wild country and somewhere there was a hidden sniper intent on seeing he never made it to the bottom of the mountain. He dug his shoulders low, letting his poles skim the surface of the powdery snow as he navigated a sudden rise. He left the ground, flew through the air for twenty feet and landed with a thump, feet together. Had he outrun the sniper...gone out of range?

The second shot gave the answer as it crackled past, sending a spurt of snow skyward less than a foot away. Falk risked a quick glance over his shoulder as he leaned away from the slope and made a fast turn across the side of the mountain.

He only saw the almost suffocating vista of powder reflecting the early morning light. Ahead was a thin grove of trees—scrubby, wind twisted pines he could use for cover. He jammed his poles deep and headed for them as if they were the finish line at the Olympics.

The sound of the skis changed to a warning rattle that indicated he was on a sheet of ice. He shifted and slid into a skidding arc toward the trees. A branch flashed overhead as he swept into the dark shadows where the snow was thicker with less crust.

He felt the skis sink deeper but they were moving well, waxed perfectly to respond to each maneuver. He made it through the scrub pines and again was on the open mountainside. The landmarks Heinz had mentioned were straight ahead. He slowed and ventured a glance back toward the trees.

Then he saw him. A blur against the dark trees, a flash, a momentary glimpse that came and went in a second. Whoever it was was dressed to kill. White camouflage suit that let him blend like a mountain goat into the snow.

Suddenly a piece of Falk's jacket parted from his shoulder. It puffed, split and he felt the tug as the bullet went through the cloth and beyond. The next shot would be the last—the fucker had his range.

Falk twisted, jabbed the poles deep and slammed down the steep slope in front of him. Then he gasped! The ground fell away beneath him... For a split second he thought he had jumped off a cliff to his death. The wind grabbed and rushed at his body as he descended through seemingly endless space. Sky and earth floated before his eyes as he balanced, arms outstretched, leaning forward into the long, long fall. He glimpsed the snowbound earth, distant trees at the border. He became suspended between fact and hope.

As he landed, snow spun in a flurry around him and he gasped for air. His skis rattled, one pole ripped from his left hand and his knuckles gouged into the snow. He'd made the greatest jump of his life and no one was there to see it.

Had he outrun the ghost in the white suit? In the distance—too far distant to be his sniper—the faint discharge of a rifle sounded. The sound spurred him to renewed action. He headed toward the row of trees Heinz had indicated. He saw the scar of rocks and followed around the edge as instructed. Alert, he eased forward slowly, skirting the trees.

The world around him was soft, silent and white until a snarling, slavering canine demon broke from the trees and lunged at him. He only had enough time to see a gaping mouth of teeth, an expanse of shaggy shoulders and eyes blazing with frenzy. The fucking thing never even barked. Instinctively, Falk leaned into a turn but the brute never reached him. It was stopped in mid jump by a thin steel cable attached to its collar. The dog jerked in the air and dropped, then feverishly renewed his mute act of frustration. Falk realized that the cable was attached to an overhead haul line running through the trees and allowed the beast restricted lateral movement.

In seconds two similar dogs joined in the snarling, leaping performance.

Falk stemmed to a stop near a clump of berry bushes a safe distance from the dogs. They hadn't barked either. Then it came to him. The animals had been debarked for security reasons so not to bark at rabbits or other small creatures in the woods.

He reasoned that the movement of the lines would alert the guards, wherever they were. Guard towers probably were spaced throughout the woods along the border, each sector with its own early-warning dog system.

Something made Falk look down. Thank God he stopped when he did. Ten more feet and he would have tripped and been impaled on a row of wooden spikes buried in the frozen earth and partly hidden from sight by bracken and snow.

It would only be a matter of time before the border guards, alerted by the haul line, zeroed in on him. He edged forward cautiously, keeping out of the deep woods as advised and skirting the dogs, who still strained at the line and snarled for a piece of him.

The snow drifted like sand in the wind from the top of the ridge he was heading for. Another rifle shot rang out in the distance and the sound bounced across the mountains. The thought that perhaps he wasn't the only one trying for an early morning crossing heartened him. Topping the rise, he saw the stream and beyond it the road... and Austria. He could see freedom.

Three more rifle shots echoed off the mountain. They were farther away now. He inched forward, every nerve taut as a bowstring, breathing in shallow gasps as if taking a real breath would give away his location.

The next dog that came at him from the side was merely a blur in his peripheral vision. He spun in time to see it leap, eyes blazing, jaw nearly unhinged with ferocity. In the split second allowed him, he also noticed the dog didn't have a restraining collar and was free to rip him apart.

Dropping to one knee, he turned the tip of his grounded ski pole up like a lance. The hot canine breath was on his face as he felt the point of the pole crunch into the furred body at the base of its throat. The jar of its weight shuddered down the pole as the dog impaled itself with a sickening shattering of bone and sinew.

For a second, Falk looked into the eyes that glared at a freakish angle. The lips pulled back, revealing long, yellowed fangs. Then the full weight slumped on the ski pole and hung like a piece of meat.

Falk began to tremble like a man with the shakes. He struggled desperately to remove the bloody shaft that finally came free. He turned from the smell of warm blood in time to see two more unrestrained dogs bounding toward him, chest deep in snow. He realized these, and their fallen comrade, were the Komondors Heinz had warned him about. There was little chance of fighting off two of them. He started forward but knew it was too late to outrun them.

Chapter 46

Falk suddenly remembered the automatic. It had a suppressor and wouldn't give away his position. For a long, terrifying second he fumbled with the zipper. Finally it came open. He grasped the gun and released the safety. His hand shook as he aimed at the nearest dog and squeezed the trigger. The gun jerked with a *phutt* sound and the dog stopped in its tracks. The shot was good—directly into the brain. Dead.

The second Komondor didn't react fast enough. Falk fired again, hitting the poor beast in the side—a "gut shot" that crippled it in a flurry of snow and blood. Stricken, it made an attempt to regain its feet but its hindquarters wouldn't function, and it slithered along, etching a deep, scarlet trail in the snow. He wasn't proud of what he had to do. Since he was a kid, he had owned dogs, cared for them and loved them. His throat constricted as he moved closer to the animal. He placed the automatic behind its ear and fired then turned quickly and jammed the weapon into his pocket. Despite the cold, sweat oozed from his palms and forehead.

He took off, never stopping until he reached the stream and leaned against a slender birch, panting. Releasing the bindings, he kicked free and, working fast, stuffed the skis and remaining pole under the snow near overhanging bracken at the base of a tree. Crouching at the edge of the stream, he knew he didn't have any cover until he reached the other side, about two hundred yards away.

He stepped into the icy water and was soon up to his knees. He removed the automatic and checked the clip. Three rounds remained.

A movement on the far bank caught his eye. A man in a hooded parka stepped from behind a snow-covered boulder with a rifle aimed directly at Falk.

Falk stood motionless. After everything he'd been through and this close to Austria, he was going to die now with his boots on. The knuckles on his hand that gripped the automatic were white.

"Doctor Falk?" the man asked.

"Yeah, I'm Falk."

The hooded man lowered his rifle. "You look like a scarecrow, Doctor."

Falk's shoulders sagged with relief. Maria said there would be someone waiting.

"Come across, hurry," the man said. "I thought the dogs had you for sure."

Falk ran, sloshing, slipping, stumbling the last few yards to shore, nearly falling into the arms of the squat, broad-shouldered man with slightly bowed legs. Slinging the rifle onto his shoulder by its leather strap, the man stuck out a callused hand and his eyes actually twinkled.

"Welcome back to Austria."

Falk shook his hand and looked back at the sweep of dark trees on the other side and behind them the mountain. It was as if it was all a dream, one he would reconstruct in sleepless nights the rest of his life.

"Come," his companion said. He pointed to a car a few meters ahead on the road and they started toward it. He removed a stopwatch from his pocket and snapped a switch on its side. "You made good time, Herr Doctor. The package Maria gave you, may I have it?"

Falk opened his jacket and handed it to him.

"Good." He pulled away the oilskin covering and exposed a small plastic box the size of a pager. Three buttons protruded from one side. One by one he depressed them. "Ach, now it's safe, deactivated."

Falk's puzzled expression was too obvious to ignore.

"Sorry, Doctor. In our business we have to be very careful. It was a time bomb set to go off one hour from the time it was given to you…would have been triggered by a radio signal had you been apprehended…"

"Hold it!" Falk interrupted, "You saying I was programmed to self-destruct?"

"Only if you were captured or I saw that you had no chance

of getting across. It would have been my job to..."

Falk didn't hear more. His adrenaline triggered a "fight or flight" reaction but he was through with "flight." He hauled off and landed a blow on the man's substantial jaw.

The poor fellow staggered back, more surprised than hurt. When he regained his balance, he studied Falk for a long minute, then burst into laughter. He rubbed his jaw and slapped Falk heartily on the back. "You know, I'd probably have done the same thing myself."

Falk walked toward the car. "One hour. How long did it take me?"

"Fifty-three minutes." He opened the passenger door for Falk. "Get in, relax."

Falk slumped into the seat; seven minutes. He had been that close to being splattered all over the mountain.

They covered a couple of miles in silence before the man said, "There's a flask of brandy in the glove compartment."

Falk opened the compartment. There was a flask of brandy there all right and it was sitting on top of the *Book of Hours.* Without taking his eyes from the book, Falk removed the brandy, unscrewed the top and took a long, slow, needed swallow then passed the container. His companion tipped it to the tune of three loud gulps and handed it back.

"It's okay. Take it out, leaf through it if you like. I understand you were interrupted the last time you were reading it."

Falk removed the missal and laid it on his lap. He turned to the driver. "What's your name?"

"Paul. Like St. Paul." He smiled as if pleased with the analogy. "We'll be in Vienna soon."

The heater was on high, the car warm. That and the brandy

made Falk feel drowsy yet he couldn't relax. He wondered about Koski and Emma. God, he hoped they were safe. One thing he knew. Treasure be dammed, his number one priority when he got to Vienna was to locate the women. Falk unlaced his boots, kicked them off and flipped open the missal. What was it about this book? What exactly was its secret?

Chapter 47

Nikolai Youmatoff almost made it down the eastern slope of Caribou Peak before the storm broke. The sky that had been gray and loaded for days seemed to descend in millions of white, minuscule pieces. What began looking like sieved sugar on the ground became eighteen inches of snow that covered southeastern Canada.

Youmatoff dug in. He could do little else. Two days later he dug out, having taken shelter in the entrance to a cave. From the depths of his haven came the sound of slow, unlabored, bearlike breathing and protracted snores. He guessed he was eight hours out of Ottawa.

He took stock of his rations. One steak remaining in a jar of rolled venison steaks that Ann had preserved near the end of the season last year. One can of yellow eyes, also homemade and preserved. A good size dab of sweet butter. Some ketchup and one can of condensed milk. This would be his last meal. He quickly corrected his thoughts—his last meal in the Canadian wilderness.

He moved on a quarter mile southeast, making sure he wasn't downwind of the bear cave, and settled in a sheltered area. He cubed the steak with his knife, putting half in the bottom of his pannikin. Atop that he layered half the can of beans and a generous dotting of ketchup then repeated all, ending with his last bit of butter. He gathered some twigs that had drifted into a pile under a large boulder and made a fire.

While his concoction heated, he sat on his bedroll and marveled at the majesty of the snowscape in the thin winter sun. "Lovely," Ann would have said. Tree shadows of elderberry hue lay like lace on the surface of the pristine snow. They were, Youmatoff thought, as real as the still, sharply etched outlines they represented and as lovely. He found himself crying. A tear fell on the weathered, hide-like skin of his hand. He would move on the minute he finished his meal. Once he reached the main highway, he'd hitch a ride to Ottawa then catch a bus to the Soviet Embassy. He wondered if he would have to tell them everything: about that night in the vault-like room, about Goering, the book he filched with the blueprint in it and the wax impression of the damnable key. Those things seemed important when he took them. Hadn't Goering himself announced that the book was "the secret to our future?" In the end they all had become meaningless to Youmatoff.

After that night he was captured and returned to prison. Only the compassion of Lego Moyzisch had saved him. The Allies sent him here to Canada, allowed him to begin a new life. For the first time in years, Youmatoff wondered about the key. When he originally arrived in Canada he had a key made from the impression—an odd key in a shape he never saw before. He wrapped the book in brown paper to protect its extraordinary cover and it served as his prayer book for years.

He did the right thing, he reasoned, sending those things to Lego. Perhaps the blueprint to the Dorotheum, which Goering had declared "Uberholt," would help Lego find the treasures and he'd become rich. Youmatoff didn't want to become rich. He simply wanted to go home to Russia to die in his own land.

When he ate the beans they were perfectly mealy and swam in a thick, brown, buttery juice that made the venison more tender. These were Youmatoff's last connection to Ann and, hungry as he was, he could barely down the last mouthful.

In his dream of dreams, Youmatoff was with Ann and they had nothing to do with material treasures. He realized that over the years he became immune to thoughts of his homeland that now atrophied. He broke camp and started out with renewed vigor.

Chapter 48

Ahead, Koski saw buildings aglow with neon lights. Herman stopped and slid down his window. A draft of icy air swirled into the car. Beside him, Koski made an attempt at nonchalance as if crossing through security after escaping from a castle was an everyday affair.

A woman glanced at Herman's papers. "Head of security saw your car, Herr Lansfeldt. He asked me to convey his good wishes for another profitable trip..." She scribbled her signature on the documents. "He looks forward to seeing you personally on your next visit."

Herman nodded amiably.

Koski was certain she heard Emma's heart pounding above her own as the woman said, "There's been a prison break in Brno. We don't know who or how many have escaped. We're getting details from Colonel Zhilin's office at this moment."

"Sounds like you'll have a busy night," Herman remarked as he rolled the window up. "See you in a few days. Good night."

Koski slowly lowered her head against Herman's shoulder and his foot eased up off the brake pedal.

The woman stood back from the car as the window slid shut.

Herman inched toward the gates beyond the neon glare and into the inky blackness of emancipation. Only when they were racing down the broad, smooth highway to Vienna did Koski sigh with relief.

"Herman, you were superb. I'm impressed."

"Ach, it was nothing." Obviously pleased with her compliment, he added, "I always see to it that the head man back there has the latest in home computers." She nodded her understanding. "When will we get to Vienna?"

"A little after daybreak. We can spend the entire day together my Liebchen."

Koski eased her head back against the headrest. She had succeeded in getting Emma and herself out of the Czech Republic. Certainly that was a victory. In the war she was fighting, however, the victory seemed more like an evacuation.

Churchill had said it after Dunkirk: "Wars are not won by evacuations." The real battle was the one waged wherever Falk fought for his freedom, one incxorably tied to her own. She knew she would go back willingly if it became necessary.

Rosie Wimmer found herself swept up and taken prisoner despite her knowledge of espionage. Such happenings do occur. John Steele, still partially drugged and strapped to a chair in the office where Pasha had taken him, had no answer to the incessant question.

"We have the key, Steele. Tell me what does it open? It's only a matter of time before we figure out its purpose and we don't have any time to waste." He brought the leather strop down across Steele's face again, lacerating the corner of his left eye.

"Don't be a fool, Steele."

"But it's true. I don't know."

"You go to the trouble to hide the key in a secret drawer, a key to... you don't know what?" He snorted. "You can do better than that. Evidently you don't put much faith in my powers of persuasion." Steele glared at him and Pasha leaned in closer. "Brasinov and I have broken many men."

"Yea, like Hitler's Gestapo once did."

"Then you understand my potential. Now tell me about the key and you'll go free."

"Bullshit."

Pasha slid the leather strap slowly across Steele's bloody, swollen lips and turned and spat out a stream of Farsi to the guards. Within minutes the door opened and Rosie Wimmer was dragged into the room.

Steele couldn't believe his eyes. Rosie was alive. She didn't die in the car explosion.

The guards pulled her across the room and stopped in front of him. She struggled between them but it was evident that she, too, had felt the sting of Pasha's strop.

"We have this Interpol agent," Pasha said, smiling malevolently. "We will kill her first then you if you refuse to give us the information we need."

Steele was silent, his eyes fixed on the floor. He remembered Emma telling him that Rosie was Irgun, using Interpol as her cover.

Rosie suddenly lashed out with her foot and caught Steele across the kneecap. "Tell him about the key, you asshole!" She turned to Pasha. "I don't know anything about a key. If you think I'd protect this bastard you have another thing coming."

"Get that fucking traitor out of here," Steele roared. "And don't expect me to save her life. As far as I'm concerned, you can kill her."

Pasha put his hand to his cheek dramatically. "How touching. A lover's quarrel."

Steele groaned and slumped against his bindings. His head hurt. He was bleeding and sick and his knee stung painfully. His resistance hit bottom. "Look, all I know about the key is that I was asked to hold it for safekeeping."

Pasha leaned closer. "By whom?"

"It was years ago. A man named Lego Moyzisch. He must be dead by now."

"Then he won't need the key. What did he say it was for?"

"I told you. I saw the man on the stairs in a hotel after we had met for a reunion in 1975. He handed me the key and asked me to keep it safe for him. When I asked what it was for, he shrugged and hurried away."

"That won't do, Steele."

"It's the absolute truth."

"He's a liar!" Rosie shrieked. She started to lunge forward but the guards restrained her. "He never did anything in his life unless there was something in it for him. That key must mean something and he knows what."

Pasha grinned. "My sentiments exactly." He motioned the guards to take Rosie from the room and she kicked and screamed all the way out.

Pasha turned back to Steele. "What makes you think this Moyzisch is dead?"

"Because he knew too much, probably knew what the key was for and wouldn't tell..." He stopped, aware that he had given the wrong answer.

"And where does that leave you in the order of things?"

Steele simply let his throbbing head fall forward and remained silent.

Chapter 49

In a noisy café on the Recht Wienzel, near the open-air vegetable market, Yakov of Czech Military Intelligence waited, seated at a marble topped table.

The café bustled with workers, stall owners and truck drivers. A thick haze of cigarette smoke filled the room and a constant chatter and clashing of dishes mixed with the smell of fried food and coffee. Yakov glanced at the wall clock. It was almost 6 a.m. He had arrived in Vienna three hours earlier, having thrown every available man into the search for Falk and Jan Michaelavitch. Sipping thick, sweet coffee, he looked around the room. Colonel Zhilin had told him that a local woman, an informant, would contact him.

When the door opened, a blast of cold air preceded a well-dressed woman. Yakov puffed a thin cigar and cursed inwardly. If she was the contact, it was a bad choice. Too many heads turned at the wild mass of red hair and the full, voluptuous figure.

Lisa Winkler scanned the room then went to Yakov's table and sat down. She lit a cigarette. "Yakov?"

He sipped his coffee. "If you prove to be other than the person I'm expecting, I'll consider this an attempt to blow my cover and I'll kill you."

Lisa took a long drag on her cigarette, reached across the table and dropped it into Yakov's coffee cup. "Look, I didn't ask for this job. Colonel Zhilin's people phoned me. I was assured I'd be well paid for my information."

"Were you followed?"

She was indignant at such a question. "I'm a professional, Yakov."

He was trying to make a point. "You took notes when you spoke to Zhilin's people?"

"I always take notes. It's my business."

"You wrote down this address?" Yakov's eyes narrowed.

Lisa nodded. "Date and time, nothing else."

"You have these notes?"

"Yes."

Yakov's fingers beckoned slowly. "Give them to me."

She thrust her hand into her raincoat pocket, pulled out a crumpled piece of paper and slid it across the table.

"Do you want me to eat it?"

Yakov took the note and placed it in the inside pocket of his coat. "First give me the information then we talk price."

"I know why the American, Falk, is in Vienna. I know he made a successful escape from your country. I can tell you where to find him, who his control is and what's going to happen when he finds what he's looking for." She relaxed against the back of the chair. "Does that interest you, Yakov?"

Yakov spoke softly "And the price for this information?"

Lisa's voice was almost a whisper. "One million American dollars in a Swiss bank of my choice."

"That will take time."

Lisa nodded. She eyed the room and wondered how many of Yakov's stooges were present.

Yakov's demeanor changed. "You also know where a man named Lego Moyzisch is hiding."

Lisa lowered her gaze and tapped on the table. "I don't understand…"

"Of course you do. You're a busybody who knows who, what, why, when and where about everybody who's anyone in Europe. You will leave this table, go to your car and drive to the place where Moyzisch is hiding. My men will follow. Once you're there, I'll be informed and will meet you. Perhaps with Moyzisch thrown in we'll have a deal." Lisa remained tight-lipped and silent.

"Go," he said levelly. "Do as I told you."

She scraped back her chair and left without looking back, cursing inwardly that she could do nothing to warn her Interpol cover. Walking to her car, she stopped to retrieve her key remote from her purse.

Kutna, disguised as a shabby merchant, came down the street pushing a handcart piled high with sacks of potatoes. He glanced at rooftops on his right and felt assured knowing that three of his best men were stationed there.

He had gone less than three feet when the roar of a high-powered engine shattered the quiet of the frosty morning and a black BMW careened down the narrow street.

Lisa was about to open her car door. She looked back as Kutna raised an arm to wave a warning. The car swerved from side to side across the narrow cobbled street, its rear wheels sliding in patches of snow.

Kutna dropped to the sidewalk. The cart tipped over and the sacks split, sending potatoes spilling into the street, across the cobblestones and under the wheels of the speeding automobile.

Three shots, like firecrackers, sounded and Lisa slumped, half turned against the side of her car, and slid to the ground. She was dead before hitting the street. The BMW screeched around a corner and was gone. The assassination took less than six seconds.

Kutna slowly beat his fist against the sidewalk in anguish and frustration. Yakov stood in the doorway of the café, his mouth agape, surrounded by shocked market workers. He was back to square one.

Chapter 50

When Eiker and Mifflin walked into Stewart's office in Grinzing, Stewart's first words were, "One of Interpol's best informants was killed on the streets this morning right under their protective cover."

Mifflin lowered his weight into a large leather armchair. "Who was it?"

"Lisa Winkler."

Eiker, who was in the process of sitting down, fell into the chair. "Jesus! How did it happen?"

"Drive-by early this morning in the central market area."

Mifflin frowned. "Do we know what she was doing there?"

"She had a meeting with a Czech named Yakov in a café on the Rechte Wienzel."

"Do we have any idea who the shooter was?" Eiker demanded.

Stewart answered, "Nothing yet."

"Who in the hell was in charge of the Interpol cover?" Stewart shook his head.

"Unbelievably, Kutna himself."

Eiker exploded. "What went wrong for Christ's sake?"

Stewart shrugged and Mifflin asked, "Can you get me Kutna?"

Stewart picked up the phone. "I need Interpol." He replaced the phone and asked, "How about a drink? I know your poison, Mifflin. What about you, Eiker?"

"Scotch, no ice."

In his office at Interpol, Kutna switched the phone to his right ear, hunched his shoulder to hold it in place and rummaged through his desk for a cigarette and growled.

"Okay, Mifflin, what now?"

"Kutna, you and your people let a damned good contact get blown away today. What the hell happened?"

Kutna sat stiff-backed in his chair, eyes half closed, lips compressed. He took a deep breath and let it out slowly. "Don't try that hard-nosed crap with me, Mifflin. I'm not the new kid on the block. When it comes to screw-ups, I have enough on you to end your career and I'd get a reward for doing it, maybe the Nobel Peace Prize for ridding the world of an asshole."

Mifflin's voice grated. "Right now I need some answers."

Kutna was having a nicotine fit. He searched further through his desk drawers, flinging paper clips, rubber bands, crumpled cigarette packs, scraps of paper with phone numbers of people who were no doubt dead.

Finally he found a battered stub and scratched a match across the top of the desk. One drag on the butt and he felt better, but he didn't allow it to favorably distort his disposition.

"Listen, Mifflin, and listen good. Lisa Winkler was a friend. I want her killers as much… much more than you do. Let me know if you have a way to apprehend those responsible." He slammed down the phone and sucked the last centimeter from the cigarette. His hand shook as he ground out the stub in the ashtray.

He picked up the phone again and dialed Rosie Wimmer. He hung up after nine rings.

Chapter 51

An early morning mist hung low over the Danube as a barge trailing smoke from its battered tin chimney churned its way upstream and Herman's car crossed the Reich Brucke Bridge into Vienna.

Koski shifted her gaze from the river to Emma, who was half asleep in the back seat, her head propped against the side window. Herman asked hopefully, "Breakfast at your place?"

Koski twisted the rearview mirror and checked her makeup saying, "Coffee first?"

Koski knew she couldn't stall him much longer. "Schatzie," Emma replied sleepily, "A cup of coffee before we get to the apartment would save time."

He sighed. "It's too early for Demel's."

"I know a place in the Ringstrasser. Take the third turn on the left," Emma said quickly.

Indeed it seemed Herman really needed coffee. As they sat in the café he gulped down his first cup and signaled for another. Koski was antsy, afraid her rising anxiety would somehow manifest.

She had checked the restroom when they arrived. There wasn't a rear exit. Nevertheless, because she believed she would manage to devise a plan to break away from the two men, she made a quick phone call outside the restroom.

"Who'd you call?" Emma asked.

"Later," Koski whispered. Back at the table she wondered at her own audacity. She had made the call and now she must think of something. Koski glanced at Herman as he drained his cup and clunked it down on the table.

"Ready?" He rubbed his stout hands together.

Before Koski could answer, she heard a loud, querulous voice behind her and turned. At the next table, a man with dark hair and olive skin berated the waiter for dousing him with coffee.

"But, sir," the waiter protested, "it was you who..."

The customer stood and continued dabbing his wet slacks with a napkin. "Imbecile! Waiter indeed, perhaps you're better suited to be a Tyrolese sheepherder."

Koski watched a thin white line rim the waiter's mouth as he compressed his lips. He was a big man with an odd mixture of refinement and simplicity, one whose appearance evoked images of the Alpine Region the other had named. Now he thrust his hands on his hips, arms akimbo, enraged at what he obviously considered an insulting remark.

"I am no peasant," he said acrimoniously. "Furthermore..."

A voice at Koski's side interrupted. "My dear departed mother and father, may they rest in peace, were born in the South Tyrol, the Upper Leach River Valley to be exact." It was Marny, standing tall. His sharp Teutonic jaw was thrust forward, his mouth set determinedly. He walked over to the table and addressed the soaked customer. "And just what is wrong with being a Tyrolese shepherd?"

Koski thought she caught a glance in her direction and a nearly imperceptible flash of bemusement in the customer's eyes. If it in fact had been there, it was quickly gone. His face darkened and he let his napkin slide to the floor.

"Let's see," he said, "if the son of a peasant who sticks it to sheep can fight like a man." He took a step toward Marny and squared off. "Or is he chicken-livered?"

Emma gasped and Koski felt Herman rise beside her. However she regarded him personally, she figured Marny was neither a coward nor a pervert.

She was right. When Marny's first blow fell like a sledgehammer Herman joined in the fray. She decided not to wait around for the count. She grabbed Emma's hand and raced out the door.

As they reached the curb Emma asked breathlessly, "Where are we going?"

Koski nodded down the street. In the distance, a taxi turned the corner and headed toward them. "You asked me who I called."

"Yes."

Koski waved and the taxi stopped a few feet from them. As they hopped in, Koski gave an address to the driver and told Emma, "A cab of course."

As the taxi pulled away, Koski smiled at the nerve of that customer who had called Marny a degenerate. Months later she would reason he was an Interpol agent who deliberately started the fiasco then went directly to a phone and reported Koski and Emma's whereabouts. For now she was satisfied with the happenstance of colossal coincidence.

"Where are we going?" Emma asked.

"To the British Embassy."

"That's what I thought you told the driver, but why?"

"Best place for you."

"And if I refuse?"

"What do you mean?"

"Koski, I've come this far. I'm in this to the end."

Koski gave her a stern, maternal look. "Listen to me. I admire your spirit, but it's simply not a good idea."

"And I suppose quitting is?"

"I'm not talking about quitting. I'm talking about using our heads. At least if you're at the Embassy you'll be safe and I'll know where you are."

"But we make such a good team."

"Yes, but now it's time to go in."

Emma looked wide-eyed. "What about Joe?"

"Now that I'm back in Vienna I can do a lot to help him."

The cab came to a halt in front of the Embassy. Emma was about to swing her long shapely legs out of the car when she said, "I don't feel comfortable doing this. What am I supposed to do here? Sit and twiddle my thumbs?" She swung her legs out. "Forget it. I'll go find him on my own."

Chapter 52

Koski sighed and pulled Emma back inside the cab. "Tell the driver to circle the block once." As soon as Emma complied, Koski said, "I've something to tell you." Her voice was barely audible.

"I'm not a doctor of archaeology. Neither is Joe. We're FBI working with American security." She had decided to tell enough truth to satisfy Emma but keep Cerberus in the loop of secrecy. "So you see why I have to continue on my own now."

"No, I don't."

"I'm a federal agent, Emma!" She tried to whisper with emphasis. "I have a job, an official assignment to do. You can't be a part of that anymore. It was only by accident that you've been involved at all."

Emma's defiant expression turned melancholy and she stared ahead. "I'm going back to England."

Koski's head rolled slightly from side to side and her green eyes flickered skyward. "What does that mean?"

"I've never really belonged in Austria. I have no family, few friends...." She turned full face to Koski with tears in her eyes. "I thought we were friends as well as partners in this."

Koski fell silent, glancing down at her hands in her lap.

Emma looked ahead again. This time she held her chin slightly higher. "I also don't think I was cut out for the antiques business. It's too dull. I'm going into a different line of work, something more exciting. Maybe I'll go into P.I. work...some field I'm good at, like operating with certain *savoir-faire* in dangerous situations; knowing how to make connections to get another agent without a passport into the Czech Republic; using my womanly wiles to entice two strangers to drive that second agent back to Austria, thus saving that so-called friend's life...like..."

"Okay, okay!" Koski interrupted. The last thing she wanted was Emma running around town causing more trouble playing amateur detective.

Emma smiled and finished her previous sentence. "Like how to tell the driver to go to my place so we can pool our resources and regroup."

"Why didn't you tell me sooner?" Emma asked as she moved around her small kitchen, splashing water into a kettle for tea.

"I wouldn't have told you now if you hadn't threatened to take off and look for Falk on your own."

Emma sat down while she waited for the water to boil. Koski fell deep in thought.

"Emma, how much did your Aunt Louise tell you about this reunion group that met at the Romischer-Kaiser Hotel?"

"She told the story many times. It was almost like a bedtime story for me." Emma went to a small desk and removed a photo album. "Aunt Louise treasured this."

She laid a battered leather album on the table and opened the pages, revealing black and white photos, some going sepia and frayed around the edges. She pointed to a group picture. "I have an enlargement of this one downstairs in a silver frame. These are some of the original resistance members."

Emma pointed out who was who. Koski looked up when she mentioned the name Lego Moyzisch.

"That's the name Horidecki mentioned when we were in Spilberg. They have his wife under protection as he called it."

The kettle shrilled its whistle and Emma filled the cups.

"Horidecki also said Lego had gone missing," Koski claimed. "Could he be in Vienna?"

"Anything is possible."

"Finding him might be the best way to either finish or halt this ridiculous hunt for treasure in its tracks." She stopped and sipped the strong, hot tea. "Think hard, Emma. Did your aunt ever tell you the group had any alternative meeting place? Somewhere other than the usual conference rooms at the Romischer-Kaiser?"

Emma was deeply pensive and then brightened. "Now that you mention it. I remember Lego said if any problem arose in the future, they should meet at a particular room at the Romischer-Kaiser, the room Horst Ekel, the owner, had used during the war to conceal refugees from the Germans. They called it simply 'the room on eleven.' I was a child when she told me. It made me think of Anne Frank."

"To your knowledge did any of the reunioners ever have occasion to use the room?"

Emma frowned. "Not that I know of, but I'm sure none would forget Lego's mention of it."

Koski immediately said, "Emma, I need you to stay here while I make a call from a public phone. Yours may be bugged."

"I have a disposable cell phone in my bedroom," Emma

replied as she sprang from her chair. "I'll get it."

Koski sipped her tea and tried to recall the phone number Stewart gave Falk and her in the car at their second briefing. That meeting seemed so long ago.

She remembered part of the number but the last four digits... association usually worked...what had she... Ah, yes, she remembered now. Christmas, December 25. The last four digits were 1225.

Waiting for Emma to bring the phone, she flipped open the photo album and looked again at the figures in the picture. She was sure her hunch about Lego was right. People in old photographs only *seemed* to reside mutely in dust-collecting albums. In fact, they sent their souls through time and space and spoke to you.

Chapter 53

The room on the eleventh floor of the Romischer-Kaiser was small and ugly. With the exception of one chair—the one in which Lego Moyzisch sat—dustsheets covered what little furniture there was. Eerie silence and an air of dampness prevailed.

Lego was slumped in the overstuffed armchair, reading by the light of a low-wattage bulb from a small table lamp. Suddenly, like an animal that has caught the scent of the enemy, he tensed. His head tilted slightly as he listened then, hearing nothing, he returned to his book. He was tired and a white, three-day stubble covered his chin. His red-rimmed eyes tried to focus and comprehend the print.

He closed the book and pushed himself stiffly from the chair, rubbing his lower back with both hands that felt thick and alien to him. He slowly kneaded sluggish circulation through his body. Shuffling to the window, he saw the fringe of a new day brighten the edge of thick, brown velvet drapes laden with mustiness.

He recalled the words he had uttered at the reunion. "In time of need for a safe haven, remember the room on eleven. It has been a refuge for many in the past."

Lego shivered slightly, tugging a woolen cardigan closer to his body. He reached out and pulled the drapes aside, allowing thin winter sun to spill into the room. He turned. What was that sound?

Without taking his eyes from the door, he backed to the chair, reached under the cushions, extracted an old Walther P38 automatic and snapped off the safety. Now the only sound was his labored breathing.

Spinning, he faced the window as if expecting to see it shatter and admit an executioner. There was only sunlight, highlighting the crazed dance of dust motes on their stage between the window and worn carpet.

He lowered the automatic, his hand shaking. "You're too jumpy," he told himself and held his wrist until the shakes subsided, then reset the safety catch.

Nothing was as it used to be. He was old and hated the fact he had lived to discover his own fears and stumbling weaknesses. Returning to the chair, he positioned it so he could see both window and door. The gun lay in his lap. He ran his tongue across his dry lips. Dr. Benson, Louise and Steele had taken a vote and decided to hear his awful secret. Now they could all be gone, taken by the evil aftermath of a war they had survived.

He vowed he would wait here as long as there was a possibility that any of the assembly was still alive and would come. This was where they had sworn to return if their life as a group was endangered many years ago.

If any were left would they remember? He looked around the

decaying room. The few tins of food were almost gone. He managed to postpone starvation by warming food on the old steam radiators he had coaxed into operation. There was no place to go. His wife would remain in protective custody in Brno until his government tracked him down and got what they wanted from him...or until he died.

He studied the gun, running his hand over the cold steel. One more day, he decided. Then he would end his waiting, perhaps place the dustsheet over both himself and the chair, leaving everything as he found it. Almost.

Chapter 54

Paul was silent as he drove Falk toward Vienna. Falk took this time to go through the *Book of Hours* resting on his knees. Page by page, he devoured every detail, scrutinized the colorful scrollwork, every loop and whorl of the magnificently formed letters. One particular picture caught his eye. It was a surreal scene of two greyhounds romping outdoors in a tiled courtyard of black and white diamond design. The spectacle was illuminated by a ray of sunlight slicing through a brilliant blue sky full of angels with raised trumpets.

The sunbeam held a dove in its saffron glow then diffused onto a fountain bordered by more angels. The light seemed to flow across the picture, touching birds, stars, jewels, silver leaves, blue feathers and small naked cherubs. One of them reached for a large Monarch butterfly. Another held a three-stringed whip on its shoulder and a sly smile played across its face.

In one corner of the picture, a cowled figure bent forward as if in prayer, head resting against the wall of the fountain. Scrolls in Latin and what looked like Arabic surrounded him. The picture was so absorbing that Falk had to force his eyes from it when the car slowed and Paul said, "Almost there."

Falk closed the book and leaned slightly to see his image in the review mirror. *My God!* he thought. A scrubby beard covered his chin and his face had cuts and scrapes. He hadn't brushed his teeth in he couldn't remember how long.

Paul swung the car into an alley behind the Kartendome and stopped. The back door of the restaurant opened and a man dressed in chef whites peered out and beckoned to them.

"Bring the book," Paul said.

As they walked to the door, two men came down the alley, got in the car and drove away. Inside, the smell of food made Falk realize how hungry he was. Fritz Lubbe bustled toward them.

"Come," Fritz pumped Paul's hand. "You two must eat."

Five minutes later Falk was scraping the bottom of the soup dish with his last slice of pumpernickel. Fritz smiled in satisfaction as if he, too, had finished the meal. "Feel better, Herr Falk?"

"Yes, thank you."

"I have good news for you. The two women are back in Vienna, your associate and the English lady."

"Where are they?"

"I'm waiting for the latest report but they are safe. You must feel better, I'm sure."

"Like a new man."

"Good." He checked his watch. "There's a taxi outside. You'll be taken to a meeting with Dr. Herschel."

"Dr. Herschel?"

Fritz, it seemed, suddenly couldn't hear. He extended his hand. "Good luck, Herr Falk. Paul will go with you." Falk thought he said it almost like he was saying, "Go with God." Fritz turned and hurried away.

Paul picked up the book as Falk said, "I have to go to the bathroom." Falk needed time out. He was back in Vienna and so were Koski and Emma. He was determined to find them before he met with anyone.

Paul smiled. "Ja, sure, down the passage, last door on the left. I'll see you outside." Paul hurried from the kitchen to the waiting taxi.

As Falk jumped onto a moving streetcar a block from the restaurant, he envisioned Paul still waiting in the cab. Paul would find the restroom window wide open when he went to find out why Falk was taking so long.

Chapter 55

Stewart answered the phone on the second ring. "Koski, where are you?"

"Here in Vienna. We went directly to Emma's antique shop. Is there any word on Joe?"

"He's back in Vienna but I don't know exactly where yet." In the same breath he said, "Listen, Koski. I want you and Emma out of there. Are you using the phone at the shop?"

"No, a cell phone." Koski turned and looked at Emma as she continued. "I think I know where I can find Lego Moyzisch. I'm going to the Romischer-Kaiser, to a roo…"

"Listen to me. I don't want you going off alone. Do you understand? You'll need backup."

"I can handle it."

"I forbid it, Koski. That's an order. You and Emma take a cab to the Hotel Ananas, a place widely used by tourists. It's located near the city center, plenty of crowds to mingle with. There's a possibility you'll be followed and you'll have a better chance of losing a tail in a crowded area.

"Split up as soon as you leave the cab. Take one of the tour buses to the Belvedere Palace. They run every fifteen minutes. I'll have a blue four-door Volvo waiting for Emma outside the Ananas. The keys will be in it. She knows the city and can meet you at the palace. She'll be in the car park next to the terrace that faces the city."

He paused. "Eiker will be somewhere on the terrace. I'll contact him to watch out for you. He's up there following a lead. Don't show any signs of recognition when you see him. Just do as he says. Any questions?"

Koski had plenty of questions but they would have to keep.

A cold wind fluttered around the great stone building and the sky seemed undecided whether to rain or snow. Eiker stamped his feet on the stone terrace of the Belvedere Palace and looked at the great sweep of gardens and the city in the distance.

The view would be spectacular in summer. The message from Stewart made it clear he was responsible for the safety of the women. According to Stewart, Koski held an important clue, one that could possibly lead to the location of the missing loot.

Two tour buses turned into the parking lot alongside the building. Eiker watched as they disgorged their passengers in the graveled area. Some gaped excitedly, readying cameras. Others moved slowly as if bored to be at yet another pile of stone to be photographed and preserved in albums that would be consigned to gather dust. Some tourists huddled against the side of the bus and lit up, their little clouds of blue smoke shredded by the stiff north wind.

Koski was the last passenger off the bus. She ambled slowly, seemingly oblivious to the tall good looking Englishman. She thought she did an outstanding job of craning her neck as if she had never seen a palace before. She turned in a circle now and then, ostensibly to miss nothing. She stopped a few feet from Eiker, her back to him.

"You look well," he said softly, aiming his long distance lens toward the distant twin spires of the Votive Church.

Koski snapped a shot of one of the many large flowerpots bordering the terrace. "Last time I saw you, you were in Nevada hightailing it in a helicopter. Falk and I almost nailed your ass."

"Ah, yes," he mumbled. "I remember it well."

"I've got a tail on the bus." Her lips scarcely moved.

He swung his camera toward the palace. "Who?"

"See the woman in the wheelchair?"

"Yes."

"She's a spotter, not sure who the real tail is." Koski watched Eiker position himself between the handicapped woman and the palace's imposing facade. The shot would include Koski.

She wanted to be sure of one thing. "Stewart says Joe made it back?"

"He did, under Mossad protection. He's safe."

She felt a wave of relief pass over her and suddenly felt like the Energizer Bunny.

"Attention bus number twenty-nine," the guide from Koski's bus called out through a megaphone. "We're leaving for a lunch stop in five minutes then on to Schoenbrunn Palace."

"Where's Emma Lewis?" Eiker asked.

Koski snapped another picture. "She's in a blue four-door Volvo near the end of the parking lot. See it?"

Eiker pointed his camera in another direction. "Got it." He

lowered his camera and looked around indifferently. "Lose the group when you get to the lunch stop. I'll be with Emma, watching for you."

When Koski boarded, Eiker was taking pictures at the far end of the terrace but he didn't miss a green BMW that took off after the bus. Casually, he crossed the terrace to the Volvo and got in.

"Miss Emma Lewis, I presume?"

Emma smiled. "Does that make you Dr. Livingstone?"

Eiker liked her right off. He grinned. "Rod Eiker."

She turned on the ignition and moved out of the parking lot.

Chapter 56

"Stay a few car lengths behind the green BMW," Eiker said. He saw the question in her eyes and liked that she didn't ask it; just followed orders.

As she navigated around a red and white, double linked streetcar, she gave Eiker a quick glance. "How did you get to Belvedere? I didn't see a car."

Maybe he spoke too soon. He believed most women talked too much. "I arrived by tram."

"Amazing," Emma said.

"Not really. I often use a tram, gets one around quite nicely in Vienna."

"No, I mean it's amazing how people communicate. Koski made one phone call and suddenly everything swung into well-oiled action."

"Not always well-oiled, I'm afraid." He nodded toward the road ahead as a car passed the BMW and suddenly they were closer. "Maintain at least two car lengths behind the Beamer," Eiker said and Emma slowed slightly. "Do you know the lunch stop the bus will make?" he asked.

"Koski said it was called Mannerheim's and that they served fine food."

"In Vienna they serve nothing else." Eiker pointed. "There's Mannerheim's just ahead on the right." He knew Koski had no idea about the BMW. He would have to cover her.

"When we get to Mannerheim's, pull over and drop me off. Then stay in the car, facing the direction from which we came and watch for Koski. Don't worry about me and don't look back. Understand?"

"Yes."

"Good."

When Emma started to pull over, Eiker was out before the vehicle actually stopped. He moved between two parked cars and casually strolled along the sidewalk, tourist fashion.

He saw Emma drive into the parking lot and turn the car around as instructed. Koski's bus was unloading. The woman in the wheelchair was the first off, helped by willing hands.

Eiker moved near a parked VW and fiddled with his camera. Inside the green BMW parked across from the bus, he spied a swarthy, dark-haired man in the driver's seat. He also saw the man slide the window down. A gun barrel appeared and rested atop the glass.

Letting his camera hang from his neck, Eiker slowly walked to the rear of the BMW. Instinctively aware that the spotter had somehow alerted the driver, he stepped aside, crouched, turned and dropped to the sidewalk in one quick continuous movement. There was no sound of gunfire but the windshield of the VW beside him shattered in a sparkle of glass shards.

Eiker's first shot killed the BMW driver. Springing to his feet, he saw Koski make it to Emma's car. He rested his arms on the roof of a red Fiat next to him and squeezed off two shots that lifted the wheelchair occupant out of the chair in a whirl of limbs and skirts.

As he dashed to the moving car, Eiker caught a glimpse of the "lady's" lower body, clad in trousers, "her" wig three feet away from the disintegrated head.

Eiker exhaled and sank heavily into the seat, sweat standing out on his forehead. "Glad you mentioned the spotter, Koski. Otherwise we'd both be history."

Koski was about to tell Emma to step on it when the car jolted as Emma pressed the pedal to the metal.

Koski turned to Eiker. "How did you know the person in the wheelchair was a man?"

"I didn't." He tapped Emma's shoulder lightly. "Nice job. I'll take over from here. Pull over."

Emma joined Koski in the back seat as Eiker drove the Volvo into traffic. He pulled to the side of the road as two police cars and an ambulance rushed past them.

"As I understand it," Eiker said, "we're headed for the Romischer-Kaiser, right?" He glanced back but saw no one following.

"Right," Koski said. "I've a hunch we'll find Lego there."

"It could be staked out."

"I know," she replied calmly. "Any ideas?"

"Maybe if you and I were to go in together and they were expecting one woman or two women…we could throw them off."

Koski obviously liked the idea but that would leave Emma alone.

"Emma," Koski said, prepared for Emma's adverse reaction,

"you'll drive to the British Embassy and stay there until we contact you, okay?"

When Emma silently nodded her assent, Koski admonished herself. She should have expected this mature reaction, should have realized that the retiring woman in the antique shop had grown into a perceptive operative of whom Quantico would have been proud. She sighed.

"Good. We'll drive once around the block and be sure it's clear. Then leave Eiker and me about two blocks from the hotel. We'll get a cab from there and you head back to the Embassy."

Emma nodded. "Well-oiled action." She shrugged at Koski's puzzled look.

"It looks clear," Eiker said. He and Koski exited the car and Emma got behind the wheel. He flagged down a cab two blocks from the hotel as Emma sped off.

Arm in arm, Koski and Eiker crossed the hotel lobby and went directly to the birdcage elevator. To an observer, they might have looked like a couple enjoying a lovers' tryst. Eiker slid open the concertina doors and Koski pressed eleven. "According to Emma, the eleventh floor is only used for storage now," she whispered.

Overhead, through the open lattice ironwork, Koski saw thick, black, greasy cables slide silently up and over the wheels, lifting them closer to another link in the entangled chain of events that began in the shadows of a world war.

"Koski, what if he's not here?"

The elevator lurched to a stop and they stepped into a dusty, unkempt hallway. As the lift jerked and descended out of sight, Koski whispered, "He's got to be here."

Chapter 57

Pasha, like a vile misrepresentation of a child, sat behind a desk too large for his needs in the third floor room of the Kanglerkrank-Zimmerstadt. He stared thoughtfully into space. If, as Steele said, Lego Moyzisch was dead, there was little Pasha could do to learn the significance of the key. Yet he was certain it held a clue to the puzzle he must solve.

"Come," he said to a knock at the door.

A tall, well-built man entered. He was light on his feet and had a disarming smile. Pasha had requested, and been given, one of the best hired killers in Slovakia. His name was Kraal.

Pasha waved him to a seat. "Report."

"When I shot the woman outside the café, I saw Kutna on the sidewalk dressed as a market worker."

"So?" Pasha hissed.

"I also saw Yakov."

Pasha tapped his knuckles methodically on the top of the desk. "Where is Dr. Falk?"

"The Israelis have him."

"Where are the British soldier of fortune and Dr. Koski?"

"He's very clever. He made contact with Doctor Falk's associate and they nearly eluded us. We trailed them to the Romischer-Kaiser Hotel. I have men waiting for them when they leave."

Falk rode the tram five blocks and jumped off at the intersection of Schubertring and Johannesgasse near the Stadt Park without paying. He had no money, no ID, nothing since they had stripped him clean in Spilberg. He had to get in touch with Stewart.

Glancing around, he realized he was outside a florist shop and a middle-aged woman was busy arranging flowers inside. Without hesitation, Falk entered the shop.

"Excuse me. Do you speak English?"

The woman looked up and smiled. "Yes."

"I wonder if you can help me. I need to make a very important phone call and I don't have any money. Would it be possible to use your phone? It's a local call. I'll have someone pick me up then I can pay you."

The woman blatantly assessed him and he was self-consciously aware of what she saw. Commercial fishermen, even after showers, smell of tuna. Teachers, once they have retired, still retain the smell of chalk.

For most of his adult life, Falk considered himself a rather clean-cut, close-shaven, shoes-shined Norman Rockwell type of guy. At this moment, however, he was unshaven, disheveled, unvarnished and unclean. Did the scent of who he truly was linger discernibly around him?

The woman produced a cell phone from her pocket and smiled. "Of course."

Falk decided that one day he would ponder further on the phenomenon he had just experienced. It was like the woman in the apartment building in Brno who saved his life by advising him not to go to the rooftop.

Falk thanked her and quickly tapped the numbers to Stewart's office. He knew it was a safe number, impossible to bug. He gave his location and Stewart told him to wait in the shop entrance. Mifflin would be right along.

In less than five minutes the limo pulled up outside and Mifflin waved from the back seat. Falk crossed the sidewalk and yanked the door open. "Give me some money."

Mifflin looked stunned. He reached in his pocket. "How

much?"

"Enough for a dozen hot-house roses."

Mifflin winced and peeled off several bills. "Damned expensive this time of year…"

Falk took the money, ran back into the store and pointed to a pail full of yellow roses that resembled spring sunshine. "Let me have a dozen."

The woman smiled. If she was surprised that an American who couldn't afford a phone call a few minutes ago now had a limo at his disposal and wanted to buy a dozen roses, she didn't show it. Falk laid the bills on the counter. "Will this cover the flowers and the phone call?"

"Yes, sir." She cradled the flowers in green tissue and a box. "Indeed it will."

Falk scooped up the box of long stems. "Thanks," he said and was out the door.

Mifflin shook his head as Falk slipped into the car beside him. "You can explain the roses to Stewart on *your* expense account."

Falk started to bring Mifflin up-to-date, including his fast departure from the café but Mifflin cut him off. "Save the details for Stewart's debriefing. Your sudden departure from the café has the Mossad highly pissed off. We've some fence mending to do. We need help from Interpol, some unit of security that knows the city inside out, despite the fact that the last person I want to ask for help is Kutna."

Stewart was sitting behind his desk when Falk and Mifflin entered. "Welcome back, Joe. You did well to escape alive."

"Tell me about it. Can you have someone put these in water?" Falk slumped into the nearest chair. "Leave them on the table.

They'll be taken care of."

Stewart turned to Mifflin. "Kutna's been trying to reach you. Call him from the other room. I want to talk with Falk."

As soon as Mifflin was gone, Stewart's voice grated. "What in the hell were you thinking when you gave the Israelis the slip?"

Stewart's eyes were hard. "They're on *our* side, Joe. They are the ones who got your ass out of the Czech Republic. You're supposed to be a doctor of archaeology, not 007."

"Sorry, Tom." He shrugged. "I decided to check in with you instead."

"Okay, well, I'll square it with them somehow but you must stay with them from here on out. The two real Smithsonian experts have been sent back to the States; too dangerous for them to be involved now."

Falk nodded. "Where's Koski?"

"She's with Eiker. They're checking out a lead on Lego Moyzisch."

Falk bristled. "Did they have to go together?"

"Yes. You weren't around," he said pointedly.

"Well, I'm back."

"I've arranged for you to meet with an Israeli by the name of Herschel. He and Eiker know each other. Seems Eiker worked freelance for him on a couple of jobs in Israel. Falk nodded. "Now," Stewart went on, "let's get down to details. Everything— from the moment you were abducted to the moment you got back."

"This is official business," Kutna said didactically when Mifflin returned his call. "Otherwise we wouldn't be on the line."

"Then get on with it."

"Interpol received information on a possible terrorist attack at the Dorotheum. All anti-terrorist precautions have gone into effect.

In addition, Yakov was reported inside the building on several occasions over the last few hours. I'm reporting this information to you because I feel it's in the best interest of both our countries."

Mifflin was silent throughout. He understood the import of the message and that Kutna could have kept the information to himself.

"Thanks, Kutna. I'll take it from here."

"Understand we have sent Interpol agents into the building as a precautionary measure. They have been instructed that everything is to be low profile."

Kutna paused and lost some of his pomposity before asking, "Has Rosie Wimmer been in contact with you?"

"No, why do you ask?"

"I've had no contact for several hours. If she contacts you, I'd appreciate it if..."

"You'll know immediately."

"Ah, Mifflin...before, I didn't mean to sound..."

"It's okay." Nevertheless, he couldn't let him totally off the hook. "So you're a *human* bastard."

Kutna mumbled something and the phone clicked off.

Chapter 58

Alone in the musty storage room of the hotel, Lego gripped his automatic and faced the door. A shiver ran through his body as he listened: three soft taps, a pause then two. Crossing the room, he stood with his back to the wall next to the door, the Walther trained on the entrance. A woman's voice called his name.

"Lego, my name is Susan Koski. I'm a friend of Emma Lewis, Louise's niece."

He relaxed for a second then recovered. "Louise who?"

"Louise Fisher," Koski replied. "Hurry. Open the door."

"Is anyone with you?"

"It's not a trap. Rod Eiker with American security is with me. It's safe."

The woman knew of Louise. Should he take a chance?

"Lego, for God's sake, open the door! If we're caught in this hallway…"

"I'm going to open the door. I'm also letting the safety off my automatic."

Koski and Eiker watched as the door opened a crack then swung ajar for them to enter. Koski slowly pushed against it.

Lego was now in the center of the room, his gun aimed directly at them as they walked in. "Over there." He jerked his weapon toward the window. "Back against the window, arms above your heads. Face the center of the room." He backed against the door, shutting it with his left foot.

Alone, Eiker might have forced Lego into further interrogation but petite, disarming Koski immediately withered his defenses. He sighed. "I had to be certain."

Koski spoke softly. "You did right." She saw him sway slightly. "Lego, you're ill…" She glanced around the room and saw the evidence of his scant rations. "You're weak." Slowly she walked to him. "Here, sit down." She steadied his frail body as he lowered into the armchair.

Leaning back, he looked up at Koski. "Where is Louise's niece?"

"She's safe at the British Embassy. We'll take you to her."

"We also need your help," Eiker interjected somewhat impatiently. "We've made contact with an Israeli archaeologist, Dr. Yigal Herschel, who can possibly help us locate the stolen treasures Goering hid under the Dorotheum."

Lego nodded. "Ah, yes, the treasures." He pulled his sweater around him. "Herschel…was he once an army general?"

"Yes. You know him?"

"I know of him. He was a good general—good for Israel." Lego shrugged. "Then so was General Rommel, who was also an archaeologist—good for the Nazis."

"Lego, we'd like you with us," Koski said. "That is unless you fear you'd be risking your life…"

"I've no more time for fears, nothing left to fear. My wife was arrested by Czech security two days after I arrived here in Vienna. They confiscated a blueprint I had that they think I can interpret."

He sighed wistfully. "I wish she still had the prayer book. It would be a great comfort to her."

Eiker stiffened. "Prayer book?"

Lego smiled. "Ja, a beautiful book. When I packed my bag before I left for the reunion in 1975, I put it in my suitcase along with the key. I doubted I'd ever live long enough to make it to the next reunion."

Koski was saddened, watching him relate his innermost feelings, still affected by loyalties formed in the latter days of the war. "Lego, you must go back…your wife…."

"They won't harm her…yet." He straightened as if calling on some lagging determination.

Koski was curious about the book. "This prayer book, was it in your family a long time?"

"Many years. I remember it came in the mail from Canada about 1955," he rubbed his chin. "There was a key taped inside."

"Who sent it?" Koski asked softly.

"The Russian Youmatoff, Nikolai Youmatoff."

"I remember," Koski said, "the man you helped to escape during the war."

Lego looked plaintively off into space. "My wife loved that book, the colored pictures...she took it with her to church every day."

Koski put her hand on his fragile shoulders and patted lightly.

"When you received it," Eiker questioned, "was there a return address?"

"Nothing."

"Then how could you be sure it was from Youmatoff?"

"Inside the cover were three Xs drawn in pencil in a row with a line through them. It was our way of signifying 'prisoner of war.'"

Eiker nodded. "What about the key? What was it for?"

"I don't know. It was a mystery to me." He shook his head. "It was small and odd-shaped. I tossed it in the back of the knife and fork drawer in the kitchen where we kept old keys."

Koski frowned. "Weren't you curious about the key and the book?"

He shrugged. "It was a long time ago. I suppose I was, but what could I do? The book made my wife happy and that was all that mattered."

Koski believed him. She also admired a man who could toss a key into a drawer and find it ten years later. "You say you took them with you when you came to the reunion here in Vienna back in 1975?"

"Yes."

"You didn't mention the book and key to the others when you told them about Goering's hidden treasure?"

"No. I wanted to ask Dr. Benson what he thought."

Koski saw that Lego was tired but she needed a few more

answers. "What happened after the reunion?"

"On the way to Dr. Benson's room I met John Steele coming down the stairs. He said Doctor David had gone to bed. I asked him to keep the key for me as I was always losing things when I traveled.

"I said I'd retrieve it at breakfast. We said good night and I went to my room. In the middle of the night I heard someone in my hotel suite, outside my bedroom. I slipped out of bed, grabbed my clothes and went down the fire escape. Had I stayed, I know I would have been killed. I never saw Benson or Steele again."

"Did you take the book with you?" Eiker asked before Koski had a chance to frame the question.

"No. I left everything."

Koski thought the package Youmatoff sent in 1955 was the book and key. Somehow they tied in with the blueprint of the Dorotheum and pointed to the exact location of Goering's cache.

Steele had the key. Who had been in Lego's suite? Whoever it was must have found the book.

Chapter 59

The sky was high blue without a cloud the day Youmatoff got off the bus and walked through downtown Ottawa. His cheeks were burnished from the wind and snow and burned more intensely with the fire from within. He had buried his snowshoes before reaching the highway and shed his wool cap and gloves since the weather had turned slightly warmer.

Was it possible he had eluded the Mounties? He was bothered by people as they passed and made him aware of himself, skittish, the city lacking the fraternity he had formed with the woods.

As the seashell held the roar of the sea, Youmatoff was certain of the smell of forest. Years ago, he heard that people who spent blocks of time in the extreme solitude of the forest become "woods queer," forgot how to act around others. He once knew a trapper who went stark raving mad in the woods. Youmatoff, caught in the maelstrom of civilization himself, moved uneasily along the sidewalk, feeling mental discomposure, out of step with unsympathetic vibrations that rose from the city.

He ran a great weathered paw through his hair that was the umber of withered fern and as dull. He was getting closer. In answer to Youmatoff's stuttered question, the bus driver indicated a building on Charlotte Street, Number 287. Youmatoff quickened his pace, knowing that the Russian Embassy—a piece of his homeland on Canadian soil—was near.

Chapter 60

When Lego, Koski and Eiker left the Romischer-Kaiser Hotel, the weak sunlight was gone and snow fell in heavy silence, muffling the sound of late afternoon traffic. Cars passed with headlights on, windows steaming, windshield wipers slashing a triangle of visibility.

Lego looked skyward, squinting against a bombardment of flakes and turned up his collar. "Ach! The city traffic will be snarled before evening."

Koski looked down at a small whirlpool of snow that swirled around her feet. "We should have called a cab, Eiker."

"I did. Called from the desk and told him to meet us around the corner just north of the entrance."

"There was a man watching us as we left," she said, impressed with Eiker's forethought.

"I know. Main reason I wanted the taxi around the corner."

Kraal, observing the three from an upstairs window of a building facing the hotel, smiled as he watched them turn the corner. As he hoped, they had led him to Moyzisch and he would be on their tail in minutes. He glanced across the street at the man he had stationed in the doorway.

Kraal was sure the threesome made his man. When Koski looked over her shoulder, Kraal toyed with various entertaining methods he might deploy to kill her when the time came. He saw his man step from the doorway and go to the curb to meet a black Volvo that was to pick him up. Kraal turned from the window and hurried downstairs to join him.

As he reached the front door, Kraal stopped and flattened against the wall in the hallway, pulling a Marakov 9mm from his shoulder holster. Through the shattered glass panel of the door, he saw that the Volvo was gone. His man sprawled across the sidewalk, his head in a pool of blood.

Then Kraal saw something that sent him racing back down the hall with only seconds to get to the rear entrance and out of the building. A hand grenade had been tossed through the broken glass panel.

He ripped open the back door and flung himself from the building as a roar and the heat of the explosion drove through it like a blowtorch and slammed him into a sooty snow bank beside a row of battered trash cans.

An admixture of the ugly stench of cordite and acrid smell of wet, smoldering wood filled the air. Wisps of smoke curled from the glassless windows of the building opposite the Romischer-Kaiser. Water from fire hoses turned to ice and slush beneath firefighters' feet.

An ambulance with its back doors open was angled to the

curb. Captain Vlad of Austrian Military Intelligence flipped a sheet over the man on the stretcher then let the paramedic close the doors.

"No need for the siren with a dead man on board," Vlad remarked as the ambulance yodeled its way into the distance.

Beside him a sergeant muttered. "They want to get back for their coffee break."

Vlad was about to concur when an excited fire chief rushed up to him.

"We've found a man behind the building," the chief said. "He's pretty badly injured but alive."

Vlad pushed him aside and went to the back. Kraal was sprawled on the ground, out cold, the back of his head burned raw. A lump on his forehead indicated a possible concussion and his left foot was blown to a bloody pulp. He still gripped the Marakov.

"I want him kept alive," Vlad said after assessing Kraal's condition. "Quick. Get an ambulance."

When the ambulance arrived, Vlad climbed in the back with Kraal and removed the Marakov from Kraal's grip. He was intrigued. The Marakov was a crib of the German Walther PP automatic, a dangerous one for anyone not thoroughly familiar with it.

It looked identical to the Walther except for one small detail: the safety catch worked in reverse. Vlad pulled down the trigger guard, snapped the slide back and up and the recoil spring slid out. Once assembled without the spring, he slid it into his own pocket. Seated next to the sedated Kraal, an attendant watched with rapt attention.

"This is military security business," Vlad said pointedly. "No mention of what you've seen. Understand?"

The attendant nodded emphatically.

Chapter 61

Mifflin rapped on Stewart's office door and entered as if, once in, his presence justified his lack of decorum. "I had a call from Vlad of Military Intelligence; could be a break for us."

Stewart eased back in his chair. "Tell me about it."

"Vlad has a man in a military hospital...thinks he could be a Muslim terrorist. He feels I might be able to find out more about him."

"They have their own people. Why call you?"

"Vlad knows I've worked Eastern Europe, on and off in Bosnia-Herzegovina. Special assignments 1992-1995 and I know how their minds work."

Stewart nodded. "Go over there and talk to Vlad."

Mifflin was perched at Kraal's bedside when the latter regained consciousness.

"What's your name?"

Kraal remained unmoving except for a flicker of his eyelids. Mifflin rasped a sentence in Farsi and Kraal opened his eyes and turned toward him. He immediately shut his eyes.

Mifflin reached out and grabbed one ear that protruded between the layers of bandages around Kraal's head. He jerked it hard and Kraal let out an agonizing moan.

"What's your name?"

"Kraal," he moaned.

"Who are you working for?" Mifflin felt the man quiver, reacting to pain and drugs. He wondered if this Kraal was the type who would rather die than tell what he knew.

"Listen," Mifflin said, leaning close to Kraal's face. "I can pump you full of drugs that'll make you tell me anything I want to know." Kraal was silent. "One phone call and I can have you shot up with so much shit you'll tell me when you had your last hard-on."

"Or," he jerked again on the ear, "you can tell me what I want to know right now and you'll stay nice and safe with the Austrians, who will most likely fly you home first class when you're well." He released his grip on Kraal's ear and smoothed the man's nightshirt over his chest. "What's it going to be, hmm?"

Kraal looked long and hard into Mifflin's steady gaze. Kraal was a terrorist. His sophistication lay in surprise, ambush attack. His role was to inspire fear. If required, to die instantly and gloriously, not slow and painful.

"Pasha," he muttered.

Mifflin brightened at the name. "That little shit! Where is he?"

"The Dorotheum," Kraal said weakly.

"That place is more popular than Disneyland these days. What's he doing there?"

"He's under it looking for Nazi treasures." Sweat glistened on Kraal's upper lip. "That's all I know."

Mifflin pushed back his chair and rose. "Just out of curiosity, Kraal, what's your cover here in Vienna?"

"Wein Neustadt, cotton exports."

"U.N. trade mission?"

Kraal nodded slightly.

Mifflin shook his head. There was something wrong with a system that allowed men like this to move freely, creating problems under the cover of a United Nations' trade mission. He looked at his watch. "When were you to report to Pasha?"

Kraal's face twisted in pain. "What time is it?"

"7 p.m."

"Then I am three hours late."

Mifflin turned and left the room. Outside, he said to Vlad, "When you're finished with him it'll be the end of the line. We don't want him back on the streets—ever."

Vlad smiled. "Nice working with you Herr Mifflin."

Chapter 62

Stewart picked up the phone and heard, "This is Kutna, Interpol. I have a message for you."

"Go ahead." Stewart wrote as he listened. *POSSIBLE TERRORIST ACTIVITY INSIDE DOROTHEUM IMMINENT. YAKOV ALSO SEEN.*

"Where did the Intel come from?" Stewart asked.

"Interpol's computer," Kutna said, "and one of our people who's been covering Yakov."

"What's Yakov doing?"

"I don't know. Interpol security forces and the Austrian police are going down there now. We're trying to keep everything as low-key as possible."

"Wouldn't it be wiser to evacuate the place?"

"Not at this time. If it's a false alarm, we'll tip them off that we got word of their plans, which could mean hostage taking…and God knows what else."

Emma was seated in a high-backed chair beside the fireplace in the British Embassy's reception area, reading a copy of the *London Illustrated News.* She looked up and glanced at an old grandfather clock in the corner. It had been over three hours since she last saw Koski and Eiker.

It was another fifteen minutes before the duo arrived with Lego. Koski went directly to a phone, called Stewart and learned Mifflin had gone to the Dorotheum following a message from Kutna.

"Any news about Youmatoff," she asked.

"Contacts in Canada report they still don't have Youmatoff in custody." Koski swore under his breath. If Youmatoff decided to go back to Russia, he could throw a monkey wrench into the works. Cerberus needed him *and* the first-hand information regarding the location they believed only he could provide. Koski hung up and joined the others.

"Ready to go?" she asked. "We have a meeting of the minds. Stewart's sending a car for us."

Koski was the first to enter the room when Stewart answered the knock. Eiker, Lego and Emma followed. Koski went straight into Falk's arms. She felt his warm breath against her ear as he bent and hugged her.

"Susan…Susan," he whispered.

They stood interlocked as the others skirted around them. She pulled back and looked at him. Handsome but older, thinner, sun and wind burned…creases at the corners of his eyes slightly more pronounced…parentheses on each side of his mouth deepened beneath a meandering mass of brown facial hair with familiar red highlights…dear…beloved…

She grabbed him again, hugging him fiercely. "Are you okay?" she asked when she finally disengaged herself and his arms reluctantly released her.

He nodded, fingering a tendril of her hair at her temple. He tenderly traced the line of her cheekbone and jaw, taking in the emotions she knew were blatantly evident in her eyes. "Thank God you're safe," he said huskily.

She sighed, suddenly aware of the others, wound one hand in his and held the other out to Lego. "Lego, come meet Joe Falk."

Lego took Falk's hand between his frail palms. "I'm happy to meet you."

Stewart ordered a hot meal for Lego and called everyone to be seated. Once he had their attention, he laid out the next move that included joining forces with Herschel.

"Falk, you and Koski will go on ahead to meet with Herschel," he said. "At some point Mifflin will join you. Due to security considerations, Emma and Lego will remain with me until cleared to join you." He glanced at Eiker then back to Falk. "Eiker will be along shortly. We have some minor details to discuss."

Beneath the Dorotheum, Pasha and two of his men led John Steele to a cell that was once a storage room, one of hundreds throughout the building.

Steele entered, walked a few feet and stopped. The first thing he saw was Rosie Wimmer.

Pasha, master of the garrote, had strangled Rosie with the leather shaving strop he used when questioning Steele. Stiff and cold, she looked almost obscene the way she was placed in the straight wooden chair. Her hips thrust forward, hands folded between her legs, head tilted back at a grotesque angle. Next to the chair was a small, wooden table with a flickering candle positioned to allow shadows to fall across Rosie's waxen face. Pasha made a sweeping gesture as if presenting her, obviously admiring his own handiwork.

Steele turned away from the final agony he saw reflected in Rosie's face.

Pasha laughed. "We completed the job you failed to do. When

I set out to kill, I don't fail." He took the candle and walked to a dark corner. "I have something else to show you." With a flourish, he illumined the lifeless body of *Faux* Monk, who was sprawled on the floor, mouth agape, two bloody sockets where his eyes had been.

"Jesus!" Steele said. "That was the man who led me to the crypt—the only person who could find his way through the passages. Without him I'm nothing to you!"

"I couldn't have said it better myself." Pasha set the candle down. "We'll let the Mossad lead us to the treasures." He walked to the door. "Yes, Steele, you're about to become nothing but unnecessary baggage—a walking time bomb to be exact."

Steele heard one of Pasha's men behind him a second before he felt the blow to the back of his head that sent him reeling into darkness.

Chapter 63

Yakov, with signs of a head cold drooping over him, stood inside the main entrance to the Dorotheum as an early afternoon crowd streamed steadily in. He stamped his feet and turned up his coat collar against the icy blasts of air that hit him each time the door swung open.

"No sign of anything, sir."

Yakov turned slightly toward the voice of one of his men in a long, leather overcoat and *astrakhan* hat. Yakov removed a cough drop from a box in his coat pocket and popped it in his mouth. "I want every inch of the building searched for possible explosives," he snapped. "Basements, storage areas, yards, sheds, offices… everything. And check every porter's ID."

Suddenly Yakov realized that the head porter was waving to

him from his small glass cubicle. Yakov refocused on his present situation. He cursed and crossed the wide hallway, shoulders hunched. He had no wish to die in a pawnshop—large or small.

The porter was Helmut Sten. Yakov had told Sten that he and his men were here to cover a story for a Czech Republic magazine. Sten held up a steaming mug of coffee as Yakov reached the cubicle.

"Please," he said as Yakov approached, "join me." He closed the door to the small, overheated office.

"Thank you, Herr Sten." Yakov pulled up a wooden chair, positioned it facing the entrance through the panorama of glass and sat down with the mug.

"Is there anything else I can do?" Sten asked eagerly.

Yakov nodded. "As a matter of fact, yes. I was about to ask if we might see how the antiques are stored and cared for prior to being placed at auction. We'd like to view the storage rooms and the underground facilities. These would be of great interest to our readers."

"No trouble. I will arrange for some of my people to guide you."

Yakov shook his head. "My men and I wish to go alone, unencumbered, so to speak. It will make for more candid shots."

"That's against the rules. No one is allowed beneath the Dorotheum without permission and a guide."

"I understand but we don't want you to go to any trouble." Yakov set his mug on a nearby table. "Just give me the keys. We'll look around, take a few pictures and be back in no time. No one will be any the wiser."

"Sorry." Sten's face reflected his uneasiness. "It can't be done."

Yakov moved quickly and Sten was facing the barrel of an ugly 9mm automatic.

"I'm out of time." Yakov spat, his gun gesturing to a row of keys on the wall. "Get those keys."

Sten's hand shook as he comprehended the situation. He handed the keys to Yakov then backed up against the wall.

"Perhaps you're right," Yakov hissed as he opened the office door. "We should have a guide. Walk ahead of me as if nothing's wrong. No heroics."

John Steele was inside a large, wooden crate labeled "Glassware" that stood in a remote warehouse area of the Dorotheum. It was coal black inside and Steele was bound hand and foot with a thin wire. One portion of it ran around his jaw and across his mouth, jamming his tongue against his lower teeth like the bit of a bridle. He breathed slowly, easing each hiss of air out between bloody, swollen lips. Steele heard someone outside the crate, a scraping sound then a click and the side of the crate snapped open and widened. It was Ali, one of Pasha's henchmen, who whispered, "I'm going to check the area."

Steele heard a sound like an old-fashioned wind up alarm clock being wound. "I'll be back before the detonator makes contact. If I'm detained, you'll die a peaceful death because the detonator will release a gas. You'll simply go to sleep." Steele felt the man pat his shoulder. "No doubt I'll return before the spring reaches contact."

How reassuring, Steele thought, as the man eased the side of the crate down and clicked it shut.

Alone with the ticking timer, Steele heaved against his bindings but the movement only caused the wire to saw more deeply into his lips. Breathing heavily, he rested his head against the rough wood of the crate. The ticking was like thunder in his ears. He had no idea how much time he had. Whatever happened, if he did get out of this he'd get that piece of shit Pasha.

Chapter 64

Kutna was already at the Dorotheum when Mifflin entered. He looked the part of a bargain hunter equal to any Viennese his age down to the battered briefcase he carried. With no wish to repeat the fiasco at the vegetable market, Kutna glanced around to make sure his men were in place. He watched Mifflin plod through the hallway, glance toward the porter's cubicle then pass from sight.

Kutna turned his eyes to the porter's office and tensed. Gut feeling told him something was wrong. He saw the porter and another man with his back to the window. The porter's face registered fear. There was something about the other man...then Kutna knew who it was.

The caretaker, followed by Yakov, left the cubicle and walked toward a door in the hall. Kutna was about to signal his men when a quiet voice beside him said, "I have a message from Mifflin." Kutna swung around to face a slim blonde in her early thirties. "Mifflin says you're to remain in place. The head porter has been taken hostage."

"I *know* that!" Kutna hissed between clenched teeth. "Tell Mifflin that I..." The woman was gone before he could finish, lost in the crowd.

A squad of soldiers, whose uniforms identified them as Austrian Military Intelligence, slowly walked the width of the hall with leashed German Shepherds, moving the public steadily toward the front doors. They closed and locked them without fanfare.

Kutna had no doubt similar squads were securing other doors. He cursed. Mifflin must have arranged it and Captain Vlad executed it. Once again he and his department were relegated to mere guard duty.

Kutna spun around and waved to one of his men at the top of the curving staircase. The man ran down the wide, marble steps and stopped in front of him.

"Get some of our people into the *Josef Saal*," Kutna ordered. "Leave enough to cover this area."

The man looked up the stairs to the tall, ornate doors of one of the auction rooms known as *Josef Saal*. "The door is closed," he said. "The auction is about to begin."

"Very well. Leave two men at the door. Detain anyone who tries to leave before the auction ends." The man scurried back up the curving staircase. Signaling to two of his men, Kutna walked to one side of the hallway.

"Knoph," he said, "stay close to me. Reinhart, I'm going to find out what's going on...cover us." Followed by the men, he went through the door off the hall into a dimly lit stairway where Yakov and the porter had disappeared.

Silently they descended three flights of stone steps bordered by a wall on one side, iron railings on the other. Reinhart, who had removed a Lugar from his shoulder holster, remained a few feet behind the others. Kutna and Knoph, crouched low, cautiously rounding each landing, alert to danger.

It did them no good. The first shot caught Knoph at the hairline, lifting his scalp like a saucer and tipping it to the back of his head. He fell on the spot in a cascade of blood and matter. A second shot, sounding almost before the first had ceased reverberating, passed Kutna's shoulder by scant inches and entered Reinhart's right clavicle, shattering his shoulder blade. As he fell to the steps, he emptied his pistol in the direction of the shots. Before he passed out, his trained reaction was rewarded when he heard a cry and the unmistakable gurgle of death.

The overhead lights went out. Cordite and the smell of insufferable closeness mixed with a sudden silence that fell on Kutna like a cloak of death tossed across a coffin. He curled into a tight ball and pressed against the stonewall.

His men were hit. He must remain silent or die. He listened, certain that Yakov and his men were there somewhere. The only sound was Knoph, taking his last breaths a few feet away. Kutna felt compelled to move. Easing away from the wall, he snaked on his belly to the center of the passageway. The sudden stuttering blast from an Uzi on full automatic filled his ears and chips of stone flaked from the wall where he'd been moments before. His instinct to move had saved his life. He would continue to play the fox. Quickly he removed his shoes. Then with a muffled yell, he let his .45 drop to the floor. He had seen the flash from the machine gun and had a good idea where the gunman was.

Scooping up the .45, he hurried silently on stocking feet to the opposite wall where he remained still, hardly daring to breathe. The weapon in his right hand was rock steady, aimed at a level two inches higher than his own belt buckle. A few seconds later he heard a slight shuffling sound. He closed his eyes to listen better. There it was again—a shoe sliding along an uneven stone surface.

He felt certain it was one-on-one now or aspects of the attack would have been different. Opening his eyes, he turned his head in the direction of the sound. He only had one chance. His finger tightened on the trigger and he stared into utter blackness, ready to squeeze off a round.

The sudden stabs of an automatic's yellow flame didn't come from his gun but from the stairs behind him! He flattened against the wall, spun his weapon upward as the lights came on.

A familiar voice said, "Okay, Kutna. Relax." But he saw no one capable of speaking. The stairwell was a scene of carnage. Reinhart, barely breathing, was draped over the stairs in a puddle of blood. Knoph was slumped grotesquely in a corner, his dead features hardly recognizable.

One of Yakov's men was propped against the wall as if taking a break. He had achieved eternal rest, eyes gazing up toward the hole in the center of his forehead.

Yakov wasn't three feet from Kutna. He wore the same forlorn expression in death that he bore in life. Beside him, head porter Sten laid still, head in an ever-growing pool of blood. He would never again drink coffee in his small, glass-enclosed office in the Dorotheum.

"Okay, Kutna," Mifflin repeated from the head of the stairs and showed himself. "It's safe to come out now."

Kutna snapped the safety on his .45 and jammed it into its holster. "Damn!" was all he could think to say and it didn't begin to cover it.

Chapter 65

The meeting between Falk, Koski and Dr. Herschel took place in the back room of an abandoned tailor shop. Koski's nose wrinkled at the smell of old wool and the faint decay of an unused area. A scowling "Saint" Paul, still unhappy about losing face at the restaurant, had ushered them in. He departed unceremoniously and slammed the door behind him.

"Delighted you made it back." Herschel got up from behind a table piled high with books and maps and walked toward them, hand outstretched. After the usual introductions, he pushed a chair to the table for Koski while Falk got his own. They sat facing the doctor.

"We shall go over the maps together," Herschel said. He set out the largest, showing details of underground sewers and passageways beneath the central part of Vienna. "We are here." He stabbed his finger at a point on the Spiegelgasse close to the Capuchin Church.

"We'll go underground near the corner. I've arranged for us to use a City Water and Power truck. We'll wear official coveralls, set up the usual caution signs around the manhole and go down under the city using the catwalks."

"The city has agreed to let us do this?" Koski questioned.

"No but by the time anyone begins to wonder about the barricade and tent over the manhole we'll be through, which could take days the way the city bureaucracies work."

Falk nodded. "Once underground then what?"

"We follow this gallery, see." He tracked the route with a finger. "It runs deep beneath the foundation of the Capuchin, cuts across and passes the east side of the underpinning of the Augustinian Church. I feel the location we're looking for is either directly underneath the Dorotheum or somewhere between the two churches." He reached to another table, pushed aside a dusty pile of fabric and produced a book.

Falk was astonished. *"The Book of Hours,"* he whispered.

Herschel nodded. "Do you think it really holds a clue for us?"

"It's possible. I need to study it more."

Koski tapped the map before her. "The Capuchin Church has

the Habsburgs urns, correct?" She looked from Falk to Herschel.

"Yes," Herschel said. "Fifty-four of them if memory serves me. Why?"

"Sadistic irony if Goering decided to conceal his blueprint for the heart of the Fourth Reich beneath the church of the Habsburgs."

Herschel's eyes brightened. "I intend to leave no possibility unexamined."

Falk studied the map again. A few hundred feet separated the churches. The passageways and galleries used by the Water and Power were well detailed down to each piece of conduit that carried cables and electrical wiring under the city.

Herschel tapped a spot beside the Capuchin. "When we arrive here I'll send one of my divers into the sewer system. You will note the waterways run parallel with the gallery. It's all part of the Danube Canal system that runs deep and fast this time of year."

"Why at that point?" Falk asked.

"I understand you were taken to a crypt beneath the church not long after you arrived in Vienna. You were left with a monk and this *Book of Hours*, correct?"

"How do you know that?"

"I have ways."

Yes, Falk thought. What the Mossad doesn't know it has ways of finding out.

Herschel continued. "Did you hear water running when you were in the crypt?"

"Yes, and the walls were wet in places."

"Good." Herschel flipped some pages back and forth, deeply engrossed, tracing, measuring and making notes.

Falk glanced down at the map in front of him. His eyes

caught sight of rows of lines winding like vines. Checking the dated legend at the bottom corner, he discovered the lines represented electrical conduits. The map was less than ten years old.

Conduits. Falk let the word linger in his mind. He stared at the map, his heart suddenly beginning to thump wildly. Latin, *Conductus*—from *conucere*—to bring forth. Vienna was a city of fountains. The *Book of Hours* pictured fountains, birds, angels, monks, churches—holy things. Good God it had been there all the time in bright, Holy Roman color! Reaching across the table, he pulled the prayer book toward him.

Koski noted the move and was about to say something but Joe quickly shook his head. At the same time his facial expression indicated that she remain silent. Koski nodded her understanding and went back to her maps.

Falk quickly checked the chart for fountain locations in the inner city where the search would take place, especially noting the area around the Dorotheum and both churches. Now the prayer book began to make sense. He flipped the pages, seeing illustrations beautifully drawn, colored pictures of monks kneeling at prayer beside fountains.

Falk's mind was racing. Was the hiding place secreted beneath a fountain? Smiling cherubs, some with whips…

A cherub, Falk thought, *is a member of the second order of angels, distinguished by knowledge and often represented as a beautiful, winged child.* Was he crazy? Goering had been master of the German Luftwaffe. A winged child indeed!

His roving index finger returned to the atlas and stopped at a fountain, bounded by both churches and the Dorotheum. "Providence Fountain," the legend indicated, "By George Raphael

Donner, built 1737-1739, more commonly known as the Donner Fountain." Reading the Water and Power notes further, Falk discovered that the Donner Fountain was sealed and capped in 1914. Beneath the fountain, clearly marked, was a stone vault dating back to Roman times and once used as a cistern, fed by a natural spring.

According to the notes, capping the spring had been necessary due to constant seepage that threatened to damage other building foundations in the area, including both churches. A more up-to-date system was presently in effect for circulating water but the cistern, a vault-like room, narrow and about thirty feet long, was still there.

Falk read more notes that were apparently prepared for the benefit of tourists. Four graceful angels, one on each corner of the fountain, represented four rivers: the Enns, March, Traum and Ybbs.

At first the river names meant nothing. He read them slowly, looking for a clue. He remembered that he had heard water on the sloping walk to the crypt, had felt it on the walls. Perhaps river water still ran through the cistern.

Was it possible it had been uncapped and the vault filled, ready to burst if anyone attempted to enter? He cursed silently. Another damned obstacle to overcome. How could he be sure if the cistern was empty?

Staring at the paper, he reread the names of the rivers, trying the most elemental formula—the first letter of each. Could it be that easy? E-M-T-Y. Empty. Yes! Imperceptibly Falk pumped his fist. Goering must have known. That's why he hid everything beneath the fountain and above the passageways. Falk felt a rush of adrenaline and scarcely prevented himself from shouting aloud. He had to get *inside* the cistern to be sure.

Herschel lowered his pencil and stretched his arms above his head. "I'd like you both to examine the route we'll be taking. Check it out, point out any changes you think we should make. Let's go over this from the minute we descend below street level."

The trio bent over the charts and maps. It was almost an hour before Falk and Koski sat back, fully satisfied with the plan they had mapped out with Herschel. The charts of passageways maintained by the Vienna Water and Power were in perfect detail down to individual light switches that were numbered and named.

Falk was careful not to let anything slip about his plan to get into the cistern beneath the Donner. He felt confident he was onto the hiding place and was ready to inform Koski when he got the chance.

Herschel still favored a location beneath the original wing that was destroyed during the last days of the war and subsequently rebuilt. Falk was unconcerned. He pondered how he and Koski could shake loose from the rest of the team and follow-up on his own lead without tipping his hand.

"I had expected the others would be here by now," Herschel remarked.

"Yes," Falk said. Although he didn't relish tramping through the sewers of Vienna with this "crew," he was antsy to get moving.

Slowly he began to formulate his exact plan. Herschel had drawn his pencil along the passageways beside the fast flowing water in the main sewer channel. The first leg ran straight then turned left for two hundred feet before hooking at a forty-five degree angle. He noticed light switches placed exactly at two hundred foot intervals. He would turn off the lights in the passage as soon as they made the right turn then and he and Koski would make a run for one of the galleries intersecting the main passageway.

Falk knew the gallery he wanted, on the right, the second one after they made the turn. Given the sudden darkness and confusion, he and Koski had a good chance of making it. The others would have to search all the galleries to find them.

Herschel excused himself to go to the bathroom and Falk took the precaution of ripping a page from the map book. It had nothing to do with the Herschel route but rather depicted details of the cistern under the Donner. Quickly he briefly outlined his plan for Koski.

Now that he had the arrangements worked out in his head and Koski was aware of their next move, he relaxed somewhat. He could afford to play Herschel's game.

"Well, Doctor," he said when the general returned, "we're in your hands. We can't really argue with your strategy."

"I'm glad we're a team." Herschel smiled a broad, genuine smile. "Remember, Emma and Lego will be safer with us than in the city. There are some people who'd like to see them as prisoners again."

They turned toward the door at the sound of voices.

Chapter 66

After what seemed like hours, Steele heard a click and the crate that enclosed him snapped open.

"You get to live a little longer," Ali said as he turned off the timer he had set earlier and pulled Steele from the crate. "Steele, you look like a fooking scarecrow."

From somewhere in the warehouse Steele heard a forklift whining toward them.

"Now we go places," Ali exclaimed and released the wire from Steele's mouth. Steele spat a bloody tooth onto the floor.

"What about these?" Steele asked and turned his wirebound wrists toward him but Ali shook his head.

The forklift, two steel fingers jutting like tusks of a long-forgotten prehistoric animal, came in from the shadows and across the wide expanse of warehouse. The whine died as the driver came up beside them. He and Ali exchanged a few words and the two tossed Steele onto the stubby rear deck of the vehicle. Ali stood at the base of one of the tusks and the driver turned the yellow machine in a tight circle and set off into the shadows of the subterranean shipping area.

If one were to draw a line through the floor from where Mifflin was standing, it would have come out within three feet of the small dingy room once used as a shipping office in the lower level; the door to which Pasha opened slightly at the sound of the approaching forklift. Satisfied it was safe, he pushed the door open and stepped out. Steele, his wrists and ankles still bound, was hauled from the machine and dragged toward Pasha.

"Good. My bait is still alive." He stepped close to Steele. "I have one more job for you."

Steele raised his head and spat. The spittle, laced with blood, hit Pasha full in the face. Ali raised his automatic, its butt ready to strike.

"Don't!" Pasha's voice trembled with rage. "You have little time to live, Steele, but I promise it will be long enough for you to regret what you just did."

Steele sneered and his bloody, swollen upper lip cracked. "Then get on with it."

Pasha wiped his face on his jacket sleeve. "Get him ready."

Ali removed the wire from Steele's wrists and ankles and snapped his wrists in handcuffs behind his back. His shirt was pulled down to his waist and a misshapen cloth bandoleer filled with explosives was strapped tightly to his body. Ali smiled malignantly as he rebuttoned Steele's shirt.

"You're primed, Steele," Pasha purred. "You're now a suicide bomber." He circled Steele like an army sergeant inspecting a new recruit. "Fits the body well." He turned to Ali. "You're certain of the range?"

"Range of the transmitter to the subject's receiver," he tapped a spot in the center of Steele's back, "is sixty meters. I intend to be a little closer."

Pasha nodded. "Remove the handcuffs. Bring him into the office." Ali took off the cuffs and he and the forklift driver shoved Steele forward.

"Here." Pasha tapped the top of a scarred wooden table. "Place his left hand in the center." Steele tried to pull away but the driver grabbed his arm and slapped it across the table.

The corners of Pasha's mouth turned up slightly. "I warned you that you'd regret spitting in my face." He reached beneath the table and came up with a thick, heavy, three-legged stool. It took both Ali and the driver to hold Steele and his hand on the table. In one swift sizzling arc, Pasha lifted the stool over his head and brought it down. The crunch of bones sounded like dry twigs being ground underfoot. Steele fell forward across the table, out cold.

"When he comes to, put that hand in his pocket. He won't need it again." Pasha replaced the stool and smoothed his shirt.

Steele was back on the forklift when he regained consciousness. His mangled left hand in agonizing pain throbbed and stabbed up his arm like a red-hot poker.

"The fooking scarecrow's awake." Ali grabbed the purple, misshapen mass that had once been Steele's hand and roughly jammed it into Steele's left pocket. A wave of nausea hit Steele and his brain fought to remain conscious.

"Take him to the gallery," Pasha ordered. "You know what to do."

"What do I do if he refuses to get close to the passageway?"

Pasha's eyes narrowed until the flesh around them threatened to engulf them. "Ali, we're men with a mission for Islam. Carry out my orders."

Ali nodded and he and the driver mounted the forklift. The electric motor spun to life. In exactly that moment, Steele came back from a hazy, REM-like void and caught sight of the one thing he coveted most in the world at that moment: Pasha's throat. When he lunged, his will denied his weakened condition, his quivering knees. With what remained of his left hand and with an almighty effort, his good right hand shot out and clamped around the scrawny throat in a bulldog grip. A gasp was the only sound Pasha made, his eyes round with fright as they shot to Ali.

"Move a muscle and he's dead," Steele rasped.

Ali hesitated at the cold, calm edge in Steele's voice. Steele dragged Pasha closer until the scrawny Arab was tight against him. In a quick shift, Steele released his grip and immediately replaced it with an arm lock around Pasha's neck. A surge of strength flowed through Steele's body. He was a Canadian paratrooper once more, oblivious to pain with the enemy firmly in his grip.

He waved his fingers for the remote Ali held in his hand. "Give me the transmitter, now. Tell him, turtle piss."

Pasha made a croaking sound. Ali leaned forward and passed the transmitter into Steele's fingers. Steele grinned, showing a gap where a tooth had been. "Throw down your weapons or I flip on this remote and we all leave...abruptly." Ali and the driver let their guns clatter to the floor. "Now," Steele said, "we get the hell outta here."

"The building is full of police and military security," Ali noted. "Better we take the galleries above the sewers."

Steele pushed Pasha ahead of him and stepped onto the base of one of the steel fingers of the forklift. "Drive real easy. I don't want to get nervous and hit the switch."

As they moved slowly toward a freight elevator, Steele listened to Pasha's harsh breathing and the soft hum of the forklift motor and thought that perhaps the life and times of John Steele were running out.

Chapter 67

To Nikolai Youmatoff, having emerged from his long woodland trek, Ottawa's sidewalks seemed the busiest he'd ever seen. It was actually a slow day, considering the approaching holiday, with relatively light pedestrian traffic. The area of the Russian Embassy was particularly deserted.

Youmatoff spied Charlotte Street ahead and he started down a side street that intersected an alley. As he passed the dark, narrow cavity between two buildings, he stopped in mid-stride. He didn't turn but looked straight ahead. He knew instinctively that a pursuer had found him and that a gun was pointed precisely in his direction.

If he twisted toward the alley, he'd be looking at his past and his future no more than six feet away. They always got their man, Youmatoff thought, and almost laughed at the irony of it all.

He waited. Apparently the Mountie was not prepared to kill

him—perhaps wound him if he resisted. Youmatoff wondered, however, why the man said nothing, did nothing.

Had Youmatoff turned and looked into the face of Sgt. Christopher Pullbrook, he still wouldn't have the answers to his questions but he might have had a glimmer of what was to come.

Sgt. Pullbrook was a graying man. He had served most of his life as part of that vast constabulary of Royal Canadian Mounted Police known as the Canadian Security Service.

From the day he entered, at less than twenty, he'd looked forward to the excitement of investigating espionage and subversion. At the time, he was six-three with a bulldog physique that bespoke his youthful determination.

Unfortunately, Sgt. Pullbrook broke his ankle during his first week of basic training—a fracture that, due to diabetic complications, never healed properly—and spent more than thirty years consigned to liaison duties requiring little involvement.

In fact, today, less than a year from the date of his planned retirement, he was doing "gofer" work, delivering a routine message to the Soviet Embassy when he saw Youmatoff. He had just come from CPIC headquarters where he saw Youmatoff's file. He noted the picture of the Russian that came over the net from Photo Service Information Center.

On one hand, Sgt. Pullbrook saw the years left to him as deserved things—ample compensation for unlived life. On the other hand, Sgt. Pullbrook, who had never mounted a horse, who—although he was issued a handgun that he usually kept holstered against his left armpit—had never gone out on what he considered a legitimate assignment, saw Youmatoff as his first and last chance for undying glory.

Chapter 68

Herschel greeted Eiker as the tall Brit led Emma and Lego into the old tailor shop where Falk and Koski waited. Shaking hands with Herschel, Lego said, "I'm honored to meet you, General."

Herschel reacted with surprise. "Thank you but that was a long time ago. I'm no longer in the Army." He greeted Emma and guided her and Lego to a couple of easy chairs, noting that Mifflin had yet to arrive. "I've been over the details with Doctors Falk and Koski. I'll take a few minutes to bring you up-to-date. I also have questions for Lego that might be vital to our operation."

Falk was disturbed they had been searched prior to entering the room and all weapons temporarily confiscated for "safekeeping." He took note that Koski nearly got by with a Beretta in her purse, no doubt issued by Stewart since her return to Vienna. She was patted down, although there was no female guard to thoroughly examine her person. Eiker, Falk noticed with surprise, readily obliged the search, dutifully emptying his pockets, offering his weapon, retaining nothing but a pack of gum and a Cartier lighter.

"Dr. Falk, Dr. Koski and I," Herschel began, "have gone over plans, charts, tourist books, blueprints and maps of the area beneath the Dorotheum and adjoining buildings, including the Capuchin and Augustine churches." He crossed to a blackboard and drew a horizontal chalk line across the center.

"Let's say this is the surface at street level. We're going under the streets and buildings by the same method the city's Water and Power people use. You'll be issued regulation coveralls, hard hats and flashlights so if you're seen no one will suspect you."

He drew a second line a foot below the first. "Here's the

sewer system's main gallery. We'll be walking in this direction." He drew a dextral arrow. "The galleries are lighted but beware: The surface could be slippery in spots. To our left will be the water from the Danube Canal, three to four feet below the level of the gallery. It runs fast and deep and at this time of the year is damned cold."

"Earlier you mentioned something about a diver?" Falk asked.

"Yes, coming to that. We'll be in two separate columns. You'll get your positions later. The first leg will be a little under a mile and will bring us directly under the old section of the Dorotheum —the wing that was destroyed in the bombing."

He placed a large X on the board and erased part of the line to make room for his next drawing. "This is the Capuchin." He drew a short line, another X and another line, continuing almost off the board. "Sorry. My scale isn't too good. This," he pointed to the second X, "is the Augustine." Finally he drew a wobbly oval to enclose both Xs. "It's my belief that what we are seeking lies within this area."

He turned to Falk. "The diver will enter a small tributary that cuts under the Dorotheum here. As you see, it crosses from the main stream, curves under the buildings and rejoins it near the Capuchin. The only other possible way anyone can get into the area we'll be searching is to follow that tributary. The diver's job is to be certain no one does. The entrance we descend will also be covered as will all others in the immediate vicinity."

"What about the city?" Eiker asked. "They could conceivably need to be down there."

Herschel nodded. "We've checked the maintenance schedule. No one will be in that section for the next three days. As you know, an Austrian schedule is exact. Nothing short of an all-out emergency can change it."

"When do we start?" Koski asked.

"Midnight, by which time Mifflin should be here." Herschel ran a hand through his thinning hair. "I suggest everyone get as much rest as possible."

He went to a door that opened onto another room. "There are comfortable chairs in there. Perhaps you can relax a while." He turned to Lego. "May I speak with you alone a moment?" Lego shrugged and they went back to the table.

The second room was once the living quarters for the family who ran the tailor shop. It contained a couch, three battered armchairs and a coffee table. Koski and Falk sat together on the couch, his arm protectively around her shoulders. Emma and Eiker faced each other in armchairs.

"Seems like a good plan," Koski said a little too loudly. She waved her arms in a gesture that indicated the room could be bugged. She continued. "Looks good on the blackboard anyway." She got up. "I need to visit the restroom. Be right back." She disappeared into the small adjoining bathroom.

When she returned Koski sank down next to Falk, pressed against him and surreptitiously slipped one hand into his jacket pocket. "So you won't feel naked," she whispered then lightly kissed his cheek.

She withdrew her hand. The weight where it had been remained and he knew the source.

"How..." he began.

She scowled to stop him and softly brushed his cheek. He felt the reverberation of her words against his skin, more than heard them. "Plastic."

His lips unmoving in a fashion that would have made a

ventriloquist proud, he softly hissed, "Where did you hide it to get it past the guards that searched you?"

"You don't want to know."

He pulled away slightly and let his vision slip into those deep green pools of speckled light. "Don't be too sure of that."

She leaned her head against his shoulder and they both closed their eyes. For nearly an hour, Falk felt like they were alone in the world.

Eiker suddenly blurted out, arousing the others. "Where the fuck is Mifflin? It's getting late. I want to get this show on the road."

Chapter 69

Kutna and Mifflin stood face to face at the top of the stairs beneath the Dorotheum. Kutna wiped the back of his hand across his forehead and said halfheartedly, "Thanks."

Captain Vlad walked up to them. "What happened?"

"Yakov and his people kidnapped the head porter," Mifflin said, "nearly killed Kutna here. Any news of other possible terrorist activity?"

"A fellow in the warehouse reported his forklift missing," Vlad replied. "We're checking it out, nothing else."

The three walked back toward the front entrance. Everything looked like business as usual, the soldiers out of sight.

"Look, Kutna," Mifflin said, "you and Vlad can take it from here. I'm late for an appointment."

Kutna nodded. "Mifflin..." he started to say but the big man waved away his thanks.

"You're welcome."

Kutna watched as Mifflin nodded to Vlad then plowed

massively across the entrance hall and out the front door. Turning back toward the main hall, Kutna wished he had some news on Rosie.

Chapter 70

Steele felt the quiver of fear running through the thin body of the man he held in a death lock. The forklift hummed at a cautious pace, the driver afraid the least bump or jar would cause the explosives strapped to Steele's body to detonate.

"Steele," Ali called, his voice low and submissive now. "I know a better way. We can stay alive...Let's make a deal..."

Steele turned his head slightly and looked at him. "No fooking deals, chum." He tightened the grip on Pasha's neck. "It's bye-bye for all of us." Pasha squirmed against him and Steele felt the bulge of a gun pressing into his side. The bastard was packing!

"Is that a gun," he questioned, "or are you just happy to see me?" He took a deep breath and jammed Pasha's head down between his legs in a leg lock that threatened to crush the man's trachea. He slid his right hand into Pasha's pocket and came out with a Beretta 9mm automatic. "How sweet it is," he said then thumbed the safety, turned and blew a hole in Ali's face. The bullet entered just above his top lip beneath the right nostril. Ali jerked back, spun sideways and was gone. As he hit the floor two feet behind the forklift, Steele shifted his eyes to the driver, who was terror-stricken.

"Nice and easy," he said, "over there next to the freight elevator." The driver headed cautiously in the direction indicated. "When we get there," Steele continued, "you get off, open the doors then drive this rig on." He grabbed Pasha by his thin straggling hair and pulled him upright to be sure the man was witness to his own execution.

He placed the barrel of the gun in the little man's ear and pulled the trigger. "Allah Akbar." Bone gore and brains splattered across the forklift and Pasha slid down and arched across the steel tusks.

They were at the freight elevator. The driver was shaking so violently he nearly fell off the machine. He opened the elevator doors, remounted the rig and slowly drove onto the large wooden platform.

Steele painfully eased from the forklift and off the elevator. He stood aside while the open latticed doors began to close. The terrified driver's face looked directly into the first bullet that took him out of his terror as the steel jacketed slug tore into his right eye. The second clipped the lobe of his left ear as he fell sideways from the driver's seat. Steele lowered the gun, reached through the lattice and jabbed a button on the panel.

"Going up," he said and headed for a side door as the elevator began its ascent.

The door led to an iron walkway known as a gallery that ran over the passageway beside the running waters of the Danube Canal and the Vienna sewer system.

At that moment Steele was three hundred feet ahead of where Falk had decided he would turn out the lights and make a run for the cistern of the Donner Fountain. Steele needed to hide, to rest. He knew his life was near its end and just once he wanted to look upon Goering's damnable stolen treasures.

If only Dr. Benson had listened to him this wouldn't have happened. They could have worked together and found the loot. It all could have been so simple. A stab of pain shot through his arm from the mangled hand. Thanks to Pasha's beatings, his head hurt and his mind weaved in and out of clarity. He reached for support but slid down the wall in a crumpled heap onto the cold iron grating. Above him, rusty iron conduits sagged like snakes. Despite his deteriorating condition, he remained filled with resolve. "If I can't have the treasure, no one will. I'll wait and when the searchers come through the passageway below me, I'll take them all to hell with me."

Five minutes after Mifflin left, Kutna glanced up the broad, curving staircase leading to the Dorotheum's upper rooms and saw Vlad double timing down the stairs. At the same time, one of Kutna's men came up to him with a startling report.

Not wanting to arouse suspicion, Kutna followed his man at a half walk, half run toward the back of the building. They made their way through endless rooms of antiques, paintings and tapestries to a freight elevator where a gathering of warehouse workers huddled. Vlad caught up with him as he stopped in front of the open freight elevator.

"Get everyone back," Kutna shouted, "but don't let any of them into the main building." Together the two men walked into the elevator. Pasha's twisted body lay slumped across the bloody steel shafts of the forklift.

The driver was slumped on the floor. The thought that flashed across Kutna's mind was that he knew something Mifflin didn't. What was it exactly and how could he use it to his advantage?

Chapter 71

When Mifflin alighted from the cab that brought him from the Dorotheum to Stewart's office he sensed things were moving fast and he was falling behind.

"What's happening at the Dorotheum?" Stewart asked calmly.

"Kutna and Vlad are handling things. Yakov and his Czechos were caught in a cross fire. Yakov's dead along with several others."

Stewart pinched the bridge of his nose and lowered his head. "There's a car waiting to take you to see Herschel. He arranged it."

"Good. Now I can catch up with Eiker."

"You can catch up with everyone."

"I'll have a tail so you'll know where Herschel and his little band are taking us."

Stewart nodded. "I'll know where you are at all times."

"Fine. I'll be in touch."

After Mifflin left Stewart leaned both elbows on his desk. He was looking forward to the end of this episode.

When he arrived Mifflin was searched and ushered into the back room.

"Glad you could make it, Harold," Herschel said. "I was beginning to think we'd have to go without you."

"Unavoidable," Mifflin muttered as he was introduced to Lego and the three joined the others in the next room. Eiker, pacing the floor, turned at their entrance.

"What took you so long, Mifflin?"

Mifflin knew there was too much to tell. He simply said, "Christmas traffic."

Herschel quickly took center stage again. "I want to run a few final details by you before we go down. Lego has given me information not shown on any of our maps or other drawings."

Two men entered carrying Vienna Water and Power coveralls and hard hats and interrupted him.

"Thanks. Put them in the corner." Herschel waited until they left to continue. "We'll form two single file teams. I'll lead one, Dr.

Falk the other. My team will consist of Lego, Miss Lewis, Mr. Eiker and one security man. Dr. Falk will lead Dr. Koski, Mr. Mifflin and a security person. The reason for the two teams is, of course, security.

"My team will go first with a quarter mile separating us. We'll be able to assist one another if an attack occurs. Are there any questions?" Since no one responded, he continued. "Very well. When my team reaches the section where a small tributary runs off from the main stream, I'll signal for the second team to join us.

"Then we'll descend below the main gallery. This could be the most dangerous part of the expedition—a descent of about sixty feet on a vertical iron ladder."

Falk was fascinated. Perhaps Herschel was onto something. Perhaps his theory was off-the-wall. No, he had to try his way. If it turned out that the fountain wasn't the place...well, he'd deal with it.

"I'll go down first to be sure the ladder's safe," Herschel explained. "When I get to the bottom, I'll flash my light three times for you to join me. It's my firm belief that we'll find the hiding place under a room that was destroyed by bombings during the war."

Mifflin snorted. "I still don't see how the room wasn't discovered at the time of the rebuilding."

"I have no idea, Mr. Mifflin. Perhaps it was. To the workers, however, it was nothing but the remains of a bombed-out building. We must assume the treasures weren't sitting in full view. The room was once the main shipping office for everything leaving the Dorotheum.

"In addition, the room was built over an old wine cellar. Most of the world knew that the wines—some of Europe's finest—like most of the riches in the Dorotheum, were removed by the Nazis and hidden in the Bavarian Alps. When the demolition crews and builders started to rebuild they figured there was nothing to find."

"Yet you expect to find the loot after all these years?" Mifflin insisted.

"Yes, I do."

"There literally must have been tons of rubble. How will you locate the room?"

"I intend to go directly to the cellar through the wall that faces the level at the bottom of the ladder."

Mifflin rubbed the back of his hand across his mouth. "It still sounds like a wild goose chase to me but..."

Herschel replied, "I had a plan where I was headed but I couldn't pinpoint the cellar until I spoke to Lego and I had to wait for him to be delivered to me."

"What do you mean?" Falk asked.

"Lego related to me how he remembered the original building, how it looked and where the shipping office used to be. I checked my plans and, knowing how Goering's mind worked, I decided it was the most likely place."

Falk shifted uneasily. Either Herschel was off by a mile or *he* was. Herschel checked his watch.

"Our transportation will be here soon. Time to get in to our coveralls." He picked up a set, checked the size and handed them to Koski. "We have small, medium and large. As you leave you'll each be given a regulation belt that contains a tool pouch and an industrial-sized flashlight. These, along with the hard hats, should let us pass easily as Water and Power workers."

Falk was the last to leave the tailor shop, following the others into a small courtyard. It was dark and a sift of snow was falling.

Light suffused over the area from an old-fashioned, wrought iron lamp above the door. He buckled his tool belt and climbed into the Vienna Water and Power truck.

Herschel hurried everyone aboard. Inside they faced each other on long wooden benches. The security men sat nearest the tailgate. Herschel went up front next to the driver. No one spoke as the truck moved from the yard and turned onto the street. All were alone with their own thoughts, Falk certain that he had the most at stake.

Chapter 72

Steele's cheek lay pressed against the cold iron railing. He shivered and slowly eased to a sitting position despite the excruciating pain that shot through his hand to his shoulder. From his perch on the totally dark catwalk he heard the gurgle of water swirling its way beneath the old city, branching off into a narrow tunnel and out of sight. What faint light there was came from the main gallery below.

His eyes were fixed on the water. Something moved. The surface rippled, bubbled and foamed and a black glistening form rose with a hiss of air.

Steele was transfixed. He'd heard of sewer rats—but this! Then there was the glint of glass as the diver pushed his mask back. Heart thumping, Steele watched the diver climb from the water, remove his mouthpiece and shrug off his air tanks and inflatable vest. A metallic clank resounded as he set them on the stone floor.

Hardly daring to breathe, Steele pulled back into the shadows as the man removed a flashlight from his belt, aimed it down the gallery and pressed the switch three times in quick succession.

Seconds later three stabs of light answered. A rendezvous in the making and Steele had a grandstand seat.

Within five minutes of the truck arriving at the manhole, Herschel had everyone down the ladder to the first level. Falk had noticed road warning signs, the tent over the manhole, reflectors. Everything was set up exactly like city crews would have done.

"We have two levels to go," Herschel said. "The next is thirty-five feet; the last fifteen. That will put us on the main gallery level one hundred and ten feet below the street. Watch your grip on the ladders, no time for accidents."

The only sound was footwear scraping on the ladder rungs as they slowly descended to the main gallery. They heard the rushing water before they saw it. Finally they were grouped beside the gallery's stonewall.

"It's like the London Underground without the train tracks," Emma whispered to Lego.

"And a damn sight colder," Eiker replied.

"Dr. Falk, get your team together. Once we start I don't want anyone using flashlights. We'll rely on gallery lighting only."

The dim lights were built into the stonewalls and covered by metal grillwork. Falk checked for the light switches to be certain he had their exact location in mind when he and Koski made their break.

Herschel checked his watch. "Dr. Falk, I have six-thirty... mark."

"Check."

"Good. When I move out give me seven minutes and then follow. I want a safe distance between us. One of my men will be at the end of your line, a sort of 'Tail End Charlie'."

Falk shot a quick glance to Koski and received an almost

imperceptible nod. They both knew the team's security man was for Herschel's safety, not theirs. It was up to Koski to take care of Tail End Charlie.

"You remember the signal?" Herschel questioned.

"Of course," Falk replied. "Three flashes and we move up and join you for the final descent below this gallery."

Herschel shook Falk's hand. "Good luck." He turned and started moving. Lego, Emma and a security guard followed.

"Damn!" Stewart slammed his phone down and drummed his fingers on the desk. Mifflin had gone to meet Herschel and now he had no way of knowing where Mifflin and the others were. One of the men following Mifflin reported he'd lost him in traffic. A few moments later a second call informed Stewart that Mifflin's backup tail was found sitting on a bus bench with his throat cut.

Chapter 73

Mifflin puffed along, following Koski, who followed Falk. Falk heard the Mossad security man bringing up the rear. Whoever was trailing me from Stewart's office, he thought, did a damn good job. I never saw anyone.

Three stabs of light flashed up ahead. Falk turned and softly called an order to stop. "Crouch down close to the wall and stay still." He blinked a response.

Mifflin heard the metallic click of a safety catch from the security man's weapon followed only by the sound of their breathing. An icy coldness drooped around them.

Herschel beamed the answering signal. "Let's move forward, slowly now." He stood as the others in his team passed. Herschel returned to the head of the column, his voice tinged with excitement. "We're getting closer to our goal. So far all is clear."

Lego slowly shuffled forward, his mind drifting back over the years to when Nikolai Youmatoff gave him the information that had dogged his life ever since. The Danube Canal rushed along at his side as if it was the years passing. He reached back with one hand and Emma grasped it. Together they were nearing the end of a mysterious journey that, for Lego, started over a half-century earlier.

After Falk responded and they started moving ahead, he knew Herschel was intent on making his way to his contact. Falk had to make his move now. They were making the right hand turn. He whispered to Koski, "Ready?" Before she could respond, he fell to his side and grabbed his ankle.

"My ankle," he moaned. "I think it's broken."

When "Tail End Charlie" moved up beside him and bent over Falk, Koski hit him across the back of the neck with her flashlight just below the rim of the hard hat. He folded forward without a sound. Falk and Koski were up and running in the direction of the second gallery on his right. Within seconds, Falk flipped the lights out and Mifflin was alone in the darkness.

The tantalizing thought that he was getting closer to his objective made Herschel increase his stride. He arrived at the location where he was to meet the diver minutes ahead of the rest of his team.

The diver snapped a salute. "All secure, sir."

"Good. Prepare the descent."

The diver knelt on the stone floor and scraped at a film of dirt and grime until he located two recessed handles in an iron manhole cover. The rest of the team arrived and Emma, Eiker and the security man formed a semicircle around him. Lego was off to one side in the shadows, leaning against the wall to gather his strength.

The diver rounded his shoulders and pulled at the handles. Nothing happened. Shifting his grip, he tried again, his neck muscles bulging with the effort. He let go and looked at Herschel. "I need something to pry..."

He gasped, his vision focusing beyond Herschel's anxious face. A peal of maniacal laughter rang out. It echoed off the curving walls to join the omnipresent sound of rushing water and sent a stab of fear through the group. Herschel turned fast, a gun in his hand. The security man crouched beside him with his Uzi whirling in all directions, seeking a target.

One face stood out to the man in the grandstand seat. "Emma, you bitch!" Steele shouted. "I should have killed you when I had the chance." The voice seemed to come from heaven and all eyes turned upward. "You two with the guns," Steele hollered, "drop them or we'll all go up together. I'm wired with explosives."

Herschel and the guard hesitated, not sure if whoever was up there was telling the truth. They raised their flashlights.

"Steele!" Emma gasped as the powerful beams illuminated his haggard face.

Steele ripped open his shirt to reveal the bulky explosive package enclosing his upper torso. His hand also held the remote transmitter, glinting in the light. He raised it over his head. "In person...I press a button and zap..." He grinned like a lunatic.

"Do as he says," Herschel commanded and the guard let his Uzi clatter to the floor. Herschel reluctantly tossed his automatic aside. It, too, resounded as it landed in the nearby shadows.

"Emma, move closer, where it's lighter so I can see you," Steele ordered. Emma did as she was told, prepared to buy some time on the chance that Falk and Koski soon would be there to help.

"You know, Emma, we could have done this together and got away with it. Just you, me and the Yank…where *is* the Yank?"

"He's not in Vienna."

"Bullshit."

"It's true. He's not here."

"Where the hell is he?"

"Last I heard he was in the Czech Republic. We escaped." Steele snarled. "We?"

"Susan Koski and I. You remember Susan, don't you?"

"Yeah. I should have killed her, too. You see it seems killing is my forte. Took them a long time to figure out how I killed our friend, Dr. Benson."

Emma gasped and staggered back a few steps.

Lego, hidden in the shadows, stared up at the man he once called a friend. A low, animal sound escaped from Lego's lips. Driven by feral instincts stronger than reason, Lego scooped Herschel's discarded automatic from the floor. Using a two-handed grip he extended his arms forward until Steele was centered in his sights. He sucked in a deep breath, held it and squeezed the trigger.

In the same instant Steele caught the movement in the shadows. One perfect shot sang into Steele's head, the bullet plowing between his top lip and nose, but not before his thumb depressed the transmitter button.

The sound of the shot didn't fade when the roar of the explosion hit the confines of the catwalk with an intensity so strong the shock wave shuddered against the walls and through the water. It caused a waterspout to rise and meet the catwalk as it crumbled in a twisted mass of iron, wood and concrete.

Yards of metal sagged, pipes split, debris showered down onto the gallery and into the water. Herschel, the security man and the diver vanished under the initial mass of falling masonry, crushed like ants underfoot. Before a chunk of flying concrete hit him, Lego lived long enough to see bits and pieces of John Steele rain down and mix with the waters of the Danube Canal.

Chapter 74

Emma survived only because Eiker had pushed her against the curving wall, protecting her with his body.

The concussion flattened Falk against Koski and she clung tightly to him. The shock wave hit the dark, narrow passage. A hot blast of air rushed down the gallery and for a moment the floor shook. The shaking stopped, replaced by an awful stillness, and the gallery filled with billows of acrid smoke.

"We're still alive," Falk rasped, spitting out sand and grit. "But we've got to go back—Mifflin..."

Making their way through the rubble, they arrived back to where Koski had struck the guard and found Mifflin flat on his back, the dead guard beside him. Falk rolled the dead man into the water. The body swirled in the stream, hit the wall then, with one arm raised as if in farewell, sank from sight.

Mifflin groaned. Koski knelt beside him, rubbing his hands and checking him for wounds. "Are you okay?"

Mifflin opened one eye. "What happened? Where the hell did you two go?"

Falk pulled him over to the wall and propped him up. "You took so long getting to the meeting I didn't have time to fill you in on our plan."

"Thanks." Mifflin stretched, testing his body for injury. "My right inside pocket..."

Falk reached in, removed a flask and passed it to him.

Mifflin took a long swig then offered it to Falk. He refused but Koski took a deep swallow.

"I've got to get up ahead and see what the hell happened." He turned to Koski. "He's still groggy. Stay here with him. I'll be as quick as I can."

The explosion had jolted all levels of the Dorotheum. Vlad cursed inwardly as he raced to meet his men in the main hall. He knew he should have evacuated the building earlier. "Cover the exits," he instructed his men. "Avert panic and make an orderly exodus."

Kutna appeared at his side, his eyes betraying his inner fears. "Terrorists?"

"Don't know yet," Vlad said. "If so they'll make demands."

"Need any help?"

"No, thanks. City police are on the way. They'll handle things outside. We're staying in the building to make sure the place is fully evacuated."

Kutna nodded and left to return to his office. He knew without a doubt that the phone lines would be overloaded with calls from around the city.

Chapter 75

For a moment Emma thought Eiker was dead. She was pinned beneath him and the pain in her leg indicated it was broken. She fought to remain calm when a small avalanche of bricks crashed to the gallery floor inches from her head.

Some lights were still burning but the dust was thick and she could only see a few feet beyond them. Her face flushed and panic began to rise within her. She stirred against Eiker's weight. "Eiker...Eiker," she coughed.

He grunted and came to full consciousness. "Bloody hell!" he rasped as he rolled onto his side then back against Emma. "Don't move. There's no floor beyond us!"

Emma groaned. "My leg is broken."

"Which one?"

"Left," she replied through gritted teeth.

"Okay." Breathing heavily, he paused, spitting out dust and grit as he quickly assessed the situation. "There are only a few feet of floor between us and the water. I'm going to move. Your left leg is against the wall. I'll do all I can to avoid it."

Another rumbling of rocks crashed into the water to their right. They both fought the smothering fear that any minute the walls, ceiling or both would bury them. He groaned in sudden pain as he eased over her body.

"Eiker, are you all right?"

His feet searched for more ground. "I'm fine." Emma was in so much pain that she decided to believe him.

The toes of his shoes found solid stone. "There's some floor remaining," he grunted. He slid onto the cold stone and fingered the floor to his left a few inches…then nothing. Unhooking his flashlight, he thumbed it on and swept the beam around the small confine. He now realized they were marooned on a shelf no more than four feet wide jutting out over the swiftly moving current. He pointed the beam down the gallery beyond his feet. What Emma saw nearly made her heart stop.

The shelf ended abruptly, blocked by a slide of rock from ceiling to stream.

"We can't just stay here," Emma groaned. "There has to be some way out."

"Your leg is broken. What do you suggest?" Emma noticed

his labored breathing wasn't subsiding.

"Could we swim?"

"You wouldn't have a chance."

She knew he was right but to lie there doing nothing... "At least try signaling with the flashlight. Do something, for God's sake."

"I'm going for help. You'll be okay as long as you stay still. Don't move at all. Understand?"

"Yes."

"Good, now listen. I'm going to remove my coveralls and shoes, attach the flashlight to my hard hat with strips torn from the coveralls. I'll turn it on and swim back upstream until I find a spot where I can get out... find help."

He paused and winced but continued. "It's possible the authorities already have teams out looking for the cause of the explosion and hopefully will see my light." He reached over and found Emma's flashlight. "Here. If you see or hear anyone yell like hell and signal them with the flashlight beam. Got it?"

"Yes."

Slowly, hardly daring to move in case he disturbed more rocks, Eiker eased out of the coveralls and slid off his shoes. As soon as he was satisfied the flashlight was secure to his hard hat, he gave Emma's shoulder a reassuring pat. "Remember now, lie still. Everything will go like a well-oiled machine."

Emma smiled weakly despite her pain and discomfort. Seconds later she heard a splash and was alone on the ledge.

Chapter 76

Falk made his way over the wet cobblestones, following the route taken by Herschel and his team. Once out of range of Koski's light, he faced nothing but thick, palpable blackness. The ever-present dust made breathing dangerous and difficult. He stopped for a moment, listening for any sound. Nothing. The silence was tomblike.

Falk snapped on his flashlight and let the beam creep over the wall until it discovered the rockslide blocking the gallery. Slowly he approached the unyielding pile of earth, stone and twisted iron. Dropping to his knees, he rested his head against the impassable barrier.

It was evident that any attempt to dig through the mass would cause the entire tunnel to collapse. He pounded a fist in frustration against the immovable blockade that separated him, Koski and Mifflin from the others—if there were others—and a trickle of stones ran down the pile into the water.

Koski had turned off her flashlight. Now she and Mifflin sat side by side in the inky blackness.

"It's ironic," she said. "So many times in Brno I thought I'd never get back to Vienna. Now I may never get out."

"Nonsense," Mifflin replied gruffly. "You'll get out. We all will."

Koski tensed at the sound of someone approaching. Then she heard a familiar voice quietly call, "It's me, Joe."

"Emma?" Koski asked once Falk was beside her.

"I don't know. A landslide has sealed the gallery. It's blocked solid. We move one rock and the whole damn place could cave in."

Koski responded with a resounding, "We have to try something."

Falk squeezed her arm. "Don't worry. We'll get her."

Falk and Mifflin stared at the rushing water by the light of Mifflin's flashlight beam, gauging its speed and depth, considering the possibility of navigating it as a means to reach the others.

Falk finally decided. "I'm going to make an attempt to get through by swimming downstream."

"Let *me* go, Falk. I'm a strong swimmer and a damn sight more buoyant than you."

"No. I'll go."

Mifflin sighed. "Then we'll go together. Koski can stand watch. If a search party shows up she can fill them in."

Koski nodded emphatically. "Go, both of you. I'll be okay until you get back."

"We'll need some dry clothes when we return," Falk said. He and Mifflin stripped off their coveralls, shoes and shirts and slid over the edge into the cold Canal.

The water took Falk's breath away as he swam with the flow, forcefully stroking to maintain his direction. For a moment he was back in the river with Jan, swimming for his life.

The current swept them along faster than Falk expected and they stroked hard to keep themselves close to the gallery's edge. Ahead the passage curved then Falk saw the beam. It was in the center of the stream, coming toward them.

"Over there...see it!" Falk called out but soon his mouth filled with water and he spat to expel it. He swam toward the light, using every bit of energy in the process. As he drew closer, he realized it was a man swimming against the stream. He was near enough now to see his face from the downward glow of the light. "Eiker!"

The Englishman acknowledged him and Falk began pointing toward the gallery. Together they swam until they saw Mifflin waving and clinging to the side of the gallery floor.

"Over here..." Mifflin yelled. "Iron rungs in the wall..."

"Ladder rungs," Falk sputtered. "See them... There."

Both men kicked hard toward the recessed rungs in the wall, reaching them in tandem.

Once on solid ground the three men updated one another on their current situations.

"Emma is the only one left alive and she's trapped with a broken leg," Eiker reported, breathing laboriously. "We've got to get her out of there immediately."

Falk nodded. "Can you find your way back to that spot?"

Eiker seemed sure he could. "Shout when I tell you and she'll signal with the flashlight."

Once again the three men entered the nearly freezing water and headed downstream.

"Emmmaaa...Emmmaaa..." The sound of her name echoed eerily in the blackness. Still there was no return light in answer to their calls.

"It should be about here," Eiker yelled as they trod water, attempting to remain in place against the current.

"Let's get in closer and try again," Falk suggested. The cold was biting through him. He knew it would only be a matter of time before hypothermia would overtake them and they wouldn't be able to rescue anyone.

"Emma!" Falk yelled at the top of his lungs. "Emma!"

Suddenly there was a flash of light through the blackness.

"There it is." Mifflin gulped, pointing back upstream. "We passed her." He was right. They had overshot her position by several hundred yards. Falk moaned and doggedly headed back, keeping his eyes fixed on the weaving beam glinting from the darkness.

Falk's light finally traced the outline of the outcrop, exposing how totally the landslide had cut them off, leaving a ledge less than ten feet long and eight feet above the water.

Falk swam closer until he felt the rocks from the landslide underfoot. Then his foot hit something metallic. He cursed softly and turned his beam downward to reveal the scuba diver's tank, harness and flotation jacket tangled among twisted iron conduits. "Herschel's diver. Poor son of a bitch."

"Up here...I'm up here." Emma's voice sounded weak and distant.

"Don't move, Emma. We'll get you down," Falk called back. Then he gingerly climbed up on the ledge with Eiker behind him.

"We're going to get you down into the water. It'll be tough going and damned cold." Falk reached out and took Emma's hand. "Think you can make it?"

"Of course," she said bravely.

"Right, love," Eiker said with a gentleness Falk had never heard before. "Soon... get you down... now."

Falk also was surprised at Eiker's apparent breathing difficulty throughout their labors. Certainly the ordeal was punishing on all of them but Eiker always kept himself in top physical condition.

Falk had seen evidence of his extraordinary stamina in the past. Why now as they suffered nearly identical physical challenges did Eiker's strength lag noticeably behind his own?

Mifflin tapped Falk's leg with a piece of iron pipe and passed it up to him. "You can fashion a crude splint, might help a bit."

Seeing Eiker's torn coveralls, Falk yanked off more strips and crudely attached the pipe to Emma's leg. She grunted with pain but didn't complain.

Eiker took the remains of the coveralls and tossed them to

Mifflin. "Wrap those around your head to keep them dry. Emma will need them when we get back. Now for the difficult part." Eiker grated as he and Falk lowered her to the turbulent water.

"Wait," Falk said. "We can use the diver's vest." He went back and picked up the inflatable lifejacket, pulled the release cord operating the air valve and the device inflated. "You're going to travel first class," he told Emma. "This is how we'll get you out of here..." Emma never took her eyes off him as he spoke.

"Once in the water, lie on your back with your head facing the direction of the flow. I'll slip the flotation jacket under your shoulder and ease it down to your hips. Keep your legs slightly elevated to take the pressure off the broken one. Eiker and I will be on either side. We'll keep you balanced and float you back to the undamaged part of the tunnel. Mifflin will be behind you at your head."

They pushed off slowly, Mifflin moving quickly into position for a man of his girth. They were no more than ten feet from the landslide area when a crack split the air and the portion of the shelf that had supported Emma seconds before broke free and sank into the water. Silently the group exchanged glances and began to swim upstream.

Koski saw the bobbing light as the three men pulled Emma through icy waters. She quickly sent three short beams in their direction ready to assist in any way possible. A sinking feeling came over her at the sight of Emma lying on her back, not moving.

Chapter 77

"She'll be okay," Falk said as he clambered onto the gallery walkway and leaned down to receive Emma. "She has a broken leg and is nearly frozen, but she'll be fine."

"Welcome back," Koski whispered to Emma as they lifted her from the Canal and eased her to the floor.

Mifflin unwound the dry coveralls from his head and passed them to Koski, who got Emma settled. Falk turned to Mifflin and Eiker. "You two stay with her. Koski and I have to go. We'll be getting into some tight spaces and I don't mean that figuratively."

Mifflin rubbed his hand across his face. He was tired and knew it showed. "Yeah. I could do with a little rest," he admitted through chattering teeth.

"No doubt half of Vienna's finest are on their way down here by now," Falk said. "If they ask what you're doing here say you were abducted by terrorists. That should make the media happy and confuse everyone else."

"Then you'd better take this." Mifflin offered his automatic. Eiker reached for it but Koski beat him to it.

"Cool Hand Koski," Eiker quipped then coughed. Falk watched the mercenary's eyes that betrayed his matter-of-fact delivery.

"Look," Eiker said hoarsely, "I was assigned as backup, to be there at the end of this caper." He made an effort to straighten to full height but didn't quite pull it off. "I'm going with you and Koski."

Falk shook his head. "No. The most dangerous part is over," he said, hoping it was true. "We won't need you from this point on." He turned again but Eiker put a restraining hand on his arm.

"I have a duty to Cerberus," Eiker announced firmly.

Falk scowled in disgust and jerked his arm away saying, "Duty? What duty? You were to be here if we needed you. We *don't* need you, Eiker. The only duty you have now is to yourself, to collect the money Cerberus owes you for services rendered."

Falk was aware that Mifflin and Emma were silent throughout this brief exchange. He figured that Mifflin, no doubt briefed on Eiker's background at the onset, would understand. Emma, on the other hand, would probably wonder what he meant. Falk took Koski's arm. "Come on. We're wasting time."

"Falk..." Eiker started but spluttered into his hand and made a fist around the spittle that ejected from his mouth. "You don't understand..." He wheezed then suddenly doubled over and collapsed.

Falk was at his side. "Eiker! What's..." Falk stopped when he saw the Brit's fist fall open, exposing blood mixed with the ejected mucus that clung to his palm and fingers. There was a trace of crusted blood at the corners of Eiker's mouth as he groaned and rolled to his right side.

"Internal injury," Koski said, echoing Falk's thoughts. She knelt beside him and saw the once powerful, intimidating man pull his knees into a fetal position, forcing a new trickle of blood to ooze from his lips.

Eiker turned his pale face toward them and whispered, "In the explosion a chunk of flying concrete...caught me and broke at least three ribs...punctured something, I'm afraid...." A paroxysm of coughing overtook him.

Falk shook his head. That explained the obvious fatigue he saw earlier. What exertion, he thought. What superhuman strength it must have taken to swim, to help guide Emma through the swift channel current. The man was phenomenal. "Why the hell didn't you tell us?"

"Listen," Eiker whispered urgently. He winced and his eyes closed. "Left leg pocket..."

Falk jabbed his hand into the man's pocket. His fingers

extracted an oilskin package.

"Open it," Eiker wheezed. "Tear the top off…"

Falk inverted the waterproof pack. Two metal spools of thin wire slid into his palm. He looked quizzically at Eiker, about to ask what it was when suddenly he knew. He heard Koski gasp beside him.

"'The Judas List,'" Falk whispered. A cold chill prickled his spine, the hair on the back of his neck rising as if drawn by a magnet.

"Stewart gave it to me…" Eiker rasped.

Falk finished the sentence, "To plant with the loot."

Falk saw it all clearly now. Tom Stewart hadn't exactly lied but, in Clintonesque style, hadn't told the whole truth. He said that Eiker had come on board in case he was needed. Oh, Stewart needed him, all right. Needed him to do exactly what Falk had, in Stewart's office during their first meeting, hypothesized that some rogue faction might do.

Doubtless this recording contained a list of names that Cerberus wanted the world to believe aided and abetted the Third Reich so a Fourth Reich could be born along with a new world order. Individuals and organizations that Cerberus needed, for one reason or another, to discredit mightily and irrevocably.

Falk didn't need to study the recording. He had no doubt that it was expertly crafted to assimilate an authentic, vintage 1940s German-made wire recording. Stewart thought of everything. The bastard!

"We've been betrayed, Joe," Koski exclaimed. "When you suggested that some unscrupulous group might make and plant such a device, Stewart said he wouldn't do such a thing."

Falk shook his head. "That's just the half of it. He merely said it probably would be impossible to generate and plant that type of a recording. He never said he wouldn't do it."

"It's up to you now, Falk," Eiker said weakly. "I can't go. You'll have to…"

"No!" Falk said harshly. "I don't fucking think so. It would be unethical, immoral…illegal."

Eiker managed a snort. "Immoral—high and mighty Joseph Falk—you and Will Rogers. I prefer Mark Twain: 'An ethical man is a Christian holding four aces.'" He stopped and choked up more blood.

"No more talking," Koski said gently. "Just lie still and relax."

He waved her advice aside. "Just doing my job, Falk, and doing it well was always my goal." He clutched the front of Falk's shirt and his head suddenly slumped to the floor as a spasm heaved through his body, pumping out a final mouthful of life.

"He's gone," Koski whispered, touching two fingers to his carotid artery.

Falk was aware of a soft whimpering. He knew that Emma, seated on the concrete several yards away, saw and recognized the throes of death. Mifflin left her side and walked over to Eiker.

"He was a good man in a way not everyone could understand," Mifflin said and crossed himself.

Falk rose and walked away from the others. It was possible that corruption could sometimes be sanctioned but not without outrage and outrage was what Falk felt when he saw the recording spools. He readily admitted he was furious that Stewart had trusted Eiker with the device. It meant that when he got back home he would need to have an honest ideological discussion with Tom Stewart and reexamine his future role in the organization.

He jammed the recording deep into his pocket, looked over at

Koski, who had covered Eiker's face with what was left of his coveralls, and said gruffly, "Come on, Koski. We've got things to do."

Chapter 78

Emma and Mifflin saw the flashlight beams bobbing crazily as the footsteps grew louder. "Here," Emma shouted. "We're over here." Three soldiers with automatic weapons at the ready hurried toward them.

"Don't move," the officer said in German.

Emma grimaced and replied in perfect German then switched to English. "My friend doesn't understand."

The officer lowered his weapon. "Who are you?"

Emma gave what she thought was an impressive account of how she and Mifflin had been walking innocently along the street and witnessed a group of masked men descending into a manhole. They had been spotted, taken prisoner and forced to go with them. After what seemed like miles, they heard gunfire then a terrific explosion in which she suffered a broken leg. The men retreated and left them here.

"Why are you wearing city coveralls?" the officer asked.

"They made us wear them." Emma's voice sounded reedy and she nervously cleared her throat. She knew they would find the yellow lifejacket next. "One of the men, a diver, went into the water over there." She stretched her slender neck upwards and aimed her blue, wide-eyed orbs directly at him. "Can you get me to a hospital? I need medical aid and I...I think I'm going to faint."

The story seemed a gross fabrication yet something caused the officer to postpone further questioning. "I will see that you get attention." He looked at Mifflin, leaning against the wall like a deflated whale. "Both of you."

Mifflin was thankful he'd had the time to slide Eiker's body over the edge into the Canal before the soldiers arrived. He also was sad at the unchristian way in which he had to clear the scene.

Captain Vlad was still at the Dorotheum when he received the call.

"See that they are well cared for. Notify their respective embassies immediately. When Herr Mifflin has changed into dry clothes tell him I'll be waiting here for him. Show him every courtesy." Vlad recradled the phone and looked thoughtfully across the main hall. Where else would he expect Mifflin to be when an explosion rocked the building but in the middle of the damned thing.

Chapter 79

"We turn left at the third slot," Falk said as they cautiously entered into a narrow, dimly lit entrance off the gallery.

"Slot?" Koski asked.

"Old inspection slots," Falk replied. "They once were used by inspectors checking the electrical conduits that are like a maze, zigzagging throughout the sewer system. Computer does it nowadays. I saw the slots on Herschel's maps, made notes and a rough sketch when he was out of the room. I also tore a page from one of the map books. Unfortunately," he stopped, reached into his back pocket and pulled out a handful of soggy pulp, "they weren't waterproof."

They were standing a few feet into the passage when Koski queried, "How far do we have to go?"

Falk grunted. "About a quarter of a mile but a tough quarter mile."

"Meaning what?"

"The passageways get narrow—very narrow—in places. The floor gets steeper the further we go. The brick roof will cause us to be belly crawling in spots."

Koski felt her stomach flip. She suffered from what she once called "discomfort in tight places." She hadn't revealed it to anyone, fearing it would compromise her chances of getting through the FBI Academy. So far she had managed to tough it out in situations where it might have surfaced. Over the past few years, however, the condition had worsened. Despite attempts to ignore it, she recognized indications that it had solidified from mere discomfort to full-blown claustrophobia. Now she would be nearly flat on her belly, deep underground in another extremely confined space…

"I'll be okay," she said with dubious conviction. "I've been in tight places before."

They moved forward in silence then Falk suddenly hissed, "Quickly…to the left!" They slipped into a recess in the wall. "Don't move…listen." They heard voices that grew louder. Hardly daring to breathe, they looked back as a parade of Austrian soldiers filed past the end of the entrance.

The squad of men never so much as glanced in their direction. When they passed, Falk whispered, "No doubt trying to discover the reason for the explosion. They'll find Emma and Mifflin and take them out of this hellhole." Eiker, he silently added, already left it.

Air noticeably lessened as Falk and Koski went deeper into the narrow passage as if squeezed between the ancient stonewalls, its life-sustaining properties lost. The ground beneath their feet turned to hard-packed earth. Once they passed the last dim light, there was only a bulb cupped by a corroded enamel shade dangling from an old-fashioned flex cable. Darkness was ahead.

"You sure this is the right passage?" Koski asked.

"Yes. From here the ground steepens to nearly meet the ceiling."

Koski was already aware that she had begun to stoop slightly.

"This passage will get narrower," Falk said. "You have to imagine a wedge of pie on its side. We must almost reach the tip before we come to the third slot on the left."

The air had lost its buoyancy and was flat and oppressive. Sweat streamed down Koski's forehead and into her eyes. Venerable dust rose from the floor with every step then resettled. Soon they had to crawl forward on hands and knees.

"Just like the monks in the *Book of Hours*," Falk recalled. "We're on our knees. To me it makes more sense every minute."

Koski shivered despite her rising body heat and the discomfort of perspiration. She merely grunted in response and crawled mechanically behind Falk, trying to gain strength from his determination.

A few hundred feet farther and they were nearly flat on their stomachs, inching forward by elbow and toe movements. The passage had shrunk drastically. Koski could scarcely raise her head without it touching bare rock. Dust swirled in her face as Falk squirmed forward ahead of her.

"Hold on!" Falk's voice came back to her, muffled and distorted. "I see a metal door recessed into the wall on my left." There was silence for a second then his exuberance faded. "Shit! There's a fucking padlock and it's rusted to hell."

In that moment Koski judged the dimensions of the surrounding passage to be no more than thirty-six inches wide and less than twenty-four inches high. The full flare of panic rose within her. She tried to move but couldn't. The walls closed in. Dizziness and lightheadedness gave way to hot, oppressive heaviness of heart and mind. Her throat constricted. She was a candle burning at both ends, dual flames dueling... inescapably approaching each other... doomed to collide, to eat each other up in tongues of exploding fire.

Primal instincts made her thrust her arms before her and clasp her hands. She wrung them in writhing, tortured undulations. Some synapse in her brain arced—or failed to—and blackness whorled inside her head.

"Koski," Falk said softly.

"Wha..."

"Koski!" Falk repeated. This time she consciously heard his voice.

"Yes."

"Are you okay?" The concern in his voice made her aware of how far she'd strayed.

"Yes." She said it stronger now, breathing deeply, having conquered nothing but undergone a lifetime in that black moment and survived. It had taken that moment to send her back to some semblance of control. She sighed again. "I'm fine."

She knew she wasn't, not entirely. She had no idea how much longer this slight revival would sustain her but she took a second to thank God for it. Her thoughts were clearer now.

"Try bashing the lock with the flashlight handle," she suggested, surprised she remembered his last words.

The sound of the attempt clanged resoundingly through the small passage. "Damn it. It won't budge." After trying everything in his tool pouch, Falk cursed again, his breath coming in high, heavy wheezes. "We have to get in!"

"The plastic automatic I gave you," Koski said impatiently. "It's a 9mm. That should do the job."

"In this small confine it'll be dangerous as hell…"

"You have a better idea?"

Falk propped the flashlight into a position that gave full beam on the padlock. "I'm going to make a side-on shot and pray that it penetrates and doesn't ricochet. Here goes."

The sound of the shot was shattering. There was a flash and the area filled with the smell of cordite. For several seconds a miniature dust squall obliterated everything.

Chapter 80

A fit of coughing came back to Koski then Falk's voice.

"It worked! Blew it to hell and gone."

Koski heard the sound of a metal door groaning on complaining hinges. Falk passed the automatic back to her. "Hang on to that. If my navigation is on track we should be at the hiding place within fifteen minutes."

They entered through the metal door and found themselves in a near duplicate of the passage they'd left. In some areas, this chamber's substratum had sagged from water seepage, leaving hollows and deep ruts. Small piles of rock and stone had fallen from the walls and they had to rake them aside with their hands. It was, however, deeper and wider, Falk noted with some relief, thinking of Koski.

"Fifteen feet to the right and we'll reach the shaft at the side of the cistern," Falk reported. He paused to catch his breath. "Then through the wall and we're inside."

"Through the wall? How?"

"There's a wooden service door ten feet from the end of the east wall. If it's rotten it won't take much to bust through."

"Did your homework, I see," she said, her voice less pinched due to the increased space between their bodies and the walls and ceiling.

"Yeah," he said, wondering if he would pass the test. Would the treasures be where he envisioned them?

Finally Falk halted. "There it is!" He steadied his flashlight on a small, wooden door set into the wall. A surge of excitement ran through him. He felt sure the cistern and Goering's plunder were behind that door.

Koski was able to position herself beside Falk now, the area allowing them to stand upright. He traced the outline of the door with his light. "Looks in pretty good condition, no sign of rot."

Koski snorted. "Sure. Where's rot when you need it?" She thumped her hand against the door and rattled the latch. "We're going to have to break it down to get in."

"Can't shoot this open. The hinges are on the inside." Falk bit his lip in concentration. There *had* to be a way. He sank to the floor, laid on his back with his feet braced against the door and kicked. Beyond a jolt to his knees, nothing was accomplished.

Koski hustled down beside him. "We'll do it together. On the count of three…" They kicked in unison. There was a creak but no visible sign of movement.

"Something could be jammed against it from the inside," Koski speculated. "Could there be another way in?"

Falk grunted. "Not that I know of. Let's try again." Their feet crashed against the door. "I think it moved. Did you feel it?"

Koski shook her head then cocked it slightly. "Listen…hear that?"

"What?"

"Sounds like water..." Koski turned on her flashlight and directed the beam back through the passage where they had come. "My God!"

Falk swung his light around and saw the earthen floor turning black—wet black. Water seeped slowly down the passage, curling and nudging into the dry earth. In the few seconds that introduced their horror, it had already started to puddle. Curving bays turned into circles and became pools as more water ran into the chamber.

They both jumped to their feet. "We have to get out," Koski screeched, the edge of panic in her voice. "We'll be trapped."

Falk trained his light on the small tunnel ahead. "I'm afraid it's not much use, Koski. Look..." A second snake of water wriggled into the area from the mouth of the escape passage.

Falk verbalized their fear. "Unless we get through the door and into the cistern, *now*..."

Chapter 81

Vlad's men drove Mifflin to the Dorotheum where he sipped a glass of cognac, sitting with Vlad in the head porter's cubicle.

Mifflin said, "There still are two members of the American team somewhere under the streets of Vienna."

"Do you have any idea where exactly?"

Mifflin took a long sip and eyed Vlad over the rim of his glass. "I'd guess somewhere between the Dorotheum and the two churches, Capuchin and Augustine."

Vlad frowned. "If memory serves that should be around the Neuer Markt near the Donner Fountain. We'll know soon if they're still down there. I have an expert from the Water and Power on the way." Vlad glanced up as someone passed the window. "In fact, I think that's her now."

The woman, escorted by one of Vlad's men, looked to be in her mid-forties with strands of gray hair visible beneath the brim of her yellow hard hat. "Captain Vlad?"

"Yes and this is Herr Mifflin, American security, working with us."

"I'm Gerda Dobbler, Vienna Water and Power."

"Have you been down to survey the damage?" Vlad asked.

"No. I understood we would go together."

They filed from the porter's office into the main hall and toward the front entrance. Three of Vlad's men followed a few feet behind.

Emma was transferred by car to the British Embassy following a trip to the hospital, where her leg was set and given a plaster cast. It began at her left knee and continued down to enclose her foot, except for her toes that were nearly the same off gray as the cast. Emma was now comfortably seated opposite Jack Blake, an assistant attaché.

Blake beamed across his desk at Emma. "It won't be too long. You'll have to wait until they take the curse off you."

"Curse?"

Blake nodded. "Our little joke. House arrest."

"They really can make me stay in here?"

"Step out the front door and you'll find out." He gave her a slightly lopsided grin. "You're safe here. Just sit tight. We'll have you on the next plane to Heathrow."

"I don't want to 'sit tight' or take a plane. I live in Vienna and I have permanent status rights. I own a business and I want to find my friends, who I believe are in danger."

"We're doing everything we can."

"Right. I'd like to know why the British Embassy sat on its backside while I was a fugitive in the Czech Republic."

The aide rubbed his chin. "I have a call out to one of our field people. When he checks in we'll see what we can do about finding your friends."

Emma glanced at the clock. "I'll give you one hour. If I don't have any news by then I'll defect to the American Embassy. *They'll* do something."

Blake raised his eyes, pushed an intercom button and asked for tea, lots of strong black tea.

Chapter 82

Falk and Koski lay on their backs. They pounded desperately with their feet against the door that Falk had trained his flashlight on. There was little time to concentrate on anything but getting into the cistern before the passage flooded.

Koski gasped.

"What?" Falk asked between tortured breaths.

"My arm. Felt like something…"

"Jesus!" Falk grunted. "There's something on my stomach!"

Two red agate eyes glowed at him and he felt the grip of quivering, rodent feet on his body. He brought the light down to reveal a rat the size of a rabbit. Its slick body glistened with moisture, its tail round and as thick as a man's forefinger. He shuddered and swung the flashlight at it but missed. It scurried into a corner, squealing with fear and desperation.

"Oh my God," Koski screamed. "It's been washed down the slots. AGGH!" She screeched again and grabbed the automatic. "Hold the light on him…" She fired and the rat's head burst and was gone, leaving a streak of vermilion gore on the wall and a twitching body floating on the water.

Falk felt the darkness closing in. Worse, as the water lapped in stinking little waves beneath his chin, he felt an awful aura of presence, a dreadful sense of countless living things sharing the shrinking chamber around him.

He turned and directed his light toward where he and Koski had entered. Dozens of terrified burgundy eyes and glossy black liquid bodies feverishly writhed over and under each other as they tumbled with water into the chamber.

Falk felt the tremor of terror that went through Koski's body. Without a word, they both resumed kicking furiously, grunting and groaning as their feet pounded the wood. Koski's screeches rose above that of their rodent companions. Finally, mercifully, there was a splintering crack and the door gave a few inches. Falk was on his knees, muscling against the stubborn old timber. It yielded with his final effort and they were through the opening like a shot.

They shoved the door back in place and Falk jammed against it. His foot touched something cold and solid as stone. Koski slumped against the wall beside him.

"That'll keep the bastards out," Falk exclaimed. However, a thin thread of water continued to inch slowly beneath the door and into the cistern.

An overpowering mustiness hit them. Falk had never breathed such air, thick as a wall and utterly still.

"Do you hear it?" Koski whispered.

"What?"

"The sleep of ages."

He did. He picked up his flashlight and its beam found three metal-shaded light bulbs hanging by cloth covered electrical flex, typical of Europe in the 1940s.

"Overhead lights," he said with relief. "Need to find the switch."

"Here." Koski was on her feet and snapped the toggles up. Two of the lights came on, casting a dim amber glow around the room and revealing the fact that Falk and Koski had indeed found what many sought.

As Falk's eyes grew accustomed to the gloom, he noticed the article he used to prop against the door was a piece of Classic Greek sculpture. It looked like it was from the east pediment of the Parthenon. His mouth fell open and he thought he said, "Jesus!" but it was Koski who spoke. Falk turned to see what she saw.

It was a scene from the caves of Ali Baba, the inner sanctum of a Pharaoh's tomb, a museum with an encyclopedic range of fine art. The long, low space seemed to flow with gold and silver.

Falk took several steps and assessed his surroundings in detail. Beside him, a deep, three-tiered metal shelf began and ran about thirty feet to the end of the room. A desk, lacquered with chinoiserie decoration in Queen Anne style, reflected the dim glimmer of the second light.

The shelf held silver and gold chalices, rows of urns and vases and ancient glazed pottery. There were Byzantine mosaics, sculpture and paintings from the Renaissance, Gothic, and Baroque —all periods it seemed. The floor space was jammed with sealed wooden crates. The black eagle and swastika on each appeared as clear as the day they were stenciled. The whole room seemed to shimmer eerily in the diffused light.

"How ironic," Koski said introspectively. "Here in the middle of all these beautiful things I only feel anger. I think of those who once owned and cherished these treasures and from whom they were stolen."

Falk nodded. "At least some may find their way back to their rightful owners." He looked around. "But now we've got to figure out how to get out of here."

Remembering the plans he had scanned with Herschel prior to leaving the tailor shop, he said, "This place was once part of a Roman water system, a bricked cistern that later became part of the Donner Fountain's original water supply." He concentrated his flashlight along the wall near ceiling level. "That's our best place to break through the ceiling. Water once flowed in there—you can see the slight difference in coloration—and exited out the other end as needed, water in, water out."

Koski made a move to follow a double row of gilt framed oil paintings stacked on a long, low bench when Falk stopped her.

"Don't move!" His voice was harsh and deliberate. "Don't touch anything. It's occurred to me that this place might be booby-trapped."

Koski remained motionless. A trickle of water continued to seep into the cistern behind them. They heard the squeal of the rats as they fought for their lives outside the wooden door. "If there *is* a booby-trap can you locate and disarm it?" she asked.

"I took a course in mines and booby-traps."

"Then we can use the explosives to blast our way out through the roof."

"Good God, Koski! I didn't say I'm a demolition expert."

"You have a better idea?"

Falk sighed. "Suppose I do find it? If I make the slightest error we'll be gone in a flash. Explosives are touchy any time, old explosives even worse."

"Better than drowning, Joe." Koski trained the beam into each corner of the room. "I've read about ancient diggings where traps were set to kill the intruder while leaving the treasures intact. Seems odd this place would be wired to destroy everything."

Falk's voice began low and rose as he spoke. "Of course. Good thinking, partner. An AHD—or anti-handling device— usually is a small, anti-personnel explosive that kills the intruder but protects the inventory." He began sweeping the floor with the light. "Remember, a small explosive trap can be a trigger for something more lethal so don't touch anything."

Falk cautiously made his way toward the other end of the room. Recalling his FBI training as a young man, he still heard the instructor, an old ex-sergeant from the Corps of Engineers, as he held up a detonating cap for the class to see. "This type of detonator is so sensitive that two flies copulating on its surface are enough to set it off." His students laughed at the time but later the sergeant's words proved to be only a mild exaggeration. Falk knew the search would be difficult and dangerous, a visual—touch and smell procedure. His instincts and training had saved his life in the past. He had to trust them now.

As Falk checked out the antique Queen Anne desk, Koski scanned the room for a possible alternate exit. She walked cautiously, stepping only where Falk had stepped, touching nothing.

Falk quickly concluded a search of the desk's exterior, carefully running his hands over the decorative lines. Once convinced it was not booby-trapped, he was prepared, grudgingly, to finish the task for Cerberus that Rod Eiker had started. Quickly he went through the desk drawers, pushing papers aside. Finally he tried the bottom right hand drawer. Locked.

Falk cursed and removed a penknife from his pocket. With a few expert moves, the drawer opened in seconds. Stewart's hunch was right. A compact wire recorder was the only thing inside. Thoughts of booby-traps again ran through Falk's mind as he reached in. His hand hovered over the piece of equipment as his eyes searched for hidden wires. All seemed clear. He lifted the lid slowly and carefully and saw the two spools of wire. Easing them from their spindles, he quickly put them in his pocket and replaced them with the ones Eiker had given him, being sure to wipe off any fingerprints.

He stared at the Cerberus replacement, knowing that he had dropped the stone into a pond of time whose ripples would reverberate for untold generations.

For a moment, he almost reached back into the drawer to remove the recoding then quickly shut it as Koski appeared at his side. They exchanged looks and immediately she knew what he had done.

"You made the switch." Not waiting for an answer, she added, "The water has eased off. Apparently the slots are filled. It's found its own level."

Falk nodded. "Yeah. I made the delivery." He patted his pocket. "I've also thought over the trigger idea and narrowed it down to one possibility based on the German love of chemical warfare, poison gas. We might have already unwittingly unleashed a silent booby-trap."

"Whoa!" Koski retorted. "An ideal way to get rid of an intruder and not harm the inventory. Could we survive by getting air from the slots until the gas dissipates?"

"Not if the gas was mustard or lewisite. Either of those old wartime chemicals can be released in mist form. It only has to touch the skin and it can enter the blood stream in seconds. You don't even have to inhale."

"We've got to break out of here now." She glanced around for something to use to batter a hole in the ceiling. Her vision fell on a ceremonial spear propped against a nearby wall. It was nine feet long with a thick, wooden shaft and a tip of hand-forged beaten iron. "I hope it's not wired to explode," she said, grabbing it.

With Koski behind him, Falk moved cautiously toward a stack of crates. He took no more than three steps when he froze in midstride. "Stop!" he hissed. "For God's sake, don't move a muscle. I've triggered a mine."

Chapter 83

The water cascading from the slots and across the gallery into the Danube Canal told Gerda all she needed to know. She stopped and called back to Mifflin and Vlad.

"We can't go any farther. Too dangerous. There's been extensive damage from the explosion and water from the inspection slots indicates breakage higher up, possibly in water and electrical lines."

The three stared at the gushing stream spewing vile-smelling water. Dobbler waved for them to follow. They returned to the surface by way of the iron ladder Mifflin and the others had descended a few hours earlier.

Mifflin felt his legs quivering as he stood in the cold air on the street level. He needed rest. He needed…Vlad passed him a hip flask.

"Thanks." Mifflin tipped it back and let the fiery liquid race down his throat. He needed brandy. He also needed to come to terms with the fact that he was definitely out of the running. It was Falk and Koski who were going down to the wire.

Chapter 84

"I felt the mine activate." Falk remained frozen on the mined flagstone. Koski was a statue behind him. Beads of sweat oozed to the surface of his skin. "A German Teller mine, I'd guess and it could be tied in to release gas when the mine explodes. It's safe as long as my weight remains on the firing pin...like holding in a hand grenade pin."

Falk grew utterly calm. A mine wasn't a rat or water creeping up and stalking you. It was a patient device that waited for you to find it. Falk would need to bring all his experience to this worthy adversary. He reasoned that somewhere in this space was a locked valve that would turn off the gas. He also knew the key to that valve wasn't in this room. It was "out there" somewhere having journeyed from Goering to Youmatoff to Lego to...who knew where?

"Koski, you'll have to gently pry the flagstone to my left. There could be a set of wires beneath it, an electrical connection to a hidden gas canister set to trigger when this device explodes. I want you to cut the wires so it won't set off the gas when I get off."

"Get off?"

"Yes. Now listen carefully. Cut the wires to immobilize the electrical circuit then we'll pull one of the crates onto this flagstone to simulate my weight and keep the firing pin in place. You'll have to work fast. I can't stay rigid like this for long."

Setting down the spear, she sank to her knees and started scraping at the edge of the two-foot slab of paving stone, trying to get a grip with her fingers. Using a screwdriver from the kit around her waist she soon had the slab loose. It was too heavy to lift. She needed something to wedge beneath it.

"Hurry, Koski," Falk urged. "Please."

She grabbed the spear again and dragged a small nearby box to her side. Using the box as a fulcrum for the spear's shaft, she pried down and the slab, at least two inches thick, lifted slightly. Grunting with effort, she angled the stone to allow her to slide it aside with her hands. She stared at the flat black earth, hard-packed and rock-smooth from years beneath the pavement. There weren't any wires.

"See anything?" Falk tried to conceal the strain in his voice.

"A small metal box sunk into the ground with a keyhole."

"Gas activating lock," Falk said grimly. "Move carefully and stay clear of it."

She gently scratched the earth's surface with the screwdriver, being careful not to dig too deep and disturb hidden wires. Her hand trembled as she traced the tip of the tool across the packed soil. Sweat trickled into her eyes. "The blade touched something!" she exclaimed suddenly.

Abandoning the tool, she let her fingers gently probe the damp earth. Neither of them dared breathe as she scraped around the object. "It feels oval, like a large egg and...there's another..." She stopped.

"What is it?" Falk demanded as he heard her swallow deeply. Her voice was small as she replied. "It's a skull. History is riddled with documented cases where the victors hid the spoils then killed those who aided them. The reason we're in this mess is because one man lived to tell tales." She paused. "I just uncovered the remains of two who didn't."

"Koski, quit the history lesson. You see any wires?" he demanded as much to refocus Koski's thoughts as to hurry the process that would relieve his cramping leg muscles and get them out of there.

"No."

"Okay...try the flagstone to my right."

She wiped the sweat from her eyes with the back of her hand, moved to the stone on Falk's dextral side and repeated the process. This time she saw copper wires when she lifted the slab. "Bingo!"

"Good." Falk fell into his groove now, his thoughts concise. "If the gas lock mechanism was keyed and gets triggered, we'll need something to cover our faces, to serve as crude gas masks. First I need a crate to counterbalance my weight. That one," he pointed.

She hesitated. "How can we be sure it's not booby-trapped?"

Falk winced from the pain in his aching limbs. "Pray and hurry."

Then the ballet began. Both were aware that the slightest jar or jolt could end their lives in a flash. Koski disturbed the six-foot tall wooden crate from its spot then pushed until it rested on the edge of Falk's stone slab. The dreadful silence of the room seemed to close in on them, broken only by the grating and rasping of the crate on stone and their harsh, urgent breathing.

Koski pressed with all her strength, willing the crate to move closer. It slid across the stone inch by agonizing inch until it touched Falk's feet.

"Okay," he said. "I'll take it from here." He tugged and pulled the heavy wooden crate into the center of the stone slab. He prayed he could get the box into the exact center to be certain the weight continued to hold the mine's firing pin in place.

Koski unzipped her coveralls and removed her shirt. She pressed it into a puddle of water to give temporary protection against the possibility of gas. Next she ripped it in half and handed a section to Falk, who stuffed the wet cloth into his pocket. Koski knelt beside the flagstone that had covered the wires.

"Which wire do I cut?"

"This will be by-guess-and-by-God," Falk rasped. "Try the one farthest from my right. A quick tap should do it. Then get up on the crates and start bashing a hole in the ceiling." He paused, looking down at her, hoping that all the words he had never said but meant to were in his eyes. "Good luck, partner."

An eerie sense came over Koski as she placed the screwdriver's blade on the wire with her left hand, an almost out-of-body experience. Her hand became remarkably steady as she delivered the first blow to the screwdriver handle with her right palm. The blade cut through the soft copper wire with ease.

For a second, a heartbeat, nothing happened. She stared up at Falk not daring to breathe. Then she heard a soft, sibilant hiss like a nest of disturbed vipers.

She broke from her spot, scrambled and clawed her way to the top of the crates. Furiously she jammed the spear's shaft into the crumbling mortar between the old brick ceiling. An acrid smell curled around her. She pressed the wet cloth against her mouth and nose with her left hand. She turned to look at Falk and what she saw unfolded in slow, agonizing motion.

Falk quickly edged around the crate that now covered the explosive flagstone and eased up the wooden side until he was standing on top. He ripped out the wet cloth and wrapped it around his nose and mouth at the same time pushing Goering's "Judas List" deeper into his pocket. Then he made a headlong dive from the top of the crate in Koski's direction. The mine exploded as his body arched through the air like a gymnast.

The blast ripped through the cistern with an erupting orange flash. The pungent smell of cordite came to Koski on a wave of piercing heat. The crate disintegrated and a discharge of dazzling color—gold coins, strings of rubies emeralds and diamonds—blew into the air and fell with Falk to the wet, stone floor.

Chapter 85

When Captain Vlad received the call about an explosion beneath the Donner Fountain he ordered his bomb squad to the scene, and his driver to take Mifflin and himself to the fountain.

The huge ornate fountain, dry and turned off for the winter, was a bustle of activity. Vlad handed his flask to Mifflin. "Stay here. Don't come any closer."

The bomb squad, already down in the dry basin of the fountain, was removing an iron grating used by maintenance crews.

As soon as Vlad neared the opening to the pumping room beneath the basin, he caught a whiff of dreadful, fetid air. Members of the bomb squad quickly put on their respirators. Vlad had one thrust at him as he called topside, demanding that exhaust fans be sent down on the double.

He slipped on the gas mask and crossed the basin. Next he descended the maintenance ladder to where two of his men worked frantically at the rusted bolt on an old iron door.

Falk lay in a fetal heap against a stack of splintered crates. A trickle of blood oozed from a gash on his forehead.

Koski kept the cloth pressed to her nose and mouth as she scrambled down to her companion. Expelling a gasp of relief, she realized that Falk, though unconscious, was still alive. She rewet both cloth masks, wrapped the torn, soggy shirt around his face again and tied it at the back of his head.

She felt her lungs searing but was thankful it wasn't the type of gas that entered through the skin or they'd both be dead.

Koski struggled back up the crates to the small, jagged hole she had managed in the ceiling. Feverishly, desperately, she worked to make the crumbling mortar wider, thrusting the spear upward with ever-weakening blows. Her head began to ring. Her eyesight blurred as dust and debris mixed with fading senses.

Soon each breath was an effort and she slumped forward onto the crate. Her eyes were closing. She thought she heard the sound of crumbling stone somewhere above her. She believed that a cool, damp, miraculous draft of fresh air flowed over her before she toppled on the edge of an almost welcome blackness. Suddenly the stone and plaster above her gapped into a three-foot wide opening and a pair of boots dangled for a second before the rest of one of the bomb squad dropped into the chamber.

Vlad beamed his powerful D6 into the darkness. Dust created by the explosion still swirled as other squad members inched forward. Vlad saw a dim, unmoving light and hurried toward it. Kneeling beside a jagged hole in the floor, he looked down into a dimly lit vault-like room that spewed the noxious air. No one could survive that, he thought.

The beam picked up the dull glint of the iron-tipped spear first then it found Falk and Koski, collapsed and still.

Mifflin stood on one of the three shallow steps surrounding the fountain. Nearby, Emma sat in a wheelchair wrapped in blankets.

Mifflin, ducking between members of the bomb squad, peered into the basin of the fountain. Utility lights were strung over the shoulder of one of the statues in the center of the fountain, past its wreathed head, over the oar on its shoulder and down into the basin.

Men scurried in and out of the manhole. Mifflin rounded his shoulders and jammed his hands deep into his coat pockets. The wind was cold and it occurred to him how very tired he was. He pushed over and joined Emma.

"Can't see much yet," he said.

"Why don't they hurry?" Emma moaned.

"Koski and Falk will be fine," Mifflin said with little certainty because he'd had a whiff of the air that boiled up from the manhole.

Emma turned to him. "What will happen if they've found the treasures?"

"I don't know. The United Nations most likely will take over. Each item will have to be inventoried and reported to the World Council down to the last nail. Everybody will be here... international organizations of every ilk, the media..." He shook his head. "I don't envy Franz Kutna being involved with the international problems that'll arise as a sidebar to all this." With his usual bulldozing tact, he added, "He lost Rosie Wimmer."

Emma nodded sadly. "I heard. So many lives have been destroyed." Yes, she thought. Rosie was gone. Steele was gone, too. For better or worse, they'd been her lifeline to Vienna. Her thoughts were suddenly interrupted by a flurry of activity at the hole.

"Hold on," Mifflin said and elbowed his way forward as Vlad emerged from the pump room. Vlad pulled off his respirator and stood aside as Koski and Falk emerged from the inner chamber. Carried by rescue workers, their faces were covered by gas masks.

Mifflin stood back as two stretchers pushed past then he peered into the basin again. Vlad raised his head and gave Mifflin a thumbs-up. Koski and Falk were alive.

Mifflin accompanied the unconscious forms of the agents in the ambulance to a military hospital in Vienna courtesy of Captain Vlad. That's when Mifflin surreptitiously removed the recording spools from Falk's pocket.

Chapter 86

It was less than twelve hours after their rescue. Koski and Falk, still somewhat pale, sat with Mifflin facing Tom Stewart in an American Embassy office.

"You did well," said Stewart calmly. "The United Nations Security Council already has the wire recording."

Falk gave an impatient nod. He still felt used. Koski quickly asked, "Did we learn anything from the German recording?"

He riffled the pages of a notebook on his desk. "Yes, although some of the information is old hat, such as the 1924 Dawes Plan that flooded Germany with an incredible amount of American capital and enabled Germany to build its war machine. The three largest loans went into developing industries, among them I. G. Farben Co. It became the largest corporation in Europe after a $30 million loan from the Rockefeller's National City Bank subsequent to the end of World War I." Stewart glanced up then back to his notebook.

"It goes on to mention that in 1939 Standard Oil of New Jersey sold I. G. Farben high quality aviation fuel. I. G. Farben's assets in the United States were controlled by a holding company called American I. G. Farben Chemical Corp."

Mifflin sighed. "What once was a dark secret has become known over time and the general public either doesn't know or care. I'd say probably a little of both."

"American funding was involved in helping the Nazis?"

Koski sounded surprised.

Stewart nodded knowingly. "Not only America, Koski. England and many others, too many to mention. War is a profitable entity to its patrons."

"So other than locating Goering's ill-gotten gains it was a waste of time," Falk said bitterly.

"Far from it, Joe," Stewart replied quietly. "The recording gave us a look into the future planning for the Fourth Reich. There were items mentioned that already have been proven true. One name mentioned jogged the memory of some of the older members at the playback session. It was Hajj Amin al-Husseini, the viciously anti-Semitic grand mufti of Jerusalem, who lived in Berlin as a welcome guest and ally of the Nazis throughout the Holocaust. Hitler had a Muslim cleric broadcasting from Berlin, who called for the extermination of the Jews.

"The mufti was useful to Hitler on another front as well…Tito was stirring up some serious shit in Yugoslavia and in 1943 the Nazis were tied up on several fronts. He sent the mufti down to Sarajevo and raised 20,000 troops. Those troops served in the SS Hanzar (Hanjar) Legion and mostly dealt with local partisan actions. Hajj Amin al-Husseini avoided indictment as a war criminal at Nuremberg by escaping to Egypt. There he received political asylum and met the young Yasser Arafat, a distant cousin. Arafat became a devoted protégé to the point where they recruited former Nazis as terrorist instructors.

"Arafat continued to pay homage to the mufti as his hero and mentor until he died. This fact gave our government's intelligence agencies a lead that radical Islam could be a direct descendant of the Nazis." Stewart paused. "Let me just say that what we found on the tape will be very useful in today's fight against Muslim terrorism."

Falk took interest. "You're saying that Youmantoff's information to Lego so many years ago will help us today?"

"Without a doubt," said Stewart softly. "The monies invested in the Nazi regime before and during World War II have gained billions in compounded interest over the years. They are now being used against the west in preparation for World War III. Remember, the Nazis first paraded themselves as only "removing" Jews from Germany then Europe."

"The Middle East, Jews and Arabs," Falk growled.

"No one ever said the Forth Reich was going to be a German entity," Stewart said. "Seems the Nazis that escaped after the war decided Europe had had enough of their organizational skills. So they hid out in various towns and cities around the world and finally agreed on an agenda to work the Muslim population. The Middle East at first then worldwide."

Falk picked up Stewart's line of reasoning. "The 'Odessa File' made that connection years ago."

"Yes, Joe, I read the book. However, Islamic fascism must be recognized for what it really is: rebirth of Nazism under a different name."

"Was there any mention of the book or the key?" Falk asked.

Stewart shook his head, rose from his chair and walked to the window. "Not a word." He moved the drapes to one side and continued staring out across Vienna before continuing. "Remember when I first briefed you on the assignment? I mentioned we'd learned via a letter from a soldier's widow who'd been ordered to give Goering a cyanide pill?"

"Yes."

"I omitted the fact that there'd been another confession, an ex-

GI named Herbert Lee Stivers. He gave his story to the *Los Angeles Times* after being assured that any charges were time-barred. He went public. This was back in February 2005 and Cerberus was aware the story was a fabrication."

"Why would anyone make up such a story?" questioned Falk.

Stewart faced back into the room and shrugged. "Misinformation. It was decided to make an attempt to clear up questions about Goering's death. The growth of the Internet over the years and bloggers beginning to ask too many questions on the subject. We were concerned the true story would come out."

"Cerberus knows the true story, right?"

"Of course."

"Then I think it's time we did, too. I'm not certain we did the right thing in switching the tapes."

"Yes, Joe. I was fully aware of your feelings. That was the reason I called in Eiker." Stewart quickly raised his hand. "Hear me out, Joe."

"Herman Goering came from a wealthy family, born to power and privilege. His personal power increased during the years prior to World War II then multiplied during the actual war years despite his Luftwaffe's inability to win the Battle of Britain."

Stewart returned to his chair. "You see, Joe, Herman Goering had planned to blow the whistle on a secret international organization. The recording he stowed away in the vault was secretly made during an actual meeting of some of the most powerful industrialists in the world. It contained sensitive material, information on their ongoing plans for world domination.

"Hitler and Goering had become part of the total power of the Rothschild organization during the 1930s and the Nazi party's rise to power; known to some as the *Illuminati*. World War III had already been blueprinted as World War II wound down.

"Goering, now a prisoner of the Allies, was bitter knowing those who had promised him everything had deserted him. Ironically he also knew many of those in power in the governments of freedom were also members of the same secret society."

"I never thought of you as someone who believed in conspiracy theories, Tom."

"I don't consider myself one either. Nonetheless, there's always a need to look closely at events of international intrigue. I'm aware that today's press would jump on what I've told you. There would be the usual denials, accusations of fake, forgery. Right-wing paranoia."

"The recording machine I saw wasn't a mini device like we have today," Falk blurted. "How could the recorder *not* have been discovered?"

"The briefcase under the table that almost killed Hitler made it into a secret meeting, Joe."

Koski and Falk exchanged glances and Mifflin spoke for the first time.

"The forces intent on killing you and Koski weren't out for the legendary war loot, Falk. They were out to locate the recordings and destroy them."

Stewart leaned forward. "You two need rest and relaxation. Tomorrow you'll both fly back home; two weeks leave, belated Christmas present."

"How about making that the day after tomorrow? Koski and I would like an extra day to recoup."

Stewart nodded. "Fine, I'll make the arrangements." He glanced at the paperwork on the desk. "Youmantoff was last seen in Ottawa. I've no doubt we'll discover a few more unanswered questions."

"Close the book on the past," rumbled Mifflin as he eased his bulk on the small office chair. "I'd like to suggest we all have dinner together tomorrow night. Emma, too, my treat, at the 'Bristol.'"

Koski glanced at Falk. "Sure, why not? Give us time to see what we learned from that old Russian fox, Youmantoff."

Chapter 87

Sgt. Pullbrook of the Royal Canadian Mounted Police stood motionless in the alley, less than two blocks from the Soviet Embassy in Ottawa, weapon poised as his lapel microphone crackled softly. He saw Youmatoff as a graying man, old and dying in a country not his own. Pullbrook lowered the gun to his side.

Had Youmatoff turned, he might have seen that Pullbrook's eyes contained a rheumy afterglow. He might have speculated why sometimes they break with tradition and don't get their man.

Youmatoff didn't turn. Years ago, a man he didn't know gave him papers that made it possible for him to avoid returning to Russia. Today another stranger was making his desired return possible. Youmatoff neither questioned nor required a look into the face of the compassionate providence responsible for delivering him into this human condition.

His chest rose then fell with a great exhalation as he continued toward the embassy. The crisp and cathartic wind off the Ottawa River whispered as it rushed by him.

He crossed Charlotte Street, slush crunching beneath his boots as he neared Number 287. He walked up to one of the guards outside the Soviet Embassy and straightened his shoulders. "I am a Russian," he said proudly. "My name is Nikolai Youmatoff. I wish to return home."

Three months had passed. Harold Mifflin was in his garden in Southern California, snipping away with his trusty Bahco pruners, working on his favorite floribundas. His cell phone chimed. "Yes," he said testily.

"Switching the tapes while in the ambulance was a work of genius," a soft voice whispered. "The society wishes to thank you for your past service and contributions to our worldwide endeavors. We feel, however, that it's time for you to retire full-time."

A dial tone droned in Mifflin's ear. Replacing the phone in his pocket, he swept away a fallen leaf. It was all over and he knew he only had a matter of seconds to live. He had no doubt he was in an assassin's crosshairs.

There was no pain as the poison dart entered his jugular. Mifflin sagged and crumpled beside his beloved roses.

The Christmas and New Year festivities had passed and Falk and Koski were back stateside. The jangle of his beside phone woke Falk. He reached across Koski's sleeping form and scooped it up.

It was Stewart. "Youmatoff's body was discovered last night in a snow bank beside the Ottawa river, a coil of barbed wire wrapped around his throat."

"So the Mounties didn't get their man," Falk grunted. Now Koski was awake.

"No. They got him only he was dead when they did. Cerberus also received word that Mikhail Brasinov was reportedly spotted in Beverly Hills."

"Brno getting too hot for him?"

"I doubt it, Joe. The Muslim Mafia paid that bastard millions to get 'The Judas List.'"

"And they got the wrong one."

"What concerns me is the sighting of Brasinov. This year's Easter Sunday service in the Hollywood Bowl is going to be a security nightmare. Religious leaders from around the world will be there as a sign of unity, including the Pope making his first official visit to the United States." Falk heard voices in the background and Stewart said, "I'll call you back."

Falk hung up as Koski asked, "What was that all about? I heard you say something about Mounties not getting their man and Brno getting too hot. What's happening?"

Falk leaned back and laced his fingers behind his head. "I'm not sure. Whatever it is could include a visit to the Hollywood Bowl."

Book Three

Dedication
To St. Francis de Sales, patron saint of writers

Prologue

With his heart fluttering, the old wino stumbled down a trash-strewn alley, desperately seeking a hiding place. His mind was fuzzy from muscatel and the fact that someone had attempted to kill him at three in the morning in his cardboard box in a shoe store doorway on Hollywood Boulevard.

He leaned against a wall and gasped for air, wondering who wanted to kill him. Not the cops. He could die on the street for all they cared.

Cocking his head, he heard footsteps: slow, measured and deliberate as a pallbearer. A cold wind flicked a crumpled newspaper down the alley and the stink of rotting garbage swirled around him. With an outstretched hand, he staggered forward, bumping along the wall until he contacted the cold iron of a dumpster.

The lid was propped open and with the last of his fading strength, the old man hiked his scrawny body up into the evil-smelling container. He was reaching up to release the bar holding the lid open when a hand grasped his wrist in a powerful grip and a flashlight beam blazed in his face. He screwed his eyes shut, his corneas reacting to a burst of luminous blue light. In the grip of his unknown assailant, he felt the sleeve of his threadbare jacket being pushed up to his elbow. A needle slid into a vein and a sudden reeling in his brain told him a powerful drug was coursing through his bloodstream. Then a voice whispered, "Don't fight it. Just close your eyes."

Chapter 1

Tom Stewart pushed aside a thick report with the name Cerberus stenciled across the cover. The file contained information he knew would elicit an immediate response from the United States Department of Homeland Security (DHS). He reached for his phone and tapped a set of numbers then drummed his fingers impatiently on the desktop waiting for Special Agent Joseph Falk to answer.

Initially Joe Falk had resisted initiation from the FBI into Cerberus but ultimately he acknowledged the need for an organization that covertly supported humankind's highest ideals. Now he and his partner, Susan Koski, belonged to a little-known cadre of specially skilled undercover agents trained to mingle with known dissidents and paramilitary terrorist groups, allowing both agents freedom for clandestine assignments. No questions asked.

Stewart wasted no time when Falk answered the phone.

"Joe, I want you and Agent Koski here in LA at once. There'll be a company plane waiting at Reno-Tahoe at 0800 hours. I'm at the Beverly Wilshire Hotel. Now move. Take off is in thirty minutes." Stewart hung up.

Falk was a thirty-something, wrapped-tight guy with a leathery tan and a brooding, magnetic face sporting a two-week-old beard. He looked at his watch. He flipped on a gray Kangol 504 Cap that had seen better days and sipped the last of his coffee as he dialed his partner. After six rings, Koski answered, panting as she ran the last half-mile of her five-mile morning run.

Chapter 2

Greg Grant was a foxy-eyed man in his late thirties. He gazed out the window of his tenth floor Washington, D.C. office and viewed the wide expanse of the National Mall and the reflecting pool in the distance. It was his first week with the DHS. The department, hurriedly created by the Bush administration a few weeks after 9/11, had been beset with problems of organization and acceptance ever since.

Grant had been an investigative reporter for the *Washington Post*. His work caught the eye of the new DHS director who offered him a position after deciding that bringing a media type on board might improve the department's image. Grant had an inquisitive mind and his thinking was always self-centered. He quickly accepted the job. Now, this morning, he was attending a briefing for his first assignment.

He sat relaxed. His slim, six-foot-two frame was arranged with the practiced ease of an actor listening attentively to his boss as he wrapped up Grant's assignment to the Hollywood killings.

"You'll head up the investigation team with two FBI agents. Being DHS, you'll be in charge. Arrangements have been made for you to liaise with LAPD."

Grant sat a little straighter. "Two FBI agents?"

"Yes. They'll act as your photographers—video and still. The Bureau has to learn sometime that now DHS is in charge of national security."

Grant's ego swelled. "I'll be *happy* to bring them up-to-date, sir."

Mikhail Brasinov cruised along Sunset Boulevard, his Slavic features softening as he inhaled the luxurious bouquet of new leather. The eight-cylinder engine of his Ferrari Testerosa purred with the promise of a growl that would occur with a tap of his toe. Glancing in the rearview mirror, he smiled and his large, yellowed teeth reflected back. Tomorrow he'd have his teeth whitened. He planned to fit in—look native when he met with Hollywood's "in-crowd."

Seven blocks north of Sunset a second victim was dead. A scrawny young woman with both arms cankered by needle scars lay propped against a stucco apartment wall on Franklin Avenue. Unlike the man in the dumpster, she hadn't fought the needle and had readily gone along with the offer of a fix. The murderer drove north to Los Feliz Boulevard, made a sharp left onto Fern Dell into Griffith Park. It was an ideal hunting place. A bubbling stream, a winding path between Pine and Cedar trees, masses of leafy ferns, waterfalls, grassy areas and picnic tables; a lovers' lane.

Voices and the bobbing beam of a flashlight alerted the murderer to remove two hypodermic needles from his case on the picnic table. He'd have to be fast to take out two at once; four in one night. His bosses would be pleased. The beam moved from side to side as his victims neared. He heard them now, a man and a woman. Then the murderer remembered his orders were to kill only derelicts and the homeless.

The beam came closer and the man said, "I hope no one broke into the Jag."

A woman laughed. "Don't worry. No one comes up here this late at night. Besides, how often do you get to make love on a picnic table in Griffith Park?"

The murderer remained in the shadows, still and silent as the duo passed.

Chapter 3

"You're late," Stewart growled as Special Agent Susan Koski ambled into the sitting room of his suite at the Beverly Wilshire.

Falk sat next to a thin, scholarly-looking man and squirmed

slightly at her tardy entrance. He'd warned her there was no time to stop for coffee when they'd dashed from the cab into the hotel.

"I needed to stop for coffee," the petite blonde said huskily. She lowered a case containing her compact digital video equipment to the floor next to a chair. At the same time, she tried not to spill the tall decaf mocha in her left hand. Stewart eyed his watch. He decided not to directly address Koski's "morning person" comment. She was the second half of Cerberus' most dynamic duo. Falk's exploits were becoming legendary. Koski's were almost mythical. Stewart intended their partnership to continue.

"Agent Koski," Stewart said, "meet Dr. Jack Wolf, Professor of Biology and Director of the Stem Cell Research Program at UCLA. He's also one of us."

Wolf was slumped in a wing-backed chair. He leaned forward, pulled his feet to a standing position, rose an inch from the seat and nodded in way of a greeting.

Stewart continued. "You'll be working with the Department of Homeland Security." Stewart knew the pair had little use for cumbersome bureaus. He held up his hand as Falk leaned forward to complain. "Hear me out, Joe. This assignment is vital to our country's safety. It's possible Mikhail Brasinov could be involved."

"He's a long way from Brno," Falk replied, referring to the Czech Republic capital where a Bosnian thug wanted for war crimes and on the run from NATO had entered into a working agreement with militant Muslims. He'd made millions. He was a dangerous man; a rich dangerous man.

Stewart nodded. "The CIA is setting up a special team as we speak."

Falk shrugged. "Why are we going to work with DHS?"

Stewart raised an eyebrow. "I don't need to tell you how the President feels about Brasinov's presence within our country's borders. You've both had first-hand experience with his organizational abilities when you were on the *Judas* case in Czechoslovakia and Austria."

Koski and Falk exchanged looks but remained silent.

"You'll both be teamed with an agent from DHS named Greg Grant. Your assignment, as far as anyone is concerned, is to assist him in investigating a rash of serial killings in Hollywood involving street people."

Stewart cleared his throat before continuing. "DHS is fully aware there are Muslim terrorist cells operating in LA and possibly linked to the murders." He paused to allow his words to sink in. "You'll be liaising with the Los Angeles Police Department as part of the ongoing effort by the federal government to mesh local law enforcement with DHS." Stewart sighed. "And we know how that goes.

"You'll go along as photographers. Grant has been briefed that you are FBI. As far as anyone else is concerned you're DHS. Being a videographer will be a breeze for Koski but you'll have to wing it, Joe."

Falk nodded. Stewart lifted a glass of orange juice and pointed to Wolf. "Doctor Wolf had been involved with stem cell biology studies long before public interest was stirred, back when the President finally decided to allocate federal funding for research. He's here to update us on the use of various bioethics and their possible use by terrorists here at home."

Stewart sipped his juice before continuing. "It's imperative *no one* learns you are actively involved in a covert operation to discover what may turn out to be a deadly tool for Islamic terrorists.

"Heightened security and active defensive measures since the end of the Iraqi debacle have done little to slow worldwide carnage by Muslim insurgents. Nonetheless, it's come to our attention that recent murders in and around Hollywood could be the work of terrorists."

"Why kill street people, Tom? What do they expect to gain?" Falk asked.

"I'll let Doctor Wolf explain further. Possibly the victims were chosen at random to test a new means of intravenous injection."

"How much do either of you know about stem cell research?" Wolf whispered.

Koski grimaced. "In the great stem cell debate, I've never given much thought to which side I was on, the stem side or the cell side."

Falk enjoyed her sense of humor as he added, "Me, too. All I know is what I read in the papers."

"Ninety percent of America's population would answer the same way," Wolf replied. "Few really care unless directly affected."

"I had a friend who would have died of diabetes if they didn't have stem cell treatment. I consider it good medicine," Koski exclaimed.

"I'm sure you do, however, as with a large element of medical research and development there are always pros and cons." Wolf paused and contemplated the scuffed toes of his cowboy boots.

"One fact most Americans *are* aware of is the cruelly commercial side of medicine; questions of funding, professional infighting, increasing cost of prescription medicine: publish or perish, corporate scrambling to be the first with the latest. *Not*, I'm afraid, always in the best interests of patients or their problems."

Wolf leaned forward, hands dangling between his bony knees. "It's possible the killer we're seeking has the ability to manipulate stem cells and by so doing change their known behavior. That in itself is nothing new. This treatment is inserted into a person's genes to enable stem cells to survive prolonged chemotherapy treatment. This is a great advantage in cases where a cancer patient benefits from additional chemotherapy after stem cell transplantation."

Koski swirled the remains of her coffee as she listened to his every word.

Wolf slowly rubbed his chin. "Normally, this manipulation would kill newly transplanted stem cells but fortified cells treated by gene therapy can survive. They give researchers another tool in the battle against inherited defects, such as anemia, sickle cell anemia and Wiskott-Aldrich Syndrome."

Koski said, "Our killer must be a medical whiz kid, Doctor."

"Yes. We're beginning to call him the Gene Genie. From what little we've learned, we've come up with a working profile of someone with a background in medical experimentation, especially stem cell transplantation. Whoever it is may have discovered a means not only to clone genes but also to add certain critical qualities to them. Smart genes from say a nuclear scientist intermixed with aggressive genes from a prizefighter or a ruthless business tycoon. Even a serial killer. There's no end to the possible combinations."

Wolf raked his fingers through his sand-colored hair. "There is also the dreadful possibility that our genius could design and create the perfect assassin—a monster that slavishly carries out orders without question."

Koski gasped. "Sounds like a modern Doctor Frankenstein!"

Wolf grimaced. "Worse. Remember the opiate used by the Russian Special Forces in the 2002 hostage situation at the Moscow theater. That reflected a new era in bio-weapons development. Since then, there have been tremendous biotech advances to degrade enemy forces while enhancing one's own troops.

"Our own Defense Department is studying the development of 'calmative' chemicals as well as 'incapaciants' and 'convulsants.' It's possible this is happening with the random killings and they, whoever they are, are experimenting with street people."

Stewart picked up the conversation. "What we have here is the ugly possibility that someone can medically manufacture a killer who can pass through any security check, no explosives and no weapons. He shows up clean on the screen. When the assigned victim is dispatched, they simply kill off the monster and create another assassin when needed."

"Sounds like a plot for a sci-fi movie," Koski muttered.

Wolf nodded. "Performance enhancing drugs are right *NOW,*

Koski. Our Air Force pilots use 'no go pills' to induce sleep...what would you think of a microchip smaller than a dime implanted under the skin of a soldier's neck and used to trigger the release of chemicals for 'body regulation' and 'rejuvenating drugs'?" Wolf asked.

Before she could answer, he waved a long forefinger in the air. "They are being studied by U.S. Special Operations Command, the Defense Advanced Research Projects Agency and other Defense Department organizations."

Stewart broke in. "We must find out who this madman is before he decides to try out his method on a wider scale."

"And we've *no* idea who we're looking for?" Koski inquired. "Could this mad genius be a she?"

"Maybe," Wolf responded. "Murder and medicine are equal opportunity employers."

Falk asked. "How do we know this person you're talking about is responsible for the Hollywood killings?"

"The Los Angeles County Coroner's office contacted me when autopsies carried out on two of the victims showed peculiarities. They both were brain dead before they died. One was found in a dumpster and the other in an alley behind Grauman's Chinese Theater. A more complete autopsy is under way. Our intelligence informs me the victims were possibly guinea pigs used to enable the killer to fine-tune the exact amount of evil concoction to inject.

"Being street people, they create less attention to the media. The next victim may well be injected with a corrected dose and become a killer by design."

"There can't be that many people with the ability to do what you say, Doctor. Surely that narrows down the list of suspects," Falk said.

"Yes. We're already checking labs, hospitals and known private industries that have the ability to produce such drugs. We're also keeping in mind that whatever is being used could have been produced offshore."

"If there is anyone with the expertise to know these persons or companies that have the capability to create such a weapon, I imagine you are at the top of the list, Doctor."

Stewart picked up the line of reasoning. "Joe, you're right. Cerberus is working through a list as we speak. Your cover liaising with DHS is just that. You'll be kept up-to-date on the tie-in with a suspected cell here locally, the Brasinov sighting, murders of the homeless. Also, from what little we've learned so far it's possible the ringleader of the cell is a big name in the pharmaceutical business."

No one spoke for a moment as the slow, tick-tock of an antique grandfather clock stretched seconds into minutes.

"What about the police?" Falk asked. "Are they aware there may be a mad scientist out there?"

"Not yet," Stewart shot back. "Let one word get out about the possibility of a mad scientist running around Hollywood injecting people with a psychoactive drug and the police will have a bigger problem on their hands trying to calm a panicked populace."

Chapter 4

Eleven thirty at night and the Hollywood freeway was

jammed. Detective Victor Young, LAPD, eyed the red taillights ahead and thought if he had a dollar for each one he'd retire. He still had six years to go.

Young lit another Camel and increased the volume on his police radio. A continuous litany of chanting monotonous voices reporting murder, burglary, robbery, domestic disputes, along with gang shootings and general mayhem; six more years in which his disenchantment with politicians at city hall would grow.

Young drove an unmarked piece of rubbish from police headquarters at Parker Center motor pool on his way out to Hollywood division. His temporary three-month assignment to Undercover Narcotics, Rampart Division, would be over in two days so forty-eight hours filling in for an injured Hollywood Narc would be a piece of cake.

The stream of stop-and-go traffic reached Vermont Avenue when a carload of gang bangers passed him driving in the emergency lane, caps on backwards, loud Rap music thumping from oversized speakers. Young almost switched on the siren then decided not to. He could stop them and be called a Fascist pig and accused of racial profiling. He ground his cigarette into an overflowing ashtray. Whatever legal aggravation he gave those punks, they'd be home tonight before he was.

Inching forward, he thought of his dad, who'd served with LA's finest when they had been just that—the best dammed police force in the nation. Back when cops kept the peace and the citizens respected their dedication to duty.

The traffic started to move a little faster and he eased across the lanes for the off ramp at Cahuenga Boulevard. He took one last look at the scumbags roaring up the emergency lane. He knew damn well his dad *would* have nailed their asses.

The wall clock showed 1:05 a.m. The desk sergeant glanced up as Detective Young entered the front entrance of the Hollywood station. He crossed the well-worn floor tiles, passed a battered wooden bench containing two drunks handcuffed to the cuff-hooks and stopped in front of his desk.

"Welcome to the real world, Victor," the white-haired cop drawled. "I heard you were coming to spend a couple of days with us. How are things at Rampart?"

Young shrugged. "My Spanish is improving."

The sergeant didn't give a damn how anyone was, especially those outside of Hollywood division. Glancing at a note on the desk, he informed Young he'd be working with Detective Bob Gulliver.

"I thought Gully was with Robbery Homicide downtown."

"He was. He got transferred to us a month ago."

Young knew a transfer out of Robbery Homicide wasn't an upward shift. Young grunted. "What happened?"

"Internal affairs. I wouldn't ask if I were you."

"Where can I find him?"

"He's waiting for you in the squad room."

Gully was seated at a wooden table, tapping a keyboard with two fingers and transferring notes to a PC. He glanced up. "Morning, Victor. Long time no see."

Young pulled a heavy wooden chair out from the table and sat facing him. "Where is everybody?"

"The brass ordered everyone on the streets. Another vic found an hour ago in the 6400 block on Fountain. A citizen called in a description, someone in a long black coat running from the scene."

"Great!" Young pushed out of the chair and crossed to the squad room coffeepot. "You want some?"

"No. I want to run our orders for tomorrow past you then go to bed."

Chapter 5

After leaving the meeting, Koski and Falk headed to a small hotel in West LA where Stewart had arranged their accommodations. They spent the rest of the day studying the latest Cerberus files on various terrorist cells and their suspected activities in Southern California.

Several hours later Falk tossed the last file aside. "Let's go eat. We need a break."

It was after eleven when they finished dessert. Koski pushed her dish to one side. "Reading those files, you'd think we'd have a better handle on illegals entering the country."

"Yeah. This country's in deep shit. Homeland Security's going to be hard pressed to *ever* cure that problem."

"So we get attached to this guy, Grant. Is he at the same hotel we're in?" Koski asked.

"No. He's staying with someone in Beverly Hills."

"How do you know?"

"I asked Stewart just before we left. You were powdering your nose."

Koski arched her eyebrows. "A woman?"

"No idea."

"Fine. I'll make it my job to find out."

"I doubt we'll have much free time." The buzz of his cell interrupted and he quickly answered. "Right. Got it. We've a beaurocar. We'll find you." Falk left some bills on the table as he rose. "Dr. Wolf. He's at the morgue."

The smell of formaldehyde at midnight can ruin a perfectly good dinner. Falk and Koski, ID tags hanging from their necks, entered LA County morgue. A stoop-shouldered janitor led them at a snail's pace through dimly lit underground corridors to a set of double doors with a row of gurneys lined up like taxicabs; the difference being that the occupants of these transporters were no longer in a hurry to arrive at their destination. Green sheeted, their big toes labeled, they waited in silence.

The shiny double steel doors whooshed open and Dr. Wolf, dressed in surgical greens, walked out. He beckoned them to follow as he re-entered the room.

Inside, they donned scrubs, gloves and masks. They had both experienced morgues in the past and unless you worked there full time, it was always an uneasy sensation being in such an environment. An icy coldness filled the room; a chill one inhaled along with the odor of chemicals and freshly cut bodies. The sibilant sound of continuous running water sluicing the granite operating slabs added another dynamic to the frigidity.

"Over here." Wolf led them past three unclothed corpses. The first table held a black man with his throat slashed open. A young girl on the second slab had been shot in the temple. The middle-aged man on the third looked as if he'd died in a traffic accident. The top of his head was peeled down over his eyes.

Wolf stopped at the fourth table. "Take a look." Falk's eyes followed the direction of Wolf's finger pointing at a scrawny emaciated old man with the top of his skull neatly removed by Wolf's cordless Stryker cranial saw. The smell of scorched bone still lingered over the table.

Koski and Falk stared at the wrinkled gray matter. The outer edges of the brain had a peculiar discoloration.

"You'll notice the bluish hue beginning to show." Wolf pointed with a thin, steel, pencil-like object at the area. "Here in the cerebrum is an indication that before he died he had lost the ability to speak or to have original thoughts."

"*Before* he *died?*" Falk echoed.

"Yes. I believe this man lived for several hours after he had been injected and programmed to carry out commands."

Wolf's eyes went to abstract speculation. "The toxic drug surged through his brain, flooding the cerebrospinal fluid, destroying the nerve cells of the cerebral cortex, inhibiting those nerve fibers from carrying signals to other cells, other parts of the brain and the rest of the body."

"An hour or two later it's possible the victim could have begun to feel ill," Wolf continued. "A feeling not unlike an unsettled stomach or the start of the flu. I'll show you evidence of other victims that have died under similar conditions and indicate the miniscule entrance wounds they suffered. This will alert you to how difficult it is to locate the puncture wound and how, in some cases, it could be overlooked altogether. God forbid this formula is ever used in spray form, as Serin was in a Tokyo subway a few years ago."

"Amen." Koski muttered.

Driving back from the morgue, Koski mused over their meeting with Dr. Wolf. "It's evident that at the moment Wolf has no idea what type of toxic material was injected into those people."

"Do I detect a tone of dissatisfaction with our latest assignment, Koski?"

"Not really. However, five unsolved murders in less than a week! Shouldn't there be a more aggressive attempt to find the killer?"

Falk felt the same way. "Murder of homeless people doesn't stir up the media enough."

Koski stared out of the car window. "Yeah. It'll have to be significant, something more exciting, an event that'll rouse the Fourth Estate to their usual frenzy to be the 'first with the worst'."

"Especially, if as Stewart said, someone big in the pharmaceutical industry is involved."

Chapter 6

Falk's doorbell rang at 6 a.m. He rinsed off shaving soap, grabbed a towel and went to the door. "Who is it?"

"Greg Grant. I'd like to take you both to breakfast. Not too early am I?"

Falk opened the door. "No problem. Come in." He indicated the couch. "Take a seat, I'll be right back." He headed to the bathroom, donned pants and a dress shirt over his tee shirt and boxers and reentered the living room.

Grant stuck out his right hand and flashed his brand new DHS badge in his left, level with his face. "Glad to meet you, Falk. I'm looking forward to working with members of the Bureau." He glanced toward the bedroom. "Agent Koski still asleep?"

"I doubt it. She's most likely halfway through a five mile run." Falk pointed to a connecting door. "We have adjoining rooms."

"Give us time to chew the fat."

Falk relaxed in one of the upholstered chairs and assessed what he saw—someone who made assumptions and was used to running the show. Arching an eyebrow, Falk asked, "How did LAPD react when they discovered DHS was about to become involved, Mr. Grant?"

"Call me Greg. DHS Washington cleared everything with the mayor's office. We'll have full cooperation with LAPD—official feedback, access to murder scenes, investigating officers, medical examiners, etc."

"Mmmm, another agency's presence at crime scenes during an initial investigation is normally against police procedure."

Grant sniggered. "Yeah, but times change. That's why the DHS was created. When you have influence, you have power. Hope we didn't ruffle any FBI feathers."

"The Bureau understands." Falk realized he was talking to someone who was already a legend in his own mind.

"Of course." Grant quickly added, "Rest assured this is not the first time I've worked with covert operators."

"Greg, I'm glad to hear you say that. How about a cup of coffee while we wait for Agent Koski?"

Grant leaned back and laced his fingers behind his head. "Sounds good, Joe."

Susan Koski ran with long easy strides, breathing the fresh morning air before the usual haze blurred the Hollywood Hills. Six-thirty a.m. and the streets began to fill with traffic. She saw their hotel ahead and hoped Falk had put on a pot of coffee.

Normally they would have run together but decided it was wiser to split up until they knew how events would proceed. Nearing the hotel, she noticed a vehicle parked halfway down the block. Her natural powers of observation noted it was a green Toyota Rav4. The man sitting behind the wheel was reading a newspaper and looked out of place. She knew the vehicle hadn't been there when she'd left the building earlier.

The SUV suddenly drove off. Instincts made her memorize the California license plate number—NTV925. She caught a glimpse of his face as he glanced back.

Once in her room, Koski jotted down the number and headed to the shower. Fifteen minutes later, dressed in faded blue jeans, a white cotton turtleneck, navy blue jacket and a pair of Reeboks, she opened the unlocked adjoining door to Falk's room.

"Ah, here she is now." Falk got to his feet.

Grant set his coffee mug on a side table and rose from the couch. "Happy to meet the other half of the duo," he said with a seemingly genuine smile. They both knew he was thoroughly briefed on both of them and fully aware of their background and accomplishments with the Bureau.

Koski took an instant dislike to the man as she said, "Nice to meet you, Mr. Grant."

"Call him Greg, Koski. Mr. Grant doesn't stand on ceremony."

"I'm taking you two to breakfast," Grant announced. "I'm

starving. Where would you like to go?"

Koski caught the twinkle in Falk's eye. "They say the Polo Lounge serves a great breakfast."

Grant's smile faded momentarily. They knew he couldn't justify breakfast at "The Lounge" on his government expense account. Then he blurted, "Great idea, Joe."

"I'll grab my purse," Koski purred. "Meet you downstairs." She returned to her room and scooped up the note containing the license plate number and headed for the elevator.

Sunlight already streamed across the crisp pink tablecloth and the waiter adjusted the blinds to lessen the glare. Service at the Beverly Hills Hotel was, as usual, impeccable. Grant nodded to the waiter with the aplomb of the archbishop to an altar boy. He dominated the conversation all through breakfast and it seemed he was not about to stop.

"There was this time in Chicago. I headed up a team investigating city hall politicians suspected of paying off teamster bosses..." He stopped in mid-sentence as his cell phone chimed. "Grant."

Koski absent-mindedly wet the tip of her finger and tapped crumbs of a jelly donut off her plate and into her mouth, enjoying the fact it had cost Grant nine dollars. She looked forward to Falk's suggestion on where to go for lunch.

Grant covered the mouthpiece. "It's the office." He continued talking on his phone. "No problems. Everyone's very cooperative. I've contacted my photographers and scheduled a meeting with LAPD at Hollywood Central this morning. I'll keep in touch."

He flipped the phone shut and beckoned the waiter as he

signed his name in mid-air.

Walking to their car Grant said, "When we meet with LAPD I'll do the talking. I know how to handle local yokels."

"We appreciate that, Greg." Koski oozed. "We really do."

Falk hid a smile.

Chapter 7

"Pease, that son of a bitch..." Paul Horn stopped in mid-sentence, turned back from the tinted floor-to-ceiling window overlooking the Pacific Ocean and wiped his brow with the back of his huge hand.

Roughly rearranging his six-foot-four, 220-pound frame on a delicate Chippendale chair, he stared across the well-appointed office of Enrico Pegmanti. "I'm sorry, Enrico. After all, Martin is your son-in-law."

"No problem." Despite his eighty-seven years and small stature, Pegmanti was still a giant in charge.

Horn continued. "I believe Martin's department was close to reproducing genes on demand. Maybe we made a mistake letting him go."

"That remains to be seen." Pegmanti leaned back and his swivel chair creaked. "I have information that Martin was lying. He wasn't just close. He *could* reproduce the germinating acceptance genes *now* if he wanted to."

Horn sat upright, the abrupt movement of 220 pounds of suddenly rearranged inertia applying a vicious torque to the chair. His eyes glittered behind rimless glasses. "Why would he lie?"

Pegmanti grasped a solid gold letter opener in his blue-veined hand and tapped the tip on the polished teakwood desk. "Paul, you've been head of our sales division for over twenty years. Perhaps in that rarefied atmosphere you've lost touch with the *inner* workings of Pegmanti Chemical Industries." He spun the letter opener in slow circles.

"Martin is keeping the progress of his embryonic stem cells and blank state cells to himself. After I'm dead, he'll announce a breakthrough. Ergo, the rewards will be all his!" Horn pushed out of the chair, crossed to the window and with his back to Pegmanti, gazed thoughtfully at the Pacific, a strange smile on his face.

Chapter 8

Martin Pease, always a clever student, had been quickly accepted at Cambridge University when he was seventeen. He had chosen to study medicine. During his years there he made tremendous strides and became looked upon as an up-and-comer in the future of medicine and sciences. Then in the summer of 1948 his world, as he had known it, came to a sudden and disastrous end.

At Cambridge he was close to home, having been born in the town of Newmarket. He was the only boy. His two elder sisters were married now. The other person in his life was Fiona, his fiancée of two years. Fiona, already considered part of the family, spent weekends at Pease's home. One weekend toward the end of term, Fiona and Pease's parents drove down to Cambridge to visit him.

After enjoying a pleasant lunch at one of the riverside pubs, Fiona and Pease strolled together, discussing plans for their future wedding. Later they said their farewells and with his father at the wheel of his car, they began their return trip. It was the last time Pease saw them alive.

A few miles outside of Newmarket, a horse transporter skidded out of control and into the family car, killing everyone including the truck driver.

Pease was inconsolable in his grief. Less than two weeks after burying his parents, he sold the family house and took advantage of a scheme offered by the U.S. government at the end of World War II. It encouraged people with certain specialties to immigrate to America.

Now twenty-two and in the first year in his chosen homeland, he knew he wanted to return to the world of medicine. He contacted his mentors at Cambridge, who gladly arranged access to the right people in California who could assist him in transitioning into research and medical science at UCLA.

Doctor Rita Massy was the first to welcome him when he entered the room of glittering personalities. He smiled wryly at the memory.

"Over here, Martin. There are people who want to meet you. I've told them all about you."

In the early 1950s, Beverly Hills overflowed with charming people; men of power and foresight; women of elegance and cunning; and those who simply bided their time and waited.

Over the next few years, Massy and Pease worked together in the field of cognitive neuroscience at Pegmanti Chemical Industries (PCI). In time, they became good friends, both passionate about their research. Theirs was a platonic relationship.

Goldie Pegmanti, Enrico's only daughter, had fallen in love with Martin and they were married. She reveled in their large house in Beverly Hills, a wedding gift from her father, and she adored throwing parties.

As the years passed, however, Goldie forgot how to love Pease because he was consumed by his work. There was never any discussion of a divorce. They were both too 'Catholic' for that. Besides, old man Pegmanti would have cut them out of his will. Although he was a mean-spirited, hard-nosed businessman, Enrico still believed in the sanctity of marriage. The old Catholic traditions from Italy were firmly locked in his soul.

Goldie and Martin simply lived in separate quarters and went their own ways. Enrico was rarely a visitor to the rambling domicile and knew nothing of this arrangement. Appearances indicated that Doctor and Mrs. Pease were a contented, middle aged couple that had found a comfortable, lasting way of life.

In time, however, Martin Pease and Rita Massy became secret lovers. Their clandestine affair was never discovered.

Six days ago, after years of research and what had become the hard labor of marriage to Goldie, he received an unexpected "Golden Handshake." Enrico Pegmanti soon realized his mistake.

Pease cleaned out his desk, collected his personal effects and downloaded *his* formula from the company computer, replacing it with a fake. He returned home and used his laptop to transfer ten million dollars from the PCI's research account to his secret Swiss bank account. The transfer was cunningly designed to be untraceable. It would be months before anyone at Pegmanti had a clue as to what had happened. Even then there was no way anyone could *prove* he was involved.

He had wrapped his cunning into the intricacies of megabytes, hard drives and a million other details of computer cleverness. A few taps on his keyboard was all it took. Despite his craftiness, Pease was an extremely worried man.

Martin Pease had rented a room in a seedy motel on Pico Boulevard in Santa Monica for a meeting with Rita Massy. He sniffed the stale air as he perched on the edge of a rickety wooden chair. He took stock of his surroundings, realizing how drastically his life had changed.

Rita was offered the position as head of research with Laser Research Laboratories in Pasadena. She left PCI and their lives had drifted apart.

Pease never had the slightest indication that Rita Massy was anyone but a talented and extraordinarily gifted scientist, deeply involved in her chosen discipline. That was the day he received a death threat. He also was informed that Rita was a third generation Saudi Muslim, a sleeper, waiting to respond to the call from those who were in power long before the formation of Al Qaida.

Massy revealed that fact at the end of a romantic dinner for two in a cozy corner of Musso & Frank's Grill in Hollywood. She explained that her father married an English woman and immigrated to the United States in the late 1920s. He anglicized his name from Abu Tala al Masry to Albert Massy. Rita was born in New York City.

Years after the WTC attack, Massy confided her allegiance to the militant faction of Islam to Pease. She threatened that Goldie and her father would be killed without hesitation unless she was given access to the latest stem cell formula he was developing along with his top-secret delivery system.

Pease rued the day he revealed his research to Massy. He had developed a system to replace the needle injection method. He'd discovered that he could distribute medication into the human system without leaving the slightest sign of penetration. He also was able to infuse from a distance that had grown from a few feet to fifty yards with absolute accuracy.

He sighed. He'd been a fool in happier days. Now his ex-wife and Enrico Pegmanti were virtual hostages. Their lives were in jeopardy unless he agreed to work with Massy and allow his work to fall into the hands of the enemy. He begged her to reconsider what she was doing. His stem cell manipulation process, used in conjunction with the delivery system, provided her with supremacy to kill or create. She was totally unmoved when Pease accused her of creating a silent killing machine.

Shocked she would even dream that he would willingly become part of such a diabolical plan, Pease had flatly refused. She scoffed at his naiveté. Was it worth the loss of two lives so dear to him?

He had learned too much too late. Now he stiffened at the sound of a light rap on the door. Quickly he crossed the shabby room. "Who is it?" There was a rustling sound. A sheet of expensive writing paper slid under the door. The paper was a signal.

Chapter 9

Martin Pease opened the door and a smartly dressed woman

entered.

"You look pale, Martin. Are you feeling ill?" Rita Massy asked.

"I'm fine."

"You've lost weight. You look like hell, frail, that's the word."

Rita Massy was green-eyed with auburn hair stylized and modern. She moved with surprising agility. Glancing with disdain at the room and furnishings, she plucked a white handkerchief from her Dior jacket pocket, flicked the seat of one of the two wooden chairs beside the window and sat down gingerly. She crossed her shapely legs and with a fingertip, moved the drab yellow drapes a couple of inches and peered down the street.

"There's no one out there," Pease said. "This place is safe."

"No place and no one is safe," she replied.

"I need a drink." Pease went to a kitchenette and returned with a Bombay tonic.

She flicked an imaginary dust mote from her tailored skirt. "We decided to let you complete your research on the delivery system—*now*."

His hand trembled as he took a long drink. Then he shook his head. "No."

"We have another target."

"You said five, not six," Pease said quietly.

"Follow orders, Martin, and you'll be able to go to Switzerland and spend your money."

Pease nervously rattled the melting ice cubes. "Why a sixth?"

"My people want a *clean* kill, one that doesn't leave needle marks."

"Meaning?"

"Doctor Wolf from UCLA was called in for consultation at the morgue. I believe you know him?"

"Of course. But why was he consulted?"

"Someone became interested in unusual findings during a routine autopsy of one of the early victims."

"What kind of unusual findings?"

"Needle marks."

Pease stared at her incredulously. "Needle marks would raise no questions on a derelict. Besides, those low-lifes are tagged and put on ice for weeks before anyone looks at them."

"Not this time." Massy got to her feet. "Your next formula delivery must be forensically clean. If it is, the arrangements for you to leave for Switzerland will be completed." She smiled, "Otherwise the seventh victim will be very well known and the method of death obvious."

Massy crossed to the door and paused. "You won't be able to spend all that money with your throat cut."

After she left, Pease refilled his glass and sat quietly in the dingy room, thinking back over the years. He had made a stupid and deadly bargain. Pease knew he must comply. Three lives depended on it.

Chapter 10

Half a block south of Hollywood Boulevard, on Vine Street, is a bar called *The Grape*. You go in through a side entrance off the bus station parking lot.

Twelve noon and the place was jammed; producers and

writers rubbing shoulders with electricians and craft workers amid loud conversations and clashing dishes.

Rita Massy found it to be the perfect place to meet her contacts. Sitting at a small table against the wall, she slapped the bottom of a ketchup bottle, applying liberal amounts to her cheeseburger.

A husky man in his mid-thirties, blond crew cut and a ready smile, pulled his plate closer. "Careful. You're going to get that stuff all over my lunch."

"Don't worry. I'm an expert." The next moment a gush of ketchup erupted from the bottle.

"Yeah, right, but not on ketchup removal."

No one would have suspected either was there to finalize a killing.

Never mentioning names or locations, Massy laid out her plan. "I want him to die on camera." She pushed a rolled copy of the *Hollywood Reporter* secured with a thick rubber band across the table.

"Everything you need is in there."

Crew Cut chomped a bite out of his BLT and chewed, thoughtfully eyeing the magazine then slid it off the table into his jacket pocket.

Massy left five minutes before him and sat in her car at the end of the parking lot. She watched Crew Cut leave. No one followed. Massy waited another few minutes then vacated the lot, drove south on Vine and hung a right onto Sunset before she realized a car behind might be following her.

She tightened her grip on the steering wheel and glanced in

the rearview mirror. Maybe it was her imagination. Suddenly she slammed on the brakes. She had almost hit the car in front of her. Damn! She was actually ruffled. She'd never had a problem before.

The car she was certain was following her went past. The driver was staring straight ahead, beating her through the green light by three seconds.

Massy sat at the stoplight and watched the car vanish among the traffic. Was she getting too old for this? The light changed and she moved forward.

Chapter 11

Chief of Police Warren Bradbury sat behind his desk in Parker Center tapping his leather-bound blotter with the tip of his large forefinger, emphasizing each slowly enunciated word. "*I... want... every... available... man... assigned... to... these... Hollywood...killings. Two mayors and the DHS are on our ass. Understand?*" Bradbury glared at the top LAPD brass assembled in his office. "Forty-eight hours. I want that bastard, whoever it is, in custody within forty-eight hours. *Get to it.*"

Captain Howard Garvey hesitated before pushing out from his chair. He wanted to tell the Chief that wasn't enough time but he knew this wasn't the time or place. He was among the last to head for the door when Bradbury called his name.

"Stay here, Howard. We need to talk. Shut the door and sit down."

Together the two men represented over fifty years of dedicated service to the City of Angels. "Go ahead, Howard. Tell me there's no way we can nab this guy in the next forty-eight hours."

Garvey noted the edge in his friend's voice. "Okay, Warren. There's no way." Quickly he raised a calming hand before the Chief could reply. "No way unless you tell me something I don't already know."

Years ago they had been partners riding a black and white when to "Protect and to Serve" was the new motto of the LAPD.

"Department of Homeland Security," said Bradbury. "We're going out as they come in. Police departments across America will end up reporting to the DHS in the near future." Bradbury leaned back in his chair until it creaked. "Cities, towns, sheriffs, State Police, even the Feds are going to feel the ripple effect. America's War on Terror is going to change law enforcement as we once knew it—forever."

Garvey knew it was true. The invisible barrier of little fiefdoms that had long hog-tied inter-agency investigations nationwide over the last hundred years had been swept away by the stroke of the President's pen when he created the Department of Homeland Security.

"Short of martial law, DHS will become the primary law enforcement agency in America." Bradbury's voice carried a note of sadness. "Howard, tomorrow three members of the DHS will be working with your people at Hollywood division. Give them all the courtesy at your command."

Koski awakened before Falk. She lay motionless, watching him sleep beside her. It was not yet dawn and the new day still un-warmed. She pulled the covers up around her ears, undecided if she would go on her run. The license plate she had written down proved to be nothing other than a driver making an early delivery to the hotel. At least that was the feedback. Nonetheless, she wasn't satisfied. There was *something* about that car.

"You running today?" Falk mumbled.

"How'd you know I was thinking about running?"

Falk turned on his side and grinned. "You'd be having a guilt trip if you didn't."

Koski was a petite bundle of energy, half asleep or not. She rolled on to her side and placed her feet on Falk's bare ass. She catapulted him from the bed. "*Your* turn to run. I'll make the coffee."

Falk twisted from the bed onto his feet and faced her, hands resting lightly on his hips. Koski pushed aside her short-fringed hair, allowing the covers to slip down and reveal her small, well-shaped breasts. "Of course you don't have to run. There *is* another means of morning exercise."

Falk felt himself stirring and his erection grew larger. Moving to the bed, he pulled back the sheets, reached down and scooped her naked body into his arms. She quickly slid her arms around his neck.

Slowly he lowered himself to a sitting position on the edge of the bed with her in his lap and whispered, "You're right. We'll work out together. You can make the coffee later."

Koski straddled him and they slowly sank back into bed.

Falk had made the coffee while Koski showered. She walked into the kitchen swathed in a yellow terry robe. "*I* was going to make breakfast."

"Decided I'd better get started in case Grant showed up."

"We agreed we'd meet him at the Hollywood station," Koski said.

"I know." He flipped a partially burnt flapjack in the air and it landed half in and half out of the pan. "Damn electric stoves. You can't control the heat like you can with gas."

"Yeah, right. Let me finish that."

"No. You get dressed. I'll fix us some eggs."

Koski headed for her room and hesitated, looking back over her shoulder at the big tough agent fumbling around the kitchen and smiled, knowing she loved that man a little more each day.

Chapter 12

Falk, Koski and Grant arrived at morning roll call in the Hollywood station and were begrudgingly accepted. DHS or not, they were still a federal team on LAPD's turf.

Captain Garvey introduced the trio, instructing the assembly to work closely with the investigators and give them every courtesy in a combined effort to apprehend the killer. Garvey then announced that Grant wanted to say a few words.

"Good morning. My name is Agent Greg Grant." He turned slightly. "Agents Joe Falk and Susan Koski, my photography team. We're looking forward to collectively investigating a possible terrorist action." He paused. "As far as the media is concerned we're seeking a serial killer; nothing else. If there are any leaks we'll know where to look. I hope I make myself clear. Any questions?"

Victor Young sat in the back of the room. He raised his hand. Grant nodded and pointed. "Yes. The officer seated in the back."

"Can you explain why the murders of these street people have a tie in with terrorists?"

"Not at this time. Any other questions?"

Again Young raised his hand. "Yes. If the DHS is watching over us doesn't that indicate the government has little trust in our ability to do our job?"

"Not at all. The government needs your expertise and your ability to work the problem at a local level. We are here to learn and to liaise with local government in a manner that will minimize any bureaucratic bottlenecks."

Another hand went up. It was Gully, Victor's new partner. "Does the DHS have any intelligence that it can share with the LAPD?"

"No, although you can rest assured anything DHS gathers will be sent immediately to Parker Center and transferred through regular channels to the field. Let me say again. We're here to assist, not hinder, your regular procedural policies."

Captain Garvey stepped forward and thanked Grant for his input. "Take over, Sergeant. Let's get on the street."

Moments later Grant, Koski and Falk sat in Captain Garvey's office. Grant leaned forward eagerly. "Okay, Captain. How's this going to work? Do we get our own black and white or what?"

Garvey shook his head. "Parker Center has deemed it wiser to assign you three one of our communication vehicles. It'll give you room for yourselves and your equipment."

"We need flexibility, Captain," Grant said. "To check out the crime scenes, question people in the area. Basic police work."

"I understand. It's been arranged for you to be taken to each crime scene. Nonetheless, we can't issue you a police car."

Grant bristled. "Why not?"

"We have no standard procedure for a federal task force being in place with us at a moment's notice, Agent Grant. We're doing the best we can to cooperate with the government."

Grant grimaced. "Very well, Captain but I assure you it won't be long before every law enforcement agency in the nation is given standard procedures on how to cooperate with the DHS." Grant checked his watch. "How soon can we get this vehicle loaded?"

Falk decided Grant had about as much tact as a Sherman Tank when it came to forging a link with LAPD.

Koski and Falk rode in the back of a police SUV. Grant was up front with the driver as they headed north on Beachwood Drive. It branched into Ledgewood, a winding road with the big Hollywood sign looming on their right.

Koski craned forward as the driver took a sharp turn and the sign went out of view. "Joe, I never dreamed I'd ever get this close to that sign."

"It used to spell out HOLLYWOODLAND at one time," the driver explained. "Originally, it was an advertisement to sell real estate up here, way back."

Grant butted in. "And possibly where one of the killings took place."

"The fourth murder in the series we're investigating, yeah, but not the first murder in the area," the driver said. "A number of homicides have occurred up here over the years; a couple of suicides, too. Young women unhappy about their careers climbed to the top of the letters and jumped."

No one spoke for a while. They continued up the hill and finally pulled to a stop.

"They found the body over there." The driver pointed toward a thicket of oleander thrusting up from the hillside onto the sidewalk. The houses on the street consisted of small to medium-sized stucco homes in white, pink, even blue.

Built back in the 1920s and 1930s, they sold for around eight to ten thousand dollars. Now they commanded prices in the hundreds of thousands.

Grant got out and pointed. "I'll take the two houses on the left. You and Koski check out those three on the right."

Chapter 13

Koski and Falk drew a blank at the first two houses. Elderly people occupied both and had no wish to answer any more questions.

The third house, the blue one, gave Koski a glimmer of hope. A curly-haired young Latino woman dressed in well-worn jeans and a t-shirt emblazoned with the letters IBM (*Italian by Marriage)* opened the door.

"Hi. What can I do for you?"

"Mind if we ask you some questions?" Koski inquired.

"Are you with the police?"

"No. We're working with the DHS doing a follow-up."

Koski and Falk flashed their DHS ID's. "Sometimes people remember little things they might have forgotten when they were interviewed the first time."

"Right. Come on in." The young woman opened the door

wide and stepped aside. Falk and Koski crossed the threshold and were immediately in a small, neat living room decorated with furniture that must have been in vogue when the house was new. "I was just brewing coffee. Take a seat." She indicated the choice of three well-worn easy chairs or a long, overstuffed couch. They opted for the couch. "How'd you like your coffee?"

"Two blacks will be fine. Thanks," Koski replied.

Falk whispered. "Is Grant still in the house across the street?"

Koski got up and peeked out the window. "Must be. I can't see him. Why?"

"I don't want him around while we're interviewing this gal. I want an exclusive here." The young woman returned and placed two mugs on a side table. "Couldn't help overhearing. Am I an important part of the investigation?"

Falk picked up one of the mugs and sipped the brew. "Good coffee. We didn't get your name."

"Nell Fynn. That's with a Y."

"Important? I don't know. Tell me. What do you know?"

"Hold on." Nell went back to the kitchen, got her coffee, returned, then folded her shapely form into one of the easy chairs, resting the mug on her right knee. She glanced from one to the other as if deciding whom to address. She chose Koski.

"I'm a writer. That's one of the reasons I live up here." She took a sip. "That and the fact I'm broke most of the time. Lucky for me this place was bequeathed to me by an aunt. She was a great lady and I bless her memory every day."

Koski leaned forward. "Nell, did you give this preamble to the cops when they were up here asking questions?"

Nell studied Koski over the rim of her mug. "No."

Koski nodded. "Then why us?"

"I want to communicate with you two."

"Why?"

"I need background on the DHS for a book I'm writing."

Koski glanced at Falk and they both grinned. "Fine, Nell, but first *we* have questions. You say you live up here and don't go out much, right?"

"I do get out but not much. My VW is almost twenty years old and I'm trying to conserve its strength. That and I'm busy with the book."

"I suppose the police asked plenty of questions so bear with us," Falk said.

Nell shrugged. "No problem. Take your time."

"On the day the body was found out there," Koski nodded toward the window, "did you hear or see anything out of the ordinary?"

"The cops asked the same question."

Falk raised an eyebrow. "And?"

"I said no. I couldn't recall anything. Then a few days later I remembered something. I was going to call them but changed my mind. I decided it was nothing."

Falk leaned forward. "Tell us, Nell."

"It was the night before they found the body. I was working late, must have been after two in the morning, and I was getting ready to turn in when I heard a car coming up the hill. We don't get too much traffic up here late at night. It was moving slowly. I could tell by the sound of the engine. Anyway, I looked out the window, you know, curious.

"At first, I didn't see the vehicle because it was driving without lights. There was a full moon and I saw it as it came past the house. Couldn't tell you what color it was but I recognized the make."

"A Rav4, maybe?" Koski asked.

"Hey! How'd you know that? Yeah. It was a Rav4. I love that little car. Soon as I get enough ahead I'm going in debt for one."

"Did it stop?"

"Don't know. I went to bed after it passed. I was bushed. How'd you know it was a Rav4?"

"Woman's intuition," said Koski gently. "Too dark to see the license plate number, right?" Nell nodded.

"You should have called the cops back."

"I suppose. I thought it might be a couple of young kids coming up here to make out."

Falk broke in. "In a Rav4?"

"Yeah. You're right." Her laugh was bubbly.

"Thanks anyway," Falk said. "You've been a big help. If you think of anything else or notice something out of the ordinary give us a call. Here's our number."

Nell took the card and studied it. "Any chance of giving you guys an interview sometime, you know, DHS and what it means to the civil rights of the average citizen?"

"Can't promise anything. We'll have to see how things go." Falk stuck out his hand and she shook it vigorously.

"I'll keep my fingers crossed, Agent Falk."

"Just one more question, Nell," Koski said. "Your t-shirt says

IBM. Are you married?"

"No. It was my aunt's. It came with the house."

As the police communications vehicle headed back down into Hollywood, Koski drummed her fingers on her knees, a habit she had when deep in thought. It irritated the hell out of Falk. He reached out and held his hand over hers. She saw the look in his eyes as he tipped his head toward the front passenger seat. They clearly indicated, "Don't say anything."

Koski went silent but restarted her drumbeat and watched the trees and bushes flash past as the driver headed to the next scene.

Chapter 14

Three minutes into reading the early evening news, the anchor died; slumped forward across the news desk. Camera One quickly cut to the weather map.

Crew Cut stood near an exit then quietly walked off the set amid the sudden confusion.

Rita Massy watched the drama on TV. She smiled and pressed the off button on her remote. This time there would be no telltale discoloration of the brain that caused medical examiners reason to suspect foul play. Her mobile rang. Massy had prearranged for the call to be brief. "Go to your place. I'll be there within the hour."

Massy parked in the street outside an apartment in Burbank, a few blocks from Warner Brothers' Studio, a white two-story stucco in need of paint. How could anyone live in such a place? She alone had paid this man enough in the last few months to enable him to live in far better circumstances.

Massy passed through the front entrance into a courtyard of

withered plants and two drooping palm trees. A small swimming pool filled with murky green water and surrounded by a chain link fence completed the picture of neglect that hung over the entire complex.

Pausing at the bottom of a set of stairs leading up to a balcony encircling the second floor, she scanned the upper units. All the apartment doors faced out onto the pool area. Number 223 was in the middle of the row.

She climbed the stairs, hearing sounds of various television shows as she passed the apartments. A child cried in the distance and a door slammed. Then she was at number 223. She kicked on the door with the side of her shoe, noting closed Venetian blinds covered the windows. Massy kicked harder. Then, taking a handkerchief from her pocket, she grasped the doorknob, turned and pushed the door open. Once inside it was apparent the place had been tossed. She closed the door with her shoulder. Whoever had searched the apartment had done a thorough job. The shabby living room was trashed with broken items. Drawers were pulled out and contents scattered. Even the cushions on the worn-out couch had been ripped open.

In the filthy kitchen she viewed a pile of dirty dishes stacked in the sink under a slowly dripping tap. She headed down the hall to a bedroom. The door was open. Crew Cut lay stretched across an unmade bed with his throat slashed and surrounded by the wreckage of another savage search.

After the initial shock of finding the man dead, Massy's brow beaded with a sweat of fear. The prototype delivery system she had passed to Crew Cut at lunch! She'd told the dead man to guard the weapon with his life. Had his killer found the device?

Massy, light-headed, heart racing, cursed the fact she should have arranged with Crew Cut where to hide the damn thing in case of an emergency. Checking the time, she realized the killing must have taken place shortly after the phone call, just over an hour ago. It was now 7:15 p.m. She had no time to waste. Someone might return.

Moving swiftly and using her handkerchief, she carefully opened the front door a crack to be sure no one was on the balcony. Satisfied, she slipped out, closing the door softly.

Two minutes later she sped up Barham Boulevard, heading back to Hollywood. *She should have taken her time, checked the body, searched for any clues that might tie him to the dead newscaster.* Damn. For a moment she almost turned back then decided it was too late. She couldn't risk someone in the building seeing her. Tightlipped, Massy shuddered at the thought of having to face the cleric and update him about the murder and losing the weapon.

Chapter 15

It was nine p.m. when the police communications vehicle pulled into the Hollywood precinct parking lot on Ivar Street. Greg Grant glanced over his shoulder. "I have an engagement tonight otherwise I'd invite you both to dinner."

The team had spent a long day scrutinizing each murder location, including the latest death at the television studio.

"Thanks. We'll get something on the way back to the hotel." Falk rubbed his hand across his chin. "Interesting day."

Grant nodded. "Yeah. We have some good footage. We'll meet here in the morning at eight. I have a couple of ideas that could move us ahead."

"What's the chance of getting an official car of our own?" Koski asked.

"I'm working on it." He swung the passenger door open. "You guys get plenty of rest. See you in the a.m."

Koski watched him cross the parking lot and climb into the passenger side of a black Mercedes parked beside the building. "Dinner dates with a woman driving a Mercedes," Koski muttered. "No wonder we're working for him."

"Temporarily," Falk replied. He pushed open the car door. "C'mon. Let's go." Falk slapped the driver on the shoulder. "Thanks for being the chauffeur in this charade today. We appreciate it."

The driver looked surprised. Grateful someone had voiced thanks. He gave a tired smile. "You're welcome. Say, if you guys like seafood try the Shack over on Cole. It's the best."

"Thanks. We'll do that." Walking to their car Koski linked arms with Falk. "That young writer up in the hills. What do you think?"

Falk shot her a questioning glance. "Meaning?"

"She said she doesn't get out much and wanted to interview us..."

Falk unlocked the car door. "I saw you jot her phone number down when we were drinking coffee. Get in, call on your cell and tell her we'll pick her up in fifteen minutes." Falk climbed behind the wheel, switched on the ignition and the car's interior filled with Mozart's Symphony No. 14 "Jupiter" as he eased the vehicle forward.

The halibut was superb. The trio finished their meal and sat in a comfortable booth at the Shack.

"The driver was right. We'll have to come here again," Koski murmured as she finished the last bite.

"My dad used to say truck drivers and cops knew the best places to eat." Nell reached for the breadbasket, pulled apart the last sourdough roll and wiped her plate clean. "And starving writers always accept a meal no matter who recommends the place."

"And investigators want the truth when they buy a meal," Falk said. "That Rav4 you saw the other night, you'd seen it in the area before, right?"

Nell stopped chewing as a surprised look flitted across her face. "How'd' you mean?"

"One of your neighbors said they'd seen a green Rav4 driving around a couple of times during the day. They remembered because it drove past slowly as if the driver was lost or looking for an address. Whoever it was also could've been scoping the area for a place to dump a body."

Falk watched as she finished eating the last of the bread then took a sip of water.

"Okay. I saw the car a couple of times."

"Why'd you hide the fact?" Falk questioned softly.

"I didn't want to get involved."

"In what?" Koski asked.

"The driver stopped outside the house several days before the body showed up on the hillside. I was out in the yard and he called to me. He said he was looking for a place to rent. Cool looking guy —said he was a musician, slept days and needed some place quiet."

Falk cut in. "Would you remember the guy if you saw him again?"

"Sure. I told him I loved his vehicle and wanted to get one like it when I had the money. He laughed. Said he'd come and see me if he ever decided to sell. He gave me his phone number."

"Notice anything about him?"

"Like what?"

"You're a writer. Describe him."

Nell looked skyward. "In his mid-thirties, dark hair and brown eyes. Couldn't tell his height since he was in the car but I'd guess five nine or so. Most Hispanics are about that height."

"You're sure he was Hispanic?"

"He looked Spanish although he didn't *sound* Spanish."

"Then why did you say Hispanic?"

"Guess it's because there are so many of us in Southern California. He could've been Italian. I don't know."

Falk pressed. "Middle Eastern perhaps?"

Nell shrugged. "That, too, I suppose. How'd you know I'd seen the car before?"

"When Agent Koski asked if you recognized the car in the darkness you came up with a Rav4 without hesitation. It's not a car most people mention as a first guess so we decided to ask you again."

"What are you going to do now?"

"Take the phone number he gave you."

"It's at home. I stuck it in my phone book. I didn't memorize it."

"Fine. You can give it to me when we get back to your place. I want you to call and ask if he'll sell the car if you raise the cash. If he says yes, find out when you can have a test ride."

Back at the house, Nell made the phone call, letting it ring several times. She glanced over at Koski and Falk shaking her head. "No answer. Like I said, he's a musician, most likely still out on a gig. You want me to keep trying?"

Falk looked at his watch. It was already past midnight. "No. Call him tomorrow. If you get him, give me a call on my cell. The number's on the card I gave you."

Falk drove back down the winding hill. "Turn the heater up, Joe." Koski nodded sleepily as the CD played softly and the warm air swirled around them. Falk concentrated on tight curves and a narrow road without streetlights when suddenly he felt something cold press firmly on the nape of his neck.

"Pull over and no heroics." Koski resisted an automatic reaction to reach for her Glock Nine and remained motionless. Falk parked the car.

"Kill the engine and lights, hands on top of your heads," a male voice commanded.

Blackness and silence filled the car. The voice continued. "Now listen up. I know who you are and why you're in town and I've something to sell."

"What?" Falk asked staring ahead.

"Information the DHS needs to know."

"How did you find us?"

"You want to buy?"

"I'll answer that when I know what you're selling."

"Fine. Drive back to your place and we'll talk."

Chapter 16

They had not attempted to overpower the young man who now sat on a straight-backed chair in Falk's living room, covering them with an automatic. Koski and Falk sat side by side on the couch. The man was olive skinned, slight of build with chocolate colored eyes reflecting that he'd learned about life the hard way; on the streets.

"I'm a gangbanger from East LA and me and a few of the gang became mixed up with a group of Middle Easterners. They said they could show us how to make big bucks, fast. It sounded easy. We thought they were drug dealers looking for local talent. The money they offered was wild. Later, when they had our trust, they told us what they really wanted."

He rubbed the back of his left hand across his mouth. "I need something cold to drink."

"Pepsi?" Koski asked.

"Yeah. It'll do."

He lapsed into silence until she returned with a bottle and a glass. He waved the glass aside and gulped from the bottle before continuing. "Turns out they wanted to use us." He took another long swig. "Mexicans can go anywhere in California and not worry about racial profiling. That profiling is a pile of shit anyway and a waste of time. Hell... Arabs can buy whoever they want to do a job. All they have to do is go where cops are hated. Easy as that."

"What made *you* change your mind?" Falk questioned, sensing the gunman was nervous despite his bravado.

"I haven't yet. I want to see what you guys have to offer."

Falk smiled. "A true patriot, I see."

The young man finished his soda. "If we make a deal it'll have to include putting me into a witness protection program in a new location far from LA with new ID and my own house."

"Ambitious plans, young man."

"I intend to improve my lifestyle."

"How did you find us?" Falk inquired.

"I'm a *thinking* gangbanger. I have my ways."

Falk nodded. "But you were fooled by a group of Arabs."

Lowering the empty bottle to the floor, the man nodded. "You're right. But I learn fast, man, and after we've made our deal I'll be living better than you."

Falk swapped a glance with Koski. "I'll have to arrange a meeting with my boss. It'll take a few days."

"I'm staying here until he comes and makes the deal." He nodded to Koski. "She'll stay with me as my guardian angel."

"You could have been followed," Koski said softly.

"Let me bring you up-to-date, lady. Nell phoned and told me you were going to pick her up and take her back to her place. I hitched up there and waited until you returned. You know the rest."

"Not quite. Tell us about Nell."

"What's to tell?"

"She's *not* a gang member?"

"No way. She's a freelance writer. She plays music to eat otherwise she'd starve to death. We met at a club in LA six months ago. I liked her music. She plays a wild clarinet. I got her a few gigs around town.

"Nell phoned me earlier and said a couple of DHS agents were taking her to dinner and then bringing her home. She was stoked, man. Said she was going to try to get an interview. I decided it would be a good time to introduce myself."

"You'd been driving around her neighborhood. You told her you were a musician looking for a place to live."

"Yeah. I told you. I met her a couple months ago at a club on Crenshaw. We got talking and she told me she lived in the hills overlooking Hollywood. Anyway, a few days ago I was ordered to look for a lonely place to dump a body and thought of the area up near her place."

"Did you tell her you were a musician *and* a gang member?"

"No."

"Who told you to look around?"

"One of the Arabs."

"Why?"

"Man, they don't tell you why. Anyway, I drove up, Nell was out in the yard and we gabbed awhile. She admired my car. We made small talk and I said I'd sell her mine when I was ready. Then I mentioned I was looking around for a place to rent."

"Did you leave your phone number?"

"Sure. Nell said she'd keep an eye open for a place."

Falk leaned forward. "You're going to have to return our weapons if you want me to call my boss."

"You said it would take a couple of days."

"I lied. What's your name?"

"Call me Marco."

"Okay, Marco. What's it to be?"

"I give you my gun. You call the cops and I'm whacked, right?"

"Not if what you have to tell us is worthwhile."

Marco lowered his voice. "It'll be worth plenty."

"Then you don't have a problem. Give it to me."

Marco handed him the automatic. "Call him. Now."

Chapter 17

Tom Stewart arrived within the hour, walked in, tossed his raincoat across the back of the couch and asked, "Where is he?"

Falk pointed. "In the kitchen. Koski's making him a sandwich." Koski and Marco entered. Marco carried a plate. He slumped into an easy chair, eyed Stewart and took a bite of his sandwich. Falk brought Stewart up-to-date while Marco chewed.

Stewart's voice was husky and his disposition edgy from having to get out of bed and drive to the hotel. He joined his fingers behind his head and leaned back. "Okay, Marco. Tell us your story."

The young Hispanic related his experiences with the Arabs, as he called them. "They needed us to act as spies, hit men, any assignment that might trigger a security check." He paused. "As long as the government continues to use its present methods of racial profiling those guys will find others to do their work."

"You don't seem to have much patriotism, Marco."

"You're wrong, man. That's why I'm here. I was born in East LA. I'm an American. You know how many people are living in

LA who *aren't* citizens—illegals working low-end jobs *if* they're lucky to find work?"

Marco's face tightened. "Some dude offers them big bucks to do something, they do it. No questions asked." Marco got up and paced the room. "I'll be straight with you, man. I knew this country was in big trouble when people like these Arabs could buy anyone as easy as buying a loaf of bread."

"What made you change your mind and come to us, Marco?" Stewart asked.

"They killed my best friend. They said he was going to go to the police."

"Was he?"

"No. It was their excuse. He refused to carry out an assignment."

"What was the assignment?"

"Place a bomb in a trash container near the snack bar at Dodger Stadium just before the end of the game. He told them he wouldn't do it, man. Didn't want to hurt no women and kids. Two days after he refused, I found him sitting in his car, dead. His throat cut."

Stewart asked. "You want to tell us who they are and seek protection, right?"

"I want to make a *deal*." He pointed at Falk. "Like I told him. I want a guarantee of the witness protection plan. A house fully paid for and a new location."

"Is that it?" Stewart questioned.

"No. I also want one million dollars. Cash."

"You're out of your mind, Marco. The government doesn't pay

out that kind of money."

"I'm not finished. I'll stay with the gang for another six months and feed you information that'll be worth more than a million bucks. Hell, every time the government dropped *one* of those smart bombs on Iraq at the start of the war, they cost that much. All the taxpayers got for their money if the missile went off track was crushed rock and some dead goats."

"What makes you think you can give us information worth a million dollars?"

Marco flicked off a few crumbs and smoothed his shirtfront. He cut his eyes to Stewart and gave a sly smile. "I don't want to be rude, but your two agents," Marco nodded toward Koski and Falk, "are working with the cops trying to find who the Hollywood serial killer is, right?"

"Go on."

"I can tell you more than the cops know right now. The killings are experimental tests to discover the best means to deliver a mind-altering drug that can turn a person into an assassin or a suicide bomber on command."

Stewart glanced at Falk and back to Marco. "How do you know that?"

"It's what I do. I keep my ears and eyes open. And these guys trust me."

"Why?"

"Good help is hard to find, man."

Chapter 18

Stewart had agreed that Marco contact him through Falk

within forty-eight hours, at which time he'd be advised whether he would become a paid informer. Marco phoned Falk the next morning at 6 a.m. They arranged to meet at a Mexican restaurant, José's, on Alvera Street, a tourist attraction near Union Station in downtown LA.

Falk hung up and looked into Koski's room moments before she was about to leave for her morning run. "Why call you so soon, Joe? He only left a few hours ago. Maybe we should go together."

"No. Contact Grant. Tell him I was called into the bureau and I'll check with him later. Stick with Grant until I join you. Gotta go."

Alvera Street is a short, quaint street of shops and small stalls selling Mexican goods, everything from jumping beans to piñatas. Falk found the restaurant—and Marco—sitting in a red leather booth facing the door.

"Coffee?" Marco asked. Falk nodded.

"Let's eat." Marco slid a plastic covered menu across the table. "I think better on a full stomach. Try the eggs and salsa. Gets the brain working."

"Coffee's fine." Falk eased into the booth. A server appeared, filled a thick mug with steaming coffee and pushed it toward him. "I thought we were going to wait a couple of days, Marco?"

"I decided to show goodwill and give you a tip."

"Why?"

"Goodwill. Understand what I'm saying?"

"No."

The server returned and placed a large plate of refried beans and eggs and a deep bowl of salsa in front of Marco, along with a covered dish. Marco tapped the dish. "Warm tortillas. You like one?"

"I'm fine."

Marco shrugged, scooped a forkful of beans into his mouth, snagged a tortilla, folded it in half and stuck one end into an egg, breaking the yolk. "You should eat, man. Breakfast's the most important meal of the day."

Falk nodded and sipped his coffee. It was strong, not bitter.

"I'll be straight with you, man," Marco continued, eating and talking at the same time. "You heard of *Jamul* right?"

Falk nodded. "The pop singer?"

"He's more than that, Agent Falk. He's a show business legend." Marco plucked another tortilla from the dish, rolled it into a tube and jabbed it into the salsa.

"He's also big with the Arabs and I don't just mean music and entertainment wise. He has homes all over the world. Right now he's at his pad in the marina. You guys at the DHS should check him out."

"What does he do for the Arabs?"

"Hey! I don't know yet. All I know is Jamul became a born again Islamic, and whatever it is he does for their cause, he does for free. It's up to your boss. If he agrees to my demands, I'll find out."

"You could have saved this information for Stewart and made brownie points."

Marco took the last tortilla, shrugged and wiped his plate clean.

Chapter 19

Crew Cut's murder received little notice from the news media. The Hollywood serial killer was still the lead story. The most concerned person was Rita Massy. She'd been called to meet with her boss and report what had happened. She parked in the subterranean garage, entered the express elevator and punched in the penthouse's security code.

Her boss was a tall, handsome man. He was on his cell, pacing impatiently back and forth across a white wall-to-wall carpet three inches thick. "She's here now. I'll call you back." He flipped his phone shut and slipped its compactness into his shirt pocket.

White slacks, a long-sleeved red silk shirt, a pair of red tennis shoes, his hair pulled into a black shiny ponytail and the man thought he looked cool. Rita Massy thought he personified a pimp. Massy's boss opened his arms like a preacher greeting his flock. "Doctor Massy, come in, take a seat. Would you like something to drink: coffee, tea?"

Both knew the dance had started. Smooth courtesy thinly covered the distrust in both their hearts. "Nothing, thanks. I'm fine."

"I see our last subject went out in grand style. No problems I take it?" He indicated a chair.

"No problem with the execution. And there'll be no questions at the autopsy." Massy leaned back in the soft comfort of the deep leather chair.

"Were you satisfied with the delivery device, Doctor?"

"Absolutely."

"This person who carried out the execution was one of your people, I believe."

Massy stiffened slightly. "Yes. I've used him on several occasions."

"Trust him then, do you, Doctor?"

"Of course," she replied.

The tall man turned toward the floor to ceiling window and stared at the view. "I had him eliminated. He's been around too long."

A wave of fear shivered into her gut and she fought to hide her reaction. She needed to move. Pushing out of the easy chair, she joined him at the window and gazed out at the panoramic view. She was the first to speak. "You did the right thing."

"You surprise me, Doctor." He turned quickly, fastened a viselike grip on her arm and led her away from the window. "You also allowed him to take the weapon back to his apartment." His eyes were slits as he moved his face close to Massy. "A foolish move, doctor. Luckily my man discovered the weapon. I have it in safe keeping."

Massy felt the grip loosen slightly then a long slender finger tapped her shoulder. "You look pale, Doctor. Sit down, relax. I won't be a moment." Massy took a deep, shuddering breath and slumped into the chair. The bastard was playing cat and mouse.

Within seconds he returned with the prototype wrapped in a towel. Placing the bundle on a side table next to her chair, he slowly unwrapped the towel and stood back to admire the killing tool.

"A wonderful device indeed," Massy's superior said softly,

any sign of his anger now gone. Both stared at the black plastic object that was the shape and size of a small flashlight. He reached down and with the solemnity of a priest raising a chalice, held the weapon cupped reverently between his large powerful hands. "So light. It feels like a toy."

Massy watched mesmerized as he turned it from side to side then took it in his right hand and aimed directly at her. "You say the new model is even more advanced, longer range, truer accuracy, even smaller! Amazing. And to think it doesn't make a sound when fired."

He lowered the weapon. "Is that the correct term, fired?"

Massy swallowed hard before attempting a reply. "Perhaps a new word will have to be coined." She felt perspiration trickling down her back. Had her boss continued with his previous fit of anger she would be dead by now.

"You will need a new assassin, Doctor."

"Yes. I have an expert in long-range work. He's already skilled with the new weapon."

He smiled and aimed the device toward the window. He held the position for a count of five then suddenly spun and stared at her. He moved in closer and placed the tip of the weapon on her nose. "I'm certain you'll see that this expert does an excellent job, Doctor."

Chapter 20

After Doctor Massy left, the tall man returned to the window and gazed out across what had been rice paddies years ago. It was now a yacht harbor surrounded by upscale apartments and known as Marina Del Rey.

Located between Venice and the Los Angeles Airport, the Marina is a place of recreation, habitation and fornication. Apartments full of swinging singles, slips full of powerboats, yachts and sailboats, all tied down in neat rows, making a city of wealth and power; floating assets.

Jamul lived in the penthouse of one of the twin cylindrical apartments that soared over the display of nautical richness. It was 9:05 a.m. Even though it was April, the sun ignored the fact and beamed kindly on the Marina. The ocean twinkled in response.

Jamul walked onto his balcony and stood facing the Pacific, focusing a large pair of binoculars on a white-hulled Grand Banks trawler as it rounded the breakwater sailing into the main channel of the Marina.

"Home is the sailor, home from the sea," Jamul whispered as the trawler cruised proudly the length of the almost deserted waterway. Jamul owned the craft along with two more identical Grand Banks. Each boat was registered under a different name. Jamul's name didn't show on any of the manifests. His name did appear, however, on one of the largest yachts in the Marina. Purchased through a broker in Gibraltar and outside EU and American waters, the vessel remained unaffected by tax considerations. The brokerage house was an establishment guaranteeing confidentiality at all times.

Elvis Presley, at the height of his success, had once owned FDR's yacht, the *Potomac*.

Sadly, it was no longer for sale and was now part of a maritime museum in Oakland, California.

Jamul had searched every major ship brokerage in the world. He finally located his dream, the sister ship of FDR's beloved *Potomac*. Jamul knew the original yacht was 196 feet long so he added another twenty-five feet. In addition, a bright blue Bell 206B-111 Jet-ranger helicopter perched on the ship's helipad.

No way was Elvis ever going to upstage Jamul. He named the craft *Caviare*. It was rarely put to sea. A full time crew whose duties were to maintain the bright work always kept the yacht in perfect condition, ready for business meetings or dinner parties at a moment's notice, whatever Jamul decided.

Jamul's position in life called for such amenities. Being adored as a demigod by those between eighteen and thirty-five from all around the world had placed him in a position of absolute power in the music industry.

His story of rising from the ranks of poverty in New York's Spanish Harlem to singer/entertainer of choice to the younger generation had been extolled ad nauseam by the world's entertainment media. With superb management, Jamul possessed a magnetic personality and a singing voice with the range of Caruso, the charm of Sinatra plus a magic of his own that no one could explain. He was a star with one name and beloved by millions.

Jamul lowered his binoculars, walked across the balcony and back inside the penthouse. He owned homes in many countries and traveled constantly, using his own private jets. Jamul had secretly embraced Islam ten years earlier. To the public he was a man with the voice of an angel. In truth, he was a man with the soul of a serpent.

The Grand Banks sailed to its mooring, tied up and no one

looked twice. Within less than a half hour of docking, Jamul was entertaining three passengers from the trawler in his penthouse. His manservant served Arabic coffee. Jamul served the three with up-to-date Bosnian passports, showing they had arrived into the country legally with visas valid for three months. United States Customs or airport security hadn't troubled the travelers. They were to join Mikhail Brasinov at his Beverly Hills apartment within hours.

Deception is an arrangement of light and dark... The people trained to see white where there is black.

Jamul was black and he could easily make Rita Massy see white.

Chapter 21

Falk's cell phone buzzed as he drove back to Hollywood from breakfast with Marco.

"Where the hell are you? You were supposed to meet me at eight." It was Grant.

"Didn't Koski phone and tell you I'd been called into the bureau?"

"No one called. I've been phoning your hotel and just located your damn cell number."

Falk's mind raced. What happened to Koski? "Look, Greg, you know the way it is sometimes. You'll have to excuse us for today. Okay?"

"DHS will take a dim view of this, Falk. We don't operate this way."

"Greg, I'm driving. You're breaking up. Can you hear me?

Hello, Greg?" He switched off and headed for the hotel.

Falk checked both suites. No sign of a struggle. Koski would have called if her plans suddenly changed and she decided not to meet with Grant. Where was she? Falk returned to his suite, thinking of the sudden request to meet Marco for breakfast; an arrangement to get him out of the way while someone snatched her?

Mikhail Brasinov studied the passports and handed them back to the two men who had arrived at the Marina. "Very good. We're working with super pros now, better than the old days, eh?" Both men nodded. "Good. Your first assignment will be to kidnap an FBI agent, a young woman. Do not harm her. She has information we need."

The burlier of the two scowled. "You want us to kidnap an FBI agent?!"

"Yes, and take her to a boat in the Marina. You'll be briefed in detail. I want *nothing* to go wrong, understand?"

Chapter 22

Koski was flat on her back in total darkness. She had regained consciousness with a splitting headache and attempted to push into a sitting position but the pain was excruciating. She flopped back onto what felt like a cot or bunk. She didn't attempt any moves other than slow deep breathing. Dampness—salt air—the smell of stale coffee and diesel oil and the sound of lapping water seeped into her consciousness.

She was on a boat. Pushing up onto one elbow, she forced herself to overcome the nausea. Still dressed in her running clothes she quickly pulled up the right leg of her sweatsuit and reached for her ankle holster. Her fingers fumbled for the .22 automatic she always carried when out alone in the early morning. It was gone.

The creaking sound of a hatch opening startled her, then a shaft of daylight stabbed into the darkness and a woman's voice called down. "Has the headache diminished yet?"

Koski shifted on the bunk, shaded her eyes and blinked up at a dark shape in the hatch entrance as the woman spoke again.

"You're not tied or handcuffed, and as long as you obey orders you won't be harmed. If you don't, you'll be killed."

Koski had experience in situations where she had learned firsthand to be silent. Say nothing. Listen. Answer questions and if they didn't already know the answers, lie.

The woman continued. "No doubt you could use a cup of coffee. Black or white?"

"Black," Koski mumbled.

Rita Massy stared through the eye slits of her ski mask at the woman curled on the bunk. Doctor Wolf, in a casual conversation with Massy, had unknowingly disclosed the interest the DHS had shown concerning the mysterious deaths and the resultant findings of brain discolorations during the autopsies.

Locating the address of two of the investigating agents hadn't been a problem. The hatch closed. Blackness returned and Koski cursed softly. One minute she had been running her morning miles and the next woke in a whorl of pain.

In the City of Angels, in an area known as Silverlake, Detective Victor Young entered his small rented house. The once bright yellow stucco had   faded to a dingy white and was surrounded by overgrown flowers and weeds.

Jacaranda trees in blue bloom next to a bright red bottlebrush were the only two living things in the garden that Victor could name. Red and green had been Jenny's colors. Green eyes, red hair. She'd known the name of every flower and plant in the garden.

Young missed her with an ache he knew would last as long as he lived. He closed the door softly.

Three years had passed since she went to the store to buy groceries on a warm summer afternoon. She never returned, having been killed in a robbery that went wrong. Young discovered later that his wife had gone to the store to get fresh garlic for her spaghetti sauce. She'd asked him what he wanted for dinner just before he'd left for work. Now he stood on the exact spot he'd been when he called back. "Spaghetti, and don't forget to put garlic in the sauce this time." They'd laughed and he kissed her goodbye.

"I won't," she said. "I'll pick some up this afternoon. Take care of yourself, Vic."

Take care of yourself, Vic. She never failed to send him off to work with a kiss and those words. Over the last three years Victor Young became an embittered man.

The winking green light of the answering machine in the living room caught his eye. He tapped the play button and heard Captain Garvey's voice.

"You have a new assignment, Detective Young." Victor noted the sound of urgency in the Captain's voice. "One of the hotshot investigators from the DHS has gone missing. Call Falk on his cell phone soon as you get this message." The Captain gave the number then the line went dead.

Young stared at the machine. Captains didn't usually call detectives at home and give them an assignment. He made the call.

Joe Falk was still at the hotel and was rechecking Koski's room for the slightest sign she might have left as a clue to her whereabouts when Young called.

"Falk."

"This is Detective Victor Young, LAPD. I've been assigned to work with you." He paused, uncertain how to phrase his next sentence. "It's regarding your missing partner."

"Where can we meet?" Falk barked.

"Your hotel, twenty minutes. I'll leave now."

"I'll be in the lobby."

Chapter 23

Falk recognized Young coming through the front entrance. "You're the guy with the questions. I remember you from the briefing. Let's get a cup of coffee and I'll bring you up to speed."

Stewart had given Falk the okay to tell detective that he and Koski were undercover FBI, not DHS photographers. He said it made for better working conditions. Stewart was right.

Young set his cup down. "I thought I was stuck with a news photographer who didn't know his ass from a hole in the ground about police procedure and I was to play nursemaid."

Falk smiled thinly. "There are a few news photographers who do, Victor."

Victor leaned forward, eager to gather facts and get started on their search. "Yeah, right. *Very* few. So the last you saw of her she was in her room getting ready to go on her morning run. You know the route she takes?"

"No. She changed it daily, for safety's sake."

"She could've been followed from the start. Let's make a few inquires," Young said.

Their first stop was a 24-hour convenience store several blocks from the hotel. The clerk remembered seeing a young woman jogging past the window shortly after he went on duty at 6 a.m. Nothing unusual. He often saw joggers from the hotel running in the early morning. When questioned further by Falk, he remembered a car drove past a couple of minutes later, driving slowly—a Rav4.

"Can you recall the color?"

"I think it was green. I'm not certain."

"Thanks." He turned to Victor. "Koski told me she saw a green Rav4 outside the hotel the other morning. She took the plate number and ran it through the DMV. Turned out it belonged to a guy making a delivery."

"You still have the number?"

"Yeah. I jotted it down." He removed a small notebook from a pocket and thumbed a few pages. "Here it is—'NTV925'."

"We'll run it again," Victor said. "Get an address and see what we can find."

Less than an hour later they had an address on June Street, a section in Hollywood consisting mainly of homes and small apartments built in the 1930s. The street number proved to be a house in the rear.

They parked out front and walked up the buckled concrete driveway. Young knocked on the door of a house with peeling brown paint on the window frames. No answer. Falk tried the bell. "No one home," the LAPD detective muttered, peering through a grimy window.

"Can I help you?" a woman's voice called.

Turning, Falk saw a heavyset woman standing on the back step of the front house. She held a yard broom across her ample chest as if it were an AK47.

"Police." Young removed his wallet and flipped it open.

The woman relaxed a little, came forward and scrutinized Victor's picture. "What about him?" She pointed the broom at Falk. Victor raised his eyebrows. Falk showed his ID. The woman looked surprised. "A cop *and* a DHS man!"

"This isn't TV, ma'am," the detective replied. "We're looking to ask the occupant a few questions." He jerked his thumb toward the peeling paint.

"He's not in."

"Know when he'll be back?"

"Never. He's dead. Killed in his car early this morning." She lowered her broom, "A wreck on the 405."

"How do you know?" Falk asked.

"Cops came by to see if he had any next of kin. Must've gotten his address from his driver's license," she said softly.

"Did he?" Falk said.

She shook her head. "None. He lived alone."

"Did he drive a Rav4?"

"All I know is it was a small green SUV."

Falk thanked the woman then they walked back to their car. His new partner turned on the ignition "We can get a search warrant."

Falk nodded. He was thinking of Koski and hoping she was still alive.

They headed north on Highland Avenue. "It'll take a couple of hours to get the warrant," Young explained.

Falk grunted, staring straight ahead.

Captain Garvey pulled the necessary strings. In less than an hour Falk and Young were on their way back to June Street with a warrant. Victor hung a left off Highland and they saw the red lights and heard the sirens of two fire trucks winding down as they turned onto June. Black smoke billowed skyward.

"That's the house!" Falk shouted. Young drove onto the curb. They leapt out and ran toward the equipment as firefighters unraveled hoses up the driveway. Two-way radios crackled as people gathered in the street. Orange flames licked through the roof of the rear house. A black and white screeched to a stop and two cops bailed out, ordering rubbernecking neighbors back.

Falk and Young flashed their IDs to the fire captain. The broom woman stood on the curb near her house as firefighters poured streams of water on the roof to lessen the chance of sparks igniting her place.

The captain wasn't impressed. "I've no time to talk. You'll have to wait until we have this under control." He turned away, rasping orders into a handheld radio.

"Whoever torched the place got matches faster than we got the warrant," Falk growled. They moved to one side, shielding their faces as the roof of the rear house collapsed sending up a shower of sparks and a shuddering wave of heat.

"We're back to square one," Young groaned.

Falk shook his head. "Not yet... Come on. I want a few more words with the broom lady over there."

She was waving her arms and yelling to keep pouring water on her roof. Catching sight of the two who'd interviewed her earlier, she scowled. "Can't you see I'm busy?"

"I think you can leave everything to the LAFD, ma'am. There's nothing you can do. We have some more questions. Let's go over there out of the way." Falk indicated a spot under a singed palm tree. "Did you see anything suspicious since we were last here?"

She glared at Falk. "Damn right I did."

"Tell us."

"You weren't gone five minutes when a green car drives up the driveway. At first I thought it was him."

"Same color?" Young asked. "Same model?"

"Yes," she answered. "Exactly the same like a twin."

"Did you get the plate number?"

"No. I thought I saw a ghost."

"How long was it here?"

"Less than five minutes. The car reversed back down the driveway and was gone. A minute later I heard a loud THUMP, saw flames inside the house and called 911."

"Thank you, Mrs.?"

"Terrabella. Molly Terrabella."

"You've been very helpful." Falk jerked his head in the direction of the car and Young followed.

Chapter 24

Tom Stewart made it official. Marco was now a paid informant for the DHS.

"You will only contact Agent Falk or me with any information you gather. Is that clear?" Marco nodded. "Any attempt to double cross or fabricate information will result in you being eliminated."

Marco sat in a molded red plastic chair opposite Stewart who had the remains of a submarine sandwich on the table in front of him. He sipped coffee from a Styrofoam cup. The meeting was in the snack bar of K-Mart Hollywood. Marco waited until the store announcement about a Blue Light Special ended.

"I get the protection plan I asked for and the money in a Swiss bank, right?"

Stewart nodded. "You have three months to earn your pay."

"I need money now, man. I'm gonna need *expense* money. I can't operate on air for three months."

"You lived okay before we met. Remember, every time we meet increases the risk of you being found out."

"People mail money. It doesn't have to be *handed* to me," Marco moaned.

"Never mail money, Marco. The dead letter office is full of mail that will never arrive." Stewart pushed his plate aside. "I'm going to give you a code word to be used only in an emergency. Place a call to the number I gave you and when someone answers simply say *ATLAS*."

Stewart slid a K-Mart shopping bag across the table. "There's a transistor radio in there. It's been paid for and the cash register receipt is inside. The radio has been modified into a GPS unit locked to a special frequency that is monitored 24/7. It plays AM/ FM like an ordinary radio. You can switch to a special broadcast frequency by pressing the case between your thumb and forefinger on one side of the speaker. That will activate a signal and transmit your exact location. You'll be picked up in a matter of minutes.

"Remember. Call the number, say ATLAS and press the radio." Stewart shoved his chair back as two yelling five-year-olds rushed past and a harried mother laden with a tray of food searched for a table. Marco glanced at the kids. When he looked up Stewart was gone.

The stressed mother quickly hooked the toe of her shoe around the leg of the vacant chair, pulled it out and plopped down as the raucous brood rounded the snack bar and headed back toward the table.

Marco made a fast retreat. So ended his initiation into the dark and dangerous world of an informant.

"Why has the Department of Homeland Security taken such a sudden interest in a serial killer?" Massy asked. Her voice was muffled by the ski mask as she delivered coffee. She studied Koski as she drank.

Koski ignored the question, finished her coffee and asked for a second cup.

Smart-ass bitch is treating me like a waitress. "It's to your advantage to answer my questions. If you prefer, I can arrange for an interrogation expert to take over. It's up to you."

The cabin was dark, the windows blacked out. Only a thin shaft of daylight cut through the partially open hatch. Koski saw nothing but a small patch of blue sky. It was time to improvise. "I'm an assigned photographer from DHS investigating the Hollywood serial killings."

"Why is the DHS interested?" Massy repeated.

"Because the victims died by unusual circumstances."

"Unusual? What does that mean?"

Koski knew she had to answer questions but intended to say very little. "The method by which they were killed."

"DHS suspects some kind of terrorist affiliation?"

Koski shrugged. "First I've heard about it."

"Why else are they working with the police? That's not normal procedure." Massy took Koski's empty cup.

"DHS is ComCen now for all law enforcement agencies to cooperate with. Do I get a refill?"

"Part of the famous, 'We'll all be one big happy security force,'" Massy sneered as she started up the wooden steps. She paused at the top. "No refills." She climbed out onto the deck and slid the hatch shut.

Koski slumped against the bulkhead in total blackness, her mind racing. She knew Falk was looking for her. How could he find her when she herself had no idea where she was? Easing off the bunk, she cautiously crossed the cabin with her arms outstretched. She'd memorized the layout of the cabin during the short session with the masked woman. She knew where the galley was.

Perhaps she could find a knife or something to break a porthole and yell for help. She had to try.

Slowly she inched in the direction of the small galley until her fingertips touched a cupboard mounted over a tiny sink. Moving closer, she bellied up to the counter, then ran her hands lightly over the surface and along the leading edge until her fingers found a drawer pull. She slowly eased the drawer open, praying it contained something useful.

Koski lightly touched the items in the drawer. She was like a blind woman in a strange house. Suddenly she experienced a surge of hope as she touched a hard rubber object, grasped it firmly and withdrew a flashlight, her thumb resting on the slide switch. Covering the lens with one hand, she slid the switch forward and her fingers glowed red. She quickly doused the light.

She knew by its heft she'd found a six D-cell heavy-duty unit. It made a deadly weapon. Unmoving, she listened for the slightest sound from above. Satisfied, she turned on the light and shone the beam slowly around the galley.

All was neat and in place. On the wall next to a built-in, one-burner propane stove were three knives: a twelve-inch carver, a ten-inch serrated and an ivory-handled eight-inch paring knife. She removed the paring knife, pulled up the leg of her jogging pants and slid the knife down inside her sock. She thrust hard until the tip sank into the inner sole of her shoe allowing the blade to remain snugly in place against her ankle. Koski was tempted to take the carving knife, too, but decided not to push her luck.

Footsteps sounded on the deck. She snapped off the flashlight. The footsteps passed overhead and all was quiet. Not wanting to tempt fate, she eased back to the bunk, hiding the flashlight beneath the blanket, somewhat reassured in knowing she had some tools at her disposal. She would wait for darkness above before making any more moves.

"*She's* no DHS photographer," Jamul muttered, lounging in an easy chair in the penthouse as he viewed a liquid crystal flat screen, showing Koski on a closed circuit, infrared telecast system. "*That* woman's been trained for covert missions."

Massy asked softly, "CIA maybe?"

"Perhaps so, Doctor."

"I can have her unarmed."

"Not yet. We need to find out more about our adversary. What do we know about her partner?"

"I had him followed after he left his hotel with someone from the police. They went to the house on June Street and made contact with the property owner, then to the Hollywood station and back to the house. By then the place was in flames and our man long gone."

"Where are they now?" Jamul growled.

They both watched as Koski slowly crossed the screen and made her way back to the bunk.

Massy glanced at her watch. "I should be getting a report any minute." The soft buzz of her cell caused Jamul's head to turn. Massy flipped the phone open. "Go ahead."

Jamul raised his eyebrows when Massy, listening, nodded affirmatively. "Don't lose them. Bring them here to the Marina."

Chapter 25

"We're being followed, Victor. Two cars: a Jeep Cherokee and a Honda. They're playing swap off."

"Who's on right now?" Detective Victor Young asked as he

made a sharp turn off Wilshire Boulevard and headed north on Fairfax Avenue.

"The Jeep," Falk said as his cell phone buzzed. "Falk."

"If you're looking for your partner, man, I know where she is." Falk recognized the voice at once. "Where is she, Atlas? Tell me."

"Slow down. Where are *you* right now?"

"Fairfax Avenue, heading north crossing Third Street."

"You're not even warm."

"Look, don't fuck with me, all right."

The Jeep was still in position three cars back. Falk couldn't see the Honda.

"You're being followed, man."

"Yeah, I know—two cars."

"They have orders to haul your ass in. Be careful. They're pros."

"Hey, communicate or I'll see your name gets spread around as an informer."

Marco obeyed. "She's being held aboard a forty-foot ketch in Marina Del Rey."

"I need a location." Falk glanced at Young, who nodded.

"'A' slip on Palawan Way. Park on Admiralty Way in the 1200 block. Walk south to Palawan. It's less than half a block. Turn left on Palawan. Four slips down on the left you'll see the ketch. It's white with blue trim named *Sea Note*. She's aboard." The phone went dead.

Falk pocketed his cell. "DHS informant. How long to get to the Marina?"

"This time of the day we can make it in less than twenty-five minutes."

"First we have to shake them." Falk jabbed his finger in the direction of the parking lot of CBS Television City. "Quick. In there. Call for back up. Park wherever you can. We're going to make a switch."

The CBS lot was vast. The Jeep driver reacted quickly to Young's sudden turn and moved fast not to lose sight of his quarry.

"He's on to us," Falk muttered, watching the Jeep as it turned off Fairfax Avenue. Young had made contact with LAPD and was told there were patrol cars in the area heading for the lot.

"Back-up coming in from three entrances. They have a description of our tails." Victor rolled down the window, jammed a magnetic base flashing red light atop the car and stomped hard on the accelerator.

The driver of the Jeep made contact with the Honda. "He's turned into the parking lot at Television City. Where are you?"

"Heading west on Wilshire just passing the La Brea tar pits."

"Move it. We have to get them."

The Honda sped up. He could be in the parking lot in two minutes.

The first police car came in off Beverly Boulevard at the north end of the lot. The second radioed its position as it entered the crowded parking complex from the Farmers' Market, an open-air tourist attraction on Fairfax Avenue. Young acknowledged their call and gave his position. A third squad car radioed they were proceeding toward CBS through Park La Brea, a tiny section of high-rise and garden apartments south on Third Street.

"You guys see me yet?" Young asked.

"Affirmative. Where's the Honda? We see the Jeep."

Falk grabbed the microphone from the detective as they wheeled in between the rows of parked cars. "No idea on the Honda, but it can't be far away."

"Roger that."

The back window of Falk and Young's car exploded as it took a hit from a shooter in the Jeep. Falk updated the cops.

"We're under fire. They're using a noise suppressor." The words were hardly out of Falk's mouth when Young swerved violently to miss a woman and small child who walked out from between a row of cars. In doing so, he grazed the rear of a parked car, glanced off and had to wrench hard on the wheel to miss the petrified woman as she stood holding her youngster by the hand. Then she pulled herself and the child back between the rows as the Jeep roared past in a cloud of dust and grit.

"Victor, a chase through here will get innocent people hurt. Stay ahead then swing across his path. We'll bail and make a run for it."

Young nodded and stomped on the gas. One of the police cars was now close behind the Jeep with siren wailing, lights flashing. Suddenly, down one of the rows ahead, came a second black and white going flat out. If both kept up their speed they would collide at the next opening.

"Spin it *now* or we'll hit," Falk yelled. Young saw the cruiser at the same time he heard Falk. He had trained to make spins and turns in defensive driving; gas—brake—pedal—yank on the wheel. It had been years ago but it all came back to Young as he automatically carried out the difficult maneuver. He swung the cruiser so the driver's side was away from the oncoming Jeep then both men leapt from the stalled vehicle. With Falk leading, they vanished between the rows of parked cars.

The Jeep was unable to stop in time and rammed into the abandoned police car, pushing it twenty feet. It turned the vehicle into a ball of twisted metal before slamming to a stop against a red Mercedes, which immediately burst into a sheet of flame. The pursuing police car screeched to a halt and both officers ran toward the scene with their automatics ready. There was no need. No one moved from inside the battered and burning Jeep.

Young turned toward the wreck ready to join the two cops.

"No!" Falk gripped his arm and pulled him low to the ground between two cars. "Look." He pointed between the rows toward the Farmers' Market. The Honda was three rows away, heading toward the fire. Sirens in the distance alerted Falk it was only a matter of minutes before the area would be awash with emergency vehicles and onlookers.

The driver of the Honda swiveled his head from side to side trying to assess what had happened. Falk could see he also was talking on a cell phone. People ran toward the smoke and flames. The Honda driver was forced to a standstill.

"Let's take him out." Before Young could answer, Falk twisted his way through the parked cars. The detective followed until they were three cars from the stalled Honda.

"We'll take his car," Falk said. "Reverse out of this mess and get back onto Fairfax."

"What about him?" Young peered around the fender of a

Chevy at the driver still talking into his phone.

"He stays...come on." They approached on either side of the Honda as people ran toward the wreck. Young was on the driver's side and almost at the door when the driver saw him. Young aimed his service automatic and squeezed the trigger. Click! A misfire!

The driver didn't panic. The other two police cars had joined in with the fire and ambulance and it was an impassable mass of officialdom. As Young tried to clear his weapon, the driver calmly removed a nine millimeter Sig Suer from a shoulder holster, tapped the automatic window button and leaned out. Falk, on the passenger side, took aim and fired a shot through the closed window.

The driver's head spun sideways. His dark, stringy hair splayed out in concert with his blood and brains as his skull exploded from the impact of a well-aimed nine millimeter Parabellum. Falk scooped up the ejected casing.

"Victor, let's move." Together they darted between the cars, moving away from the fire and confusion. "We'll steal a car, one closer to an exit, and then head for the Marina."

Young nodded, gasped his thanks and pointed across the lot. "We'll head for Beverly Boulevard. Follow me."

No one bothered them and within a few minutes they were beside a Subaru Outback. The doors were unlocked.

"This'll do fine," Falk said. "Hot wire it and let's go."

Victor Young wasted no time. Soon he had the ignition wires joined and the engine running. He drove sedately, not wanting to attract attention. Falk drummed impatiently on the dash as they exited onto Beverly Boulevard and headed west. He eyed the gas gauge noting it was down to a quarter of a tank.

"How far do we have to go?"

"About twenty miles."

Falk checked the side mirror. "Okay. When we get to the Marina drop me off on Admiralty Way. I'll walk down to Palawan Way. Stay far enough back to make sure I'm not being followed. I'll locate the boat and check it out."

Young turned the Subaru south on La Cienega. "We could involve the cops at the Marina. They'll know the area better than we do."

"Not unless I run into trouble. Right now all I want is to get aboard that boat and find Koski." Falk leaned back and wondered if Marco's information was for real or a trap.

Chapter 26

Koski was starving. She hadn't eaten for hours and decided to rummage around in the galley. She slid off the bunk and crept amidships, carefully shading the beam of the flashlight. Once in the galley area, she aimed the shaft of light at a hanging cupboard to the right of the sink and tugged the door open to find a few canned goods, an open box of soda crackers, a jar of strawberry jam with the top missing, and several slices of individually wrapped American cheese held down by a jar of horseradish.

She wolfed down three crackers, tore open a slice of cheese, wrapped it around a cracker, stuck her finger in the jam and wiped it on the cheese. It tasted like heaven. As she munched the last cracker, she heard footsteps crossing the deck. Clicking off the flashlight she returned to the bunk, licked her fingers, wiped her hands down the sides of her pants and waited.

Then the sound of voices caused her to investigate. Koski moved cautiously to the bottom of the steps beneath the hatch. She eased upward one step at a time. The conversation was barely audible but she was able to recognize the voice of the woman who had served the coffee.

"I received a call from the towers to be ready to move out of the Marina."

"Where to?" a male voice asked.

"Don't know. Orders are to be ready."

"What about her?"

"We go, she goes."

Koski knew if they sailed out of the Marina her chance of an escape was slim. She reached up and tried to move the hatch. It was closed tight.

It was early afternoon when Falk climbed from the stolen Outback and walked along Admiralty Way. LAPD Detective Victor Young drove off as arranged but kept Falk in sight and remained in the background.

A store, The Skipper's Locker, caught Falk's eye. A modern day ship's chandler. He quickly decided that a nautical appearance while scouting the Marina would be good cover. He crossed the street and entered. Electronic depth meters and navigational aids were stacked beside radio transmitters and hand-held GPS units. There was rope and line of all styles. Chrome and brass fittings, rustproof screws, nautical hardware for anything that sailed. He wondered what an old time sailor would have made of the place.

He headed toward a section devoted to the well-dressed

sailor. Noticing the prices on various merchandise, he was reminded of the answer a friend of his had given when asked what it was like to own and operate a sailboat.

"That's easy, Joe. Just imagine standing in an ice cold shower in your most expensive suit and tearing up one hundred dollar bills."

Falk purchased a canvas carry all, the type with pull strings and easy to sling over your shoulder. He also picked up a pale blue zip front windbreaker, a pair of deck shoes, also light blue, and a navy blue cap with a golden anchor emblazoned above its shiny peak.

In a small dressing room, he packed his shoes, tie and jacket in the canvas bag, shrugged into the windbreaker and laced his new shoes. He checked in the mirror to make sure his shoulder holster didn't bulge, and placed his cap at a jaunty angle, making a mental note to dirty it up a little when he got outside. He didn't want to look like a complete rube.

He paid cash and was about to leave when he noticed an eight-foot aluminum boat hook with a paddle on one end and a hook on the other. The clerk happily rang up the sale. Falk slung the canvas bag over his shoulder along with the boat hook and almost whistled a sea chanty as he headed out the front door.

Once on Palawan Way, he curbed a natural urge to rush. Drawing attention was the last thing he needed. The layout of the various slips was his target. He passed one of the self-locking gates in the heavy duty chain link fence separating the public from the slips. He knew he had a problem.

He stopped in the pretense of tying a shoelace and quickly

checked the lock. He relaxed. It was a standard type widely used in low security areas. On the dockside of the fence, a steel cover protected the twist lock, supposedly to stop anyone from reaching through and turning the security device. He'd opened similar locks with ease when he was a kid. To be sure, he pushed his hand through the fence and made a test run. His forearm had grown in the last thirty years and there was no way he could reach around the security shield. He even had a hard time removing his arm.

Damn it! He had to get down to the dock.

As he neared the gate of slip four, he saw the white and blue ketch. A burly man on deck seemed out of place. Falk felt certain he was security. In case he was questioned, Falk had prepared a cover story saying he'd promised to do a favor for a pal by cleaning the brass fittings on the vessel next to the *Sea Note.* It was a small sailboat with a blue tarpaulin tied down fast and pulled over the boom protecting the deck from the weather.

He toyed with the idea of calling down to the *Sea Note* to say he forgot to get the gate key from his pal. Yeah, right. Burly would tell him to go to hell. He was almost at the gate when a car pulled up and a young woman got out. She opened the trunk and lugged out an ice chest.

She called to the driver. "Don't forget to bring the cell phone after you park, honey." She slammed the trunk lid shut and the car drove off. The woman went to the gate, set down the ice chest and unlocked the gate.

Seeing his chance, Falk moved forward as she pushed the gate open. "Hey, let me help." Without waiting for an answer, he scooped up the ice chest and indicated with a nod that she go ahead. She smiled with Falk close behind her. For a moment he thought she was going to the *Sea Note* but she turned right at the bottom of the ramp and stopped beside the sailboat with the blue tarp. "Thanks. That was very kind of you."

There were only two boats in the dock. He had to come up with something fast. Burly now standing in the stern of the *Sea Note* watched their arrival with unguarded suspicion.

"Are you with the *Sea Note*?" the young woman asked as she began undoing the ties holding the tarp.

Falk looked around as if for the first time seeing the two boats. "No. I'm... I'm—this *is* slip four?"

"It is."

Falk continued his act. "Panay Way, right?"

"Oh, no. You're on Palawan Way. This is basin E. You need basin D."

Falk shook his head. "I feel like such a fool. I was supposed to meet my friend who has a boat in slip four. I'm not familiar with this Marina. Only been here twice and both times he drove. I better get going." Falk turned away and headed for the ramp when she called to him.

"Wait. My husband will be here soon. He has a cell phone. You can call your friend and tell him where you are. That's if he has a cell phone on board."

"That's a good idea. Let me help you get the tarp off." As he worked, he noticed the man on *Sea Note* had lost interest in their activity.

Falk had almost finished folding the tarp when the young woman pointed to a man coming down the ramp holding a canvas carryall. "Here's my husband now." She waved. "I bet he wonders who you are." Falk had no doubt he did.

"Hi, hon. Didn't forget to bring the phone, did you?"

The man shook his head and patted his back pocket. "It's right here." It was obvious he wanted to know who was standing on his boat with his wife.

"I said he could use our phone. He's lost." She turned to Falk. "Sorry. I don't know your name."

"Bill Moore," Falk answered quickly.

"Mr. Moore helped carry the cooler down to the boat then discovered he was at the wrong slip and the wrong dock."

Setting the carryall down, the man stuck his hand out. "Bob Curry. This is my wife, Jean."

Falk shook hands with them. "I know I must look a damned fool." Movement on the *Sea Note* caught his eye. A woman moved into sight next to the guard. They stood amidships near a hatch cover talking earnestly. The woman waved her arms as he spoke and pointed toward the twin high-rise towers across the basin.

Curry said, "Could happen to any of us. I have the same problem sometimes when I'm in a new Marina. I bet it happens often in one this size." He reached into his pocket and pulled out his phone. "Go ahead. Give him a call."

Falk tapped in numbers and two rings later Victor Young answered. "Jack, this is Bill. I've ended up on the wrong slip. I'm on Palawan Way. Yeah, I know, but I did get the boat hook you wanted. No. That's okay. I'll walk. How far did you say? Then I'll wait right here, slip four. You sure you don't mind? I'm with a couple that let me use their phone. I'm next to a blue and white ketch with two people on board." Falk turned away and spoke softly. "The woman on the ketch is just leaving and another man is going aboard."

Falk turned off the cell and handed it back. "He'll come and get me in the dingy; said it was a long walk." Falk knew Young picked up on the mention of the two on the ketch and would move in to give him cover. He could only stall for so long. Now she stuck her head out of the hatch and announced she was making coffee and would he join them?

Curry was forward of the mast securing a line as Falk said he'd enjoy a cup. Pretending to be on the lookout for the imaginary dingy, he kept an eye on the *Sea Note,* carefully checking the physical layout of both slips.

The ramp ran from the dockside gate to a jetty structure jutting out into the channel. Each slip notched into the jetty and a large storage box allocated to each vessel. There was room for the boats to maneuver and navigate into the main channel then head out to sea. From where he stood, he was less than twenty feet from the ketch.

It was a jump from the deck to the jetty, a short sprint and he could scramble aboard in seconds. Falk looked up to the road at the sound of an engine and saw the Outback. Its motor revved and slowed, making erratic progress along Palawan before coming to a shuddering halt opposite the two boats.

Young got out, opened the hood and leaned into the engine compartment. A minute later, he went to the rear, lifted the hatch back, rummaged under the tire well and returned with a handful of tools. Falk had his backup in position. Now it was up to him.

Koski had strained to hear snatches of conversation on deck. She climbed the stairs again. This time she pressed her ear against the hatch and was able to hear a few words. The woman was speaking.

"Keep an eye on the sailboat next to us. Take 'em out if they make any moves toward this boat."

Koski's heart fluttered. There was someone on a boat next to them! She knew that an inboard motor powered a boat as large as the one she was on. Grabbing the flashlight, she quickly moved back to the galley. The place to look for an inboard was below deck amidships.

The beam from her flashlight caught a quick glint high up on the bulkhead in the corner over the sink. The bastards had her under video surveillance! She killed the light and scrambled up onto the sink, reached into the cupboard and grabbed the jar of jam. She stuck two fingers of her right hand into the jar, scooped up a glob, and with her left hand felt along the edge of the bulkhead where it met the deck. There it was—a recess. Her fingertip felt the lens. After smearing a thick coating of jam across the glass, she eased back onto the floor. She turned on the flashlight and continued her search for a floor hatch to an engine compartment and bilge area. Within two minutes she found the hatch.

She grasped a metal ring, yanked hard and shone the light into the bilge area. The sudden stench of oil and dead air was a slap in the face. The beam of light fell on a sign in red paint with two arrows pointing in opposite directions. OPEN/CLOSE was stenciled above a black painted iron handle. Immediately she knew she must turn the handle to OPEN and the seacock would allow a flow of seawater into the bilge.

Aiming the light around the engine compartment, she located the inboard diesel. She was undecided whether to sink the boat. It would pose a threat to her life if someone didn't arrive before it sank. On the other hand, she could fill a can with diesel oil and rags, ignite it and cause black smoke to billow from below deck. That would gain attention. She decided to put the second plan into action. After all, there *were* people on the next boat.

Chapter 27

The antibodies transmitted by the biolog laser injector killed the CEO of Majestic Films instantly. He died on the back lot, crumpled in the dust of a western street set.

Grant arrived at the crime scene as the victim was being examined by the ME inside a cordoned off area. Captain Garvey was talking with several detectives outside one of the false fronted buildings.

"What happened, Captain? Who's the victim?"

Garvey grimaced slightly, remembering the words of the Chief about cooperation between the police department and the DHS.

Garvey sighed. "Head of the studio. He was inspecting the back lot with his security chief when he simply buckled and fell down dead. That was it."

"Sounds like a heart attack or stroke," Grant retorted.

"Yeah but at the moment he died his secretary was on the phone being told her boss would be killed on the back lot." Garvey paused. "He was dead before she could contact him."

The medical officer straightened and walked toward them.

"The *killer called* to tell her what was going to happen!" Grant exclaimed.

"Evidently whoever it was wanted her to know it was murder, not a heart attack."

"Why would anyone do that?"

Garvey rubbed his chin as the doctor joined them. "Let's hear what the doc has to say."

The ME quickly reported his findings. "Can't find a mark on him. Might have been a sudden heart attack. That's all I can tell you at the moment."

"What about the phone call?" Garvey asked. "Whoever called knew he was going to die. That doesn't sound like a natural death."

"Can't help you there. That's your department, Captain."

"How long before we know how he died?"

"Seeing the DHS is involved, I'd say an autopsy will possibly be performed later today."

Grant pushed forward. "I'm from DHS, Doctor, and I want to be present at the autopsy. Any problem?"

The doctor glanced at Garvey. "None at all. See you there." He nodded to the Captain and headed back to his car.

Grant and Garvey watched as the coroner's men bagged and loaded the body into an ambulance, slammed the doors shut and drove down the western street and out of sight.

Grant gazed at the wooden sidewalks and false fronted buildings. "For a minute there I expected to see them load the corpse onto a horse-drawn buckboard."

"I know what you mean," Garvey said. "I'll go with you to the morgue. By the way, what happened to your videographers?"

"They're on temporary reassignment," Grant mumbled.

"She's found the camera." A scrawny individual in shorts and tee-shirt sat hunched in front of a television screen. A second man reading a magazine glanced up.

"How could she?"

"Dunno. Look for yourself." He pointed to a blurred screen. He picked up a phone and called Jamul, who immediately gave orders to get Koski off the boat.

The men on the ketch already had their hands full. A column of black smoke curled from around the hatch cover.

Burly saw the smoke first. "That stupid bitch set the boat on fire!"

Falk turned at the commotion and saw smoke and two men tugging at the hatch. He grabbed the boat hook and leapt from the small sailboat to the jetty. Within seconds he was on the deck of the ketch. "Let's try this." Falk jammed the boat hook under the edge of the hatch but one of the men shoved him back and Burly started to pull out an automatic.

Falk quickly whirled, bringing the eight-foot pole hard against the side of Burly's head, knocking him senseless to the deck. The second man, shocked at the sudden deadly action, hesitated a split second too long. Falk rammed the oar end into the guard's stomach. The impact drove him backwards across the deck where he teetered for a second at the rail before vanishing overboard.

Wasting no time, Falk pounded on the hatch with his pole

yelling Koski's name. He jammed the pole under the edge of the hatch and started to pry. The smoke continued to curl from below deck as he worked. Suddenly someone was beside him with an axe.

Bob Curry swung the axe into the center of the hatch, twisted the blade and repeated the action several times until he had a gaping hole. Falk dropped to his knees and yelled into the dark, smoky gap. He saw the can of burning rags and knew at once what Koski had done to attract attention. Falk called her name again and was suddenly relieved to see her dirty, smoke-grimed face peering upward toward him.

She quickly unhooked the storm locks and Falk pulled the damaged hatch onto the deck. She reached up, took Falk's hand and was yanked up into the fresh air.

Flinging her arms around Falk's neck, she kissed him long and hard before saying, "I knew you'd come."

He scooped her into his arms and carried her to the side of the boat. Curry jumped to the dock and held his arms up to take her. Once ashore, Jean appeared with Falk's ditty bag slung on her shoulder and handed a bottle of water to Koski. She took a fast swig then urged Falk to get everyone off the dock and up onto the road—FAST.

Victor Young's voice boomed from the road telling them to hurry.

Burly, still flat on the deck, crawled under cover of the thick black smoke pouring from the hatch to where his automatic lay. Young had the engine running as the four ran up the ramp to the road. Burly grabbed his weapon, got to his feet, squinted across the dock and opened fire. Rounds zipped into the ramp as Falk pushed everyone through the gate and into the car while a great sheet of yellow flame ripped skyward from the *Sea Note.*

"What in the hell happened?" Curry exclaimed.

Koski replied, "It's okay. The boat'll sink before the fire can spread." Turning to Falk she said, "When I heard you call out 'Down the hatch', I lit a match and touched it to a trail of paint thinner I'd laid from the galley to the bilge. I found the thinner when I was looking for the sea cocks."

"Sea cocks!" Falk echoed.

"Yeah. I also scuttled the boat."

"The U.S. government will cover any damage to your sailboat," Falk assured the Currys as Young drove them back to their car.

Chapter 28

Rita Massy slumped in an easy chair, gazing through the picture window of the penthouse. The spiral of smoke from the ketch slowly diminished, swirled by an onshore breeze. The wind did little to diminish Jamul's anger that he hurled at the unfortunate man reporting what they had discovered when they arrived at the slip.

"None of you went down to the boat? No one went aboard to see if anyone was there!" His voice grew louder and his black face, if it was possible, seemed blacker.

"The Coast Guard showed up. Then a fireboat and cops were arriving." The nervous man tried to explain. "We got the hell out."

"I told you to bring back the woman, not to get the hell out."

Jamul turned away in disgust. In his heart he knew they had done the right thing. No way did he want to become involved in anything that might lead him to become part of any type of investigation.

Massy's voice was calm. "I'd say someone beat us to it, Jamul. Whoever it was no doubt rescued the woman and fled."

"Yes, Doctor, and I'll be ridiculed as a fool for not foiling the rescue."

Massy smiled. "Perhaps not. We can make the incident work to our advantage."

Jamul sat down. "Go on."

"We let it be known the escape was intended to happen. You planned the kidnapping as a means to test the ability and strength of DHS and its operatives."

"No one in the organization is going to believe that!" Jamul spluttered.

Massy lightly clenched her fist, extending her index finger skyward. "Let me finish. We now know the woman is *not* a DHS photographer. Neither is the man who rescued her. We have stronger and wiser adversaries to contend with than we thought—a more *unorthodox* agency, an enemy who uses tactics not unlike our own.

"Brasinov will identify them, whoever they are, and alert al-Qaida of their existence. You'll be a hero and stronger than ever. Trust me, Jamul. Everything will be ready by Sunday and then all of Islam will celebrate our latest strike against America."

"*Everything* better be ready, my friend," Jamul said as he rose and stalked from the room.

Chapter 29

The unexpected and forced detention in a house located on Rockledge Road, high in the Hollywood Hills behind the Hollywood Bowl, took Marco by surprise.

"You've been chosen for an important task, Marco. You were recommended as a man with smarts, who wishes to get ahead in life. Is that correct?"

Rita Massy asked the question sitting opposite Marco, a long oak table between them. The high beamed ceiling and oak paneled walls reflected the Spanish décor so popular in fine homes in Hollywood during the 1920s and 1930s. The afternoon light seeping through the lead lined windows was fading fast.

"Who wants to know?" Marco muttered.

"Who I am matters not, young man."

"Why was I brought here?"

"Instructions," Massy purred. "You and selected members of your gang are to become landscape workers. You will remain here each day after work until our task is complete."

A door at the far end of the room opened. A man entered and switched on an ornate floor lamp casting a yellow glow through its tasseled silken shade.

"You're aware that when any member of your gang is assigned to carry out an order we expect complete compliance. Disobey and the punishment is swift."

"Yeah. You kill them," Marco said softly.

"In your case I've been assured you are a man with ambition and leadership qualities, right?"

Marco nodded.

"For the next few days you'll be working with a landscaping crew in the Hollywood Bowl, preparing the grounds for the Easter Sunday Services. Each worker will be cleared by security and issued a pass.

"At the end of each day, a truck will return all workers to the landscape company headquarters. Your crew will be transferred here to stay overnight and return to the company each morning for the trip to the Bowl."

"What do we tell our families?"

"Say it's a job out of town, nothing else. Each of you may bring a change of clothes and a few personal belongings. Advise your compatriots this house is heavily guarded. They'll be shot if they attempt to escape."

Massy pushed back from the table. "There's a car waiting to return you to the Barrio." She gave an icy smile and walked from the room, high heels rapping the hardwood floor.

Marco watched her leave. His hands were clenched on the tabletop. He'd be sure he had a small AM/FM radio among his personal items. "Bitch."

Chapter 30

On the drive from the Marina to the hotel, Koski removed the paring knife from her shoe then curled up on the back seat and fell asleep.

"Hell of a gal," Young said, nodding at the knife. "What was she going to do with that?"

"Don't ask," Falk replied. "We should get our stories in synch about what just happened back there."

They decided that Young's report explaining their exit from the parking lot fiasco on Fairfax should include Falk receiving a tip saying Koski was a prisoner aboard a boat in the Marina. The resultant blaze and sinking of the boat shouldn't be part of the report. Falk took responsibility for any repercussions by saying it had been in the interest of national security.

Koski had showered, eaten a steak dinner delivered by room service and was now on the same page as Falk.

"The only person I talked to on the boat was a woman in a ski mask. She brought me a cup of coffee and asked questions."

"Anything about her voice?" Falk questioned.

"Educated, knew I was with DHS. Later I tried to listen in on a conversation up on deck discussing something about a penthouse. I got the impression they were waiting for someone to come to the boat to interrogate me. I also was under surveillance on a hidden, infrared closed circuit TV."

"What did you do?"

"Smeared jam over the lens."

Falk grinned. "Interesting."

"I wondered if they'd got you, too, Joe."

"They tried." He quickly brought her up-to-date on the events leading up to the Marina rescue. Falk got up from the table. "Whoever these people are, they've got state-of-the-art equipment. Time to relocate. I'll update Stewart."

Koski knew in cases like this it was standard operating procedure for Cerberus to send a couple of doppelgangers. They were operatives with similar physical appearance, who'd stay at the hotel, allowing them the opportunity to move on.

Falk finished his conversation with Stewart.

"Where're we going?" Koski asked.

"The Marina. Stewart says there's a Taswell 43' all weather Raised–Saloon cutter tied up next to the Coast Guard station. It belonged to a drug cartel, was seized and is now government property with modern *everything*. The Coast Guard is waiting to pipe us aboard. It'll be our temporary base of operations."

Koski blew out her cheeks. "Oh, boy!"

For security reasons, they made the journey to the Marina in the back of a laundry truck Stewart had sent to the service entrance of their hotel.

It was dark when they walked up the gangplank and were met by a Coast Guard lieutenant, who snapped a salute.

"Welcome aboard. I understand this will be your office for awhile."

"Correct, lieutenant," Falk replied.

The officer gave them a familiarizing tour of the cutter's layout. "We have a skeleton crew to take care of maintenance and security. They've been informed of your arrival and will stay out of your way."

Returning to their starting point, he pointed to the lighted windows of the Coast Guard station less than a quarter mile away. "You're hooked into our communications center. Here's a card with phone numbers and radio frequencies in case they're needed."

"Thanks. We're going to need a car. Can you handle that?"

"Already taken care of, sir. Mr. Stewart said to tell you there'll be a black Ford Mustang dockside in an hour."

"Thank you, lieutenant."

"Goodnight, sir, ma'am."

As a brisk wind blew up the channel, Koski huddled her arms across her chest. "Let's get warm." Falk slipped his arm around her waist and led her across the deck and into the salon.

"Nautical and nice," she remarked, taking in the décor and comfortable surroundings. "A lot better than the last boat I was on."

Falk said, "I'm going to take another tour around the boat to be sure I know the pointed end from the blunt end, okay?"

"Fine, and remember, I can show you how to sink her if you like."

Chapter 31

Shortly before 11 p.m. a cab dropped Martin Pease off at the home of Paul Horn in Pacific Palisades, a well-heeled community overlooking the ocean. Horn lived alone in a rambling house far too big for him. His wife had left him three years earlier for a younger and richer man. Horn had married late in life and his young wife had promised she'd love him forever then changed her mind.

Horn answered the door, holding a snifter of brandy. He was amazed at the sight of Pease on his door step.

"Relax, Paul. Let me in. I need a drink."

"Martin! I thought you'd..."

Pease pushed past and entered. "Well, you were wrong." He held up his right hand as if stopping traffic. "I wasn't followed. No one knows I'm here."

Somewhere in the house a clock chimed midnight as Pease finished telling Horn everything that happened since he left Pegmanti Industries.

Horn whispered softly, "If your formula does what you claim, al-Qaida isn't simply gaining another tool in its 'Arsenal of Evil' but a weapon it will embrace implicitly."

"Money and power, as usual, *are* the all-embracing commodities in this case, Paul."

"Enrico believes you could reproduce the germinating acceptance genes now if you wanted."

"He's right. He has no idea, however, what else has developed from my research. Only two others know the full capabilities."

Horn sipped his brandy. "Why are you telling me?"

"I need someone inside Pegmanti Industries I can trust."

Horn's eyebrows arched. "And you trust me? How touching."

"I don't trust you. I never did but I know your weakness for money."

"What kind of money are we talking about?"

"Put it this way. I'm giving you the opportunity to remain alive. If I were to inform a certain person that you knew about this weapon you'd be dead within the hour.

"We'll discuss money after I find out how much you're worth to me on the inside. Now listen carefully. This is what you tell Enrico."

Rita Massy sat alone in her car parked on Mulholland Drive, staring down at the lights of the San Fernando Valley twinkling like scattered diamonds. She needed quiet and time to reflect on the last few hours.

She was back in favor with Jamul due to her successfully arranged murder of the studio head on his own back lot. The autopsy showed no indication of foul play. Marco and his crew were safely under the control of al-Qaida by day and secure in the safe house at night.

It was almost midnight. She started the engine and turned up the heater. March could be a cold month in California. The radio murmured the late news as she eased the car onto Mulholland and toward her destination—the house on Rockledge Road.

The meeting would be pivotal to al-Qaida continuing as a leading presence in the terrorist world. The deaths of Saddam Hussein and Osama bin Laden, and the continuing relentless pursuit of their followers by U.S. and U.K. forces, caused al-Qaida to lose influence and control in many Islamic communities, along with others in the world who used the evil powers of terrorism for their own agenda.

Massy knew the day was fast approaching when the world would know that al-Qaida could still make the Western world reel. The Easter Sunrise Services at the Hollywood Bowl was a multi-religious ceremony designed to unite the world by showing respect to every religious sect.

The gathering of clerics from around the globe would represent every religion. The Governor of California and representatives of a dozen other world governments would stand as one in the white domed amphitheater. The soft dawn light of an Easter Sunday would slowly cast its pink glow across the thousands of souls packing the Bowl as countless millions around the globe watched on television. There was even the possibility the new Pope would be present—his first visit to California.

Security would be tighter than any other time in the Bowl's history. Massy slowed the car. She took the sharp downhill turn toward the Tudor stone house on Rockledge and moved toward a single light shining from a window overlooking the curved gravel driveway. The car crunched to a halt and a dark-suited valet opened the driver's door.

"Good evening, madam." Massy stepped from the car noting two armed men standing in the shadows. She nodded and walked up three wide stone steps to the double door entrance that swung open as she approached.

Once inside, she handed her coat to an attendant and was led across a parquet tiled reception hall. The servant opened a tall, ornate door and with an upturned palm indicated Massy should enter.

A huge stone fireplace at one end of the long oak-paneled room held a log fire burning brightly. Two high-backed armchairs framed the hearth and mantle. As Massy walked toward the fireplace, a voice from one of the chairs greeted her.

"Good evening, Rita."

Massy stopped beside the chair and softly replied, "Good evening, Mr. Pegmanti."

"Please, sit down." Enrico Pegmanti motioned to the chair beside him. "We're the early ones. We get the best seats in the house."

Massy settled into her seat, feeling the warmth from the fire glow around her. She had been to the safehouse several times before but never to one of their meetings. She wondered how many times Pegmanti had chaired secret enclaves in the fine Tudor mansion high in Hollywood Hills.

Massy had known for years that Pegmanti Industries made millions supplying various terrorist groups with chemical warfare poisons. As far as Enrico was concerned, money was money no matter where it came from.

"How are your Mexican American friends, Rita? I hear you have a bright young man by the name of Marco working for you. Didn't one of his friends have to be eliminated not too long ago?"

It never failed to amaze Massy how much knowledge Enrico amassed. It was seemingly endless.

"Yes. Marco and the others are kept here every night and assigned each day to the Bowl gardening staff making preparations for the Easter Services."

Enrico shifted in his chair and stretched his thin white hands toward the flames. To Massy, they seemed like vulture talons reaching for dead flesh.

Enrico stared into the flames. "What assurances do you have that he won't attempt some sort of retaliation for his friend's death? I understand Mexican culture leans toward revenge for such deeds."

"He's well aware that if he makes the slightest wrong move he and everyone else will die."

"Perhaps he's been smart enough to take advantage of that possibility."

Massy bristled. "What do you mean?"

"It's possible he already made arrangements with the police to be a paid informant. It happens."

"Do you know something I don't?" Massy was startled at the suggestion.

Enrico lowered his hands and rested them on his knees, continuing to gaze into the flickering fire. "I think you should be very careful. Test his loyalty. If you have any doubt, kill him."

If it had been anyone but Enrico Pegmanti talking Massy would have dismissed the idea of Marco being a possible informer. "How can we be sure?"

"Take this Young Turk aside and give him misinformation he might feel important enough to reveal. You'll know soon enough if the information leaks to the police. I'll leave it to your active imagination as to what you tell him."

A murmur of voices and the sound of others entering the room stopped any further conversation. A group of men approached the pair at the fireside. Several servants quickly arranged chairs close to the warmth.

Jamul, imposing in a scarlet hooded robe that emphasized his tallness, took a dictatorial stance facing the assembly. Feet apart, the glow from the fire radiated like a holy aura around him.

Brasinov was grim-faced and still stinging from the abortive attempt to kill Falk in the CBS parking lot and the loss of two of his men. He clenched his fists as he listened to Jamul.

"Welcome to you all. Tonight we formulate the final details of a long-anticipated dream for the nation of Islam; an occasion that will be forever burnt into the history of the Western world as an apocalyptic event."

Chapter 32

Millions of dollars sat waiting in Martin Pease's Swiss bank account. Nevertheless, secretly finding a way to leave the country was difficult due to tough airport security and customs. Both were formidable barriers even to those with nothing to hide. Pease had little doubt his passport information was already a "no go" in the international computer systems.

An analytical person, he reasoned the only one he might trust was an old acquaintance, Doctor Jack Wolf.

Pease waited until Wolf finished a lecture at UCLA and was walking back to his office, then fell into step beside him. Pease spoke softly. "Good afternoon, Jack."

Wolf spun around. "Martin!" He was genuinely surprised to see his old friend. "What the devil are you doing here? It's been years since we've seen each other."

Pease indicated a bench at the side of the path. "Sit with me a moment, Jack." He touched the edge of Wolf's sleeve.

"Let's chat in my office," Wolf glanced at the sky. "It's getting chilly."

"No. Here is better for us both. Please sit down, Jack."

"What is it, Martin? Are you ill?"

"Nothing like that." Wolf seated himself next to Pease.

"My life has been threatened."

"Good lord! Threatened by whom and for what?"

Pease glanced around before answering. "My formula. I suppose you know I'm no longer with Pegmanti."

"I heard you retired."

"I suppose I did in a way. I was given the golden handshake."

"Why?"

"Enrico Pegmanti believed I was stalling on my research, holding back until he died so as to claim all the fame and resultant monetary rewards."

"Were you?"

"The thought *had* crossed my mind. I decided against it when I discovered my research was going in a different direction than my original stem cell experiments."

Wolf forgot the coldness of a late March afternoon. "Different direction?"

"It was quite by accident. It was during a test on cell division and transplant. I took cells from a ferocious Rottweiler and transplanted them into an old, rather arthritic Golden Retriever that was expected to die at any time. Next morning, the Retriever was energetic and snarling at its keeper to a point where she could not approach the animal."

"Obviously a reaction to the transplant," Wolf replied.

"That's what I thought at first. Nevertheless I continued with transplants from aggressive animals into placid subjects. It became obvious it was possible to pass aggression and placidity back and forth, similar to brainwave synchcronization experiments."

"You were able to calm an aggressive animal by transplanting cells from a peaceful one?"

"Exactly, but that's not all. Over months of in vitro experiments I developed a serum from the cells. Through a simple injection I obtained the same results as a complete Yigal transplant."

Wolf felt as if an electric shock had gone through him.

"Martin, you sound light years ahead of us here at the

university."

"Working for Pegmanti Industries I was sworn to keep my discoveries secret."

"Surely you're free to share your research now?"

"Let me finish." It grew colder and a chilling wind began to cut across the campus. "I went further. It's not widely known but the company also has been experimenting with laser ray systems. I became friendly with a bright young scientist several years ago when the laser lab was first established. I was frustrated having to sedate an aggressive animal prior to the injection.

"I didn't want an opiate or anesthesia to dilute the effectiveness of my serum. I needed a method to safely inject a savage animal. That's when I learned of the young scientist's discovery. He'd developed a delivery system far improved over a regular injection syringe. His system is why my life is in jeopardy."

Pease moved a little closer to Wolf and lowered his voice. "Thanks to the laser system, my altered cells have the ability to kill and leave no sign of an entrance wound or cause of death."

Wolf heard the thud of his own heart. "How's that possible?"

"The cell serum is delivered to the target by a means never before used. Laser technology combined with what I call a biolog laser injector or BLI. I discovered I can transmit any other biological monoclonal antibody drug over a quarter of a mile."

Wolf was stunned. "How?"

"Jack, trust me. It can be done."

"You're playing God, Martin! If your discovery falls into the wrong hands, bioterrorism could be the end of the world as we know it. What about this laser scientist you were working with?"

Wolf's mind was racing. He had to get Martin Pease to Stewart.

"He left Pegmanti three months ago, recruited by Laser Research Labs. Rita Massy has a prototype of my delivery system and has used it to demonstrate its lethal ability to an Islamic group. My latest model is even more effective."

Wolf exploded. "Have you contacted the authorities?"

"No."

Wolf couldn't believe what he was hearing, "Why not, man?"

"Enrico Pegmanti and his daughter would be murdered."

"And Doctor Massy has your BLI model!"

Pease glanced around, startled by Wolf's outburst. "The prototype model. I have the latest BLI safely hidden. I'm the only one who knows its location."

Wolf had to get Pease to Stewart. "Doctor Rita Massy involved with terrorists! Martin, you can't just leave it hidden. Someone is sure to find out. Look man, I'll get you governmental protection. You can collect the BLI and keep it out of the hands of terrorists."

Removing an automatic from his pocket, Martin pressed the barrel into Wolf's side. "No. I need a safe place to hide *now*. Sorry, Jack. Let's go."

Chapter 33

The Department of Homeland Security was rife with problems. None of the merging bureaucracies, including the CIA and FBI, owned computer systems that could speak to each other. There was no mandate or funding in the nearly 500-page Homeland Security Act to change that. The DHS was originally designed to unify law enforcement agencies nationwide under the direction and guidance of a federal security tsar.

Nevertheless, infighting between various agencies, differences between trade unions, and leadership questions continued. Once acclaimed as a major tool in America's fight against terrorism, it was turning out to be a bureaucratic nightmare.

Shortly after 1 a.m. Chief Bradbury was slumped in the back seat of his chauffeur driven car on the way to Parker Center. Falk and Koski were off the DHS team. Grant had a broken leg. Three more deaths in the Hollywood area and the city politicians were putting the squeeze on the Chief.

Bradbury had called an emergency meeting of his top people at 3 a.m. at his Parker office. He had contacted Garvey, asking him to be there a half hour ahead of schedule. He wanted a one on one.

Garvey sipped hot coffee from a thick thermos mug when he arrived at police headquarters. It was 2:35 a.m. when he entered the main entrance, flashed his ID and headed to the elevators.

Bradbury's secretary, seated at her desk in the anteroom outside the Chief's office, looked up. "Go in, Captain. He's expecting you."

Seeing the secretary signaled to Garvey this was going to be an all-stops-out operation.

"Morning, Howard. Come in and sit down. I see you have your coffee already."

Garvey raised his mug slightly. "Never leave home without it."

Niceties over, Bradbury got down to business. "When the media get the news of the latest deaths—and the now non-existent

DHS team—they're going to raise hell." Bradbury leaned back in his chair, the incandescent glow of the desk lamp accentuating the dark circles under his eyes. "What do we have on the latest vics?"

"Medical examiner's report shows no outward signs of cause of death. I'm awaiting updates from the morgue."

The Chief grunted. "The early killings showed a pinprick entrance wound, now, nothing. I'm getting feedback saying the perp is possibly testing a new killing device."

"I know. It's a refinement on the Bulgarian umbrella technique."

"A *hell* of a refinement," Bradbury muttered.

Garvey stared into his coffee cup. "I've got my best people working around the clock."

"That ruckus in the CBS parking lot included one of your men, right?"

"Yes, sir. Detective Young was assisting Agent Falk in a search for his missing partner. Young's report stated Falk received a tip to proceed immediately to Marina Del Rey while they were in the lot."

"Did that call result in the boat fire at the Marina?"

Garvey shook his head. "Nothing in his report to that effect."

"Have Young verbally update you on every minute he spent with Agent Falk; where they went, who they spoke to, everything."

"Young's due to return to Rampart division today."

"Not any more. He stays with Hollywood until this thing is over. Team him up. Get him out on the street and keep tabs on him at all times. Damned DHS."

Garvey was already mentally matching Young with Gully.

"Right, Chief."

A wall clock chimed three. "C'mon. Let's get to the meeting room. I gotta chew ass."

Chapter 34

Falk paced the deck of the cutter, mulling over the events of the last few days. He'd passed Marco's tip about Jamul on to Stewart, who advised him Cerberus was aware that Jamul, like numerous Hollywood personalities, leaned toward peace and aid to the under privileged, no matter what their political views toward American policy were.

In his own mind, Falk felt the information from Marco carried a message, a warning that more than friendship and understanding of other people's plight was at stake. Stopping in the stern, he gazed toward the lights of the twin Marina towers. One of the penthouses housed Jamul and he intended to seek him out.

Koski looked up as he entered the warm salon. "I thought you were going to stay out there all night."

"Come on. We're moving. Dress warmly. We'll be gone awhile."

The pungent smell of burnt wood and plastic still hung in the air and a thick fog rolled in across the Marina. Falk quickly opened the gate and nodded to Koski to go ahead down the ramp.

It was well after midnight and the opaque fog sucked light from the street lamps. They could still make out the faint outline of a mast and part of the deck jutting from the wreck of the *Sea Note*.

Falk nudged Koski forward toward the Curry's sailboat. "I've a key for the hatch."

"What if they come back?"

"They won't. They mentioned they were going up to Lake Tahoe for the weekend."

"How'd you get the key?"

"There were two spares hanging on a key board in the galley. I'll lift the tarp and you crawl under." He passed her the keys attached to a floatation device. "It's the red one. The green is for the gate." Koski vanished under the tarp. He heard her fumbling to unlock the hatch. He lifted one corner.

"Don't turn on any lights when you get into the cabin." She finally got the hatch open and slipped inside, felt for the edge of a bunk and sat down, thinking this was getting to be a habit. A few seconds later Falk scrambled in beside her.

"We took all our stuff onto the cutter, Joe. All we have is what we're wearing."

"We're still armed. I've a hunch we were watched going aboard. It's only a matter of time before they come after us."

"We had Coast Guard security and a skeleton crew. So what do we do now?"

"Get some rest and wait for Wolf to call me back."

Falk had left messages with Doctor Wolf's exchange before leaving the hotel. Wolf, however, had made previous arrangements with Stewart. As long as he was active in the ongoing investigation, they should have a safety signal between them. Stewart was to call his cell every night at midnight. Wolf was to answer "wrong number" and hang up. If Wolf failed to answer, Stewart would know the doctor was in trouble.

Three minutes later Falk's phone buzzed. He answered

immediately. "Doctor Wolf?"

It was Stewart.

"Tom, what's up?"

"Doctor Wolf's missing." He filled Falk in on the nightly signal arrangement. "Intelligence reports indicate something big brewing in the Los Angeles area within the next few hours."

"Yeah," Falk said. "Easter Sunday service at the Bowl. It's been a security nightmare for months."

"DHS is running security. Your job is to find who is responsible for zapping homeless people and studio heads and why."

"Any word from Marco?" Falk asked.

"No, and FYI Greg Grant's in the hospital with a compound fracture of his right leg. You and Koski are still at the Marina, right?"

"That's affirmative."

"Good." Stewart's phone cut off.

"Why didn't you tell him we'd left the cutter? Stewart will find out when the USCG updates him."

"No need for him to know yet. Grant's in the hospital with a fractured leg."

"When did that happen?"

"Don't know. Didn't ask."

"That'll cheer up Bradley."

"If I know Grant he'll be back one way or another."

Falk had blacked out the windows and made sure no light was showing. Now he sat at the small table in the galley and tried for the fourth time in an hour to reach Marco.

Koski glanced up from a paperback she'd found in a small mesh hammock hanging beside her bunk. "He could still be out playing a gig. Nell said he played most nights."

"He has to take a break sometime."

"Maybe she knows where he is."

Falk pushed a set of plastic salt and pepper shakers around in a circle. His face was set in deep thought.

"Yeah. She said she worked late on her book." He quickly made a call. "Nell? This is Agent Falk. Remember me?"

Nell was wide awake. "Absolutely. What's happening? Are you going to give me my interview?"

"Not now. I called to see if you might know where Marco might be. I've been trying to contact him."

"I haven't talked to him in a week. Anything I can do?"

"Maybe. From what you told us about your sporadic gigs around town, I thought you might pick up some info here and there."

"I play and listen, pick up pieces of this and that. In fact, I earn a dollar or two as a stringer for a columnist here in town."

"I can't offer you money, Nell."

"I didn't mean it that way. I just wanted you to know I have contacts."

"What we need might be a bit out of your line."

"Try me."

Falk brought her up-to-date on Dr. Wolf—who he was, where he taught and that he'd vanished. "You still have my cell number?"

"Next to my heart," she said brightly.

Falk smiled. "If you come through you'll have an exclusive

interview."

"I'll have fresh batteries in the tape recorder. Bye."

Falk disconnected and glanced at Koski. "What's that you're reading?"

"*The Saint Steps In*. It's about a guy named Simon Templar."

"Great. Get some sleep. We're going to be leaving the Marina before daylight."

Chapter 35

Enrico Pegmanti watched as Paul Horn paced back and forth in front of his desk. "Sit down, for God's sake, man. Security is equipped to protect our secrets. They have for years. Why should it be any different now?"

Horn, hollow-eyed and pale, turned to Pegmanti. "If Martin's formula gets into our competition's hands, it'll cost us millions." He lowered into the Chippendale chair and it creaked under his weight.

"You've no idea who phoned you last night?"

Horn shook his head. "Other than it was a man, none whatsoever," he lied.

"Tell me again what was said."

Horn leaned back and fluttered his eyelids closed. "The call came in around 11:30. I was just getting ready to turn in. At first I thought it was a wrong number. The voice was hesitant. He mentioned Pegmanti Industries and called me by name. I asked him who he was and what he wanted. That's when he said someone within the Pegmanti organization was about to sabotage our stem cell research program. When I asked how he knew the phone went dead."

"That was it?"

"Yes. I think we should alert the DHS."

"Don't be a fool," Pegmanti snarled. "We notify those bastards and they'll be all over us. We'll take care of our own security. If it'll make you feel better, you can work with the head of security to be sure everything is handled to your satisfaction. I'll give orders you have total clearance in the labs." Pegmanti dismissed him and informed his secretary to have the chief of security see him at once.

Falk and Koski left the Marina before dawn. They drove northbound on the 405 Freeway until they reached the Sunset Boulevard off ramp, then headed east toward Hollywood.

"I could use some breakfast. How about you?"

"Soon as we collect Nell," Falk replied. "We'll treat her to breakfast." Koski shrugged and hunkered down deeper into her seat. If she had her way, the car heater would be up all the way and she'd have her coffee by now.

The sun highlighted the top of the Hollywood sign as they reached Nell's house.

"Stay in the car. I'll get her." Falk headed up to the front door and rang the bell. He rang three times before she answered.

Nell looked surprised. "Good morning, Agent Falk. Something wrong?"

"Plenty. That's why I thought we'd get an early start."

"Come in."

"No time. Get dressed. We're taking you to breakfast."

Nell took a sip of coffee. "After you called me last night I made some calls. No one knows where Marco is but you said the doc who went missing teaches at UCLA, right? I have a friend who works in maintenance. Those guys know everything that goes down on campus." She checked her watch. "He should be arriving at work about now."

Traffic was heavier now as Falk drove to UCLA. Nell talked. "He works out of the science building. He's not a floor sweeper any more. Sam's graduated to electrical lighting. He keeps the fluorescent lights glowing night and day."

After finding a parking place and walking along what seemed to be miles of corridors, they arrived at a cubbyhole office deep in the bowels of the building.

Sam was unpacking a box of fluorescent tubes. He looked up in surprise at the sudden appearance of the trio and then recognized Nell.

"Hey, Nell. What's happening?" He glanced at Falk and Koski with suspicion before engaging her in a hip-hop handshake.

Nell told Sam the agents needed help tracking down Dr. Wolf.

"I saw Doctor Wolf walking with a guy late yesterday afternoon."

"How late?" Falk questioned.

"Later than usual. I get off at five but yesterday I didn't get out until almost five forty-five."

"Can you describe the man with him?"

"Old like the doc, medium height. They walked toward the faculty parking structure. I didn't take too much notice."

"Anything unusual?"

Sam thought for a minute. "Come to think of it, the guy

walked real close to the doc."

"Did you see them get into a car?"

"No."

"Do you know what make of car the doctor drives?"

"Dark blue Volvo. He keeps the car in good condition, uses a dust cover when parked in the lot."

"Thanks." Falk gave Sam his card. "Call me if you hear anything about Doctor Wolf." The trio left Sam with his light fixtures.

Falk asked, "Which way to the faculty car park?"

Nell pointed. "Over there. Come on. I'll show you."

"You know your way around the campus pretty well," Koski remarked.

"I should. I spent four years here getting my degree."

"In?"

"Master of Arts in Film/Television and Digital Media," Nell chirped.

Falk gave a low whistle. "Plus writer/musician and a stringer for a Hollywood columnist. You're a busy woman, Nell. What other talents do you have?"

"I do great interviews." Nell pointed. "That could be his car."

They approached a vehicle shrouded in a dust cover. Nell lifted a corner and peered under. She was right. It was a dark blue Volvo with doors locked. Falk had a door open in seconds. He and Koski quickly checked the interior.

"No sign of a struggle," Koski muttered as Falk rummaged through the glove compartment. "Whoever was with Wolf decided on a different mode of transportation."

Stewart called Falk as they drove back down the hill after dropping Nell off at her house.

"One of Doctor Wolf's associates suggested we contact a Doctor Martin Pease, head of research at Pegmanti Industries. Wolf and Pease worked together years ago. Contact him and see what you can find." Stewart gave the address. "Why did you move from the cutter?"

"Developments, sir."

The phone clicked off.

Enrico Pegmanti instructed his security chief that Horn was to have free access to the research laboratories. He also expected a daily report on all of Horn's daily activities. Pegmanti leaned back in his chair and created a steeple of his long bony fingers then rested his chin gently at the apex. Paul Horn had to be eliminated.

Chapter 36

Rita Massy attached the latest biolog laser injector beneath her forefinger. "Good work, Paul. Where did you get this?" Massy was impressed with the lightness and balance of the compact weapon.

"I checked every outside contractor doing work for Pegmanti," Horn said. "It was a long and arduous task but it proved fruitful on my twenty-second phone call. It was in storage at Celeste Castings in Torrance."

Horn discovered that Dr. Pease had arranged to store a metal box in their warehouse. Horn lied to Celeste Castings, explaining that Pease and the lab needed the contents of the box to continue with an important experiment. It arrived special delivery.

"It cost a bundle to run that baby down but I'm sure your people will reimburse me."

"No problem." Massy, with forefinger outstretched, sighted across Horn's living room. "You have the nomenclature on this weapon?" Massy took a handwritten manual Horn passed to her. Once she'd read it and made a few trial tests they'd be ready for the service.

"You did a great job, Paul. You'll be paid well. The difference between the two weapons is amazing. Let me show you." Massy opened a case containing the original prototype. "Just look."

She passed the device to Horn who held it awkwardly, not knowing what to do. "This looks like a large penlight to me."

Massy took the weapon and placed it in its case. "Go sit in your chair and I'll perform for you."

Horn obediently crossed the room and lowered into his upholstered armchair.

"Now, say I was going to point at that oil painting above your head." Horn looked worried. "Relax, Paul. I won't harm the painting." Massy gestured toward the artwork.

"Now it looks as if I'm simply pointing at the picture, right?" Horn nodded. "Good. Attached beneath my index finger and snugly hidden in the palm of my hand is the new micro mini weapon. If I were to fire it there wouldn't be any sound or indication I had done anything except point across the room." Rita Massy narrowed her sea green eyes as she studied the artwork. "That's a nice painting, Paul. Should I know the artist?"

Horn slowly stiffened in his chair. His eyes widened with fear.

Massy turned and pointed directly at Horn and clenched her fist. Her finger was still pointing at him as a recessed trigger in the body of the device activated the laser. A split second later Horn slumped forward in his chair.

"I said I wouldn't harm the painting." Massy gathered up the original prototype and opened the door. She glanced back at Horn's crumpled form, paused a moment, then walked back to the body. Less than a minute later she closed the door softly behind her.

Paul Horn's housekeeper discovered him early the next morning. Tom Stewart contacted Falk on his way to Pegmanti Industries.

Finishing the phone conversation, Falk glanced at Koski. "Paul Horn, an executive of the Pegmanti Empire, has been found dead in his home with no apparent signs of how he died. Let's go."

Koski turned up her coat collar and rubbed her hands together. "Southern California is supposed to be warm. It's almost April and we're down at the beach. Go ahead and turn the heater up."

Nell received a call from the Hollywood columnist, tasking his stringer to investigate a story about a DHS agent who broke a leg in a fall at the city morgue and was now in St. Vincent's Hospital. Nell immediately thought of Agent Falk!

Carrying a towel-covered tray and dressed in floral scrubs, Nell looked cute as she entered the room. There were three beds, two of them empty. Grant lay with a stack of pillows behind him, his leg in a splint suspended by pulleys. Nell had expected Falk and her face dropped upon seeing the scowling countenance of Grant.

"Whatever you've got on that tray, I don't want it. Get out of here."

"I thought this was Agent Falk's room."

Grant's eyes narrowed. "Wait a minute. Come here." Nell moved closer. "I was told there was a DHS agent in here with a broken leg and I thought..."

"You thought what?"

"I know Agent Falk and wanted to say hi."

Grant's investigative reporter instincts kicked in. "When did you meet him?"

"He and his partner were investigating a murder and I mentioned I'd like an interview." She paused. "I'm not really a nurse. I'm a writer and wanted some inside information about the DHS for my book."

"Did you get your interview?"

"Not yet."

Grant knew he had a winner. "What would you say if I told you I'm his boss? If you'll work with me, I'll give you an in-depth interview that *TIME* magazine would die for."

"What do I have to do?"

Grant didn't intend to screw up his first assignment. He couldn't strut his stuff with a broken leg but he sure as hell could get around if he had an electric scooter.

Grant called a medical rental supply company and ordered an electric scooter. Then he signed himself out and assigned Nell as his personal assistant.

Twenty minutes later he zipped through the corridors of St. Vincent's on a bright red scooter with Nell trotting to keep up.

Greg Grant was back on the job.

Chapter 37

Despite the many security procedures put into effect across the United States since 9/11, there were still numerous gaping holes in the system. Bridges and dams, airports and docks teemed with bureaucratic experts claiming their program was foolproof. Some used words such as watertight and impregnable.

The sad fact was most of the posturing related to protecting their jobs, an action 180 degrees counter to what the nation needed. America fell over itself in its desire to become terrorist proof. In doing so, they knocked large gaps in their hastily organized security screens, a case in point, the Hollywood Bowl.

Preparations for the Easter Sunday Services were ongoing. Every vehicle checked in and out—no exceptions. No one was permitted to enter the area without a thorough security check and every worker carried an official ID.

Marco, hands stuffed deep in his jacket pockets, stood with the other workers in the back of an open truck. Nonetheless, Marco, alone the last few days, had unknowingly hidden six bombs in the roots of trees in and around the stage area where the dignitaries would assemble.

The truck inched slowly forward into the nursery zone at the rear of the huge acoustic shell. A large part of the re-landscaping project had included planting new saplings. Unknown to anyone, and cunningly hidden in the root ball of each sapling, lay a small and powerful plastic bomb wrapped in sacking. Each passed through stringent hands-on security checks and electronic wands.

They never registered a flicker on the security equipment. The sniffer dogs were foiled by the addition of agricultural composts, chemicals and soil surrounding the roots.

When triggered, the deadly devices would hurl ball bearings at waist level into the audience. At the same moment, the biolog laser injector, with laser accuracy, would zap celebrities on stage. A second assassin, using the original prototype weapon, was primed to fire airborne bacterial laden shells set to burst over the audience as the tree bombs exploded.

Marco climbed down from the truck and stamped hard on the ground to restore his circulation.

"Hey, Marco. How many more trees we got to plant, man?" one of the gang members asked.

Marco shrugged. "When we're finished we go back home, okay?"

Marco carried the radio Stewart had given him and increased the volume of a Spanish music station. He always carried it, even going through security. So far, not one security guard bothered to examine the cheap-looking radio. To them, if it played it was a radio. Marco eyed a pile of new saplings stacked against a wall of the nursery, estimating at least two hundred and two days until Sunday.

Massy watched the crews receive their assignments. She decided this was a good time to test Marco's loyalty.

Feeling a sharp tap on his shoulder, Marco turned quickly. "You won't be digging holes today, Marco. You're working inside the nursery. They're a man short."

Marco's street smarts immediately went into overdrive but he remained silent.

"You're getting an opportunity to prove your worth to us."

"Meaning what?"

"Keep your eyes and ears open. The Department of Homeland Security has added a command center inside the nursery as part of the security coverage. I need to know how many people are on duty at all times. You'll report to a man named Fred and be watched every minute. Now get going."

Marco had gone only a few feet when Massy called out. "One other thing, I notice you carry a radio everywhere you go. Leave it with me. Fred doesn't like Spanish music."

Massy drove out of the Bowl, stopped at the corner of Hollywood and Highland, picked up a male passenger then continued toward the Santa Monica Mountains overlooking Malibu. Forty minutes later they arrived in a lonely, boulder-strewn canyon. Massy parked the car and swept her gaze over a rugged landscape of sparse vegetation and a few stunted Manzanita trees dotting the hillsides. Satisfied they were alone, Massy switched off the ignition.

"Let me have it." The passenger obeyed and she snapped the device under the forefinger of her right hand. "You must be totally familiar with this weapon before Sunday. Follow me and bring the cages."

Massy's companion walked quietly beside her toting two wire mesh cages, each containing two cats. He'd been called on in the past to complete assignments requiring a certain talent not easily found. This one would prove to be difficult.

"I've no doubt you'll master this weapon within a few hours."

Massy held her right hand up beside her face, palm outward. The plastic object was clearly visible attached snugly under her forefinger.

"A friend of mine, trained by the British Army during WWII, told me that during pistol training they fired at wooden dummies designed to spring up as they walked the firing range. Soldiers were taught that when a target appeared to simply point and shoot."

"I've heard that one before. I still prefer the Weaver Stance," her companion said.

"I'm sure you do," Massy said silkily. "Forget that when using this weapon. You're going to be using one never seen outside of the laboratory where it was designed."

The duo was now a half mile into the canyon. Massy scanned the harsh terrain. Her shooter must learn to use a piece of equipment unknown even to the U.S. Armed Forces.

"There'll be no sound or recoil. Once you get the hang of it you'll feel as powerful as Zeus hurling his thunderbolts."

Her cohort remained silent as he watched Massy walk forward and point toward a boulder jutting from the side of an outcropping. "See that odd shaped boulder?" He nodded.

"Set one of the cages on top. Leave one cat inside, put its companion in the other cage and keep it with you."

The man trudged up the rocky slope, set the cage in place and glanced back down to Massy.

"That's fine," Massy called. "Get back down here." When the man returned, Massy asked, "How far away would you say our target is?"

"I'd guess about fifty yards."

"Good." Lightly clenching her right hand into a fist but with the forefinger extended, Massy pointed toward the cage, tightened her clenched fist and then lowered her arm. "Bring me the cat. Leave the cage where it is."

The man hiked back. He could see the cat through the wire mesh as he approached. When he reached the boulder, the cat was apparently unharmed, seemingly fast asleep.

Officer Robert Gully opened the cage door and removed the animal. It didn't move. Gully stared at the still feline. The damn cat was dead. It was at that moment Gully realized the immensity of the situation. He was about to use an instrument of death that would soon allow terrorists to wield unprecedented power in political assassinations worldwide.

"We don't have all day, Gully," Massy shouted. "Get back down here. Today's Friday. Unless you're perfect on Sunday you'll be a dead man. You still need a lot of target practice."

"Damnedest looking weapon I've ever seen," Gully muttered.

Massy watched Officer Gully, the man she had chosen to commit an act of terrorism against his own country, examine the BLI. Over the next few hours, Massy explained in detail the workings of the biolog laser injector.

Finally, in late afternoon, Massy was satisfied with the skill and accuracy Gully had attained in such a short span of time.

"You've excellent control of the weapon, Gully. I suppose I have to thank the LAPD for the hours of extensive weapon training they give their officers."

For the first time since he'd agreed to be the shooter, Gully felt a shiver tingle his spine. He'd sold his soul for promised riches.

Anger and frustration had turned him into a hired assassin.

It all began when Gully wrote up his partner, a rookie fresh from the Academy. During an investigation the rookie had inadvertently handled a piece of crucial evidence that later ruined any chance of a conviction.

His partner's error also ruined Gully's long-awaited promotion. As officer in charge, he failed the system by allowing it to happen. Gully protested, saying the man was incompetent. His captain advised Gully that charges of racism might possibly enter in if he protested the outcome. The rookie was a young black man.

Gully swallowed his pride and remained with the force. Less than ninety days after his transfer, Massy contacted him and painted a picture of riches if he considered becoming an informer.

Gully received a huge amount of money upfront. The agreement videotaped without his knowledge. Two days later, Massy played Gully the tape, advising him the video might show up at the DA's office if he ever decided to change his mind and stop obeying orders. Now, almost two years later, he stood in a rock-strewn canyon, learning to use a weapon of frightening possibilities. Will what he was about to do go into the history books along with past traitors who had caused world wars through their actions?

The bodies of four cats lay stretched on the ground. Massy nudged one with the toe of her shoe. "Can't see any marks. Not even a veterinarian can say how they died. You see, their own body killed them the instant the frequency transmitting the chemical particles penetrated their system. It works the same with any living body. Biocomplexity. Death is instantaneous. No apparent internal damage and marks on the body. It's a perfect killing tool."

Massy remained silent on other features of the weapon, such as the ability to project mind-altering drugs or other dedicated opiates. Giving too much knowledge to an assassin was never a good idea even when you had decided he'd die at the scene.

The shadows grew longer and a salty Pacific breeze snaked through the canyon.

Massy snapped, "Come on. Get the cages back to the car."

Gully's Easter Sunday assignment was LAPD security—helmet, goggles, and gloves. As he lugged the cages back to the car, Massy instructed Gully to modify his right hand glove to accommodate the biolog laser injector.

Marco stacked the last hundred pound sack of potting soil onto a wooden pallet and stepped aside as the steel tusks of a stubby yellow forklift hoisted the load skyward. It spun around and wound its way across the concrete expanse of the indoor nursery. It was almost quitting time.

"Learn anything, Marco?"

Massy stood beside him, face slightly tanned, wearing scuffed and dusty hiking boots, her usually clean fingernails dirty.

Marco nodded. "Yeah. It's easier digging holes out there than hauling sacks of horse shit in here."

"There's more to learn in here." Massy nodded toward the security area in the far corner of the warehouse.

Marco grunted. "I couldn't get within fifty feet of that place. A couple of guys at lunch said the entire Bowl is swarming with security, night and day."

"Tomorrow's Saturday. It's our last chance to gather

information."

Marco shrugged. "Boring as hell in here. Let me have my radio. I won't play Spanish music. I need something to keep my mind off dried horse shit, peat moss and potting soil."

Massy shook her head. "I'll keep it until our work here is done."

Chapter 38

Like most of the homes they passed on the drive up the steep twisting roads, the mansion was equal to the best. It was a three-story Tudor, gray slate roof tiles and two sets of twisted red brick chimneys. Grant's second call from the hospital was to his friend in Beverly Hills who had arranged for a handicapped-equipped van to be waiting outside. Nell brought the van to a crunching halt on the thick gravel driveway and turned to Grant.

"You've got rich friends."

Grant nodded. "Old money. Lower the tailgate."

Nell opened the back doors and pressed a switch unhinging the tailgate from a vertical position down to the van's floor level. Grant had already moved his scooter to the back of the van and smoothly inched forward onto the elevator. Nell pushed another button lowering him to street level.

"C'mon. Let's get inside." Grant switched on and whirred toward the front entrance.

The entrance hall was huge. A black and white checkered marble floor and wide, curved staircase led to the upper floors. Nell walked beside Grant across the entrance hall and into a cavernous room furnished with heavy antique furniture. Thick damask drapes were pulled closed across leaded windowpanes. A deep seated couch covered in umber colored satin was in sharp contrast to the bright blue dress of a small, wizened woman seated demurely at dead center.

Grant swerved to a halt in front of the couch. "I'd like to introduce my new personal assistant, Nell Fynn with a Y. Nell, this is my aunt, Ms. Agatha Coleman."

Agatha looked to be in her late eighties, white hair and piercing blue eyes that still sparkled with a zest for life.

"What's he got you doing, my dear? He's not to be trusted. Ditched college and broke his mother's heart. Went off to be a newspaper reporter."

"Investigative journalist," Grant said. "Now I'm with the DHS."

"Even worse," Agatha said. "He's been staying here with me while looking for murderers. Now he's driving around with a broken leg on a senior citizen's electric scooter. Tell me. What exactly is a personal assistant anyway?"

"I'm not sure yet. I just started today."

"She's going to keep me up-to-date. Nell has contacts and I think I can make use of them."

"What sort of contacts?"

"Skills and contacts," Grant replied. "Nell's also a writer."

"Well! With those qualifications she might even solve your case, Greg."

"I'm doing all I can to get two of my agents back who were transferred from my team. Nell's in touch with them."

"And what are you going to do confined on that contraption

with a broken leg?"

"Run the show from here using the wonders of electronics and Nell on the outside."

Agatha turned to Nell. "He's turning you into a remote controlled private eye. You'll end up like that young woman in the detective novels. What's her name? She's in those books with a single capital letter for a title."

Nell laughed. "Oh, you mean Sue Grafton's Kinsey Millhone. I should be so lucky."

Chapter 39

Martin Pease called a cab from UCLA that took him and Dr. Wolf to spend the night in a Westwood Motel. On Saturday Pease rented a car and drove east on Sunset as Wolf's mind worked overtime trying to think of a means to contact Stewart.

The local news was on the car radio and Pease suddenly reached over and increased the volume. "Listen."

The reporter said, "Paul Horn, an executive with Pegmanti Industries of Southern California, was found dead in his home early this morning. The police are treating the death as a possible homicide..."

Jabbing the off button, Pease shouted, "*Now* do you believe me?"

Wolf had never doubted him. He remembered Massy from the short time, years ago, when he worked for Pegmanti. Massy had befriended the young Englishman upon his arrival at the company. Perhaps even back then Massy saw Pease's potential.

"For God sake, Martin. A terrorist cell with a futuristic

delivery system *you* designed!" He must contact Stewart immediately. "I can get you help."

Pease gave a harsh laugh. "Who? Someone with the government?"

"A person I've known for a long time."

"He can get me out of the country?"

"Yes."

"You can reach him by phone?"

"Yes."

"Here's my cell. Call him."

Wolf quickly tapped Stewart's number. "Tom, this is Jack. Yeah. I'm okay. I'll be at your place in twenty minutes. I have someone I'd like you to meet."

Falk drove north on the Pacific Coast Highway heading to the Pegmanti address when his phone chirped. "Falk. Okay. We're on our way." Checking his side mirror, he made a screeching U-turn.

"What's up?" Koski grabbed the armrest as Falk pushed the car way over the speed limit.

"Stewart. He wants us back at his hotel. Doctor Wolf's with him."

Forty-five minutes later they entered Stewart's suite.

"You both know Doctor Wolf." Wolf raised an arm in greeting and Koski saw how tired he looked. "And this is Doctor Martin Pease."

So began the debriefing.

Two hours later Pease ended his story.

"Where can we find Doctor Massy?" Falk asked Pease.

"I don't know. She always contacted me."

"Koski," Stewart ordered, "contact Laser Research Labs in Pasadena. They'll know."

Koski had directory service give her the number. "This is Agent Susan Koski, FBI. Listen carefully and take down this number. Have someone in authority phone me back immediately. They'll be screened through by an FBI operator. Tell them Agent Susan Koski told you to contact her. You'll be routed to me at once. Do you understand? Good. Now do it."

The room was silent for what seemed like an eternity. In reality it was less than seven minutes before Koski's cell rang. Identifying herself, she asked where Doctor Rita Massy could be located. She listened, raised her eyes and stared at Falk. "You mean there is no way she can be reached? Yes. I understand. Thank you." She snapped the phone shut, "She's on a month-long sabbatical somewhere in the Amazon rainforests."

"Rubbish!" Pease snorted. "She's *here in town*."

"You've no idea where we can find her?" Stewart asked.

"No. We agree over the phone to meet in various places of her choice. I never know where until an hour before the meeting."

"We can get a warrant and search her house," Falk suggested.

"You'll find nothing," Pease said bitterly. "Rita Massy is far too smart to leave any incriminating evidence."

"Then where *does* she operate from?"

"I've no idea."

Falk wondered aloud if it were possible that Jamul had Massy as a houseguest during the planning stages of a forthcoming attack. Pease shrugged.

Stewart had assigned a surveillance team to Jamul's place

immediately after Falk reported his breakfast meeting with Marco. The stakeout confirmed the fact that Jamul had a yacht moored at the Marina, which he also placed under surveillance. Having no information on Massy at that time, the watchers had simply videotaped everyone entering and leaving the building and the yacht.

"We have video on every person who went in and out of the towers and the yacht, right?" Falk asked.

Stewart nodded. "Yes. For two days."

Falk sighed. "Massy could be in the towers, on *Caviare* or any place in the Marina. If Jamul is involved he's keeping a low profile. I suggest we get technicians to go over the tapes, frame by frame, with a picture of Rita Massy beside them."

Chapter 40

Falk and Koski scrutinized Massy's employment files at Laser Research Labs in Pasadena. Falk came across a black and white photograph attached to a company security document taken several years earlier. He passed the form to Koski.

She matched the picture with a blowup from video surveillance. A small frown creased her brow. "That's the woman who interrogated me on the boat!" she said softly.

Falk looked over her shoulder. "You said she wore a ski mask."

"She did. It's the eyes. I'll never forget them."

Falk flipped through the background information in the dossier. Education degrees, publications awards, hobbies. "Says Massy's hobby is sailing," he read aloud.

"And I'm sure she was in the Marina when I was being held," Koski grunted.

"Call DMV. If she does have a boat registered they'll have it on file."

Koski phoned, using the same procedure she used when contacting Laser Research. Within five minutes she had the information. A Dr. Rita Massy was the registered owner of a Grand Banks 46 Classic.

"DMV doesn't have any information on individual slips but they have the registered owner's home address. Massy's is 2109 Avondale Road, San Marino," Koski said quietly.

"Let's check it out," Falk replied.

San Marino is an upscale conclave of mansions and historic homes sedately set amid trees, half-acre lawns and security walls. It's backed by a police department dedicated to the serenity of its residents.

Built at the turn of the century by powerful industrialists, politicians and other movers and shakers of the time, the area was designed for the rich. Today, their descendants retained the same lifestyle.

"Massy must have been doing well to live around here," Falk muttered as he drove along Euston Road, passing the Huntington Library and Art Gallery.

Koski, engrossed in her map book, looked up. "Yeah. Hang a right on Woodstock."

The Avondale address turned out to be a large, two story Spanish hacienda with the customary red tiled roof. It sat back from the road behind a pair of ten-foot high decorative iron gates.

It was secured by a thick chain and a padlock the size of a dinner plate. Two infrared security cameras covered the approach to the gate.

"Wait here." Falk inspected the padlock, brass, old-fashioned but effective. He turned quickly when Koski tapped the horn and a police car rolled up beside him.

"Anything we can do, sir?" a polite but commanding voice asked.

"Yes, officer. We want to talk with Doctor Massy." He indicated the padlock and chain. "Seems she's not at home."

The officer slid from behind the wheel. His partner was already out and watching Koski. "Keep your hands where I can see them, sir." The officer removed his automatic and held it at his side. "Slowly remove your ID." The cop held his weapon away from his leg.

"We're from the Department of Homeland Security."

"That's fine, sir."

Falk removed his ID and held it to view.

"Tell your partner to hand her ID through the window." He jerked his head toward the other cop.

"Do as he says, Koski."

Satisfied with the IDs, both cops relaxed. "What does the DHS want with Doctor Massy? She's been away for almost a month."

"We need to talk to her."

"When she left, Agent Falk, she informed the station she'd be gone for six weeks. We keep a close watch on property when any of the residents around here leave."

"We'd like to get in and look around," Koski said.

"You'll need a search warrant."

Falk had no time to waste. "Fine." He put away his ID and returned to the car. "Call Stewart. Bring him up-to-speed and tell him we're going back to the Marina."

Koski nodded and transmitted.

Falk and Koski entered the Harbor Master's office in Marina Del Rey. After a brief explanation and ID presentation, they waited in a pleasant room overlooking the main channel.

"I can see the cutter we almost spent the night on." Koski said, craning her neck for a better view of the large craft.

A middle-aged woman entered the room. She carried a thick leather book and angled into a chair facing them. She thumbed the pages without saying a word. Satisfied, she marked the page physically with her right hand and closed the cover. "We don't usually give out information like this."

"We understand," Falk responded.

"Seeing it's for the DHS the Harbor Master is making a concession."

"Thank you."

The woman tilted the book toward her chest as if afraid they might see something they shouldn't then slid her hand from between the pages and read aloud.

"Doctor Rita Massy, Grand Banks 46 Classic, slip number 1443 Bora-Bora Way, Basin A."

Koski had swiftly jotted down the information.

"Thank you, ma'am," Falk replied. "The agency requires me to advise you it's against the law to disclose that the Department of

Homeland Security requested this information. If for any reason the person we're seeking is given any indication that could in any way be detrimental to our investigation, that party will be charged with breaching the Securities Act in a time of war. Any questions?"

Wide-eyed, the woman whispered, "I understand."

Upon leaving the Harbor Master's office, Falk said, "We'll cut through Fisherman's Village and check out Jamul's boat. It's too long for a regular slip."

Once through the collection of shops and restaurants and onto the walkway adjacent to the main channel, Falk pointed. "There she is. Wow! Looks like something Onassis might have owned."

They leaned on the walkway rail like tourists watching the activity of the crew working topside, scrubbing the deck and polishing the shiny teak rails and brass.

"Check out the helicopter," Falk said, indicating a bright blue Bell 206B.

Koski shaded her eyes and scanned the far side of the channel. "According to the map on the wall back in the Harbor Master's office, Bora-Bora Way is directly across from where we're standing."

"It is," Falk agreed, "but right now I want a closer look at *Caviare*."

Jamul had boarded his yacht Friday night under cover of darkness. Now, seated at a custom-built console of electronic wizardry, he could observe any part of the yacht on a large flat screen monitor. The equipment enabled him state-of-the-art satellite send-and-receive capabilities. The sophisticated equipment, under the guise of business use for his worldwide interests, used an especially designed code that was cunning yet simple. He used words and phrases widely accepted in show business jargon but with different meanings when matched to the decoding manual.

A smaller screen beneath the monitor flickered to life. Massy's image filled the screen and her whispery cold voice filtered through concealed speakers.

"The woman who sank the boat is standing dockside accompanied by the man who rescued her. Two of my men followed them when they left the Harbor Master's. Send backup from the yacht. We'll take them out."

"I'll have them ashore at once," Jamul rumbled.

Massy nodded as the image faded.

Mikhail Brasinov's first venture to the U.S. as a skilled Islamic warrior had been a complete failure. So when Jamul suddenly ordered him and another man ashore to go after Koski and Falk, he was determined to prove his worth.

Brasinov's reputation was well-known. He had no need to be concerned. He had killed many and disrupted dozens of the NATO troops' plans to bring peace to Bosnia. Many lauded Brasinov's claim that NATO and U.N. troops had hidden all the dead bodies and that had been their only means of keeping peace.

His present assignment to the cell chosen to represent Islam's next blow against the U.S. on American soil was a great honor for a young man born to peasant stock in Eastern Europe. Growing up with war and hatred, he quickly learned to kill or be killed. He'd made the choice. His future was with radical Islam.

Chapter 41

Jamul knew nothing must disturb tonight's black tie affair. This was a pivotal part of the overall operation. Easter Eve vigil would begin at sundown and be celebrated aboard the *Caviare*. A grand gesture on Jamul's part, designed to show his deep concern for world peace and his embracing of all religions. The idol of millions, however, still had important duties to carry out to remove him from any suspicion of being associated with a planned terrorist attack.

He closed down the console and shrugged into a flight jacket. He flipped on a baseball cap and tugged down the bill, went topside and walked aft. Two mechanics were finishing their final flight check on the Bell as Jamul put on dark glasses and climbed up to the helipad.

"All ready?" Jamul asked, knowing the aircraft had been standing by for at least twenty minutes. Assured all was in order, he eased into the Perspex cabin, settled in the pilot's seat and began his pre-flight check.

Jamul was a skilled copter pilot with five years experience. He glanced at one of the mechanics and twirled his right hand in the sign for takeoff. The rotors came up to speed. The mechanic's overalls fluttered from the down draft as the helicopter slowly lifted from its pad. It hovered over the main channel for a few seconds, swooped left, climbed and headed toward Hollywood.

He was flying to the Bowl to supervise final preparations of the audio and lighting systems. As usual, he was in charge, as he would be Easter Sunday morning. He would be standing center stage as the sun rose, leading a massed choir in singing Handel's

Messiah. Audiences worldwide traditionally rose from their seats at the first stirring notes. Tomorrow the powerful hymn would be his signal for the violence to begin.

"Two on our tail," Falk whispered as he glanced back toward the Coast Guard station.

Koski looked toward the *Caviare* and spotted two men running down the gangplank, darting glances as if seeking someone. "Make it four." Seconds later the small blue helicopter clattered skyward from the fantail.

Falk grabbed his cell from his jacket pocket. "We're aft of the *Caviare.* Okay, make it fast. We'll fake a medical emergency." He closed the phone. "Okay, Koski. Faint and stay down."

She responded as if cued by a film director. A small crowd started to gather and Falk quickly ordered them back.

"Give her air." Glancing over the knot of onlookers, he saw that the Coast Guard had responded to his call. Three Coast Guardsmen, one pulling a gurney, ran toward them from the nearby USCG office.

"Step back please. Nothing to see here," a commanding voice ordered as a corpsman knelt beside Koski. Falk scoped the area to see if he could spot the followers. They'd vanished.

The medic rolled Koski onto the gurney and Falk fell into step with them as they carried her back to the Coast Guard station. It had worked...for now at least.

The same lieutenant who showed them around the cutter was on duty when they arrived.

"Welcome aboard." He grinned. "Good ruse."

"Yeah, but we're going to need a way to leave here *without* being followed." Falk tapped Koski's shoulder. "Oscar winning performance."

She got to her feet. "Thanks."

"Seeing you're such a good actor," Falk quipped, "I've an idea on how we can expand your role."

Chapter 42

Rita Massy had been gone less than ten minutes when two men walked up and hustled Marco from the nursery building into a waiting car and drove him to the safe house. No one spoke on the short ride. Now, handcuffed and sitting on the floor of an empty room on the top floor, Marco felt dazed by the sudden change of fortune.

Twilight filtered through a grimy window at the end of the room. He struggled to his feet and shakily crossed to the window. He leaned against the frame and stared down to the grounds, aware that they were swarming with unseen guards.

Enrico Pegmanti, assisted by the butler, shrugged out of his thick overcoat as he entered the safe house and demanded, "Is he here?"

"Yes, sir," the butler answered.

"Bring him to me." Pegmanti walked through to the same room where he and Rita Massy had met. He lowered slowly into a chair beside the fire. He was already wearing his tuxedo for the black tie event aboard the *Caviare* later in the evening.

A log in the hearth flared a gas plume of sapphire blue. Pegmanti watched it with a childlike fascination. The house was silent except for the soft hiss of the burning wood. It seemed to soothe the old man until the sound of a door opening broke the spell. Pegmanti continued staring into the flames as footsteps came closer to his chair and stopped.

Pegmanti cast a sideways glance at the man and Marco at his side. "Leave us alone," Pegmanti ordered.

The man nodded. When the door had clicked shut, Pegmanti indicated a chair opposite him. "Sit down, young man."

Marco had no idea who the old man was but knew instinctively he was in the company of a man of power. Slowly he folded himself onto the edge of the chair. Still cuffed, he sat stiffly, his arms pulled behind him.

"What caused you to become a traitor, Marco?"

Marco was stunned. What had he done to cause suspicion?

"I'm not a traitor."

"You don't consider working for a group of foreigners determined to overthrow the American way of life not traitorous!"

Marco blinked rapidly. The old man was talking about the Arabs, not him being an informer. Quickly his mind spun into action. "I did it for the money."

"Were you born in the United States or Mexico?" Pegmanti asked.

"I was born in East Los Angeles."

"Even worse, Marco. You sold your birthright *and* you're a traitor." One of the logs burnt through and fell, sending a shower of tiny sparks spiraling up the chimney.

"Many years ago I also became a traitor, not by selling out to the enemy but by leaving my country in 1931 when it needed every able bodied man." He turned his head and looked at Marco. "Like many other Italians, I came to America a penniless immigrant. I was seventeen." Pegmanti paused and rubbed his left hand over the top of his right, as if trying to increase his circulation. "Over the years I made a fortune and tripled it during World War Two," his voice almost a whisper. "Then I became a traitor a second time. Hearing about you has changed my mind."

"Why me?"

"You're aiding a terrorist group. The same as I've been doing. I'm an old man looking for forgiveness. I've decided to make amends on this Easter Eve, the great vigil before Easter Sunday morning."

Marco tensed. Why is this old guy telling him anything? "Who are you, mister?"

"It matters not. I ordered you killed."

Marco sat straighter on the chair edge and swallowed hard before asking, "And now?"

"Admit that you'll agree to work against these people and I'll see you leave here alive and you can complete your mission."

Marco knew the old man could have him killed, the same as they killed his best friend. "I joined for the money. I don't care what the Arabs do."

"You'd make a lot more money if you gave the government information that could break up a terrorist cell." Pegmanti reached into his jacket pocket. "I believe this is yours. I'm told you don't go anywhere without it." He switched on the radio and a music program was in progress. Snapping it off, he continued. "I know what this really is, Marco. When I tripled my fortune during the war, part of my company was manufacturing such devices for the government, perhaps not as sophisticated back then, same idea though."

Marco was defiant. "All I can tell anyone about this job is I've been digging holes and planting trees."

Pegmanti nodded slowly. "Very well...now listen carefully."

Chapter 43

After several phone calls, one of them to Chief Bradbury, Grant had gathered enough information to decide the best place to begin looking for Koski and Falk. He was determined to get back into the action. That crazy dame had sunk a boat in Marina Del Rey and now they'd been seen snooping around in the Marina again. That was all he needed.

"We'll dress as medics," Falk said crisply. "I'll need a volunteer to replace Agent Koski on the stretcher and a USCG ambulance to drive to Daniel Freeman Hospital. Once the 'patient' is delivered to emergency, Koski and I will walk through the hospital and out the front entrance. A car will be waiting to take us to Bora-Bora Way, slip number 1443. Any problems, Lieutenant?"

"Can do, sir," he answered.

"Then let's do it."

Daniel Freeman Hospital was less than two miles from the Marina. Upon arrival, Koski and Falk rushed the gurney into the emergency entrance. They turned everything over, including the scrubs they'd worn, to two Coast Guardsmen who had gone on ahead to await their arrival. Then they vanished into the hospital corridors.

Koski, slightly out of breath, walked across the main lobby

and out the front door.

"Good plan, Joe."

"Keep moving."

A Coast Guard vehicle rolled into view and they quickly crossed the sidewalk and ducked into it. The lieutenant was at the wheel and quickly pulled out onto Lincoln Boulevard and headed back toward the Marina.

"Next stop Bora-Bora Way," announced the lieutenant. "We'll have to go all the way around to the other side of the Marina. It won't take long."

"What do you know about the large sloop docked near Fisherman's Village?" Falk asked.

"The *Caviare* belongs to the pop singer, Jamul. We don't see him very often. The sloop sits there most of the year with a skeleton crew. Waste of money if you ask me."

"There's going to be a big party on board tonight. A bunch of bigwigs, politicians and foreign visitors are gathering before the Easter Sunday Services at the Bowl. I guess you'll be part of security."

"Yes, sir. Absolutely. We received orders to increase our presence along the dockside near the *Caviare*. Show the flag and make everyone feel safe and sound. Main security will be undercover DHS."

Koski caught a glimpse of a street sign as the car turned left onto Admiralty Way.

"Almost there, ma'am," the officer said. "Any place in particular you'd like to be let off?"

"Basin A, slip 1443," Falk answered.

"Okay. That's on the south side of Basin A. You want me to wait?"

"No. We'll be okay. I've got the USCG phone number in my cell if we need assistance."

"Fine. Here we are."

Meanwhile, Jamul had completed his preliminary checks at the Bowl, visited with and instructed his stage crew, joshing with them in his usual breezy manner. He made sure as many people as possible saw him at the Bowl then made ready to return to the Marina. He headed back to the helipad, assuring everyone he'd see them early Sunday morning.

Once Falk and Koski were out of the car, they looked down into Basin A and the neat rows of boats. Koski pointed across the channel. "I was right. We're directly opposite the *Caviare*."

"She sure looks pretty all lit up," the lieutenant remarked. "Take care now." He turned the car and headed back.

Falk stared across the channel toward the yacht. Light bulbs strung from stem to stern added a festive touch.

"I think I see Massy's trawler, Joe."

Falk followed her pointing finger. "I didn't know you were an expert at recognizing boats."

"I'm not. There was a boating magazine in the Harbor Master's waiting room and it featured a Grand Banks on its cover."

"Point out a couple of other boats so it's not obvious we're looking for a Grand Banks trawler. I'll go down and check it out." They both tested their communication equipment, adjusting the earpieces and testing the mikes.

"Hear me okay?" Falk asked.

"No problem."

"Stay down and cover me."

Walking in the shadows, he headed toward the dock gate. One or two lights glimmered from a few boats. The trawler was dark. He glanced up as the reverberation of an incoming helicopter shattered the stillness. It swept low across the channel, approached the stern of the *Caviare* and settled gently onto the helipad.

At the dock gate, Falk removed the key he'd taken from the Curry's and quickly opened the lock and started down the ramp toward the Grand Banks. One gate key fit all.

There were no lights showing and Falk needed to be certain there was no one aboard. The design of the trawler was such that it was easy to see into the top cabin from dockside. He kicked off his shoes and stepped aboard. Then he padded across the deck to the channel side, bending low, making himself less noticeable from the road. If not for the sound of lapping water and the ping-ping of wire halyards strummed by a light wind as they tapped the aluminum masts of nearby sailboats, it was dark and silent.

He checked the cabin door—locked. He quickly used a lock pick and within seconds was inside. Street lamps cast enough radiance to enable him to see without a flashlight. Moving forward to the bridge, he checked the controls and quickly familiarized himself with the layout.

Falk was experienced with powerboats and knew many of them had similar controls. He crossed to a set of steps and went below into the main salon area. Nothing out of place. If Rita Massy lived aboard, she was a fastidious housekeeper. He checked the sleeping area, same thing, neat. His earpiece came alive as he entered the main cabin. "Joe," Koski whispered. "Someone just parked up on the road."

"Are they still in the car?"

"Yes." Falk left the cabin, scooped up his shoes, jumped ashore and swiftly hunkered down behind one of the large storage bins assigned to each boat. Then he heard the sound of the gate opening and footsteps descending the ramp.

Rita Massy had intended to go directly to the *Caviare* from the penthouse communications room after warning Jamul. When she learned they had lost sight of Koski and Falk, she remained in the control room, monitoring communications and hoping they'd report finding the duo. Finally, fuming at their escape, she opted to return to her trawler and dress for the party.

Falk watched Massy board and go below.

"I'm going back aboard," he hissed into his mike. "Stay where you are."

Koski's voice whispered in his ear. "Be careful."

Chapter 44

Officer Robert Gully rolled down the window of the police car, allowing a stream of air to enter as they cruised down Hollywood Boulevard.

"Jesus. I'm whacked," Gully grunted.

"You volunteered for Special Services."

"After my demotion I went out for the special squad 'cause of the extra pay."

"You've been acting kinda strange, too."

"What do you mean, strange?"

"Edgy," Victor Young said. "Anything bothering you?"

"Nothing's troubling me, pal. Just tired is all."

"After the Bowl we can go home and get some sack time."

Gully felt a sudden surge of adrenaline run through his body. This time tomorrow he'd have committed the act.

Rita Massy began to change into her dress, hurrying, wanting to be across at the *Caviare* before the main guests arrived. Facing a mirror, she made a third attempt to get her hair exactly right. Suddenly, halfway through her task she stopped and listened. Someone was on deck.

She backed away from the mirror and eased the cabin door open. Every nerve was alert for the slightest sound. It could have been a seagull or perhaps the wind. She opened the door a little wider until she could see down the short corridor. No one there. She left the door ajar, went back to where her black satin dinner jacket was hanging, reached into a cunningly designed holster built into the inner lining, and removed a Glock 17 with a loaded magazine.

She kicked off her black pumps, slipped into a pair of rubber soled deck shoes and moved into the corridor.

Falk knew he'd accidentally banged against the wheelhouse and could have been heard. Quickly opening the wheelhouse door, he entered and eased it shut. He crouched between the Captain's chair and the control panel and waited.

Chapter 45

Marco sat opposite the old man and knew his only chance of remaining alive was to go along with him.

As he started to speak, Pegmanti held up his thin bony hand. "You're wondering why I'm offering you a chance to live. Correct?"

Marco nodded.

"I've discovered there is a plot to kill my wife and daughter." He stared at the flickering flames in the hearth. "I'm not concerned about me. I deserve to be killed after the life I've lived." He turned toward Marco. "But not my daughter."

Pegmanti shifted his frail body in the chair and continued. "There is an assassination plot to kill the pope along with other religious leaders from around the world. It will happen during the Sunrise Service. I want you to get the message to whomever it is you work for."

"How can I? I'm a prisoner in this house."

"When I leave you will come with me. My driver will exchange places with you. When he's found, he'll say that you overcame him and forced me to go with you."

"No one will believe that."

"I think they will when they find my driver tied up and unconscious." Pegmanti slipped a cell phone from his pocket. "I've contacted him. He knows what to do."

"Does your driver always come inside the house when he picks you up?"

"Of course not but he will today. I told him to bring me a thick scarf I left behind. I've had a nasty cold and don't want to catch pneumonia."

Marco was impressed. So the old bastard had it all figured out. "When's he coming?"

"In a few minutes. We have to be ready."

Five minutes later the door opened and the driver entered carrying a thick woolen scarf. Placing the scarf beside Pegmanti, he crossed to the drapes, removed a tasseled cord and placed it on a chair. Then he went to Marco and unlocked his cuffs. Next he removed his peaked chauffeur's cap and coat and turned his back to them.

Pegmanti ordered Marco, "Tie his hands behind him with the cord. Make them secure and hurry."

Marco obeyed and within seconds had the driver securely tied. Pegmanti handed Marco a leather sap.

"He must look as if he was attacked." The driver looked at Pegmanti and nodded.

Marco took the weapon and quickly carried out orders. The driver slumped to the carpet without a sound.

Pegmanti arched his thick white eyebrows. "You've used one of those before, young man. Put on his coat and cap and hurry. Turn up the collar and stay at my side until we're at the car then open the rear passenger door. Once I'm in, close it, get in and drive away. Don't speed. I don't want to raise suspicion." Pegmanti wound the scarf around his neck.

Marco shrugged into the coat, pulled on the hat, tugging the peak low, took a deep breath and stood at Pegmanti's side. "Let's go."

No one saw them as they walked to the front door. Outside, one of the guards nodded as they went down the stone steps to the car. "Good night, sir."

Once behind the wheel, Marco had to restrain himself from

tromping on the gas as he drove away from the house. Once through the gate he turned and headed down Rockledge Road, headlights sweeping through the curves.

"When we get to Sunset, I'll give you directions to my home in Bel-Aire. I shall remain in hiding until I'm certain you have contacted your superiors and I know my wife and daughter are safe."

Pegmanti reached into his pocket, removed Marco's radio and leaned forward. "Keep your eyes on the road and reach back and take this." The radio went from hand to hand. "Many lives depend on you, Marco. Don't fail."

Chapter 46

Grant and Nell arrived at the Harbor Master's office. Grant, in his usual swashbuckling manner, threw his weight around flashing his badge despite being seated on an electric scooter. He demanded to know if any of his agents were asking questions.

The woman who gave Falk the information about the location of Massy's boat was ashen-faced. "I can't tell you anything. I was warned I would be committing a federal offense against the Securities Act in a time of war."

Grant looked at her in utter amazement. "They told you that?"

"Yes."

"*I'm* in charge of the DHS task force. They work for me."

"I still can't discuss our conversation, sir."

"There will be trouble if you don't."

"Not as much trouble as having a federal charge against me in a time of war."

"Oh for God's sake, woman..."

The woman glanced across the room as the door opened and a ruddy complexioned man entered. "What's the problem, Marge?"

Marge moved closer to the newcomer. She quickly updated him.

"I'm the Harbor Master and what this woman told you is true. She reported the entire meeting between the two agents to me."

"Fine. She's seen my credentials and I want to know what they wanted and where they were going after leaving this building. You can call Washington and verify who I am."

The harbor master was a tall, well-built man who eyed Grant with a withering look. "I did twenty-five years in the Navy, young man. I know what it is to disobey orders or federal regulations."

"Then pick up the phone and call this number."

Grant reached into his pocket, removed a calling card and handed it to the harbor master. "Make it fast. A lot of people are in imminent danger of a terrorist attack. We don't have time to waste."

The harbor master heard the harsh tone of urgency in Grant's order. "Marge, call this number and let me know when you get through." She took the card and scurried from the room, happy to be away from the argument.

Grant drove the scooter to the window and glared out across the channel.

In less than five minutes Marge and the HM were back in the room. "Washington wants to speak with you." Marge handed the phone to Grant.

"This is Grant. Who's this?" Grant's face tightened. "Yes. I understand, sir." He listened to his boss bring him up-to-date on who Koski and Falk actually were.

The voice in his ear continued. "Allow them to continue whatever they've arranged regarding this case and for God's sake give that woman a written note telling her she won't be prosecuted by the government." There was a pause and Grant heard a sigh. "I heard you had a broken leg and were in the hospital. What the hell are you doing at the Marina?"

"I have an electric scooter, sir, and I wanted to get back on the job."

"Your entire handling of this operation so far has been a cock-up, Grant." His boss hung up.

This was Grant's debut assignment for DHS, and his boss was all over him. He considered his operation a complete failure. He *had* to make some good points…and fast.

Jamul exited the helicopter. Seething, he went directly to his suite. He'd been unable to raise Massy on the radio and it was almost time for the first guests to arrive. Rita Massy was the official greeter, allowing Jamul time to make his grand entrance.

He called her cell phone again. Still no answer. Jamul was not only angry, a tinge of fear entered his thoughts. He must remain calm. There was too much at stake. He contacted the yacht's captain, instructing him to be prepared to greet the guests and continue as host until Massy arrived.

On the other side of the channel, Koski watched the trawler intently for any sign of movement. She knew Falk had gone back on board after Massy. Moving a little closer but still hugging the shadows, she gazed across the channel at the lights of the *Caviare*.

Her main task was to be sure Falk was okay. A slight crackle in her ear indicated Falk had switched on his phone. She waited for his voice—nothing. Koski tensed then realized his phone was open. He was broadcasting to keep her up to speed. Falk was in trouble.

Massy crept closer to the wheelhouse. She pressed back against a wall when a commanding voice told her to drop her weapon. Throwing herself to the deck, Massy fired three shots toward the voice and heard breaking glass.

"Unless you want to bleed out on your boat, lady, throw your weapon up here." Falk could dimly see a darker mass down in the salon.

Massy obviously had no intentions of dying. "Don't shoot!" She tossed the Glock into the wheelhouse and heard it clatter across the wooden planking.

"Stay where you are, Koski. I'm okay," he whispered. He knew she'd heard the shots and was already down on the dock next to the boat. He saw her crouching beside one of the lockers. Her eyes never left the wheelhouse.

"Okay, Doctor. Come out with your hands on your head," Falk ordered as he eased up from behind the helm controls.

Massy crawled into view, her hair still a mess.

"Over there." Falk indicated with the barrel of his automatic. "Back against the wall. Keep your hands on your head." He checked her for any other weapons. "We're going to the Coast Guard station. You have a lot of questions to answer. But first, you're going to clear our lines and if you try anything I'll drop you on the spot. Understood?"

Massy nodded. She went out the door onto the deck. Falk

followed close behind. She jumped to the dock, went forward, let off the bowline, turned and went aft for the stern lines.

Falk watched every move as he heaved the lines onboard. "Okay, back onboard and make it quick."

In the seconds it had taken Massy to go to the forward line, Koski had nimbly crossed the dock and was on deck in seconds, crouched behind a hatch.

"Nice work. Stay out of sight." She smiled and readjusted the earpiece. Falk had seen her.

"You did well, Doctor Massy. Now get over here and start her up."

Massy fired up the engines and started to flip toggles.

"Forget the lights," Falk ordered. "Move across the channel and find a mooring close to the Coast Guard station."

"We can't cut across the channel without navigation lights. Marina Del Rey takes a dim view of breaking the rules of the road."

"I'm sure they do but we're going to break them now so move out."

Massy spun the wheel and eased the boat away from the dock. Falk picked up a pair of binoculars and focused in on *Caviare*, secure in the knowledge he had Koski as backup. He could see guests on the deck sipping drinks and enjoying the evening.

Massy thrust the throttles forward. She spun the wheel, causing the boat to heel to starboard and knocking Falk off balance. At the same time she kicked him at the base of his spine.

Koski leapt into the cockpit and slammed a karate chop into

Massy's carotid artery. She staggered across the deck, hit the rail and went overboard. The trawler was now under full power and churned out across the main channel. It streamed a phosphorus wake and narrowly missed a sailboat heading up channel.

Yells from the sailboat were lost in the roar of twin diesels as the boat continued an out of control rampage across the channel. Falk clawed to his feet, grasped the helm and fought to get command of the bucking vessel. At the same time, he desperately reached into the darkness for the throttle controls.

Chapter 47

A flashlight beam swept across the control panel and Koski's voice called out, "Back off the throttles, Joe."

"They're jammed. They won't move!" Koski was at his side in seconds. Together they attempted to pull back on the controls but they remained locked at full throttle. Pounding across the channel at full speed with no lights was akin to taking a chance driving the wrong way in the fog on the interstate. Falk reached for the ignition key and turned off the engine. The sudden silence after the roar of the motors and the slowing of the forward movement was sweet. The Grand Banks slowed to a wallowing motion in mid-channel.

"Get that beam on the panel, Koski. Find the light switch before we get run down." Koski located the switches and a second later the cabin and navigation lights came on. Red and green never looked so good. Falk realized they were closer now to the *Caviare* and that people had watched the mad dash across the channel and the sudden stop and were crowding the rails wondering what was going on.

"Hit every light switch you can find. Get below and turn on the main salon. Light this boat up."

Koski quickly carried out the order as Falk called the Coast Guard station.

Nothing happened. He redialed. Still nothing. The phone was useless. He yelled to Koski. "Something's wrong with my phone. Could have happened when I fell. Let me have yours."

She tossed him her phone.

"This is Agent Falk. Put the lieutenant on and make it fast." Within seconds he was speaking with the officer.

"We need your help, Lieutenant. We could do with a tow, two scuba diving suits and double tanks for both. I'll fill you in when you arrive."

Passengers on the sloop found the trawler a point of interest. The excitement grew when a searchlight from an approaching USCG cutter stabbed through the darkness as it neared the drifting craft.

It was more than excitement that surged through Jamul's body when he recognized Massy's trawler. Returning to his quarters, he snapped on a two-way radio and tried to raise Massy. No answer. He could see the USCG cutter going alongside, lines thrown across the decks as several men jumped aboard. Damn! What happened to the fool? This was the last thing he needed. Grabbing a pair of binoculars he focused in on the action and saw the boat was about to be towed in.

Each of Jamul's trawlers was fitted with a self-destruct system. Despite the thoroughness of security on each craft, there was always a possibility that some forensic evidence could lead back to him. If someone had boarded Rita Massy's boat, it had to go.

Jamul dialed a preset frequency on his radio to trigger the explosive device system that would disintegrate the vessel and everyone aboard with a touch of his finger. He had to be certain the USCG hauled the boat far enough away from his sloop before triggering.

He watched as the crew got the trawler in tow and headed back toward the USCG dock.

Passengers on the *Caviare* lost interest as the boat moved away. Jamul watched; his finger hovering above the switch that would obliterate Massy's folly. Jamul had a perfect view of the port side of the Grand Banks up-channel twenty feet behind the cutter. What he didn't see were the two scuba divers who slid into the water from the starboard side and dove deep as the doomed boat wallowed its way to eternity.

Koski's phone rang continuously as it sat on a bunk next to her clothes in the cabin.

Tom Stewart cursed, tossed his phone aside and addressed Wolf. "I can't reach Falk or Koski, Doc. We have a problem."

Chapter 48

They came for him as he knew they would. He was ready. A small suitcase sat on the floor next to the front door. When the bell chimed Pegmanti opened the door himself.

Two men stood at the top of the steps. One of them showed his ID and asked, "Mr. Pegmanti?"

"Yes." He picked up the case. "My wife and daughter…?"

"They're safe, sir. Come with us."

Enrico Pegmanti walked down the steps, stopped and looked back at the house, wondering if he'd ever see it again. Shaking his head, he turned toward the car, an agent's hand on his elbow. His wife and daughter were safe. He'd made his decision. There was no looking back. It was time for his last confession.

One of the agents held open the passenger door and the other took his suitcase. Suddenly the sharp crack of a high-powered rifle seemed to make the world stand still. Two more shots fired from the direction of a group of trees near the house hit Pegmanti in the face and neck.

Enrico Pegmanti, a man who had lived his life on his own terms, died without a sound.

After calling for an ambulance, one of the agents called Stewart. "He's dead, sir. Sniper—happened in a matter of seconds. Pegmanti had a small suitcase with him."

"Bring it in right away," Stewart snapped.

Deep below the icy channel, Falk glanced at the luminous dial of his wrist compass. He swam ahead of Koski as they headed for Jamul's sloop. Koski, to his right and slightly behind, followed in the wake caused by his flippers. The water was inky black. Falk had requested the lieutenant send the compass as part of the scuba equipment along with an innovative piece of underwater hardware, a multi-node miniature transmitter. It was smaller than a pack of cigarettes and designed to attach to metal by a powerful magnet.

The transmitter emitted a signal to allow a receiver ashore to log an exact location up to a distance of several hundred miles via satellite hook-up. Perhaps its greatest asset was that an onshore operator could activate the receiver section of the underwater transmitter any time, sending a mega-high frequency signal through the metal of a ship's steering mechanism, disturbing all electronic flow on board. This totally disabled the electrical system. Controlled by an onshore operator, it was equal to reaching out and cutting the boat's main power switch.

They weren't using flashlights in case someone on deck noticed a glimmer of light beneath the surface. Koski moved in beside Falk as he located a site on the *Caviare's* metal rudder. He'd arranged with Koski that he would signal when the time came to back away from the vessel.

Swimming as a team was standard operating procedure and in many cases had proved to be a lifesaver. Now, Koski was close enough to make out his shadowy presence as he clamped on the electronic device and tested it to assure it remained in place. He was turning; ready to give the signal to follow him back to the dock where the Coast Guard lieutenant had promised to be waiting with the car.

Koski saw Falk's signal and turned. Suddenly a rib crushing THUD and a water amplified concussion wave flung them both hard against the side of the sloop. Ten feet beneath the waters of the channel, they were swirled like dolls. Koski's mask ripped from her face and for a few seconds she didn't know if she was facing up or down. She was totally disorientated by the violent turbulence. The swirling darkness and the need for air caused her to grab wildly for her mask and mouthpiece.

Falk fought hard to remain upright, knowing Koski was in

trouble. She had been close enough when he gave the signal to move out. Suddenly she cartwheeled past, her mask and mouthpiece torn from her face.

Frantic he reached toward her but she wasn't there! Ignoring the mind-altering ringing in his ears, he dove even deeper. His arms and hands were outstretched in a desperate attempt to find her.

On the surface, those on the deck of the *Caviare* were shocked to see the Grand Banks trawler suddenly erupt in an orange fireball. The stern lifted high out of the water as the shattering roar of an explosion rent the quiet evening.

Jamul watched the trawler, now blazing from stem to stern, roll onto its side, spewing black clouds of oily smoke. Within minutes it slid beneath the waters. The tow cable from the Coast Guard cutter thrashed the turbulent waters like a hungry sea serpent. Fast action by one of the Coast Guard crew in cutting the cable saved the cutter from going under.

Jamul remained at the porthole. No one would find anything in the remains of Massy's boat. He left his cabin and went topside to share his supposed shock with his guests.

A fat man with a drink in his hand stood at the rail amid a crowd of nervous guests as Jamul walked up beside him.

"What in the hell happened?" the man asked. "Was it a terrorist attack or something?"

Jamul shook his head. "I doubt it. An engine room explosion I'd guess."

"You'd think the Coast Guard would have known something was wrong before towing the vessel," the fat man said indignantly.

"I think they were as shocked as we were." Jamul didn't recognize the man but knew he was doing the right thing, mixing and acting as mystified as the others. Then he saw the mayor plowing towards him. This man he did know.

"Jamul," the mayor rasped. "We were almost blown out of the channel. What's happening?" The mayor's fat face was gray with fright and he licked his thick lips with every other word he uttered.

"Good evening, Mr. Mayor. Glad to see you're okay. Seems the craft the Coast Guard was towing blew up in mid-channel. We're lucky they weren't any closer to us. It could have caused major problems."

"We need better security, damn it. If this is any example of the security being supplied by the DHS to a group of people like us tonight, I have little trust in them."

"We can't blame the DHS, Mr. Mayor," Jamul stated.

"We can and I do. You have some very important people aboard your yacht, Jamul. DHS is going to hear from me and I'm not the only one aboard who will raise hell. I've already considered contacting the President and cancelling tomorrow's Sunrise Service."

"But Mr. Mayor, it's a long-standing tradition. We can't let something like this cancel tomorrow's event. Think of all the dignitaries who have traveled from around the world to stand together; so many religions showing a unity never before known. The world will think they don't have the faith to pray together."

Jamul laid it on thick and the mayor, his political mind tuned to every word, nodded in agreement. "Perhaps you're right. Nonetheless I will insist that security at the Bowl be doubled."

"A wise decision, Mr. Mayor," Jamul purred as he moved toward another group of VIPs on deck. The majority of his guests acted calmly although he knew many were worried. Acts of terrorism had become a way of life no matter where you went.

"Was that a terrorist attack, the explosion out there?"

Jamul turned to see an elderly woman point across the channel with her champagne glass as she looked up at him from under a mass of white curly hair. He recognized her as one of the city council members but her name escaped him.

"Of course not," Jamul said. "Rest assured we have the best security on and around the boat. I can promise you the evening won't be spoiled in any way."

A tall, gaunt man joined them. "Gussy, I'm sure Jamul will see that we remain safe here tonight and tomorrow."

Jamul recognized Assemblyman Jason Grainger and his wife. Jamul immediately took over. "There you are, Mrs. Grainger. Your husband knows I will do everything in my power to see that you and everyone aboard tonight have a wonderful time, and a safe and memorable Easter Morning Service. I've heard there's a possibility the Pope himself will be present."

Gussy smiled demurely and with practiced skill deftly lifted another flute of champagne off a passing tray. "I suppose so but in my position on the council I have to be sure all goes well."

"I assure you it will. Now you must excuse me. I have to be certain all is ready for our dinner below."

Mr. and Mrs. Grainger sipped and smiled as Jamul headed across the deck.

"What a wonderful man," Gussy sighed. "I knew from the

first moment I met him, he was just what we needed in this city. I told the mayor..."

Jason nodded. "Yes, yes, dear. I'm sure you did. I see someone over there I have to say hello to." He moved away from his wife, leaving her standing on the deck with a faraway smile, trying to see where the waiter and the drink tray had gone.

Chapter 49

Koski quit trying to claw for her mask. She knew she was going to drown. As a young girl, she overheard an aunt say that drowning was a peaceful way to go. Now, with her lungs seeming ready to burst through her rib cage, she knew her aunt was wrong.

As Koski sank deeper into the numbing ice cold water, she lost the will to fight. She wanted to open her mouth, suck in and speed up the inevitable. Her downward drift stopped abruptly and a hand clamped her nostrils shut. Something pushed into her mouth and life-restoring air rushed from Falk's breathing apparatus in a cloud of bubbles. He wrapped one arm around her waist and kicked hard for the surface.

She breathed again and automatically kicked toward the surface. Falk quickly removed the mouthpiece, sucked air and returned it to her. He dove deep to get her and they'd have to share his air on their assent. The darkness and uncertainty of how many feet he had to cover before getting to safety depended on his self-control and strength.

After what seemed an eternity they broke the surface. He gratefully breathed in the night air, shaking his head to clear his vision and settle the nausea rising in the pit of his stomach. They were several hundred feet behind the *Caviare's* stern and close to several small sailboats at anchor. The boats afforded them shelter from the lights along the walkway of Fisherman's Village.

Koski gasped as Falk removed her mouthpiece and pulled her into the shadows of a dingy tied behind a sailboat.

"You're okay. Spit it out. You're okay."

Her face was deathly pale and her short blonde hair plastered to her head. She opened her eyes, sputtered and coughed. "I thought I was dead."

"Few more seconds and you would've been."

"I'm so cold, Joe."

"First, help me get you into that dingy. Can you do that?"

She nodded weakly. He pulled her to the side of the craft and passed her a rope running from the boat. "I'll go aboard from the stern so I don't tip the boat then I'll haul you in. You okay?"

Koski's teeth chattered. "Yeah, but hurry."

Falk was in the dingy in seconds. Even the heavy tank and equipment hadn't slowed him. He turned and reached for Koski. He yanked her into the boat and covered her with a piece of tarp he found stuffed under the wooden seat. He slipped off his tank and laid it beside her, placing the mouthpiece in her hand.

"Take a drag as you need it. I'll be fast as I can."

She nodded. Falk squeezed her hand, slid over the side and swam silently to the dockside to locate a ladder. He was fully aware that suddenly climbing out of the channel in a wetsuit after an explosion was cause for one of the many security people around the area to shoot first and ask questions later.

When Pegmanti's suitcase arrived, Stewart snapped it open.

Dr. Wolf was at his side.

"Let's see what he was carrying," Stewart said as he took out a thick manila envelope and laid it on the table before removing an old cigar box. Stewart tugged the envelope open and removed a sheaf of typewritten papers. "Business correspondence between Pegmanti Industries and some of its customers." He thumbed through the pages quickly.

Wolf looked over Stewart's shoulder. "Yes. I recognize some of the company names. Why was he carrying those?"

"We'll know soon enough. I'll have a team go through them at once. Go ahead, Doc. Check out the cigar box."

Wolf released a small metal clasp and lifted the lid. A plump human finger with a diamond ring attached lay on a blood-soaked paper towel.

"My God," Wolf whispered.

Stewart peered into the box. "Paul Horn's ring finger was amputated. The police haven't revealed that fact. It's part of the ongoing investigation."

"You think it was sent to Pegmanti as a warning?"

Stewart nodded. "Yeah and the motivating factor that made him decide to use Marco as a means to escape."

Wolf looked up. "Where is Marco?"

"I don't know. I'll have to get in touch with this Nell woman."

Despite repeated attempts, Stewart was unable to reach Nell or dig up any information from DHS in Washington on the whereabouts of Agent Grant. He hung up and the phone rang at once. "Stewart." It was Grant's boss in Washington.

"I'm calling to give you a heads up. I had a call from Agent

Grant. He has a broken leg and is trying to operate from a goddamn electric scooter. Haul his ass in."

Stewart grunted. "Where is he?"

"The Harbor Master's office in Marina Del Rey."

"Give me his number. We'll get right on it. In the meantime, tell your people working security for the *Caviare* to evacuate everyone. *Right now.*"

Falk located ladder rungs built into the dock wall so boat owners could access their small craft. He slipped off his fins and hooked them onto his equipment belt and then carefully started to climb. He used the glow from the dockside lights as a guide and carefully raised his head above the dock's edge. All clear. He was about to complete his climb onto the walkway when he heard someone coming. He remained motionless as the sound of footsteps grew closer. He had to get help for Koski. If he suddenly appeared on the dock a trigger-happy security guard might shoot him. The footsteps stopped a few feet from the top of the ladder. Damn!

He gripped a rung with one hand and unhooked one of the fins, took a deep breath and hurled it far out into the channel. The splash caused the person above to immediately turn toward the water and lean forward. Falk, moving with the speed of a striking viper, grabbed the man's leg.

The man reacted in terror. Something coming out of the darkness was the last thing he expected. Falk was up and over the edge of the dock. One fast blow with the side of the remaining heavy flipper into the security officer's neck was all it took.

Falk dragged the unconscious man into a darkened

entranceway of one of the stores and waited. He heard the distant sound of music coming from the sloop. He slipped out of the scuba equipment. He removed the guard's uniform, secured the man with his own handcuffs and pulled on the uniform. He made sure the guard's nine millimeter automatic was cocked and loaded then strode toward the *Caviare*.

Chapter 50

"Sorry to break up the party early folks." The voice of the officer in charge of security came over the speakers of the *Caviare*. The music stopped. Jamul was dumbstruck. No one had informed him of any impending announcement. Standing beside the mayor there was little he could do except listen.

"Due to safety precautions we must ask you all to leave in an orderly fashion. No need to panic. Members of the Coast Guard and Department of Homeland Security are standing by to assist in your departure. Thank you."

Jamul excused himself and went topside. Once on deck he was shocked to see so many armed security personnel. The dockside was swarming.

Jamul approached one of the ranking officers. "This is an outrage. Who authorized this? I'm entertaining very important people."

"Direct from the President, sir," the officer replied.

Jamul began to speak but the officer cut him off. "Sorry, sir. Orders." Jamul was fuming. He didn't intend to let tomorrow morning's event turn into a failure.

The security personnel and the passengers leaving the sloop

made perfect cover for Falk. Within minutes, he was in the Coast Guard station arranging for assistance for Koski. Two medical corpsmen left at once.

Falk stood in the deep shadow of a building close to the sloop as the passengers filed down the forward and aft gangplanks. Now that Koski was well cared for he moved forward. He walked up one of the gangways with a group of security personnel. It was the perfect chance to check out the sloop.

"You three guys." Falk turned as an officer ordered, "Get below. Be sure everyone's off this boat." Falk didn't need a second invitation. As he followed the two men ahead to a companionway, he saw a tall black man in an argument with a security officer. He recognized Jamul immediately. Once they were below, the two security men stayed together and went forward. Falk went aft seeking the captain's quarters.

As Falk clattered below with the other two men, he missed seeing Agent Greg Grant carried down the gangplank. His scooter was hauled off between two security men while his assistant, Nell, followed. Grant tried unsuccessfully to assure the two burly guards that he was from the DHS as he reached for his ID. Once off the ship, he found himself plunked dockside. The two guards turned and went back aboard, thinking whoever it was must have been nuts.

"Nell, back to the Coast Guard station," Grant fumed. "This is ridiculous." She had to trot to keep up with him as he recklessly drove along the dockside through the crowds leaving the sloop.

Color slowly returned to Koski's cheeks as she sat wrapped in a red blanket, sipping a mug of hot chocolate in the Coast Guard station. She heard raised voices in the vestibule. She recognized Grant's voice immediately.

"I was carried off the boat. I insist you let me back onboard. I'm investigating a very important case."

Koski leaned forward, not wanting to miss a word. The lieutenant's voice cheered her to no end.

"The order came from the top to evacuate the boat, Agent Grant. Orders are being carried out." He paused. "Are you *sure* your superiors know you're working with a broken leg and riding an electric scooter?"

"Yes, damn it, they do."

Koski opened the office door. With the blanket draped around her shoulders, mug in hand, she made an imposing figure. "Greg! I thought I recognized your voice. Nell! What are you doing here?"

Grant glared. "Where's Falk?"

"It's a long story." She held up her mug. "Either of you want cocoa?"

Nell shook her head. "Koski, you look pale."

"I just got hauled out of the channel…"

"You were on the boat that blew up?"

"We got off before it actually exploded."

Greg wheeled in closer. "So where's Falk?"

Koski knew he'd keep badgering her until she told him. "On the yacht is my guess," she said calmly.

Greg's eyes narrowed. "It's being evacuated. No one's allowed aboard."

Koski shrugged. "Then I suggest we stay here until we get updated."

"Not me," Grant growled. "Come on, Nell. We've places to go. Let's move it."

Koski took a swig of her hot drink then peered over the rim. "New job, Nell?"

"I'm his aide, part-time." Nell was quickly discovering that being this guy's aide was crazy. She seemed glad when the lieutenant told Grant he wasn't going anywhere.

The area below deck was tight. Falk moved aft with caution. The other two guards going forward gave him the perfect opportunity to check Jamul's quarters.

"Can I help you?" Falk spun around. Jamul was standing behind him.

"Security. Orders to clear the yacht," answered Falk.

"I heard the orders, officer."

"Agent, sir; DHS."

Jamul's eyes flashed. "Excuse me, agent?"

"Captain, I have orders to be certain the ship is clear of passengers and crew."

"Fine. I'll accompany you but first I need something from my cabin." Jamul led the way to his quarters. Falk followed, somewhat surprised at the unassuming manner. A few minutes earlier he'd seen him arguing with a deck officer.

Was this tall, gregarious man truly a born again Muslim, craving to be instrumental in arranging an opportunity for world religions to come together or was he a major player in a terrorist plot?

Jamul stopped, unlocked the polished mahogany door of his cabin then waved Falk inside. Jamul sauntered in behind him, headed to a built-in wardrobe and removed a leather flight jacket. "There are so many details and so little time."

Falk stood in the large cabin and eyed an amazing array of electronic equipment.

"My hobby, Agent Falk," Jamul drawled. "Modern day equivalent of Ham Radio. Electronics have come a long way since those days." He nodded toward the wall. "Transmitter-receiver, television-radio and computer technology all combined. Worldwide satellite capability, too, of course." Jamul smiled, opening his arms wide. "Show business tools of the twenty-first century."

Falk studied the array. "Captain, we're due topside. Once you're ashore DHS can finish its sweep of the sloop."

Jamul nodded. "Of course and I must fly to the Bowl and oversee last minute details."

Falk remained silent as he followed Jamul out of his cabin.

Chapter 51

Koski was edgy as she watched the passengers and crew stream past the Coast Guard station windows in full evacuation.

"Why is everyone being taken off?" Nell asked. "If the boat is in danger and we're this close don't you think we should be moving out, too?"

"Precautionary procedure," Grant muttered. "We'll have to wait here for a heads up." Grant's boss had instructed the USCG that Grant remain at the station.

Koski had no idea where Falk was. She knew he'd made it to shore and arranged for her to be picked up. Was he on the yacht?

She craned her neck to get a better view. There were no more passengers going down *Caviare's* gangplanks. The vessel had an empty look. Why would he remain behind? Something was wrong. She had to locate him.

Koski casually mentioned she had to go to the ladies room.

"I'll come with you," Nell said. Koski gritted her teeth.

"Don't take too long, ladies," Grant called as they went out the door. "We may have to move at a moment's notice."

"How do we find the washroom?" Koski asked.

"First door down the hall, on the left," replied a young Coast Guardsman.

Once in the bathroom, she turned to Nell. "Stall for me. I don't want Grant to know I'm gone."

"Gone where?"

"To find Falk," she said softly. "Stay here as long as you can. If anyone asks, make up a story. Give me as much time as possible."

Arriving topside, Jamul located the officer in charge and informed him he was flying to the Bowl to check out last minute details and security. Jamul's lips were set in a grim line as he lifted the copter off. He glimpsed the last of his evacuated guests shuffling back to their waiting cars.

At the foot of the gangplank, Koski flashed her badge and security gave her clearance to proceed. She caught sight of the Coast Guard lieutenant and called, "I'm looking for Agent Falk. Have you seen him?"

"I just came aboard. I was dockside overseeing the evacuation. What makes you think he's aboard?"

"A hunch I guess." Koski's face brightened. "Hold it. There he is." She moved swiftly across the deck to where Falk was speaking with the deck officer who told Jamul to obey orders and leave the boat.

"Hey. You're supposed to be recouperating in the Coast Guard station," Falk said.

"I've recouped, Joe."

Falk put his arm around her shoulders. "This is my partner. She's supposed to be on light duty."

"Nice to meet you, ma'am," the officer replied, touching the peak of his cap.

"We were discussing Jamul," Falk explained. "He's taken off for the Bowl. I was with him in his cabin."

Koski nodded eagerly. "And?"

Falk shook his head. "Other than seeing his array of electronics—zilch."

"Security is checking them out as we speak," the officer added. "Everything's normal."

Falk rubbed his chin. "I suggest every piece is checked out closely. Haul everything over to the Federal building in Westwood. The Feds have the tools and personnel."

"We'll get on it right away," the officer replied. "Nice meeting you, ma'am." He turned and headed aft.

Chapter 52

A debriefing by an expert is a harrowing experience. Marco blew out his cheeks and sighed. "Man! I've answered all your questions. What more do you want?"

"You're doing great."

A wooden table and a plastic cup of Coke separated Marco from his inquisitor. The agent finished his cigarette and stubbed it out in an overflowing ashtray. "I must be sure you haven't forgotten any small detail about Enrico Pegmanti that might help us."

"Unless you have a new stack of questions, man, I've said it all. I was with him less than an hour, including the drive to his home."

The agent looked up as he lit another cigarette. "I do have a few more. Once we're through you'll see Mr. Stewart." Marco watched the man studying his notes. He wondered if telling Stewart he could gather information that would break up a terrorist cell had been such a good idea. He sipped the Coke, glad he was still alive. He knew, however, that things would never go back to what they were.

The phone rang and Marco's interrogator answered, "Agent Martin." Glancing at Marco he said, "Almost through." Hanging up, he started the tape recorder beside him again.

Tapping his notebook he said, "When you've answered these you'll be on your way."

Gully was ready. He'd practiced for hours concealing the plastic bio weapon he was going to use at the Sunrise Service. No word from Massy. Not that he expected any. That bitch was a stone killer. If anything went wrong tomorrow, he knew he would be among the first to die.

Now, standing before a full-length mirror in his bedroom, he repeated the movements. He raised his arm and pointed at a crucifix on the wall, making sure the plastic weapon remained hidden in his gloved hand out of sight. He nodded back at his reflection. Perfect. This time tomorrow he'd be on a plane winging to Rio with enough money to live the rest of his life in the sun.

The house on Rockledge was no longer useful as a safe haven. The Marco and Pegmanti escapade had seen to that.

Jamul's helicopter tilted a 180 and headed out over the coastline toward Catalina Island. Jamul's destination was a small souvenir shop in Avalon named Catalina Curios. For over twenty years it had served tourists, creating a steady stream of customers. It was easy for anyone to enter and exit without suspicion. A perfect set up, run by a husband and wife who'd lived on the island for as long as they had owned the shop.

The community knew them as a friendly couple in their late sixties, spending their twilight years on the island. In reality, their income came from a Syrian cartel in Damascus.

Jamul leaned back, clenching his jaw tightly as he thought how the centers of control in the Middle East had shifted since the Iraqi conflict. American presence had shaken the once complacent regime of various terrorist organizations worldwide, from the green countryside of Northern Ireland to the desolate mountains of Afghanistan and Iran and across to the shores of Gaza, Lebanon, Syria and beyond.

Tomorrow's operation *must* go perfectly. It would show the world that al-Qaida could still select a target and carry out the plan despite the boasting of Americans at home and abroad. This attack was meant to make the highly touted Department of Homeland Security look inept. It also would rekindle a flame in the breast of Islam, igniting like a band of fire around the Arab world.

The helicopter began its descent and Jamul concentrated, guided by a single light below. There was a car waiting for him. He allowed himself an hour, less if possible, to make the visit and be back at the Bowl before two a.m. The soft thud of landing skids on grass announced his arrival.

Three Middle Eastern men sat in a small back room office of Catalina Curios. They looked up as Jamul entered, escorted by a bodyguard.

"Welcome, Jamul." A small, wizened man rose from his chair at the table. "Allow me to introduce my friends."

"Thank you," Jamul's deep voice rumbled. "That won't be necessary. It's better if I know as little as possible. You understand."

The man smiled. "We understand." Nodding to the guard the wrinkled man indicated a chair be placed at the table.

Jamul slid onto the seat and folded his arms. "There have been problems at the Marina. We might have to cancel the event."

The men straightened and a murmur of disbelief rose as Jamul continued. "I assure you it will be a last resort if such a thing were to happen. Nonetheless, too many unordinary occurrences over the last few days have alarmed me."

"We arranged the deaths of Pegmanti and Horn. No suspicion will fall upon you, Jamul."

Jamul shook his head. "Doctor Massy's boat was hijacked and her with it. I was able to destroy the boat before the Coast Guard searched it."

"That's very good, Jamul. You did well."

Jamul grimaced. "Perhaps, but I have no assurance that

Doctor Massy went down with the boat. She may have been picked up. She could be questioned..."

The man slid the cuff of his jacket back and checked his watch. "We're only hours away from an enormous display of strength; a strike against the infidels that will demonstrate to the rest of Islam that we are not beaten. We will never stop. Despite whatever worries you have, we must go forward, Jamul. It's too late to stop. Go now. The safe house here on the island knows to expect you after the attack. Continue your work for our cause and may Allah shower his blessings upon you. Allah Akbar."

Jamul was aware that the Imam sitting before him could be the next President of Iraq. He could be voted in by popular demand and sanctioned by the United Nations. He also was aware that the cell on the island would continue to be a secret place to plan future attacks against America. He had his instructions. It was time to leave.

Chapter 53

Jamul landed the helicopter in an area designated for the LAPD skywatch copters. The police aircraft would continuously circle the Bowl throughout the service. Jamul had previously arranged with the mayor to have his aircraft use the landing pad. The city was always gracious to those who helped fill the coffers of commerce.

Now, stalking across the helipad, Jamul waved to the guards, who grinned and returned the salutation. He had given out over a thousand of his latest CDs to key personnel in the last two days. Everybody loved Jamul.

Arc lamps shone harshly across the stage, reflecting the white arch of the domed shell. Stagehands and technicians swarmed. They were pulling cables and calling orders, moving electronic equipment in one last effort to have everything in place.

Jamul watched from the seated area where in a matter of hours hundreds of worshippers would take their seats. He turned, scrutinizing the hills behind the last seats in the massive amphitheater. Few lights glowed, indicating the remoteness and seclusion of the homes.

Security constantly patrolled the Bowl. Jamul was aware that, despite the number of guards in the area, there were infiltrators. Massy's walking zombies, thoughtless obedient monsters of Islam. Armed and programmed to use their bio-lasers, they lay motionless in the darkness beneath special gauzy black cloths. They waited for their moment to kill before their transition to hell.

A chilly wind stirred through the Cahuenga Pass from the San Fernando Valley, rustling the leaves of the newly-planted saplings. The bombs, cunningly nestled amid their root balls, awaited the transmitted signal to detonate.

Jamul planned on remaining at the Bowl for the rest of the night. He'd keep busy with last minute details. He planned to greet the famous as they arrived, pay homage to church leaders and curry favor with the various religious clerics. After opening the service as lead singer with the massed choir from all nations, he'd fade into the background before the assassinations and the dreadful roar of exploding bombs. Then he'd reappear and rush to help those in need.

Jamul moved toward the feverish activity on stage. A smile

creased the edges of his lips as he recalled the words of Massy when she last reported on the serum's progress.

"They will walk among their own—unsuspected—infidels killing infidels. What more can we ask for?"

"Hey, boss, everything's ready for a final check." A brawny man in blue jeans sporting a gray ponytail waved from the stage.

Jamul returned a mock salute. "Be right there, my man."

Koski and Falk returned to the Coast Guard station with the lieutenant. Falk said, "We're going to need a car, lieutenant."

"Agent Grant's SUV is in the parking lot."

"He's here?" Falk exclaimed.

Koski interrupted. "Joe, I was going to tell you…"

"That's okay. Let's get the vehicle. Lieutenant, I'd appreciate it if you don't mention who took it."

The officer led them to the SUV. "Wait here. I'll get the keys." He was back in a few minutes and gave the keys to Falk. "I told Grant we had to move it. It was blocking another car."

Falk slipped the ignition key off the key ring and handed the ring back. "Let's hope he doesn't miss the key until later."

"I'll stall him as long as I can."

"Thanks, Lieutenant. You've been a great help. I'll see it gets reported to the right people. One more thing." Falk scribbled a phone number on a piece of paper. "Have someone keep calling this number. When they get through, tell him to meet me at the Hollywood police station."

The officer nodded. "Good luck."

Falk turned on the ignition and headed for Hollywood.

Chapter 54

A little past three in the morning and activity at the Bowl was still intense. Jamul went about his usual routine before a concert, checking everything on stage, yet his mind kept returning to the *Caviare*. Was he under suspicion for his fast departure? Was he being watched?

He signaled the sound technician that he wanted a test on the main mike. He watched as it lowered toward the stage. It stopped at a predetermined spot where he would be standing when leading the choir. He beckoned to his soundman and gave him new orders. The man nodded and returned to his controls. Some workers noticed and stopped their activity as Jamul stood center stage, head tilted and eyes staring into the darkness.

The first tremulous note of an organ sounded. It was reed-like at the beginning then grew in tone and tenure, filling the massive speakers, swelling and expanding as the first bars of the opening hymn rippled through the night.

Then the organ stopped. There was a crash of silence as Jamul's mellow-toned voice picked up the note the organ left in midair and took it to a new dimension of a solo performance. Each word of the hymn was clear, sweet and amplified. Spreading out across the seating area, it caused guards at the very back, close to the hill behind the Bowl, to stop and listen in awe.

The workers on stage remained rooted in place. When he had finished they rewarded him with applause.

The test had relaxed him. He felt more in charge, more self-assured. The orders he'd given his soundman were to record the opening hymn, then, if need be, play it back in case of any last minute hitch that might keep him off stage. Already preparations were underway to let in the early arrivals. In a few hours the sun would begin to rise.

Stewart, Pease, Wolf and Marco had gone directly to the Hollywood station after the call from the USCG lieutenant. Now they were studying a large-scale map of the Hollywood Bowl with Falk, Koski and Captain Garvey. Garvey jabbed a stubby finger in its center. "I have men throughout this area, here, and going all the way around the Bowl's parameter. The DHS has their people and the FBI. Any unusual movement and we'll have them."

"Captain," Stewart's voice had a hard edge. "Our intelligence reports that the danger may already be in place." Hours of debriefing with Marco and Pease had intensified the realization they were up against an imminent danger that could cause worldwide repercussions.

"We can cancel the service," Garvey said. "Instigate another massive search, bomb squads, sniffer dogs, the works."

"This is a gathering of religions from around the globe, Captain. Perhaps for the first time in history so many diverse religions have agreed to come together and participate in a religious service. We blow the whistle and cancel this, America becomes known as the devil's handmaiden. Besides, as long as Jamul is there and we keep an eye on him, I think we still have a chance."

"I hear you, Tom but there's no guarantee Jamul will be there. Trust me. We should take him out—now." Falk spoke the words passionately.

"I know how you feel, Joe. We pull Jamul off the stage before the service starts and it'll be called everything from racism to an anti-religious, capitalistic sentiment by the rest of the world."

Falk remained silent before turning to Marco. "Marco, tell us where you were in the Bowl every day when you were working."

Marco waved his hand over the map. "All over. We were assigned different jobs when we came in every morning. I worked on a crew planting saplings and in the nursery stacking bags of steer shit. Things like that."

"Were you ever working on the stage, near it, under it, close to it?"

"No. Just hard labor, man. Lifting, digging, hauling stuff around outside. Like I said, only time I was inside was when I humped manure."

"Show me on the map the area you and the other guys worked in."

Marco stared at the map, walked around the table and squinted at it from a different angle. "That's the stage, right?" Falk nodded. Marco traced his finger around the side of the structure to where the nursery yard was located. He tapped his finger. "In and around there. We'd collect a bunch of saplings, load them onto flatbeds and haul them out to the job."

"Where was the location?"

"Different each day. We started there." He tapped the map again. "We worked our way back up the side of the Bowl, on the other side of the seating area—over here." He ran a finger in a circle. "We had to dig every hole with a post digger. Hard slow work."

Falk nodded. "I'll bet. How many did you plant each day?"

"Twenty of us on the team. We each planted about ten or fifteen I guess."

"Notice anything about them?"

"They were trees, man. That's all."

Falk rubbed his chin slowly. "Planted all along this side of the Bowl, right?"

"Yeah, and down along that side, across the back and down here."

Falk watched Marco trace an arc beyond the last row of seats then back toward the front of the Bowl."

"That's a lot of trees, Marco."

"Tell me about it."

"If your team each planted ten a day that's two hundred trees!" Koski exclaimed.

"We were told we were planting a new forest that one day would be a living monument to the Easter Sunday when the world came together and prayed."

Falk slapped his hand down hard on the map. "Let's move, Marco. We're going to dig up…"

"Joe, what the hell…" Stewart cut in.

"Those trees could be part of the plot. They surround the audience on both sides and at the back, possibly booby-trapped to detonate by remote radio transmission."

"So where does the mind-altering serum come in? What about the so-called zombies, Joe, and the Hollywood murders? How does all that fit in to the Hollywood Bowl?"

"I don't know. But we've got to check those trees."

Martin Pease spoke for the first time. "Someone will be out

there with a biolog laser injector—possibly several of them."

Chapter 55

Falk, Koski and Marco flew to the Bowl in a police helicopter. Martin Pease had brought everyone up to speed on the chemical weapons most often used if any terrorist action was to take place. Upon landing, security led them to a small office next to the amphitheater.

The head of security, a tired-looking man in his fifties, pored over a detailed map of the Bowl with three DHS personnel. He looked up as the door opened. "Agents Falk and Koski." He eyed Marco. "Who's he?"

"Special witness, sir," Falk replied gruffly. "He's been cleared by Stewart."

"I'm Bob Sorenson. Glad to meet you." They shook hands.

"We have very little time, sir." Falk said.

"Yes. Stewart filled me in. He said your special witness helped plant the trees." He looked directly at Marco. "Were certain trees rigged?"

Marco shook his head. "Don't know. They all looked the same to me."

Sorenson cursed. "There are hundreds of trees and no time to start digging them up. Besides, they could be booby-trapped."

Falk's mind raced. Scores of bombs exploding simultaneously would kill hundreds, plus there would be others slain by biolog laser injectors. It didn't make sense. Why would Jamul remain on the stage if that was about to happen? The Pope and other church leaders would also be on stage. If any of them became casualties it could ignite a worldwide religious war. An incident of such massive proportions occurring on American soil would make the United States an international villain, responsible for any repercussions that might follow.

Falk spoke up. "We have to close the Bowl, Sorenson. The service must not go on, no matter how many religions we upset."

Sorenson spun around. "Special tactical teams plus my people are in place. DHS security and LAPD are covering every possible angle. We take control of any tree bombs. We can carry on."

Marco interrupted. "When we were held each night at the house on Rockledge, I could see the entire Bowl, the seating area, the amphitheater, everything."

"Go on," Falk said.

"I also got to see other things."

"Like what?"

"A bedroom full of electronic equipment, radios, computers and stuff. I got talking to one of the house cleaners and she told me it was an amateur shortwave station. Belongs to the owner. But it wasn't."

"How do you know?"

"My cousin, José, is a Ham operator. Been doing it since he was a kid. I knew him and his equipment. What I saw at the house was state-of-the-art digital."

"And they could transmit a signal to detonate bombs in the root balls, right, Marco?"

"I guess, but today you can detonate an explosive device from a cell phone."

Falk nodded. "True. Nonetheless, we're going up to the house.

Sorenson, I suggest you assign several of your men to be with Jamul at all times, plus some he doesn't know about—just in case."

"Okay. I can spare a couple of men to go with you."

"Thanks. That won't be necessary."

Chapter 56

The house on Rockledge was dark. An air of emptiness hung about the place as Falk slowly drove past. "You said the grounds were patrolled at all times, right?"

"All the time," Marco answered. "There were lights on in the house and grounds 24/7. We had lights until ten then it was lights out for us."

Falk turned the car around, switched off the headlights then started slowly back along the road. "I don't see any sign of light in the house or on the grounds."

"Maybe they've gone," Koski whispered. "They'd have no need to hang around after the attack."

"I can take a look," Marco said.

"Wait. You and your crew were locked in the attic every night?"

"Like a jail," Marco snapped.

"Stay in the car with Koski. I'll check out the house."

Koski opened the glove compartment and removed a flashlight. "Take this."

"Go around back," Marco hissed. "There's a window next to the kitchen door that's easy to open, old-fashioned lock."

"You don't miss much, Marco."

"It's a hobby of mine, man."

Falk grunted and vanished into the darkness.

A sallow-faced man quietly sipped coffee in the attic. The only light was a dim glow emitting from a shielded dial light on a portable transmitter. His assignment was to detonate the tree bombs.

From his vantage point, he could clearly see when the first streaks of dawn glowed in the east over the Hollywood Bowl. When the lights dimmed and the sun crested the hills, he would open the window and listen to the strains of the opening bars of the organ followed by the voice of Jamul. Then the choir would merge into the famous Hallelujah Chorus. When the hymn ended and the religious dignitaries walked on stage, Jamul would slip away, and that would be his cue to detonate.

After the explosions, mass panic would grip the survivors. Gully would eliminate the VIPs on stage. Jamul would then appear heroically through the smoke and carnage to aid the wounded and dying. He'd be seen on worldwide television as a brave and caring person.

The man smiled thinly and poured a second cup of coffee from a thermos. Unlike Officer Gully, who would fly to Rio, he would remain in Los Angeles, where he'd retire and continue living in the small house in Silverlake. Maybe he'd buy the place. He would have enough money. He nodded and sipped. Yeah, he'd buy the house…like he and Jenny had once dreamed.

The memory of her voice floated in his mind, soft and sweet. "Take care of yourself, Vic." Just the way she used to when he left for work each day.

Chapter 57

Marco was right. The window slid open with little resistance and Falk climbed into a large, old-fashioned kitchen. He stood motionless. Except for an occasional drip-drip from one of the taps over the sink, all was silent.

He removed his shoes and set them on the windowsill. Next, he snapped on the flashlight, shielding the beam to a mere slit with his fingers. He carefully crossed to the door and pushed it open.

Moving with caution along the wooden planked corridor, he headed toward the front of the house. Where was the stairway? He paused, tilting his head from side to side, listening for the slightest sound. The building might be empty now but someone may return at any time. He picked out the outline of a banister and the lower steps of the staircase, carpeted in thick pile. He had the advantage of moving silently.

He carefully made his way to the second floor landing, stopped, paused, before turning right and softly opened the first door he came to. A bedroom, everything in order, as if it had recently been cleaned.

He checked three other rooms. Each was neat and clean. He looked into the remaining rooms. The fifth was different. Heavy drapes hung at the windows. Falk quickly closed them, making sure no light leaked out, then shut the door and switched on the light. At once, he saw the room was a workshop. Coils of electrical wire lay on the floor in a corner. A toolbox and soldering iron along with several schematics were piled next to it. Whatever had been there was long gone. Falk rapidly checked the rest of the room but found nothing significant.

Victor Young drained the last of his coffee from the thermos into his cup. It wouldn't be long now. He was dressed warmly. Nonetheless, the cold had crept into his bones. He needed to go down to the kitchen and make another thermos of coffee. He had time.

As he opened the attic door, Victor Young thought he heard a sound. Sliding a suppressed nine millimeter Colt from a shoulder holster, he stood on the landing. It might have been the wind, but he had to be sure. His investment was too great.

Young had lost his ambition when Jenny died. From that moment on he simply went through the motions of living. The police psychologist had worked to help him deal with his loss but sometimes, no matter how much assistance someone gets, he simply gives up.

Officer Young had given up. It then he'd been approached to become a stringer, an informer, someone who knew the inside workings of the LAPD. That included everyday procedures carried out by uniformed personnel. He'd been told the feedback was for an author wanting information for a book.

Young agreed. He realized he was going nowhere within the department and began to feed back bits of information. It was two years before he was informed whom he really was reporting to. By then it was too late.

His sudden assignment with Falk was a worrisome time. He wasn't about to let anything get in his way. The cell looked after their own. Each person was unto themselves, each a separate unit taking orders but never knowing the other members.

He had no idea that his friend, Officer Gully, was destined to be a featured part of the morning's horrors. Like many throughout history, two men had decided to betray for pay.

Young crept down the stairs, one hand holding the thermos, the other his nine millimeter. He stopped on the second floor landing and listened. All was quiet. It must have been the wind. By the time Victor reached ground level Falk was slipping on his shoes and sliding out the kitchen window.

Less than thirty seconds later Young turned on the kitchen light, crossed to the sink and filled a kettle with water. He set it on the stove and turned the heat on high.

Chapter 58

The blow that Koski administered to Massy on the trawler hadn't carried its full effect. The boats pitching and tossing had everyone off balance. As a result, the chop sent Massy reeling back against the rail and over the side. The moment she hit the water it was swim or die. A lifelong swimmer, she kicked off her deck shoes, struck out for the dock and merged into the darkness.

Fifteen minutes later, she dragged herself onto the dock a few yards from where they'd set sail. She lay shivering, gasping in great gulps of air. Finally getting to her feet, she staggered along the dock to her stowage locker, retrieved the hidden key from its place under a nearby ledge and opened the lid.

After drying herself as best she could on an old piece of rough canvas, she rummaged deeper among the collection of miscellaneous items that had gathered over the years. An old pair of blue jeans and—best of all—a thick, woolen, paint-splattered sweater. Quickly she shrugged it on then pulled the jeans on over her dress pants. No shoes, no problem. Her car was parked on the road. A spare key in a magnetic tin box was tucked under the front fender.

A thunderous roar and a vivid flash of flame abruptly lit up the dark channel. Massy shaded her eyes against the sudden glare. She knew at once that Jamul had triggered the doomsday switch on her boat. So much for the two meddlesome bastards from DHS.

Live-aboards on nearby boats came out on their docks and huddled in groups discussing what happened. Massy kept to the shadows as she made her way back to her car.

Once in the vehicle, she watched as the flames finally flickered out and the wreckage of her boat sank from view. She started the car and headed onto Bora-Bora Way.

Massy was aware that Jamul knew she'd gone to her boat to dress for the evening aboard the *Caviare*. Yet the bastard had triggered the doomsday switch. Hatred for Jamul swept through her as she gripped the wheel. Jamul was an upstart compared to the work she'd carried out over the years for the cause. *She* should have been the one chosen to head the West Coast cell, not a crazy jumped up pop singer. She was well aware that Jamul was chosen because of his popularity with his millions of fans. He was a man who worked unsuspected behind a facade of adoration. It was then that she made up her mind to kill him.

She drove toward basin E near Palawan Way. Her intention was to board one of the other Grand Bank trawlers Jamul kept docked and ready for an emergency. She'd have no problem boarding. She'd simply tell the guard she was on a special assignment and needed to change into dry clothes before heading to the Hollywood Bowl.

Dressed and possessing a somewhat soggy, laminated security pass she'd retrieved from her dress pants, she was ready to enter the Bowl. The guard waved her through. Once inside she'd locate Gully and assign him an extra target—Jamul.

Massy had made herself well-known to most of the security and DHS personnel at the Bowl when the trees were being planted. She knew where Gully and the special security squad were assembling. Glancing at the dash clock, she knew they were already in place. She had one stop to make before going inside.

Falk was only a few yards from the house when Young flicked on the kitchen light. So there *was* someone in the house! He hugged the wall and eased back toward the lighted window. Whoever it was didn't seem to care if anyone saw the light.

Falk could see a man in the kitchen, his back to the window, standing at a stove. The man moved out of Falk's vision for a moment. Falk watched until the he reappeared with a jar of instant coffee. With his back still to the window he scooped three spoonfuls into a thermos. He reached for a steaming kettle and filled the container, screwed the top on, flipped off the light and left the kitchen. Falk headed back to the car.

Koski rolled down the window when Falk tapped on the glass. "Marco, come with me. There *is* someone in the house. I need a guide. I'm taking no chances that whoever it is will get away. Stay with the car, Koski. We may have to move out fast."

Koski grumbled, admitting she would rather go with Falk but knew it made sense to use Marco's knowledge of the inside layout of the house.

"We won't be long," Falk said. "Keep the engine running."

Koski watched them disappear into the estate's grounds. Sighing, she sat back. It was getting cold. She turned on the engine and switched on the radio and heater; might as well be comfortable.

Rita Massy knew the house on Rockledge was empty except for Young. Now she was going to pay him a visit and change his schedule. The original plan was for Victor to trigger the tree bombs using three separate frequencies set one minute apart.

To be certain Gully had a chance at Jamul, she wanted the sequence changed to two frequencies one minute apart, a thirty-second pause then the third frequency. This would be unsettling to Jamul, whose timing would be off as to when to reenter the stage.

She also didn't have her cell to call Young. It was water-logged and she'd left it on the boat. She slowed the car and turned onto Rockledge.

Falk and Marco made their way down the side of the house and arrived at the now dark kitchen window.

"You first. Wait in the kitchen," Falk whispered. Marco nodded and quickly and silently opened the window and nimbly entered. Falk followed, closing the window partway behind him.

"I found the room on the second floor where you saw the radio equipment. Whoever's inside must be on the ground floor or the third floor."

"Or in one of the attics," Marco whispered. "There's four, two at the front and two in the rear."

"Do the back attics have a view of the Bowl?"

"Yeah. We were in one and I could see it."

"Kick off your shoes and follow me, Marco."

Massy was about to slow at the gate when she saw a car parked opposite. Immediately her adrenaline warned her of danger. She continued driving Rockledge, taking a quick glance in the car as she passed. It was too dark to be sure but it seemed there was someone in the driver's seat. To be certain, she drove a quarter of a mile along the road and pulled onto the shoulder and partway into a large growth of mulberry. Dousing the lights and killing the ignition she sat and waited. She removed a suppressed automatic from the glove compartment and opened the door. She'd been sure to arm herself while dressing. She stayed off the road and walked back along the grassy shoulder toward the parked car.

Chapter 59

Koski was listening to the radio when Massy's car swept past. She watched the taillights vanish around the curve ahead. What a desolate spot. She wondered why anyone wanted to live up here. Privacy, she supposed. She glanced at the dash clock and noted that Falk and Marco had been gone fifteen minutes. She grew edgy. Maybe she should go check. They both had cell phones. Falk would have called if there was a problem. She settled back in the seat.

The low sound of the radio, the hum of the motor and the warmth from the heater were too soothing for her to stay keenly alert. She turned off the heater and cranked the window down a bit.

As Massy neared the parked car, she realized the engine was running and there *was* someone inside. There could be more than one person. Crouching, she inched her way closer until she was sure the first shot would hit the front tire. Leaning against a tree for support she aimed and squeezed. Phutt...a muffled cough and the nine millimeter slug slammed into the tire. Massy waited motionless.

Koski felt the tire collapse then the car dipped its nose to the right. A blowout without moving! For a second she wanted to open the door and see what happened. Instead, her training and instincts made her quickly grab her weapon and snap off the safety.

Falk whispered, "Marco, are there any other stairs leading up to the attics?"

"Yeah. Back stairs from a yard. We had to use them every night. Didn't want us tramping mud through the house, I guess."

"Fine. Take me to them."

The house was from an era when there were live-in servants and the back stairs were typical of the day. Falk opened a door and shone his covered light onto the bottom step, uncarpeted.

"I bet they creak, right?"

"Never noticed. We were always talking and kidding when we came back."

"All the same, I think we'll go back to the carpeted stairs," Falk muttered. As he closed the door, he noticed an old-fashioned key in the lock. He removed it and put it in his pocket.

Falk waved a halt on the third floor landing. All of the rooms they'd checked were empty. Only the attic remained.

"Wait here. I'll call if I need you. Okay?" Marco nodded and Falk slowly mounted the attic steps with his automatic at the ready.

Koski, with her weapon cocked, suddenly realized a tire

doesn't blow out on its own. Someone shot it out. Without hesitating she jammed into drive, stabbed the accelerator to the floor, skidded out onto Rockledge and barreled down the road on the flat tire. She fought to keep control as the car bucked against the rim on asphalt.

Massy was shocked at the sudden action. She pressed back into the bushes as the car's front right fender swept past her, missing by inches. The rear tires kicked up clumps of grass as it sped into the darkness with its lights off. It all happened so fast. Son of a bitch! She didn't even have time to shoot at the vanishing vehicle. It wouldn't get far with a flat. The driver had been waiting for someone and whoever it was was still in the house and had no way to escape. Massy quickly crossed the road and entered the gate.

Sparks flew from the front wheel rim as Koski wrestled the steering. She knew she had to stop or risk going off the road. She noticed a car pulled off to the right, parked almost out of sight in a stand of mulberry bushes. She had seen a car pass her a short while before the tire blew. Was there any connection? She pulled to a shaky stop behind the vehicle, got out, went to the front and felt the radiator. It was still warm. It could be the car. She tried the door. Locked.

Koski reached into her purse and removed a small wallet of lock picks. Ten seconds later the door swung open. Using a pen light from her purse, she swept the narrow beam around the car's interior until it landed on the glove compartment. She opened it and rummaged around until she found the registration papers. She gave a small gasp as the beam lit up the owner's name. Jamul. The address was the penthouse at the Marina. Koski slammed the car door shut and ran back toward the house.

Arriving at the gates, panting for breath, she stopped. No sense in barging into the grounds. She must catch her breath and be ready for anything. She was in peak condition. It took but a few seconds and she breathed steadily as she ventured toward the house. Remembering what Marco said about the kitchen window being an easy entry, she cautiously headed down the side of the house searching for it.

Falk was halfway up the attic stairs when he heard voices on the landing below. He stopped. Someone was talking to Marco; someone who seemed to know him. Easing down one stair at a time, he strained to hear.

Massy had silently entered the house by using a key at the front door. She heard voices on the stairs and with weapon drawn she started upward.

The voices stopped and Massy continued. In the graying darkness of the third floor she saw a shadowy figure leaning against the wall. Massy's hand slid along the wall until she felt her fingers touch the light switch. *Click.*

The sudden bright light caused Marco to cover his eyes for a second. When he lowered his hand, Massy exclaimed, "Marco! What are you doing here?"

Marco used all of his streetwise cunning. In a split second he answered, "I came to rob the house."

Massy stared at him in disbelief. "You kidnapped Pegmanti?"

"Sorry, lady. He fooled you. He used me to escape. It was a set up. I came back here with a friend. I knew there were some nice pieces I can sell."

"Who were you talking to?"

"My friend," Marco replied.

Massy looked around the empty landing. "Where is he?"

Marco nodded down the corridor. "He's checking out the rooms."

"Who was in the car?"

"Three of us. Two of us came in and José waited in the car."

Massy still held the gun on Marco. "José had a flat tire so you don't have a ride now, Marco. Tell your pal down the hall to join us."

Falk heard the conversation and knew he had to make a move.

Massy eased to the bottom of the attic stairs and called up while keeping an eye on Marco.

"Victor, get your ass down here. We have company."

Falk was stunned. If someone came down the stairs there would be no place for him to hide!

"Who the hell's down there?" Victor Young called.

"It's me, Massy. Get down here now!"

Falk waited until the footsteps were almost at the bend in the staircase, then ran down the stairs, leapt the last few and landed on Massy sending her crashing to the floor. Massy's automatic slid across the landing. Marco scooped up the gun while Falk threw all his weight into a punch to Massy's jaw. Her head snapped sideways and she went limp. Falk turned as Young came down the last few steps, his automatic spitting flame.

Dropping to the floor, Falk rolled behind Massy's crumpled

form. She took all three shots in the chest.

Marco held Massy's gun steady with both hands and squeezed off three rounds before Young could re-aim. One in the chest, one in the throat and the third between the eyes dropped the man at the foot of the staircase.

Falk scrambled to his feet. In the last seconds before Victor fell, he'd recognized him. For a moment he thought everything had gone wrong. Falk winced at the sight of Victor. What caused a man like him to become a traitor?

Koski heard the shots and headed up the last flight, her gun at the ready.

"All over, Koski. Take it easy. Marco just saved my life."

Falk and Koski found the transmitter in the attic. Falk stared through the window at the lights down in the Hollywood Bowl.

"Perfect view from here," he said.

"Yeah. When the sun came up he'd have been able see every tree we planted," Marco whispered.

"We still have to get counterinsurgency forces to evacuate the early arrivals. No doubt they're already in their seats." Falk punched Stewart's cell number as he spoke.

Chapter 60

The darkness of night shifted to the dim grayness of predawn. Jamul was in his element, ordering people around, being important, needed and adored.

He crossed the stage to oversee some detail and happened to glance out across the seating area. A shock of adrenaline surged through his veins. There was a light on at the house, shining from the attic. The house was supposed to remain in total darkness. Victor Young's orders emphatically stated—the house must be dark.

"You okay, boss? You look like you seen a ghost out there." Jamul turned to see one of the electricians standing next to him.

"I'm fine. This historic event is going to be a great moment for the world." Jamul glanced over to the international and American television crews carrying out their last minute duties. "Over ninety-five million people will be viewing the service that will show the world that it is possible, with the right leadership, for all religions to come together in unity and harmony."

Jamul's mind raced. *Something is seriously wrong*, he thought. He could fly out in the helicopter and leave now, but then how would he explain his sudden departure before the massacre? His grandstanding act as an angel of mercy to the bomb victims would be gone. He paced the stage, pretending to be checking the directional microphones as he struggled with the new situation.

In a flash of genius, Jamul's unique ability to think under pressure kicked in. During his scheduled absence after the opening hymn, he'd make it to the landing pad, board the chopper and trigger the tree bombs from a pre-set back up transmitter on board. Then he would double back and re-appear on stage as the angel of mercy after all.

The explosions would, as designed, signal the drug-injected, mind-altered zombies to use their bio weapons on the audience while Gully took out religious leaders on stage.

A feeling of elation swept through him. Everything was going to go as planned. Then, as quickly as the euphoria enveloped him, it vanished., replaced by a sense of cold reality as he saw columns of camouflage-clad soldiers, in full battle gear, trotting around the outer perimeter of the amphitheater. They stood in a line, shoulder to shoulder, M4/A1 rifles slung at the ready.

A group of civilians walked across the wide stage toward him. Jamul recognized the mayor and several city council members. "Mr. Mayor, this is an unexpected pleasure." Jamul was the genial host. He gestured toward the assembled troops. "I see we are to have tight security on top of the already tight security."

The mayor looked tired and pale under the lights of the arc lamps. His entourage was grouped around him. "The Department of Homeland Security canceled the service, Jamul. The Holy Father's plane has been rerouted to a military Air Force base where it will be refueled and return to Rome."

"That can't be true!" Jamul exclaimed. "The world is awaiting the greatest gathering of religions ever held."

"We have red alert. Imminent danger of a terrorist attack here in the Bowl. Everyone must be evacuated."

Jamul shook his head. "We can't allow a rumor to stop the service."

"DHS doesn't consider this a rumor."

Jamul's mind flashed back to the lights in the attic and the Army's sudden appearance. Soon there would be a mass evacuation of hundreds of early worshippers. He must prove that al-Qaida can attack even when a red alert is in effect. There was still time to cause damage.

"I understand we must obey the evacuation order, Mr. Mayor." Jamul's voice was calm.

"However, I feel it my duty to remain on stage and sing the opening hymn as the authorities conduct an orderly evacuation. On this Easter morning, it is the least I can do under the circumstances."

Perhaps they wouldn't be able to cause the catastrophic damage and death as planned. But if he moved fast he could get to the helicopter, trigger the tree bombs and start a chain of events that would show the world they could still strike. The television crews would waste no time in showing the damage to a world waiting to view a meeting of peace. Instead they would witness total disaster.

The mayor desperately wanted his city to appear in the best light possible under the most drastic of conditions. Millions of international viewers weren't going to see the religious gathering they hoped for or be able to listen to the choral groups singing the praise of Easter.

Jamul's voice would soar high across the Bowl. It would be a tribute to all who believed in freedom of religion and a perfect cover for his vanishing act.

Chapter 61

Falk pocketed his cell. "Stewart says the Bowl is being evacuated. The Sunrise Service is now officially canceled." He looked at Victor Young's body and shook his head. "Let's move."

Koski dropped to one knee beside Massy and started going through her pockets.

"What are you looking for?"

"I need her car keys, Joe."

"Why?"

"Our car is out of commission."

"What happened?"

"Long story. Here they are." She got to her feet and started down the stairs. Falk and Marco followed.

Koski filled them in about the blowout and her escape as they made their way back to Massy's car.

Highland Avenue was a sea of vehicles and crowds of people on foot. Horns blared and police bullhorns crackled. It looked like a riot.

"Damn." Falk pulled to the curb more than a half mile from the entrance. "We're going to have to hike in."

Two police helicopters circled overhead. Falk looked up at the persistent eyes in the sky and remembered Jamul had flown from the *Caviare* in his copter to the Bowl.

"Marco, do you know where Jamul lands his helicopter?"

"Not far from where we worked in the nursery area."

"Lead the way."

"You'll have to climb through brush and over some walls. We can get to the back of the nursery by cutting through the intersection of Highland and Cahuenga near the Hollywood Freeway."

"No problem. Let's hustle."

As in the earlier rehearsal, the giant organ played an opening chord that quickly changed to a sustained note of pure joy then flew high through the early morning air. Next Jamul's magnificent voice entwined with the now fading note until only his resonance filled the amphitheater. Outside and in, the crowds became mesmerized by Jamul's singing as it trickled through the assembled masses. Such was the power of his talented voice—even though it was a recording. People who moments before had been pushing and shoving, edging on the verge of panic, began to slow. Some even stopped to listen, unaware that Jamul was slinking through the shadows toward the helipad.

Falk and Koski exchanged glances as Marco led them through thick brush and high grass. She nodded, feeling her skin tingle at the sound. How could someone who sang with such amazing sweetness design plans of mass destruction and assist in carrying them out? She thrust through the brush wondering if sweetness was only a hair's breath away from evil as was genius to madness.

Marco pointed. "Over there. You can see the roof of the nursery building."

Falk nodded. "We go over the fence?"

"No," Marco answered. "Stay close."

Like an infiltration squad, the trio wended their way between trees, bushes, old crates, lawn mowers and coiled hoses. Marco held up a warning hand. "There's a hole in the chain-link fence. Follow me."

"Marco, the place is crawling with security," Koski hissed.

"They're busy with the crowds." They were in the nursery yard now with no one around.

"Which way to the helipad?" Falk asked.

"Just beyond the trees we planted."

"With bombs in the roots, right?" Koski muttered.

"So they say."

"Koski, you and Marco move around to the amphitheater. Stewart said he was near the stage. Tell him I'm going to cover the helicopter pad in case Jamul decides to leave early. Advise him to be watchful for anyone with a bio weapon. It'll be small and probably hidden in one hand. Anyone pointing in an aggressive manner could be a shooter."

When the organ music faded, it was the cue for the choir to sing as a unit, allowing the massed voices their own moment of glory. Jamul dreaded the moment. There wasn't going to be a choir. Everyone had been ordered to leave. The organ had faded when suddenly the sound of two clear and strong voices reached Jamul's ears. Looking back, he saw the young women in white cassocks slowly walking on stage.

Two more entered from stage right then three and four, singing and growing stronger in voice as the choir grew. They were coming back in groups, slowly getting into their position as a choir —defiant to any terrorist threat. The organ softly picked up the melody.

The television cameras jockeyed for position to air the dramatic scene. The announcers were excitedly telling the world what was happening. Their voices reflected the dramatic moment as the singers grew in numbers until almost the entire choir was in place singing like they never had before.

Koski and Marco watched the choir's amazing appearance as they walked toward the front of the stage.

"I thought everyone was ordered to leave," Marco said.

"They were," Koski mumbled as she saw Stewart waving to them to join him.

Stewart's first words were, "Where's Falk?" Koski brought him up-to-date. Stewart looked tense.

"Jamul's gone. No one can find him."

The first bomb exploded and earth and rocks rained down as people screamed and ran. The choir, who only moments before were blissfully singing, now crouched in horror as they shielded themselves from falling debris.

The roar of explosions turned hundreds of people into a pushing and shoving mob fighting their way out through the main entrances. Few noticed the zombie-like figures pointing randomly at the exodus as they triggered their deadly bio guns. Mind-altered and confused, not seeing their targets on stage, they blindly fired at anything that moved.

Gully, with the special police detachment, saw them and immediately knew what was happening. Their targets, the religious clerics, were gone, hustled out at the first warning. Gully knew he'd never be paid in full. He'd been abandoned, left to fend for himself. The pope had been his target.

More deafening explosions roared in rapid succession, shaking the Bowl. Those inside the amphitheater fell as shrapnel, rocks and pieces of trees scythed through bone and flesh. The result was far more devastating than had been expected. Rather than being a means to panic people while the mind-altered zombies took out the clerics, the bombs had created a massacre.

Falk was almost at the helipad when red and orange geysers erupted from the ground a hundred feet away. First the blast, then a furnace-like heat blew him to the ground. Jamul had made it unseen to the copter. He snapped on the back-up transmitter and triggered the last sections of trees then started the engine for takeoff. He planned to say he'd been forced at gunpoint by one of the terrorists to fly him out of the Bowl.

Falk shook his head, trying to clear his vision and the ringing in his ears, then staggered to his feet. The clamor of the blades slashing through the air and the whine of the engine spooling up told him Jamul was getting away. Sucking in drafts of cold morning air, he ran toward the helicopter as it started to lift. Quickly he leapt onto the landing skids and jammed himself into a position that allowed him to grasp a stanchion protruding from the underside of the cabin. Blade rotation increased. The sound screamed in his ears as the chopper rose, swaying slightly before gaining altitude then moved through the air with surging speed.

Falk looked back on the chaos below, praying Koski was safe.

Jamul banked the helicopter in an arc toward the coast. If Jamul was heading to his yacht, it was only a matter of minutes before he set down on the stern. If he decided on going further abroad, Falk knew he'd be in deeper trouble.

Chapter 62

Koski, Marco and Stewart had dropped to the ground as the first bombs exploded. Koski gazed skyward as a helicopter lifted off, already vanishing into the smoke from the explosions. If she hadn't been aware that Falk was near the helipad she might never have noticed it.

The semi-darkness made it impossible for her to see someone hunched beneath the cabin. Then the copter was gone, the sound of its engine diminishing as it vanished into the clouds of black smoke rising from the trees.

"That could be Jamul," Koski yelled to Stewart. "Contact the police helicopters."

Stewart squinted up. "Too late, Koski. They're on a secure frequency. By the time we got through he'd be long gone."

"He's already long gone. We have to do something. Joe could be in that copter."

Stewart realized she might be right. If Falk had gotten close enough, he'd have made every effort to board the aircraft. If he had, he'd have stopped Jamul from leaving.

"Let's get over to the pad," Stewart rasped.

After searching the area, they knew Falk was gone. "Jamul could have forced him on board at gun point."

"Jamul would have shot him like a dog," Marco said. "He's not the kind to take prisoners."

"Not unless he needed a hostage," Koski said quietly.

Stewart leaned more toward Koski's theory and quickly reached for his cell phone. Within seconds, he was in contact with the Coast Guard at the Marina.

"This is Stewart. Put me through to the officer in charge immediately." He looked back at the shattered ruins of the seating area and the medical teams at work. "Lieutenant, has the helicopter returned to the *Caviare?*" Stewart's face tightened. "*Caviare* sailed over an hour ago?" Clicking off, he turned to Koski. "Your theory could be right. You two follow me."

Fog hugged the Pacific and reached inland like a gray wrinkled blanket. They should be over the Marina by now. How would Jamul make a landing? Falk stared down at the thick swirling vapor. The copter stayed on course, not attempting to descend. Where was the damn fool going? A rendezvous at sea?

The chill factor troubled him. His grip was weakening and he had to concentrate every second to stay in place as icy numbness slowly crept through his body.

There was a break in the overcast for a few seconds and he glimpsed the Pacific and knew they had flown long enough to pass over the coast. There was only one place to head for in such a small aircraft—Catalina Island, thirty miles west of the Marina. He knew he couldn't hold on much longer, then he heard a sweet sound. The engine pitch altered slightly and he felt a change in speed. Jamul was preparing to land.

Seconds later they were in deep wet clouds. The rotors were swirling the opaque murkiness around him until suddenly everything became clear and the rising sun welcomed them back to normalcy. Below, Falk saw the top part of Catalina Island as Jamul swept over the western edge of the coast. It was a lonely stretch far from Avalon and the hustle of tourists and commerce.

A two-lane road ran along the edge of the island. No sign of life among the scrub brush. Jamul had chosen a deserted landing place. Gently, like a butterfly, the copter touched down without a shudder. Falk couldn't move. He wanted to roll off, find a place to hide. It was no use. He could hardly release his grip from the stanchion.

The rotor's blades wound down and he heard the cabin door click open. The whoosh-whoosh of the blades sounded like a giant scimitar twirling over his head ready to execute anyone in their area. Falk watched as Jamul's legs came into view, then stood beside the copter. He immediately dropped into a squat and stared at Falk.

"Enjoy the ride did you?" A nine millimeter automatic rested casually on his knee. "I don't think you can raise your hands so stay as you are. A car will be here in a few minutes and we'll take a ride into Avalon. I have friends waiting."

Chapter 63

Stewart led Koski and Marco back to the security point inside the nursery. Koski, trotting eagerly to keep up, reminded him of the equipment she and Falk had installed beneath the water line and attached to the sloop's rudder. "We can transmit and cut electrical power—stop her dead in the water."

"I don't want to stop her yet. I want the yacht shadowed." Stewart's cell chirped. "Stewart here. Right. Get a fix on the call. I'll get back to you." He pocketed the phone. "DHS received an anonymous call saying Jamul and an agent by the name of Falk were being held hostage."

"Held where?" Koski asked.

"They didn't say and we didn't have time to get a fix on the call."

"Trail the boat until they're in international waters then attack," Marco suggested.

"No. We can switch it off like a toy whenever we want," Stewart replied. Koski knew he was right.

"Jamul was tight with the Arabs, like I told you. Why take him hostage?" Marco asked.

"Jamul's tight with everyone from the President down to his

fan clubs," Koski muttered.

Marco snorted. "It could be a trick saying Jamul's been taken hostage. How do we know? They could say that to give him an alibi, make him look like a hero. Hey, man, the world would rather believe he's a hostage than an al-Qaida terrorist."

"I like your thinking, Marco." Stewart slapped him on the shoulder.

"If the world finds out Jamul *is* part of al-Qaida his career is over," Koski added.

Stewart shrugged. "Maybe he's ready to receive adoration from a different section of the world. He still has money and power to hide anywhere, live unseen, like Bin Laden and others did. People like Jamul live only to cause problems in the name of Islam. We have to get them both back any way possible."

A car drove up the deserted coast road and stopped. Falk sat in the grass beside the helicopter. A man exited the car, moved quickly across the open ground and exchanged words with Jamul. He walked over to Falk and kicked him in the ribs. He pulled Falk's arms behind his back and snapped on a pair of handcuffs then calmly walked to the copter and climbed in.

"Go to the car," Jamul ordered. Falk got stiffly to his feet as the sound of the chopper winding up rattled through the air.

Jamul followed, covering Falk with his automatic, and opened the back door of the car. "Get in." Jamul entered the front passenger seat, the barrel of his gun aimed at Falk's chest. "Sit back and enjoy the ride."

Chapter 64

Koski paced anxiously in front of the security desk. Marco was slumped on a chair with his eyes half-closed. He opened them at the sound of Stewart's voice.

"When Jamul's helicopter took off, we know he headed west. That's all we know. Fog has socked in the coast. He could be anywhere."

"West could mean Catalina," Marco offered. "How far could he go in that little bird, man?"

"West also can mean any of the Channel Islands. He may have headed west then turned north up the coast. We have a full alert out for *Caviare* and the copter."

"That damn boat could be a decoy to make us do just what we're doing—tracking it—while Jamul and Joe head in another direction," Koski added.

"Understood," Stewart said edgily. "We'll have to wait."

Stewart earnestly updated Koski and Marco.

"Seemingly, the *Caviare* was infiltrated during the evacuation when security was recalled for duties at the Bowl, leaving only a skeleton crew. As it stands, the focus is on getting the dead and wounded out of the Bowl. No official word on Jamul's whereabouts yet."

"Are they going to say he was taken hostage?" Koski asked.

"Yes."

"I still think Jamul nailed Falk and hauled his ass off to Catalina," Marco muttered.

Koski turned angrily. "Agent Falk is not in the habit of having his ass hauled anywhere he doesn't want to go, Marco. Remember that."

"Yeah, well he might have this time. There's heavy fog over the coast. No sign of them since the fog lifted. I bet Jamul hightailed it to Catalina. As a hostage, he'll have the public on his side and rooting for him to be found. He lays low for a week or two then lets someone find him and it's welcome home, Jamul."

Stewart grunted. "I have a helicopter taking two DHS specialists to Catalina from the Marina to join others on the island. I've ordered they stop here first. I want you and Marco on board."

Koski brightened. "You know where they are?"

"No, but I agree with Marco. Catalina is a good place to start."

Marco cut a glance to Stewart. "I like the way you think, man."

The sound of a copter landing out on the pad stopped any further conversation.

"Let's go. That's them now," Koski said.

Greg Grant had raised hell at the Coast Guard station after his car was stolen. He phoned his boss in Washington, complaining of no cooperation in assisting him with his investigation. His boss told him he was off the case until fit to work. No way was he going to represent the DHS sitting in an electric scooter with his leg in a cast.

Nonetheless, Grant was determined to prove he wasn't going to fail on his first assignment. Now, with the carnage at the Bowl, he wouldn't give up. He pocketed his cell. No one would know he was off the job.

"Nell, I've been ordered to the Bowl to do whatever I can to help."

"We don't have a car," she reminded him.

"Tell me about it! You and that Koski woman go to the john, she leaves you locked in, my car's stolen and we're stuck here while the Hollywood Bowl is blown apart." He glanced out the window in time to see two uniformed security guards entering the building.

"Follow me." Grant wheeled out of the room to the front office as the men entered.

"DHS," Grant announced. "We're on special assignment and need transport to the Bowl. Can you guys help us?"

One of the men, a burly sergeant, looked surprised. Grant waved his ID. "Check it out."

A Coast Guardsman came around from the front desk. "He's for real, scooter and all. She's his aide," he said, indicating Nell.

"Jesus! I've heard of walking wounded but this takes the cake."

"Well, can you help?" Grant asked.

"We've just been ordered to board a Coast Guard helicopter and fly to Catalina with one stop at the Bowl. You're in luck."

"Let's go."

Koski and Marco stood at the edge of the landing pad as a Sikorsky VH-60N chopper touched down amid a whirl of dust. The door slid open and a uniformed man waved, indicating for them to get aboard.

They ran across the concrete apron. Koski grabbed the soldier's hand and he hauled her inside. A second later Marco was on the floor beside her and the door slammed shut. Koski felt the aircraft shudder as it swayed upward. She shrugged into a safety harness, buckled up and settled with her back against the bulkhead.

When Koski finally checked out their surroundings, she couldn't believe her eyes. Lashed on the opposite side of the copter sat Greg Grant, an electric scooter beside him! Marco's eyes widened as he recognized Nell sitting a few feet away. The noise was too loud for them to converse. All four stared at each other in disbelief.

Chapter 65

Officer Robert Gulliver's only contact with the plan had been through Massy. Now, standing in the Hollywood Bowl amid the aftermath of the explosions, he knew he'd been a cop too long to think his part in the plan would be forgotten. He was a marked man. Marked by whoever had masterminded the Easter morning carnage.

The bio weapon attached to his finger felt cumbersome inside his riot glove. His squad had moved to one of the exits to oversee the exodus of those able to walk out of the Bowl.

Massy had treated him like a servant, overbearing and cynical of a cop who sold out. She had underestimated Gully's ability to uncover a few facts about her. Cops had means and he used them to his advantage. He learned the doctor somehow was associated with Jamul. She frequently visited Jamul's Marina Del Rey penthouse and owned a boat at the Marina. She'd get her money if she'd survived the bombings. If she didn't get paid she'd use blackmail. Celebrities hated bad press.

Jamul's car drove five miles along the coast road before it turned onto a narrow road and headed inland. A few miles later, it came to a stop in front of a decrepit house with a red tiled roof that had turned an ugly orange color over time.

Falk surveyed the place. "Hope that dump has a toilet. I've gotta go."

Jamul led the way through several nearly empty rooms to a kitchen at the back of the house. "Take his cuffs off," he told the driver. "Show the way. Stay outside and leave the door open."

Falk eyed a tiny window with a grimy cracked pane set high in the whitewashed wall of the washroom and knew there was no escape. He noticed a slither of dried up soap on the floor as he was washing his hands. He scooped it up and put it in his pocket.

When Falk exited the restroom, he was surprised to see a gray-haired Jamul dressed in a natty business suit.

"We're ready, Falk. You'll be in a wheelchair."

Brasinov pushed an old wheelchair toward Falk. "Sit down." They all left through the back door and walked toward a minivan parked behind the house.

"Cover his legs." Jamul tossed a blanket to the driver. "Snap these cuffs to the right-hand arm rest, down low." The driver obeyed and yanked Falk forward and to one side as the cuffs snapped low on the armrest, almost at seat level. With the rug covering any sign of the metal manacles, to a passerby he looked like a twisted cripple.

"We mustn't forget his hat." Jamul slipped a size large LA Dodgers cap onto Falk's head. It slipped down, resting on the bridge of his nose. "Perfect. Let's go, Mikhail."

Mikhail Brasinov moved forward, gripping the wheelchair handles, and followed behind Jamul.

Chapter 66

Catalina has only one airport. The Airport in the Sky was a quarter mile from the Sikorsky as it settled down onto a restricted pad located away from general air traffic.

As the rotors slowed and it became possible to hear, Grant yelled, "I can have you arrested for running out on me. You know that!"

"Yeah, right," Koski replied. "If I'd have known you were on this aircraft I'd have waited for another one." She turned to the two DHS men.

"Let him get off himself. He's on sick leave and a little out of his mind. If you take any orders from him you'll both be up for aiding an incompetent in time of a national emergency." She jumped down from the aircraft and Marco followed.

"Stay with him, Nell," Marco shouted over his shoulder. "You heard what she said."

As Koski and Marco left, they heard Grant bellowing threats at the top of his voice.

"Is what you just said true?" Marco asked.

"Don't know. I had to say something to keep him from tagging along."

A tall man, a major with the Army Corps of Engineers, walked toward them and touched his cap in salute. "Agent Koski?"

"Yes."

"Tom Stewart asked me to meet you and," he looked at Marco, "Marco, right?" Marco nodded. "Follow me. I have a car waiting."

The major brought them up to speed on the drive into Avalon. There was a security team at the airport checking all incoming and outgoing aircraft. The Coast Guard and local police were already checking every boat that was at anchor or tied to a mooring, and, following airport procedure, all incoming and outgoing sea traffic.

"This is going to be a time-consuming job as you might have guessed. Easter, the town is full of tourists and college kids, swelling the population by thousands. If the terrorists have landed on the island and are holding Jamul and Agent Falk hostage, it'll be difficult to find them."

Koski stared out the window. Catching a brief glimpse of the harbor, she saw what looked like a floating forest. If the authorities were going to check every boat they were in for a tough job indeed. As if reading her mind the major said, "As I mentioned, Easter is always a busy time in Avalon."

Koski motioned to the crammed harbor, "How do you expect to check every boat? There must be hundreds."

The major gave a short laugh. "Very carefully. And don't forget aircraft up at the airport."

"You think Jamul and Joe are being kept hostage here on Catalina Island, major?"

"No one knows. DHS is checking several other possible locations."

Viewers around the globe watched the televised reports from the Hollywood Bowl in disbelief as explosions gushed amid the exiting crowds with sickening detail. Vatican City announced the Holy Father's survival as a miracle.

The abduction of Jamul and a government agent from the

Bowl by the unknown terrorist group and the declaration he was now a hostage mystified everyone. Why are terrorists holding a man like Jamul hostage? He was a recognized Islamic working closely with religions around the world to bring peace and understanding to all. The Easter Morning Sunrise Service was to have been his crowning moment in bringing the world together in an understanding of cooperation between Christian diversity. Nations wondered who had planned and carried out such an evil attack. Was Jamul alive or dead?

Jamul watched the television coverage with mixed feelings. It was not up to the cell's original expectations. Nonetheless, millions now knew that America was still vulnerable to an attack, anytime, anywhere. Playing a hostage was perfect cover for his part in the deadly act. He planned to remain out of sight until he organized and staged a dramatic escape from his captors and emerged a hero.

Two weeks before the Bowl attack the cell had made arrangements for Jamul to enter a private convalescent home for the mentally impaired. This was an expensive retreat in the hills overlooking Avalon, where families of the rich and famous hid away their embarrassing relatives. Jamul's stay was to be in a lavish private section of the home.

Chapter 67

Officer Robert Gully was aware the bio weapon was worth plenty. He'd never see the other half of the money he was promised, but if he sold the weapon to the right people it would more than compensate the loss.

Gully, present when the bio weapons used by the "zombies"

to fire the gas into the crowds were collected by the police, took a silent delight in seeing LAPD experts baffled about what they were. He stood among his fellow officers with the latest model of the biolaser strapped snugly under the index finger of his gloved right hand. He knew it was only a matter of time before the word got out about the new tools of destruction. Then they would remain under heavy guard in the LAPD weapons lab.

Certain people in the LA underworld would be very interested in a demonstration.

The major clicked off his cell as the car came to a stop outside the Coast Guard station. "No helicopters landed at the Catalina airport during the time Jamul's copter was hijacked. Authorities are checking the surrounding areas for possible sightings."

Koski nodded as she viewed the crowded harbor. The sun was up and the fog had burned off, heralding what promised to be a bright sunny day. Bright for some, she thought as she followed the major toward the office. In all the confusion at the Bowl, the helicopter could have gone in any direction. They might be miles from the landing place. The thought nagged at her as they entered the building.

Marco remained silent throughout the journey. Now he knew the reason Stewart went along with his suggestion that they check out Catalina. It happened during his debriefing with Stewart after the escape from the house with Pegmanti. He mentioned his conversation with Massy and the time when she refused to return his radio, saying he might be assigned to a place where the buffalo roamed.

Not until they were at the site of Jamul's vanished helicopter at the Bowl and he'd mentioned the copter might have headed for Catalina did he recall a school trip to the island. He'd seen a herd of wild buffalo roaming the hillsides. Marco had caught the sudden realization in Stewart's eyes when he mentioned Catalina. Now here they were.

"Marco, you look like you're going to fall asleep." Koski's voice brought him back to earth.

"Uh, yeah. I was thinking, that's all."

"Stay alert. We're going to a briefing."

A hastily arranged meeting room was set up in the Coast Guard station. Several people were already seated when the trio entered. Koski and Marco sat at the rear of the room as the major walked to a battered podium and introduced himself and the others.

"As you are all aware the country is on high alert. I've been sent to organize search parties to go through every water craft in the harbor." A groan of disbelief filled the room.

"I know. Naval personnel from Long Beach and Marines from Camp Pendleton will comb the hills and valleys of the island. Houses, stores and businesses will be searched by local police and a detachment of Military Police being flown in from the Embarcadero in San Francisco.

"DHS will also be working the same venues. The reason Catalina was picked as the most likely location of the terrorists holding Jamul and probably FBI Agent Joseph Falk is because of a clue received during a debriefing several hours ago. Nothing is for certain but it's the best we have to go on at the moment."

Koski leaned in to Marco. "*You* were debriefed by Stewart.

Was it you?"

Marco whispered, "Later."

Koski glowered but kept quiet.

The major ended by saying they had a lot of ground to cover and no time to waste. He glanced at his watch. "We'll meet back here in one hour."

The major rejoined Koski and Marco. "Arrangements have been made for you two to stay at the Hotel Villa Portofino on the sea front. I doubt you'll have much time to spend there. When you do, you'll each have a room in which to catch some sleep. In the meantime, we can grab a bite of breakfast from the Coast Guard. C'mon."

Koski and Marco followed as the major fell in step beside a Coast Guardsman who led them to breakfast.

"Tell me what you know, Marco," Koski hissed. In the space of time it took to get to the mess hall, Marco filled her in. "That's a hell of a slim clue! I can't believe Stewart went for it," Koski muttered.

"It's all we have. If we didn't have that we'd be still wondering where to start."

Koski knew he was right.

Chapter 68

Falk was in the wheelchair, strapped in the back of the specially fitted minivan, unable to speak. He'd been drugged with a strong opiate after being loaded aboard. Jamul still acted the part of a white-haired old man as he sat next to the driver. The rear of the van was windowless. The drive took under an hour. Finally they came to a stop and the back door was flung open.

The driver operated an electric lift and lowered Falk to ground level. Jamul said a few words to Brasinov who nodded and shoved Falk up a ramp and through the entrance of a fine-looking old building. Falk was able to catch a quick glimpse of the harbor in the distance and a view of the famous casino near the harbor wall.

Two nurses dressed in white and a distinguished-looking man in a pinstriped suit, Dr. Victor Richardson, greeted them with much bowing and scraping. Immediately Falk knew they were in a very private, very expensive nursing home.

"Good morning, Mr. Rashantan. We are honored to receive you," Richardson gushed as he leaned over Falk. The nurses beamed their welcome, stopping just short of a curtsey.

Jamul quickly said, "Mr. Rashantan is lightly sedated at the moment. My name is Mr. Saba. You will communicate through me at all times."

"We have everything in order, Mr. Saba, as instructed by your people in Johannesburg," Richardson purred.

Jamul smiled, thankful that his friends at the curio shop had made the arrangements. The preparations demanded absolute secrecy.

"Mr. Rashantan and his party aren't to be disturbed under any circumstances. Mr. Rashantan is here in the United States for top-secret government meetings that are to take place later in Washington, D.C. The layover on Catalina was designed to keep the media out of the picture and the need for top security."

Dr. Richardson was more than happy to oblige when

informed how much he would earn for his cooperation.

"Of course, Mr. Saba. I understand," he replied. The doctor quickly assured Jamul all was under control. They would be in a wing that was totally apart from the general population.

Falk bent and twisted in his wheelchair, his hands and feet covered by the heavy rug. He wanted to yell at the doctor to call the cops, DHS, anyone.

Marco finished his breakfast, sat back and wiped his lips. "If Jamul is faking his abduction and hiding somewhere on the island, I'll bet it's first class."

"What do you mean?"

"That dude just does things like that—best of everything."

"And if he is a hostage where is he?"

"Don't know. No one does, right?"

"I think Joe tried to stop Jamul and something went wrong."

"You got pissed when I said that."

"Well, I've had time to think."

"Good. You want more coffee?"

The major came to their table. "What do either of you know about a guy called Grant, says he's DHS?"

Koski shook her head. "Oh, no. Why?"

"I got a call saying he's raising all kinds of hell at the airport. He says you're supposed to be working for him."

"Call Tom Stewart. He'll put you straight. Okay?"

"I don't have time for this, Agent Koski."

"Just one call. Trust me." The major blew out his cheeks and stormed across the room.

"C'mon, Marco. Time for us to move out." She pushed back

her chair. Marco shrugged, gulped down his coffee and followed her.

Koski looked at the passing tourists enjoying their Easter holiday. "We passed an airport bus on the way down. Take it and find out where Grant and Nell are. Get her on her own." The sun was warming the air and moving the morning on. "You'll have to find where to catch the bus."

"No problem. What'll I do when I get Nell?"

"Both of you get back on a bus, go to our hotel and stay there. Grant will be on his own with the scooter. It'll at least slow him down. You do still have the cell phone Stewart gave you?" Marco tapped his shirt pocket. "Good. Give me a call when you get back to the hotel."

Marco mingled with the tourists and headed down the street toward the waterfront.

Marco was right, Koski thought. Jamul *would* seek a luxurious place to hole up in. Koski shivered slightly and fatigue swept over her. It was a little after ten. How long since she'd had a full night's sleep? At the Academy, they taught that sleep deprivation led to mistakes. She'd return to the hotel and instruct the desk to call her at four. Six hours sleep would make all the difference, bring her back up to speed. Besides, there were plenty of aggressive people out there searching.

Koski took a cab back to the hotel. Leaning back with her eyes half-closed, she was on the edge of sleep when the cab braked for a red light. Koski glanced over to a vehicle stopped beside them. The driver's face brought back a picture as sharp as if flashed onto a screen. It was the guy who was sitting in the Rav4 outside the hotel in West LA when she returned from her morning run.

"Driver, follow that Land Rover next to us. Let him get ahead then stay back. I don't want him to know he's being followed."

The cabby was startled and half-turned to look over his shoulder.

Koski held up her badge. "Do it now." Luckily there was little traffic and the driver quickly followed her orders.

"Driver, stay at least three cars back." They drove along a winding road leading into the hills. "Where does this road lead?" Koski asked.

"Heads out of town, past the Wrigley Mansion. You can see it up on the hill there."

She craned her neck and snatched a glimpse of the old house once owned by the chewing gum magnate. The traffic in front of them was thinning.

"What's up ahead?"

"Older houses, a couple of hotels then nothing until you get to the airport."

Koski leaned forward. "Deluxe hotels?"

"No. Mostly older houses that were converted into hotels over the years. Tourist hotels, you know."

Koski still saw the Land Rover about a quarter mile ahead.

"You part of the big search we're having?" the driver asked.

"I came over for some R&R. That guy ahead looks like my ex. He owes back pay on my alimony. I want to be sure."

The driver's eyes looked at her in the rearview. She knew he didn't believe a word.

"Could be your lucky day and here I was thinking the FBI

could find anyone, anytime."

"Not true. We wouldn't need a most wanted list if it was."

The driver grunted and sped up as the Land Rover vanished around a bend ahead. Once through the curve, Koski saw the road ahead was empty.

Chapter 69

Falk sat on the bare wooden floor of a small stuffy attic. He was handcuffed to the foot of a metal-framed bed still shackled by leg irons. One hand was free from the manacles to allow him to eat and drink a meager lunch of bread and cheese. He'd taken stock of his surroundings and knew he was in a formidable prison with a thick oak door to the side, and a small skylight window above, the skylight ten feet overhead mounted flush in the ceiling.

The house was a stoutly constructed building from the days when stone and oak were the main materials and pride of workmanship mattered.

Falk had seen the luxury on the floors below in Jamul's quarters as he was hustled up to the attic. Now, as he chewed the remainder of his lunch, he knew he must escape. The longer he was a prisoner, the less chance he had of staying alive.

He sipped a mouthful of water from a tin mug. Falk removed the sliver of soap from his pocket, held it in the palm of his hand and spat a little of the water on it. Moving his free hand close to his cuffed one he tipped the water and soap into his upturned palm and rubbed both hands together, softening the soap. Then slowly massaging the slimy mixture onto his shackled wrist he started to manipulate it, pulling back slightly to free his hand. He repeated this several times, gritting his teeth against the pain.

There was only a little soap left but his hand was almost free. A few more tugs and he'd be out. The skin was raw and bleeding when he finally slipped loose. He washed the blood from his wrist with the last drop of water. Wasting no time, he tilted the bed nearly vertically against the wall beneath the skylight. Using the bed as a ladder, he inched upward, the leg irons slowing his movements.

The bed was shaky. Each movement made it shimmy. It could slide sideways at any moment and crash against the wooden floor, alerting those below. Inch by inch Falk eased upward, his eyes fastened on the glass skylight. Every fiber of his body was centered on getting to the window. He reached up, his fingers scant inches below the edge of the frame. The bed creaked and for a moment Falk thought it would go over. He reached out, touched the wall and waited. It held. He inched upward again. This time his fingertips touched the frame but he still needed at least another foot so he could work on the skylight and open it.

He saw the iron bar used to push open the window. Three holes were punched into it to enable someone to adjust the airflow into the attic. He needed to stand on the top of the bed. There was no room for error once he reached out and grabbed the iron device. He had to get the window open, pull himself up and through the opening.

He took a deep breath and steadied himself against the wall then reached up, grasped the iron lever and pushed. Nothing. It was jammed. Evidently the window hadn't been opened for years. Falk closed his eyes. His body ached with tension and fatigue. He had to open the son of a bitch—he had to.

He thought of smashing the glass with his shoe. No good. He could lose his balance and the sound of breaking glass was out. Holding the lever with one hand, he reached up and used the heel of his hand against the wooden framework. Flakes of dried paint dropped past his face. He hit against the frame three, four, five times and felt it move ever so slightly. Switching hands, he tackled the other side of the frame and felt it move a little more.

Encouraged, he thumped harder. The window opened half an inch then he felt a draft of air flow past his face. He pushed. Slowly the window yielded. With a final shove, it flung wide open, back against the roof. His fingers grasped the frame's edge as he sucked in cool air. He remained that way for a few seconds, gathering his energy for the arm-wrenching pull up and out of the window.

Focusing all his strength into his arms and shoulders, he took a firm grip and pulled himself up through the small opening until he had his head and shoulders outside. He slid onto the slate roof. He lay flat against the tiles a few feet from a brick chimney stack and sucked in lung-filling gasps. He crawled to the stack and sat with his back against the structure. He'd made it onto the roof but it was just the beginning of a dangerous journey to the ground and his escape.

Cursing the leg irons, he reached down and removed his leather-soled shoes. He tied the laces together and hung them around his neck. He needed secure traction. Confinement of the leg irons gave little room for error on a slate rooftop. In a crouched position, he moved to the ridge top and inched to the far end of the house, away from the rooms containing Jamul's entourage. He moved down the roof toward the edge at the back of the building that overlooked a large garden thirty feet below.

He quickly scanned the area. On the right was a kitchen garden with what looked like a tool or storage shed. Several rakes leaned against the wall. A wooden door was set into the brick wall. From his point of view he could see it led into a formal garden and beyond that a row of oak trees. He turned his attention to the immediate problem of getting off the roof in one piece.

Falk was relieved when he saw a sturdy iron gutter. He followed it along the eaves until he came to a drainpipe. Lying face down on the roof, he reached over, grasped the gutter and shook it. Solid as a rock. He gave silent thanks to the days when building materials were made to last.

Slowly he turned his body so he faced up toward the ridge, carefully lowered his legs over the edge, moving his feet as best he could in their restraints, trying to locate the drain. Inch by inch he lowered himself until he felt the drainpipe with the toes of his stocking feet, and edge of the iron gutter across his stomach. A few more inches and he'd be over the edge. Gripping the gutter, Falk lowered his body further until his feet were on either side of the drainpipe, the chain between the anklets conforming to the cylindrical pipe.

Grasping the gutter-to-drain connection with both hands, he started down. Suddenly he felt a tug and looked up to see one of his shoes jammed in the gutter. Quickly he reached up with one hand and tried to free it. There wasn't time, so he rotated his head and neck until the other shoe was swung free and dangled over the edge.

"Damn it." He started his descent hoping no one was in the garden to see him or hear the rasp of the chain as it slid down the pipe. When his feet touched the soil of a flowerbed, Falk shuffled toward a row of bushes and hunkered down.

Chapter 70

"We lost him!" Koski exclaimed, scanning the empty road ahead.

"I don't think so," the cabby replied. "See that row of trees ahead on the right? There's a driveway leading up to a private hospital. He must have turned in there. There's no other way he could have gone."

"Are you sure? I don't see any hospital."

"Yeah. I've been there a couple of times. Very secluded. The driveway is over a half mile long, big old house. Locals say it's a high-priced loony bin."

"Are there outside guards at the house?"

"Don't know. Never saw any when I was there. They do have closed-circuit television cameras at the gate. Do you still think that guy was your ex?"

She shook her head. "Guess not. I can't see him in a place like that."

"Like I said, it's high-priced."

"How high?"

"Folks say you could get a week at Betty Ford for what it costs for a day in that place."

"Then it wasn't my ex. He couldn't even get a job in a place like that. Let's get to my hotel."

Once in her room, Koski called Marco. "Where are you?"

"On the airport bus, almost back in town. We'll be at the hotel in five minutes."

"Fine. Come up when you arrive."

The excitement of what might turn out to be Jamul's possible hideout had removed all thoughts of sleep. She headed for the bathroom and a quick shower.

She was drying her hair when there was a knock at the door. "That you, Marco?"

"Me and Nell."

Koski opened the door and Marco and Nell entered. "You sounded excited," Marco said.

"I am. Sit down and listen up." She brought them up-to-date, including about the man in the Rav4.

"You think Jamul could be hiding out in that place?"

"I do. That guy in the Land Rover was my tip-off. He was outside our place in Hollywood then turns up here on Catalina and drives to a secluded place in the hills."

"You see him drive onto the grounds?"

"No." She twined the towel into a turban. "He was in front of us and when we went around a bend his car had vanished. The only place he could have gone was up to the house. Even the cabby thought so."

"And now you want to call in the troops and head out there?"

"Not exactly. If we go busting in with troops and police, and Joe is being held prisoner, his life wouldn't be worth a damn.

They'd kill him."

"*You* want to go in and find out, right?"

"You're close. I need you and Nell as a diversion to allow me to get in and look around."

Falk glanced up at the roof and he saw his shoes hanging from the rain gutter. Crawling and keeping bushes between himself and the house, he wormed toward a wooden shed. A place to hide, take stock, and, if he was lucky, find something to cut the damn chain off the leg irons.

The door wasn't locked and several seconds later he was inside. It took a few moments for his eyes to adjust to the gloomy interior as he squinted around. He knew once they discovered he escaped, all hell would break loose.

There was the usual collection of garden tools and a small workbench. As he checked a dark corner, he noticed a set of bolt cutters half hidden behind a sack of mulch. He snatched them up and after three attempts with the cumbersome tool he was free.

On the back of the door was a set of raunchy-looking, mud-splattered Bib and Brace overalls. A straw gardening hat with a wide brim hung over them on the same nail. He decided he could make an escape disguised as a gardener. What better way than to wander through the grounds with a rake or hoe.

Falk unhooked the overalls, shrugged into them and pulled on the hat. Now he needed tools to look the part. He found a hoe and a rake then the best item of all, a pair of Wellington boots. He tipped them over to make sure there wasn't a spider's nest inside, shook them and noticed they were a size bigger than he usually wore. He pulled them on and stuffed the severed chains down among the old tools in the workbench drawer. At least now he could move in a more normal fashion.

Tugging the brim of the hat low across his forehead, he cracked the door open and looked outside—all clear. He shouldered his tools, stepped out into the garden and trudged around the side of the house toward the main entrance. Had no one noticed he'd gone?

Glancing up he saw his shoes still hanging in the gutter. Then he saw the man who'd driven them to the place. He was with another hulkish-looking character. They both looked agitated as they rounded the side of the building looking every way at once.

Falk stopped and began working on a flowerbed with the hoe, head down, paying close attention to his work.

The driver pointed toward Falk, said something and they parted. Hulky headed toward Falk, the driver going off in the opposite direction.

"Hey. You see a guy around here in leg irons?" the man yelled as he got closer to Falk, who didn't look up. He just kept on working, his heart beating faster than normal. Then Hulky was next to him. Falk glanced at him as if he'd just become aware someone was there.

"You deaf? Did you hear what I said?"

Falk shook his head and played dumb.

"Did a man go past here? Leg irons?" Hulky pointed to his own ankles thinking he was trying to communicate with some foreigner whose knowledge of the English language was somewhat lacking.

Falk grinned, nodded, looked at the man's ankles then back at the man and grinned inanely again.

"Dumb shit." Hulky shook his head and pushed past Falk who was once again busy hoeing.

Falk needed to get away from the private wing area. He waited a few minutes then slowly sidled his way toward the front of the building, raking and hoeing as he went. Keeping his eyes on his work, he finally arrived close to the front entrance.

Quickly scanning the car park, he noticed an old pickup truck parked alone, away from a group of up-to-date expensive automobiles. Shouldering his tools, he ambled to the lonely vehicle, threw the rake and hoe into the bed, opened the driver's door and got in. No yells or shouts. The owner of the truck was nowhere around and there wasn't a key.

Falk expertly hot-wired the engine to life, checked the gas gauge, released the hand brake and moved out. He was halfway down the long driveway to the main road when he saw a car approaching. Tugging the brim of his straw hat a little lower, he increased his speed. As the car passed, he took a glance at the occupants and almost swerved off the road. Koski was at the wheel. Both cars screeched to a halt. He saw her turn the car around and pull up beside him.

"Joe! I can't believe this. Get in. Quick."

Falk was in the car in seconds and she had the car in motion before he could close the door. Marco, in the back seat with Nell, leaned forward. "Hey, man. You look like a picture of my mother's brother when he was doing stoop labor in the San Joaquin Valley back in the fifties."

"Thanks."

Koski asked. "Where's Jamul?"

"Back there. Private wing of the hospital." Falk checked the rearview. "What were the odds of you finding me here?"

"A million to one. And if it hadn't been for a comment by a cab driver and a guy in a Land Rover, I'd still be looking."

"Stop the car," Falk ordered.

"What?"

"Stop the car. I don't want to leave the truck standing in the middle of the drive. Soon as they see it abandoned they'll know I was picked up. I'll follow you in the truck."

Chapter 71

The reports to Stewart's office on the mainland from around the island were dismal. DHS was still in a major search mode but with no results and no contact from Koski.

"Jack, every hour that passes diminishes our chances of finding them."

Wolf nodded and looked over at Pease, half-asleep on a sagging couch.

Pease opened one eye. "You said you were going to get me out of the country."

"Well, you'll have to wait a little longer, Mr. Pease. I have some pressing problems at the moment."

Pease sighed and closed his eye.

Marco made a suggestion. "It'd work out better if Nell and I drove the truck and followed you two back to the hotel. That way, if they show up, Nell and I can go off in a different direction while you and Agent Koski get the word to Stewart."

Falk agreed that what Marco said made sense. "Okay, Marco. Let's do it."

There still was no sight of any one heading down the long drive as Marco and Nell got into the truck. Marco was behind the wheel when Falk called out. "Hey, I forgot to mention there was no key. You'll have to…" Before he could finish Marco had the engine running.

"No problem." Marco waited until Koski turned left onto the road then started down the driveway. Glancing into the rearview, he saw a fast-moving Land Rover come suddenly into view. Marco stepped on the gas and turned right at the end of the drive.

The Land Rover was gaining on him and Marco knew he'd be overhauled in minutes.

"They're gaining on us," Nell murmured. Then the rear window shattered as a bullet went through the cab and out the windshield. Pulling to the right, Marco skidded to a halt on the dusty soft shoulder and a cloud of dust obliterated the truck.

"Get on the floor and stay there," Marco yelled. "Don't move."

A thin man and Hulky climbed from the Land Rover and walked toward the truck before the dust settled. That was when Marco backed up fast, hitting both men hard. They went down like chaff.

Marco leapt from the truck. Both men were groaning. Hulky groggily aimed an automatic at Marco who kicked it from his hand, scooped up the weapon and shot the man in the head. Thin man was face down, groaning. As Marco approached him he rolled over—an automatic in his right hand—and fired.

Marco stopped in mid-stride as the impact of the bullet into his right shoulder spun him to one side. Thin man took aim again but Marco, despite the agonizing pain in his shoulder, flung himself at the man on the ground as a second shot grazed his cheek. Marco's knee connected hard into the man's groin. He wrested the weapon from the man's grip with his left hand and shot him in the kneecap.

"Amigos, when the cops arrive tell them you were shot by an Islamic terrorist then show them your green card. Adios."

Nell was out of the truck at the sound of the second shot. She saw Marco getting to his feet and ran toward him.

"I said wait in the truck," Marco yelled.

"I know. Now it's time I got out of the truck. Look at you!"

Marco nodded toward the Land Rover. "Can you drive one of those?"

Nell held him around the waist and walked to the vehicle. "Sure, I can."

"Good. Let's get back into town and update Falk."

"You killed one and kneecapped the other!" Koski exclaimed as she examined Marco's flesh wound. "Another inch to the right and it would have shattered your collar bone."

"I know."

"It happened so fast, Koski. I've never seen anything like it," Nell said breathlessly.

Falk, cleaned up and wearing a change of clothes, came in from the bedroom. "Good job, Marco. I'm proud of you. There's a corpsman on his way over from the Coast Guard to patch you up."

"*I'll* feel proud when I have my money in a Swiss bank."

"I just got off the phone with Stewart. There'll be just a few details to clear up."

"Like what?"

"When Jamul is brought in and we find out who's behind all this."

"Man! Bringing him in won't do a thing except get a lot of big time lawyers into a pissing contest to see who can prove him innocent."

"He has to stand trial, Marco," Koski said.

"Do what you have to do, okay?"

Falk nodded. "You and Nell are going back to the mainland. Stewart's arranged protective custody for you both until we get Jamul. He also assured me he would see you get the original conditions you asked for. You've done a hell of a job, Marco."

The corpsman finished his work, and Marco was strapped into a sling and seated beside Nell.

"Koski and I are heading back to the Coast Guard station," Falk explained. "See you two on the mainland."

Once outside, Koski asked, "What's at the Coast Guard?"

"We're not really going there."

"Where are we going?"

"I know where Jamul is. If we get a task force charging into the hospital he'll simply say he'd been held captive by a terrorist who got away and the public will believe him. That's why I'm going to make Jamul a martyr."

Koski took a deep breath. "You mean…"

"Kill him. The report will read that his militant Islamic captor killed him. Think how the people will react. Their hero murdered."

Koski exclaimed, "You mean it, don't you?"

"Stewart has sanctioned the plan to be carried out by Cerberus, too much chance of a leak if done any other way."

"Where do I fit in, Joe?"

"Other than knowing the plan, you stay with DHS at the Coast Guard station. Stewart's orders."

"We're a team, Joe…"

"You'll have to sit this one out."

Koski's lips tightened. The idea of setting off to kill a man in cold blood worried her. Had Cerberus joined the rest of the world in casual "Wet Jobs"—removing people and manipulating the results to look like murder by someone else? Evidently, the answer was yes.

"When does it happen, Joe?"

"Tonight. I know the inside of the building." He tapped his cell phone. "I'll be notified if he tries to leave."

"I don't like it, Joe."

"I'll be fine." He put his arm around her waist and pulled her close. "I'll be okay." They embraced and kissed. She rested her head on his shoulder and wondered if he'd *asked* to go alone and not involve her in a premeditated murder.

Chapter 72

Officer Robert Gully went off duty while police, fire and emergency crews were placed on red alert until further notice. He returned to the Hollywood station, changed and headed up the San Diego Freeway to the San Fernando Valley. Local news constantly updated details of the attack.

As usual, experts said they had expected something like this. The government hadn't been vigilant and the DHS was unprepared. Gully snapped off the radio.

"Dammed media," Gully said aloud. "When will they learn they're preaching to the choir?"

As he topped the hill on the 405 and started down into the Valley, he checked the time. It was a little before five p.m. Harry Greenwood would still be at his place in Encino. Gully touched his jacket pocket, reassuring himself the bio weapon was safe. Harry would wet his pants when he saw what he had for sale.

The Rainbow Gold and Coin Exchange was on Ventura Boulevard in a two-story stucco office building. Greenwood told his clients he chose the location because it was safer than a storefront.

Customers knew it was for security reasons. Everybody had to buzz to get through the front door. The door opened into a steel cage with three security cameras. Someone on staff verified each client's name and checked it off in the appointment book. No one got past the cage without an appointment.

Gully parked on Havenhurst Avenue and walked down to Ventura. He thought it smarter to stay out of parking garages. They recorded in and out times, and license plate numbers were often captured on video, and he wanted neither.

He skipped the elevator and walked to the second floor. Greenwood's place was at the back of the building, last door on the right. He pushed the button and was buzzed into the cage.

"Hey, Bob. How you doing?" a tinny-shounding voice asked.

Another loud buzz and Gully walked into a thickly carpeted

place of business.

Harry Greenwood was a heavyset man in his fifties. He stood at the glass counter next to a no smoking sign, a double-Corona cigar gripped between his large yellowed teeth. The cigar was unlit.

"Doing okay, Harry," Gully replied. "Like I said on the phone, I've got something to sell."

"You shoulda maybe told me what it was, like I asked you. You may have wasted a trip."

"Don't think so. We need to be in private."

Greenwood's thick eyebrows form a "V." "I can give ya five minutes."

"Fine."

"C'mon." Greenwood opened another electronically operated door and the two went into his office. The staff had already left for the day. Gully waited until Greenwood sat behind his gigantic oak desk. Reaching into his jacket pocket, Gully removed the bio weapon and laid it in the center of the desk.

Greenwood leaned forward in his chair. "What the hell's that? Ya playing games?"

"That, Harry, is worth millions."

"I don't have time for dumb jokes…"

"Wait. Let me demonstrate." Gully moved the weapon around on his forefinger until it was correctly positioned. "Now point at something in the room I can use as a target."

"Hold it. Whaddya mean, target?"

"Something you don't care about like that vase full of imitation flowers on the side table. They look like shit anyway."

Greenwood looked over at the vase and scowled. "Okay. Get to it. I ain't got all day."

Gully wasted no time. He simply pointed at the vase, touched his thumb on the recessed trigger and squeezed. The vase disintegrated.

Greenwood opened his mouth and the cigar fell in his lap. "What the fuck? Whaddya do?"

Gully shrugged. "I just gave you a demonstration of a weapon of mass destruction. It's yours for only $500,000—cash. With your connections you can triple that."

"I'll need details, Bob."

Gully told him all he knew about the weapon. Greenwood could sell it to the Russians or Chinese, who would take it apart and make their own.

Greenwood was impressed. He knew what Gully had would be easy to sell and offered the man $300,000, finally agreeing on $450,000. "Wait here. I'll have to go to the vault. I suppose ya want me to validate yer parking ticket, too," he rasped.

"No need, Harry. I didn't use the parking garage." Greenwood nodded and left the room.

Gully never heard the suppressed .45 Colt that sent a bullet through his head.

Harry Greenwood reholstered his weapon. He'd have one of his boys remove the body. It was good luck for him, and bad for Gully that no one saw Gully enter. He'd locate Gully's car and have it disposed of somewhere across town where it would look like some street punk had stolen and vandalized it. Greenwood picked up the bio weapon and slipped it into his pocket. He'd also make sure Gully's name was removed from the appointment book.

Chapter 73

As the nine millimeter slug went through Gully's head, Joe Falk walked through the main entrance of the private hospital he'd escaped from only hours before. This time he was dressed in suit and tie and carried a slim briefcase.

He crossed to the reception desk and introduced himself as Joseph Stewart, an attorney retained by a family in Pasadena. He was to personally check out the nursing home, meet with the director and confer in detail on all levels of the operation. The family sought assurance of complete secrecy in all matters. Falk handed his card to the receptionist. He had the card made less than an hour earlier at a local print shop.

"I'm sure dropping in unannounced is not the way you usually conduct business," Falk said with a smile. "May I speak with the head man?" He paused. "Or is it head lady?"

The receptionist smiled. "Head man is correct. Doctor Richardson. Doctor Victor Richardson. Please take a seat, Mr. Stewart. He's with someone. It shouldn't be too long."

Falk glanced in the direction the woman indicated before walking over to some couches and chairs arranged around a large fireplace. He noticed an old-fashioned elevator with an ornate iron pointer above the door. The pointer stopped on two.

Eventually the elevator door opened and Richardson stepped out. He paused a moment, saw Falk and headed toward him.

"Good evening. I'm Doctor Victor Richardson. How can I help you?"

Falk unfolded from the chair. "Joseph Stewart. I appreciate you seeing me without an appointment."

"Not at all, Mr. Stewart," he replied. "Let's go to my office."

Once seated, Falk began his speech. "I represent a family who needs to place their aging father into a private facility. The man is a well-known figure in the business world. His family doesn't want anyone to know he's here. The multinational corporation he heads would lose millions if the stockholders even thought their investment was in a company with a sick man at the helm."

Falk continued. "The story being released is that he's going to be fishing in the far west and will be unreachable."

The doctor had heard many reasons over the years and this was as good as any.

"So we're looking at least a month. Correct?"

"Possibly six weeks. It all depends on how much security and secrecy you can provide."

"Of course." Richardson looked as if he was mentally toting up the cost.

Falk took out a small pad and pen. "I jotted down a few questions. I'll ask the questions and make margin notes. It'll be easier for both of us." Falk didn't want him to see the questions were nothing but scrawl he'd jotted before leaving the hotel.

"Fine. I'll walk you through the facilities and you can ask questions as we go."

"Good idea, doctor."

The receptionist glanced up as they walked past, quickly picked up her phone and then tapped a few digits. "We have someone taking a tour with Doctor Richardson. The visitor's business card says he's a lawyer. Do you want me to check out the number?"

Jamul's face darkened. "No. Whoever answers will know we have doubts about him. I'll take care of it." Jamul put down the phone. "He's back," he said softly.

Less than an hour after moving into the private quarters at the hospital, Jamul's men had visited the receptionist and other key personnel. He made them an offer they couldn't resist. They were to report any unusual visitor activity and would be well paid.

Now the call from the front desk was paying off.

"I can get backup," Brasinov said.

Jamul shook his head. He needed to keep a low profile. As long as he had someone with him whom he could kill and say he was the terrorist that had abducted him, he felt secure in fooling the authorities.

"What do I do if it's the agent?"

"Kill him. Find Falk's partner and bring her to me," Jamul said calmly. He went into the bedroom, took a bio weapon from his bedside table and adjusted it beneath the forefinger of his right hand. He removed his old man wig and beard and again was his imposing self.

"As you can see," Richardson suggested, "in no way do we resemble an ordinary nursing home. We think of our patients as guests." He was right. The interior had little resemblance to an institution. It looked more like what it once was—a gracious home.

"Our security is non-intrusive. We have a silent alarm system that is directly connected to police headquarters in Avalon."

They approached a graceful wooden staircase curving to the

upper floors. There were oil paintings of stern-faced men gracing the wall and staring with disdain at anyone using the staircase. Richardson noticed Falk eyeing the portraits as they ascended.

"Past owners. They came with the place."

"Interesting." Falk's mind tried to figure the location of Jamul's quarters from where he was standing. They'd walked down long corridors with many twists and turns and he was no longer sure of his bearings.

"My client instructed me to inquire about private quarters away from the general populace."

Richardson stopped on the stairs and looked over his shoulder. "All of our guests have total privacy. They can remain in their quarters as long as they wish. We have all the amenities possible to take excellent care of them."

They continued and Falk knew as soon as he got the opportunity to look out of one of the upstairs windows he'd be able to orient himself as to where he'd been when he made his escape.

"I was asked to look at rooms with a view, preferably facing south."

The doctor smiled. "Ah, a view of the ocean. Good choice. This floor is perfect." He nodded toward one of the windows. "Allow me to show you." Standing side by side Richardson pointed out details like a tour guide.

"We're located on a high point on the island that's surrounded by over three hundred acres of native land, wild and unspoiled. Buffalo herds, bison to be exact, roam freely. They've been breeding since their transfer from Wyoming in the 1920s to make a western movie. The magnificent beasts remained after the film was completed and over the years became native to the area. We're very proud of them."

In the distance, the Pacific twinkled in the evening sun. Falk recalled catching a glimpse of the sea as he worked his way along the roof ridge before descending the drainpipe. He knew immediately where Jamul's quarters were.

"Another important factor is the lack of traffic or noise. We are five miles from Avalon via the canyon road. Guests can walk or be wheeled about without breathing tainted air. " The doctor's mobile chirped. "Excuse me." Richardson moved away, leaving Falk time to solidify his plan. Jamul was on the third floor of the maximum privacy wing. Evidently Jamul had not attempted to leave after Falk escaped. He must have been secure that he arranged everything so he could remain in seclusion despite any search of the house. If they did close in on him, he could always say he was being held hostage.

"Sorry about that, Mr. Stewart."

Falk waved his hand. "I understand. You're a very busy man." He glanced at his watch. "I wonder if I'd be allowed to wander around on my own to get the feeling of the place. I have hard taskmasters to report to."

"I can have one of my security people accompany you. I'll instruct them to stay back, not bother you but still have you in sight. You do understand?"

"Of course, Doctor. I'd be concerned if you hadn't suggested it. In fact, I'll be sure to mention your concern for your guest's safety and security when I complete my report."

"Very well. I'll see to everything at once." The doctor opened his phone and spoke rapidly. He looked up with a smile. "All taken care of. He's on his way."

Chapter 74

Falk and Richardson gazed out across the hills. They heard footsteps. Turning, Falk saw a pleasant looking young man approaching, late twenties, medium build.

"Here's Keith now," Doctor Richardson said. "He'll answer any questions you have. I'll be in my office if you need me."

"Thanks, Doctor. I won't take long."

"No problem. Regulations you know." Richardson headed to the elevator.

"Are all the rooms on this floor occupied?" Falk asked.

"Most of them," the young man replied. "Let me check. I have a list." He removed a sheet of paper from his pocket. "There are two vacancies on this floor."

"I'd like to see inside to get an idea of the size. The people I work for will have a lot of questions."

"Sure. Which one would you like?"

"Sea view, definitely."

"Okay." He indicated a door down the hall on the right. Removing a bunch of keys, the man opened the door and stood back. "Go ahead. Take your time. Look around."

Falk went straight to the back of the apartment and checked the rear windows that looked out on to well-kept gardens and wild countryside. Moving slightly to his left, Falk could see the edge of the wing he had escaped from. It was one floor higher and much further back from where he stood.

Now he had a better understanding of the layout. He'd have to get rid of the security guard and find a way to get into Jamul's quarters. The heavy drapes still in place gave him an idea. Pulling them aside, he checked the stout cords that opened and closed them. He took a penknife from his pocket, reached up as high as he could and cut the cords down. He wrapped them around his waist and buttoned his jacket. Falk waited so it looked like he was checking all the rooms before he rejoined the guard.

"Nice apartment," Falk said, "but not private enough. Is there anything more remote from the rest of the house?"

"All the apartments are safe and secure, Mr. Stewart."

"I have no doubt. My people want *absolute* privacy. Let's keep looking. Perhaps the top floor will have something to offer."

"Full, sir, I'm afraid. It's always full. They have the best views."

"I noticed there's a wing attached. I saw it from the back windows of the apartment I was just in. Is that part of the hospital?"

"Old and drafty staff quarters. No guest would want to stay there."

Falk shook his head. "Seems like a waste. I'm sure it has a great view and is very private. I think Doctor Richardson is missing a bet not using it for his patients."

"You'd have to talk to him about that, sir."

"I will. I'll walk through the third floor and that'll be all, I think." Falk pointed to the elevator. "Let's ride up."

The man pulled open the elevator door and stood aside. Falk stepped back in the car and unbuttoned his jacket. He removed the cord from around his waist as the man busied himself closing the door and attending to the old manual controls. It happened fast. The cord looped up and over the young man's head and tightened around his throat. "Relax. I'm not going to kill you but you will be out of sight for awhile."

Falk applied just the right amount of tension to the cord until the man passed out and slumped to the floor. He wound the cord under the man's arms and around his chest. The elevator was at the third floor.

Looking up, he saw the escape hatch on top of the car. He took one end of the cord between his teeth. He jumped up and grasped the ledge of the opening. Falk placed the soles of his shoes against the wall and stretched until the top of his head was touching the grillwork of the hatch cover, then pushed. The grill moved and Falk continued pressing through until he was on top of the elevator looking down at the guard. Using all his strength, he grasped the guard's collar, dragged him through the hatch, and laid him on the car roof.

Gasping from the exertion, he removed the cord, cut it into lengths and bound his victim's hands and feet. The man groaned and Falk knew he was going to be okay. Nonetheless, Falk removed a handkerchief from his pocket and stuffed it into his mouth. The light from the elevator illuminated a ledge set into the elevator shaft. It looked like a work area for the repair technicians. He pulled the guard onto the ledge and pushed him as far back as was possible.

"If you can hear me, remain still. Don't try and move or you could fall three floors. I'll tell the authorities where you are. When the time is right, you'll be rescued."

Falk then dropped a length of the cord through one of the holes in the escape grill, let it fall into the car and then lowered himself down. He eased the grill cover back into place by jerking on the cord then pulled the cord free and stuffed it into his pocket. Glancing up he made sure everything looked normal before pressing the button for the ground floor.

Leaving the elevator and glancing toward the reception area, he saw a man seated at the desk. His head was down and he appeared to be engrossed in paperwork. Evidently the shifts changed while he was on the upper floors. Falk walked across the foyer and down a long corridor toward the wing containing Jamul's apartments.

Two nurses approached, laughing and talking to each other. They didn't seem to notice someone wandering the corridors. Perhaps the suit and briefcase made him appear legitimate. He nodded as they passed. So much for Dr. Richardson's so-called super security.

The polished tiles beneath his feet suddenly ended. It was replaced by wall-to-wall carpeting that was thick, soft and expensive. He recognized the place where Jamul and his party had stood when Dr. Richardson and the nurses greeted him as he sat twisted in the wheelchair. Now the place had an unearthly quiet like a church at twilight.

Jamul turned the bio weapon on and off with his thumb as he slowly calmed down and glanced up at a flat plasma screen television hanging on the wall. The picture was in sharp, crisp color and showed the corridor leading to the door of his suite. One of his men covered Jamul from the bedroom. Anyone entering the suite put themselves in a deadly crossfire zone.

On the second floor of the wing Falk suddenly felt a shiver run through his body. It was his personal built-in alarm, an endowment that had saved his life several times. He was being watched. He glanced back then retraced his steps to a door marked Dispensary. In seconds, he picked the lock, entered and switched on the light then locked the door behind him.

It was a small, windowless room. Falk ran his eyes over the shelves of chemicals and bottles. Six oxygen tanks stood in a row against one wall. He examined their gauges—full. Then he checked a natural gas outlet attached to a Bunsen burner. A telephone stood on a desk. Falk quickly memorized the number. He turned on the gas, opened the valves on all the canisters and once he heard the steady hiss exited the dispensary.

Falk backtracked to the ground floor and left by a side door. Dusk had turned into night and he silently moved around the side of the house and stood in the deepest of shadows.

The guests were at dinner and the security guard was safe on his ledge. Falk took out his cell and called the number of the phone in the dispensary. He kept the cell at his side and concentrated his gaze on the second floor wall near the dispensary.

Suddenly a dull thump came from the building, followed immediately by a blinding flash as the wall split apart into a gaping hole. A gush of yellow orange flame leapt into the darkness. The fire alarms clamored throughout the building. Lights came on, shining from every window. Falk knew Jamul had to come out and was ready for him.

A. G. Hayes

The floor heaved beneath Jamul's feet when the huge explosion blew the dispensary wall across the gardens below. A second later, his bedroom door flew open and one of Jamul's men staggered into the living room and leaned against the wall. Jamul pointed and thumbed the recessed trigger on the bio weapon. The man's eyes widened for a second before crumpling to the carpet.

Jamul walked into the bedroom and retrieved his white wig from the dressing table. He put it on and checked in the mirror. It was time for Jamul to leave—alone.

Moving quickly, Jamul went into the corridor and ran in the opposite direction from the cloud of billowing smoke. Ahead he saw a lighted sign above an emergency exit. He pushed the bar, thrust through and started down a set of stone stairs.

At the second floor he was suddenly among other guests trying to make it down the last flight and to the safety of the outdoors. He immediately transformed into the bent-shouldered old man. No one could recognize him as the famous Jamul. He would be even less noticeable once outside.

Falk watched the guests stream from various exits and stand in huddled groups as the nurses and orderlies checked on those in need. He had picked the right fire exit, knowing Jamul would head away from the original source of the disaster. He saw him, head and shoulders taller than the rest.

Staying in the shadows, he moved closer. In the distance, he already heard the sound of fire and emergency vehicles. Jamul had edged his way toward the far side of the building. He was going to run for it. Why? Falk wondered. Now was the perfect time for him to come forward and claim he escaped his captors.

763

Falk saw Jamul look over his shoulder as if undecided whether to return, then he started to move in the opposite direction. Perhaps he sensed Falk was nearby and decided to postpone his grand entrance for a later, safer time. It was at that moment their eyes met over the crowd. Falk saw a quick flash of a smile as Jamul turned and vanished into the darkness.

Police and ambulance personnel wheeled their vehicles around the building, screeching to a stop in an untidy group in front of the hotel. Red and swirling blue lights added to the confusion as two TV trucks rolled into the scene.

Pushing his way through the crowd, Falk followed. Jamul was already out of sight, somewhere in the blackness of the wild open land surrounding the hospital.

Falk took out his nine millimeter, clicked the safety off and moved forward into the blackness.

Brasinov, standing apart from the crowd, watched Jamul and Falk vanish into the night.

His orders had been to bring the agent's partner to Jamul. He always obeyed orders.

Chapter 75

Stewart wasn't able to contact Koski. Calls to Coast Guard, Avalon over the last two hours reported the same. Stewart wondered if he'd made a mistake in separating his two best agents. It was possible that Falk had disobeyed orders and taken Koski with him to kill Jamul. They had both bent a few rules in the past.

Stewart tapped a rapid tattoo with his fingertips on the desktop, wondering if the serenity of his own retirement would even match a small part of what Pease could look forward to. Pease had agreed to give full details of his bio weapons to the U.S. government in exchange for protection by the Federal Witness Protection Program and a home in Switzerland.

A saying from Stewart's schooldays ran through his mind. *"The extremity of justice is extreme injustice."* As he tried to recall who had written the quotation, his phone rang.

"Stewart." He tilted back his chair and closed his eyes as he listened to the voice. Then he let the chair return to all four legs. "Goddamn it, Grant. I've had it with you. No. I don't know where Falk is and if I did I'd warn him to get as far away from you as possible.

"You and that damn scooter are being recalled to Washington, under close arrest if need be." He listened to the splutter and blather from the other end. "Grant. Take my advice and go home. Take workers' comp for a few weeks."

Slamming the phone down, he muttered, "Take a prick out of the news media and put him in the DHS and you have a prick in the DHS."

Coast Guard Catalina phoned Stewart and informed him of the explosion and fire at the convalescent home. Stewart immediately arranged for his party, including Pease, to get over to the island at once. Stewart felt hampered by having Pease with his group but knew safety called for him to be under Cerberus protection at all times.

They crossed by high speed Hovercraft from Marina Del Rey. Due to FAA rules, The Airport in the Sky on Catalina closed at sundown.

The radio crackled and the voice of the major in charge of the search reported that a security guard was rescued from inside an elevator shaft at the hospital after an anonymous phone call had given his exact location. The man suffered ligature marks on his neck and a major sore throat but otherwise was in good health. He said he'd be able to identify his attacker.

Standing beside the radio operator, Stewart made a mental note to be sure the man and Falk never meet face-to-face. He reached for a microphone and toggled the switch.

"Are all the residents accounted for, major?"

"I was informed there are two dead, sir. One by a gunshot wound and the other was an apparent heart attack. An African diplomat also is missing."

Stewart pinched the bridge of his nose. "Diplomat? What do we know about him?"

"Very little at the moment," the operator replied. "The doctor who runs the place is hesitant to say too much. Says his guests, as he calls them, demand privacy at all times."

"Did he now. Well, he's going to find out that during a nationwide red security alert, he'll be fully debriefed and *will* answer *all* questions. Get right on it. Let me know the outcome." Stewart went on deck and squinted through the darkness and flying spume as the boat raced toward Avalon's glowing lights.

Falk trailed through the darkness after Jamul. He was able to catch an occasional glimpse of his quarry but never close enough to be sure he didn't miss when he fired.

Suddenly the smell of ozone filled his nostrils and a branch above his head snapped and fell to the ground. For a moment Falk thought the tree had been struck by lightning. There was no rain or sign of a thunderstorm. Then it came to him. Jamul had a bio weapon! The ozone smell was the particle beams from the high frequency laser blasting through the damp night air. There wasn't any sound but the dampness could have caused the odor when the weapon fired.

Falk squinted trying to see any movement ahead. Nothing but blackness. A wisp of fog swirled in from the Pacific to add to the problem. He sank into a crouch and waited. Jamul had the advantage. He was a black man on a black night with a weapon that made no sound to give away his position. Falk realized he'd been suckered into the chase—a chase that wouldn't end until one of them was dead.

When Jamul faded away from the crowd at the hotel, he moved toward town. Falk could see the soft glow of Avalon in the distance. Jamul had to move. As long as Falk remained hunkered down Jamul could make his escape.

Falk laid flat on the earth and belly crawled to an oak tree on his right and again peered into the darkness. At least he had something between him and the bio gun. How far did it shoot? Could its particle beams penetrate a tree?

Then he heard a sound. A snuffling and crunching that was slow and deliberate. The sound got closer, moving in on either side of him. The darkness was suffocating. He couldn't see anything. The sound was nearer now and an even darker mass loomed beside him. He felt the sudden warmth of hot breath and animalistic snorts. He remained rigid as four huge bison, their humped shapes looming, slowly grazed their way through the grass. Falk felt his blood run cold. If provoked, one of those brutes could stomp him to death in seconds.

Now the smell of ozone mixed with the pungent odor of the beasts. One of the bison stopped in mid movement, buckled at the knees and heeled over, crashing to the ground a few feet from Falk. The others made a deep rumbling sound, pawed the ground and charged forward at an amazing speed for such ungainly-looking brutes.

Staring ahead, Falk saw a figure, backlit by the distant glow of light from the town. It rose from the ground and ran crashing through the brush and thick grass. Falk noted Jamul had gotten rid of his wig to guarantee complete camouflage in the darkness. The ground around them shook and vibrated with the thud of charging bison as others in the herd came bursting through.

Quickly Falk went around the oak and stayed on the lee side as the rest of the herd streamed by. As the last animal passed, Falk ran across the side of the hill toward town. In the distance, he saw car headlights as they drove up the canyon. Falk scrambled down the steep slope toward the road, grasping tufts of thick grass to stop himself from sliding headlong into the canyon. The bison were nowhere in sight. He wondered how such large beasts could vanish so quickly.

Falk grunted as his ankle connected with a thick clump of gorse and a sharp pain ripped up his leg almost toppling him. He regained his balance and made it to the roadside.

What was Jamul's plan? Announce he'd escaped his captor during the evacuation at the hospital? Falk watched for any sign of movement alongside the canyon. Cars passed, their headlights momentarily lighting the sides of the highway. Keeping in the shadows, he edged his way down the narrow canyon road toward Avalon.

The road was about five miles from town. Both men were in good shape. They could be in the heart of Avalon in less than an hour. Falk lengthened his stride, gritting his teeth, and trying to ignore the growing pain in his ankle.

Chapter 76

Stewart stepped ashore dockside in Avalon and headed straight for the Coast Guard station. Crescent Street was awash in tourists enjoying the evening. He noticed the famous Casino Ballroom ablaze with lights. The building had once been the mecca of the big bands since the 1930s and 1940s and continued entertaining young people and their choices of music to the present day.

A large poster in a store window announced the music of the 1940s would be playing that very evening at the Casino.

Stewart pushed through the doors of the Coast Guard station and found people moving in all directions. He saw the major in conversation with Falk and immediately joined them.

"Tom, we've got zilch," the major growled.

Stewart secretly wondered if perhaps he'd made a mistake in concentrating on Catalina. Jamul could've gone almost anywhere. "What did you hear about the African diplomat?"

"All we know is he was listed as 'Mr. Saba and party'."

"And party?"

"Yes. The doctor finally came clean. He said there were five in the party, all men, one of them in a wheelchair."

Falk grimaced. "That was me. Now all we have is two dead men; one supposedly dead of a heart attack."

"Damn it, Major," Stewart said. "Jamul escaped from under our noses. Hundreds are combing the island and he still escapes!"

"There was a new report of two men, one shot dead and the other kneecapped. The police are questioning the wounded man as we speak. Jamul can't get off the island without us knowing," the major said defensively.

"Right. There are several thousand people out there, major." Stewart jabbed his thumb over his shoulder in the direction of Crescent Street. "They'll all be going home after an Easter weekend by ferry, private boat, airplane, you name it. You think we can check all of them?"

"We can try, sir."

"Trying isn't good enough. We have to nail his ass before the tourist exodus starts tomorrow morning. You've had all boats checked, shops, private homes, anyplace anyone can hide out, right?"

"Including some places that we might hear from later who want to sue us for invasion of privacy."

"Let them. Okay, Falk. Bring me up-to-date."

Chapter 77

Stewart boiled after Falk finished his story. "You let him get away!"

"I didn't *let* him, Tom. A bison stampede and utter darkness can throw one's aim off."

"Well, you'd better get that ankle taped up. We still have a chance of finding him. Then you can finish what I sent you to do."

A Coast Guardsman came by with two cups of coffee and handed one to each of them.

"Thanks," Falk muttered and grimaced as the tape grew tighter around his ankle. He placed his weight on it. The corpsman had done a good job. The pain had lessened.

"He can't be too far away. I wasn't far behind him when I lost him." He checked his watch. "Now he's about twenty-five minutes ahead of me."

The crowds were still heading toward the Casino Ballroom. Stewart nodded out the window. "Big night tonight at the Ballroom. That place will be full. They can handle over three thousand five hundred on the dance floor."

Falk glanced toward the famous landmark. It was lit up with hundreds of bright twinkling lights, a beacon attraction for music and lovers. He turned to Stewart.

"What's going on there tonight?"

"Big Band music," Stewart answered. "A salute to the music of the 1930s through the 1950s and a pain in the ass for security. We're checking everyone who enters. Why?"

"A hunch," exclaimed Falk. "Jamul made his debut as a singer in New York City years ago in an amateur contest at Radio City Music Hall. It was his first step into big time. He sang a Frank Sinatra classic, won first place and never looked back."

"You think he's hiding in the crowds at the Ballroom? He'd never make it through security."

"No. I think he'd purposely go there to make a statement. He wants to show everyone he's escaped from his Islamic captors, strut in the limelight and be adored by his fans."

Koski had returned to her hotel after Falk left on his assignment. She was flipping through old magazines in the foyer. Killing time wasn't one of her usual pastimes. Finally she went up to her room and watched late breaking news on TV until she tired of the sameness of all the talking heads.

She tried reading a paperback but tossed it aside after a few chapters. Instead she decided to freshen up, change and go down for an early dinner. She was almost through with her dessert when a man pulled a chair away from her table and sat down.

Koski froze and her heart beat faster. Brasinov sat opposite her, his black eyes glinting and a thin smile on his thin cruel lips.

"Good evening, Ms. Koski. Where is Agent Falk?"

"He wasn't hungry. What do you want?"

"Please, don't let me interrupt. Finish your dessert then we can talk about our days in Vienna."

Koski didn't want to talk about the time she and Falk had been involved with Brasinov on one of their assignments in Austria.

"Actually, I'm here to take you to someone who will make you a household name."

"I don't want to go anywhere with you." Koski set down her fork and spoon.

"As you would guess, I have a gun aimed at you. Please, no heroics. We'll leave together like a civilized couple."

Koski knew she had no choice. When they sauntered from the dining room, she felt the hard metal snout of an automatic touching her ribs.

The melodious beat of the band already oozed throughout the ballroom by the time Falk arrived at the stage door. Stewart called ahead and advised DHS security that Falk was to liaise with them backstage.

Once inside, a surly stage manager met Falk. "I hope you're the last one. I have a show to tend to." Falk assured him he was. "Good. I'll give you a quick tour then you're on your own. C'mon."

Together they walked through what seemed organized chaos to Falk. Cables snaked across the floor, ropes and scenery. Everything had an odd, temporary look about it—a circus waiting for the last act so they could pack up and move out.

"Up there are what are known as the flies." The stage manager pointed upward and Falk gazed at a maze of wires, ropes with sandbags attached, motorized rigging equipment and a rack of spotlights attached to a catwalk fifty feet above their heads.

"No one's working up there tonight. Having just the bands we've no need for backdrops or scenery. C'mon, you can see the band on stage now." Falk heard the brass blaring as they neared the wings. The stage manager tugged Falk's sleeve. "Wait here." The stage was brightly lit and members of the orchestra were hard at work. Falk tried to squint out across the footlights but the glare made it impossible.

"Where are the others from DHS?" Falk asked.

"Dunno. I told them to do whatever they had to do. Just stay out of my way." He looked over his shoulder toward the ropes and scenery then checked his watch. "I gotta go. You look around. Be careful. It's easy to get hurt if you don't keep a sharp eye open."

"Thanks." Falk again looked out into the darkness beyond the footlights then into them. Was Jamul out there? Where was Koski? Was it possible Jamul had her? The singer's plan began to take shape in Falk's mind.

The band started up with a new number. At the first few notes the audience clapped and whooped then settled down to enjoy the thumping rhythm. "Chattanooga Choo-Choo" was leaving track twenty-nine as Falk eased back into the shadows. He quickly called Stewart's cell phone to tell him it was possible Koski had been abducted by one of Jamul's men.

Fifty feet above, he reviewed the catwalk with its sandbagged weighted ropes and pulleys. He knew that was the place to be; a bird's eye view. He moved deeper into backstage. *"Nothin' could be finer than dinner in the diner,"* the vocalist crooned, as Falk found the permanent ladder attached to the wall that enabled him to ascend to the catwalk. Rung by rung, he made his way upward, his eyes fixed on his destination fifty feet above.

Pulling himself onto the narrow walkway, he heard the singer belt out the last few lines...*"until I tell her I'll never roam— Oh, Chattanooga Choo-Choo carry me home."*

The audience cheered and whistled. They enjoyed the trip back through the Golden Age of Big Band music. Falk edged to the center of the catwalk and looked down. He had the best view in the house amid a faint smell of grease, paint and dust. Five minutes to intermission.

Shortly before intermission, a four-seater electric golf car whined along Crescent Street to the Casino Ballroom. Jamul was seated next to the driver, a wide brimmed straw hat pulled down low across his forehead. In the rear, Brasinov sat next to Koski, a gun pressed into her ribs.

The driver pulled the golf cart into a parking lot and Jamul handed him a wad of cash. "Find someone backstage who'll open the stage door for five hundred dollars or whatever it takes. We'll wait there."

Jamul held Koski's arm in a steely grip outside the stage door and inhaled deep breaths of cool sea air. "This place holds thousands of people. We'll go on stage during the intermission, announce I've made an escape and introduce you as my savior. They'll go crazy. Enjoy the adoration when it sweeps across the footlights, Agent Koski."

Koski remained silent, her hair ruffled as wind from the Pacific swept around the building. She shivered and pulled her jacket tightly around her.

Five minutes later they were inside looking up at the huge art deco ceiling. Recorded music played and the crowds milled around waiting for the second half of the show. The next of the Big Bands readied themselves behind the stage curtain. Three minutes to show time.

Chapter 78

Jamul was excited. The tiredness and stress that had plagued him since leaving the convalescent hospital was gone. Now, amid the magic of the music and the electrical vibes from the huge assembly, he came alive, anticipating when he would move forward, mount the stage and announce his escape.

Nodding to his driver, Jamul pushed forward. Koski was still held in his grasp beside him. Inch by inch they moved closer to the stage.

"Now," Jamul said calmly and without hesitation walked up a short flight of steps at the side of the stage. It happened so quickly and smoothly no one seemed to notice until Jamul was center stage with Koski. Jamul's driver had also gone on stage behind the curtain. Seconds later he appeared with a floor mike and set it in front of Koski and Jamul. Jamul removed his hat. With a flourish he skimmed it out into the audience and tipped the mike closer.

"Good evening, ladies and gentlemen. This is Jamul speaking. I am back."

For a few seconds the audience was stunned. Some who had been heading for the bar stopped and turned at the sound of his voice. Those still in the ballroom recognized the tall powerful figure at once. It *was* Jamul!

"I am no longer a hostage of the militant Islamic Jihad. I am free thanks to this tiny person beside me. Agent Susan Koski, FBI." Koski stared at the floor. "I came here at once to announce my escape."

He paused with the skill of a smooth politician. He saw the audience was over the shock of his sudden appearance. They leaned forward, hanging on his every word.

"How'd you get away, Jamul?" a voice from the audience called.

"Let me just say that Agent Koski was my savior. You can read the details later."

"Sing for us, Jamul. *Sing*," a voice called. Within seconds it became a chant. "Sing for us, sing for us…"

Jamul wore a smile of joy on his face. He shook his head and waved his arms. It was no use. They wouldn't take no for an answer. Jamul leaned into the mike.

"Okay. Just one song." The chant had shortened to "sing, sing, sing." The curtain slowly opened as the musicians scrambled to their seats, eager to play for Jamul. The audience stomped and cheered when they saw the band on stage.

Jamul waited as the audience settled down. "Thank you. Thank you. It was a night such as this many years ago when I stood for the first time in front of a large audience in an amateur talent show backed by a Big Band." He turned and indicated the orchestra, at the same time giving them a deep bow. Then facing the audience, Koski still at his side, he continued.

"I sang a Sinatra ballad that night, 'Luck Be a Lady Tonight.' It turned out to be lucky for me back then. Later, it became my signature tune. I'd like to sing it for you tonight."

Thunderous applause, cheers and whistles slowly quieted as the orchestra started the introduction. Jamul looked down at Koski and began singing. Falk had witnessed the unbelievable scene below as if it were a dream. Jamul was on stage with Koski at his side! He was only fifty feet away, yet so far. He couldn't just shoot the man in front of thousands. There also was Koski to think about. Jamul had her in close beside him. He would have to wait.

Jamul finished to a wild applause. He held his arms out wide as if embracing the audience. At the same time he threw his head back and looked up to see Falk staring down from the catwalk. Jamul's mind, the satanic side, immediately went into action. With automatic reaction he thumbed the trigger on the bio weapon as he held his arms wide. The first shot went wild, missing Falk by several inches. As the laser zapped into the wall he scrambled for cover, causing the catwalk to swing wildly.

The smile was gone from Jamul's face now. He signaled for the curtain to close as shouts from the crowded ballroom called for more. Koski twisted free from Jamul, jumped from the stage into the crowd and vanished. She had seen him fire upward and for a moment had even caught a glimpse of Falk as he threw himself down on the catwalk. She had to get backstage.

Chapter 79

Jamul had to kill them both. He didn't want anyone to dispute his story of getting free from the fake hostage situation. He hurried into the wings to the sound of wild applause, followed by Brasinov and the driver.

"Falk's up there." Jamul pointed and ordered Brasinov, "Kill him." He turned to the driver. "Find the woman. She mustn't get away."

DHS agents came swarming toward Jamul as the two men vanished to carry out his orders. Jamul immediately went into his hero role.

Koski jostled and pushed her way through the crowds, working her way back toward the wings. When she finally squeezed backstage, she saw Jamul surrounded by well-wishers from the DHS. She knew at once she'd be wasting her time if she tried to communicate with them. They were as charged up as the damn audience.

Slipping unnoticed past the admiring crowd, she moved along

the wall looking up at the catwalk to see if Falk was still there. That's when she saw Brasinov halfway up the ladder. She started up after him.

Brasinov was concentrating on the long climb and never knew Koski was behind him until he felt a grip on his ankle. He jerked around, looked down and tried to kick her free.   Taking a chance, Koski reached with her other hand and grabbed his waistband. She was now thirty feet up holding on to nothing but the man. If he fell, they'd both go crashing to the floor.

Brasinov held the ladder with one hand and reached for his gun with the other. Koski saw the muzzle aim toward her as he tried to steady himself for a shot. Releasing her grip on his ankle, she grasped tight to the ladder and removed her hand from his waistband. She reached between his legs, grabbed his balls and pulled down with all her strength. Brasinov growled like a wounded animal and dropped the gun as Koski held on like a vise.

The man was in agony and tried to reach back and grab Koski. When he did, she snatched his arm and pulled him off the ladder, leaning inward, head tucked in tight as Brasinov plummeted over her, landing with a sickening crunch on his head.

Trembling, Koski continued her climb, pulled up onto the catwalk and lay gasping for breath.

Falk was at the far end of the long catwalk and turned quickly when he felt the movement. Then he saw it was someone laying flat. Koski.

She clung to him as he spoke softly. "I have to finish my assignment, Koski." She nodded.

"If Jamul leaves here he'll still be useful to the cell, no matter what we try and prove. His fans will believe him. You heard them just now. They idolize that swine. Think of all the other millions around the world."

She nodded. "I know. It has to be now."

"Go down the ladder at the far end of the catwalk." Falk pointed. "It's close to an exit. Wait there and stay out of sight. We're going to have to move fast when I join you. Okay?"

"Be careful, Joe. Jamul's driver's down there and he has a gun."

"Okay. Now hurry. Call Stewart and tell him to have a car at the back of the ballroom when we come out." He handed her a phone. "Call just before you go down the ladder. Now move out."

She took the phone, kissed him and made her way along the slightly swaying catwalk.

Falk watched until she reached the end, made the call and vanished down the ladder.

The driver stood on the outer edge of the DHS men as they milled around Brasinov's crumpled body. He'd seen Koski on the catwalk then lost sight of her but knew he had to obey orders and stay with Jamul. He caught Jamul's eye for a split second but it was enough for him to catch the almost imperceptible shake of Jamul's head that indicated he abort the order to hunt down Koski. The driver turned and left the building as Koski crouched, hidden behind a piece of scenery.

Falk removed two items from his pockets that Stewart had supplied him with prior to leaving the Coast Guard station: a smoke grenade and a long barreled .44 Magnum fitted with a sound suppressor. He checked the smoke grenade and replaced it in a side pocket. The time had come. Moving to the middle of the catwalk, he steadied himself against the railing and stared down. Jamul was in the center of a crowd. Not an easy shot.

Removing the grenade from his pocket, Falk hooked it onto his waistband, took a couple of deep breaths then riveted his eyes on his target. Curling his finger around the trigger, he took careful aim and squeezed. A muffled "spit" and Falk saw Jamul's head snap back in a spray of blood. He scooped the grenade from his waistband, pulled the pin and tossed it into the center of the group.

Falk scurried along the catwalk and down the ladder to the exit. Thick smoke from the grenade filled the backstage area as Koski pushed the door open. Together they burst into the cold night air as Stewart pulled up in a car. In seconds they were both aboard the vehicle and Stewart drove out of the lot and headed into a maze of small back streets.

Stewart glanced in the rearview. "There's a helicopter on the way. We'll rendezvous at a prearranged spot near the center of the island."

Koski moved closer to Falk as the car roared through the darkness. Falk had carried out his orders; assignment complete.

Worldwide Media had covered Jamul's shooting. Talking heads discussed the event non-stop. Messages poured in from around the world praising God for sparing Jamul's life. Medical reports went into detail on how close he came to death. A half-inch closer and Jamul's carotid artery would have been severed and he would have died instantly.

There was no mention in the first medical bulletin that the bullet had severed his larynx and he would never be able to speak again. Jamul was destined to live out the rest of his life as a mute and his fans would forget him. The Islamic cell had no further use for his fame as cover. Now he'd live forever taunted by the memory of the opening verse of the last song he sang to his adoring fans.

They call you lady luck
But there is room for doubt.
At times you have a very
Un-lady-like way—of running out.

A military helicopter lowered to its pad at the Van Nuys Airport in the San Fernando Valley. Koski and Falk were heading back to the FBI office in Reno.

"The story that Jamul had escaped, been hunted down and shot by the terrorists held together well," Stewart said. "I suppose shooting from a shaky catwalk fifty feet above the target was the reason you weren't able to get a perfect head shot. Right, Joe?"

The helicopter touched down amid a cloud of dust. They bent their heads against the backdraft as Falk and Koski prepared to dash for the aircraft.

Falk yelled to Stewart, "Absolutely, Tom." He gave a quick wave and grabbed Koski's elbow. They dashed across the apron, heads low, and climbed aboard. They both had their headsets on by the time the copter swooped across the San Fernando Valley, gained altitude and headed toward Reno.

Koski glanced back toward Los Angeles. "Glad we were able to give Nell her interview. She earned it."

"Yeah and Marco got his Swiss bank account and into the witness protection program."

"Nell told me she was going to get the Toyota Rav4 she always wanted as soon as she sold her article."

Falk grunted. "Marco said he and Nell were going to get married. Maybe he'll want a Ferrari. He can afford it."

The helicopter leveled off and the landscape below changed to rugged hills. The snow-capped Sierras glinted in the distance.

Koski snuggled close to Falk and rested her head on his shoulder.

"Do you think Stewart believed you, Joe?"

"About what?"

"Missing a head shot at fifty feet?"

"A very difficult shot from a shaky unstable platform, my dear."

"Yeah, right," she said softly.

Stewart watched the helicopter dwindle into the distance then snapped his fingers. "Grafton."

"Who's that?" his driver asked.

"I've been trying to recall who wrote a certain quotation and it just came to me. Her name was Grafton. Sue Grafton. It was in a detective novel. Her protagonist paraphrased the famous Roman orator Cicero, who said, '*Summum jus, summa injuria*'. 'Extreme justice is extreme injustice'."

Lawyers are being murdered by laser-driven arrows. The FBI believes that someone is training Native Americans to take over the US economic system. Joe Falk and Susan Koski are assigned to find the hired killer and The Fox, the real force behind the killings.
GREAT SOUTHWEST BOOK FESTIVAL AWARD
AMAZON KINDLE GENRE BESTSELLER
Now included in THE COMPLETE KOSKI & FALK Volume I.

A 700-year-old prayer book, a key and a faded blueprint came to light and begin a search for Nazi Herman Goering's treasure. In modern day Vienna, American agents Koski and Falk must locate the treasure and the Judas List—a compendium of individuals and organizations that financed WWII, and intend to bring about the Fourth Reich.

PACIFIC RIM BOOK FESTIVAL AWARD
Now included in THE COMPLETE KOSKI & FALK Volume I.

Jamul, an adored American pop singer, dreams of a grand show of Islamic Jihad power, intending to use a biological weapon to eradicate religious leaders at an Easter service at the Hollywood Bowl. Cerberus agents Joe Falk and Susan Koski must stop the next brutal terrorist attack on American soil.

LOS ANGELES BOOK FESTIVAL AWARD
Now included in THE COMPLETE KOSKI & FALK Volume I.

A stolen weapon of mass destruction hidden years ago on board the Queen Mary has remained there undisturbed. Up to now. Agents Falk and Koski are called in to evacuate the ship and somehow locate the bomb. Risking their lives to locate the weapon, they discover that a Girl Scout has strayed from her group during evacuation and is hiding in the ship.

PACIFIC RIM BOOK FESTIVAL AWARD
Now included in THE COMPLETE KOSKI & FALK Volume II.

Koski and Falk come up against what very well may prove to be their most complex and dangerous case yet: The Quantum Death Machine. Each faces mortal peril, while, at the same time, their smoldering relationship begins to heat up.

AMSTERDAM BOOK FESTIVAL AWARD
Now included in THE COMPLETE KOSKI & FALK Volume II.

Published after QUANTUM DEATH, its prequel:

Long-ignored computer genius Kate Keenan has designed a computer program that will put Hollywood and Bollywood out of business. Suddenly everyone wants her…and her program. To stay alive, Kate goes into hiding, barely keeping ahead of a lethal hoard of pursuers with only one thing in mind: *Finding Kate* and possessing or destroying the program.

Now included in THE COMPLETE KOSKI & FALK Volume II.

"We chose the place for its neutrality. The Brits opted for its inaccessibility and the Israelis agreed because of its impregnability," Agent Joseph Falk's voice crackled in the earphones of fellow Agent Susan Koski as she swept her binoculars across the vastness of the dark green sea below to focus on the jagged black rock that comprised the home of Flangenan Lighthouse, a lighthouse clinging tenaciously to the rocky outcroppings three miles west of Tiree Island for over one hundred years. Then she spied a concrete bunker recently added to the west curve of the lighthouse, and yet another built into the east face of the rock cliff...

Now included in THE COMPLETE KOSKI & FALK Volume II.

From a little known address within the Vatican, operation "Eternity" is launched, ultimately redefining the world's intelligence services and their strategic plan for global cooperation. It all begins with a humble Pope with a different plan for this and the next world. "68 VIA CONDOTTI: Eternity Ltd." is the third of five Kate Keenan Special Assignment books in a serialized read not unlike watching a 1950s movie serial. A simple realization in the mind of God's Hand on Earth ultimately reaches beyond this time and world.

CHANG THE MAGIC CAT is a rollicking, adventurous screenplay-novel set in merry old England. It follows Chang, the wise, mystical, magical, all-knowing cat through his adventures with bumbling humans as they search to discover the rightful heir to Briersly Manor.

About the Author

A. G. Hayes studied television writing at UCLA. He has published short fiction for CBS TV and other television production companies. He lives in the Sierra Nevada Foothills and spends his time writing and traveling to nearly every part of the world. He has used personal experiences gained during service with the British intelligence in Eastern Europe and the Middle East to enrich the characters of his protagonist teams. He is the multi-award-winning author of *Who's Killing All the Lawyers* (Savant 2011), *The Judas List* (Savant 2012), *Imminent Danger* (Savant 2013), *The Chemical Factor* (Savant 2015), *Quantum Death* (Savant 2016) and *Finding Kate* (Savant 2016), *The Solar Triangle* (Savant 2017) and *68 Via Condotti: Book One - Eternity Ltd.* (Savant 2019) as well as the delightful vaudeville-style screenplay-novel, *CHANG the Magic Cat* (Aignos 2017).

If you enjoyed *The Complete Koski & Falk,* consider these other works from Savant Books and Publications:

Essay, Essay, Essay by Yasuo Kobachi

Aloha from Coffee Island by Walter Miyanari

Footprints, Smiles and Little White Lies by Daniel S. Janik

The Illustrated Middle Earth by Daniel S. Janik

Last and Final Harvest by Daniel S. Janik

A Whale's Tale by Daniel S. Janik

Tropic of California by R. Page Kaufman

Tropic of California (companion music CD) by R. Page Kaufman

The Village Curtain by Tony Tame

Dare to Love in Oz by William Maltese

The Interzone by Tatsuyuki Kobayashi

Today I Am a Man by Larry Rodness

The Bahrain Conspiracy by Bentley Gates

Called Home by Gloria Schumann

Kanaka Blues by Mike Farris

First Breath edited by Z. M. Oliver

Poor Rich by Jean Blasiar

The Jumper Chronicles by W. C. Peever

William Maltese's Flicker by William Maltese

My Unborn Child by Orest Stocco

Last Song of the Whales by Four Arrows

Perilous Panacea by Ronald Klueh

Falling but Fulfilled by Zachary M. Oliver

Mythical Voyage by Robin Ymer

Hello, Norma Jean by Sue Dolleris

Richer by Jean Blasiar

Manifest Intent by Mike Farris

Charlie No Face by David B. Seaburn

Number One Bestseller by Brian Morley

My Two Wives and Three Husbands by S. Stanley Gordon

In Dire Straits by Jim Currie

Wretched Land by Mila Komarnisky

Chan Kim by Ilan Herman

Who's Killing All the Lawyers? by A. G. Hayes

Ammon's Horn by G. Amati
Wavelengths edited by Zachary M. Oliver
Almost Paradise by Laurie Hanan
Communion by Jean Blasiar and Jonathan Marcantoni
The Oil Man by Leon Puissegur
Random Views of Asia from the Mid-Pacific by William E. Sharp
The Isla Vista Crucible by Reilly Ridgell
Blood Money by Scott Mastro
In the Himalayan Nights by Anoop Chandola
On My Behalf by Helen Doan
Traveler's Rest by Jonathan Marcantoni
Keys in the River by Tendai Mwanaka
Chimney Bluffs by David B. Seaburn
The Loons by Sue Dolleris
Light Surfer by David Allan Williams
The Judas List by A. G. Hayes
The Path of the Templar by W. C. Peever
The Desperate Cycle by Tony Tame
Shutterbug by Buz Sawyer
Blessed are the Peacekeepers by Tom Donnelly and Mike Munger
The Bellwether Messages edited by D. S. Janik
The Turtle Dances by Daniel S. Janik
The Lazarus Conspiracies by Richard Rose
Purple Haze by George B. Hudson
Imminent Danger by A. G. Hayes
Lullaby Moon (CD) by Malia Elliott of Leon & Malia
Volutions edited by Suzanne Langford
In the Eyes of the Son by Hans Brinckmann
The Hanging of Dr. Hanson by Bentley Gates
Flight of Destiny by Francis Powell
Elaine of Corbenic by Tima Z. Newman
Ballerina Birdies by Marina Yamamoto
More More Time by David B. Seabird
Crazy Like Me by Erin Lee
Cleopatra Unconquered by Helen R. Davis
Valedictory by Daniel Scott

The Chemical Factor by A. G. Hayes
Quantum Death by A. G. Hayes and Raymond Gaynor
Big Heaven by Charlotte Hebert
Captain Riddle's Treasure by GV Rama Rao
All Things Await by Seth Clabough
Tsunami Libido by Cate Burns
Finding Kate by A. G. Hayes
The Adventures of Purple Head, Buddha Monkey and Sticky Feet
by Erik and Forest Bracht
In the Shadows of My Mind by Andrew Massie
The Gumshoe by Richard Rose
In Search of Somatic Therapy by Setsuko Tsuchiya
Cereus by Z. Roux
The Solar Triangle by A. G. Hayes
Shadow and Light edited by Helen R. Davis
A Real Daughter by Lynne McKelvey
StoryTeller by Nicholas Bylotas
Bo Henry at Three Forks by Daniel Bradford
Kindred edited by Gary "Doc" Krinberg
Cleopatra Victorious by Helen R. Davis
Navel of the Sea by Elizabeth McKague
Entwined edited by Gary "Doc" Krinberg

Coming Soon
Truth and Tell Travel the Solar System by Helen R. Davis
Honeymoon Forever: Find Love, Keep Love by R. Page Kaufman
Leon and Malia's Island Music (music CD)

and from our *avant garde* imprint, Aignos Publishing:

The Dark Side of Sunshine by Paul Guzzo
Happy that it's Not True by Carlos Aleman
Cazadores de Libros Perdidos by German William Cabasssa
Barber [Spanish]
The Desert and the City by Derek Bickerton
The Overnight Family Man by Paul Guzzo

There is No Cholera in Zimbabwe by Zachary M. Oliver
John Doe by Buz Sawyers
The Piano Tuner's Wife by Jean Yamasaki Toyama
Nuno by Carlos Aleman
An Aura of Greatness by Brendan P. Burns
Polonio Pass by Doc Krinberg
Iwana by Alvaro Leiva
University and King by Jeffrey Ryan Long
The Surreal Adventures of Dr. Mingus by Jesus Richard Felix Rodriguez
Letters by Buz Sawyers
In the Heart of the Country by Derek Bickerton
El Camino De Regreso by Maricruz Acuna [Spanish]
Diego in Two Places by Carlos Aleman
Prepositions by Jean Yamasaki Toyama
Deep Slumber of Dogs by Doc Krinberg
Saddam's Parrot by Jim Currie
Beneath Them by Natalie Roers
Chang the Magic Cat by A. G. Hayes
Illegal by E. M. Duesel
Island Wildlife: Exiles, Expats and Exotic Others by Robert Friedman
The Winter Spider by Doc Krinberg
The Princess in My Head by J. G. Matheny
Comic Crusaders by Richard Rose
I'll Remember by Clif Mc Crady

Coming Soon:
The City and The Desert by Derek Bickerton
Till Then Our Written Love Will Have To Do by Cheryl R. Woods
The Edge of Madness by Raymond Gaynor

Aignos Publishing | an imprint of Savant Books and Publications
http://www.savantbooksandpublications.com

www.ingramcontent.com/pod-product-compliance
Lightning Source LLC
Chambersburg PA
CBHW070340030726
47504CB00001B/13